WINTER IN PARADISE SQUARE

'My younger daughters, Evelyn Hermione, whom we usually call Eve, and Charlotte Rose, whom we call Lottie.' It took just a moment to realise her mother was speaking French. 'Madame Katarina Komovskaya.' She had a blurred impression of a dark-haired woman who had a fine but ageing beauty, a solemn young boy who was fair-haired and only a little shorter than her, of an identical boy but much taller than her, and of a man in his middle twenties, as fair as his younger brothers but taller and wide across his shoulders.

Like his brothers he took her hand, bowed, clicked his heels and introduced himself. 'Peter Igorovitch Komovsky at your service.'

He kept his eyes on hers, and his lips did not simply brush her hand in a polite kiss, they lingered as though he was tasting her. And when he lowered her hand he did not release it immediately. He held it a moment longer than was polite, and below his wide, brushed moustache, his lips parted in a smile which made her blush.

Also by A. R. Davey

Autumn on Angel Street

About the author

Winter in Paradise Square is the second novel by A. R. Davey, who was born in North London in 1945 and now lives in Wellingborough, Northamptonshire. It is the sequel to *Autumn on Angel Street* which was published by Hodder & Stoughton in 1995.

Winter in Paradise Square

A. R. Davey

CORONET BOOKS
Hodder and Stoughton

Copyright © 1996 by A. R. Davey

First published in Great Britain in 1996
by Hodder and Stoughton
A division of Hodder Headline PLC
First published in paperback in 1996
by Hodder and Stoughton
A Coronet Paperback

10 9 8 7 6 5 4 3 2 1

British Library C.I.P.

Davey, A. R.
    Winter in Paradise Square
    1. English fiction – 20th century
    I. Title
    823.9'14 [F]

ISBN 0 340 66602 1

Printed and bound in Great Britain by
Cox & Wyman Ltd., Reading, Berkshire

Hodder and Stoughton
A division of Hodder Headline PLC
338 Euston Road
London NW1 3BH

With love to my father, Thomas Charles James Davey,
who introduced his young son to books and gave him a typewriter,
and who died far too soon.

PART 1

CHAPTER 1

———————

London, winter 1912

Lottie Forrester peered down the dark street and trembled. The lamps were not lit. Why did this street, of all streets, have to be dark?

She hesitated, wondering if she could find another way to the underground station, but she didn't know the district well and there were so many streets and dark alleys and riverside paths. She might get lost and that would be even worse.

The wind whipped rain along the street, and pushed her, gently and then hard as if it was challenging her to go the way she always did, challenging her not to be scared of the dark, not to let her imagination run away with her.

Was it her imagination, though, or had someone really followed her last week? Was it a trick of the shadows, or did someone stop when she did, and walk when she did?

And why?

Why would someone stay close enough to be seen but far enough away to disappear before she reached the main road leading to the station?

Why had they not approached her, grabbed her, tried to steal her bag? Why else would they follow her? She told

3

herself it was her imagination, it was all to do with the dockland atmosphere, the fogs, the smells and sounds, and the emptiness of the place.

She shivered, cold as well as scared, and walked into the darkness. She walked quickly, the heels of her ankle-boots ringing against the paving stones, the sound echoing between the high warehouse walls on either side of the narrow street. The echo comforted; it told her she was alone.

The wind pushed her on. It played with her hat and blew rain onto the new green coat she had been given for Christmas and tomorrow's birthday, her twentieth, and she knew her mother would complain because she had worn the coat for work and not kept it for church and other best wear as she had been told to do.

The coat made her look stylish and fashionable and its deep green emphasised the copper colour of her hair, but she had worn it mainly because it helped to prolong the magic of last week's Christmas and carry it into an ordinary, dreary working day.

The wind blew her hat loose and she stopped to fasten it. And she heard a single heavy footstep.

Lottie stood still, skin tingling, scared to move, scared by the danger, scared by the spell the wind and the rain and the dark all cast.

She looked back down the street. Rain lashed into her eyes, blinding her, and the wind carried a smell, a sharp smell of strong tobacco smoke or it could be the scent of spice from a warehouse.

The wind eased. She saw a shape, large and dark. The rain blinded her again – she shielded her eyes, and there was nothing, only an empty, dark street.

She turned and instinct made her walk silently, on tiptoes, as if she were creeping away. Moments later she heard footsteps. There *was* someone. She *had* smelled tobacco smoke.

She walked faster, almost running, legs trembling, fear making her notice every smell, every sound, and the loudest sound seemed to be his footsteps as he matched his

4

speed to hers. He did not come any closer. He kept his distance, but why?

The street led up a rise and turned to the left. She followed it. Up ahead there was a junction with a streetlamp lighting the corner. She reached it and crossed the road. There was no one she could call for help. She rushed on, legs aching, heart knocking, her breath becoming ragged.

She glanced back. A man in the lamplight, now thirty or forty yards behind her. He was wearing an overcoat and brimmed hat and he was tall, and limped as though there was something wrong with his left foot.

Was he the man who was following her, or could she ask him for help? She saw him hesitate and she knew he must be looking for her. She stepped backwards, away from him, and knocked over a stack of wooden crates left near a gateway.

Now Lottie ran. She ignored the change in her breathing, the first sign of the ever-lurking asthma, turned right into another dingy, dark street, looked back and saw the man lurch around the corner, closer now.

She ran faster, as fast as her long skirt and wet coat would allow, glanced over her shoulder and saw he was struggling to keep up with her. She stopped and looked back again just before she reached the next junction. She could not see him, and that frightened her even more because she did not know where he was or where he might come from.

She ran into the lamplight on the street corner but instead of taking her usual route she turned right down a sloping street. It was dark and unfamiliar, enclosed by a high walled carter's yard on her side and a warehouse on the other. She could hear and smell the cart horses in their stalls behind the wall but she could not hear voices or the sounds of anyone working.

She could hear someone running, unevenly, half dragging one foot, and seconds later she saw him outlined against the light from the corner streetlamp, hesitating, unsure where to go. She pressed her back tight against the

5

carter's wall. She was not wearing gloves and the rough bricks scratched at her hands as she moved along the wall.

Her fingers felt wood, and she edged herself against the gates which must open into the yard. She pushed against them but they were locked. She looked back towards the corner and saw the man walk across the road as if he was going to carry on, but he then paused and peered towards her. She pressed herself hard against the gates and prayed that they might open.

A train rattled over a nearby bridge and hooted into the dark. The wind lashed rain across the street and somewhere water gushed from a broken pipe or gutter. Then, out from the curtain of sound she heard his heavy footsteps coming closer.

She burst away from the gates, ran, blundered into a dustbin, sent the bin clattering in one direction and the lid rolling like a hoop in the other, and jumped between them. Behind her she heard another clatter and a thud and a curse and guessed the lid must have tripped him.

She smelled the river, found she was at the top of a flight of stone steps and clattered down them, her heels catching the hem of her long skirt. She almost tripped, jumped the last three steps, slid on wet cobbles and ran along an unlit alley that led downwards. Now the river smelled even stronger.

Boots crashed down the steps behind her. Her heart burst the air out of her lungs. Her chest tightened, her breath rasped. Asthma.

She slipped, steadied herself and pitched onwards into the dark. Heard boots slamming on flagstones behind her, closer than before.

'Don't let him catch me! Don't let him . . .' Something hit her stomach.

She toppled forwards, grabbed whatever hit her and realised it was an iron bar, a railing. Water slopped below, and echoed. Fear, and wreaths of river-smelling fog chilled her.

She followed the railing, steadying herself above the unseen river, until her foot stumbled against a step, a wooden step. She moved forwards carefully. The secure railing gave way to a loose chain, and she found she was on a narrow plank bridge. She picked her way across to the far side, and trod on grass. Silent, life saving grass. She ran soundlessly, heard a thud and gasp behind her and guessed whoever was following her had reached the railing.

Then she heard his boots thud across the wooden bridge.

She heard him curse when he trod on the grass, and she crouched down to make herself as small as she could, invisible in the low-lying fog. He trod about, his boots squelching on the marshy ground, and she stayed still, hardly daring to breathe, praying he would not hear the wheezing breaths she did take. She listened to his curses, his ragged breathing and held her breath. He was standing so near she could have reached out and touched him. Then he spat, missing her by inches, turned and squelched away. She heard him thud back across the wooden bridge and then lost his footsteps as, she supposed, he walked back into the alley.

Lottie did not move. The water slopped and she saw lights from boats and ships as they moved along the river. She saw them, watched them move past, heard half-distant shouts and engines, the wash of moving water, but she did not move.

The cold crept through her coat and into her until it froze her muscles and reached her bones. It made her shiver but she could not move away. She was terrified.

And then she saw the rats moving up from the river's edge.

Suddenly her feet were thudding across the bridge and she was in the alley, running up the mossy slabs towards the steps, away from the river with its cold and its fog and its rats.

She reached the top step and looked around. Her eyes were well adjusted to the dark and she could see the fallen dustbin lying in the roadway, its lid yards from it, but she could not see the man who had followed her. The street seemed to be deserted.

Her breath came in erratic bursts which weakened her

and she found it difficult to walk up the sloping street but she did so, slowly, all senses alert for anything which might warn her he was still there, waiting.

She reached the corner and peered both ways along the poorly-lit street which led towards the station. There was no one about and the only sounds were made by the wind and rain. She turned right and felt the wind on her back again, pushing her towards the station and safety, and home. She was trembling and she walked for five minutes before her arms and hands stopped shaking. As the trembling reduced she found it easier to breathe, and the added fear of an asthma attack waned.

She did not rush anymore, she was too tired, and anyway there were a few people about and she sensed the danger was over, for today.

But what about tomorrow? And what would her mother say about her new coat? And what would her father say about her keeping her job in the shipping office?

None of the family had wanted her to take the job because they all said she would not like the amount of travelling, she would find the job too hard, and she would not like the dirty surroundings.

And they were right, but she did not want to admit they were.

Two long walks at either end of an underground railway journey were tiring but at least the train gave her time to rest before she had to walk again, and her breathing had improved so the walks must be good for her.

Also, she did find the job difficult, as they said she would, but only because she could see ships sailing to and from foreign ports and it was much more interesting to think about what their crews had seen or were going to see, than to concentrate on typing tedious letters and cargo manifests.

Finally, of course, the docks and the surroundings *were* dirty and poor which was precisely why she wanted to work there. She never expected to be allowed to do the same things as her elder brother, Jamie, but she wanted to prove to everyone that she did not need to be protected or

treated any differently than her twin sister, Eve, or Helen who was Jamie's twin. Unlike her, Eve and Helen were allowed to help the Hoxton Women's Mission which their mother and Aunt Lizzie ran by actually visiting the slums and meeting the families the mission set out to help. All she was allowed to do was sit in the mission office and type letters because, unlike Eve who was tall and dark like their Aunt Lizzie, she was far too small and pretty to risk going into some of the buildings; and when she argued that she was the same in size and looks as her mother and Helen they just told her she was different in other ways, and that she should not worry about it.

But she did worry about it. *She* had always been treated differently, was still being treated differently, almost as though she were still a child and often in a way which made her feel lonely and not even a part of the family. She hoped, if she stood up to them all and proved she could do this job they might think differently about her.

She would prove she was as *capable* as any of them even though she knew that in one way she was different to all of them. They were all happy with the way they lived, and she did not blame them for that, but she wanted more from life. She wanted to do things other than washing and cooking. She wanted much more from life.

She did not want a palace, as they all said when they teased her but she did want a lot more than a house like the one in Angel Street, her Aunt Lizzie's house where her parents had lodged ever since they were married, where she and the others had been brought up. Ideally she wanted to live in something more than a three storey working-class terrace. She would like a large house where her family was not crammed on top of each other, where she could have a full-sized grand piano to play rather than the short upright they had at home now. The house would be in a garden square that she could look down to from her window and see Nanny watching her children as they played in a safe garden, a garden with railings around it.

She did not want to worry about money the way her parents sometimes did, and she wanted to have the time

and money to help people in her own way, just as she had been told her rich Aunt Catherine had before she died.

And she knew she could have all that, eventually, when she married Albert. Verney's Bank was one of the most respected in the City and Albert's grandfather had promised him a Directorship when he married.

Mrs Charlotte Rose Verney. It *sounded* grown up, so perhaps next year, when she was married, she might be treated as a grown up.

Perhaps, then, she might begin to feel she was part of the family. After all, she would be twenty years old tomorrow and she would like to be accepted by her family before she went off next year to perhaps start one of her own.

She heard a heavy step behind her and spun around.

'You all right, miss?' A man carrying two babies stared at her and half turned as his wife tried to manoeuvre a pram through the narrow front door of a house and down two steps to the pavement.

'Yes, thank you. You startled me, that's all.'

'Sorry, miss. I slipped and nearly dropped these two. Could you hold them for me so I can help my wife with the pram?'

She took the babies and shuddered. She hated feeling anything against her palms, even gloves, and she did not like touching anyone. And if anyone touched her she cringed.

'Thank you, miss, that's real kind of you.' The babies' mother thanked her.

'Not at all.' She handed the children back and rubbed her bare hands together as though she were washing them clean.

She liked children when they were older. If only it was possible to have them without going through all the inconvenience of pregnancy and babies. Even more important, if only it was possible to make babies without mating like dogs, like Kitchener, the scruffy mongrel she and her brother Jamie used to take for walks on the local wasteland near their home.

She shuddered as she always did when she remembered

the last time she had gone out with Kitchener. One moment she had been petting him and the next he was riding up on the back of a friendly spaniel. She had tried to pull him off and he turned on her, snapping and growling, then went back to the spaniel until it yelped in pain and ran away. Kitchener had come back to her then, still dripping, and rubbed himself against her, asking to be petted and forgiven.

She never did forgive him, especially after a woman who had stood watching it all, roaring encouragement and laughing all the time it was happening, told her that one day she would want a man to do the same thing to her, and that was how babies were made. She remembered running home, crying, telling her mother about the awful lies the woman had told her, and seeing the look on her mother's face which told her the woman was not lying.

The asthma and the nightmares seemed to start soon after that. She never touched Kitchener again, or anyone if she could avoid it. And she hated the thought of anyone touching her, especially men.

Albert was very good about respecting her, but she knew that would have to change when they married and that was why she was forcing herself to allow him to touch her more and more.

She shuddered and rubbed her hands together again, and realised that she was not carrying her handbag. She must have dropped it during the chase. She half turned, instinctively, to walk back, and stopped dead.

He was watching her. A few feet away.

She began to run, not even thinking of shouting for help. Her hearted hammered fast, knocking air out of her lungs. She could see lights ahead, the main road, and she knew she had only to cross it to reach the railway station. She passed a couple walking slowly and still did not think to ask for help, she had to get away, get away from this man who was tormenting her.

The main road seemed to come at her, traffic heavy, no opportunity to cross. She stood still, feet tapping, scared to stand and unable to run. Then she turned and saw a gap in

11

the traffic, ran to the middle of the road, saw another gap and ran all the way across.

She joined the crowd in the station and realised immediately that her purse was in her lost handbag. She had no money. She would have to walk all the way home. All that way with him out there, following her.

She began to panic, then a hand gripped her shoulder.

She screamed.

'I'm sorry I startled you.' A woman said and glanced uneasily at the man who was with her. 'You ran past us a few minutes ago but while we were waiting to cross the road a gentleman asked us to return your handbag to you. He said you dropped it and he's been trying to catch you. He has a bad leg.' The woman said, as if that explained everything.

'Thank you.' She accepted her handbag and noticed the suspicious look in the woman's eyes. 'Thank you very much.'

She clung to the handbag, walked back to the station entrance and looked out across the road. The man was standing on the far pavement. A motor-bus growled past, blocking her view, and he had disappeared.

He had not been trying to catch her to return her bag, he could have called out if that was his real intention, but she had seen the look on the woman's face and she knew people would think that was all he wanted to do. Even her parents would not believe what had happened to her.

She turned back into the station, bought her ticket and as she waited for the train she checked there was nothing missing from her bag. Everything was there although she knew someone had rifled through it and even read a letter she had received that morning – it had not been properly returned to its envelope.

Why? Why had he not grabbed her in the first street, where it was dark and there was no one about? Why did he wait for her after he had left her by the river? Why did he go to the trouble of returning her handbag? Why had he read her letter?

She sat in the train and tried to think of possible answers,

12

and failed to find even one. It was a complete mystery, and somehow it had already begun to seem remote and unreal. If it were not for the grass and mud stains on her new coat she might have thought she had imagined it, but she knew she had not.

She left the station in the midst of a crowd, feeling safe and glad that in twenty minutes' time she would be home. The streets were busy and well lit and as she turned up Mile Hill, the last street before Angel Street where she lived, she glanced into the pawnbroker's shop and saw all the clocks stated the same time, half past seven. She was half an hour late. Only half an hour? So much had happened she was sure it must be much later.

'Lottie!' A coster who worked one of the barrows on Mile Hill called her as she passed. 'Look at the state you're in, gel? Thought you worked in an *office* down the docks, not on the wharf. Bin unloading cargo all day, then?'

'I feel as though I have.' She forced a smile on to her face and kept walking so she would not have to explain how she came to be so dirty.

'Wotcha, Lot.' Another man yelled. 'Gissa smile, ducks.'

She gave him the smile he wanted and saw him grin back. These were nice people, friendly and harmless, helpful and concerned if someone was in trouble. She liked them even if her own ambitions were for much more than they would ever dream of, and they seemed to like her even if what they called her 'la-di-da' accent, inherited from her mother, did seem to put her classes apart from them.

Eve Forrester could not believe what Mr Dobbs had said. 'Mr Dobbs, do you understand what I've just told you? Polly, your daughter, is dying. I've come from the hospital to tell you and I'll be glad to take you to her before it's too late.'

She stared down at the man who sat slumped sideways in his wheelchair, and waited for his answer. He did not look back at her. He looked at the small black kitchener, intently as if he was inspecting it for dirty marks, then scratched his days'-old grey stubble and turned his face away to stare through the narrow window where rain obscured the view of his shared back yard.

She took a deep breath and explained once again that although she was not a fully-trained nurse she had become friendly with his daughter because they were the same age and Polly seemed to have taken a particular liking to her. And she explained that the hospital had not sent her, she had come in her own time because Polly had asked her to.

'Nah.' He shook his head and used his elbows to pull himself a little more upright in the wheelchair that was meant to replace the legs he had lost in an accident at work. 'She deserted us, me and the gels, and now she wants me to say it's all right and I won't. Besides, 'ow can I get to the 'orspital, eh? Me, like this?'

'I can get you there, Mr Dobbs. Will you come?'

He seemed to hesitate, then he settled and a hard look came into his eyes. 'Nah. She can stew, after what she did to us. Leaving 'ome like that. Leaving us to get on with it all ourselves.'

'Doesn't she deserve something, Mr Dobbs? After all, she did look after you and her sisters when your wife died, and she went out to work every day to support you all. She did everything for you, Mr Dobbs.'

'Yeah, and she buggered orf when it suited 'er, didn't she?'

'Only because she was sent to prison, Mr Dobbs, and even then she came back to take care of you as soon as she was free. Mr Dobbs, Polly didn't just abandon you and it's not fair to—'

'She bloody did! She did! She left us to take up with those fancy women. Bloody suffragettes! Trouble makers, all of 'em. Ought to leave things alone, that's what I say. Never do any good, none of 'em. Nothing wrong with the way things are. Mrs Pankhurst, huh! And that other woman, the bloody Braithewaite woman. She needs lockin' up, she does, an' the bloody key throwing away!' He was so agitated he writhed about in his chair and flecks of saliva sprayed out of his mouth.

14

There was no point in arguing any more. She had failed, just as Polly said she would. He would not come back to the hospital with her and from what Polly had told her about the way he treated the other girls she was sure they would not come. They would be too scared of upsetting him.

'I'm sorry you won't come, Mr Dobbs, but if you change your mind you know where Polly is. A taxi-cab will take you there, and here's the money for the fare. I'll leave it on the side, here.' She took some of her own money out of her purse and left it on the sideboard. 'It'd make all the difference to Polly if you'd come, Mr Dobbs, and may even save her. She cried when I told her I'd ask you to come and see her .'

She opened the kitchen door and almost fell over the six girls who were waiting outside. They stared at her, silently, and she identified Louise who was the oldest. Polly always called her Lou.

'Louise? Lou?'

The girl nodded, but did not speak.

'You heard what I said to your father?'

Lou nodded again.

'Polly loves you and him and she really wants to see him, and all of you. I've left enough money for a taxi-cab to take you to the hospital and bring you home again. Try to persuade him to go, please. It could make all the difference to Polly, not to feel he's abandoned her.' She was tempted to ask if they would go without him, but she guessed that would only make matters worse.

'I'll see what I can do,' Lou said without enthusiasm. 'I'd better get on with our tea. Thank you for coming, miss. I'll see you out.'

Eve walked down the short, tiled front path and stepped onto the pavement. She shut the front gate and looked back at Lou who was still watching her from the front door.

'Bye, Lou. Polly really would like to see him.'

Lou nodded. 'I 'eard 'ow you stood up for Polly being a suffragette, miss. Are you one, too?'

'No.' She was embarrassed to say she was not.

'Why not? You talk as if you are, so . . . ?'

'I don't have the time to do that and learn to be a nurse.' That was the coward's answer, she knew that and she knew why she was not a suffragette – her parents thought the movement was wrong to break the law – but to admit that would sound lame after all she had said in Polly's defence.

She walked towards the Thames, half a mile north of the street where the Dobbs' lived. The evening had come on quickly and now it was dark and raining hard and the wind had a sharp, cold edge to it.

She had left most of her money with Mr Dobbs, so she would have to walk all the way back home and that could take her two hours. She reached the bridge across the water and saw an illuminated clock hanging from a shop front. It showed the time was half past five.

She stepped out, her long legs carrying her quickly across the lantern lit bridge, her pace warming her. As she walked she thought about Mr Dobbs and Polly, and wondered how she was going to tell Polly her father would not come to see her.

The costers were packing up their barrows as Eve reached Mile Hill.

'Blimey, Eve. Wot've you an' Lot bin up to? Right pair o' drowned rats, boaf of yer!'

She grinned at the boy she and Lottie had been to school with, a boy who was a young man now, running the barrow his father and grandfather had run before him. 'You've seen Lottie?'

'Couple o' minutes ago. Just up ahead.'

'Thanks.' She had enough energy left to sprint and she caught up with Lottie as she reached the corner of Angel Street. 'Evening Angel!'

Lottie turned, startled. 'Eve?'

'It's all right, I didn't mean you, I was talking to him, up there.' She nodded towards the gilded wooden angel sitting in its niche on the corner of the Angel Inn. The angel, battered and cracked and with its paint peeling, looked uncomfortable advertising the ale house it belonged to. She often spoke to it when there was no one around to laugh at her.

She thought Lottie seemed very quiet and as they walked under a streetlamp she saw the state of her new coat. 'Lottie! What on earth happened to you?'

Lottie started to explain, but she was almost incoherent and within seconds she started to sob and gasp for breath.

'Don't worry, don't worry. Let's get you indoors and sorted out.' She wrapped her arm around Lottie, the sister who was twenty minutes older than her but whom she thought of as much younger, guided her up the front path and knocked on the door.

CHAPTER 2

Rose Forrester sensed an urgency in the way the door-knocker was rapped and when she opened the front door she understood why. Both her younger daughters looked as if they had been thrown into the Thames and dragged out again, but Lottie looked the worse by far.

Eve's height and broad shoulders, her sheer angularity, made her look ungainly and awkward, untidy even when she was not, and the impression of untidiness was usually emphasised by long hanks of her heavy black hair which could not be tamed by anything less than a tight net or a skull cap. In contrast Lottie always looked small and neat, beautiful and delicate as a porcelain figure, and even when her long copper curls were left free to tumble over her shoulders they always did so decorously.

Now, her hat was askew, her hands, face, new dark green coat and her boots were all streaked with mud and slime and her hair was lank and pressed hard to her head. And her pale grey eyes were red with broken blood vessels.

'What ever's happened?'

'Lottie's been attacked by a man,' Eve said coldly.

She went numb with shock. 'Lottie?'

'He didn't touch me, Mama.'

'Are you sure?'

'Yes. Yes!' It was only when Lottie broke into sobs she realised they were all still standing by the front door.

'Come in, go into the kitchen and I'll bring the bath for you.' She hurried them both into the kitchen, the small room behind the front room, the room where they cooked on the kitchen range which gave them all their hot water, where they ate and where they usually sat and talked and seemed to spend most of their lives. 'Take your clothes off. There's plenty of hot water and I'll fetch the bath.'

'Papa? Jamie, Joe?' Lottie asked about the men who might come in unannounced. Joe was Helen's husband and like Jamie he worked for her father, Edward, painting and decorating.

'They've already eaten and gone back to work to finish a job. Get undressed.' She walked down the three stairs which led to the scullery in the back addition and through the back door into the yard.

The bath was kept hanging from a nail in the back wall, where it had been kept since Elizabeth had brought Rose to this house nearly twenty-five years before. Elizabeth used to bathe in a lean-to shed in the yard in those days, delousing herself after visiting the slums. It seemed a long time ago, and now they had proper baths in the mission in Hoxton.

She took down the bath and collected a bucket, carried both back to the kitchen, then used the bucket to fill the bath with water from the kitchener. Lottie had removed everything except her underclothes so she asked Eve to help her collect the dirty things and they left Lottie alone to bathe in private.

She and Eve inspected the clothes in the scullery. She was angry about the coat, but too worried about Lottie to even think of scolding her for wearing it.

'It's mainly mud, Mama,' Eve said encouragingly. 'It might just rub off once it's dry.'

'Maybe, but those green stains won't.'

'At least they're green like the coat, Mama, but the smell. It's awful.'

19

Rose sniffed the coat and agreed, and wondered exactly what had happened to Lottie. How much had actually happened and how much had been imagined? How much had been an over-reaction to an innocent situation?

Rose and Eve listened to Lottie's story as they all drank tea. Her story did not make sense, and Rose said so. Lottie burst into fresh tears.

'I know, Mama. I don't understand it either, but it did happen. It really did.'

'All right, Lottie, all right. I'm not saying I don't believe you, simply that it doesn't make sense. Now, what shall we do about tomorrow?'

'I wondered if someone could go with me, and meet me after work?' Lottie asked timidly.

'I'm sure we can arrange something, Lottie, but how long can we keep that up? Wouldn't it be best if you simply found another job, something nearer home or at least away from that area?' She wondered if all this was simply a story Lottie had invented as an excuse to leave her new job without losing too much face.

Lottie shook her head. 'Even if I did leave he might find me again, Mama.'

'But why should he, Lottie?' It was obvious Lottie would need someone to look after her but it was hard to imagine the man, if there really was one, was anything more than someone who had simply chanced on her and followed her because he knew she would be alone. Anyway, if it was true it was possible that he was as frightened of getting himself into trouble as Lottie was frightened of being followed again. 'He'd only have followed you for two reasons, Lottie. Either he wanted to grab you or your handbag. He didn't touch you and he even returned your handbag. I think he was just a silly man, lonely or even drunk, who was sorry for what he had done and returned your bag because he didn't want to get into trouble.'

Lottie shrugged and suggested they tell the police.

'No,' Rose said quickly. 'I don't think that's a good idea.'

'Why not?' Eve asked in her usual blunt way

'I just don't think it is. We don't want the police interfering in our lives.'

Eve bridled. 'It's hardly interfering, Mama! They're here to protect people and . . .'

'I said no!' Rose said sharply, sure Edward would agree with her. 'Your father won't want the police involved. He'll want to take care of Lottie himself, and Jamie and Joe'll both want to help.'

She reached across and patted Lottie's hand. 'Don't worry, we'll sort it out, and even if there is someone following you he won't hurt you.'

Lottie pulled her hand away. '*Even* if, Mama? Even if? There *was* someone. Really, I'm not making it up.'

'Of course. I meant to say even if he follows you *again*.' She covered up her mistake, still not sure how much of Lottie's story to believe, not sure how much of it was her vivid imagination or an excuse.

Rose could not help thinking it was almost the same story Lottie told when she wore a new frock to school and accidentally ripped it. That day she had come home late and in tears and told them she had been chased by some dogs and tore the frock trying to get away from them. It was weeks before she admitted she had made the story up.

'Is my coat ruined?' Lottie asked nervously and wiped her eyes. 'I'm sorry I wore it, Mama.'

'I'll look at it tomorrow, once it's dried out.' She looked at Lottie and tried to decide what was happening in her head, then she turned to Eve, keen to change the subject before she voiced any more doubts about Lottie's story. 'Eve, how did you get on with Mr Dobbs? Is he going to visit Polly?'

'No.'

She listened as Eve told her how Mr Dobbs lived and what he had said. That was another story which was difficult to believe, and once again she said so.

'I know it sounds unlikely, Mama, but he's very bitter because Polly joined the suffragettes. He seems to think she was enticed away by Lady Braithewaite and I think he blames her for everything that's happened to Polly.'

'The family's obviously very poor, Eve, and I suppose he feels Polly's first duty was towards them, not the suffrage movement. Especially considering Polly joined Lady Braithewaite. What do the newspapers call her? Lady Bee and Violent Violet? She is the one to blame for what's happened to Polly!'

'Yes, I suppose you're right, Mama. Does Aunt Lizzie still go along to listen to Sylvia Pankhurst?' Rose could tell from Eve's tone that the question was not quite as innocent as it sounded.

'Yes, to some of the public meetings!' She was careful not to say too much until she knew what Eve was leading up to.

'It's strange, isn't it?' Eve stared down at her empty teacup. 'We're all socialists, to some extent, and we all believe in women's suffrage but none of us actually does anything about it.'

'When would we have the time? We're too busy leading our own lives, Eve. You're nursing, your aunt and I are running the mission, your father's running his business and preaching in the church on Sundays, Helen and Maisie have got husbands and children to look after and Jamie and Joe work all hours to make ends meet. Lottie works too, of course, and she helps at the mission when she can, and you or Helen come out with Lizzie and me when we need you. We're actually doing a lot more than most people, and practical things at that.'

Eve nodded. 'I know, Mama and I know you said you could understand Mr Dobbs feeling Polly shouldn't have joined the suffragettes, but what would you say if I joined them?'

So that was it. 'Are you saying you will?'

'I'd like to, Mama. One day I'd like to look back and think I'd played my part in helping us get the vote. I've been thinking about it for some time.'

'Oh yes?' She tried hard not to sound too dismissive but she was sure Eve would not have thought seriously about joining the suffragette movement if she had not met Polly Dobbs.

When Polly was admitted to the hospital Eve had talked

22

about her almost non-stop for days, telling stories Polly had told her about how she had joined Lady Braithewaite's suffrage movement and had developed from simply handing out pamphlets to passers-by to going on the marches Lady Braithewaite organised. Then she had graduated to smashing windows and throwing eggs and flour bags at politicians who opposed women's suffrage, and finally she had been arrested.

Eve recounted the stories in a way that suggested Polly thought of being arrested as an honour and being force fed her greatest achievement, but according to Eve that was the beginning of the end for Polly. Years of hard work and not having enough food had already weakened Polly's heart long before she went on a deliberate hunger strike. The final torture of being held down while a tube was thrust down her throat and soup was poured into her was enough to cause a seizure, and then another, and another.

Polly might have thought what she had done was right, but she was dying because of it and she was barely twenty years old.

The thought of Eve going the same way made Rose shudder.

'Mama?' Eve persisted. 'What would you and Papa say?'

She paused to consider what to say because she was sure Eve would stretch any concession to its limit. 'If you honestly feel you must join the fight then we wouldn't stop you, but we'd prefer you didn't.'

Eve leaned forwards, fire in her eyes. It was almost frightening how much she resembled Elizabeth thirty years ago, when she was about Eve's age and still full of reforming zeal. Eve did not only look like Elizabeth but over the years she had begun to act like her and even had similar mannerisms.

Rose had been looking at Eve but something in Lottie's face caused her to look closely at her other daughter. Lottie's eyes were gleaming as much as Eve's, but not with enthusiasm. She had seen this look in Lottie's eyes before; Lottie was jealous. But jealous of what?

'Are you all right, Lottie?'

'I think I'm simply tired,' Lottie said and smiled her special smile, the one which detracted from her eyes, the one which said she was unhappy but did not want to discuss her feelings with anyone. 'I think I'll go to bed.'

They said good night to her and waited until she was out of earshot before they spoke again.

'What do you think about Lottie's story, Eve? About being followed?'

Eve shrugged. 'I'm not sure. It doesn't seem very likely, does it?'

'So, you're saying you don't believe her?'

'I don't know, Mama, but even if it didn't happen I'm sure Lottie believes it did. I think she spends so much time dreaming she can't always tell what's real and what's in her imagination.' She paused and tried to find an example. 'She's going to marry Albert, for instance, and she's convinced they're going to be happy, but they hardly talk to each other because they've almost nothing in common, and she can't stand him even touching her.'

'I think you're exaggerating, Eve. They do talk, not about serious things, perhaps, but they're happy in their own way. He's very fond of her and I'm sure he'll take care of her. They certainly won't be short of money.' She hesitated, wondering if perhaps, in her way, Eve was jealous of Lottie. Also, as their mother, she was unsure if she was being disloyal in discussing one daughter with another.

'I don't think I am exaggerating, Mama. I've watched the way Lottie tenses whenever Albert gets close to her. I think you should let her spend more time helping the women at the mission. It might help to bring her down to earth.'

'You may be right.' It was a good idea, in principle. They all protected Lottie too much. They had always protected her far more than they had Eve, but Eve had always been big and healthy whereas Lottie was the smallest of all the children, and her asthma had made her the most delicate and the most in need of care. Perhaps it *was* time for the caring to stop, time to make her stand on her own feet.

But there was just one thing that worried her, one thing which told her they should protect Lottie even more.

24

It was late, the mission was quiet and Elizabeth had dozed off at her desk.

'Mrs Hampton! MRS HAMPTON!'

The Night Supervisor's shouts pulled her awake and she rushed from her office and onto the dark landing.

'Get out! Get out, NOW!' She heard Mrs Murphy shouting at someone, then she heard a crack and a sharp grunt as though Mrs Murphy had been hit.

She bounded down the stairs to the dim hall and saw the front door left wide open and Mrs Murphy crumpled on the hall floor. 'Kathleen!'

She could see blood pouring from Kathleen's nose and mouth, and then she saw someone move in the shadows under the stairs.

A man stepped out from the dark. 'I've come to take Florrie and my kids home.' He stank of beer.

Florrie Biggs had come to the refuge two days ago because her husband had come home fighting drunk, then beaten her and thrown her down the stairs when she told him he was frightening their children who slept in the same room.

Elizabeth pointed to Kathleen, who looked dazed but was clambering to her feet. 'Did you hit her?'

'I've come for Florrie.'

'I don't care.' Elizabeth's heart thumped with fear. 'Did you hit her?'

'I've come for—'

'Get out of this house now and don't come back.' She pointed towards the door and stepped out of his way. 'Go. Now!'

'I said—' His words were drowned by a deep and furious ringing sound as Kathleen Murphy pummelled a gong. Suddenly the hall filled with women brandishing rolling pins, saucepans, frying pans and anything else which could be used as a weapon.

Elizabeth saw the man's expression change. 'I said get out. Now, please,' she said quietly.

One of the rougher and bolder women shoved him. 'Or we'll do worse to you than you did to 'er.'

Elizabeth walked to the door. 'Come on, we don't want any more trouble.'

He walked towards her and stopped. 'I'll do fer you, yer bloody cow,' he said very quietly and spat in her face.

She did not react, simply waited for him to pass through the door, then slammed it shut, and wiped her face with her handkerchief. 'How badly are you hurt, Kathleen?'

'I think he broke me nose, Mrs Hampton.'

'Yes, I think you're right.' She looked closely at the injury. 'I think you ought to come home with me so Eve can look at it for you.'

'No,' Kathleen shook her head slowly. 'I'm not leaving here tonight in case he comes back. And if he does he'll be sorry, for sure. I'll be waiting for him next time, Mrs Hampton. You can be sure o' that, you can.'

Florrie Biggs stepped forwards, shaking visibly, and burst into tears. 'I'm sorry Mrs Hampton, Mrs Murphy. Sorry for causing all this trouble.'

Elizabeth put a hand on the woman's shoulder. '*You* haven't caused any trouble, Florrie. Your husband's responsible for this, not you. You came here to be protected and I can understand why.'

'But he'll be back, Mrs Hampton. I know he will. He's vicious when he's drunk.'

'And I'm stubborn when I'm sober.' Elizabeth tried to sound reassuring, but she had to fight to stop herself trembling.

A second later a window smashed, then another and another, glass falling like a cascade and cold air rushing through open doors and creating draughts. She ran into the drawing room next to the hall and saw the rain slanting in through three large window-panes which were shattered. Seconds later the patterned glass in the front door fell inwards.

'I'll get you, yer bloody cows. I'll get the lot o' yer!'

Elizabeth rushed to the smashed window and saw Florrie's husband staggering away down the street, then heard front doors crash open as the neighbours came to see what had happened.

'Are you all right, Lizzie?' Bill Crabb, a police sergeant,

in his fifties who lived in a house opposite rushed across the street.

'Yes, thank you.' She explained what had happened.

'Right! I'll sort him out first then I'll be back to help.' The fact that he was off duty did not seem to worry Bill, the biggest man she knew, and he turned and ran down the wet street like an athlete.

She saw him catch up with Mr Biggs, saw Mr Biggs try to throw a punch, and saw Bill hit him just once in his stomach. Biggs fell onto the road and Bill pulled him onto the pavement before leaving him and running indoors. He was back moments later, lifted Biggs onto his shoulder and carried him back to the mission where a half basement was enclosed by railings. Within seconds the bully Biggs was sitting handcuffed to the railings.

She walked through the front door as Bill turned to the crowd which was growing in spite of the rain and addressed several of the men. 'Right, David, you're a builder. Have you got anything you can use to board up these windows for the night? And Jim and Henry, can you get something to hold all the glass once we've picked it up?'

The men said they would help and moved away, except one man, Stan Butcher, who pushed to the front of the crowd and said his piece. 'None of us ever minded the mission just for the 'omeless being 'ere because we never 'ad no trouble from it, but now we got this refuge for all these women wot get bashed up, we've 'ad nothin' but trouble from men coming to get them back.'

Elizabeth stepped forward as she heard some murmurs of support. 'That's not true. We've been running the refuge for three months and this is only the fifth or sixth time we've had trouble.'

'Yeah, but it's getting worse,' a woman shouted back. 'Stan's right. We 'ad the mission all those years and nothing 'appened, and then six fights in three months.'

'Six? More like ten,' a man shouted out.

Elizabeth held up her hands to quell the rising shouts. 'I'm sorry there's been any trouble at all, but you've seen what this man's like, and the others were just the same.

What d'you think they're like at home where they can do what they like to their wives without being seen?'

'Wives?' another man shouted. "Arf of 'em ain't married anyway, so I've 'eard. An' 'ow do you know they don't deserve it?'

'Deserve it?' Elizabeth screamed back. 'Deserve having teeth knocked out, ribs and noses or fingers broken? Being thrown down stairs? And it's not just women we're trying to protect. We've young girls whose fathers've been raping 'em for years!'

'So you say! So you say!' The man dismissed everything she said.

'Look! Look!' Elizabeth was so angry she could not think what to say, but Bill took over before anyone could say or do anything more.

'It's gone ten and it's far too late to have a public meeting tonight. Now, if you're willing to help, then please help, and if you're not then please go home.' He turned to her, an anxious look in his eyes. 'I'm sorry, Lizzie, but I reckon it'd be best if you left me to sort things out and you went and had a nice cup of tea. And I'll get someone to come and collect our friend.'

She could see the sense in what he said and did as he suggested.

Half an hour later, after she had persuaded everyone to go to bed and she was alone in the scullery at the back of the mission, Bill Crabb joined her.

'I just wanted to let you know everything's shuttered up and safe. Biggs has been locked up for the night so you won't have any more trouble from him. Why don't you go home, Lizzie? You look worn out.'

'I feel it. The chairman of the Trustees is coming tomorrow and I've been trying to catch up with everything he might want to look at. He's not going to be happy, seeing all the damage that's been done. He wants to cut down on our funding, not increase it.' The mission was fully dependent on a charitable trust and Biggs's actions could not have come at a worse time.

28

'Things'll look better in the morning, Lizzie, they always do after you've had a good sleep.' Bill smiled and nodded towards the door. 'Come on, I'll see you get home safely.'

'It's very late. What about Gladys?' Gladys was Bill's wife.

'She was the one who told me to make sure you got home all right.' He smiled and opened the door into the hall, urging her to leave.

Once again she saw the sense in what he said but before she committed herself she asked if Kathleen felt well enough to be left alone for the night, and was told quite clearly, in calm Irish tones, that it would take more than a drunken man and a broken nose to stop her doing the job she was paid to do.

It was a long walk from the mission in Hoxton to the house in Islington, and it was a wet and cold walk but it had its compensations.

Bill was a good man and as someone she had known for over twenty years he was close to being a friend. He and his wife, Gladys, lived on the top floor of a three storey house they shared with his married daughter and her husband and children. Gladys had a curved spine and a weak heart which kept her bedridden, and all she saw of the outside world was a segment of parkland which was just visible from her third-storey bedroom window.

It was a miserable life for Gladys who had been a cashier in a local greengrocer's shop until it was impossible for her to work any longer, and Elizabeth sensed it was an equally miserable life for the uncomplaining Bill who saw his wife imprisoned in a deteriorating body which would only release her by dying.

They talked as he walked her home, incessantly and about anything which came into their heads. He told her about his retirement in a few years and how he was both looking forward to it and at the same time dreading the amount of time he would have on his hands, and he told her how he wished he could afford a small house in the country so Gladys could look out and see trees and fields all around, or a place by the sea. He said Gladys loved to watch the sea.

29

In turn Lizzie told him about her hopes and fears for Edward and Rose's children and grandchildren, her fears for the way the world was moving and her hopes for the mission and the refuge.

'You sound like an old-fashioned reformer.' He smiled, and took her arm as they crossed a road.

'There's so much that still needs to be done, Bill. You live and work in the East End and you must know how people live. It is getting better, I think, but there's still an awful lot to do.'

'And your mission's the answer?'

'No. The mission's been there for nearly forty years, Rose and I have run it for twenty-five, and it's not the answer but it does help a few women and children who'd be destitute without it. That makes it worthwhile, but we do need social reforms which make missions like ours unnecessary.'

He nodded. 'There, I said you were a reformer.'

'No, I'm not. Not really,' she disagreed. 'I admire the socialist reformers and the suffragettes, and even though they sometimes break the law, I'd love to do what they do, but I don't have the time, the energy, or, quite frankly, the courage.'

She shrugged, and they both realised their arms were still linked from when they had crossed the road. They parted instantly, and consciously walked a little farther apart.

Seconds later she saw her brother, Edward.

Edward had ignored the couple walking towards him until he saw them part quite suddenly. The move was so unnatural it attracted his attention and when he recognised his sister and Bill he felt uneasy.

Edward loved Lizzie. He was grateful that life had brought them together and kept them together throughout all their trials, and he was sorry for her because although she filled up her life she seemed lonely at times.

She had married Richard twenty-four years ago and buried him a year later after he died trying to stop a runaway cart ploughing through a group of children. That in itself was ironic because the shock of his death caused

Lizzie to lose their baby. She miscarried the day before Richard was buried.

And Edward liked Bill Crabb, it was almost impossible not to. Bill was an honest man, tough but gentle, and he was devoted to Gladys and their family but he also seemed quite lonely at times, and Edward sensed Lizzie and Bill's mutual feelings of loneliness could overcome their better instincts.

'Bill, Lizzie.' He greeted them affably. 'You're a bit later than we expected, Lizzie, so I thought I'd better come over. Just in case there was any trouble.'

'You're a bit too late, Edward.' Bill told him what had happened and about their conversation. 'I reckon Lizzie'd soon put the world to rights if she had the chance. Pity there's not more like her.' Edward thanked Bill for taking care of Lizzie and they parted.

'I reckon we've discovered another reformer tonight. Rose tells me Eve wants to join the suffragettes,' he said cagily, and wondered what Lizzie's reaction would be.

'And what did you say about that?'

'Rose and I both told her to be careful.'

Lizzie leaned towards him. 'Well, Edward, I must admit I admire her. And Eve can take care of herself. If it were Lottie . . .'

Now the conversation had turned to Lottie, he told her what Lottie had said happened to her.

'It does sound odd,' Lizzie said, 'unless for some reason someone's deliberately trying to frighten her.'

'But why, Lizzie? And who?'

CHAPTER 3

Elizabeth lay awake even though she knew she needed to be well rested and alert when she met Mr Buddelscome, the Trustees' Chairman, later that morning.

She listened to the house creaking, just as she had ever since she had arrived there as Evie Roper's lodger twenty-seven years before. Twenty-seven years! So much had happened in that time.

She thought about the night she had found Rose hiding with her babies in a damp, fly-infested room no larger than a linen cupboard. She remembered that Rose had been so badly beaten she did not recognise her at first. She had not only been beaten, but abused in other ways, tricked into taking opium until she was half addicted to it, and her spirit had been broken so she was no longer able to make even simple decisions or care for herself or Helen and Jamie. Hubert Belchester, Rose's husband, had tortured her and tried to destroy her.

She remembered the night a few years later when Rose was taken away to hospital, thought to be dying of consumption, and the autumn afternoon Edward appeared in Angel Street and saved her life simply by going to her and giving her hope. Hubert Belchester was largely responsible for Edward having been away for so long.

She remembered good things, too, things that had nothing to do with Hubert. Jamie had grown up to be just like Edward, and Helen like Rose. Lottie had grown up as a mixture of both with Rose's looks and Edward's imagination and reticence, and Eve . . . Well, Eve had grown up just like her, perhaps just like the daughter she had lost when Richard died, and there was some compensation in that but there was worry, too. Of all the secrets that Elizabeth, Edward and Rose shared, there was one which she did not share with anyone, the one secret which would explain why Eve resembled her so closely. And that was a secret she wanted to take to the grave. She sensed that if she ever had to tell the awful truth it would tear the family apart.

She turned over and thought about the other truths that could harm the family.

They were all so respectable. Edward had built up his own business, albeit a small one, and he preached in the Angel Street Methodist church most Sundays. Helen's husband Joe was a vicar's son and Jamie's wife Maisie had been a teacher before their two boys were born. Eve was training to be a nurse and Lottie was about to marry a banker. And, of course, she and Rose ran the mission.

What would happen to all that respectability if the truths came out? If people found out that Edward had been to prison, even worse if they found out why he had been sent to prison? What would people think if they found out that Edward and Rose were not married? What would the children think?

She twisted onto her back and stared into the darkness. It was ridiculous. She did not think of Hubert Belchester for weeks on end, sometimes for months, but as soon as something odd or unexplained happened both she and Rose immediately wondered if Hubert had found them, and was manipulating their lives again.

'Damn you, Hubert Belchester. Damn you for everything you've ever done, and for making us all wonder if you're behind every bad thing that's ever happened to any of us. Damn you for the curse you've put on us.' Then she turned over again, angry with her own restlessness and blaming Rose for ever having married Hubert Belchester in the first place.

When Elizabeth sat down to breakfast the next morning she wished Lottie and Eve happy birthday, and saw they were anything but happy. Lottie seemed genuinely frightened about being followed, which seemed strange if she had made the story up, and Eve was clearly worried about how she should tell Polly Dobbs that her father would not go to see her.

'Good luck with the trustees, Aunt,' Eve said as she put on her cloak, ready to leave for the hospital.

'Thank you, and good luck telling Polly. Perhaps it won't be as bad as you imagine.'

Eve grimaced and nodded, listened as Rose told her not to be late home because everyone was coming to celebrate her and Lottie's birthday, called goodbye and disappeared into the hall. Moments later Eve was back, kissed Lottie on her forehead, told her to take care, and banged out through the front door.

'Are you as frightened as you look, Lottie?'

'Yes, Aunt Lizzie. Papa's coming with me this morning and he and Jamie are both meeting me tonight, but I'm still scared.'

'Don't worry, they'll make sure nothing happens to you.'

'I know, but I'm just as worried that something'll happen to one of them.'

Lottie was serious, but the comment sounded funny. She was thought to be in danger and she was worried about her bodyguards, and with good reason. Lottie, Rose and Helen were all a little over five feet tall, and Edward and Jamie were no more than five feet six inches.

Elizabeth finished her breakfast as Edward came back from telling Jamie and Joe to delay starting their new job until they had been to the mission to repair the damage from the night before.

34

'If we can get it done before Mr Buddelscome arrives you might not have to tell him, Lizzie.'

'Unless someone else tells him first.'

'Pessimist,' he shot back and she thought things had changed a lot since the days when she regularly accused him of being a pessimist. Now he was optimistic about everything, to the point where she sometimes thought he was too convinced that everything would turn out right. She supposed it had something to do with his faith, but although she and Rose tried to match his unfailing belief in God's ability to finally make everything come right, they both fell short of his conviction.

'Realist,' she said after a moment's consideration, and went to the scullery to help Rose and to confirm their movements for the day.

Mr Buddelscome was uncharacteristically late arriving and Jamie and Joe had ample time to repair the damage. They left just before someone told Elizabeth Sergeant Crabb was asking to see her.

Sergeant Crabb? That meant he must be in uniform.

She tidied her hair and ran downstairs.

He was waiting in the hall and a tall, fine boned woman was standing behind him. She held a young boy tightly by the hand.

Bill did not introduce them immediately. Instead, he nodded towards the single pane of gold-coloured glass which sat in the door where there had been a set of multicoloured glass patterns. 'I thought someone said you had some trouble here last night, but there isn't much evidence of that this morning, Lizzie.'

'No.' She smiled towards the woman and her sombre looking boy.

'Bill, are you going to introduce us?'

'Mrs Hampton, please meet Mrs Komovskaya and her son, Paul.'

'Mrs Komovskaya?' She struggled with the name and guessed she pronounced it correctly when the woman smiled. 'Is that a Russian name?'

35

'Yes, it is Russian, Mrs Hampton.' Mrs Komovskaya had a warm and rather husky voice, and she spoke slowly as if she was having some difficulty with the language. They shook hands and she prompted her son to follow suit. 'Paul, say good morning to Mrs Hampton.'

Paul offered up a small, cold hand, and introduced himself in a light but gruff voice. 'Good morning, Mrs Hampton. I sincerely hope I find you well.' He bowed and clicked his heels together in an attempt to be even more formal.

Bill said simply. 'Mrs Komovskaya and Paul have been sleeping in the open.'

'Why?' she asked.

'We have room which my sons Peter and Sasha pay rent for, but man who owns, he want more than rent.' Mrs Komovskaya cast a sideways look towards her son as if to suggest she did not want to say too much in front of him. 'I think all other women in house do what he want but I not. He break down our door and window so the wind and the rain blow all through. Then he steal things. I frightened, for me and Paul, so go.'

Elizabeth nodded. It was a familiar story. 'Why didn't your other sons help?'

'Not know where to go.'

'We've found them, Lizzie. They work in a hotel in Mayfair. Mrs Komovskaya knew the name but didn't know where it was. I've taken the liberty of asking them to come here this afternoon. I hope you don't think I'm being presumptuous but Mrs Komovskaya does seem to need the sort of help you offer.

She agreed, asked Mrs Komovskaya to sign the register and immediately arranged for a room to be allocated. Minutes later the Chairman of the Trustees arrived, quickly followed by Rose.

Mr Buddelscome asked detailed questions about their missionary work in the slums and seemed concerned that they believed there was still considerable work to be done.

Elizabeth reminded him why the charity was formed. 'Mr Buddelscome, we're here to offer the destitute and near destitute shelter and an opportunity to recover some dignity and find work with which to support themselves.'

She saw Buddelscome bridle. 'I don't need to be told how to suck eggs, Mrs Hampton.'

'I wasn't presuming to, Mr Buddelscome, but—'

'Your refuge,' he interrupted her. 'How many women are there now?'

'Five. And ten children.'

He stared at her for a moment. 'Has the refuge caused any further trouble, Mrs Hampton?'

'None at all,' she lied, grateful he had not seen last night's damage.

'That's not what I understand from a Mr Butcher who lives across the road. He even has a notice in his window demanding this place be closed.' Buddelscome smiled as he sprung his trap. She despised him for it but kept herself composed. 'Mrs Hampton, this mission isn't your personal property. It was formed solely to help destitute and near destitute women and children and not those who choose to leave home for whatever reason. The mission's supported by an independent charity. Independent, Mrs Hampton, means no allegiance to any particular church, business or political organisation.'

She was insulted. 'Do you seriously believe I've run this mission for twenty-five years without being fully aware of that, Mr Buddelscome?'

'I'm not sure. How much have you collected in donations during those twenty-five years, Mrs Hampton?'

'Very little, but I'm not expected to collect—'

'But I am, Mrs Hampton and I can tell you that it's becoming more and more difficult. We rely heavily on an established register of charitable donors, wealthy men who believe in traditional values such as self-improvement, helping the unfortunate, respecting family life.'

'I'm also well aware of that, Mr Buddelscome.' She wondered what point he was preparing to make.

'It appears that many of our donors are aware of your refuge, Mrs Hampton, and feel that it encourages wives to leave their husbands.'

'But that's rubbish. We *don't* encourage them to leave, we simply offer them somewhere to come to when they feel they can't stay in a home where their husbands beat them.'

'That's not how it's seen, and you must understand that our benefactors' displeasure has caused a reduction in donations received,' he snapped. 'Now, you must either do as instructed and close the refuge or we will remove you both from this office.'

She was too stunned to respond but Rose reacted strongly. 'That is ridiculous nonsense, Mr Buddelscome. Are you honestly saying that if a woman puts herself and her children out on the street we can offer help, assuming we find them before they starve or freeze to death, but if she wants to bring them directly here we must refuse them shelter?'

'That is the benefactors' preference, Mrs Forrester,' Buddelscome replied in a sharp tone.

'Then they're fools,' Rose said hotly.

Mr Buddelscome sighed with apparent exasperation. 'Mrs Forrester, please try to understand that their money supports many missions, and without it every mission would have to close.'

'I do understand, Mr Buddelscome, but it's evident that neither you nor these benefactors understand real life,' Rose retorted.

Buddelscome ignored Rose's anger and pointed to the last entry in the register. 'This woman. Komovskaya? What's she doing here?'

'She and her eight-year-old son were found sleeping in a baker's yard. They're homeless,' Elizabeth explained.

'Is she foreign?'

'Russian.'

'Why doesn't she go back to Russia?'

Before Elizabeth could say anything Rose had turned on him. 'Probably because it's a bloody long walk, Mr Buddelscome.'

It was the first time she had ever heard Rose swear, and from his reaction she guessed it was the first time Mr Buddelscome had heard any woman swear. His Adam's apple worked furiously as he gobbled air and his eyes seemed to bulge. When he finally spoke it was in a high voice which somehow emphasised his weaknesses. 'I must tell you, Mrs Forrester, Mrs Hampton, that I find your attitudes unpleasant and obstructive. I caution you to be rather more respectful because your attitudes might well influence the Trust to accept a very interesting offer to purchase this building. A very interesting offer indeed, and one that it is considering.'

Elizabeth was not sure she had understood correctly. 'What, exactly, are you threatening us with, Mr Buddelscome?'

'We might decide to sell this site for a substantial sum which would help support the missions in other cities.'

'You'd close the Hoxton mission?' She was aghast.

'It would make financial sense, Mrs Hampton,' Buddelscome said coldly, shut the register with a bang that smacked of finality, and stared directly into her eyes. 'And not only financial sense.'

Elizabeth stared back, returning his challenge, and only half heard him say he must leave. He had walked half-way to the office door when she spoke. 'Mr Buddelscome, we've devoted more than half our lives to the mission, and there are women and children here who depend on its help and support. Are you serious about selling it or was that simply a threat to make us nervous?'

Buddelscome was already on the landing and he started down the stairs and did not bother to answer until he had reached the front door and pulled it open. 'Mrs Hampton, I must warn you that although the final amount has not yet been agreed we have been promised a very generous figure which is guaranteed to secure the future of every other mission.'

'No final amount? So, you don't know how much will be offered?'

'No.'

'That's rather unusual isn't it? May I ask who the purchaser is?'

'We've been approached by a bank representing a

company which already owns substantial amounts of land, Mrs Hampton. That's all I can say.'

'When will we know our future.'

Buddelscome replied calmly. 'You've ample time before anything happens. It'll be months before we know the final figure and have to commit ourselves.'

Elizabeth was growing tired of his vagueness. 'Mr Buddelscome, I'm not accustomed to financial dealings but this all sounds rather unusual to me. Can't you simply tell us a date when we'll know what's to happen? Please?'

'Yes. The proposed purchaser has been very precise about that. If the sale proceeds he wishes to purchase on the sixth of September.'

She heard Rose take in a deep and ragged breath, and when she looked at her she saw a look in Rose's eyes which she had not seen for years. Rose was scared.

They said hasty and almost acrimonious goodbyes to Buddelscome and the moment the door was closed she turned to Rose. 'What's wrong?'

Rose gave a small shrug and said haplessly, 'The sixth of September, Lizzie? That's the day I married Hubert.'

It was a moment or so before she understood what Rose meant. 'Are you suggesting Hubert's behind all this?'

'Why not? You said it seemed an unusual way to go about business. Why wait from December until a specific date in September?' Rose paused, obviously expecting an answer. 'Well?'

'Rose, there may be other reasons we're not aware of. You can't assume everything that goes wrong is Hubert's doing.'

'It is him, Lizzie.' Rose's voice was flat, emotionless. 'He's found me and he's toying with me, just as he used to all those years ago. It is him, I know it is, and I don't know how to stop him.'

She saw Rose already slipping away from her, back into the horror that once nearly consumed her, and the thought made her furious. 'Well, if it is him he's got a fight on his hands. You're not alone, Rose, and this time we'll beat him. We've plenty of time, over eight months.'

'Perhaps,' Rose said without spirit and turned away.

* * *

Rose found her spirits were lifted in the most unexpected way.

She went to Mrs Komovskaya's room to ask if there was anything else she needed and heard her talking to Paul in French. French! Her maternal grandmother was French and her mother had been educated in France. French! She had taught all her children to speak French even though they never had any reason to use it, and now they had someone to practise on. She took advantage immediately by introducing herself using her best formal grammar.

Mrs Komovskaya looked surprised, and then smiled, and it was the full warmth and trust of the stranger's smile which lifted Rose's spirits.

They talked without stopping for an hour, and during that time Rose learned about all the important events in Katarina Komovskaya's life and was so enchanted by the woman that she invited Katarina and her three sons to join her family for that evening's celebration of Lottie's and Eve's joint birthday.

Lottie guessed the office supervisor had a reason for leaving early because the bell was rung at ten to six and everyone was told to leave.

The other girls rushed to get away, to take advantage of the early release, but she tidied her desk slowly and took her time wrapping up in her coat, scarf and hat. Her father and Jamie were not due to arrive before six and she did not want to leave until she could be sure they were there to protect her.

She had wanted one of them to walk with her but her father insisted they follow at a distance so that they would not frighten off the man she said had followed her previously. She was not enthusiastic about being used as bait to draw her tormentor into the trap, but she agreed it was better to catch the man than to simply frighten him away and then worry that he might return.

She stepped out from the building and stood in the dark street. Drizzling rain blurred the light from the gaslamps so

41

they looked like a row of giant dandelion clocks receding down one side of the long street. The drizzle held the light high so it did not reach the pavement and left long patches of impenetrable darkness.

The other girls had left, walking in the opposite direction to her, and the street was quiet, and empty. There was no sign of anyone, not even her father and Jamie.

She pulled her collar tight to her neck, took a deep breath, and walked away from the safety of the office door. After five minutes she reached the corner where she had hesitated the night before and saw that half the streetlamps were lit. They gave dim light to the first part of the narrow street but the rest was still in darkness. She looked back, saw no one, turned and walked towards the first lamp.

She counted the lamps as she passed them, four, five, six, seven. Two more and she would be in darkness. This was where she had heard him before. Was he waiting?

She stepped past the last lamp, into the darkness. Her ears listened for any sound, any indication that he was there again.

She found herself walking faster, faster and faster until she was almost running. She reached the bend where the street turned and began to lift up the rise. The slope slowed her, made her breathe more heavily, and above the ragged sound of her own breath she thought she heard something.

She stopped. One footfall behind her.

She ran, up the slope, past the lamp on the corner at the top, and along the next two streets, and she heard someone behind.

'Lottie, stop!'

It was Jamie.

She turned as he ran up to her. 'Where's Papa?'

'Two streets back, exhausted,' Jamie panted. 'Why'd you run?'

'I heard someone.'

'Yes, Papa. He called when you started running. Didn't you hear?'

'No. I wasn't even sure you were there. Did you see anyone else?'

'No one. No one at all.'

She was sorry. If they had seen someone following her they might or might not have caught him but at least they would have known she was telling the truth. Now she had to go home knowing nothing had been resolved. Nothing had changed.

A clock sounded the half hour as Jamie settled one side of her and her father walked on the other, and they walked towards the railway station.

Rose always kissed Edward when he came home in the evening, and he always kissed her back, on her lips, and they always murmured that they loved each other. It was a routine but it was not something done simply out of habit. They did it because they meant what they said and they were always grateful that each of them had survived another day without mishap. They had not always led such safe lives.

Tonight, when he returned with Lottie Rose kissed him as usual but clung to him for a few moments longer than normal, to tell him she wanted to talk in private. Then she walked up to their bedroom, the only place they could guarantee complete privacy. He followed.

'What's wrong?' he asked, shutting the bedroom door behind him.

'I think Hubert's found us. I think he's going to buy the mission.' She told him what had happened and she could see he was worried even though he tried to reassure her.

'It's a coincidence, that's all, sweetheart, and if you're really that worried we just need to find out who the real buyer is.'

'There are three hundred and sixty-five days in a year, Edward, so it's an enormous coincidence that particular day should be chosen, especially this far in advance. Anyway, how can we find out who's behind it without drawing attention to ourselves?'

'There must be a way.'

'Perhaps, but I know it's Hubert because he's not only going to wreck everything we've done by closing the mission but he's playing with us, too.' She started to cry even though she was trying hard not to.

'Oh come on, sweetheart, I think you're tired and overwrought and . . .'

He tried to hold her but she pushed him away to emphasise her point. 'Edward, it's typical of Hubert. He's like a cat with a mouse, he enjoys manipulating people, tormenting them, and he doesn't care about hurting innocent bystanders. He wouldn't approve of our refuge so he's forcing us to close it, but that's not enough for him. He's going to make us careful not to upset the Trustees or they'll close the rest of the mission early rather than risk losing his money. He'll be manipulating us all the time until he finally buries everything we've worked for over the past twenty odd years.'

'Perhaps we could try to raise enough money to buy the building ourselves,' Edward suggested.

'How could we? We live almost from day to day, always have, and even if we did raise enough he'd simply increase his offer. That's probably why he hasn't confirmed exactly how much he is willing to pay.' There was another aspect of all this, and she hesitated before she spoke. 'Besides, if we beat him over this he might be even more vindictive in other ways.'

Edward held her, his mouth close to her ear. 'Perhaps it's time I went to see him.'

'And what good would that do?' she asked quickly, scared of the consequences. 'He'll lie to you, or cheat you or bully you, or all three. At best you'd only let him know he was hurting us, which is what he wants to do, and at worst . . .' She stopped, realising she had said too much, touched on the one subject they never, ever, talked about.

Edward's face stiffened and she clung to him, apologising without speaking, but he spoke, saying what she had stopped short of saying. 'At worst I might kill him and go back to prison, or be hanged.'

'I'm sorry, darling. I'm sorry.' Her tears changed to sobs.

His hand smoothed her hair. 'Don't be sorry, Rose, I still think of it most days even if we don't talk about it. But it just

44

goes to show how he already influences our lives and always has. Perhaps you're right and this is all Hubert's doing, but it may be as well to get it all out in the open at last . . .'

'No. We mustn't tell anyone. Promise me you won't. Ever.' She watched him hesitate and could see him thinking. 'Promise me, Edward. I won't let you tell because it'd hurt everyone we love, and it would mean he'd won after all.'

'He might tell them, Rose. That could be his final revenge.'

'No.' Edward did not really know Hubert. Their secrets were Hubert's best weapon and he would not tell, not when he could use them to torment. 'He won't tell. Promise you won't either.' She guessed he felt he was failing her because he could not protect her properly, but she could not help him. 'Edward, promise me you won't tell anyone. Ever.'

'All right, Rose, I promise I won't tell!'

'I'm sorry, Edward. It's all my fault.'

'No, it's Hubert's fault and you mustn't ever forget that. I knew the risks when I came back and found you, and we've had twenty odd years free of him. Long enough to raise a good family, and I'll not let anyone tear us apart now.'

She kissed him firmly and felt his arms close even more tightly around her. 'Nothing's ever going to separate us, Edward. Not again. Not like the Komovskys have been separated.'

'Who?' He released her.

'The Komovskys. They're Russian.' She told him what Katarina had told her, then reminded him that a little later the family were coming around to celebrate Lottie's and Eve's birthday. 'And I've invited Katarina and her sons.'

He nodded and smiled, then kissed her again.

Eve's shift had ended. She said good night to Sister and went to fetch her cloak and handbag, but as she returned to the corridor she found a few visitors had arrived early and were waiting outside the ward. Prominent among them was a tall, poised, dark-haired woman in her mid-fifties

45

who looked exactly as she did in the photographs the newspapers printed.

Eve stopped. She had never been face to face with someone famous, or infamous as Lady Violet Braithewaite was usually described.

'Excuse me, madam, but have you come to see Polly Dobbs?' Eve asked.

'Yes, Nurse. I understand she's registered on this ward.'

'I'll take you to her, madam, but I'm afraid she's very ill. She's asleep at the moment and shouldn't be woken.'

'I see.' The woman nodded and hesitated, clearly waiting to be shown the way to Polly's bed. 'You said she's *very* ill?'

'I'm afraid she is. She had another seizure today and she's not expected to last much longer.'

'Oh. In that case perhaps I shouldn't stay. Her family must—'

'Her family don't visit her, won't visit her. I called on her father yesterday, to ask him to come to see her before she dies, but I don't think he will.'

'A very difficult man, Nurse. He once told me I was a witch and said I should have been burned at the stake.' Lady Braithewaite shrugged.

Eve was surprised by the response, and further taken aback when Lady Braithewaite asked if she would stay with her for a while.

'Certainly, Lady Braithewaite. Of course.'

'You recognise me, Nurse?'

'Yes, and I'm honoured to meet you, my Lady. I've read so much about you, heard so much—'

'Most of it exaggerated,' Lady Braithewaite interrupted her. 'And please don't bother with all that "my Lady" stuff. I like to be called Lady Bee because I try to work hard and sting even harder or even just Bee because it doesn't set me apart from any other women in the country. Lady implies things which simply aren't justified, my dear.'

They arrived at Polly's bed and sat down, one each side. They continued to talk very quietly but Polly stirred suddenly and opened her eyes. 'Eve? And Bee?'

Lady Braithewaite smiled at her and touched her hand.

'Yes, old girl. You're in a bit of a mess, so I hear?'

'It seems so.'

'Perhaps we can get you out of here and down to the White House in Eastbourne. A bit of sea air—'

'Won't do any good,' Polly interrupted, gasping. 'Too late for that, Bee, much too late for that.'

'You'd be more comfortable, my dear.'

'But dad couldn't get to Eastbourne.'

'He might not get here,' Lady Braithewaite suggested in a kind voice.

'He will.' There was a hint of defiance in Polly's voice. 'Won't he, Eve? You did go to see him?'

'I went, Polly.' She realised Polly did not remember being told her father would not come. Polly sighed and lay back, thanked them both for coming to visit her, and slipped back into sleep.

Lady Braithewaite released Polly's hand and sat for several minutes before she spoke, very quietly. 'Well, the last time I saw her she was in prison, had refused food and drink for three days and was beginning to hallucinate. I wish these young girls wouldn't do it. They don't have the constitution, especially the slighter ones like Polly. But they do have immense courage.'

'I don't think I could do it,' Eve admitted. 'It must be awful.'

Lady Braithewaite smiled tolerantly. 'Awful? That doesn't begin to describe how you feel. Your mind and body are at war with each other. You have to force yourself not to think about the physical pain at the time, but you feel it all the more when it's over.'

'Then why do you do it?'

'Because it's the only way left to continue our protest.' Lady Braithewaite leaned closer and continued in a whisper, her eyes always on Polly. 'We go to prison as political reformers but we're treated as though we're common criminals. We wear prison clothes with convict arrows, have to do quite degrading tasks and submit to humiliating personal inspections and sanitary routines and we're locked up alone most of the time. Finally we're

47

expected to accept what we're given to eat but although we have to submit to the other things we can refuse their food. It's a symbolic refusal of their right to imprison us.'

Eve was surprised to hear Lady Braithewaite talk quietly and rationally about submission and symbolism, it seemed to belie what the newspapers and her parents said about her.

Lady Braithewaite hesitated and her expression which had been calm and reflective hardened. 'They don't force feed people like me, not if they know who we are, but they don't care about the likes of Polly. It's torture, binding someone so they can't stop a tube being pushed down their throat. Shock makes them vomit up most of what they force into you so the process isn't only cruel but also ineffective.'

'Then why do they do it?'

'It asserts their power, Nurse. It asserts their power over you as an individual woman. I think of it as rape.'

Polly slept on, restlessly, snuffling or breathing deeply. A far-off clock marked the end of visiting time.

Eve stood up as the Night Sister joined them, looked closely at Polly and suggested they leave. 'I don't think she'll wake up just yet. You may as well leave her alone.'

Lady Braithewaite rose, ready to leave. 'She seems very peaceful, poor child.'

Eve turned to follow Lady Braithewaite. 'Goodnight, Polly.' She whispered the words, too softly for Polly to hear and be disturbed.

As Eve walked away she felt tired, and guilty because she was glad to be going home and leaving Polly in someone else's hands.

Lady Braithewaite walked beside her as they left. She appeared to be thinking, and then seemed to reach a decision. 'Do you live far away?'

'Not far. It takes me about forty minutes to walk home from here.'

My motor-car is waiting. It'll take you home, Nurse.' Lady Braithewaite pulled on her gloves and walked a little faster so Eve found it quite difficult to keep up with her.

'That's very kind of you Lady Braithewaite but there's really no need. I can walk.' She ran down the stairs a few feet behind Lady Braithewaite.

'Of course you can but I'd like to talk to you, if you don't mind.'

'Of course not, but you don't have to take me home.'

'I won't. I live quite close by and Perkins can take me home first and drive you afterwards.'

'Oh.' Somehow that seemed even more of an ordeal, but when they reached the front doors and she saw the rain beating down she changed her mind and accepted the offer.

She had never ridden in a motor-car before and the vehicle standing outside the hospital looked big and comfortable. She hesitated on the pavement, unsure what to do, until a man wearing jodhpurs, knee-high boots and a grey uniform jacket and cap suddenly appeared, greeted Lady Braithewaite and opened a door for them both to step into the motor. Eve was ushered in first and she did not see the man sitting in the dark on the far side of the carriage-like seat until she touched his knee.

She screamed with surprise.

'I'm sorry,' an exceptionally deep voice apologised. 'I was asleep.'

'I'm sorry, it was my fault.' Eve said quickly to the shadow she could barely see.

'You've met Robert, my son. I'd quite forgotten he was waiting.' Lady Braithewaite said vacantly as she climbed in beside Eve. 'Robert, this is . . . I'm terribly sorry but I don't actually know your name.'

'Forrester. Evelyn Forrester.'

'Well, Miss Forrester's learning to be a nurse and she's a friend of Polly Dobbs. You can accompany her when Perkins takes her home.'

Eve felt her hand gripped and gently shaken, the man apologised again, and then the motor-car moved away.

She settled back into the soft seat and smelled the leather and began to relax until the driver steered the motor around a corner and threw her against Robert Braithewaite.

'I'm sorry,' she apologised again.

He didn't answer. He was already asleep and she had not woken him.

Lady Braithewaite spoke on her son's behalf. 'Please excuse Robert but he's a doctor and when he isn't working he's sleeping. Now, Miss Forrester, you recognised me and you asked questions which suggest you have an interest in women's affairs. You may care to know that there's a meeting at my house on Friday evening.'

'A meeting?' she asked nervously, remembering the conversation she had had with her mother.

'The Women's Freedom League, Miss Forrester. May I expect you?'

'Yes, of course.' The words came out as a polite response before she had time to consider what she might be committing herself to, but having promised to be there she could not immediately think of an excuse not to go.

The car turned into a large square and stopped outside an elegant house lit by large gas lanterns. 'Until Friday, Miss Forrester. Give Perkins your address and he and Robert will see you safely home. Good night to you.'

The driver, Mr Perkins, opened the door and Lady Braithewaite was gone, only the fragrance of her scent remaining.

'Where do you live, miss?' Perkins had returned to the driving seat and he spoke through a window which separated him from the passengers.

'Towards Shoreditch, please. Angel Street.' She saw the way his face changed for just a moment, and guessed that like so many people he had misjudged her background because she had inherited her mother's middle-class accent. 'I can direct you when we're in the neighbourhood.'

'Thank you, but there's no need. I come from Hackney, myself. Lived there forty years before I joined her Ladyship. Angel Street's off Mile Hill, isn't it?'

'Yes.'

'Thank you, miss.' He smiled, slid the window shut and made the motor-car glide away.

Robert Braithewaite appeared to be asleep still, even

when he spoke to her in rumbling tones. 'Miss Forrester, I think my mother's intrigued by you, so make sure she doesn't lead you into trouble.'

'I beg your pardon?'

'You heard me, Miss Forrester. My mother has untold potential for causing trouble, particularly to people who intrigue her.' He stretched his long legs and spread himself against the back of the seat, hands clasped behind his head. 'To intrigue – now what does that mean to you? To fascinate or puzzle? To use secret influence? To carry on some underhand plot? It can mean all those, you know, and I sometimes think my mother can't actually distinguish between any of them. There is one meaning, however, that she does not understand at all.'

She waited for him to continue but he did not, and when she looked closer she could see he was watching her and waiting for her to answer. 'I understood your mother to mean she was puzzled by me, although I can't understand why.'

'Because she's misjudged you, Miss Forrester. That's why she's intrigued by you!'

'Well I don't know why I should intrigue her. If anything, I'm intrigued by your mother. She's nothing like I expected, and I'd like to try to understand her better.'

'Well, if you ever come close to understanding her, will you promise to explain her to me? I've been her son for thirty years and I don't understand her, yet.' He stretched and sat up properly. 'I apologise for being such poor company but I'm rather tired.'

'Your mother said you are a doctor?'

'Family trade.' He rubbed his eyes. 'Father was a surgeon, I'm not that good.'

'General practice?' she asked and when he nodded she gave her honest opinion of a General Practitioner's place in medicine. 'Then you're part of the vanguard. You see symptoms to cure. In hospital all we see are ailments to treat. I don't think there's anyone so important as a good GP. If more people had symptoms correctly diagnosed—'

'If only it were that simple, Miss Forrester. There are

congenital illnesses, accidents, birth defects... and children who could never have been diagnosed as *ill* even though they might be crippled or dying.' He slumped back and looked through the window. 'I don't find it very rewarding.'

'What's the White House in Eastbourne?' She remembered his mother had offered to take Polly there.

'That's the Women's Freedom League's official head-quarters and rest home. A few nurses look after the worst cases when they're released from prison. I occasionally go down there at weekends if I'm not on duty in the practice.'

'Your wife must be very understanding, Doctor.'

'My wife?' He sounded puzzled. 'I live with my mother.'

He yawned, apologised once more, and promptly fell asleep again, his head resting against the back of the seat and rolled over to his right shoulder.

After several minutes his mouth dropped open and he snored, deeply asleep even though his head was rolling from side to side with the car's motion. If his mother was interesting, then so was he.

It was too dark to see him clearly and she was trying to study his face when his eyes opened and she was caught, unable to look away without seeming foolish. He did not speak, simply studied her for a moment or two, gave her a beaming smile which showed his teeth white in the darkness then fell asleep again.

The motor-car slowed and turned, and as she looked out she saw the little wooden angel outside the Angel Inn. She was almost home.

Robert Braithewaite stirred and woke up when the car stopped. He peered out of the window. 'I really think I ought to warn my mother that you're not what you seem, Miss Forrester. More to avoid embarrassment for you than anything else.'

She nodded. 'Perhaps you should, but would you like to come indoors and see how we savages live?' She hoped he would, and wondered whether or not she dare try to blackmail him into coming indoors by telling him it was her birthday.

'I share a practice close to the docks, Miss Forrester, and my surgery's in a house far worse than anything in this street. And my surgery's better than most of my patients' homes.'

'I'm sorry, I assumed—'

'Please don't apologise. I can't come in because I have an early surgery and must go home, but I hope we can soon meet again. I've enjoyed talking with you.'

'Yes.' She was astonished to find she had enjoyed talking to him too, even though she hardly knew him.

'I'll see you to your door,' he said and moments later she realised she had thanked the driver and was standing on her front step, Robert Braithewaite towering above her, sheltering her from the rain which was slanting down. 'Beware of my mother, Miss Forrester, she's a very determined and persuasive woman. She may lead you into things you'll regret.'

'Like Polly Dobbs?'

'Like Polly! I don't really know her but I do know her brother,' he said.

'Her brother? She didn't tell me she had a brother.'

'Ah, well,' he said as if he was chiding her. 'Couple of years older than her. Fine chap. Docker, when he can get work.'

'You met him through Polly?'

'No, professionally, as a healer of the sick so please don't ask me any more questions about him. Ask Polly why she didn't tell you she had an older brother.'

'If she's still alive to ask,' she said, aware that Polly may have died already.

'Don't feel guilty about Polly Dobbs, or any other patient for that matter, Miss Forrester. We're not gods, or angels. We're just ordinary human beings trying to do our best, which often isn't good enough.'

She looked up into his face and nodded, and he looked back at her, his eyes fixed quite openly on hers when the wind caught the rain and threw it over his shoulder and into her face. She took out a handkerchief but before she could wipe her face with it he took it from her and dabbed several spots dry then handed it back. It was a strangely intimate thing to do but it did not seem wrong or out of place – it seemed surprisingly natural.

'Well, Miss Forrester, I'd better bid you goodnight. I certainly hope we can meet again, soon,' he added, then he was gone.

She stepped the two yards to the front gate and watched him walk around to the far side of the car. Her heart was pounding and she could hardly catch her breath. Would he look back, pause to say goodnight, wave to her? Or would he simply get into the motor-car without acknowledging her any further? How would she feel if that was what he did?

She wanted to call out, say goodnight, oblige him to respond, but that would not tell her anything except that he was polite.

She waited, ridiculously anxious that he should turn towards her.

He did. He stopped, looked back at her, and gave a salutary wave. 'Goodnight, Miss Forrester. Don't get too wet out here.'

'I won't.' She waved, and as he was about to climb back into the car she remembered something she wanted to ask him. 'You said there was another meaning to the word intrigue, but you didn't say what it was.'

'To have a secret love affair, Miss Forrester.' He seemed to hesitate, then he nodded and settled into the motor-car. It moved away and she waved after it until the rain hid it from view, then she turned towards the front door but she did not knock immediately.

She needed just a few moments alone, to think and try to organise her thoughts. Once more she stepped back along the short path and stared into the darkness where the motor-car had been, but that only left her more confused as to why she should be feeling as she did.

CHAPTER 4

Lottie told Eve she did not feel like celebrating their birthday and she was not surprised when Eve admitted the same feeling, but they both knew how much these family gatherings meant to their mother so they washed, brushed their hair, dressed in their second-best clothes and pretended enthusiasm.

Lottie thought her mother looked drawn and preoccupied, but she seemed to recover as the family closed around her. Maisie and Jamie arrived first, with their twins Edward and Adam, and Helen and Joe arrived with little Josephine a few minutes later. The boys, a little more than three years old, concentrated first on swaddled up Josephine, and later on the feast of treats laid out on the front room table.

The sound of family talk spread through the front room, the kitchen and the scullery, quiet, sustainable conversations that had been going on for years. Opinions were exchanged, or reinforced because they rarely changed, memories were brought out and common hopes repolished. Daily business was discussed, the subject of Lottie's being followed, the sense in her changing her job, and when would Albert suggest a firm date for the wedding?

Lottie listened and joined in the conversations as far as she thought she was allowed to but she did not feel part of it all, even when she was being discussed. She saw herself as two people, the caricature they saw whom she hardly recognised, and herself looking out at them, trying hard to touch them but being warded off with misguided kindness and sympathy.

It was her birthday, she was twenty years old and engaged to be married and they made her feel like a child, so she decided to escape up to her room. Everyone would understand if she feigned illness or said she was tired through worrying about the man who had followed her. Besides it was rather dramatic, her leaving the party meant to celebrate her birth; it might make them realise she was telling the truth about being followed.

'Lottie?' She started so much that her mother apologised for frightening her before asking if Albert was coming.

'I think so, Mama. He said about nine.' She had half forgotten about Albert, who enjoyed her family occasions much more than she did.

'Well, I hope he arrives soon because there's a surprise and I'd like him to be here first.'

'Surprise? What sort of surprise, Mama?'

'I've invited some more people, new friends I hope. I think you'll like them, Lottie. They're rather different.'

She ignored the inference that she might not have liked them if they were normal and asked why they were different.

'They're Russian and they've been treated very badly since they came to England.' Her mother's voice was drowned as the whole family gathered around her to ask questions which she refused to answer. She quietened everyone by raising her hands. 'I want you all to welcome these people because they need to feel they have some friends. Mrs Komovskaya's husband died and she was forced to leave Russia very quickly. I'm sure they'll tell you all you want to know, but please be kind towards them, and don't judge them too harshly. You don't know what they've been through.'

Lottie found her interest was refreshed.

* * *

She opened the door to Albert as the front-room clock struck nine.

'Happy birthday, Charlotte.' He smiled down at her and his hands reached out but did not touch her. She smiled, glad to see him, pursed her lips and saw the relief in his eyes before his hands gripped her arms and his lips pressed against hers.

She held herself still and willed some warmth to pass through her lips, but it would not. Albert pulled away, released his grip on her arms, smiled as if he was apologising for wanting something which was unnatural, and changed his smile for one he used to greet her mother.

'Good evening, Mrs Forrester. I hope I'm not too late but I couldn't leave earlier. Father wanted to talk about business.'

'How are your parents, Albert? Well, I hope?'

'Very well, and they send their regards to you and Mr Forrester . . .'

Lottie heard the conversation drift away as Albert was consumed by the family he would soon be part of. She had worried for weeks before she had introduced him to them, the rich banker's son meeting the poor decorator's family, but there had been none of the embarrassment she had expected. Albert had not simply been accepted, he had been absorbed and in turn he had adopted her brother and sisters as the siblings he did not have.

She watched him talking to Jamie and was amazed how the two men had become friends. They had completely different backgrounds, completely different prospects and yet they found enough in common to interest and respect each other. Albert had almost instantly achieved something she had failed to do in twenty years, but it did not comfort her, it worried her.

It made her feel even more lonely, as though she had lost him to her family, and in her heart she wondered if, as an only child, he wanted them more than he wanted her. Perhaps she was simply an introduction to a way of life which appealed to him.

She turned as she heard a rap on the front door.

'I'll go, Lottie.' Her mother fluttered passed her to open the door, and moments later the hall was filled with giants who were quickly ushered into the conveniently empty front room.

She was so astonished she could not speak other than to murmur the usual polite greetings as they passed by, and a moment later Aunt Lizzie shepherded her into a queue ready for formal introductions.

She looked up at Albert and saw a wariness in his eyes, but then he saw her looking and he smiled, indulgently.

'My younger daughters, Evelyn Hermione, whom we usually call Eve, and Charlotte Rose, whom we call Lottie.' It took just a moment to realise her mother was speaking French. 'Madame Katarina Komovskaya.' She had a blurred impression of a dark-haired woman who seemed taller even than Eve and who had fine but ageing beauty, a solemn young boy who was fair-haired and only a little shorter than her, of an identical boy but much taller than her, and of a man in his middle twenties, as fair as his younger brothers but taller than his brother and wide across his shoulders.

Like his brothers he took her hand, bowed, clicked his heels and introduced himself. 'Peter Igorovitch Komovsky at your service.'

Unlike the little boy, Paul, and his brother Alexander, he kept his eyes on hers, and his lips did not simply brush her hand in a polite kiss, they lingered as though he was tasting her. And when he lowered her hand he did not release it immediately. He held it a moment longer than was polite, and below his wide, brushed moustache, his lips parted in a smile which made her blush.

'I'm pleased to meet you, Mr Komovsky, or is it Komovskaya?' she said in French, but he replied in fluent but accented English.

'I am Komovsky, Miss Forrester, because I am a man but my mother is Komovskaya because she is a woman. We

Russians are very concerned with gender. We pride ourselves on knowing a woman from a man.' He sounded serious but his lips and his dark eyes smiled and she blushed even more as she realised he was teasing her.

'Mr Komovsky, please allow me to introduce Albert Verney, my fiancé,' she said primly, hoping to embarrass him in turn, but he grasped Albert's hand and congratulated him on having captured such a beautiful woman to marry, and then turned, instantly, to business.

'You have no connection with the bankers named Verney?'

'My family business,' Albert said proudly. 'I'm something like a great, great, great nephew of Jacob Verney who founded the bank, Mr Komovsky. My father's one of the Directors and I manage investments for some of our London customers.'

She noticed the smile had gone from Peter Komovsky's face now he was talking to Albert and she turned away, only half hearing Peter explain that he was once an agent for a Russian bank and his position required him to help develop foreign trade by travelling throughout Europe.

She moved to Peter's younger brother who looked lost among so many strangers. 'It's Alexander, isn't it?'

He answered in a voice which was surprisingly deep for a young boy, and although she spoke to him in French, he replied in English which was only a little halting and showed no signs of a foreign accent. 'I am usually called Sasha, Miss Forrester.'

'And I am usually called Lottie.' She smiled up at him, noticed how pale his tobacco-coloured eyes were and how smooth and unshaven his face was. She guessed he was only fourteen or fifteen, still a boy, and thought there was a large difference in the sons' ages.

She was embarrassed that she could not think of anything suitable to say and was grateful when he excused himself and joined his brother Peter, and Albert.

She looked at them standing together and she was struck by the differences between them all.

Albert, tall and rather portly, smartly suited and neat with his well-trimmed dark brown hair and moustache was the epitome of a respectable banker. Peter was even taller and broader than Albert but he was leaner, his body more muscular. His moustache was wider than Albert's and his fair hair longer so it straggled over his weather-battered face. His well-worn trousers, collarless red shirt, open at the neck, and his loose black waistcoat made him look more like a bandit than anyone respectable. Sasha had even longer straw-coloured hair, and although he was a little taller than Albert he was not so broad. In fact his white shirt enveloped him and fell in loose folds where it was tucked into the waistband of his black trousers. A soft black bow sagged around his shirt's too-large collar and gave the impression he was an artist of some sort.

She understood, now, why her mother had asked them all not to judge the family too quickly, turned away from them and studied Mrs Komovskaya who was talking to her mother and Helen.

Mrs Komovskaya's beauty and bearing were chillingly perfect, but the warmth of her voice and smile overcame the impression of coldness, and her insistence that everyone call her Katarina confirmed her friendliness.

She was tall, and her thick hair, black but turning to silver and pulled into a smooth dome on top of her head, made her look even taller. She had a fine boned face, high cheekbones and a deep forehead which emphasised large, intelligent eyes. A grey, layered lace blouse, which fastened tight around her neck and wrists, draped from her broad shoulders and was tucked into the narrow waist of a plain, darker grey skirt that covered hips which hardly existed, and then fell in gentle folds to within an inch of the floor.

The conversation flowed in French, talk about small and inconsequential matters, and Lottie tried not to take a part. She preferred simply to watch Mrs Komovskaya, to study her and look for clues which might explain some of the mystery her mother had suggested would intrigue her.

Although Mrs Komovskaya wore no jewellery and her clothes were old and worn to the point of becoming shabby, it was obvious that Katarina Komovskaya was not accustomed to living in cheap furnished rooms. She stood with her back straight and her chin lifted. Her voice was low and well modulated and she sounded confident and interested in what was being said. But her bearing and voice and attitude did not reveal as much as her hands. They were long and thin, so thin that her bones and veins showed through the skin, and they moved constantly. When Mrs Komovskaya was talking her hands flowed to emphasise her words, but when she was listening the thumb and fingers of one hand stroked the fingers of the other, obviously seeking comfort by touching familiar rings which were no longer there.

Lottie watched her father listening to a conversation held in a language he could not understand and wondered once more at the tolerance that flowed between him and her mother. They had totally different backgrounds; her mother's father was a bank manager so her mother grew up in a comfortable home, but her father was brought up in a working-class mining family somewhere in the north of England. Apart from her Aunt Lizzie all her grandparents, and aunts and uncles were dead now, and had died even before Helen and Jamie were born.

Perhaps that was what held them together, made her mother so willing to accept the way they lived. Perhaps that was what made her own family so important to her mother.

She wondered if she and Albert would be as happy as her parents, whether they could learn to adapt to each other as well as her parents had.

'Lottie!' She came out from her dream and realised she was standing in everyone's way, preventing them from reaching the food they had all been invited to eat.

Her mother was helping Katarina, Helen was looking after young Paul, Peter had disappeared but Sasha obviously needed help so she pulled him to the table and loaded a plate for him.

There was nowhere to sit so she led him to the kitchen, which was just as crowded, and finally to the scullery where they perched on stools by the scrubbed table.

She looked up into his tobacco eyes, framed with long

golden lashes, scanned his face and wondered how old he really was. He was very good-looking, there was no question, but he was not manly, not in any obvious way other than the surprising deepness of his voice.

He looked up and caught her looking at him. 'Mr Verney, your fiancé, will not object to us eating alone, Miss Forrester?'

The thought of Albert objecting to her eating alone with a young boy amused her. 'No, I don't think he'll object, Sasha. And please call me Lottie, not Miss Forrester. I know I'm older than you but that makes me feel too much older.'

'It is your birthday anniversary today? You are twenty, I was told?'

'Yes.' She did not bother to pretend she was offended that he knew her age.

'I was twenty last November, so I am actually a few weeks older than you. So do you think Mr Verney—'

'No. It doesn't matter, Sasha,' she interrupted him, so surprised he was twenty that she allowed her surprise to show.

He must have noticed because he smiled and said, 'I was born twenty years ago, but my face does not understand this and everyone thinks I am much younger. I shave every day, like my friends, hoping that will make my beard grow faster. Sometimes I shave twice each day even though my friends tell me that once a week would probably be enough. They are kind, my friends, but they like to make fun out of me, and I like that because it stops me becoming too serious. My friends in St Petersburg say that I have the mind of an old man and the body of a young boy.' He smiled and she smiled back at him. 'I tell them I think that is better than the other way around.'

'You all speak very good English, Sasha. How did you learn?'

'Thank you. My father's mother was English and we lived with her for many years until she died, but Paul and I both won scholarships to a music academy and we were tutored in English so that we could travel abroad. My older brother, Peter, speaks English well although he learned only from our grandmother and then from travelling.'

She noticed a little wariness when Sasha mentioned Peter, and although she wanted to know more she did not ask any questions about Peter. Instead, she asked Sasha about his musical education.

He seemed eager to talk. 'Paul is the really talented one. He plays violin beautifully, like my mother. Peter also plays the violin, but fast and clumsily, like a gypsy. I play the piano, which is not so easy to carry as a violin, so I compose and play the tunes in my head. Very large, my head. It can seat a full orchestra.'

She laughed. 'You enjoy music?'

'It is my life. If I could not compose and play I would wish to die.'

'Then will you go back to study?'

'To Russia? No.' His mood turned dark in an instant and she saw him withdraw into himself.

'I'm desperately sorry, Sasha. I spoke without thinking,' she said quickly, embarrassed at the effect her question had.

'It's fortunate you're not in Russia, then. No Russian should speak without thinking. The Tsar would prefer it if no Russian thought at all, unless it was to agree with him.' He growled the words almost as if he was talking to himself rather than to her.

She did not know how to respond. She was scared to ask anything that he might construe as personal in case she made his mood worse, but she sensed he might want to explain what he had said. 'I thought the Tsar was kind. Isn't he called the father . . . ?'

'Batyushka. The Little Father, the Big Father being God, but the Tsar thinks he is also the Big Father, Lottie.'

'Is that why you left Russia?'

'We left because it was unwise to remain. The Tsar had already killed my father and—'

'The Tsar killed your father?'

'His Secret Police did.'

'When?'

'We were told two months ago, but it could have happened before then.' He paused and must have noticed

63

the confused expression on her face because he explained more without her asking. 'He was in prison. Convicted for throwing a stone at the Tsar's carriage. Killed for such an enormous crime when the Tsar orders the Cossacks to hack off people's heads in the streets.'

'Did he throw the stone?'

'Lottie, my father wore spectacles that thick.' Sasha held up his hand, his forefinger and thumb a quarter of an inch apart. 'He could not even have seen the Tsar's carriage from where he was supposed to have been standing. Anyway, the carriage was empty at the time. He died because someone said he threw a stone at an empty carriage he could not even see.'

She shivered. 'But why would anyone do that, Sasha?'

'Perhaps because he had been voicing his opinions too loudly, his political opinions. In Russia we have the Tsar, the Bolsheviks and a few democrats. The Bolsheviks don't trust the Tsarists, the Tsarists don't trust the Bolsheviks, and no one trusts the democrats, so it is better not to give a democratic opinion.'

'Your father was a democrat?' she asked, and saw Sasha nod. 'And you, Sasha? Are you a democrat?'

'No! I am nothing. I observe and I compose. I do not allow myself the luxury of having an opinion. I suppose I thought that would protect me.'

'But you still had to leave your home?'

'Oh yes. You see, my father was a kind and reasonable man with no ambitions other than to be a very good polisher of fine musical instruments. He was not political but he thought like a democrat and he must have said something which was overheard by the wrong person. He had twice survived consumption, my father, but one mild attack of opinion killed him.'

'You sound very bitter, Sasha, but I think I would be bitter, too. Anyone would.'

He hunched himself forwards, his eyes locked onto hers. 'The Tsar's Secret Police were watching us, Lottie, after they killed my father. They were waiting for any one of us to do anything which they could pretend was against the Tsar, and then they would have arrested us too. We heard they were coming to our apartment so we left quickly, within ten minutes of being warned. We wore our warmest clothes and carried very few belongings so as not to arouse suspicions among neighbours who might be spies.'

He stopped, staring at his hands which were resting palms down on the table, and without thinking she reached out and stroked the fingers on his right hand. He continued without looking up at her. 'We were hidden by friends and we learned later that the police arrived half an hour after we left. They broke down our door, found we were not there and took what they wanted, cutlery, pictures, beds, even my piano. They smashed everything else to spite us for escaping.'

'But why did they do all that, Sasha? I don't understand.'

'You don't understand because you are English, Lottie. In Russia rumours can ruin lives and for some reason the Secret Police believe we are dangerous criminals, or perhaps revolutionaries like my father was supposed to be. They would kill us all if they found us, which is why we came to England. England is a very free country. You do not die for having the wrong opinion in England.'

She thought Eve would argue that Polly Dobbs was dying because of her opinions, but she didn't say anything about Polly, and although she wanted to know still more about Sasha she did not want to hear any more about his father or politics. She wanted to talk about his music and his life before his father was arrested. 'I've read that St Petersburg is a beautiful city.'

'Some say it is the most beautiful in the world. It's wonderful in the summer but I prefer it in the winter.' He leaned forward excitedly, his eyes shining and his deep voice suddenly light and energetic. 'It's most beautiful in the winter when the ice decorates the buildings with delicate lace, Lottie, and when the river freezes and we skate under coloured lanterns and to the music of good bands. In the winter you can hear bells ringing everywhere. Big bells from churches and small ones on the sleighs.'

'It sounds wonderful.' She could see it in her mind and

she wished she could go there to see it for herself.

'It is wonderful, Lottie, and whenever I feel sad or lonely I dream I'm back in St Petersburg in winter. I dream I'm a great composer who's captured all the city's beauty in a grand symphony. I can easily hear the music in my head when I'm dreaming, but then I sit at my desk and try to remember it and I can't. It makes me afraid that the city is too beautiful to be captured by anything, even music. It is too beautiful to be captured by anything except the winter itself.'

'And are the winters long in St Petersburg?'

'Yes, and I think they will grow longer.' He slumped back, no longer in his beloved city, no longer dreaming. 'I think that soon there will be a long winter all over Russia. It is coming, and when it has come I will never go back.'

She reached out, took both his hands in hers and looked deep into his eyes, so deep she thought she must be able to see his soul, but all she saw was a young man who had not yet come to terms with losing his father and the home that he loved. He was young and immature, like her, and like her he coped with life's trials by escaping into dreams.

It occurred to her that although she had known Sasha for less than an hour she already had more in common with him than anyone else she knew. 'I have enjoyed talking with you, Lottie, but perhaps we should go back to Mr Verney and your family?'

They stood up, still holding hands, and she wanted to hold him, to comfort him and tell him he could come and talk to her any time he cared to, but she did not do any of those things. She released his hands and looked down at the floor, too embarrassed by her own feelings to look into his eyes in case she had embarrassed him too.

When he did not move she did look up, and then she saw his serious face. 'I have enjoyed talking to you, Lottie. I hope I haven't bored you too much.'

'Not at all, Sasha.'

'Well, thank you for listening. And for giving me food.' He bowed formally and opened the door for her but she asked him to go ahead while she quickly tidied the table where they had eaten.

She watched him leave and realised she was trembling. She was not sure why she was trembling but she knew she liked the feeling.

The door from the back yard opened and Peter Komovsky stepped into the scullery. A different feeling surged through Lottie, a feeling she did not like.

'Miss Forrester.' He greeted her with a nod. 'Please excuse me but I wished to smoke and I thought it was more polite to do that out of doors.'

'Thank you, Mr Komovsky. That's very considerate of you.'

He waved his hand as if wafting away her thanks. 'Peter, please, Miss Forrester, and I apologise for playing with you earlier. I did not realise you were engaged to be married.'

She deliberately waved away his apology. 'Don't let that worry you, Peter, and please call me Lottie.'

'I was watching you through the window,' he said.

Without thinking she reached across the large stone sink and quickly drew the curtains. When she turned back to him she saw him smiling again, but coldly, and it was so disconcerting that she stumbled and would have fallen if he had not grabbed her. His grip was so fierce she looked into his eyes and saw pure anger in them.

'A little too late to close the curtains, Lottie. You cannot undo what's already done.'

'I don't understand what you mean.'

He had pulled her into him so her chin was against his chest, and with one slight twist he pulled her even tighter against him, her breasts pushed against his hard stomach. Then he let her go and stepped back from her.

'I'm sorry, I didn't mean to frighten you, but please understand, Miss Forrester, that Sasha is still very young and he is lonely. You are very beautiful but you have a fiancé. I would not wish to see Sasha suffer any more disappointments.'

'He won't.' She rubbed her arms where he had grabbed

her and thought that tomorrow they would be bruised, but she did not resent what he had done. She found it comforting that he wanted to protect his brother, and wished she had someone so passionate to protect her. 'Don't worry, Peter. I'll make sure he doesn't misunderstand my feelings for him.'

It was only after she had said the words that she realised they could have an entirely different meaning to the one she had meant to convey, but she deliberately did nothing to clarify her meaning.

She heard someone start to play a classical piece on the piano in the front room and guessed Sasha had been made to perform, and that everyone would be expected to play something before the evening was over.

'I think I'll smoke another cigarette. Outside.' Peter said, half cocking an ear to the music. He stepped back out into the yard and closed the door behind him.

She stopped tidying the scullery and went to the front room where the table had been removed and everyone was packed together on the settee and in the two armchairs, on dining chairs wedged into free spaces, or were simply standing wherever there was room. Sasha was seated at the upright piano and Katarina was standing beside him. They both smiled at her as she entered the room and she stood just inside the door, entranced by Sasha's playing.

The old upright had never sounded quite the same and when he finished his first tune everyone applauded and asked him to play more. He played a variety of short pieces, mainly slow and introspective, and he settled a quiet mood which did not reflect the birthday celebrations but did seem appropriate to the last day of a year which had changed the Komovskys' lives.

When he stopped Katarina reached for a violin case which was resting on top of the piano. 'All I have left of my husband are our sons and my violin. He put on polish to make it shine. He lived this way, by putting polish on violin, viola, cello. He was a gentle man.'

Katarina took the violin from its case and held it as if it

were a young baby. It was a warm amber colour, beautifully marked and flawlessly polished. She tuned it quickly, tucked it under her chin and caressed it with her bow. Perfect sound. She played a slow, poignant piece Lottie did not recognise.

The last note seemed to hold everyone spellbound for several seconds and when they recovered enough to applaud Lottie felt compelled to speak. She did so in French to ensure Katarina Komovskaya understood exactly what she said. 'It's a wonderful violin, Mrs Komovskaya, with an exquisite sound and you play it most beautifully.'

Katarina smiled at her and Lottie noticed how her eyes glistened as she answered, also in French. 'Thank you, Lottie. It is a wonderful instrument and it was given to me by a wonderful man, Igor Petrovitch Komovsky. He spent many hours smoothing and polishing the wood and every time I play it and feel the polish he applied next to my skin I feel I am close to him. It is he who makes me play well.'

Suddenly Katarina offered the instrument to her. 'Now, Lottie, you play something for us.'

'I can't, Katarina. I can't play your violin. I wouldn't feel right.'

'Then bring your own,' Katarina insisted, so she had no choice and ran upstairs to fetch her own instrument.

She felt daunted as she tucked her dull violin under her chin. 'I don't play at all well, so please don't expect too much.'

'We don't,' Jamie said, smiling.

She made her first nervous pass with the bow. The instrument squeaked discordantly.

'I told you I wasn't very good.'

Katarina took the bow, tightened it, applied resin and asked for the violin. She drew the bow a few times, tightened strings, did something to the bridge, played a few notes and handed the instrument back. 'Try again, but hold the bow lightly, like a feather and move you fingers like this.'

Lottie felt Katarina's fingers guiding her own, drew the bow, and felt the instrument vibrate.

'There!' Katarina said, smiling.

'But I didn't hear anything.'

'You felt something?' Katarina asked, once again talking in French. 'Then listen with a different ear. Your heart's ear.'

She tried again and heard the thinnest, lightest notes she had ever played lift away from the strings and float away across the room.

'Again,' Katarina ordered.

She played a full scale up and down several times, found the instrument's and the bow's balance, and experimented with them, listened with her mind but found her heart was leading her into combinations of notes which pleased her.

'Good! Good!' Katarina Komovskaya paced around the crowded room, leading her on with her arms, never quite touching her but inducing her into movements close to a slow dance which led them both forwards and backwards and turned them in gentle circles, the music playing all the time. 'That is good, Charlotte. Forget your arms, forget your fingers and play it only with your heart.'

The random notes tumbled into a melody she knew from memory, a melody her mother loved, and she saw her mother smile before her eyes closed in concentration.

'Romance,' Katarina Komovskaya softly breathed the word, 'romance.'

Lottie played softly and with feeling, her emotions focused inwards by not seeing anything outward, heard Katarina whisper that the music was Russian, Tchaikovsky, Canzonetta, the second movement of the concerto he wrote in Italy, heard the door open and shut quietly, but did not look, did not want to lose the feeling she had in her mind and in her heart.

She played on and on, reaching through the movement, soft and lyrical one moment and vital and fast the next, the moonlight music of lovers and the fireside spirit of gypsy dancing, lost in a magic world of emotion and solace.

She heard a deep murmur of appreciation, recognised Sasha's voice, heard him say quietly, 'She plays like an angel.'

She threw herself at the final notes with a gypsy-like flourish.

'No, Sasha,' another, even deeper voice said. 'She plays like a Russian.'

Her eyes opened and she saw Peter smiling at her with his arrogant expression. He stood feet apart, hands on slim hips. He looked the brigand of story books, the robber baron of operetta; daring and dangerous, and she noticed his soft leather knee-high boots shuffle as his feet wanted to dance.

He snuffed his heels together and bowed very formally. 'My full respects to you, Miss Forrester. You have my undying admiration. I would die for someone who brings Mother Russia into my heart so sweetly.'

He spoke English, for all to hear, and once again she blushed.

'Let us dance,' he said suddenly. 'In the yard. Play, Mama. Play like a gypsy. Sasha! Paul! Come on, both of you. Now!'

He was impossible to resist and he led the exodus to the back yard. Someone demanded candles and candles were found.

Katarina played and her sons danced; Paul haltingly, Sasha gracefully, but Peter violently – throwing his body into wild contortions, yelling, clapping his hands and shuffling his feet so fast and so high that he seemed to defy gravity.

Lottie found herself caught up in the excitement and rhythm and although she avoided Peter's constant invitations to join in the wild dancing she swayed with the sound, tapped out the rhythm with her feet, clapped to it with her hands and swung her head as she sung out wordless sounds. The atmosphere was exotic, intoxicating, and she was lost to it, her blood pulsing faster and faster, her hands clapping ever louder, ever more frantic.

In her mind she was no longer in Angel Street, she was in a gypsy camp deep in Russia.

'Charlotte?' she heard Albert and the dream was shattered.

'Yes?'

'It's late and I must leave.'

'I'll see you out.' She waited until he had said goodbye to everyone and was almost drawn into the dancing by Peter who seemed to have endless energy, and she walked to the front door with him.

'I love you very much, Charlotte. You do know that, don't you?'

'Yes, of course I do.' She wondered why he had chosen this moment to tell her something he hardly ever mentioned.

He kissed her cheek, opened the door, and left without commenting on her birthday, without saying whether or not he had enjoyed himself and without wishing her a happy New Year. She ran the few steps down the path and leaned on the gate, watching him stride away, but he did not look back and she did not call after him.

She heard the front-room clock strike eleven and realised how little time she had spent with him during the last two hours. Then she realised she had not told him about the man who had followed her. She had not even thought about the man since the Komovskys had arrived, and she had hardly thought about Albert since they arrived.

She walked back indoors, a little unhappy because she felt she had been disloyal to him. She found the music and dancing had stopped and everyone was trailing back into the house.

Her mother slipped one arm around her and the other around Eve. 'Have you enjoyed your birthdays?'

'Oh, yes, Mama,' she said honestly and hoped her enthusiasm would hide Eve's quieter response.

Suddenly it was midnight. The Komovskys looked on cautiously as doors were opened back and front and lumps of coal were carried in and the whole family rushed out into the road to see if they could find a chimney sweep who might just happen to be passing in the middle of the night. Neighbours also gathered in the street, every bell in London seemed to join in repetitive peels, and everyone milled about kissing everyone else, not something Lottie enjoyed until she suddenly faced Sasha.

'May I kiss you, Lottie, as a friend?'

She nodded, felt his hands hold her arms much as Peter had held her but gently, and saw his face come towards hers. She meant to allow him to kiss her cheek but something distracted her and she turned her face at the very last moment. His lips touched hers, lightly, momentarily, too briefly, but she felt them and felt the warmth surge through her own lips. He pulled away. She smelled the tang of strong tobacco before she saw Peter watching her kiss his brother.

Something she did not understand made her skin tingle with excitement.

She lay awake. Even though the house was silent she could hear music; lyrical, plaintive music or fiery gypsy tunes. She did not see Albert, she saw Sasha's and Peter's faces. She walked to the window and looked down into the dark yard and saw a gypsy camp, raised her eyes to look over the roofs opposite and saw St Petersburg's skyline.

She told herself it was ridiculous. Albert could give her everything she ever wanted, a gracious home, money, respectability, and all without demanding too much in return.

What could Peter or Sasha give her?

Nothing. Except excitement.

Peter scared her. She was sure he was a bandit who would take everything he wanted and give little in return, but there was something about him that made her feel different, something which made her scared of what *she* might do if she was free.

Sasha charmed her with his honesty and his dreams, but that was all they were, dreams. One day he would grow up and put his dreams away, just as she knew she would have to, and what could he offer her then? Nothing. Nothing at all.

So she tried to forget him and tried to go to sleep thinking of Albert, but she could not.

In her head she heard nothing but a great symphony which had not yet been written.

CHAPTER 5

London, 1913

It was the first day of 1913, and Eve was astonished to wake up to the sound of Lottie singing. Various choruses drifted up to her as Lottie moved from the scullery to the kitchen, rattling plates and crockery as she helped prepare breakfast.

She slipped into her dressing-gown, padded downstairs and grimaced as Lottie sang an off-key version of 'Waiting for the Robert E. Lee'.

'You sound happy this morning?'

'I feel happy.'

'Any particular reason?'

'That's exactly what Mama asked. I woke up feeling happy, that's all.'

'Good.' Eve took some warm water up to her room, washed and dressed, and by the time she came down for breakfast everyone else was gathered around the table, everyone silent except for Lottie whose bright mood was irritating the rest of them.

She was surprised to find Lottie so cheerful because she had overheard the short conversation she had had with Albert as they parted the previous night and it was obvious

74

to her that Albert was not happy with the way Lottie had been behaving towards Sasha Komovsky. Albert sounded unusually abrupt with Lottie and it was quite clear that he was angry enough to call off the engagement. She thought that would have left Lottie in a miserable mood, not a happy one, and she wondered if Lottie even realised how much she had upset Albert.

Also, yesterday morning Lottie had been stiff with the fear of being followed. The danger was still there if the threat was real, and Eve wondered once again if the threat was imagined.

She jumped as someone touched her arm.

'I'm sorry, dear, I didn't mean to startle you,' her mother apologised.

'Sorry Mama, I was miles away.'

'Thinking about young Polly Dobbs?'

'Yes.' She lied to save embarrassment and took the opportunity to excuse herself by saying she was eager to find out how Polly was.

Lottie envied the way everyone treated Eve as she left to find out whether or not Polly Dobbs was still alive. 'No, it isn't a good way to start a new year,' she heard her aunt say flatly, and assumed she was talking about Polly Dobbs, so she made a sympathetic remark.

'Pardon?' her aunt said and everyone stared at her.

'I said it must be awful for Eve to see someone our own age die.'

'We were talking about the refuge, Lottie,' her mother said impatiently. 'Weren't you listening?'

'No, I was thinking about Eve.'

'Oh,' her mother said without asking why, and turned back to Aunt Lizzie. 'We'll have to pay Kathleen a week's wages but she may as well leave today so she can look for another job. It's fortunate she didn't live in or she'd be another one who'd have to find somewhere to live.'

Lottie was even more confused. 'Is that Mrs Murphy? Why're you sacking her?'

This time her father explained, after sighing impatiently.

'Are you deaf or still half asleep, Lottie? The Trustees are insisting the refuge is shut down.'

'Why?' She was astonished when they told her, even more so when she learned that the mission might also be closed later in the year. 'How many women are in the refuge at the moment?'

Aunt Lizzie answered. 'Five, and ten children, but we think we know of a house they may be able to rent. And we're thinking of asking Mrs Komovskaya and Paul if they'd like to move in here and sleep in the top back room for a while. The Trustees want her out of the mission.'

A tremor of excitement ran through Lottie. If Katarina Komovskaya moved in Sasha would visit her, and that would be fun!

'I can see you like that idea,' her father said flatly. 'But don't think it'll be all parties and violin playing. Once Mrs Murphy's left someone's going to have to spend nights at the mission, and that means your mother, Lizzie and maybe Eve, so you'll have to help more around the house, my girl.'

'Couldn't I help at the mission?' She grabbed at the chance to be treated like Eve.

'To avoid working in the house?' her father asked sourly.

'No! To take my turn helping at the mission.' She saw the way they all looked at each other and knew they would not agree.

'And what would you do if there was any trouble, Lottie?' her father said in an exasperated voice. 'We've enough trouble looking after you as it is, walking you to and from work. There's no point in asking for even more trouble by sending you over to the mission, is there?'

'No, I suppose not.' She always wilted under his bullying, and as there was nothing she could do to help she did not see any point in listening to the rest of the conversation.

She slipped back into herself and hoped she had not upset Albert too much. He seemed to be her only hope of ever escaping from this house and the family which not only did not trust her to do anything responsible but did not seem to believe her when she told them she was in danger.

76

Albert had left in a bad mood last night, but she told herself he would come back and probably apologise to her. Albert was predictable, and kind, and he did not expect too much from her. She knew he would always treat her in much the same way as she used to treat her favourite childhood doll.

Lottie heard the supervisor's bell ring to mark the end of the day, tidied her desk, wrapped herself up in her coat and hat, and stepped out into the dark street. A match flared and died, and then another, her father's signal that he was watching her.

She turned and walked through the badly-lit streets. She especially noticed the smell of the river and felt the evening mist freezing her face, but she thought that must be nothing compared to the winter cold in St Petersburg, and having had the thought she could not remove it from her mind.

The streets all looked similar in that they were dark and deserted and the mist closed around the few streetlamps and stopped them spreading their light. The pavements were wet and the roads slippery whether they were made of cobbles or wooden blocks, but although she noticed it all she did not pay any attention to it. Her mind was in St Petersburg and she was straining to hear the music she had heard the night before in her sleep. She forgot to listen for footsteps which might be following her, and even forgot that her father was there to protect her.

She forgot him so completely that, for just a moment, she was surprised to see him standing behind her on the underground station platform.

A train stopped and she stepped into the nearest carriage, her father behind her, and when she reached the station near their home she left the train and he followed, still without speaking. He followed her all the way up Mile Hill and did not approach her until they had passed under the little angel on the street corner.

'Still no sign of anyone, Lottie?' her father said sharply as he walked by her side.

'No, Papa.' She saw him nod and knew he did not really

77

believe she had ever been followed.

A few minutes after they reached home her father confirmed her thoughts. She overheard him telling her mother that he was wasting his time.

The evening passed very slowly. No one said very much, either to each other or to her, and she felt the strained atmosphere was her fault because she had upset her father.

She hoped Albert would come and apologise for leaving so abruptly the night before, or even to give her an opportunity to apologise to him – but he did not call and that simply added to her misery.

She tried to escape from the atmosphere and her own mood by reading, but she could not concentrate so she went to bed early.

Being alone made her feel worse. Her bedroom was directly above the kitchen where the others sat and every time she heard a murmur of conversation she strained to hear if they were talking about her.

After everyone else had gone to bed she still lay awake, scared that she might be followed again and frustrated that no one believed her story.

She tried to console herself by thinking that everyone would have to believe she was telling the truth if she was attacked by the man who had followed her. The thought did not console her, it made her feel worse and it frightened her so much she listened to every creak the house gave. Imaginary figures climbed the stairs to her bedroom and crept into her dreams.

She fell asleep and did not know she was screaming until her father was standing over her, and when she saw the look he exchanged with her mother she could have screamed again.

She was telling the truth. She *was*!

CHAPTER 6

———————

Eve heard Lottie scream, but before she woke fully she thought it was Polly Dobbs, and that thought kept recurring throughout the night.

She woke early and rushed to the hospital to be told that Polly Dobbs had died in her sleep, and that Polly's brother and one of her sisters were waiting downstairs and wanted to talk to her.

She went to see them immediately and found them sitting on a bench near the hospital's public entrance.

'Lou?'

'Morning, Miss Forrester.' Lou stood up, and the young man at her side unravelled his long legs and stood with her. 'This is Tom, my big brother.'

Eve shook the man's strong hand. 'Good morning, Mr Dobbs. I'm pleased to meet you but I'm terribly sorry. You're too late to see Polly.'

'It's all right, Miss Forrester, I know. I would've come sooner but Polly wouldn't have wanted to see me. We didn't get on.' He looked her straight in the eyes, on a level with hers and shrugged his wide shoulders. 'I can't stand me dad so I shoved off to sea as soon as I was old enough, and Polly never forgave me.'

'You're a sailor?' She remembered Robert Braithewaite had said Tom Dobbs worked in the docks.

'Was. I'm a lighterman now, down on the docks. Gave up the sea so I could keep a bit of an eye on Lou and the girls after me mum died. Lou kept in touch with me although Polly wouldn't.'

'Tom gives us money,' Lou said, and squeezed her brother's arm. 'We couldn't manage without him.'

Eve noticed the pride in Lou's voice and the sadness in her eyes, and told her, 'Polly's been taken to the mortuary and I don't know if they'll let you see her.'

'We don't want to,' Lou said flatly. 'A policeman came and told us Pol was dead and Dad sent me with a letter for you, Miss Forrester.'

Eve took the letter, a pencilled note on a folded scrap of paper which Lou pulled from inside her cheap coat. She read it quickly, and because it did not seem that either Lou or Tom knew what it was about she read it out to them. 'Dear Miss Forrester, can you please get the Parish to do the burial. There will not be any mourners. Mr Dobbs.'

Tom Dobbs sighed. 'Typical! I'll do it, Miss Forrester, we can't expect you to.'

'I don't mind, Mr Dobbs. Really, I don't.' Far from minding she was eager to help.

'Perhaps we can do it between us?' he suggested and she nodded.

Lou offered her some coins. 'The money you left, Miss Forrester, for the cab.'

'Keep it, Lou, for the children. I'd forgotten all about it.'

'I'd rather not, miss, if you don't mind.' Lou pushed the coins into her hand. 'You left it for me dad to come and see Polly. He didn't use it even though he should have, and now it'd seem wrong to use it for anything else. Now it's too late.'

She saw Lou was close to tears so she put her arm around her shoulders. 'Come on, Lou. Let's get you and Tom something warm to eat and drink.'

Lou shook her head. 'Thank you, miss, but I can't stop.

I've got to get off to work, you see, but you will help Tom bury Pol, won't you? Without letting me dad know because he'll go up the wall if he finds out I'm seeing Tom?'

'Of course,' Eve nodded. 'But surely he won't mind Tom—'

'He would,' Tom Dobbs interrupted her. 'Dad's got no time for me, Miss Forrester. Never has had.'

'No.' Lou looked up at her. 'Especially after Tom stopped Dad from putting me in an asylum.'

'Pardon?' She was not sure she had heard properly, but Lou quickly explained what had happened.

'I got raped at our old place, Miss Forrester, when I was fifteen. The boy was sixteen and he lived upstairs with his mother but, of course, they said he hadn't done it and when they knew I was pregnant they spread stories about me going with half the men in London. Lies, like, but Dad believed them and he wanted to get me committed. Anyway, Tom stopped him and Pol found us the new place to live, south of the water where no one knew us. I stayed indoors with Dad 'til I had the baby.'

'Oh, Lou.' She squeezed the girl's shoulders. Lou shrugged. 'Little girl, she was, very *small*. Ever so pretty. Pol found someone to give her to, miles away so it'd never get traced back.'

Lou burst into tears and Tom wrapped his arms around her. 'Dad still blames Lou for letting him down, Miss Forrester. Never lets her forget it, and he's never forgiven me for stopping him having her put away. And Pol never forgave me for not being there to take proper care of Lou. And I don't reckon I'll ever forgive meself for not sticking around to look after them all.'

Eve nodded, shocked by everything new she had learned, and she promised Lou she would keep the funeral arrangements secret. She agreed to meet Tom the next day to make the arrangements and just as they were all about to part she suddenly remembered something. 'Flowers, Lou? What flowers did Polly like?'

'Violets. She really loved violets. That was our mum's name, Violet.'

'It's Lady Braithewaite's name, too.'

'Yes.' Lou's expression changed. 'I sometimes wondered if that's why she thought Lady Braithewaite was so good. Anyway, goodbye, Miss Forrester, and thanks for all you did for Pol.'

'I didn't do much for her, Lou. Not enough, anyway.' She shrugged, shook hands with Lou and Tom Dobbs, then turned and reported back for work.

It seemed a long day, and in the middle of the afternoon Sister handed her a brown-paper parcel which held Polly Dobbs's belongings. She was supposed to pass it on to the family but the paper was not really big enough and she could see Polly's suffragette sash poking through one of the joins.

Eve remembered how proud Polly had been of the sash and felt it deserved more than being thrust into a paper parcel, so she took it out, folded it carefully and put in her cloak pocket when she left for home.

Eve turned towards home. The pavements were busy with the early evening rush and the roads were crowded with carts and wagons, motor-cars, buses and trams. Above the traffic noise an organ grinder churned out an erratic rendition of Alexander's Ragtime Band. The charred odour of roast chestnuts and the homely smell of baked potatoes mixed with the traffic fumes.

It was all very ordinary, sights and smells that made up a part of her everyday life, but Polly Dobbs who had been no older than her, would never see or hear or smell any of this ever again.

She put the thought away. She was tired and did not want to think about anything so she walked fast and concentrated only on avoiding the other pedestrians and not getting run over when she crossed the roads.

The blustery evening air was damp, threatening rain, and when the rain did come it came quickly. A sudden squall whipped Eve out of her reverie. She came to instantly and the first thing she saw was Holloway Prison, the women's prison.

She walked passed it every day and had always accepted it as a building where criminals were locked in.

Now she saw it as something else.

It was also a building meant to keep people out. There were complaints about forced feeding reported in the newspapers, and questions raised in Parliament. Men and women campaigned to have it stopped, and foreign governments sent writs criticising the British Government for allowing it to continue, but the torture was continued not in the open but behind the thick stone walls which muffled the women's screams and where the public could not see what was happening.

She looked at the high wooden doors with their black metal studs reinforcing the thick planks, and as she stared the doors trundled open.

A small black van drawn by a single horse cut through the heavy traffic. The police driver seemed to leave the horse to steer itself towards the prison gates while he constantly twisted around in his seat, presumably watching for any troublemakers who might attack him or try to free his passengers. Meanwhile his passengers waved their hands and lace-edged handkerchiefs between the bars fixed over openings in the van's sides. Occasionally a flash of green and white and violet revealed a suffragette sash being waved defiantly, its last outing before it was confiscated by the warders.

She felt Polly's sash in her pocket and was tempted to take it out and wave back, but common sense and an even stronger feeling not to offend the law stopped her. Then, above the sound of the traffic, she heard women singing.

'La Marseillaise', the international anthem sung by everyone who saw themselves fighting for freedom.

The van passed through the gates and they closed behind it, snuffing out the sound of the women's voices.

She squeezed Polly's sash, and made a decision. 'It's wrong,' she said out loud.

'Pardon, miss?' A man's voice asked, and she turned and saw a policeman.

'Nothing,' she said. 'I was thinking out loud.'

'Well, I'll 'ave to ask you to move along please, miss. You've been standing 'ere too long. Outside the prison, like.'

'I'm sorry, Constable. I didn't realise there was a law against standing still,' she smiled.

'Now, now, miss. There isn't, but we don't want any trouble, do we? Not 'ere. Not outside the prison.'

'No, we don't want any trouble, Constable, especially not here, outside the prison.' She turned to leave and as she did so her cloak swung open and revealed her nurse's apron.

The policeman noticed and apologised immediately. 'I didn't realise you were a nurse, miss. I thought you might be one o' them suffrygettes.'

'I am, Constable. I'm both.'

He looked uneasy, as if he was not sure what to do. 'How long 'ave you been a suffrygette, miss?'

'I should think for about a minute, Constable. But don't worry, I'm not about to burn anything down or smash any windows. I'm not that sort of suffragette.'

'I'm very pleased to 'ear it, miss.' He smiled and she smiled back. 'Now, miss, can I 'elp you across the road? It's a bit dodgy in this rain.'

'Thank you very much.' She let him take her arm and lead her across the double junction opposite the prison, and she thanked him again when they reached the far side.

'My pleasure, miss.' He touched the rim of his helmet. 'Now you carry on being the sort of suffrygette what don't smash an' burn things, an' don't cause trouble, eh?'

'I'll try,' she said honestly, squeezed the sash again, and walked away towards home.

With any luck she would not need to burn and smash things. The suffragettes had called a truce because the Government had all but guaranteed the vote for women. With any luck all she would have to do was sign petitions and go to public meetings, but she knew that if the Goverment did not keep its word she would burn and smash things and do all she could to win the vote.

Winning the vote was only the beginning. The right to elect whoever they wanted to represent them in Parliament would bring women into politics, make the men who made the laws listen to women's views.

It was 1913 and the country was changing. And Eve wanted to be a part of a movement which would influence that change. She walked home with a new sense of purpose, inspired by Polly's example and fuelled by Lady Braithewaite's invitation to a Women's Freedom League meeting

Her mother opened the door to her and helped her off with her wet cloak. 'There's a large bunch of flowers in the kitchen. A young man brought them for you.'

'Flowers? Young man? Who?'

'A doctor. Doctor Braithewaite. He told me about Polly Dobbs dying, dear, and said the flowers might help you to feel a little better.' Her mother looked sad. 'I'm sorry about your friend. Was it awful?'

She was so surprised by the flowers and Robert's kindness that she hardly heard her mother's question.

'No, she died in her sleep. During the night.'

'Did her father come?'

'No, but he sent Polly's sister Lou with a note asking me to arrange for Polly to be buried. On the Parish, as he put it.'

'And will you?'

'I'll help the brother, Tom. Mr Dobbs doesn't want anything to do with him, either. Neither did Polly apparently.'

'Very sad, dear.' Her mother ruminated for several moments, then seemed to dismiss the Dobbs family and concentrate on her own. 'I assume this young man's a doctor from the hospital?'

'No, Mama, he's not from the hospital, but you can see he is very kind and thoughtful.'

'And when will you see your doctor again?' Rose asked in a teasing voice.

'He's not *my* doctor, Mama. He's simply *a* doctor.'

'But you are blushing, Eve.' Her mother smiled, a little triumphantly.

Eve was blushing because she was flattered that Robert Braithewaite had thought about her and gone out of his way to deliver flowers to her. She had never been given flowers before and they had evoked emotions which she thought Robert Braithewaite probably had not intended to evoke, but in spite of herself she hoped he had.

'I only met him two days ago, and I only met him then because his mother came to visit Polly.'

'Doctor Braithewaite?' her mother frowned. 'I see. He's Lady Braithewaite's son. The woman we were talking about the other day?'

Here was an opportunity to bring everything out into the open. 'Yes, Mama. I met her two nights ago and she seems very nice. She's not at all like the woman the newspapers write about.' Eve paused. 'She's asked me to go to a meeting at her house tomorrow night.'

'And are you going?'

'I'd like to, but I know how you feel about her.' She shrugged.

'Just be careful, dear. We've enough to worry about at the moment and we don't want any more. We closed the refuge today. Your Aunt Lizzie's been out all day telling people we can only help the genuinely destitute and that doesn't include women who want to leave violent homes.'

'I'm sorry, Mama. That's awful, after all the work you've put in.'

Her mother sighed. 'It'll be worse if we have to turn someone away from the doors.'

Eve shuddered at the thought. 'Will you really have to do that. How're the Trustees to know if you let someone in?'

'They will, dear. They will.' Her mother frowned. 'The Trustees know much more than they should, Eve, so it's obvious someone's watching us and telling them what's happening.'

'But who?'

Her mother shrugged. 'I know Mr Butcher spoke to Mr

Buddelscome, but I don't think the Trustees would rely totally on him.'

'Then who else is there, Mama? And why would they do it?'

Her mother shrugged again and would not say, but this time Eve had an odd feeling that her mother knew exactly why.

Eve looked up from the book she was reading when her father brought Lottie home and they joined her in the kitchen. 'Everything all right, Papa? Did you see anyone, Lottie?'

'Nah!' Her father snorted dismissively.

The next day Sister allowed Eve to leave work early because she had promised to help Tom Dobbs arrange Polly's funeral. Tom was waiting for her outside the hospital, but after he had taken her on a bus and explained his plans she realised that he did not really need her help.

'Polly and I didn't get on, Miss Forrester, but I'm not having her buried like a pauper just to please Dad. I'll see if I can get her buried next to Mum, they'd both've liked that.'

He took her to a shabby undertakers on a dirty back street in Stepney, and after the arrangements had been made they went to a corner tea house which seemed clean and quite refined and totally out of character with the rest of the area.

It was clear that the women who ran the shop knew Tom and with very little pressing he admitted he lived around the corner.

'I lodge with an elderly couple, Sid and Cissie Jackson. Well, I wouldn't call it lodging, not really. They treat me more like their grown up son. Keep trying to marry me off.' Tom laughed quietly.

'You've never felt like marrying?' she asked for something to say and not really sure why she did not feel comfortable in his company.

'Never found the right young lady,' he said simply, looking her straight in the eyes. 'Don't want to make the same mistake as my Mum and Dad. They spent their whole lives arguing. Well, more than arguing, they had full blown rows.'

Eve thought the Dobbs's parents could not have spent all their time arguing because they had raised a house full of children, but although she did not say anything Tom seemed to guess what she was thinking.

'Giving Mum kids was Dad's way of keeping her down, Miss Forrester. He overdid it and killed her in the end, then went on the bottle, had an accident at work and crippled himself. I reckon it was God's way of paying him back for what he did to Mum when she was alive.'

'So you believe in a vengeful God, Mr Dobbs?'

'Yeah.' He nodded and looked serious. 'If God wasn't vengeful He'd allow us to forget things we don't want to remember, Miss Forrester, but He doesn't. He makes sure we remember all sorts of things we'd rather forget.'

'That's conscience, Mr Dobbs,' she said.

'No, it's spiteful, Miss Forrester.'

She shrugged. She could not argue with his point of view because she had not had time to think it through, but she was impressed that somehow, in spite of their differences and poverty, Mr and Mrs Dobbs had managed to raise a family of thinkers.

'Miss Forrester, would you care to come and meet Sid and Cissie? I'm sure they'd make you welcome and you could eat with us. Then, perhaps, we could go out together for the evening.'

'No, I can't.' She did not think to soften her refusal, but she realised her abruptness was rude and she owed him some sort of explanation. 'I've already arranged something for this evening.'

'Tomorrow then? It's Saturday?'

'No. I'm working, and then—'

'Sunday?'

'Church. And the mission in the afternoon.'

'Monday?'

'No.'

'Tuesday?'

'I'll see you at the funeral on Tuesday.'

'And afterwards?'

'I don't think so, Mr Dobbs.'

'Any other day? Any other time?'

'I don't think so, Mr Dobbs,' she said again firmly, but politely.

'Oh,' he said, not at all offended and seemingly resigned to her refusals. 'Shame. I think we'd get along fine.'

'Perhaps we would, but I just don't have any time at the moment, Mr Dobbs.'

'You can call me Tom, Miss Forrester. That doesn't mean you'll have to marry me, you know.' He grinned and suggested that if she was ready to go home he would see her to a station or bus stop.

She smiled, accepted his offer, and called him Tom.

Lady Braithewaite's house was so large and opulent that it daunted Eve and made her acutely conscious of the surroundings she herself had grown up in.

An overly formal man opened the door to her and ushered her into the grand hall just as Lady Braithewaite ran down the stairs and saw her.

'Nurse Forrester! So pleased you could join us. Follow me.'

She did as she was told and followed her into the large, plant-filled conservatory, where a woman in a domestic uniform bobbed a brief curtsey.

'Tea for Miss Forrester and myself here, in the garden salon, Carter. And tell Doctor Robert to come down and introduce himself in an hour, not before. Miss Forrester and I have things to discuss.'

The maid disappeared.

During the next hour Eve was introduced to six well dressed women who arrived at intervals and were shown through to the garden salon. Between the interruptions she answered all the questions Lady Braithewaite asked and quietly defended her opinions when her hostess or any of the other women challenged her replies.

She had the impression she was being interviewed for some unknown position, an impression borne out when Lady Braithewaite cast an enquiring glance at each of the other ladies present, an enquiry greeted unanimously by silent nods.

'Well, Miss Forrester, we had planned a meeting to discuss further tactics but the possibility of your coming caused us to reconsider certain aspects of our current philosophy. Would you care to join our leadership committee?'

She was stunned, unsure what she had done to warrant the invitation.

'What would joining your committee entail?'

'Actively trying to make this Government see sense and give women the right to vote, explaining the issues to women in a way they can readily understand, and helping us to plan campaigns for future issues once we have the right to vote.' Lady Braithewaite had ticked of the issues on her fingers. 'You see, Miss Forrester, far too many women see the campaign to win the vote as an end in itself. It isn't, and unless we decide exactly what needs to be changed and educate women to use their votes to effect those changes as soon as possible the movement will lose its impetus and all the struggles and sacrifices will have been wasted.'

'I agree.'

'Then allow me to welcome you to our committee.' Lady Braithewaite smiled, and all the other women murmured their own words of welcome.

Eve found herself in an awkward situation; she had simply meant that she agreed with Lady Braithewaite's views, not that she agreed to join the committee. Her parents would not approve and the hospital Board might make her resign if they found out. She took a deep breath and prepared to explain, but everyone was distracted as Robert came through the door and the moment was lost.

'Miss Forrester's agreed to join our committee, Robert.' Lady Braithwaite greeted him with the news, and Eve saw her opportunity fade even further.

Robert nodded and cast her a concerned look, and she realised how attractive he was, and how working on his mother's committee would provide further opportunities to see him. He greeted the other ladies as he crossed the floor, but she was the only one whose hand he shook.

'Miss Forrester, I warned you not to allow my mother to lead you astray, but you obviously did not listen. Now, I don't think I should offer you congratulations so much as commiserations.' He smiled but his eyes were serious.

'I'm too surprised to accept either, Doctor Braithewaite,' she said, and his mother applauded her reply.

'Spoken like a natural politician,' Lady Braithewaite laughed. 'And that could be your destiny, Miss Forrester.'

She looked at Robert's mother, astonished by what she had said. 'I rather doubt that, Lady Braithewaite, but if I was to become a politician I'd be a socialist.'

'You mean you wouldn't be one of us, Miss Forrester?' Lady Braithewaite asked calmly.

'Yes.' She nodded, and eyed the assembly for individual reactions.

The only clear reaction came from the oldest lady, dressed in different shades of grey and green which gave her a mellow, almost forest-like aura. 'We're part of the *Women*'s Freedom Movement, Miss Forrester, not the Liberal Women's or Tory Women's or even the English Women's Freedom Movement. Because we all come from similar backgrounds it's difficult for us to promote that concept, and quite frankly we couldn't ask most girls of your background to join us because they'd simply look, feel and sound out of place. You don't. That's why we *need* you. No one else will do.'

Eve would have mistrusted anyone else who told her that, even Lady Braithewaite, but she was sure this woman was speaking the truth. Quite suddenly she trembled with excitement.

'You'll find the Committee will encourage you to raise any items which interest you and we'll all ask for your opinions on matters where you should be better informed than the rest of us, Miss Forrester. We'll teach you how to speak at meetings and ask you to join marches and protests and take part in some other activities, but not bombings or fire-raising since you object to those tactics.' Lady Braithewaite smiled.

'If the Franchise Bill is passed there'll be no need for any more protests anyway,' Eve said confidently, and saw Lady Braithewaite's expression change.

'*If* it's passed, Miss Forrester. Don't rely on that too much, we're all quite sure the Government'll find a way to avoid the issue.'

Eve turned as Robert spoke. 'Pray the Government sees sense, Miss Forrester, because if they don't Emmeline Pankhurst and my mother plan to wage war on them. Isn't that so, mother?'

'Of course. I'll fight them as I would any enemy.'

A tea-trolley was wheeled in and all talk of politics was overwhelmed by social chatter.

She thanked Robert for the flowers he had given her and told him about the Dobbs family and the Komovskys, and found he was very easy to talk to.

The first time she had met him it had been too dark to see him properly but now she could see him clearly. He was tall and broad and looked around thirty years old. His curly hair was dark brown like his eyes, his finely featured face was open and honest. As she studied him his eyes suddenly locked onto hers. She felt herself blush, and saw him smile. He leaned towards her and looked slyly to the left and right. 'Let me know when you're ready to leave and I'll arrange for Perkins to drive you home, Miss Forrester.'

'No, I couldn't put him to all that trouble.'

'It's what he's paid for, Miss Forrester. Besides, it'll give me an excuse to come with you so we can talk some more.'

She nodded, and suggested they leave immediately.

The journey home seemed to take no time at all and she was sorry when it was over. She had told Robert all about herself, and her family and the mission, and given him details of Polly's funeral so he could pass them on to his mother whom she thought might want to attend. She had told him so much about her life but he had told her nothing about his.

He accompanied her to the front door and once again refused her invitation to come inside, apologising and explaining that he had an early surgery to attend and needed to go home to bed.

When they parted she walked back down the short path and hoped again that he would turn back and wave, which he did, and once more she watched the car until it was out of sight.

She walked back to the front door, her heart and stomach and senses bubbling with a strange excitement, and found it hard to stop herself smiling.

She realised now why she felt so at ease with Robert Braithewaite but uncomfortable with Tom Dobbs. Tom was a nice man, honest, straightforward and quite good-looking, but she was not in love with him.

CHAPTER 7

It was late on Sunday afternoon and Eve was alone with her aunt in the mission office.

'It's not been a good week, has it, Aunt Lizzie?'

'I've known worse. Things are sorting themselves out. Mr Buddelscome seems satisfied with what we've done here, Florrie Biggs and the other women are all safely ensconced in a house right over in Lewisham and Mrs Murphy's already found herself another job. Katarina's moving in with us tomorrow and, would you believe, Mr Butcher's been over to apologise for causing such a fuss. Bit late, of course, but at least it's something.' Her aunt spoke without looking up from the file she was reading.

'Do you trust him?'

'Why not?'

'I think Mama believes he might be spying on you and reporting back to Mr Buddelscome.'

'Well, there's not much to report back now, is there? And in future we're going to make sure we don't do anything to upset the Trustees. Maybe, if we're good girls, we can persuade them not to sell.' Her aunt finally looked towards her, over the top of her spectacles which had slipped almost to the end of her prominent nose. 'Talking of being good girls your mother tells me you've joined the mad Women's League. When are you going to burn down Parliament?'

'I'm not. At least I hope I'm not.'

'So do I, Eve. Your mother's got enough to worry about as it is. She doesn't need you to bring even more trouble home.'

'I'll try not to. Anyway, if the Franchise Bill goes through—'

'It won't,' her aunt said flatly. 'They'll find a reason to reject it.'

'You sound disappointed, Aunt.'

Her aunt took her glasses off. 'Well, of course I'll be disappointed if it's rejected. I support the suffrage movement in principle and I'd like to be more active but I'm responsible for this place and the two don't go together. If the Trustees even suspected that I, or your mother, were actively involved in politics they'd throw us out of here quicker than you could blink. And if they suspected we were using this place for any political activity they'd close it down. They've made it clear they can't afford to upset the benefactors, who're men who wouldn't support the suffrage movement or the Socialist cause. That's another reason why I want you to be careful. What you do could rebound on us here. And it could cost you your job if the hospital find out.'

'Yes, I know,' she said.

Lottie breathed an enormous sigh of relief when she opened the front door and saw that Albert had come after all.

'Come in, Albert. You're later than usual.' She almost dragged him into the hall, called out to tell her mother he was there, and guided him into the front room as the clock struck four.

She waited for him to take his coat off, but he did not.

'I'm sorry I'm late, Charlotte, but I've something important to say and I've been walking about trying to find the right words.'

Finally, she thought, he is going to set the date for our wedding.

But he did not; and she stared at him before repeating what he had said to make sure she had understood him. 'You think we should suspend our engagement until we're both sure we really want to get married?'

He looked uncomfortable and nodded.

'But I thought you were sure, Albert?'

'So did I, Charlotte, but the more I think about it the less sure I am.'

'Why? Is it because . . .' she faltered, and blushed.

'In part, Charlotte.' He saved her the embarrassment of mentioning her difficulties. 'I can't go through life waiting for permission to kiss you or touch you, but it's not only that. It's also because I'm not sure you love me, at least not as much as I love you. I'm not sure you'll be happy with me.'

'I do and I will. I know I will.'

'I'm not so certain, and it's a big step to take if we're wrong for each other.'

'Oh, Albert?' She could not hold back tears which formed quickly and tumbled out of her eyes. 'We're not wrong for each other. We're not . . .'

She heard the door open, sensed someone had come in, heard her mother apologise and the door close again.

'I really feel we need more time, Charl—'

She threw herself into his arms and smothered his mouth with hers, but she knew that was a mistake even before their lips touched.

Even under these circumstances she felt nothing. No thrill, no warmth, no comfort or enjoyment.

Albert explained his decision to her parents and left soon afterwards, not even stopping for his usual Sunday tea. He left her with only a vague promise that he would be in touch in a week or two. Or three.

She spent the evening service praying that he would be waiting for her when she left the church but he was not, so she went to bed early and cried herself to sleep, sensing she was trapped for ever in a half life that would only make her more and more miserable.

She woke in the dark early hours and tried to console herself by thinking about Sasha, but somehow she could no longer see him as a romantic composer who would one day write a brilliant symphony about the beautiful city he loved. Now she saw him quite clearly as he was; a poor Russian waiter who dreamed about going back to a country he was scared to return to, and of writing music even he had said was beyond his ability.

She realised suddenly that she was facing reality. She did not like it, but she was determined not to run away from it, and she promised herself she would do all she could to avoid taking refuge in her dreams.

Monday morning was cold and miserable, the wind spattering rain against the kitchen window and blowing draughts between the sashes so the curtains twitched as though they were nervous.

'What's wrong, Lottie?' Her father noticed she was twitching as much as the curtains.

'I didn't sleep much, Papa.'

'Thinking about Albert?' he asked in a matter of fact way.

She nodded.

'Sensible fellow.' Her father flicked his newspaper to fold it better. 'Best be sure before you marry. As sure as you can be, anyway.'

His words did not give her much comfort, and moments later he made matters worse.

'About tonight, when you finish work. You know Mrs Komovskaya's moving in today, up on the top floor? Well, Lizzie's decided she'll move into the back room so Mrs Komovskaya and Paul can share the bigger front room, but it means we've got to shift a lot of furniture about and bring in a couple of beds and other bits of furniture for the front room. We might be late meeting you, so can you hang around your office if we're not there in time?'

She listened to what he said and guessed why he was giving her so much detail – he was really saying that they all had enough to do without bothering with another fruitless expedition to follow her.

'Well?' he persisted, and she knew she should tell him not to bother to meet her, that she would make her own way home.

'Yes, Papa, I can wait.' She did not look at him as she spoke, but seconds later when she did look up she saw the scorn in his eyes.

She felt scared all day, especially as the temperature fell and the rain turned to icy pellets which the wind pelted against the office windows in sudden bursts. The hail would take the light from the lamps and make the streets even darker to walk down.

The supervisor told them all to stop work a few minutes before six, and as she cleared her desk she looked down into the street, hoping to see her father, or Jamie or Joe, waiting where they always did, but the hail was too thick for her to see across the street.

The other girls had left by the time she reached the front door and stepped out onto the pavement. She squinted across the road and thought she saw someone in the shadows where her father always waited, but she was not certain so she waited in the light cast by the lamp over the office door.

A match flared, she thought, then another. She sighed, surely whoever had come to meet her, her father, Jamie or Joe, could have crossed the road and walked with her for once? Surely there was not much chance of the man they wanted to catch coming after her in this weather?

She waited a moment longer, hoping they would give up and walk with her, but another match flared. She suspected her father was waiting for her and he was becoming impatient.

She turned and walked, her back to the wind, and heard it carry the sound of a boot scuffing the cobbles as her father stepped out from the shadow and followed some way behind her.

The worst part of her walk was where she had been frightened twice before, and almost predictably the wind had gusted into the street lanterns and blown half the flames out. She turned into the dark street, her heart thumping as it always did at that point, and walked from poor light into dark shadow.

She heard the boot scuff again, a long-drawn-out scuff that sounded like a foot being dragged, not lifted.

She looked back, fear already half closing her throat, and against the white hail curtain lit by a streetlamp there was the silhouette of a man who was much taller than her father. A tall man, who was broad, and walked with a limp. The man who had followed her before.

She ran without thinking, without looking, blundering against walls and dashing across streets. She did not look for help – there was none, the streets were empty except for her and the man who was chasing her.

Safety was the railway station, where there were people.

A slope slowed her. She tried to run faster but her legs ached, her boots slipped on the slush.

Suddenly someone pushed her. Fingers clutched at her coat.

She wrenched herself away and ran blindly into the street.

She did not look back, she was too frightened, but she heard him curse and knew he was behind her again because the wind blew the sounds of his boots and his heavy breathing into her ears.

She saw the station, and a street filled with traffic before it.

She did not stop at the kerb. A gap opened between the buses and cars and wagons and she ran on, through the divide and into the station. And he followed her, lurching awkwardly through the crowd.

She saw the man clearly, dark, heavy-browed with a red scar cutting across his left ear and cheek, across his left eye, and stopping above his nose.

She turned and leaped for the stairs, holding her coat and skirt up so she did not trip as she threw herself downwards into the underground tunnels.

A crush of people followed her, protecting her from the scar-faced man but pushing her to the edge of the platform.

She stared down at the shiny rails, her heart pounding, the asthma wrapped even tighter around her throat and chest. She felt faint, tried to move backwards, away from the rails but the crowd was solid. It would not let her move.

'Excuse me, I must stand back. Please let me through. Please.' She turned to face the impersonal wall of bodies but there were no gaps. 'Please. Please let me get through.'

A rattling sound echoed along the tunnel and an incoming train pushed the air before it. The crowd surged. She turned quickly and her toes slipped over the edge of the platform.

She saw the train rush out of the dark, felt a man's hands on her back, just as she had before.

'No!' She screamed but the rattling train was almost in front of her, dazzling her, deafening her, drowning her shout.

Her legs buckled. She fell. Heard a woman scream. Then nothing.

Edward rattled the office doors but they were locked for the night and there was no sign of Lottie.

The motor-taxi he had taken from the underground station to save time chuffed and clanked away on the far side of the road. He walked back to the driver. 'I'm only fifteen minutes late but it seems my daughter didn't wait.'

The driver muttered something about the young being too impatient, but he tried to give Lottie an excuse for not waiting. 'No, she suffers from asthma so maybe this cold wind started playing her up. You'd best take me back to the station, but drive slowly, will you? We might see her on the way.'

They drove slowly, the motor-car's dim lights hardly penetrating the hail. They did not see Lottie so he paid the driver then made his way down to the platform to wait for the next train towards home.

He noticed someone had lost their hat and a train had run over it, leaving it partly shredded and lying across a line.

Lottie heard the rattling train, felt it against her back, and

100

opened her eyes. She saw a carriage ceiling and realised she was lying on the floor.

An elderly, silver-haired man with a neat beard stared down at her. She thought he looked as though he could once have been quite beautiful.

'How do you feel, young lady?' His voice was velvet, and as he brushed her hair from her face she noticed his hands were cool and soft and she did not mind them touching her.

'Did I faint?'

'Yes. Fortunately I caught you but I'm afraid you lost your hat and one of your shoes.'

She noticed that he called them shoes even though they were boots.

'They don't matter,' she said as steadily as she could. 'Thank you for saving me. I might have fallen under the train.'

'My pleasure, my dear. Now, let me help you get up onto a seat. You can't lie there for the rest of your journey.'

He slipped his hands under her and lifted her bodily, then set her down gently on a seat between two women who asked how she was and fussed over her while he stood back, interested but not interfering. She wished the women would keep quiet so she could talk to the man who had saved her, but she satisfied herself with studying him for a few minutes.

Now she could see him clearly she realised he must be around sixty years old, older than her father, slender, fine-featured and quite – beautiful – there was no other word for it. He was well dressed, well manicured and brushed and he put her in mind of an exotic silver cat she had once seen in an oil painting.

She smiled at him and he smiled back and once again his velvet voice asked her if she was quite recovered. He had a quaintness, an old-fashioned quality which was not out of place with him and which calmed her, and she realised that the asthma attack, if that was what it was, had ended without her noticing.

Her two unofficial chaperones left the train at the next station and he asked if she would mind him sitting next to her. They talked easily, about everything and nothing, she forgot each topic immediately. Their arms rubbed against each other and occasionally their hands touched but she did not mind.

When she reached her station she excused herself and stood up, awkwardly with only one foot booted.

'I can't imagine how I could have lost that boot.' She looked down at the other boot still laced tightly up to her ankle. 'Not without losing my foot with it.'

'Simply pretend you're Cinderella, my dear, and maybe one day a handsome prince will call with the shoe magically turned into a crystal slipper.' He followed her onto the platform. 'Meanwhile please allow me to arrange for a carriage to take you home, not a coach drawn by white horses or even a pumpkin dragged by white mice, but a motor taxi-cab as befits a modern young lady.'

She tried to tell him it was not necessary but he overwhelmed her, called a taxi and paid the driver in advance. It was not until the taxi had turned the first corner and she could no longer see him waving to her from the pavement that she realised he had not told her his name.

She knocked on the front door and was taken aback by the stunned look her mother gave her when she opened it.

'Lottie? Where's your father and what on earth's happened to you?'

'I was followed again,' she said, and suddenly the fear clamped around her. She could not breathe, and seconds later she fainted.

When she opened her eyes she half expected to see the silver-haired man again, but she saw her mother and Katarina.

'Don't talk,' her mother ordered and helped her to sit up and then propped her up on a chair so she could hang her arms over the chair back to ease her breathing. 'Don't talk until you're ready.'

She heard the front door open and close, and seconds later her father's voice. 'What's happened?'

Her mother answered for her. 'She was followed again.'

'How did all this . . . ?'

'I don't know, Edward. She'll tell us in a minute.'

She saw her father kneel down in front of her, hail melting on his shoulders, worry creasing his face. 'I came for you, Lottie, even hired a taxi-cab to save time. Why didn't you wait?'

'Thought I saw you, Papa,' she gasped.

'Don't try to speak,' her mother said again, but she had to tell them now, while she was still sure of everything.

She spoke slowly with long pauses to gather her breath, and was glad when she had finished.

Her father helped her turn around so she was sitting properly on the chair. 'So you lost a boot?' he said carefully, a worried tone edging his voice.

She nodded and looked down as he tugged at the remaining boot, still laced tightly around her foot, and seconds later she knew he did not believe her.

'I'm surprised you lost it, Lottie, if it was laced as tight as this one, not without breaking your ankle. Are you sure about all this?'

'Yes, Papa.' Her chest tightened again.

'Really? I think your mother had better take off your stocking and see to cuts or grazes. It must have hurt you when it came off and we don't want your ankle festering, do we?'

He moved away and she rolled down her stocking until it slipped off her foot. Her ankle was as slim and pretty as it always was, neither bruised nor skinned.

'What really happened, Lottie? Really, now?' he asked quietly, and she saw the glance he exchanged with her mother.

'I told you, Papa. I don't know. When I woke up in the carriage my boot had gone.' The words left her gasping for air.

'All right, all right,' he said reassuringly, but she knew what he really meant was he thought she was making it up.

Edward lay beside Rose in their front bedroom on the first

floor and listened to Lottie crying in the next room.

He wanted to go to her and hold her and tell her not to worry, but there were two reasons why he could not. She had not let him hug her for years, not since she was little more than a baby; and it would not be fair to tell her not to worry when he was so worried himself.

Rose's father had fits of madness which he had hidden until just before he died. Rose never knew about it, and Edward did not want her to know she may have passed the madness on to her own daughter.

He had hoped he was wrong, hoped that Lottie was dreaming too much or just seeking attention, but her problem was worse than that. Her boot could not have fallen off, and it could not have been wrenched off without injuring her. She must have taken it off and thrown it away, but why?

The story she told was Cinderella, so perhaps she hoped a handsome prince, or even Albert, would arrive with her boot and ask her to marry him. The elderly man with white hair and a beard was so like Santa Claus that he wondered if she hoped he would come and bring her a new coat to replace the Christmas present she ruined the week before.

He did not know what to think. Perhaps Lottie needed treatment, but madness could not be cured like a childhood illness. The treatment might mean locking her up in an asylum and that might drive her completely mad, so perhaps she should be left to live as best she could to enjoy her periods of sanity. They would have to cope with the times she slipped into a dream world.

He realised that if Albert decided he still wanted to marry her he would have to be told they should never have any children. That was the only way to stop anyone else suffering.

He felt the bed heave as Rose sat up. 'I can't bear to hear Lottie cry and do nothing. I'm going to her.'

'Tell her I love her,' he said, a lump in his throat.

He listened to the murmured voices coming through the thin walls, voices which sounded quieter and softer as the minutes passed.

Rose came back after a long time. 'She's a little better. Says she's sorry she's caused so much trouble.'

Rose lay down and fell silent so he asked what was wrong, and heard her cry as she answered. 'She's going to Polly Dobbs's funeral tomorrow, in case no one else does, and she said she wished Polly could have lived, and she could die.' Rose took a ragged breath and Edward slipped his arms around her and held her tight. 'I'm scared, Edward. I'm scared what she might do to herself. And I keep wondering if Hubert *is* behind it all!'

CHAPTER 8

The sun shone the day Polly was buried. Eve was glad, it made the occasion seem a little less grim, and she was pleased that Mr Dobbs's assumption that there would be no mourners was wrong. Twenty people came.

Lottie came and Tom brought Lou and Sid and Cissie Jackson who he lodged with. A dozen women who knew Polly and had been to prison for their beliefs also came to pay respects to the young woman who had given more than any of them. Finally, Lady Braithewaite and Robert appeared.

Eve had not been able to buy violets so she draped the cheap coffin with the suffrage sash Polly had been so proud of. Lou said she thought the sash was even better than violets and Polly would have appreciated having it buried with her.

Eve found the burial upsetting and she was glad when Robert gripped her arm and eased her away from the graveside.

'Come on, Miss Forrester. There's nothing more to do and it's time to go. She's dead and buried now.' He walked beside her, his left hand supporting her as they walked across the soft ground and back to the road.

'Dead but not forgotten, Doctor, and she never should be.'

He nodded as if to say he understood, then he shrugged. 'The dead shouldn't be forgotten, Miss Forrester, but they often are. Unless there's a reason to remember them.'

'Then I'll have to find a reason to make sure Polly's remembered.'

'I'm sure you will.' He tightened his grip on her arm. 'Lou said Tom's invited us to a tea-shop. Let's go.'

She turned her head and saw Tom Dobbs looking at her. He nodded to Robert. 'Morning, Doctor.'

'Good morning, Tom. I'm sorry about your sister.' Robert held out his hand, and Tom took it after a moment's hesitation.

'Thank you, Doctor.'

Tom looked at her, a question in his eyes. She did not understand until she saw him glance down to where Robert had linked his arm with hers. He was asking her if Robert was special. She looked away rather than commit herself to an answer.

The suffragettes and Sid and Cissie went home, but the rest of them walked to the little corner café Tom had taken her to the previous week, and there they toasted Polly's memory with tea.

'May she not have died in vain,' Lady Braithewaite added when everyone else had spoken.

Robert looked across the table at his mother. 'More important, I'd say, is to ask that she didn't *live* in vain.'

'It's the same thing,' his mother snapped.

'I don't think so, Mother. It's not the same at all,' Robert persisted, and drew an embarrassed silence around the table.

Eve felt uncomfortable as the silence continued. Robert looked sad, and she wondered if he was sad because of something remembered and now past, or if it was sadness for the future.

He looked back at her, directly into her eyes, and she smiled but he did not react. Then she realised he was not looking *into* her eyes, he was looking through them as though he wanted to see into her mind, to know what she was thinking.

Suddenly he stood up, still with his eyes on hers. 'I'm sorry to leave so abruptly but we must go, Mother. It's time.'

'Yes. Yes.' His mother sounded distracted. 'I'll be in touch with you, Miss Forrester. In a day or so. About another meeting.'

'Thank you, Lady Braithewaite.'

'No. I don't like all this Lady this and Lady that. You're with us now. Call me Violet.'

'Only if you'll call me Eve.'

'No, thank you, Miss Forrester. I abhor this appalling modern habit of abbreviating the English language. I imagine you were Christened Evelyn and that is what I shall call you.'

Robert turned to her and without changing his expression he asked a favour. 'And, Miss Forrester, may I also call you Evelyn? I'd be honoured if, perhaps, you'd call me Robert.'

'Of course, Robert.' Her heart beat so hard she stammered his name and blushed at her clumsiness. He nodded and she watched him help his mother out to the street and she wondered if he would look back at her.

He did, and she felt her colour deepen, and she wondered what he thought about her. If he thought about her.

His mother's motor-car arrived as if by magic and stopped outside the tea-house. Perkins alighted, opened the door, and moments later mother and sad son were whisked away.

'That was a bit embarrassing,' Lou said, then added quickly, 'you've joined Lady Bee's League, Miss Forrester?'

'Yes. Why?'

Tom spoke before Lou could answer. 'Then I think you're foolish, Miss Forrester.'

Lou looked her brother in the eye. 'I think that's Miss Forrester's business, Tom. Anyway, I want to join, too.'

'No. Polly's dead, isn't that enough?'

'I don't want her to have died without reason, Tom,' she heard Lou argue.

'She didn't, Lou. I'll make sure of that,' Eve said.

Tom turned to her. 'Why? It's not your fight, Miss Forrester.'

'But it is. I'm a woman and I want to have a say in how this country's run. Anyway, I feel I owe Polly something.'

'Why, Eve?' Lottie spoke for the first time. 'You did all you could for her so why do you think you still owe her something?'

'Because she risked her life to make all our lives better and I'd feel I was letting her down personally if I didn't do all I could to win the fight.'

'A matter of honour?' Lottie seemed to understand.

'Yes, Lot, and I'd be a coward not to carry on the fight.'

The cups rattled as the table shook. Tom was standing up, red-faced and agitated. 'And you couldn't stand being called a coward, could you, Miss Forrester? You'd rather die, I suppose?'

'I'm sorry, I—'

'Don't bother.' He waved his hand. 'I couldn't expect you to understand. We're a long way below you, Polly and Lou and me, so I'll thank you again for all you've done. It really is appreciated. Enjoy your tea, it's all paid for. Goodbye.'

He was gone before she had time to recover from his outburst. She half rose but Lou stood up and stopped her.

'I'm sorry about that, Miss Forrester. He's a bit hotheaded, you see.'

'But I don't understand what I did to upset him?'

'You said the forbidden word. Coward. That's what Polly always called him for leaving home. She said he ran away because he didn't have the guts to stay.' Lou pulled on her thin coat. 'I'll go after him, and then I'd better go on home. Thanks for all you did for Pol. I really do appreciate it, and so does Tom, really. I hope we'll meet again some time. On a march, perhaps, or even in prison. Bye, Miss Forrester.'

Eve turned to Lottie. 'I suppose we should go, too.'

'In a minute.' Lottie looked down and concentrated on slowly spinning the teacup, the tip of a finger against the cup's handle. 'I need to talk.'

'I'm listening,' Eve said quietly. 'Go on.'

Lottie looked up at her and then looked out of the window, but did not say anything for a while. When she did speak she looked away, at her cup, the window or at the precise lines her finger nails made on the table cloth. Her voice was a little husky and her eyes glistened with small tears which spread into her eyelashes but were not big enough to roll down her face. 'I've never really fitted in, have I? I know you all think I'm different. Weak and stupid and unreliable and not grown up, and I am trying to be different but I'm not mad, Eve, no matter what anyone thinks.'

'Not *mad*, Lottie?'

'Well, you don't really believe I've been followed, or that the man on the train helped me, do you?'

'Be reasonable, Lottie. It's difficult for us to understand why the man who followed you and the man on the train would have behaved as you say they did, or how you could have lost your boot without hurting your foot.' She paused, hoping Lottie would look up instead of hiding her face by looking down. 'Come on, Lottie. Whatever did or didn't happen, you have to admit that none of it seems very plausible, does it?'

'But that doesn't mean it's not true, Eve. And it doesn't mean I'm mad.' Lottie paused for a few seconds, then looked up and asked plaintively, 'Does it?'

She was scared to say she thought it might indeed mean Lottie was mad, so she smiled and shook her head. 'No, Lottie, and as for not feeling part of the family, I do understand what you mean. I sometimes feel like an outsider, too. There's something special between the rest of them. I suppose it's because we were the last to come along and a lot happened before we were born, things we can never be a part of.'

'Do you really mean that?' Lottie's eyes shone with hope.

'Oh, yes. Mama treats Helen and Jamie differently. I don't think she loves us any less than them, but it's different somehow.'

'And Papa?'

'I've noticed the way he looks, at times, and it's almost as if he doesn't know what's happened to bring us all together. I think he sometimes feels uncomfortable that he isn't the sort of man Mama would have married if her parents hadn't died when they did. It's not his fault, of course, but he hasn't been able to give her the sort of life she might have had.'

Lottie nodded absently. 'No. I suppose Mama would have married someone like Albert.'

She hesitated. This was the first time Lottie had mentioned Albert since the weekend. 'Do you mind him suspending your engagement? Really mind?'

Lottie grimaced. 'I'm not sure.'

'Well, whatever happens, Lottie, I can't think you'll ever grow old and lonely. You only have to smile and men almost fall at your feet. Look at Peter and Sasha!'

'That was fun, wasn't it? But it was only fun, Eve. I was just enjoying myself and I didn't mean to upset Albert. I'm sure that's what caused the trouble although he didn't actually say so.'

Eve smiled again, consolingly, and thought Lottie and Albert really did not understand each other at all. Lottie did not realise that Albert had no idea of what fun was, and he had not understood how naive she was even though it should have been obvious to him.

It was probably a good thing that Albert had suspended their engagement, and it would probably be best for both of them if they did not get married, but that was not really her business so she did not tell Lottie what she thought.

That evening Eve told her mother that Lottie did not feel part of the family, and without telling Lottie they asked Jamie and Helen and everyone else to treat her less like a child who needed protection and more like an adult.

They had all spent so long making allowances for her that at first it was surprisingly difficult to remember to treat her differently but they persisted, even when Lottie seemed puzzled or suspicious by their different attitude towards her. Eve was especially pleased that she was able to

111

persuade her mother and Aunt Lizzie to agree to Lottie joining her overnight at the mission when it was her turn to stay. Having company made the chore more enjoyable, and it gave her an opportunity to learn more about her reclusive twin without having to ask obvious questions.

It was interesting to see how Lottie changed and became more confident, more adult, even to the point of asking their father to stop following her to and from work.

'Are you sure, Lottie? After what you said happened last time you came home on your own?' Her father stopped eating his breakfast and Eve watched him look from Lottie to their mother and then to her, almost as if he was begging them to ask Lottie why she had changed her mind.

Neither did, but she saw a determined expression on her sister's face. Lottie was scared, that was obvious, but she was clearly trying to overcome her fear.

'Are you sure, Lottie?' their mother repeated their father's questions.

Lottie nodded. 'We haven't seen anyone for weeks. I think whoever was following me has given up.'

'Well, if that's what you want.' Her father shrugged, and returned to his food.

After Lottie had left for work he sat back from the table. 'I think we'll still watch her for a few days, without her knowing. Jamie and Joe can help me by hiding themselves along her route where they can keep an eye on her.'

Eve was surprised he suggested doing anything more after he had complained so much about the need to follow her in the first place. 'Does that mean you believe she was followed, Papa?'

'No, not at all, but if she's as scared as she looked when she left here I'd like to be able to help her if she needs me. I'd rather do it openly than have her making up another daft story and worrying the life out of us all.'

They spied on her for three days. Lottie did not see them and they did not see anyone else. Lottie, unaware she was being watched, did not seem perturbed that she was walking alone.

'That's it, then,' their father said after the third day, rubbing his hands together as if he was brushing off dirt. 'No trouble and no daft stories. I reckon it's done with now and we can all get back to normal.'

Eve smiled and thought it was typical of her father to want to get back to what he thought was normal. He hated change of any sort and usually preferred to ignore things until he was forced to face up to them.

Eve noticed how her father told her in one breath that he admired her for wanting to play a part in the suffrage debate, but in the next breath he warned her not to take any risks. He never showed any interest in the meetings she went to, until she came home afterwards, and then he wanted to know as many details as she could remember.

He was also quite dismissive when she told him Lady Braithewaite wanted her to stand on the platform and make a five minute appeal at a small public meeting in a local hall, but on the night she noticed him and her mother in the audience, faces alight with pride.

That was her first experience of public speaking and as she returned to her seat at the rear of the platform she noticed the smile on Lady Braithewaite's face. 'You're a natural orator, Evelyn. I was watching the audience while you spoke and everyone here was concentrating totally on what you were saying. Did you enjoy it?'

She paused before she answered, wondering whether to be modest or truthful, and decided on truthful. 'Yes, I did. I was nervous, but I enjoyed it.'

'Good. Ten minutes next time. Next Sunday evening?'

She nodded, keen to do something other than help paint slogans on banners and make placards for other women to demonstrate with. Besides, Robert might be there.

She had not seen him since Polly's funeral and although she had thought about him every day she still was not sure if she had misread the signs which suggested he might be interested in her as anything more than a woman who sat on his mother's committee. Perhaps if they could meet again, for a little longer and alone if possible, they could talk and she could understand him better.

Another speaker had started so she did not ask about Robert, and when the meeting ended there was too much happening for her to bother Lady Braithewaite with personal trivialities.

Sasha and Peter came to dinner on that Sunday, almost two weeks after their mother and Paul had moved into the house. It was the first half day they had been allowed to take off and they both wore suits, bought second-hand, which their mother promised to tailor to make them fit better.

Eve noticed Sasha's embarrassment when he first met Lottie again, and her returned embarrassment as he told her his mother had written to him saying how his and Peter's actions may have offended Albert. 'I'm very sorry, Miss Forrester. I'll do anything you wish to make amends. If you would like I will go to Mr Verney and explain that any blame should be—'

'No, Sasha. All I'd like you to do is to play the piano for me. Something you have written.'

'Certainly, Miss Forrester, but I think—'

'No, Sasha.' Eve saw the determination on Lottie's face, noticed how firm her voice was, and noticed that Lottie had actually taken Sasha by his arm. 'Please play something for me, and call me Lottie. Nothing should change between us, Sasha, no matter what Mr Verney may think.' Aunt Lizzie was at the mission so the table in the kitchen was extended to seat the eight of them, and Eve, her mother and Lottie served up Sunday dinner. Peter and Sasha looked tired, and it was either their fatigue or a warning from their mother which made them much quieter than they had been during their previous visit, but even though they were quiet they were eager to talk and she learned that Peter was interested in British politics and was particularly interested in the votes for women movement.

Conversation inevitably turned to the subject, and shortly after the pudding was finished Lottie and Sasha excused themselves and went to the front room to play the piano.

Sasha's music stopped the conversation in the kitchen.

'His concerto,' Katarina said proudly. 'He has not yet finished it, but it is beautiful.'

It was beautiful, astonishingly beautiful and romantic and so peaceful that no one seemed moved to leave the snug kitchen for the more comfortable front room. Eve heard a knock on the front door, and as she was nearest she went to answer it.

'Albert. How nice to see you. Come in.'

He thanked her, stepped into the hall and nodded towards the front room. 'Sasha Komovsky?'

'Yes. He and Peter came to dinner.'

He nodded, and her mother came up behind her and welcomed him, then told him to go straight into the front room where everyone was about to gather. Her mother went back to clear the table and Eve ushered Albert towards the front room.

He opened the door and stopped.

Sasha was seated at the piano with Lottie standing close behind him, her hands resting on his shoulders, her mind somewhere other than Angel Street.

'Good afternoon, Charlotte.'

'Albert!' Lottie came out of her dream and smiled, then seemed to realise where her hands were and removed them jerkily from Sasha's shoulders. 'I didn't expect you.'

'Evidently,' Albert said tartly.

Sasha stood up quickly, greeted Albert with his customary formality, and immediately apologised. 'Mr Verney, I would not wish you to believe there is anything improper in my friendship with Miss Forrester.'

'Wouldn't you?' Albert growled ungraciously. 'Alone together in this room? Playing the piano?'

Eve was annoyed by Albert and sorry for the embarrassment he was causing both Lottie and Sasha so she intervened. 'And playing it beautifully, Sasha. We were all listening to you, in the next room, too entranced to come in here. Now your mother's living with us I hope you'll come more often. I'm sure Mama and Papa would love to hear you play more regularly and no doubt the practice would help you, too.'

'Your mother's living here?' Albert sagged visibly, and moments later Mrs Komovskaya appeared and paused to be reintroduced.

The afternoon passed politely and formally. Albert was clearly embarrassed by his own unannounced arrival, an embarrassment probably made worse by everyone's acceptance that as Lottie's fiancé he had a right to be there. It seemed he stayed only because it might have been even more embarrassing if he had left too quickly. Peter and Sasha left a little after five o'clock and Albert departed at half past five, awkwardly, formally shaking hands with everyone except Lottie whose cheek he kissed. If he had wanted to spend any time alone with Lottie he had failed to do so, mainly because Lottie made it quite clear she did not want to be left alone with him.

'Well, Lottie?' their mother asked after he had left. 'Is he coming back again?'

'I think so,' Lottie answered without much sign of concern, 'but I asked him to arrange his next visit in advance to avoid any further embarrassment, Mama.'

Eve knew then, for certain, that Lottie had changed.

Eve was pleased that Robert came to the meeting she was speaking at that night. He waved to her from the back of the hall and his mother told her it was the first meeting he had ever attended.

Lady Braithewaite launched the evening and then introduced Eve as the first speaker. She should have talked for ten minutes but she had not rehearsed properly and she was actually on her feet for fifteen. No one seemed to mind and when she finished the applause and shouts of support from both men and women left her stunned and shaking.

'I said you were a natural orator, Evelyn.' Lady Braithewaite smiled. 'Twenty minutes next time?'

She grinned, wondered what Robert thought of her oratory, then settled back to listen to the next speaker.

The meeting collected more funds and recruited more members, and suddenly she was in the Braithewaites' motor-car, being driven back to their home where several of the committee members were going to have drinks.

She was disappointed that Robert was not in the car. She was told he would come home later, and she hoped he would not be too late as she would not be able to stop at the house long before she had to leave.

In the event she became so overwhelmed by the other members' response to her speech that she did not see him arrive and it was only when everyone's attention passed to something else and she could extricate herself from the throng that she realised he must have been watching and listening for some time.

'Congratulations, Miss Forrester.' He was holding a glass of whisky which he half raised as a toast.

'Thank you. I thought we'd agreed on Evelyn.'

'Ah, yes, we had, but that was before you became famous.'

'I'm hardly famous, Doctor.'

'But you will be, Miss Forrester.' He sipped his whisky and studied her over the rim of his glass. 'You will be, Miss Forrester.'

'I'm not sure I want to be.'

'You don't have to be sure, Miss Forrester. My mother's sure and that's enough. You just have to do as you're told, like the rest of us. Welcome to the club.' He drained his glass and reached for a decanter to refill it.

She placed her hand over his to stop him. 'I hoped we might talk.'

'What about?' He looked her straight in the eye.

'Well, there's the Manchurian caterpillar poaching crisis. That's a fascinating subject, I've heard.'

'Only to Manchurians or caterpillars. There must be something far more interesting than that.'

'Then you choose,' she said, still returning his stare.

'No. You want to talk, I just want to drink, and you're stopping me.'

She freed his hand but kept her eyes on him. He looked away, unstoppered the decanter and lifted it to pour, then lowered it. 'No, I've thought of something, now, but it can

117

only be discussed away from here. I'll get the car and take you home.'

She assumed he meant Perkins would drive and he would ride with her in the back but he astonished her by helping her into the rear seat and then driving the car himself. She felt uneasy then, particularly as he had been drinking but she was even more concerned fifteen minutes later when he turned the motor-car off the road and bumped it across some uneven ground before stopping it in the pitch dark where there were no lights to be seen.

He did not speak as he left the driver's seat and even when he opened the rear door and sat down beside her he did not say anything.

'Where are we, Robert?'

'Hampstead Heath.'

'What are we doing here?'

'You wanted to talk and I gathered you wanted us to be alone. We are, now.' His logic was rather disconcerting. 'What did you want to talk about? Surely not the Manchurian caterpillar crisis?'

'No.' She laughed softly at the way he was teasing her, but now she had the opportunity she did not know what to say. How could she say she thought she loved him and wanted to know how he felt about her, without embarrassing them both and possibly ruining the opportunity of anything ever developing between them? 'You left the funeral in rather a hurry. I hope it wasn't anything serious?'

'We had to visit someone in hospital. It was all rather sudden and,' he paused as if he was trying to find appropriate words, 'they were very, um, ill.'

'Oh, I'm sorry. I wouldn't have asked if I'd known.'

'Of course not.' He smiled, then added in a hard tone. 'You wouldn't have needed to if you'd known.'

She shrank away from him, offended by what he said, logical or not.

'I'm sorry, Miss Forrester, Evelyn. That was very rude of me. I'm afraid I'm rather, well-attached to the person and we thought she was dying. It was a great shock and it's still a worry.'

118

'But she's still alive at the moment?'

He grimaced. 'That rather depends upon one's definition of alive.'

He was upset so she looked away, out into the darkness, and tried to think of something else to say, something which could not upset him any further. 'You and your mother have a beautiful home, Robert.'

'I hate it! Always have!' His venom shocked her. 'It's a beautiful house, but it's not a home, Evelyn. Never was. It's a showpiece meant to impress impressionable visitors. It's like my mother, really. Her function is to impress people, and she's very good at it. So good she's even begun to believe the image she's created is real.'

'That's a strange thing to say.'

'But it's true, Evelyn. It's her way of coping with life since my brother died. One of her ways. The suffrage movement was a Godsend to her because it allowed her to invent a fantasy character and the newspapers helped by giving her character a name, Lady Bee or Violent Violet. She's become that character. A figment of her own and the newspapers' imagination, but she wasn't always like that.'

Eve sensed the subject was dangerous, but that he wanted to talk. 'When did she change?'

'Three years ago, when Arnold,' – he paused almost imperceptibly – 'died. Up until then she'd been a socialite, an intelligent and cultured socialite, perhaps, but she lived just for pleasure. She was never a motherly sort of person. We had a nanny to bring us up and we hardly ever saw Mother at all. I think she only had us because it was something which was expected of her, and that rather goes for my father, too. He was always more interested in his racehorses than he was in Arnold or me. Not that I'm complaining. One shouldn't speak ill of one's dead father or one's live mother but I never found either of them particularly pleasant company, and other than realising that they have made me rather insular I've no regrets about not being closer to them.'

That might explain his remoteness and his frequent sharp temper, but there was something which puzzled her.

'If you hate the house and don't much like your mother, why do you live there? Surely you could live on your own?'

'I did, for a while. Up until Arnold . . .' He leaned towards her, went to say something, hesitated and then sat back before he continued. 'After Arnold died Mother changed and wouldn't leave me alone. She kept coming around to the house I had, saying how sorry she was about the way she'd treated me as a child. She simply wouldn't go away so it was easier for me to move back into her house. Also, up until then she'd been a happy, passive soul, but she became very bitter and aggressive towards everyone, including herself, and I was scared she might try to kill herself unless I was there to stop her.'

'That's awful. How did your brother die – do you mind me asking?'

'Not at all. He had a motoring accident in France. He was driving in the dark, must have miscalculated a bend in the road, left the road and hit a tree at speed. His pocket-watch was smashed at six o'clock and they weren't found until ten the next morning. A Sunday morning.'

'They?'

'Oh, yes.' Robert looked awkward, sad and bitter. 'Lydia. She was pregnant and the baby also died in the crash.'

'And Lydia?'

'No, she lived but the experience affected her mind. She has to live in a home now. It was her we went to see after the funeral.'

Now she understood why he was so upset and why he made his comment about the definition of life.

'It's quite harrowing, visiting her.' He spoke quietly, not looking at her but looking down at his hands resting in his lap. 'It's all one can do. That and pray that some day she'll recover.'

'Do you see her often?'

'I try to see her every week. She often doesn't react to me being there but she knows if I don't go, so I try to see her every Sunday.'

'You went there today?' That might also explain his earlier mood.

'This afternoon.'

'You must be very fond of her,' she said softly.

'Yes, but of a memory really. How she was. It's worse than death you know, madness. Death takes but it also gives. It gives freedom to those who are left to carry on with their own lives. Madness doesn't. Madness just takes. It takes and takes and takes.' He stopped suddenly and changed his mood. 'Come and look at the view.'

'It's pitch black! There isn't a view.'

'There's always something to see if you know where to look, or how to look,' he insisted softly, then added in a brisk tone. 'Come on!'

His hand gripped her elbow and she had to choose between making a fuss or doing as she was told. She did as she was told.

He helped her out from the car and did not release his hold on her as he guided her across the damp grass and up a slight hill. Then he ordered her, 'Close you eyes until I say you can open them.'

'You're very,' she sought for the right word, a word which would both make it clear that she was only obeying him because she wanted to and one which he might find mildly amusing, 'commanding.'

'Yes. I get that from my mother. Eyes shut?'

'Yes,' she said, and found it strangely exciting to be led through the dark with her eyes closed, by a man who was confident enough not to mind her criticising him.

'Good.' He made her stand still. 'Keep your eyes closed, look up at the sky, count to twenty and open your eyes. I'm letting you go, but you're quite safe.'

His hand slipped away. She did as she was told.

'Twenty.' She opened her eyes, and saw more stars than she had seen in her whole life. Then she looked down and saw London laid out. The myriad of lights seemed to reflect the heavens above her. 'It's beautiful.'

Robert was not with her, and she realised he had moved away so she could enjoy the scene on her own. She did not call out or even turn to look for him, he would come back in his own time, she thought, and while she was alone she would enjoy the rare treat of actually being left alone.

Bells peeled far away and a dog barked. Otherwise there was silence. She stood still and enjoyed it all, reached up and removed her hat so the wind could run through her long hair.

'You see?' Robert came back after several minutes.

'I see,' she said.

'I'd better take you home now.' He sounded reluctant to leave.

'Can we stay for just a little longer? Just to stand here, or talk?' she asked.

'Of course.'

He stood beside her and as the silence lengthened she wished he would take her arm or her hand, or even put his arm around her waist. She suddenly wondered if he wanted to kiss her. She had never been kissed properly, and sometimes she wondered if it was something which would ever happen. And she thought, deliberately, unlike Lottie she wanted it to happen.

She lifted her hand and combed her hair with her fingers, freeing it so she could feel the wind on her scalp, and as her hand dropped back by her side it brushed his. Their knuckles pressed together for a few cautious moments then she felt his fingers interlock with hers. Moments later they each had a firm hold on the other's hand, but they did not speak, did not look at each other.

For the moment it was enough just to hold hands.

The wind buffeted them harder and they stood closer. She could feel the warmth from his arm against hers, and she could feel her heart knocking against her chest.

'The show's nearly over,' he said and she saw an edge of cloud cutting the sky, hiding the stars.

They stood longer, still and silent.

The clouds were building up, scudding fast before the wind. She turned her head and saw where the moon glowed through a cloud worn thin. It emerged full and misty through the ragged end of the cloud that had hidden it.

'It'll rain tomorrow,' she said softly.

'I think I'm falling in love with you, Evelyn,' he said as softly, and without looking at her.

'And me with you,' she said, her heart beating so fast it made her voice tremble. Her eyes were shut tight, trying to capture the emotion so she could remember every detail to enjoy again later, and she did not see his face come down over hers – she simply felt the warmth and pressure of his lips on hers and she turned her body into his, felt his arms around her, and thought this was the most wonderful feeling she had ever known.

'The show's nearly over,' he repeated quietly.

She looked up at the sky. The moon was free now, and the clouds which had hidden it were now covering the stars as if they were putting them away until another night. The pitch black which had hidden the heath had been replaced with a pale light from the moon, silhouetting the trees and making the bushes look like shadows.

There was no one on the heath except her and Robert, and for that moment it seemed they were the only people in the world.

'Time to go,' he said.

'Yes.' She did not move.

'Evelyn?'

'I'm sorry. I don't want to break the spell.'

'Then save it, Miss Forrester, save it. I keep a special place in my heart for spells I don't want to break, and sometimes, when I'm alone, I take them out and look at them, and enjoy them all over again.'

'That's a very honest thing to say, Doctor Braithewaite.'

'Honest?' He shrugged, reached out and took her arm. 'Let me take you home, Evelyn, before you catch cold.'

She looked up into his face, never closer to hers than it was now, expecting to see him looking happy, but the moonlight showed her a sad man. A man who was so deep in sorrow that she knew she should not ask why.

CHAPTER 9

The following evening Eve was at the mission with Lottie when Lady Braithewaite arrived.

'Evelyn, can you join a raiding party tomorrow morning? Meeting at four? Wearing quiet shoes?'

Quiet shoes? Her stomach churned. 'A raiding party? To do what?'

'I've hundreds of members organised for a mass fly-posting raid. I want posters pasted up on buses, trams and buildings along all the main routes into the City and Westminster by the time people start going to work tomorrow morning. We want them to see Votes for Women posters everywhere they look. Can you come, Evelyn? Lou Dobbs is coming though you shouldn't meet her because she's working for a different centre.'

'Is that wise? For her family, I mean. If she's arrested there'll be no one to—'

'She insisted, Evelyn. If she doesn't join us she'll join Mrs Pankhurst. At least I can try to keep her out of trouble.'

'Yes, I suppose you're right.'

'Of course I am.' The impatient response was snapped. 'Now, I have a lot to do. Can you join us tomorrow, or not?'

'Where do we meet?' Eve committed herself and tried to control the tremble in her voice.

Eve hardly slept and she was glad when it was time to get up. It was still dark when she peered through the curtains and noticed there was a friendly fog but no rain. She dressed in warm clothes and was surprised to find Lottie was already downstairs, hot tea brewed, ready to see her leave.

She ate the toast Lottie had prepared for her, swallowed the tea and pulled on her long coat.

Lottie followed her to the door. 'Good luck, Eve, and take care. Please.'

'Don't worry,' she called back, already worried herself, scared about what she was going to do, that she might let the others down, and scared of the consequences if she was caught.

Lottie was too frightened to go back to bed so she sat in the large room which was used as a drawing room and waited for Eve to return.

She heard the back door bang and called out, 'In here, Eve,' and recoiled when her dishevelled and breathless sister burst in and hugged her.

'Lottie, it was the most exciting thing I've ever done! We put up hundreds of posters and then the police almost trapped us. I escaped along the canal but one of the policemen fell into the water and couldn't swim so I went back and threw him a life-belt. I nearly got caught for it, but he was all right and a Sergeant saw what I'd done and let me go. It was wonderful!'

'Does that mean you'll do it again?'

'No. It's too dangerous. For the mission. If I was caught the Trustees might decide to use that as an excuse to close it down.'

'Well, I suggest you get washed and changed before anyone else sees you,' Lottie said.

'Yes, but look at this first. It's one of the posters we pasted up.' Eve flattened a poster on the table and read the slogan out loud. 'Convicts and Lunatics and Women have no Vote for Parliament.'

125

The words were printed in red across a picture of women dressed as convicts doing various household chores.

'I've never thought of it like that, Eve. It isn't fair, is it?'

'No, Lot. It's not fair,' Eve said. 'It's not fair at all. And now I must get ready for work.'

The bell rang and Lottie opened the front door, expecting to see her mother or Aunt Lizzie. She did not expect to see Sergeant Crabb, and she hoped she hid her surprise as she welcomed him.

'Good morning, Miss Charlotte. Is Miss Evelyn here?'

'Yes. She's upstairs, preparing herself for work, Mr Crabb,' she tried to sound unconcerned but her mind whirled with fear and concern for her suffragette sister.

'Will she be long?'

'No. Would you like to come in to the drawing room and wait?'

He nodded and she led him towards the drawing room, and it was not until she stepped aside for him to enter that she remembered the poster still spread out on the table. She could not stop him seeing it.

'Interesting poster. Where did it come from?' he asked.

'It just appeared,' she said.

'Just appeared?' he mused, and looked directly at her. 'Your sister wouldn't have anything to do with it, would she?'

'I'm afraid you'll have to ask her about that.'

He picked up the poster and flicked it with his free hand. 'The trouble is, Miss Charlotte, that there's a lot of truth in this, and a lot of us sympathise with these suffragettes even if what they're doing's illegal. But they're breaking the law.'

'Good morning Mr Crabb.' She had not noticed Eve watching from the doorway. 'Who's breaking the law?'

'The women who're posting these up.'

She watched Eve walk over to him, take the poster and read it as though she had never seen it before. 'There is some truth in what it says, though, isn't there?' She admired Eve's composure as she handed the poster back to Mr Crabb, treating it as though it was something he had brought in with him. 'Did you call for anything special?'

'I just wondered if you could pop in and see Gladys when you've got a moment. She's none too well and I reckon—'

'I'll come over now, if you like. I've got about twenty minutes or so before I need to leave for work.'

'Fine.' He seemed grateful, and carefully returned the poster to the table. 'I wouldn't let your mother or your aunt see that, Miss Charlotte. They've got enough on their plates at the moment, without worrying about harbouring suffragettes in the mission.'

Lottie blushed and wondered how Eve could possibly stay so calm. 'Please give my love to Mrs Crabb.'

He smiled at her and she thought she saw a twinkle in his eyes as he thanked her and promised he would.

'Mr Crabb said you weren't feeling too well?' Eve said as soon as she saw Gladys. She left the question open, expecting Gladys to tell her about some new symptom.

'Shut the door dear, and come over here so I can talk quietly, without Bill hearing.'

Eve did as she was told. 'What's wrong?'

'Is there any way I could go into hospital, lovey? Bill needs a break and he's not going to get one if he has to keep looking after me day and night.'

'It may be possible, but are you sure?'

'Yes. Could you find out for me? I don't want to ask Bill because I know he wouldn't do anything about it. He'd say he'd tried but there wasn't anywhere for me to go.'

'I'll try, Mrs Crabb, but I can't promise anything.'

'There's a good girl. And you won't tell Bill?'

'Not if you don't want me to.'

'I don't.'

She said goodbye to Mrs Crabb and left, nervous about what Mr Crabb would say when he found out what she had done.

Eve and Lottie had volunteered to spend the Wednesday night at the mission and they had just finished their evening meal when one of the women told them Mr Crabb was asking for them.

'Please ask him in.' Eve thought he was probably paying one of his frequent social visits, but when she saw the expression on his face she knew she was in trouble. Gladys! He must have found out. She opened her mouth to explain but he raised his hand to stop her, and immediately took her to task.

'Your aunt and your mother both trusted you to stay here and not cause any trouble, and what have you done? You've gone out running with the suffragettes, Miss Evelyn. A bloke I know recognised you and told me to warn you that if you hadn't saved one of his lads from drowning he would've arrested you. So far he's not told anyone, but he doesn't agree with your lot and if there's any more trouble he'll be straight round here to sort this place out. Do you understand?'

'Yes, thank you, Mr Crabb.'

His expression softened. 'Please don't let your aunt or your mother down, Miss Evelyn. They've done a lot for both of you.'

She nodded and promised him she would be more sensible in future, and then she saw him out.

The following Monday Lou Dobbs appeared at the mission door and asked if she could stay because she had nowhere else to go.

'Your father's thrown you out, Lou? Why?' Eve asked.

'He saw me with a boy, a young man, and jumped to the wrong conclusion, Miss Forrester. We weren't doing anything. Really!' Lou shifted her bag of belongings to her other hand, then dumped it on the floor. 'He's just a boy from where I work and although I think he does fancy me a bit I've tried to show him I'm not that keen because I knew it would cause trouble. He lives with his parents and they've just moved in close to us so he insisted on walking home with me. Dad saw us and—'

'Have you tried to tell your father all this?'

'I tried, but he wouldn't listen, said I was lying. He found out that I'd gone to Pol's funeral, see, and I'd told him I didn't. He said if I'd lie about that I'd lie about anything.

And then he found out I belonged to the Women's Freedom League and he went off his rocker. I wondered if you could let me stay here for a few nights. Just until I can find myself somewhere permanent.'

'Of course, but it'll have to be in a dormitory.' Eve wanted Lou to understand that she could not expect any special treatment because they knew each other. 'In fact I can find you a bed now. Lottie and I are doing our bit as supervisors tonight.'

Lou beamed. 'That'd be wonderful, Miss Forrester. I've got a chance of getting me old job back. The one I had before . . .' She paused. 'Well, you know. Before we had to move away.'

'A fresh start, Lou? And not too far from Tom. I'm surprised you didn't go to see him?'

'There's no room there, Miss Forrester, but he sends his respects to you. And his apologies for the way he behaved a few weeks back, after Polly's funeral.'

'Tell him I'd forgotten all about it.' She picked up Lou's bag and told her to follow, then turned on her to make one thing very clear. 'You're free to come and go as you please providing you're indoors by ten o'clock each evening, Lou, but you must promise not to involve yourself in any WFL or suffrage activities while you're here. We can't afford any trouble and if you bring any to us I'll throw you out onto the street. Do you understand?'

'Sounds a bit unfriendly, Miss Forrester.'

'Not unfriendly, Lou, just blunt. Do you understand?'

'Yes, Miss Forrester.'

'And you promise to follow the rules, whatever Lady Braithewaite tries to persuade you to do?'

'Yes, Miss Forrester.'

'Good. I'll show you your bed.'

Eve saw Lou leave for work the following morning, and had an uneasy feeling that she had made a mistake by allowing her to stay in the mission. She was so unsure of what she had done that she told her mother and Aunt Lizzie the moment they arrived.

Her mother looked horrified, but not for the reason Eve expected. 'The man's inhuman, Eve. First he allows his eldest daughter to die without going to see her, then he refuses to go to her funeral, and then he throws his next daughter out onto the street because he thinks she may have a boyfriend.'

'That's not all, Mama.' She told her about Mr Dobbs's attempt to have Lou certified insane because she was raped.

'Of course you did the right thing by taking her in, Eve. I understand your worries about her suffrage activities but I assume she won't let you down?'

She shrugged. She did not have any way of knowing whether or not she could trust Lou Dobbs other than remembering that Lou had given her back the taxi fare she had left for Mr Dobbs to visit the hospital.

Eve saw Robert the moment she left the hospital that evening and ran to him, suddenly eager to have him kiss her. 'Robert! It's lovely to see you.'

His kiss was peremptory and disappointing. She pulled away from him, concerned that he had changed his mind about her.

'You haven't heard, have you?' he asked urgently.

'Haven't heard what?'

'The Franchise Bill's been withdrawn, Evelyn. No votes for women. Mrs Pankhurst and my mother have declared war on the Government, starting tonight. They're threatening to smash and burn and bomb everything they can, even Parliament itself. My mother's gone into hiding because the police are already looking for her and you must be careful what you do and say because there's a rumour that the Government may bring in emergency powers which'll give them the right to arrest and imprison anyone they even think may cause serious trouble. You'd best not make any rousing speeches for a while.'

'Are you serious?'

'About prison? Yes.'

'No. About not making any speeches?'

'Of course I'm serious. They could put you in prison, Evelyn.'

'But it's now that I need to make those speeches. Don't you understand that? They can't be allowed to intimidate us into silence.'

'No. You'll just have to wait for the vote, Evelyn. Get another Bill presented, a Private Member's Bill or something. There are ways if you're patient.'

'Just how patient do we have to be?' she stormed at him. 'We've been waiting years for the same rights as men and the men keep denying us those rights. They promised us this time they'd pass the Bill and they haven't. We have to fight or we'll lose all the ground we've won.'

'You're wrong, Evelyn. You've been spending too much time with my mother and now you're beginning to sound like her. Good God! One of you's enough. I can't stand two of you!'

She did not know what to say so she turned away without saying anything, and when he called her back she ignored him. If he wanted her he would have to run after her and apologise for what he had just said.

He did not run after her, but he did call out three words.

'Be careful, Evelyn.'

CHAPTER 10

Eve was careful. In everything she did and said.

She did not try to find Lady Braithewaite, even though that would have given her a possible excuse to speak with Robert, and she was careful to make it clear to everyone who asked that she did not know where Lady Braithewaite was. She was formally polite to the policemen who attended nearly every public WFL meeting, and she constantly advocated determined but not violent pressure to achieve the objects she set out.

She was pleased to hear her audiences respond to her and astonished when one of her speeches was reported almost verbatim in a newspaper. The Committee was impressed and decided she should be given more prominence at future meetings.

'Evelyn, look at these.' Maud Whitton-White, Lady Braithewaite's deputy, opened a small parcel which the printer had delivered earlier that day. 'What do you think?'

Eve could see by its shape that the parcel contained printed sheets which the women called sashes because they were made to be pasted across other posters, but she did not see what was printed on them until she took one and turned it over.

Evelyn Forrester
Votes without Violence

She stared at the four-inch-high letters which spelled her name and at the smaller letters which spelled out her policy. 'I don't know what to say, Maud. Whose idea was this?'

'The Committee and I thought we should take advantage of your popularity by advertising your presence at future meetings. We believe you can attract the sort of people we want to join us, particularly now the other groups are actually upsetting some of their supporters by increasing their militancy.'

'What did Lady Braithewaite say?' she asked, conscious that Violet Braithewaite was eager to increase the level of violent protests in the hope of forcing the Government to present another Franchise Bill.

'We didn't ask her, Eve,' Maud said. 'She may not like what we've done, but she'll have to accept the Committee's decision. We all support your arguments, Evelyn, and we'll all stand by our decision to take advantage of your popularity with the public.'

The following night she stepped down from the rostrum after making the meeting's main speech, and came face to face with Robert.

'Very good speech, Evelyn. I see you haven't been arrested yet.'

'No.' She tried to judge his mood and his feelings for her, but the crowd jostled them and moments later two newspaper reporters interrupted with questions.

She saw him scribble a note and managed to take it from him before they were pushed apart. She thrust the note into her pocket. She would read it later, but now she had to answer the reporters.

'Do you know where Lady Braithewaite is?' The usual question.

'No, I don't.'

133

'Is it true that you've taken over leadership and moved it away from militant policies?'

'I haven't taken over. Lady Braithewaite's still our leader.'

'Then where is she?'

'I don't know,' she said again and tried to keep her balance as the crowd swelled around her like a sea and pushed her and the two reporters together.

'You work in the East End. What do you think about Sylvia Pankhurst being imprisoned again?'

'She wouldn't be in prison or even threatened with it if we really had a free society.'

'Miss Pankhurst has threatened to hunger strike. What are your views on hunger striking?'

'It's abhorrent but perhaps the only means left for us to show we mean business.'

'Would you hunger strike if you were arrested?'

'Of course.' The crowd pushed them all again and she stumbled, but two policemen held the crowd away and helped her to clamber back to her feet. She thanked them and turned back to the reporters. 'I really must leave.'

'One last question, Miss Forrester. Would you ever resort to fire-raising or using bombs?'

'No. I personally wouldn't want to risk endangering anyone's life.'

She allowed herself to be hurried out to a motor-car belonging to one of the committee members and was happy to be driven away from the boisterous crowd and the newspaper reporters' questions.

'Well, you certainly roused some support tonight, Evelyn,' she heard the man who was driving call over his shoulder and his wife, sitting beside her, agreed.

'Yes, but will it do us any good? Will just talking actually have the effect we want?'

'It's better to talk than fight,' the woman beside her said quietly.

She nodded, and remembered to read Robert's note. It consisted of three words: *Mother is back.*

* * *

The next day Eve heard that a huge explosion had devastated Lloyd George's new house in Walton Heath. She had just enough time to wonder if Violet Braithewaite was behind the plot before attention focused on Emmeline Pankhurst.

Eve's father looked serious as the whole family discussed the development. 'It's a bad day for this country when people think it's all right to explode bombs to get what they want. And to have come to it already, only three weeks after the Bill was withdrawn.'

Was that all it was? Only three weeks! She had made so many speeches it seemed like months.

Her mother suddenly reached out and clutched her hand. 'You won't get involved in all that, will you, Eve?'

'You haven't been listening to my speeches, Mama,' she said softly, meaning the comment as a reassuring joke, but her father had his own views.

'You be careful, Eve. You've done well and we admire you for it but all the things that have gone right for you could turn against you just as quick, you know.'

Eve and Lottie had volunteered to spend the night at the mission and while she was checking all the doors and windows were secure she overheard Lou discussing the bombing of Lloyd George's house.

'I'd blow 'em all up, one by one. Not just their houses either. I'd threaten to blow each one of 'em up until there wasn't any Government left. That's the way to get the vote. Scare it out of 'em! And you could all help if you came along to some of the meetings and supported the bombings.'

Eve's stomach churned. This was exactly what she had been scared might happen if Lou came to stay. She put her head around the door, 'Lou? Can I speak to you, please? In the office?'

She ran upstairs to the office and waited. Lou arrived a few minutes later.

'Lou, I warned you that I couldn't allow you to bring politics into the mission.'

'I was just discussing the news, Miss Forrester,' Lou said in an injured voice.

'No you weren't, Lou. You were advocating violent policies and inciting the women to do the same at public meetings.'

'I was only doing what you do, miss. You go out and make speeches at least three times a week.'

'Yes, but I don't advocate violence and, more particularly, I don't bring my politics back here!' Lou's defiance made her angry.

'But I heard you did, miss,' Lou said smugly. 'I heard you went out on a poster raid, threw a copper in the canal to avoid arrest, and then hid back here where you thought you wouldn't get caught.'

The accusation stunned her, and she admitted it before she thought of the consequences. 'How do you know about that?'

'I can't say, miss. I gave my word not to,' Lou answered truculently.

'Well, Lou, when I agreed to take you into the mission you gave *me* your word that you wouldn't introduce politics. You've broken that word so I'd like you to leave. Now!'

'Come on, miss. At this time of night?' Lou laughed, a little nervously.

'I mean it, Lou. Tell me or get out now. I won't have you or anyone else putting the mission at risk.'

Lou tugged at her hair, looked around the office, and finally conceded. 'I heard it from someone who works for the *London and National Cryer*. He said they're going to print some stories about the suffrage leaders.'

'The Pankhursts and Lady Braithewaite, maybe, but not me. I'm nobody,' Eve said, aghast at the thought of her story becoming public and her aunt and parents knowing what she did.

'You're not much at the moment, miss, but who knows how far you could go if you wanted to.'

'When are they going to print these stories?' she asked, wondering if she could admit to what she had done before the newspapers printed the story.

Lou scoffed. 'They won't print them, miss. Lady Bee's seeing to that.'

'How? How can she stop them?'

'Dunno,' Lou shrugged.

'You must know!'

'I don't! Perhaps she's taking out one o' those things you get from the court.'

'An injunction?'

'Perhaps. You could always ask her tomorrow.' Lou shrugged again. 'Can I go to bed now, miss, or d'you still want me to leave.' Wind and rain rattled against the window as Lou asked the question. 'No, you can stay, but I don't want any more politics brought in here. I'll talk to you again, tomorrow, after I've spoken to Lady Braithewaite.'

She watched the girl turn and walk away, and she was sure a sly smile spread over Lou's face.

Eve went to the room she shared with Lottie and told her what had happened. Lottie listened, and suggested she should visit Violet Braithewaite the following day and ask how she intended to stop the newspaper publishing the stories.

Eve went to bed but she could not sleep for worrying about what might happen. The wind grew stronger and blew more rain against the front of the house, and downstairs the hall clock struck eleven, then half past eleven, and then twelve.

And then she heard the front door lock click!

She rose instantly and rushed onto the landing but she could not see anyone in the hall. She ran downstairs and switched on the electric light, half expecting to see one of the women with a man she had let in, but there was no one in the hall but her. She turned to the front door and saw it was no longer bolted. Then she noticed the key was not in the lock.

She was momentarily puzzled because she had locked and bolted the door herself, and then she realised that someone had gone out and taken the key.

'Lou!'

Eve ran upstairs to the dormitory Lou shared with seven other women and checked Lou's bed. It was empty, but

Lou's belonging's were still there. She obviously intended to come back but why had she gone out in the first place? Especially on such an unpleasant night like this.

'What's going on?' one of the women woke up and asked.

'Lou's gone out. Do you know where?'

'No,' the woman said, shaking her head, then added, 'but just before she turned in tonight I saw her tear a page out of a little notebook she uses and stuff it in her coat pocket.'

'What did she do with the notebook?'

'Put it back in her cabinet, I think.'

Eve opened the cabinet beside Lou's bed and found the notebook tucked under a suffrage sash, identical to the one she had buried with Polly. She took the book to the office, looked at it under her aunt's desklamp and found lists of well-known people and what appeared to be their addresses. Various dates were pencilled alongside the names, and as she glanced through the pages it occurred to her that when Lou told the women what she would do to politicians who opposed suffrage she might have been hinting at plans she had already made.

But Lou had torn a page out, so what was written on that?

Eve flicked through the pages quickly, eager to find anything that might help, and found the ragged remains of the torn page behind all the lists. It was the last page to have been written on so she held the next page up to the light in the hope she might read any indentations. There were none.

Frustrated, she tossed the little book down on the desk. Where *had* Lou gone? And what was she doing?

She stared at the book and pleaded with it to give up its secret, and noticed one page was slightly crumpled, as though Lou might have had her thumb on it when she ripped the missing page out. She read the addresses on the page and stopped at one which seemed extraordinarily significant: *The London and National Cryer – Printers*. She looked at the opposite page and read the firm's address, and alongside it she noticed a faint mark which looked a little like an onion. Or a bomb?

Was that how Violet was going to stop the newspaper publishing the stories, by blowing up the printers?

She rushed back to the bedroom, woke Lottie, and explained what she thought was happening.

'I'm going after her, Lottie, to see if I can stop her. I know the way from here.'

'And if you're wrong, Eve? You'll be giving them an even better story to publish?'

'Maybe, but we can't risk lives, Lottie,' she said, and dressed as fast as she could.

'How will you get there? It must be two miles away and Lou must've left ten or fifteen minutes ago?'

'I'll walk. And run.'

She ran for as long as she could, and then walked quickly. Apart from the noise made by the wind and rain she could hear nothing other than the sound of her own footsteps echoing along the dark and empty streets. She was alone, and uncertain she was doing the right thing.

Perhaps she should have gone back to bed and allowed things to run their course. Perhaps she should not be interfering and making matters worse for herself. Perhaps she was completely wrong and Lou was simply meeting someone who had nothing to do with bombs or politics?

The printers were in a turning off to her right. She ran across the road, turned a corner, and heard the rattle and whine of presses printing. She ran down the street and was grateful to find an open door which led directly into the print room.

'Can someone help me? I need to speak to the man in charge,' she almost shouted at the first man she saw, a large man with thick, strong arms showing below his rolled up sleeves.

'That's me. What's up?'

'I think someone from the Women's Freedom League might try to explode a bomb in here,' she gasped.

'Oh yeah?' the man said suspiciously. 'And what makes you think that?'

'It's just something I heard. I came to warn you.'

'It's more likely you came to start a fire yourself. Out! Go on. Get out. Now!' he said and pushed her towards the door, his strength easily overcoming hers.

'Please! Please believe me!' she argued but he took no notice, pushed her out into the street and locked the door behind her.

She walked to the corner of the street and waited, sheltering in a recessed doorway. She waited for a long time, and then she saw two figures come out from a shadowy entrance opposite the printers and move into light shining out from a ground floor office window.

'Stop! STOP!' she yelled and raced towards them.

One figure looked at her then fiddled with whatever she had in her hands. The taller figure came towards her, arms outstretched, and shouting, 'No, Evelyn. NO!'

Eve grabbed Lady Braithewaite and half dragged her a few yards towards Lou who had swung her arm back, ready to throw something. 'LOU!'

Lou looked at her and stumbled, caught her foot on the kerb and fell. Her arm snapped forwards. Something crashed against the brickwork just below the office window.

For a moment the only noise was the wind and rain.

'RUN!' Lady Braithewaite yelled and wrenched herself free.

'Bomb?' Eve heard a man say loudly. 'Bomb? Is this a joke?'

Lou scrambled to her knees and screamed at Lady Braithewaite.

A moment later the bomb exploded.

Eve was knocked flat as Lou crashed against her. Then a fountain of flame seemed to lift over her and settle in a ring all around. She saw Lady Braithewaite stumble and rise again, with her coat and hat on fire.

Then everything seemed very quiet and she had an immense pain in her head.

She could not breathe.

Then nothing.

PART 2

CHAPTER 11

London, 1913

Lottie stood quite still and tried not to shiver as the wind whipped the cold through her coat and into her bones. She stared past the grave, past the mourners standing on the other side of the gravel, and tried hard to hang on to reality, the reality she was learning to cope with until the bomb blew the family's life apart.

It would be so easy to slip back into a dreamworld where she could make-believe everything was perfect but she would not be slipping into a dream, she would be slipping back into a nightmare, isolated from her family and scared she was going mad.

She heard the words which were intoned as the coffin was lowered, and looked at Tom Dobbs, white-faced, still shocked by his sister's death, and the only member of his family to see her buried. Then she looked at her own family, genuinely grieving for another wasted life and also worried about Eve who was alive but injured, and waiting to be arrested for bombing the printers.

Lou had been closest to the bomb and had died instantly but she had saved Eve from anything worse than cuts, bruises and concussion. Eve had been unconscious for two days and even now, three days after waking, she still had a severe headache and was shaking from shock.

Lottie agreed with everyone who said Eve was lucky to escape relatively unscathed but she still thought it was so unfair! Eve had been involved because she was trying to stop Lou exploding the bomb. Now she was hurt and being blamed for everything, and everyone said that when she came out of hospital she would probably go to prison.

'Come on, little sister.' Jamie slipped his arm through hers and led her away.

They all gathered outside the cemetery gates, where everyone had gathered after Polly's funeral, but this time they did not go off to the cosy tea-shop. Tom and the Jacksons shook hands with everyone, Tom thanked them all for coming, and they all went home, too cold and tired to do anything else.

The moment Lottie walked though the front door she noticed Sasha's long black overcoat hanging from the hallstand.

Before she could take her coat off Katarina, who had been looking after the children, came out from the kitchen and offered to make tea. Moments later all the children appeared, eager to show everyone the pictures Sasha had helped them to draw. Each picture was similar, always of onion-domed churches and families skating or riding in sleighs.

She turned and found Sasha standing behind her, the children clustered around him. 'Do you like children, Sasha?'

'Of course, Lottie. Very much.'

'Why?'

He thought for just a moment, then said simply, 'Because they believe in fairies and magic.'

She smiled. It was the sort of answer she should have expected.

He frowned. 'You look very tired, Lottie. Are you unwell?'

'No, not unwell, Sasha, but I am tired. Very tired.' She had not been sleeping well.

She turned her head as her father placed one hand on her shoulder and the other on Sasha's. 'If you want to practise on the piano, Sasha, then go ahead.'

'Oh, no, sir!' Sasha looked horrified. 'I came to visit my mother and to offer my condolences to you and your family, not to play music. That would be wrong.'

'Rubbish!' her father said bluntly. 'We wouldn't see it as being disrespectful, and we'd actually find it comforting to listen to you. Go on, lad. Take Lottie into the other room and play something for us.'

She saw Sasha was still hesitant so she squeezed his hand to encourage him and led him through the door into the front room.

Sasha played beautifully for half an hour, always suitable music, always Russian music. Lottie drank her tea English-style and he drank his with heaped spoonfuls of sugar and slices of lemon.

After a while she stood behind him as she often did when they were alone, her hands resting on his shoulders and her mind suspended in a world and mood that his music evoked. It was not until he turned and looked up at her that she realised she was crying.

'Lottie? Lottie? What's wrong?' He was on his feet, his hands holding her elbows.

'I don't know, Sasha. I don't know.' She looked up into his soft eyes. 'Hold me, Sasha, please.'

His arms slid around her, wrapping her up, squeezing her to him, shutting out the world. She was safe, snug and warm, and something inside her stirred.

She lifted her face and pursed her lips, hoping he would understand, hoping she would feel the same thrill she felt when they kissed accidentally on her birthday.

His face came down, she shut her eyes, and warm emotion poured through her. She held him tight as he kissed her again, then felt his hands running over her back, pressing her tighter and tighter to him so she could hardly breathe. Feelings overwhelmed her and she kissed him again and again, firmly, slowly, almost melting with the pleasure she felt.

'LOTTIE!' her aunt said coldly. 'How could you, when there's Albert?'

'I—' She stepped away from Sasha, unable to excuse herself, unwilling to attempt to explain.

'It's my fault, Mrs Hampton,' Sasha apologised and accepted the blame.

'It's both your faults,' her aunt said sternly. 'I think you'd best come with me, Lottie.'

Her hand was grabbed and moments later she was in the kitchen with the rest of the family who did not seem to have heard what had been said in the next room.

Sasha followed moments later, avoided looking her in the eyes and made an excuse to leave. He spoke to everyone in turn, a slightly different message for each, and he came to her last. He spoke formally, as he always did, but although his eyes said far more than his words she was not sure what they *were* saying. Was he apologising for compromising her, or was he saying something else? It was impossible to know, so she tried to tell him how she felt without telling everyone else.

'Thank you for playing for me, Sasha. Thank you for everything. It was wonderful.' She saw her aunt glare at her, and hoped Sasha understood as well as her aunt did.

Half an hour later she was washing up in the scullery when Aunt Lizzie came in and closed the door.

'Please don't give your parents any more to worry about, Lottie.' Her aunt sounded stern.

'He was just trying to comfort me and we—'

'Comfort can lead to all sorts of problems, Lottie, and you shouldn't expect Sasha to provide it. He's a young man, a very young man, and he could well misinterpret your feelings. You could even be misinterpreting your own feelings, considering all that's happened lately, but you mustn't forget that you're still engaged to Albert.'

'Yes, Aunt.' It was obvious that Aunt Lizzie had forgotten what it was like to have strong feelings for someone.

'Please don't say "Yes, Aunt" like that, Lottie. You might think I'm old-fashioned and stuffy but you must remember you owe Albert your loyalty unless you're prepared to tell him that you won't marry him. Anyway, you'll only make yourself feel guilty if you go behind his back.'

She almost asked her aunt what she would do under the circumstances, but she knew her aunt would tell her to marry Albert as she had planned. After all, Albert could offer her everything she wanted, unlike Sasha who had nothing.

But Albert could not make her feel the way Sasha could.

Rose heard the postman deliver the afternoon post and went into the hall to collect it, but Lottie had already picked it up from the mat and was sorting through it.

'I thought Albert might have written, Mama. I sent him a letter about Eve.' Lottie had the letters fanned out in her left hand, and she suddenly frowned and plucked at one. 'This one's wrongly addressed. It's for a Mrs R. Belchester, Mama.'

Rose tried to speak but could not. Hubert! *He had found her.*

Lottie reached for the door. 'If I can catch the postman I'll give it back to him.'

'No! Give it to me.' She snatched the letter away from Lottie, realised she had over-reacted, and tried to excuse herself. 'It's for someone else. Someone staying at the mission.'

'Then why wasn't it sent there?'

'Lottie! Do you have to question everything I say and do? Do you think I'm lying or talking because I like to hear my own voice?'

'No, Mama!'

'Then accept what I say, once in a while, and don't be so irritating.'

She took the letters into the kitchen where she could be alone, and heard Lottie run upstairs, snivelling.

She sat still and looked up to the ceiling, almost as if she could see through it and into Lottie's bedroom, and she imagined Lottie lying on her bed, face buried in her pillow to muffle the sounds of her crying.

The letter had caused trouble before she had even opened it.

Hubert! She had sensed his presence for weeks, almost wished he would appear, and now that he had, even if it was only in the form of a letter, she was scared. Having the letter was like having him come uninvited into the room. He was no longer part of her life, but he was there, invading it.

She glanced at the kitchener. She could burn the letter unopened and that way it could not harm her, but that would not stop Hubert knowing where she was. He would simply write again or, even worse, come to the house.

'Why, Hubert, why? It was all over years ago.'

She sat still and slowly gathered up her courage until she had enough to reach out and open the letter.

My Dearest Rose,

I trust that you are of reasonable health in the face of the considerable problems you currently face. It appears that you have passed your wilfulness to your daughter, Evelyn.

I would not have located you but for Evelyn's activities. The name Forrester is synonymous with my memories of you. Simple enquiries revealed that you are living with Forrester as his wife and have four children and three grandchildren.

I, of course, have nothing. My father died several years ago and my mother last autumn.

I must confess that I feared you may have died also and that I was a widower, but in the hope that you were still alive and may one day wish to return I have remained as faithful to you as I would have wished you to remain to me.

I must congratulate you upon your ability to disappear so well. Even your brother, John, appears unaware of your circumstances, although his drinking is of a level which renders him unaware of many things, including his wife, Lillian.

I have disposed of the coastal estate in Dorset and the London house you know so well and I now spend much of my life in Jerez where I manage the sherry and manzanilla production. However, I still have interests to manage in

England and while here I reside at my club or in a hotel.

I have taken meticulous care of all your personal belongings, and ensured your clothes are kept clean and aired and ready for your use should you wish to return to me, your husband, and resume our life together.

I feel that in that regard there are matters which require discussion and I would ask you to meet me for tea at the Savoy, our usual table, next Saturday.

I am sure you will agree, and not render me any further disappointment,

Your Loving Husband,

Hubert

He knew all about her and her family, and he wanted to meet her, but not immediately. He was giving her several days to think about it, to worry about it, to consider the consequences of going and the possible consequences of not going. He had not changed, he was still like a cat with a mouse, tormenting it before he finally bit into it and left it to bleed to death.

She folded the letter, returned it to its envelope and hid it in her pocket. She had to think carefully before she did anything, told anyone. A mistake could be disastrous.

Eve found it strange to be a patient in the very ward where she had worked under Sister Brewer's watchful eyes, and she found it hard to lie down quietly when she was normally so active.

Although the ward was dark she was wide awake. A clock ticked away the minutes and although she could not see it to read the time she could hear muted noises that identified the hospital routines. She guessed it was around ten o'clock.

Ten o'clock! Was that all? She shifted in the bed, uncomfortable but without any real pain apart from an aching head, bored and eager to get on with whatever was going to happen to her.

When her parents had visited her that evening and told

her about Lou's funeral they had both seemed very strained, suddenly much older, and she had felt responsible for bringing so much trouble into their otherwise relatively ordered lives. She had apologised to them and they had told her she should not worry because it was not really her fault. But it *was* her fault. If she had simply warned the police it would have been possible to arrest Lady Braithewaite and Lou before they exploded the bomb and no harm would have been done. Now, her parents were desperately worried about her, Lou was dead and Lady Braithewaite was injured. All because she thought she could stop them by herself.

She turned her head as the door opened, and heard Sister Brewer quite clearly even though she was whispering. 'It's terribly late, Doctor, and most irregular.'

'Please, Sister. I'll be very quiet and I won't stay for long, I promise.' It was Robert. This was his first visit since the accident, as she preferred to think of it. Her heart skipped and made her head throb even more, but she did not mind. He had come to see her, and that was all that mattered.

Sister Brewer hesitated, then said patiently, 'Come along then, but be quiet now. We'll see if she's awake.'

'How are you feeling?' She could not see him but she could tell from his voice that he was worried.

'Headache, but that's about all.'

'Seems as if you were lucky.'

'Yes, I suppose I was, really.'

He hesitated, then told her he had seen her while she was still unconscious.

'Oh, I didn't know. Thank you.'

He said how relieved he was to see she was recovering, and then a tetchiness crept into his tone. 'Evelyn, what did you think you were doing? You should have called the police.'

'I know, but I didn't, Robert. Anyway, perhaps it was fate. It's all too late now,' she said, already resigned to the situation. 'How's your mother?'

'The right side of her face, her right shoulder and her

right hand are all badly burned. Fortunately Perkins knew where I was and brought her straight to me. I gave her some emergency treatment, then we took her down to the White House in Eastbourne and across to France the following morning.'

'France?'

'A friend of mine has a very small hospital near Rouen. He specialises in burns. She'd have been arrested if I'd taken her to a hospital in England.'

'Like me, you mean?' she said, trying not to sound bitter.

'I didn't know you were involved. I thought mother was acting alone.' He shook his head. 'I did warn you that she'd get you into trouble. How long will it be before they let you out of here?'

'Just in time to be arrested and go to court, I should think.'

'I shouldn't think they'll bother, Evelyn, and even if you are arrested I can't imagine the case going to court. Not when the printers corroborate your story that you were trying to stop the bombing.'

'I'm not going to ask them to do that, Robert,' she admitted quietly.

'You'll have to. You might go to prison if you don't,' he said in a shocked voice.

She explained why his mother bombed the printers, and the agreement she had come to with the newspaper. 'You see, Robert, this way I can claim I went there to stop Lou bombing the place without involving your mother or saying why the printers was being bombed. In return for my efforts to stop the bombing the newspaper has agreed not to print the story about my exploits during the poster raid. It's the only way I can keep everything secret and not harm the mission. It's actually a better solution than your mother's because if she had succeeded in wrecking the printers the newspaper would simply have printed the stories in a later edition.'

'But you could go to prison, Evelyn,' he insisted.

'There's a small risk, but I'm known for arguing against violence. My campaign slogan's *Votes without Violence*.'

'Your *compaign slogan*? Evelyn, I think my mother's right about you. You are a natural politician.'

'And one without the right to vote.'

'Good God, woman! Even after all this, when you're lying there like that, you're still making speeches. A suffragette through and through. Don't you ever think of anything else?'

'Yes, but at the moment my main thoughts are about getting the vote.'

'And me?' he asked quietly.

'And you, Robert. And you.' She smiled and thought he was about to kiss her, but Sister Brewer rustled up to the bed.

'Doctor Braithewaite. Surely I don't have to tell you about a patient's need to rest?'

'No, Sister,' he said contritely. 'Goodnight, Evelyn.'

She smiled, and thought his visit had done her as much good as all the treatment.

Elizabeth passed a letter across the desk for Rose to read, but Rose said she was too tired to read it and asked her what it said.

'Mr Buddelscome informs us that at the last meeting of the Trustees a motion was proposed and seconded that both you and I receive a severe written reprimand for the way in which we run this mission, and in particular for our negligence in allowing certain parties with known political affiliations to use the mission as a shelter for illegal acts. We are also reprimanded for jointly allowing the mission and the Trust to be brought into disrepute, and would have been removed from office had it not been for our long and previously faithful service. And because they have decided to close us down in preparation for the premises being sold to raise finance for the other missions.'

She watched Rose's face and saw very little reaction, just a *small* grimace of acceptance. That did not surprise her because Rose seemed to have become almost immune to shocks since the day Lou Dobbs was buried, presumably because she was simply so thankful that Eve had not been killed by the bomb that she was prepared to accept whatever else life threw at her.

There was one consolation. 'Well, Rose, apart from Eve's predicament things can't get much worse.'

'They already have, Lizzie.' Rose took an envelope out of her bag and pushed it across the desk.

The envelope was address-side down so she turned it over and immediately understood what Rose meant.

'Hubert?'

'Yes. Read it. He wants me to meet him tomorrow. For tea at the Savoy. *At our usual table.* He's acting as though we're still married, Lizzie.'

'You are, Rose,' she reminded her, and leaned forward to read the letter. It left her cold. 'When did it come?'

'The same day as Lou Dobbs's funeral.'

So that was what had changed Rose's mood. 'Have you told Edward?'

'No. I'm not sure how he'd react, but he'd probably cause even more trouble.'

'Are you going to meet Hubert?'

'Yes. I don't want to but I will.'

'D'you want me to be there, just in case?'

'Just in case of what? He's hardly likely to abduct me from the Savoy, is he? Anyway, I don't want him thinking I've brought someone along because I'm scared of him.'

'But you are, aren't you?'

Rose nodded. Neither of them spoke for several minutes, and when they did they both spoke at once, expressing the same view. Hubert could not be involved in the purchase of the mission if he had only just found them so the date must simply be a coincidence. Also, if there was any truth at all in Lottie's stories about being followed it clearly was not anything to do with Hubert.

'So, Rose, if he's not trying to manipulate your life as you thought, why are you so scared?'

'Lizzie, if I knew I'd tell you, but I don't,' Rose gasped, and minutes later she was in the throes of a full asthma attack.

It was two hours before Rose had recovered enough to be taken home, and even then she could not be hurried. It was dark by the time they reached Angel Street and Lizzie took Rose up to her bed and made sure she was comfortable before going back downstairs to draw the curtains and light the fire in the front room.

They had rarely used the front room before Katarina and Paul came to stay, but now, with so many people in the house, the room was used every evening. Lizzie lit the fire and the gas mantle and was about to draw the curtains when someone knocked at the front door.

She left the curtains, opened the door and saw Bill Crabb standing on the step. 'Sorry to disturb you, Lizzie. Can I come in?'

'Of course.' She led him into the front room.

He looked pale and ill, unsure of himself, and when he did not speak she was sure he must have come to tell her Gladys had died.

'Oh Bill,' she started to say, and moved towards him with her hands outstretched but he interrupted her, engulfed her hands in his and held them gently.

'Lizzie, I've just heard Miss Evelyn's been arrested for the bombing and she's been moved to the prison infirmary.'

'What?' She felt unsteady and as she swayed his arms slipped around her waist and held her.

'It's worse. She's denied it but says she has no defence. She could go to prison for years, Lizzie.'

'Oh, God! I can't tell Rose that.' She clung on to him, her face pressed against his chest.

'Easy does it,' he said gently. 'Easy does it. Rose'll cope. You'll see.'

'How, Bill? How do you cope with everything when it keeps going wrong?' She sobbed and was glad for the comfort that came from holding someone and being held in return. 'How do you cope with your life, Bill, with Gladys, day in, day out?'

'I cope because I have to, Lizzie, not because I want to, not any more.' He spoke heavily and she felt his chin rub against the top of her head. 'And I cope because I don't

154

think too much about it, and try not to think about how I'd like to be living, Lizzie, what I'm missing because . . .'

Still holding him tight she looked up at him when he stopped. 'Go on, Bill. Go on.'

'I think, maybe, you know.' He looked down at her and as he did so his lips brushed her nose.

She did not flinch, looked him straight in his eyes, inches away from hers, aware that his lips were even closer to her lips. She wanted to be kissed, needed someone to be tender towards her, and she could guess how he felt about her now he had admitted how unhappy his life was.

'Oh, God, Lizzie, this is wrong,' he breathed, but did not move.

'I know,' she said and shut her eyes, and waited.

It was the first time a man had kissed her on the lips since Richard had died over twenty years before. The feeling overwhelmed her. Sap rose up. She clung to Bill's neck and pulled his face down harder against hers, only half believing what was happening, scared it would end, scared it would not happen again. She was determined to wring every grain of enjoyment out of it before reality encroached and made her feel ashamed of herself.

She was grateful he reacted the way he did, clamping her against him so she had difficulty drawing breath, kissing her again and again on her lips and face and neck and throat.

He stopped suddenly, loosened his grip. 'Lizzie, this is wrong.'

'Of course it is. I'm sorry.' She stepped back and could no longer look him in the eyes. 'I'm sorry I took advantage of you like that. It was wrong of me.'

'Is that what you did?' he said gruffly.

'I think so.'

He levelled his eyes into hers, and shrugged, his face holding an expression of unhappy resignation. 'I thought I'd better let you know to save you going to the hospital, but I reckon I'd better go now.'

'I suppose so.' She did not want him to leave but it would be unwise for him to stay.

Lottie arrived home and wondered why the front room curtains were left open when the lamp was lit, so before she knocked on the door she stepped up to the window and looked in.

'Aunt Lizzie?' She was astonished, and then angry.

Her aunt was doing far worse than she had done. At least Sasha was not married.

Rose was glad she was alone in the house because if anyone had been there to see her dressing to meet Hubert they would have gained the wrong impression.

She prepared herself meticulously, determined to give him the impression that Edward left her wanting for nothing. Unfortunately that meant dressing herself as attractively as she could and she suddenly felt much as she imagined a young woman might feel when she was getting ready to meet a man she cared for.

The ridiculousness of the situation made her smile, something she had not done for days, even weeks, and the reflection she saw in the mirror contrasted so much with the one she had become used to that she realised how much she had aged. She had been proud of her beauty in the sense of being grateful rather than vain, but now her beauty had disappeared under lined skin and sagging jowls, and her heavy copper-coloured hair was thin and grey.

She was glad that her figure was still there, although she knew her breasts were not so firm now and her waist and hips were thicker than they had been, but at least she could still see her beauty passed on in Helen and Lottie. If anything Lottie was more beautiful, her grey eyes softer and more loving than the vivid green she and Helen shared.

She dressed in her favourite clothes; an ankle-length moss green dress covered by a calf-length coat in dark grey wool, and a wide-brimmed hat trimmed with ruffled dark green lawn and speared by an amber-tipped hat pin. An amber brooch fixed to the throat of her dress's high collar completed her decoration.

She deliberately chose not to wear any rings other than the brass one Edward had given her years ago to wear on her wedding ring finger. She was proud of that ring, proud of all it stood for, all she and Edward had gone through to be together. Nothing would make her hide it or feel ashamed to wear it.

Finally, she selected a small handbag and a pretty parasol-type umbrella, and spent a moment checking her reflection in her full-length mirror.

Yes, she was satisfied that she was quite presentable, even for tea at the Savoy.

She sat alone for an hour, edgy, strained, constantly looking for someone she could recognise as Hubert, resenting the dark, neatly-bearded foreign man on the next table who insisted on smoking a pungent cigar, and the lady with him who smoked equally pungent cigarettes. A uniformed waiter kept glancing towards her, anticipating her order and embarrassing her so much she thought of leaving before deciding that would not be wise.

Then an official wearing a morning suit arrived and bowed subserviently.

'Excuse me, madam, but I've been instructed to inform you that Mr Belchester has telephoned our reception and asked us to apologise to you on his behalf for his absence and explain that he has been unavoidably detained and will not now be able to meet you as arranged. He suggests that you take tea with us against his account and promises that he will be in touch with you in due course to make further arrangements.'

She smiled, thanked the official, and left.

She was sure Hubert was there, watching her, and she was determined to exit in a manner which would show him that he could not intimidate her with his tricks. Once outside she stepped into a taxi-cab and asked the driver to take her to Trafalgar Square. She thought Hubert would be impressed to see her ride rather than walk away, but she knew she could not afford to ride too far.

She caught a bus from the Square, eager to arrive home

and change into normal clothes before she aroused any of the family's suspicions.

Lottie was pleased to be allowed to finish work early but disappointed when she arrived home and found no one there to answer the door. She thought her mother or Katarina might be next door with Maisie and turned to go as her mother opened the front gate.

'You're early, Lottie. Anything wrong?' She could tell that her mother was anxious.

'No. The supervisor felt ill and decided to close the office early,' she explained absently, distracted by the way her mother was dressed. 'You're all dressed up, Mama? Been somewhere special?'

'Just someone I had to see.' She saw her mother blush slightly, a sure sign there was more to her appearance than she wanted to admit.

'Someone who smokes cigars. He smells rich, Mama,' she said as a joke, and instantly regretted it.

'Don't be ridiculous.' Her mother spoke too quickly, too sharply, then tried to justify herself. 'It's not what it seems, Lottie. Please believe me, and don't tell anyone. That's important.'

'No, Mama,' she said quietly, and as she stepped aside for her mother to open the door she smelled not only the cigar smoke but her mother's best perfume, the perfume she used only for the best occasions.

Lottie watched her mother run upstairs and come down minutes later, changed out of her best clothes but still wearing a guilty expression, and an awful suspicion sowed itself in her mind.

If Aunt Lizzie was having an affair with Mr Crabb why should not her mother be meeting someone? A man who was rich enough to smoke expensive cigars?

After all, it was a constant source of wonderment that a woman with her mother's background should have married a working-class man like her father.

She also realised, quite coldly, that the only certainty in her life had been the assumption that her parents would always be there, together. They were the pillars of trust that supported her life.

Suddenly the pillars did not seem so firm, and without their support she sensed that her determination to hold on to reality would soon slip.

A moment later she made a decision.

If reality was as awful as it seemed she had to find a way to make it bearable, and that required money. Obtaining money was simple. She would marry Albert.

CHAPTER 12

———————

Eve liked the barrister the Women's Freedom League retained for her. He was elderly, affable, blunt and realistic, and he summed up her situation in two sentences during their first meeting.

'Miss Forrester, if you plead guilty and offer no evidence in your defence you will go to prison for a period. If you plead not guilty and offer no evidence in your defence you will go to prison for an even longer period.'

'I'm not guilty and I refuse to plead otherwise, but I've already said I will offer no defence so please do whatever you can to keep my sentence to a minimum. I can't afford to spend too much time locked up if we're to get on with the fight.'

'Quite. I'll see you in Court.'

It was that simple and almost that quick when she came to Court. The hearing took thirty minutes and the Court sentenced her to two years in prison.

Then she was loaded into a van and taken away to Holloway, where she found the peculiar sensation of unreality that had enveloped her since the accident suddenly torn away.

'Forrester! Strip naked and wash yourself with this in there.' A used bar of carbolic soap was thrust at her, someone else's hairs embedded in it, and she was shown a row of baths in a long, grey-tiled room. 'Wash yourself properly, mind, or we'll have to come and do it for you.'

The senior wardress, large and loud, bellowed the orders and laughed.

The water was nearly cold and the soap reluctant to lather but she managed to wash herself all over, stood up and dried herself on an inadequate towel. When she returned to the room where she had left her own clothes she found they had been taken and replaced by durable prison clothes. She dressed fast, to cover her nakedness and because she felt cold, and it was not until she picked up the overall-style outer garment that she saw the arrow pattern.

It reinforced what she already knew. She was a convict.

She felt sick and sat down on the bench that had held the clothes.

'Forrester! Stand up. Stand up and finish dressing!' The large wardress glowered at her.

She did as she was ordered.

'Right! Hair. Any infections? Any visitors?'

'No.'

'No, madam! No, madam! Remember who you're talking to, Forrester.'

'Yes, madam.'

'Right. Lean over and let me look at your hair.'

'It's clean and I don't have any—'

'I'll be the judge of that.' The wardress's fingers snaked into her hair and a vicious tug made her wince as her head was yanked low enough for the officer to make her inspection. 'Clean, you reckon? Well I don't think so, Forrester. Quite a little farmyard you've got in there, my lady.'

'I don't think so. It's perfectly clean.'

'Clean enough to satisfy you, maybe, but not us. We don't want you infecting everyone else in here just because you can't be bothered to take proper care of yourself.'

'I am clean. I'm a nurse and—'

'Silence! Forrester, you do not speak unless you are spoken to, and even then you watch what you say. Understand? UNDERSTAND?'

'Yes, madam.' There was no use in arguing. She had lost more than just the freedom of movement when she was sentenced; she had also lost her right to argue, to be an individual. Now she was wholly in the power of others.

'Right, sit down on that bench again. Scissors!'

Someone brought scissors and there was tugging and then snipping sounds. She saw chunks of her hair fall around her, pieces of her taken away from her without her consent.

'Into the other room and we'll wash your head properly.'

She was virtually frog-marched back into the room with its baths and sinks and her head was thrust over a sink so the edge pressed against her throat, almost choking her. Foul-smelling disinfectant was poured neat onto her hair and rubbed into her scalp until it burned and then it was washed off with cold water which carried lengths of her hair with it. Her hair clogged the plug hole so the water could not run away. It rose up in the sink until it covered her mouth and slopped against her nose.

She tried to pull her head up so she could breathe but each time she was pushed back again, nose and mouth pushed and held under the water. She blew bubbles to show she could not breathe but the wardresses ignored her and poured more water over her head, filling the sink even deeper. The disinfected water stung her eyes, flowed through her nose and into her mouth so she could taste it. She forced her head back against the wardresses hands and spat the liquid into the sink.

'That'll do,' the big wardress said flatly. 'I reckon she understands what we mean by clean, now.'

She coughed and spluttered and did not resist as they led her along a dimly-lit, cold corridor. A door was opened, she was pushed through into darkness and the door grated shut behind her.

She stood waiting, but nothing happened. She was alone

in what felt like a cave, a dungeon.

It took her several minutes to realise the cold, echoing cave was her cell, her home for the next two years. She lurched around in the dark and found a cot-like bed with a thin mattress and a thinner blanket. A stool, a bucket, a wooden chest and a rickety little table completed the furnishings. She sat on the bed, wrapped herself in the blanket, and tried to imagine what her life was going to be like for the next hundred weeks.

A voice called through the door. 'You're going to spend the next few days locked up in here, Forrester, so you'll have to live with whatever you do to the place.'

She heard footsteps stride down the corridor, a grill clang shut, a lock turn, and then silence.

'Wotcha in fer?' a coarse voice called from the next cell.

'I exploded a bomb.' Best not to claim she was innocent.

'Jesus Christ! D'yer kill anyone?'

'No.' Best not to complicate the answer.

'Suffragette, are yer?'

'Yes.' Best not to say too much about herself.

'So'm I. All of us are on this wing. On'y just moved us 'ere 'cos we smashed up our last lot o' cells. We're doing this lot at nine. You'll 'ear the clock strike. Smash yer windows and yer stools and anyfing else yer can manage. Right?'

'Right.'

It was all dark and foreign, and much harsher than she thought it would be. And now she was expected to invite even more trouble by smashing up her cell.

She did not have much choice. She had no friends with the wardresses, that was obvious, and if she did not join in with her fellow prisoners she would have no friends there, either. She could not spend months here without someone to talk to, confide in. It was not possible.

Her eyes had begun to adjust to the dark and high up on the wall opposite the door there was a patch of darkness which was not quite so black as the rest. She used the stool to climb up to it and felt glass. That was her window and she was going to smash it at nine o'clock.

She wrapped herself in her blanket again, lay down on the bed, and shivered. She was cold even fully dressed and wrapped in her blanket, with her window still in place! What would it be like when she smashed it?

There were sounds outside in the corridor and her neighbour told her their food was being delivered. A voice shouted at her to stand back even though she was lying on the bed, and the food was shoved through a slide in the door and left on the floor for her to collect. A tin dish of gruel and a tin mug of flavourless but foul-smelling liquid which might have been tea. She could not face either so she left them where they were. Half an hour later someone came to collect the tins.

'You haven't eaten it?'

'No.'

'You won't get any more 'til the morning.'

'I don't mind, I'm not hungry.'

'Right.' The tins were taken away.

She turned onto her side and wondered if it would get better as time passed. Perhaps she just felt particularly vulnerable at the moment. Perhaps she would get used to it.

Perhaps she would not. It might get even worse. She shuddered. She was weakening already and she had only been there for a few hours.

She heard a clock strike, counted, and was relieved when it stopped at seven. Still two hours to go before she joined in the protest against suffrage convictions and made herself even more uncomfortable.

She lay back in the dark and listened, noticed some similarities with the hospital at night and thought it must be something to do with grouping large numbers of people together in big buildings.

She must have dozed because she woke up as a clock struck. She listened, too late to hear each strike, and wondered what time it was. The clock's mechanism seemed to settle, the reverberations of the last strike humming into the night, then silence.

It lasted seconds.

The sudden uproar scared her and took her breath away. Glass smashed, women screamed and shouted and wood splintered. The volume of noise was so terrifying it unnerved her, and it was added to by the staff ringing bells and running along the corridor hammering on the cell doors and yelling at the women to be quiet.

She pulled her cot over to the window wall, climbed up and swung her stool at the window. It smashed instantly and cold air blew in. She jumped down, took her empty bucket and smashed it against the cell door, shouting and screaming like the rest, building up a frenzy that made her feel better and warmer.

The row went on and on and during the few lapses on her wing she could hear prisoners on other wings also joining in the protest. Someone outside her cell opened the cover to a spy-hole and she put her own eye to it, saw someone looking in at her and saw the dimly-lit corridor as they pulled away.

'Will you be quiet, Forrester?'

She banged the bucket against the door. That was her answer.

'Last chance, Forrester. Will you be quiet?'

She banged the bucket again and again and again, eyes shut, shouting and screaming with the other women. Suddenly the door came open and her feet were hooked away. She fell awkwardly on her elbow and screamed with pain but something cold punched her in the chest, knocked the breath out of her and rolled her over and over. She was slammed up against her cot, and every time she tried to protect herself her arms were forced away.

Suddenly she could not breathe. She was suffocating, but whoever was holding her quickly let go. She reached out, rolled over, and something hit the back of her head. It shoved her face against the iron cot-frame. The pressure moved away from her head and ran down her back, and numbed by the shock and cold she realised it was water. She had been hosed, knocked breathless and soaked.

The water stopped, the cell door slammed shut and

seconds later she heard a whoosh as the woman next door was given the same treatment. Then that cell door slammed and she heard another opened up.

'They're hosing us, the bastards,' the woman in the next cell shouted from her window, and kept yelling until the women next to her joined in and then another and another.

She did not join the shouting from the windows. She was in too much pain from her elbow, still weak from so long in a hospital bed, and too shocked to protest any more.

The treatment had demoralised her already and she wanted to crawl into a small, warm nest and be alone with her pain and misery and know that in the morning things would seem better.

But there was no nest and there was no warmth and not even anything which was dry. And things would not be better in the morning.

Everything was soaked and the wind was blowing cold in through the smashed glass. The best she could do was try to cover the window with her dripping blanket and sit on her stool all night. The mattress was sodden and the floor was cold and wet; in her condition a night spent on either might be fatal.

She sat on the stool and felt the water draining off her and her soaked clothes sticking, chilling her through.

She grew stiffer each hour, chilled so much she was glad she was shivering because she knew that might just keep her alive, and she listened to the total silence that accompanied the total darkness.

The prison night did not sound like a hospital night now, it sounded like something she had never experienced before, something she did not want to experience again. She had seven hundred nights of this and the thought made her wonder if she would still be sane when they let her out.

A clock which stood somewhere outside the prison walls where normal life still went on struck each hour through the night. She heard it strike each one. As it struck five her cell door opened. She cowered back, scared what would happen next.

'Forrester?' Dim light shadowed a large form.

She tried to answer but she could not. Fear and cold made her jaw rigid.

'Come on.' Hands reached out, she flinched but they gripped her gently and helped her to stand, her joints cracking as she did so. 'We've another cell for you. Don't smash this one.'

'The others?' she managed to ask, but clumsily and quietly through uncontrolled lips.

'And them. You're first because you're at the end.'

She started as the wardress grabbed her injured elbow. 'Cracked it.' She managed to say.

'Just a bruise, probably,' the officer said.

'Cracked. I'm a nurse,' she mumbled.

'No, you're a prisoner, Forrester. We'll get it looked at in the morning.'

She did not argue, the thought of dry clothes and somewhere soft and warm to lie was too enticing.

When Eve woke up she realised that what she thought had been a nightmare was real. She knew she had to get out, and there was only one way to do that even though it was dangerous.

Breakfast was pushed through the door opening but she did not even look at it. Half an hour later someone came to collect the tins.

'You haven't eaten anything? Are you ill?'

'No,' she said unsteadily, 'apart from an elbow which was cracked when I was hosed last night.'

'Then why haven't you eaten?'

'Because I am a prisoner being illegally detained by His Majesty's Government as a consequence of my committing a purely political act and I am invoking my rights not to accept your food or drink.'

'You're going on hunger strike?' the anonymous voice said succinctly.

'I am a prisoner being illegally—' The slide slammed shut before she could repeat the full statement. She noticed the food and drink had been left inside the cell.

Around midday she heard the other prisoners' food being delivered, and their loud complaints about its flavour and quantity. She did not receive anything; not until the tins had been collected from the others and then a bowl of steaming and spicy stew was slipped through the opening in the door. Not just the stew but a tin mug of strong coffee. The smell of both made her mouth water.

She calculated that she had not had a drink for nearly twenty hours and the saliva was welcome. She kept it in her mouth, rinsing it around and around but the instinct to swallow was strong and after she had swallowed it a foul taste clung to her tongue and gums. This was just the first day, there was far worse to come.

She knew that after four or five days a gang of them would attack her, push a tube down her throat and force food into her.

But she also knew that by the time that happened she might not be in any condition to care.

CHAPTER 13

———

Rose told Lizzie that Hubert had asked for another meeting. Because both Lottie and Katarina were at home that day, she took her best outfit to the mission and changed there.

She dressed exactly as she had before, but this time she was less scared of Hubert than she was of being seen by her own family.

She arrived late at the Savoy, a deliberate ploy to show Hubert she was not totally subservient to his demands. An official greeted her and showed her to a table, and when she recognised several waiters from before she hoped they did not also remember her.

If they did they were too gallant to let her know, even when they served her tea which she ordered against Hubert's account. Once again he kept her waiting and once more he sent a message, finally, apologising for being detained and suggesting they meet at a future date.

Once again she was polite to the man who brought the message, and again she sensed Hubert was there and watching her.

She decided this was the last time that she would come. She was not his puppet, and the next time he pulled the strings he would find she did not react to his demands. What would happen after that depended on the circumstances at that time, but she would not be made a fool of again.

She went back to the mission and changed back into her ordinary clothes, glad that no one other than Lizzie had seen her.

She did not know that Lottie had watched her leave the mission, then followed her until she had taken a bus.

The following afternoon, after church and after the midday dinner, Lottie settled Albert on the settee in the front room and explained why she had written and asked him to visit for the day. 'I've considered all the things I wanted to think about, Albert, and decided I really do want to marry you. As soon as possible.'

She could see he was surprised, and it showed in his voice when he asked the inevitable question. 'Why, Charlotte? Why have you suddenly decided that's what you want.'

She gave him the answer she had rehearsed, even snuggling against him exactly as she had rehearsed when she was alone in her bedroom and using a propped up pillow. She kept her face hidden from his eyes. 'I wanted to test my love for you, Albert, by not seeing you regularly and not knowing when, or even if you were coming to see me again. All that's made me realise how much I need you. How much I've come to depend on you and your strength and guidance, Albert. I want to marry you as soon as possible before you change your mind and decide you don't want to marry someone as silly as me.'

'You're not silly, Charlotte, just a little sheltered and naive, and I rather like that. It's part of your charm.'

'Then you do still want to marry me?' she asked, trying not to sound too coy.

'It's what I've always dreamed of, Charlotte.'

'How quickly can we make the arrangements?'

'Well, I don't know. I should ask your father—'

'He'll agree. He's expecting it.'

'But then there's the wedding to plan and a house to find and furnish, and we have to consider Eve, of course.'

'I don't want to wait until Eve's released from prison, Albert. I just want to get on with it.'

'All right but we can't get married in less than six months. There're guests to invite, the wedding breakfast to arrange, and I'll have to talk to your father about payment. Mother and Father'll expect quite a function and we can't expect your father to pay for it.'

'No we can't, but we can't embarrass him either. Besides I don't want a big function so let's just run away, go to Gretna Green, wherever that is. It'll be terribly romantic.' The romance of running away to get married suddenly occurred to her and a new, warm dream was born. 'Let's decide on the date.'

'No, Lottie, we can't do that either.'

'But why not. It's only the two of us. No one else matters.'

'They do, and you know they do. We can't run away and we must have a large wedding because it's expected in my circle.'

'In which case I'm not sure I want to marry you at all!' She left him and ran up to her bedroom.

If she was going to leave home she wanted to do it now, while she still thought of it as home and before her father found out that her mother had met another man on at least two Saturday afternoons.

It was all so distasteful, and hypocritical, especially as both her mother and Aunt Lizzie had accused her of lying when she was telling the truth about being followed.

Edward heard Lottie rush upstairs. 'Sounds like trouble, sweetheart. Perhaps we'd better go and talk to Albert?'

He ushered Rose into the front room. 'What's the matter with Lottie?'

'She's decided she wants us to get married, Mr Forrester, but she wants to do it in a matter of days, weeks at the most, and she's upset because I've told her that's not possible.'

Edward could not hide his surprise. 'I'd be very happy to see you and Lottie married, Albert, if that's what you both want, but what's the rush? I thought you'd both agreed to let things settle for a while?'

'We had, Mr Forrester, but Lottie's changed her mind and she doesn't want to wait. I don't know why, but it's almost as if she's scared that something may happen if we don't marry very soon.' Edward noticed a trace of perplexity in Albert's voice, and immediately wondered if Lottie was in a hurry because she was pregnant. It was unlikely, but these things did happen. If she was expecting a baby he was sure it was not Albert's, but had she and young Sasha found a way of spending time together alone?

If that was the case it would be unfair on both men if she married Albert, but at least he could take care of her, give her the things she wanted, and give her stability. That was Albert's greatest contribution as a prospective son-in-law; he was as stable as Lottie was unstable.

'Albert,' he saw Rose take Albert's arm and guessed she was having the same thoughts as him, 'are you really sure you want to take Lottie on? I know she's very pretty and can be loving and sweet but she can also be very difficult. Very difficult.'

'She says she really does want to marry me, Mrs Forrester, and I certainly want to marry her.'

Edward realised that Albert had missed the point of Rose's unusually vague approach and he spoke more directly. 'Albert, you'll remember all the trouble Lottie gave us recently with her stories about being followed? Stories we think she made up to draw attention to herself? Doesn't that worry you, just a little?'

'She has a very strong imagination, Mr Forrester.' Albert smiled a little thinly.

'Yes, but she supported her stories by ruining her new coat and throwing away a perfectly good boot which she insists just fell off even though it was laced up above her ankle?'

'May I ask what you're trying to say, Mr Forrester?'

'Simply that Lottie's gone through a lot over the past few weeks, and especially during recent days, and although she seems to have stood up to it all her mother and I are concerned that this sudden rush to get married might be something to do with all that's happened.'

Albert nodded again. 'What do you think I should do, Mr Forrester?'

'Well, for a start I don't think you should rush into marriage just because Lottie thinks she wants to. A few weeks or months isn't going to make much difference at your ages. Second . . .' His courage faltered, then picked up again. 'Her mother and I were wondering if she ought to see a doctor, a special doctor. Someone who could advise on her moods, like.'

Rose spoke up to support him. 'Lottie's very highly-strung, Albert. She always has been, and she's been telling stories, exaggerating things, all her life. We love her dearly and would like to see her happily married, but you ought to be sure what you're taking on.'

Albert was silent for a minute or so, and then he seemed to come to a decision. 'I appreciate what you've told me, but I really do want to marry Lottie and I don't think anything that's been said would stop me. But, I'd hate to do anything which might make her worse, and I'm wondering if I could get some advice. From a professional?'

Edward felt relieved that Albert was taking the problem seriously, but he could still see a problem. 'The difficulty is, Albert – how do we arrange for her to see someone? I haven't the heart to suggest—'

Albert interrupted him. 'I know a doctor who might help, Mr Forrester, and we might be able to organise things so Lottie doesn't even know he is a doctor. Perhaps I might take her for a meal to celebrate our proposed wedding, and by chance meet a friend whom I'd have to invite to join us?'

Edward nodded, glad to be spared the agony of telling Lottie what was on his mind. 'That means you'll have to set a date.'

'Yes, of course.' Albert nodded. 'With your permission I'd suggest six weeks from today. People are sure to draw their own conclusions about how hasty we're being, but then we can prove them all wrong, can't we?'

Edward hoped Albert was right.

* * *

When she left her office Lottie had so much on her mind that she hardly noticed the way the evening fog closed around the streetlamps and made the dimly-lit streets even darker. She was worried about her parents, about Eve and the possibility that Eve would do herself irreparable harm by hunger striking, and she was excited and nervous about her wedding in six weeks' time, particularly the thought of living in a hotel while they found, decorated and furnished a suitable house.

Her dreams were all about to come true. It had been so long since she had last been followed that she did not bother to keep looking back. She had not bothered for several weeks, but when she was no more than five minutes from the station something instinctive made her turn around.

A shadow moved and stopped.

Her heart and mind lurched. He was there, in the darkness behind the nearest streetlamp. She stood very still and listened, trying hard to ignore all sounds other than the hissing gas lamps. Then she turned and walked away, listening all the time. And she stopped. He did not. He took two steps more than her and then he stopped.

She did not bother to look back again, she just ran.

She clattered blindly from streetlamp to shadow to next streetlamp, one hand clutching her hat and the other grasping her handbag, the noise of her heart and breathing drumming out the sound of the man chasing her.

She came to a junction, saw a motor-car coming, judged she had time to cross in front of it, jumped into the street and ran across the road. Behind her there was a squeal of tyres, a shout, and more shouts but she did not stop.

She wished the car might have knocked him down, even killed him, but she knew it had not. She saw the crowded station entrance and safety just across the main road, hesitated for a moment, saw a gap open in the traffic, dashed across the road and plunged into the crowd at the station. She leaped down the stairs and reached the platform just in time to jump into a train which was about to leave.

The door was closed behind her, the carriage began to move, and as she looked out of the window she saw him; the silver-haired man who had helped her before, and whose existence even she had begun to doubt. He was standing at the rear of the platform, apparently waiting for someone.

If she had not leapt onto the train she would have met him again, but if she had not leapt onto the train the man with a limp might have caught her.

She sat down, trembling but glad no one was taking any notice of her and wished her silver-haired man was there to help her again instead of being on the platform behind her. She even thought she might leave the train at the next stop and wait for the following train in the hope of meeting him again, but she dismissed the thought. It was more sensible to go home and tell her father that she had been followed again.

Then it occurred to her that she could not do that. She could not tell anyone she had been followed again because they had not believed her before and they certainly would not believe her now. But as she stared at her reflection in the darkened window another, more comforting, thought came to her.

She could tell Albert that the walking was too much for her now the riverside fogs were becoming worse, that they were affecting her breathing. He was sure to insist that she give up her job immediately and although she would argue, she would allow him to win, just as a subservient wife should.

That would please him no end. And her, now she was about to be married and did not need her job any more.

Lottie was surprised to find Albert waiting outside the station, and even more surprised when, uninvited, he kissed her cheek and wrapped an arm around her waist.

'Lottie, we're going out tonight, to a restaurant.'

'Why?'

'Come along and you'll find out.' He grinned at her and added quickly, 'I've asked your father and he's agreed so

175

there's no reason for you to say no. The table's booked, and a motor-car to take us there and collect us. Just the two of us, some very good food and a little wine.'

'But why?'

'I told you, come and you'll find out.'

Albert was already wearing formal evening dress under his overcoat and the realisation that he was taking her to a grand restaurant left her undecided what to wear. She told him she wished her mother was there to advise her, and wondered if she should ask Helen, but Albert already had her dress in mind.

'When we went to the Christmas dinner with my parents you wore a green dress. Wear that. You look beautiful in it.'

She did as she was told, and began to feel that either Albert was changing or she had misjudged him. Perhaps, now he knew they were to be married, he would continue being more assertive. She hoped so; she did not want to spend her life with a man who seemed almost scared of her.

The green dress was a heavy cotton and well lined, which made it ideal for wearing in a warm restaurant or theatre. Deep green, it was simple and demure. A high neck fastened with four pearl buttons, tailored shoulders and tight sleeves fastened at each wrist with four more pearls, it flowed smoothly over her bust, clung to her waist, spread loosely over her hips and hung in folds shoe height from the floor.

She borrowed her mother's pearl earrings, pearl dress-ring, two large mother of pearl combs to hold up her thick copper hair, and a simple silver-grey shawl made from fine wool to wrap around herself if she felt cold, and she presented herself before Albert.

He did not speak, but for a moment she thought he was going to cry. When he did find some words they were few, and spoken quietly, 'You're a vision, Charlotte, and I don't think . . .'

He stopped and refused to finish what he was going to say. Moments later the front door-knocker banged. The motor-car he had arranged was waiting for them.

The restaurant was large and noisy and well lit by splendid chandeliers. A small orchestra played without pausing and the dance floor was busy with happy couples enjoying themselves. The round tables were set with starched linen, sparkling crystal and highly-polished silver, and all the plates and bowls were fine porcelain. Everyone seemed friendly, the patrons, the waiters and the musicians.

Albert ordered for her without stinting on either food or wine, and every time she asked why he had taken her there he promised to tell her later.

'Albert, I'm not complaining but this must be costing an absolute fortune!' she said when they finished their last course.

'You're worth it, Charlotte, this and so much more. And, although it's not the reason I've brought you here, I can tell you now that my father's promised to give me a substantial share holding on my next birthday, so our future is assured, my dear.'

The surroundings and the laughter and the wine overcame her, 'Oh, Albert, I do love you.'

'That's what I hoped to hear,' he said and his hand came across the table to grip hers, but there was something hard in his palm.

He released her and she turned her hand over and saw an exquisite ring, one diamond in a cluster setting. A moment later he had taken the ring back and was by her side, slipping the ring onto the second finger of her left hand.

'I know I've already given you a simple engagement ring, Charlotte, but I want you to have this one to show everyone just how much I really do love you.'

'Albert, it's beautiful.' Without asking he kissed her on the lips and she realised, after he had pulled away and returned to his seat opposite her, that she had enjoyed it.

She started as something behind her popped, and suddenly a glass of foaming wine was presented to her. 'Champagne, madam, sir.'

The waiter left the bottle at the table and Albert poured her some more.

'To us, Charlotte, whatever the future holds.'

'To us,' she replied, and was distracted as an attractive middle-aged gentleman stopped by the table.

'Albert, old friend! Haven't seen you for . . . I can't remember.' The man had a pleasant Welsh accent and an easy smile and even though she knew he was going to intrude on them she did not mind.

He was Evan Pryce-Jones and he had, he assured her, the most boring job the Government had ever created and certainly was not something to talk about. Instead they talked about Albert and Lottie and Lottie's family, and the crises which had occurred over the past weeks. They did not talk about her being followed, she thought Albert seemed almost at pains not to mention that, but they talked freely about Eve being in prison and her own efforts to support Eve.

'Do you enjoy an exciting life, Charlotte? Do you enjoy things happening outside your control?'

'I'm not sure. Sometimes I think I might, other times . . .' She shrugged.

The orchestra started up with a new tune and Evan Pryce-Jones was on his feet. 'Albert, may I ask Charlotte to dance?'

'Certainly.' Albert also rose and gave her no option but to allow his friend to lead her on to the dance floor.

Evan danced beautifully, and he complimented her on her own ability. 'You dance wonderfully well, Charlotte. You must spend a lot of time dancing to be this good.'

'Hardly any, I'm afraid.'

'Wouldn't you like to? Wouldn't you like to be a princess, or perhaps even Cinderella, to be whisked off by a handsome prince to live happily ever after?'

'Do you know a woman who could honestly say she wouldn't?'

Her answer seemed to startle him and he was silent for a minute or so. 'Where will you and Albert live when you're married?'

'He wants to move into the new suburbs in Walthamstow.'

'And you?'

'It seems a sensible thing to do.'

'But what would you really like to do?'

'I'd like a big house in a garden square where the nurse could take the children and I could look out at them and be satisfied they were safe.'

'D'you like children, Charlotte?'

'If they're polite and tidy.'

He laughed. 'Babies? D'you like babies?'

The tune ended before she answered. She thanked him for the dance and began to make her way back to Albert, Evan close behind her.

'Good evening, Doctor,' she heard someone say and did not take any notice until she heard Evan respond.

She turned, saw him smiling at the elderly group around the table, and then his hand was on her elbow, guiding her away.

'Very pleasant people in many ways,' he said, 'but terribly boring.'

'Doctor? Are you a doctor?'

'Yes. Of philosophy. A doctor of philosophy.'

'I see.'

She glanced back as she heard another call from his friend's table. 'Read your latest paper, Doctor Pryce-Jones. Fascinating study. Fascinating.'

'Thank you,' he called back. He seemed eager to get her back to Albert and once there he seemed to be in a hurry to leave the restaurant.

She said goodnight and watched Albert walk with him to the cloakroom, and then return to her.

'A charming man, Albert. Shame he had to leave so suddenly, we were having an interesting conversation.'

'I'm glad you like him, Lottie. Perhaps we can meet him again.'

'Yes. I didn't know he was a doctor.'

'A doctor of philosophy, not a medical man.'

They drank a little more of the champagne and she excused herself to go to the Ladies Room. She was looking into a large mirror, replacing one of the combs in her hair, when another reflection moved into view.

'I hope you don't mind me interrupting you, my dear, but everyone at our table noticed that you and your young man appear to be celebrating something. Your engagement, perhaps? I simply wish to pass on our best wishes if that is the case.'

'Yes, thank you. That's very kind of you.' She turned and now she could see the woman properly she realised she was one of those who knew Evan Pryce-Jones. 'We're having a proper family celebration some time later, but Albert wanted tonight just for the two of us.'

'And Doctor Pryce-Jones.' The lady smiled.

'Oh. no. He was here anyway and just joined us instead of leaving earlier.'

'Oh, we didn't notice him earlier and we've been here all evening.' The lady frowned, then smiled again. 'Brilliant man, isn't he? So modest for someone so eminent in his field.'

'Philosophy.' She smiled back and tried to sound as though she knew the doctor better than she did.

'Philosophy? No, psychology, isn't it? Or do I have it wrong? All these new things, well, new to my age anyway though I expect you young things understand them all. I thought I had it right, though, psychology? Well, the study of the mind, anyway.'

It was difficult to smile and be polite to the kindly woman who had wished her well in her future marriage. Lottie excused herself and walked back to the table, sat down and refused the final dregs from the champagne bottle.

'I understand the doctor is a doctor of the mind, Albert. Did you know that? Is that why he joined us? Why we spent the evening talking about me and my family?'

He did not answer.

'Did you think the wine would make me talk more freely, Albert?' She had been feeling a little fuddled, but her mind was very clear now.

'Listen, Charlotte, your parents and I—'

'*My* parents, Albert? You're sure it's not your parents who're worried about who, or what, you might be marrying?'

180

'No, Charlotte! Your parents told me they've been worried about you for a long time. They decided ages ago that you might need some sort of treatment to help your mind.'

She sat still, stunned by what he said. Her clear mind was jumbled now and it took her several minutes to piece together her thoughts and translate them into words. 'And Doctor Pryce-Jones? What does he think?'

'He thinks you definitely need help, Charlotte. Professional help.'

'He's wrong, Albert.' She had not told him about the man who had followed her earlier that evening and she knew she could not tell him now. It might further condemn her as being mad. 'He is wrong, Albert. You're all wrong!'

'I don't think so, Charlotte. He's very experienced.'

She felt deflated, betrayed, even dishonoured, and she did not know what to say or do. She sat back and closed her eyes. 'Take me home, Albert. Take me home.'

She pushed her father aside the moment he opened the front door, rushed past him and up the stairs without speaking. She heard Albert briefly explain why she was upset and her father say that her mother was staying overnight with Aunt Lizzie at the mission. She heard what he said and almost ran back to tell him what she knew about her mother seeing another man, but suddenly she did not care what any of them did. She wanted nothing to do with any of them, not any more.

They had all betrayed her, and she could not live with that. Or them.

She closed her bedroom door quite carefully, took her mother's earrings out of her ears and threw them hard against the skirting board. They smashed and the little trails of strung pearls rolled across the painted floorboards around the edge of the room, the smaller beads falling through the cracks. She stared at them, took out the mother of pearl hair combs and threw them down so they broke, then she dropped onto her bed and sobbed.

Downstairs she heard Albert and her father talking

quietly, the murmured sound confirming that Albert, her mother and her father had conspired to betray her. They had made her believe they were taking her seriously when all the time they were deceiving her, planning to have her examined by a doctor who treated mad people.

Thank God for the lady who had told her who Evan Pryce-Jones really was. That anonymous lady might have saved her from being sent away, committed to an asylum.

Minutes later she heard Albert preparing to leave and her father telling him not to worry about her because she was only in a mood and would see sense in the morning.

Her father did not come up to see her for an hour, and when he knocked on her door she pretended to be asleep and did not answer.

The following morning Lottie packed two changes of clothes and a few personal items into a carpet bag, took what cash she had saved from a miniature wooden chest, put the rings from Albert out of sight in a drawer and left the house early and without having breakfast.

She would prove to everyone that she was capable of looking after herself by taking a room somewhere, perhaps in a YWCA hostel and finding a new job. She was leaving home and she would never go back. Never.

As she turned out of Angel Street for the last time she fingered the letter in her pocket. She had written to her parents, explaining why she had left and what her plans were. She would post the letter that evening so they would receive it tomorrow morning when she would already have left her job and they would have difficulty finding her.

Lottie worked as best she could during the morning but it was difficult to concentrate because her mind was too occupied with what had happened the previous night, the plotting which had been going on for weeks before, and what she was going to do tonight and with the rest of her life.

The supervisor was ill so the office manager, Mr Grundley, had come into the office to supervise the work and he was in one of his bad moods.

He was an elderly man, tall and bony. He wore small round spectacles that always looked as though they might fall off the end of his nose but he was not a comic figure. He had red-lined lecherous eyes and bent fingers that would sneak out and grab the girls' arms so hard they would bruise, and sometimes he would come into the office and stare at them or stand in a doorway so the girls were forced to brush against him as they passed through.

She told him she wished to resign her position and he agreed to give her a reference if she worked her last full day without pay.

'Miss Forrester, I'd like that typed now, please. It's urgent.'

He gave her a long document, four pages of figures and detailed descriptions which she typed as fast as she could but before she could check her work Mr Grundley sent the office boy to collect it and take it to him in his glass cubicle. Lottie put the next piece of work into her typewriter.

'Miss Forrester!' Mr Grundley roared and everyone stopped and turned to look at her. 'Come here. At once!'

She ran to the cubicle and stood beside him as he jabbed his pen through all the mistakes she had made, and without apologising destroyed one page which was perfect.

'This is rubbish, young woman! Pure rubbish!' His gesticulating hand touched her breast twice and then he grabbed her arm so hard she winced. He pulled her close to him and glared into her eyes. 'Do it again, and quickly. I've already told you it's urgent.'

She did as she was told and this time she read it through to be sure it was perfect.

'Don't just stand there reading it, give it to the boy!' Mr Grundley roared again and shouted at the office boy to collect the papers.

The boy was so scared he dropped them and trod on one sheet which needed retyping. She did it quickly and made a mistake she did not notice, but Mr Grundley did.

'Miss Forrester!' The shout went up again. 'Do it again! And I'd like it this week, preferably today if you think you can manage that.'

She began to type again as the shipping manager came into the office and demanded the document which was now delaying the loading of some cargo.

'It'll be finished any day now,' she heard Grundley mutter to his colleague. Then she heard them snigger together and make quiet comments about her being beautiful but brainless and only good for one thing.

Her embarrassment and humiliation made her hands shake so much she had to type slowly. She prevented herself striking the wrong keys by resting her fingers on each one before she pressed it, but it simply endorsed what Grundley was saying about her and finally he insisted she hand the work to another girl who typed it fast and perfectly.

She worked through her dinner break, trying to reduce the pile of work which had built up because she had wasted so much time and because she did not want to face the other girls who now seemed to share Mr Grundley's opinion of her. The harder she tried the more mistakes she made and the worse things became.

'Miss Forrester!' Mr Grundley yelled for her four times during the afternoon, and each time he pulled her close to him as he sat at his desk, so close she could smell the beer and spirits he had drunk during his dinner break. When he called her into the cubicle for the fifth time she burst into tears. 'Stop snivelling, girl, and do this again.'

'I'm sorry, I can't. I can't do any more today.'

'Do it now, and well, or I'll sack you without a reference, and then you won't be able to work anywhere!'

Threatened, she sat down and typed the work again, and continued even though the bell rang and the other girls and the office boy went home.

She did not know Mr Grundley was behind her until she felt his hands rest on her shoulders.

His touch frightened her so much she jumped, but he pressed down hard to keep her in her seat. 'Let me read it before you take it out, Miss Forrester.'

He peered over her head, his hands slowly sliding from her shoulders to her chest and down to her breasts. She froze.

'Now, Miss Forrester, I really can't condone the standard

of your work in this office, but perhaps there's another job which is more suitable to your talents.' His hands squeezed her.

She tried to struggle but his hands held her tight and he moved his forearms down to trap her upper arms. She felt his head rub against hers and smelled his alehouse breath waft across her cheek. 'I'm not asking you, Miss Forrester. If you want references you'll—'

'I don't, Mr Grundley.' She placed her hands, palm down, on the edge of her desk. Her heart was pounding and she was trembling with fear. She knew she would have to fight him off.

'I don't think you understand my offer, Miss Forrester.' He breathed so heavily she had to turn her nose away.

'I think I do, Mr Grundley,' she said quite calmly, then stood up quickly, using her hands to add force. She snapped her head back as she did so.

She felt a sharp pain and then a warm rush of his blood on her neck before she turned to look at him. He was holding his hands to his face. Blood was pouring through his fingers. She guessed she had smashed his nose.

She grabbed her coat, hat and bag, rushed out into the street and turned the way she always turned out of habit but it was the direction she had to walk in anyway. She had to go to her usual station and take her usual train but leave it three stops earlier if she was to go to the YWCA hostel.

As she walked, feeling hot in spite of the damp fog, she realised that in one day she had lost her family, her home, her fiancé and her job, but she had gained some confidence and self-respect.

She walked quickly, leaving Grundley and the shipping office further and further behind her. She would find another job and never go back again, never walk along these fog-bound grimy little streets again, never be scared of being followed again.

Then she heard the footsteps, running up behind her.

She half turned, someone hit her, then a hand covered her mouth.

She was yanked off her feet, shoved against a wooden door which crashed open, and pulled into an alleyway. The door slammed shut behind her.

She dropped her handbag and the carpet bag, but the man had his arms around her so she could not move. She smelled his beery breath and felt his hands clawing at her breasts as he dragged her backwards along the alley. Mr Grundley!

He swung her around and pushed her forward, still holding her from behind, as he had in the office, and then she felt her feet slip over the edge of a step.

She reached out and her right hand touched an iron rail. She grabbed it, pulled sharply and at the same time swung her head back just as she had earlier.

'Oh, no you don't, Miss Forrester!' he growled, squeezed her roughly and tried to pull her off the rail.

She held on tight, felt his breath on her neck and swung her head back a second time.

Pain!

He let go of her and a moment later he was falling, over and over. Suddenly there was a loud crack and he was not falling any more.

She peered into the dim light and saw him sprawled across the bottom four steps, his head at a sharp angle to his shoulder. He did not move.

'Mr Grundley? Mr Grundley?'

He did not speak, did not move. She sensed he was dead.

She had killed him!

She began to shake, moved away from the top of the steps in case she fell down them, walked past her spare clothes which had spilled out of her bag and now littered the ground, and leaned against one of the walls which enclosed the narrow passage.

'Oh, God,' she pleaded, needing help, needing to be told what to do.

No help came.

She listened, hoping to hear him move or groan, but he did not. She pushed herself away from the wall, stood still for several minutes to make sure her legs were steady

186

enough to carry her, picked up her clothes, with hands which shook, and stuffed everything back into the carpet bag. She hesitated again, still unsure what to do, walked back to the top of the steps and listened. There was no sound from the figure lying at the bottom of the steps.

She turned and walked away, back out into the empty street.

Everything seemed normal, and that seemed unnatural. She had killed Mr Grundley and when his body was found and she did not go to work and the girls told the police what had happened today and how they had left her alone with him . . . Her mind raced, and ahead of her she saw the underground station.

She stood on the edge of the platform and wondered if it would be painful to throw herself on the lines as the train came in. Even if it was, the pain would not last for long. Dying might be less painful than living with what she had done, less painful than going to the police and confessing.

'Good evening,' a pleasant voice said, and she turned and saw a man's face and thought perhaps God had answered her prayer with a miracle. Her gentle, silver-haired man had appeared just as he had before. 'Are you quite well now?'

'No, not exactly.' She trembled.

'Oh, I'm sorry to hear that.' He half turned, as if he did not want to become involved with her again, then stopped, touched the back of her collar and stared at his fingers. 'Blood? Are you hurt?'

'I'm not sure. I've been attacked.' She felt faint and as she dropped her bags he grabbed her and half carried her to a bench.

'Sit here for a few minutes. We don't want you falling down again, Miss . . . ?'

'Forrester,' she said as a train rattled into the station.

'Miss Forest?' he said and she was about to correct him when he left her and went to retrieve her two bags from beneath the feet of people who were boarding the train.

As the train left he placed the bags beside her on the

bench and looked along the empty platform. 'I think, perhaps, you'd better allow me to look at your neck and head to see if you've been badly cut.'

She removed her hat pin and hat, bent her head forwards and pulled her hair up so he could look for any injuries.

She felt his fingers gently parting her hair before he spoke. 'No, Miss Forest. The back of your head looks a little swollen but there's no other damage to you, but your hair's sticky with blood so I hate to think what you did to the man who attacked you.'

She sat back and looked at her hat which had blood both inside and out. 'I think I broke his nose the first time.'

'The first time! How many times did he attack you?'

'Twice. Once in the office where I work. Worked. And then again as I was walking to the station.'

'And you fought him off twice? How?'

'He was holding me from behind, on both occasions, and I butted him in the face both times.'

'And he ran off the second time?'

'No.' She thought, perhaps, she should have told him that Mr Grundley had run away, and wondered if it was wise to tell him any more.

'Well, if he didn't run off, what did happen?'

'I think I killed him.' The words poured out before she could stop them.

'Very unlikely, I should think. What happened?'

He was so reassuring that she wanted to believe he was right and she told him everything that had happened since she had made her first typing mistake.

He listened carefully at first, and then as the platform began to crowd with passengers he suggested they should go to a local tea-shop where it would be easier to talk. 'Unless you feel you should really be getting home, Miss Forest?'

No, she did not feel she should be getting home.

The tea-shop was small and empty of customers, and a table in an alcove gave her and Mr Joseph, as he had introduced himself, complete privacy. In half an hour she told him everything that had happened since the first time she had been followed. When she finished she sat back and looked at him, waiting for him to comment, tell her she was ridiculous, advise her to go home, go to the police, go to Doctor Pryce-Jones for help, or to make his own excuses and leave her alone with her fear and misery. Instead he reached out, took both her hands in his, and smiled.

'Yours is a rather confusing story, Miss Forest, and a very unlikely story and I can understand your parents thinking you may be a little, um, odd? But I believe you. I believe you completely and I can assure you I've heard of far stranger stories than yours, and they've all been true and proven.'

'Really?' The relief was enormous.

'Oh, yes,' he said airily. 'I've recently retired from the Bar and as a barrister I heard stories like yours every day when I was in court. I heard the most unbelievable stories and, of course, some of them were lies, total fabrications, but I learned how to tell if people were lying to me, or if they were a little odd. I can tell that you're as normal as me or anyone else, Miss Forest.'

'But Doctor Pryce-Jones said—'

'Believe me, Miss Forest, the only help you need is rest, complete rest and an opportunity to allow the strain to dissipate. And it will.' His smile turned to a frown. 'But there is a problem. Your fiancé couldn't have chosen a worse man to turn to than Doctor Pryce-Jones. He's considered brilliant in many ways, but he has a weakness for beautiful young women and I suspect that's why he hoped to prolong his contact with you. Also, there's another, more serious problem.'

She watched him as he sat still, clearly trying to find a way of breaking bad news without upsetting her, and in the end she told him to say whatever was on his mind and not worry about her feelings.

'He does a lot of very good work with the police. His evidence alone has convicted many men and women, several of them for murder. Some have been hanged, others have gone into asylums which is worse than being hanged, Miss Forest.'

'I don't understand, Mr Joseph.'

'I'm thinking ahead, Miss Forest. First, I'd like to go to the alley where you were attacked to ascertain the position. Then, if you'll permit me, I'll give you my considered advice as to what you should do.'

'I can't go back there.' The thought made her feel sick.

'Of course not,' he said soothingly. He was still holding her hands and now his thumbs stroked the backs of her hands and had a peculiarly calming effect. 'Tell me exactly where this alley is and I'll go alone. You can stay here and wait for me to return, and then, as you quite clearly can't go home, I'll help you to arrange suitable accommodation and ensure your parents know you're quite safe.' His kindness was overwhelming and when he left she was sure he would come back alone, not with the police.

He was gone forty minutes and when he returned she could see from his expression that things were not well.

'What's happened?'

'Several things and none of them good, Miss Forest. You said you were going to the YWCA but you can't, not with all that blood in your hair. A casual passer-by won't notice it, the waitresses here haven't seen it, but anyone else will. I suggest you come to my house. I have staff who live with me, so we won't be alone, and you can bathe and change your clothes in privacy before going to the YWCA, or whatever you decide to do. But I think we should go now. I have a taxi-cab waiting outside.'

She wanted to ask more, but there were several other customers now sitting at nearby tables and his glance warned her not to say anything else.

Rose was worried. She stared down at the broken hair combs and what was left of her earrings, and quickly searched Lottie's wardrobe and chest of drawers. Her daughter's old carpet bag was missing, and so were a few clothes and some personal belongings Lottie treasured.

She opened another drawer and found two rings; one Albert had given her as an engagement ring and another which was a splendid concoction of jewels. The rings, more than anything else, told her that Lottie had run away.

She ran down stairs as Edward came home from working late. 'Lottie? Have you seen her?'

'No. Not since breakfast.' He paused. 'No, I didn't see her then. She'd already gone, but that was probably because she'd been in a mood last night, made a fool of herself and didn't want to face me this morning.'

'What happened last night?'

He told her and she was so scared she called him a fool for not realising how upset Lottie really was, and within moments they were having a blazing row about his unsuitability as a father and her insistence on always putting the mission first and the family last.

He turned around and slammed out of the house, saying he would go and look for Lottie who was probably safe with Helen or Jamie, and she started to call him back, but stopped.

She knew that if she called him back she would tell him about Hubert, and now was not the time to do that.

Something in her, some instinct, suggested that somehow Hubert was involved in all this.

It was not logical because Hubert had said in his letter that he had only found them after Eve had attracted his attention, but Hubert did not always tell the truth.

CHAPTER 14

Mr Joseph ushered Lottie into the taxi, dumped her two bags on the floor and then spoke to the driver in his exposed seat. She sat back, her hands clasped together, waiting to learn what Mr Joseph had seen. He joined her and moments later the taxi pulled out into the traffic stream, the driver leaning forwards over his steering wheel and peering into the thickening fog.

'It should take us about half an hour, Miss Forest.'

She almost corrected him, but then decided not to. He had called her Miss Forest so often that it would be embarrassing to correct him this late. Also she sensed there might be some safety for both of them if he did not know her real name.

'You're wondering what's happened?' he asked, and she nodded. 'A man *has* been found dead in that alley. What did you say your Mr Grundley looked like?'

She described him, hoping that by some miracle his was not the body which had been discovered, but once more she could tell from Mr Joseph's expression that her hope was unfounded.

'It's even worse than that, Miss Forest. I'm afraid you

were seen by someone who claims he saw you lure this man into the alley and leave alone a few minutes later.'

'But no one could have seen me! The street was empty. There was no one about.'

'The police have a witness who described you very well, even down to the clothes you're wearing at the moment so he must have seen you. The man was still there because he had called the police and taken them back to the scene. Fortunately I know the inspector who's investigating the case and he pointed out his witness to me, Miss Forest, and he sounds like the man you said first followed you. Tall man, club foot.'

'It doesn't make any sense. Why would he—'

'You were late leaving work, Miss Forest. Perhaps he grew tired of waiting. Perhaps he saw the other man follow you and he followed you both. It doesn't matter what happened, simply that it did. If you go to Court the police'll put this man up to give evidence against you. And if you tell the Court that he'd been following you for weeks and Evan Pryce-Jones gives evidence to say he thinks you're unstable you'll not only be found guilty of murder but you'll be committed to an insane asylum.' He took her hands in his. 'And if that happens you *will* go mad, Miss Forest, I assure you.'

'But what can I do?' She realised she was wailing.

'Nothing,' he said, simply.

His answer confused her for a moment, and then she felt relieved. Of course, she simply did not have to do anything.

'Except go away for a while,' he added unexpectedly, 'because the police will interview your office colleagues and when they offer the witness's description your colleagues will identify you and the police will know who they're looking for. That won't happen until tomorrow, so I suggest that tonight you write a letter to your parents telling them that you've left home because you're unhappy, you've resigned from your job, and you're going away and will write in due course. Nothing more than that. Something both to reassure your parents who, I'm sure, do care for you, and something they can show the police as evidence that they're not hiding you or were involved in what you did.'

'You mean commit murder?'

'No, I don't believe that's what you did. You've been systematically terrorised by a man who's followed you, and you've been intimidated and technically assaulted by a man you worked with. Ultimately you had to defend yourself against this man. The circumstances simply suggest, very strongly, that you committed murder, but you and I know you didn't. So long as you accept my protection, Miss Forest, I'll ensure no harm comes to you.'

'I've already written a letter, Mr Joseph.' She explained what her letter said and told him the office boy had put it in the post together with the office correspondence.

She was resigned to her situation by the time the taxi-cab stopped in front of a large house in a formal square. 'Where are we?'

'Not far from Kensington Gardens. I strongly recommend you stay here as my guest, Miss Forest. As I mentioned, I have resident staff, and it seems to me that you need a little time to yourself.' The driver opened the door and she accepted his help to step out of the taxi.

The fog smelled of smoke and it caught up in her throat and made her gasp. She explained to Mr Joseph that she suffered from asthma.

'I've just the cure for that. My late wife had a similar problem and I've some of her medicine indoors. And I've an even better remedy than medicine.' He carried her carpet bag up the steps to the front door. 'I've a house on the Norfolk coast and when I retired I had all my old files taken there, with the intention of removing any important documents which may have been overlooked and then destroying what was left. I'm planning to go back there tomorrow and my housekeeper, Mrs Miller, has planned to come along to look after me. Perhaps you could come too, and help with the files and perhaps type some letters for me. It'd actually be very helpful to me and it would give you the chance of breathing some clean sea air. Why don't you think about it while you bathe and change into fresh clothes.'

'Yes, I will.' She followed him into his large house, the sort of house she had always dreamed of, but her life had been changed so much, so suddenly that her dreams seemed irrelevant.

'Good evening, sir, miss.' A plump and pretty woman in her fifties or even sixties, who looked and sounded as though she was a West Country farmer's wife, came into the hall and bobbed a hurried curtsy.

'Good evening, Mrs Miller. Please allow me to introduce Miss Charlotte Forest. She's the daughter of an old friend of mine, up in London on her own and she's had a small accident, I'm afraid.'

'Oh dear.' Mrs Miller frowned with concern.

'Nothing too serious. I've invited her to stay with us for a few days. She may even come to Norfolk to help me with the files and correspondence. I've telephoned her parents so we have their blessing.'

Mrs Miller, whose frown had deepened, smiled when she heard Mr Joseph's reassurances. 'Would you like me to run a bath for you, Miss Forest.'

'That would be nice, Mrs Miller. Thank you.' Mrs Miller had led her halfway up the first flight of stairs before Mr Joseph called out, 'Use my wife's room, Mrs Miller. It'll give Miss Forest a little more privacy.'

'Yes, sir.'

'Oh, and Miss Forest, you'll obviously want to change into clean clothes and I imagine yours will be rather spoiled so I suggest you take whatever you need from my wife's wardrobe. I think you'll find she was about your size.'

Mrs Miller took her to a bedroom which had both a dressing room and a bathroom attached. 'There you are, my dear. You get yourself nice and clean in here and I'll leave some of Mrs Joseph's clothes out there for you to choose from. She had some lovely things so I'm sure you'll find something you like. They've all been cleaned and aired recently so they shouldn't be musty or anything.'

'Mr Joseph seems very kind. How long has he been a widower?'

'I don't know, my dear. It seems that when Mrs Joseph died he closed this house down and went off to live in the house he's got in Norfolk. He's only just decided to use this one again and he had it all done up, and then employed new staff only a few weeks ago. His wife's things were here still so he got me to have 'em all cleaned up ready to give 'em away, but when it came to it he couldn't, you see?'

'That's very sad. He must have loved her terribly.'

'I think he did, my dear. He still mopes about some days, and he admitted to me, once, that he's taken down all her pictures because he couldn't stand to see them, her being dead and all that.' Mrs Miller had been running water into the bath and dripping in salts and fragrances so the steam filled the air with the scent of a summer garden. 'There you are, my dear. You just leave your clothes on the floor and slip in there. You'll feel better in no time.'

Lottie did as she was told, glad to be rid of the blood-stained clothes but unable to take her eyes from them as they lay crumpled on the floor. Coming indoors from the fog had helped her to breathe more easily and the steam helped even more, but the crumpled clothes reminded her of the way Mr Grundley had looked when she saw him lying at the bottom of the steps. The bath water turned pink as his blood washed out of her hair. Her chest tightened and stopped her breathing.

She could not move.

There was a knock on the bathroom door. 'It's Mrs Miller, Miss Forest. Do you want anything?'

'Come in.' The shout left her gasping for more air and she saw Mrs Miller looked frightened. 'Asthma, Mrs Miller. I can't breathe.'

'Asthma? You get asthma? I remember Mr Joseph saying his wife got asthma. Oh, my dear, you just sit there and I'll be back in a minute or two. Meanwhile, you pull the plug and refill that bath with clean water, Miss Forest.'

Mrs Miller was gone for several minutes but when she came back she brought a small glass half filled with a brown liquid. 'Now, drink this, my dear. It'll help you feel better.'

Lottie drank the liquid which tasted of iron and thought it might be one of the tonics her mother sometimes used, and she began to relax almost immediately. Mrs Miller was right, it did make her feel better.

The bath cleaned her and relaxed her even more and she felt surprisingly calm as she looked at the choice of clothing Mrs Miller had laid out on the bed.

The clothes were a very good fit, if rather old-fashioned in style, but she felt Mrs Joseph's choice of colour suited her exactly. She chose a plain dress of royal blue wool with white lace at the collar and cuffs. The colour contrasted with her copper hair and made it appear to flame under the electric candelabra.

Mrs Miller appeared moments later. 'Mr Joseph's medicine does seem to have helped your breathing, Miss Forest, but you do look tired, my dear. Why don't you lie down for a few minutes, before you go down to dinner?'

'Thank you, Mrs Miller. I think I might.' She did, fully dressed, convinced that after two or three minutes rest she would feel more alert.

'Miss, miss,' Mrs Miller was gently shaking her. 'It's nine o'clock, miss.'

'Nine o'clock!' She leaped off the bed, confused and not sure what to do. 'Nine o'clock? Are you sure?'

'Yes, miss. There's some food downstairs. Mr Joseph's waiting for you.'

'Food? I don't think I could eat anything, Mrs Miller.'

'Try, miss. It's very light and, anyway, I'm sure Mr Joseph'd like your company. Especially looking like you do, miss, if you don't mind me saying.'

Then she heard Mr Joseph call up the stairs. 'Everything all right, Mrs Miller? Does our young guest need anything?'

'No, sir, everything's all right and she doesn't need anything more,' Mrs Miller called out loudly.

Lottie followed Mrs Miller downstairs and into a large dining room where a big polished table had been laid with two silver and crystal dinner settings.

'I hope you don't mind dining informally, my dear.' Mr Joseph was looking out of the window and he spoke without turning, but when he did turn he stopped dead. 'My God!'

His expression alarmed her. 'Is something wrong? Would you prefer I didn't wear this dress?'

'No, not at all.' He sounded nervous and as he walked towards her she could see his mouth twitch slightly. 'It was simply that, from a distance, you reminded me of my wife. It was a shock, rather like seeing a ghost.'

'I'm sorry.'

'Please, don't be sorry.' He held her arm and guided her to a seat then sat on the opposite side of the table. 'It's just your colouring. You don't actually look much like my wife except for your size and colouring. Please don't feel you should apologise for being beautiful, Miss Forest. There are too few beautiful people and things in this world.'

'Thank you.' She smiled at him. 'Thank you for everything, I don't know what I'd have done without your help.'

'Please, please, please, Miss Forest,' he said in a begging tone. 'You've more than repaid me already. You've made me feel useful again, something I haven't felt for months, and you've exorcised a fear I had.'

He paused and looked down at the cutlery, absently played with a spoon, and spoke without looking at her. 'You see, I felt I had to come back to this house but I was scared of how I'd feel because my wife and I were so happy here. Now, you've come here with me, used her room, worn her clothes and made it easier for me to bear her death. I shan't be afraid to sleep here tonight, and that's because of you, Miss Forest. You've actually done me by far the biggest service by dispelling some of my loneliness. I should be thanking you, not you thanking me.'

'Not at all, Mr Joseph. All I've done is accept your help and hospitality.'

'Which I'm privileged to offer you, Miss Forest and which is why I'm a little reluctant to remind you that although I've offered you accommodation either here or in

Norfolk, you haven't yet accepted. I'll understand, of course, if you feel you can't, but I'd be honoured if you would. I can assure you that Mrs Miller will be your constant chaperone.'

His old gentlemanly quaintness made her smile. 'I'd like to stay, Mr Joseph, and to go to Norfolk with you, if I won't be too much trouble.'

They ate a light and delicious meal and talked about art and travel and recited their favourite poems to each other.

Suddenly she yawned. 'I'm sorry, Mr Joseph, but I suddenly feel terribly tired, as though I could sleep for a week.'

'I understand, Miss Forest. I'm going to read for a while but you please yourself what you do and treat this house as you would your own home. If you wish to go to bed, then please do so. Use the rooms you used earlier. I'm sure Mrs Miller will be pleased to help you find all you need and you'll find a key inside the bedroom door. Please use it. It's important that you feel safe.'

Elizabeth was surprised when Edward came banging on the mission door after midnight. She listened carefully as he told her that Lottie appeared to have run away.

'She hasn't told us where she is, Lizzie. The way she slipped out this morning, and now this – it's as if she's scared of me.'

'She probably is. What d'you expect her to do after what happened last night? She probably thinks you want her committed.'

'I don't! She's not mad as such, just a bit too inclined to turn in on herself at times.'

'Then you should've told her that last night. It's too late now she's gone missing.' She paused, aware that she was blaming him totally although she knew they were all partly responsible for what had happened, both to Lottie and to Eve.

She looked at him, adopted brother and sister thrown together in yet another crisis, and she realised again just how much she loved him, and Rose, and the rest of the family. There were times when she could happily strangle any of them, but once the irritation was over those times simply made her love them all the more.

Lottie did not lock her bedroom door as Mr Joseph had suggested because she thought that after all he had done for her it would have been churlish, a sign of mistrust. Even though no one would ever know she felt it was a matter of honour not to turn the key.

She chose one of Mrs Joseph's plain white linen nightdresses, marvelled at how well it fitted her, and snuggled down into the comfortable bed. The bedroom fire had been lit, the bed had been turned back to air and lavender water had been sprinkled on her pillow to calm her and help her sleep.

She turned off the electric lights and opened the curtains so she could lay in bed and see the moon, then lay down and fell asleep instantly.

She woke several times when she thought she heard noises in the room, but although she always sat up, she soon slumped back, aware that the only noises she could hear were the ticking of a clock, the shifting of coals as the fire died and the sound of timbers creaking as the house cooled.

The fire was dead, cold ash, when the nightmares started.

She was back in the office, Mr Grundley tearing at her clothes, his mouth slobbering over her body, and the shipping manager was there, watching and laughing, encouraging him. Then she was in the alley, choking, hands clutching her throat.

She woke, instantly alert, realised it was her own hands on her throat, her usual reaction when she sensed an asthma attack was starting, but she did not feel asthmatic.

She relaxed, dozed, and slipped back into the alley, trying to stop Mr Grundley from falling but he was too heavy. She heard his head hit the paving, and saw it crack open.

She screamed.

'Miss Forest? Are you all right?' Mr Joseph's voice.

'Come in, please. The door's open.'

Seconds later he was there, the light was turned on, the curtains closed. 'Miss Forest, whatever's the matter?'

'I was dreaming. Dreaming.' She dragged breath into her lungs.

'Asthma?' He sat down on the side of the bed and she lunged towards him. His arms went around her. 'I really think Mrs Miller should be doing this, my dear.'

'No, I want you to hold me.' She gasped for air.

He did, even when Mrs Miller came to see what the fuss was all about. He held her while Mrs Miller gave her another glass of the relaxing medicine, until Mrs Miller suggested they should all try to sleep and they both left. It was Mr Joseph who held her all that time, Mr Joseph who convinced her it was just a nightmare and who kissed her forehead and told her he hoped she would sleep well for the rest of the night.

In the morning she awoke to someone knocking on her door. She slipped out of the bed and wrapped herself in a woollen dressing-gown, slid her feet into felt slippers, and opened the bedroom door.

'Mrs Miller! How nice of you. Good morning.' She opened the door wide and stepped aside as Mrs Miller carried in a tray loaded with breakfast.

'Not too early, I hope, miss.'

'Not at all.' The little gilded clock sitting on the mantelpiece showed it was ten o'clock.

'Mr Joseph had to leave early this morning but he'll be back before luncheon and he asked me to tell you he'd like you to eat with him.'

'I'd like that.' She looked at the amount of breakfast and wondered if she would be able to eat luncheon.

Mrs Miller leaned forward, lowered her voice, and said in a confidential tone. 'I hope you don't mind me saying this, miss, you being the daughter of Mr Joseph's friend, but having you here's changed him already. He was smiling when he went out this morning. That's the first time I've seen him smile properly since I've been here and that's several weeks now.'

Lottie was pleased to hear that she had made the lonely Mr Joseph smile again. He was, without doubt, the kindest man she knew and she had felt safe ever since she came into his house.

'What's the Norfolk house like, Mrs Miller?'

'Oh it's very remote, miss. Isolated. You could do whatever you liked up there. No one would know.'

Rose heard the post fall through the front door and rushed to pick up the pile of letters. She sorted through them quickly, then stopped when she found Lottie's letter.

Her heart pounded so hard she could hear it.

She opened the envelope with her finger, fumbled out the single sheet of writing paper and unfolded it.

Her spirit sank as she read what her daughter had written, but she could understand why Lottie had left home, and why she said she would keep moving on if they tried to find her.

CHAPTER 15

Mr Joseph smiled at her. 'You seem remarkably at ease, Miss Forest.'

'I feel very much at ease, Mr Joseph,' she said, astonished by how calm she was considering the circumstances she faced.

'I'm very pleased, Miss Forest.' He smiled. 'Is there anything special you wish to do before we leave?'

'I would like to write another letter, to my sister, Eve, to explain to her why I've left home.'

'But you won't say anything about the,' he paused, '*accident* you had?'

'No. I don't think that'd be very wise, especially as Eve's already in prison.'

'In prison? What for?' His face creased with surprise.

She explained what had happened to Eve and he looked even more concerned than he had previously. 'Miss Forest, I can only endorse everything I told you yesterday, but even more fervently. If you're arrested for what was an unfortunate accident and the Court finds that you have a sister imprisoned for exploding a bomb, you'll be condemned before the trial begins. I assure you that the police will find some way to use your sister's situation against you, even though they shouldn't.'

Lottie wrote her letter to Eve and handed it to Mr Joseph to be posted, then went up to his wife's room and with Mrs Miller's help chose several outfits warm enough for wearing on the east coast in winter.

Eve was glad that for once there was no one trying to persuade her to eat or drink. Someone had been there all day, pleading or cajoling, saying anything to persuade or entice her to try just a little of the food or a sip of the drinks they brought in every half hour or so.

It had been difficult to resist someone who pretended to be her friend, who sat with her, ate sparingly and offered to share her food. Someone who drank noisily while reiterating the futility of what Eve was doing by denying herself. It was difficult to resist the persuasive logic of the doctor who told her that as a nurse who had seen Polly Dobbs die she must be better placed than most women to understand how her body craved for water because it was dying.

The voices had gone on and on, until at last there was silence, but after several hours of silence she began to hear other voices – voices that were inside her own head or appeared to come out of the walls and the floor, voices that called to her from a great distance or made her turn her head quickly to see who was behind her.

Voices that whispered or shouted or sounded concerned and said she had made her point and should stop before she did herself too much harm to be any further use to the movement. Concerned voices that reminded her she had a mother and father who did not deserve all the worry she was causing them.

Treacherous voices, too, that said no one would know even if she did sip just a little of the cold, clean water from the big enamel jug, or eat just a taste of the meat and onion stew left in a straw box to keep it warm.

No one would know. No one *else* would know, but she

would so she closed her eyes and put her hands over her ears and prayed for *real* silence.

She could not think of anything but drinking the water, the feel of it on her tongue, swilling around her teeth, pouring down her throat. She swallowed, reacting to the mental picture.

Her dry throat cracked and made her cough.

Edward ate his midday meal at a table which was untypically silent. Katarina had offered to earn her keep and relieve Rose by working at the mission each day, and so he ate alone with Rose. They usually talked about work, the mission, the family or general news, but she had not spoken since they sat down and the only sounds were the creaking kitchener and the rattle of rain against the back window.

He looked at her across the table and noticed how Rose's vivid green eyes which used to sparkle with vivacity now looked dull. 'You look tired. Ill, almost. Anything wrong?'

'What do you think? One of our daughters is in prison and on hunger strike and another's run away because she's scared we want to put her into an asylum. How do you expect me to feel?'

'Oh, lass, I'm sorry.' He reached out to touch her hand but she pulled away, and left him feeling clumsy and foolish.

Eve had done what she did for her own reasons but Lottie was his fault, he knew that. Lottie would never have agreed to see a doctor and the only way seemed to be to trick her. It *was* for her own good.

He had not meant to upset her and when she came back that night he had desperately wanted to go to her but he knew she would not talk to him. She never had. Never talked to him and never came to him for a cuddle. Never treated him as her father. She had cut him out of the family, and now Rose was doing the same, and he could not blame her.

He knew his nervousness showed because his voice had slipped back into the north-east dialect he grew up with. It was strange how he always slipped back to his roots when he was really worried. It was as if he secretly wished he had never left, and in his heart he occasionally wished he had not. He sometimes wished he had not done a lot of things, including spoiling Rose's life.

She deserved better than him, a better life than he had given her, but he could not imagine how he could live without her.

He started as someone knocked on the door. Rose did not stir, just sat staring at nothing, and she did not even react when he stood up and went to see who was there.

'A telegram for Mr Forrester. Are you Mr Forrester?' a uniformed boy asked brightly in spite of being whipped by the wind and rain.

'Yes. Thanks.' He opened the envelope, took out the telegram and read it.

'Any reply, Mr Forrester?'

'No. Thank you.' He gave the boy a penny and shut the door.

Rose was still sitting alone at the table and he touched her shoulder gently, almost scared to disturb her. She looked up at him but did not say anything.

'It's from the prison, lass. Eve's not eaten or drunk for four days. They want us to go to see her and persuade her to give up before she makes herself ill.'

'I'll get my coat and hat.' She sounded tired, defeated, and she moved slowly as though she was worn out, but he was scared to say anything more about it in case he provoked another row which would only exhaust her further.

He helped her down from the bus which stopped directly opposite the prison doors. 'Are you all right?'

She nodded, and as the bus pulled away they stood on the kerbside, waiting for the heavy traffic to part so they could cross. He wanted to hold her hand for comfort but she was standing far enough away from him to make it obvious that she did not want to share her unhappiness with him, so he concentrated on the traffic racing along the wet road, watching for a gap and ready to guard her as they crossed.

'Mr Forrester?' He turned and saw Sister Brewer walking

towards him, obviously on her way to the hospital. 'Here to see Eve?'

'Yes,' he stepped back from the kerb, 'we had a telegram asking us to come and—'

Tyres screamed. He turned. Heard a thud. Saw a brown sack fall onto the front of a skidding motor-car. Saw it thrown off as the motor hit another car.

Then he saw the sack was Rose, and as her head smacked against the road he saw her blood.

Lottie was looking up at the moon as it seemed to race across the sky, and then the car turned a bend and the moon disappeared. She looked ahead and saw the sea, cold and almost flat with the moonlight glittering on small grey waves. It disappeared behind a bank of sand dunes and suddenly Mr Joseph slowed the car and turned towards the beach.

'We're here,' Mr Joseph said, stopped the car and turned off the engine.

The sea was a little way ahead, visible through a gap in the sand dunes, and alongside her was a square, solid-looking house with flint walls. The house was two storeys high and the moonlight glinted off six windows in the front wall.

She climbed out of the car and stretched her legs and back which were stiff from hours of being cramped up and hardly able to move. The wind carried grains of sand and the smell of the sea, and with the smell it brought a soft sound, the soothing sound of small waves lapping against the shallow beach.

Mr Joseph smiled at her and took her arm in his. 'Come along, my dear, you'll soon feel at home.' He spoke in the quiet, confident voice that had calmed her weeks ago when he took care of her in the train and once again he made her feel safe.

She realised quite suddenly that she felt more than safe. With her arm in his she felt comfortable and relaxed as though she had known this man for years. With their arms linked and his promise soon to have the house feeling like home she felt almost as though she was married to him.

He guided her to the front door, opened it and led her into a large hall where he lit an oil lamp on a small table.

'It's lovely!' The words escaped before she could hide her surprise.

She had expected something drab and forbidding but the hall looked pretty and homely and she imagined the rest of the house was the same. Within a few minutes Mr Joseph had lit lamps in the other ground floor rooms and she found they were all as welcoming as the hall. Even better than pretty and welcoming, she found each room had a fire laid and ready for lighting and even the kitchener was prepared for use.

The house was not damp and it warmed up surprisingly quickly. Mr Joseph carried all their luggage to their rooms and placed a small box of essentials in the kitchen.

Mrs Miller made cocoa and went to bed, but Lottie took her own and Mr Joseph's cocoa to his study, a small room lined with books and furnished only with a writing desk and captain's chair and two easy chairs placed by the fire.

She found Mr Joseph sitting back, half hidden by the wings of his chair, with the room lit only by the fire's flames. He looked tired but he smiled as she handed him his cocoa.

When she thanked him again for everything he had done, he waved away her thanks. 'Please, Miss Forest, I've already told you that you're giving far more than you're taking. Now, I think we'll devote tomorrow to buying stores and to recreation. Then I'll take you for a long walk along the beach. The air's sure to do you good, and I'm sure you'll appreciate the isolation this place offers. You can walk for hours without seeing anyone at all.'

'Thank you. I'm sure I'll enjoy that, Mr Joseph.'

'Yes, I'm sure we both will, but we must also decide how to address each other. *Mister* Joseph makes me feel so old, old enough to be your father. Even your grandfather!' He smiled again and his face creased in the fire light. 'I'm sure that when we know each other a little better we'll both feel much more at ease in each other's company.'

'Yes, I'm sure we will.' Tired, she found herself short of breath and he reminded her to take more of her medicine before she went to bed. She thanked him once more, and kissed him, just lightly on his cheek, but it pleased her and she thought it pleased him, too. He was older than her father, but in some ways he seemed to be only a little older than herself. It was strange.

She took her medicine and slept well in her bedroom facing the sea, lulled by the waves lapping against the shallow beach.

CHAPTER 16

Edward sat on the hospital bench, and tensed as the doctor who was attending Rose walked towards him. 'She's still alive, Mr Forrester, but only just, and you shouldn't expect too much.' The doctor's words permeated his shock, and he nodded to show he had heard what was said.

He heard Sister Brewer tell Helen and Jamie the same when they arrived an hour later, but he also heard the extra words she whispered, words she probably thought he could not hear. 'Her skull has been fractured and she is deeply concussed. Her brain could have been badly damaged and the doctor believes that even if she does live she might be a complete invalid, blind, deaf, crippled, even deranged.'

Rose, oh, Rose! He reached out to her in his thoughts and tried to creep into her mind, to know what she was feeling, and tell her he was with her and that if she died he would die, too, in spirit if not in body.

He could not imagine life without her. She was his life, his only reason for living. The children were important to her but not to him. He cared for them, even loved them, but not as much as he loved her and he would always have given up the right to have children just to have her. He had both, and he thanked God for that, but he would never forgive God if He took her away.

His faith was strong because God had brought him and Rose together. Loving Rose was his true faith and without her he would have nothing.

A terrible fear swamped him as he sat in the soulless corridor and already felt he was alone.

'Let's go home, Papa.' Helen took his arm. 'It's nearly midnight. You look exhausted and we're doing no good by staying here.'

He told her and Jamie to go and leave him with their mother but the Night Sister agreed with them and told him to go home and rest in case he was needed tomorrow. 'If Rose does recover consciousness we may need you to talk to her to see if she recognises you. We don't want you falling asleep because you're too tired.'

It seemed to make sense so he allowed them to lead him away.

They walked home through the sharp wind and the drizzle it carried. The streets were empty and quiet and he was glad because he knew he would have resented seeing people going about their normal lives when Rose might die at any moment.

It was night and the cell was dark.

Eve sat up and vomited bile. She kept it in her mouth and forced herself to swallow it. It made her vomit again and again but each time she forced it back down her gullet. She could not afford to lose any fluid if she was to stay strong enough to win her fight. She had not taken any food or water for five days now, and they would come to force feed her at any time.

Every part of her body hurt. It was a battle of wills, a matter of pride not to allow her body to betray her mind, not to drink just a little of the water which smelled so sweet. It was a matter of pride not to give in. A matter of pride to embarrass the Authorities into releasing her.

She made herself a vague promise she would die before she admitted defeat and condemned herself to the same sentence they had condemned her to. She reminded herself that she was a political prisoner, and had been convicted of a political crime.

She retched and swallowed the bile again. It occurred to her that she had joined a small band of women who had suffered in order to win the right to vote.

'Votes for Women' she thought, and wondered if she could have those words carved on her headstone if it came to that.

Somehow she knew her mind was drifting but that did not matter. All that mattered was she did not drink, and she did not eat.

She noticed grey filter through her small window, and turned, crossed-legged on her bed, to look at it. She was cold, cold all through, so she pulled the blanket around her, over her head and tight under her chin, and stared out through the high window and watched the day coming.

The sun bore down on her, warm on her face, and the flowers smelled sweet as the bees blundered among them. Lottie was drinking golden lemonade, draining her glass and pouring more from a jug. 'Here you are, Eve.' The glass was offered, she grasped it and tipped it up.

Lottie and the glass and the garden had gone.

She woke up, and heard a metal trolley rattle along the corridor.

The forcing trolley.

A door grated open and a woman whimpered. Another woman cursed her coarsely. 'I don't want to force you. Eat, or drink some bloody water, you stupid woman!'

Eve crawled off her cot and across the floor, pressed herself against the cell door and pushed herself upwards. She clung to the door and strained to hear the first woman answer, willed her to have enough strength to refuse.

Then she heard a man's voice 'Examine her, Doctor, and please tell me if she's fit enough to take food.'

The answer came a few seconds later, too quickly for a proper examination. 'She's fit enough.'

The woman's whimper turned into a whine. It stopped as a scuffle started.

Then, 'No! No! NO! Please, NO!' The howl ranged down the corridor.

More scuffles. A tin basin fell onto stone flooring, rolled around and around, quicker and quicker until it shuddered, then silence for a moment.

'NO! No! Please, no, PLEASE!' The cell door grated and thudded shut, but it did not muffle the howl, the choking sounds and then the gurgling noise a drowning woman makes.

The gurgling went on and on, for much longer than anyone could hold breath. It stopped.

Silence dragged on. And on.

It went on for too long. No sound, but there was a smell. Soup. Onion soup. That was what they had forced into her.

Still no sound. They must have filled her lungs instead of her stomach.

She retched with shock and with fear. It was her turn next.

She stared down at the floor. She had retched but not vomited. Her stomach was empty.

Then she heard the sound from along the corridor, the soft sound of another woman retching and the slap as the soup came up and hit the floor. And the splattering noise as she vomited more and more soup, the coughing and sneezing as she cleared her gullet and nose of the liquid meant to save her.

Then the scream, the awful scream of a woman who had been violated, and the awestruck silence of all the other prisoners who were unable to help.

A door grated and the trolley rattled again. It was coming for her, bringing the metal gag to force her mouth open, the rubber tube to be pushed down her throat. She heard voices and footsteps. The officer, the doctor and the four wardresses.

She pressed herself against the door as the trolley stopped outside. The key turned in the lock. She felt faint, wanted to faint, wanted to be unaware of what they were going to do to her. Then she felt the door move against her body.

She stood still in the doorway, swaying on her weakened legs, her arms hanging loose at her sides, her head so heavy her chin rubbed against her chest.

'Forrester?'

She grunted.

'This is your final opportunity. Are you going to eat? Drink?'

She hauled her head up and stared beyond the man, the officer sent by the Governor, and tried to see something better than this squalid moment and what was to come. Then she shook her head.

'Examine her, Doctor, and please tell me if she's fit enough to take food.' She heard the officer's order and the doctor's questions – questions asked too fast to be understood let alone answered, and felt the doctor's stethoscope on her chest.

Then she heard the doctor's verdict. 'She gives me no reason to think . . .' He rattled on, his words chosen not to incriminate him in the torture he authorised, but his voice sounded hollow.

She could not stop them physically so she tried to argue but her voice would not rise above a whisper and she could see they were not listening to her. She was disregarded, and all she could do was repeat her argument in her mind, tell herself she had not answered the doctor's questions, tell herself she was unwilling to endure forced feeding when this was abhorred by foreign governments who condemned Britain's Government for authorising the torture.

She felt herself lifted and thrust backwards into a chair which see-sawed her legs up and her head down. A woman's warm, plump legs and even warmer rump sat on her shins and forced her feet down until her ankles burned with pain. Hands clamped onto her thighs and thumbs poked into her soft flesh until they shocked her muscles into a spasm.

Pains exploded into her head but she clamped her mouth shut, determined not to scream, not to make their job easier, determined not to accept the gag until they forced her.

A pad covered her eyes and a strap burned across her forehead, tearing out wisps of hair, banging her head against the chairback. Her arms were wrenched out and back. She felt the hard grip the wardresses had on her wrists and shoulders, then the intimacy of women's breasts pressing her arms flat, and then the women's chest bones and ribs as the pressure increased.

Her cracked elbow pulsed with hot pain which made her feel sick, but she still kept her lips shut.

'Pinch her nose,' the officer said calmly. 'And put the pad over her mouth.'

She could not move, she could not see, and she could not breath. The dark turned red. Her body throbbed with pain, and fear.

She could not breathe! Wriggle! Fight! They were going to smother her, going to kill her! She tried to fight but she could not. They held her too tight. She was too weak.

The pad came off her mouth.

She gulped air, cool, fresh air, and something hard jabbed into her mouth and trapped her lips against her teeth.

Her jaw hurt, she could not close it, could not breathe because it was open too far. Something clicked, metal on metal. It forced her mouth open wider, forced her lips against her teeth. She felt her teeth forced into her flesh and jar against the metal gag as they bit all the way through her lips. Tasted blood, felt teeth break, could not breath. Felt someone pulling her tongue and air rushing down her windpipe.

'Tube,' the officer said.

She fought, but only in her mind because the women held her too tight for her to move. The man pushed a rubber tube into her body, violating her just as he had the woman before her, and all the women before her.

Her gullet closed and retched but the tube was pushed deeper and deeper into her, invading her as nothing else could, disobeying nature and discarding her dignity.

Then she felt warmth in her throat and gullet, and liquid spilled into her, unwanted and indigestible. It laid in her, filling her up, but not entering her stomach. It rose up outside the tube, filled her gullet, and she realised what

215

would happen when it reached her mouth. It would choke her.

She tried not to breathe when the soup filled her mouth, and she felt it spill out, slide down her chin and throat and seep, warm and slippery, over her chest and breasts.

Her head was exploding with the need for air but the refusal to breathe was the only choice she had left. They had taken away every other right she had as a human being. They could take away her freedom to leave, make her wear whatever they wanted her to wear, make her spend her days alone, destroy her dignity and they could force food into her but they could not force her to breathe. That was all that remained, her only weapon to prove she would not be beaten.

The effort of not breathing numbed all the other pains and cleared her head. The world she knew did not exist any more, not for her. The family which had always helped and protected her could not help her now and therefore it did not exist for these moments. She could see she was alone.

All that existed was her spirit, and she sensed that put her apart from people who led normal lives and had never experienced this acute sensation of loneliness, the awareness that in the moments before death, when you have absolutely no more life to live, you are totally and completely alone.

And she realised that if by some miracle she lived she would never be the same again.

'She's full,' someone said calmly.

She was pulled upright, the gag was released and suddenly she was on her hands and knees and the soup was flooding out of her mouth and nose. The chair was pulled away and the trolley rattled towards the door.

'Eat, or tomorrow we'll be back and we'll make you swallow. We'll keep on until you do.'

The door slammed shut, and a key turned in the lock.

She vomited and vomited again and again until she had rid herself of everything they had poured into her, but she could still taste the soup, and smell it and feel it on her clothes and in her hair, and it would always be in her mind.

What they had done to her amounted to rape. She had

been raped officially, on behalf of the Government.

She collapsed on the floor, lying in the mess that had poured out of her body, and knew that tomorrow it would happen again.

Edward sat by Rose's bed and all he could see of her was her face, as white as the bandages and plaster that encased her skull and neck and spread down over her shoulders. Her bloodless colour shocked him, her whisper-light, erratic breathing frightened him. It was three days since the accident and she was no better.

'And no worse,' Sister Brewer reminded him, and once again he was thankful that she had been there to help Rose immediately after the accident; a sign, surely, that God did not mean her to die?

He prayed silently, his lips moving with the concentration, and he asked God to do what he liked with him but save her. God could have anything he wanted if he saved Rose.

'Come on, Father, they want us to leave.' Jamie held his shoulders and half lifted him away from the bed.

'Just a minute, lad.' He leaned over Rose and kissed her forehead, lightly, just enough for her to know he was there, if she knew anything at all. 'I love you, Rose. I'll see you tomorrow.'

Edward could not sleep and spent most of the night sitting in the cosy kitchen, trying to distract himself with a novel. He crept back to bed at dawn and then slept heavily until the middle of the morning. When he woke up he found a note from Jamie beside his bed. It suggested he spend the day at home or at the hospital. Jamie and Joe could manage work without him.

He decided they could not and he was dressed and ready to leave when he remembered an argument he once had with his father. Ma had been very ill but she was recovering and his father refused to go to see her because it would make him late for work. Now he was behaving in exactly the same way.

He shivered. The thought of turning into his cantankerous father frightened him. He buttoned his coat and went to the hospital.

Rose had been moved into a small room off the main ward.

He guessed it was the room Eve sometimes referred to as the dying room, and he sat beside Rose and held her hand and pleaded with her not to die.

Lottie stopped walking, ignored the wind tugging her loose hair, and turned to stare out at the sea.

She did not know what day it was, how many days she had spent here, and she was not concerned. The sea and the sky and the house and Mr Joseph's company had a tranquillising effect which made days pass in an unhurried and unchecked way. She enjoyed a stream of time which absorbed her and flowed around or over obstructions and things which should have worried her, a stream of time which promised to flow gently and easily onwards and onwards for ever.

The flint-walled house was built immediately behind a gap in the sand dunes where a small stream burbled and fanned out across the sands, and the beach curved away gently to the north and south, forming a shallow bay.

As he had promised, Mr Joseph took her for long walks on the firm sands. They strolled north and saw no one, and south and saw no one. It was as if they were living in their own private world. The air smelled of the sea, clean and clear, and the sun shone so the dune-sheltered beach was warm.

By standing on top of the dunes it was possible to see for miles; see how the coast curved and the way the waves frilled the sand, and turning inland see across open flat country or look up and wonder at the size of the sky.

She was used to seeing the London sky, etched with chimneys and churches, but here even the churches kept below the horizon so the sky could expand. The big sky entranced her. Cloudy or clear, dawn or dusk, its colours and its impression of freedom were intoxicating.

She had lost track of time and lost track of herself.

She had changed. Mr Joseph had changed her, or at least allowed her to change herself.

She did not worry any more and she had found out, at last, what it was like to feel wanted. To be happy.

She was learning to be herself and to enjoy the simple life Mr Joseph was showing her on walks like these when they were alone for hours and sometimes did not speak for hours, but still enjoyed being together.

'Look! Look! Mr Joseph, there! The bird, catching fish!' She pointed excitedly as a bird skimmed a shallow wave, swooped and rose with a silver fish flopping from its beak.

'Yes, I see it!' He seemed as excited as her, but as the bird flew away he chided her. 'Does it still have to be *Mister* Joseph? You make me feel like a character in a Brontë novel. Most people call me Joseph.'

'It's difficult for me to think of you as anything other than Mr Joseph – my guardian and benefactor.' She giggled as she added the final description and he pretended to be offended and walked a little way ahead of her.

'Now you've made me feel more like someone in a Dickens' novel – Miss Forest,' he called back.

'I'm sorry,' she pretended contrition, and added, 'sir!'

'Enough!' he roared above the sound of the sea. A scavenging gull turned its head and stared at him as if it was offended by the noise he made. Mr Joseph turned to face her and walked backwards, the wind flapping his coat around his knees, and he pointed to the gull. 'You see, now you've made me upset one of our neighbours. Call me Joseph, Miss Forest, I insist.'

'Certainly, but only if you call me Lottie.' She saw him wrinkle his nose in disapproval, and made another suggestion as she walked faster to catch him up. 'Charlotte?'

'A lovely name but rather long.'

'My second name's Rose?'

'Yes! Oh, yes.' He seemed pleased and edged around to walk a foot or two away from her. 'I very much prefer Rose. It's short, to the point, and very English. Rather like you.'

He had turned the joke on her, and she was glad he had.

She blushed and he came close. His arm slipped around her shoulders.

'I do like Rose, seriously. Would you mind if I used it?'

'Of course not. It'll remind me of my mother.'

'Do you miss your parents? Being with your family?'

'I know this'll sound awful, but no, I don't. Perhaps that's because of what they tried to do to me. Anyway, I don't want to forget them but if they were all dead I'd have to live without them, and that's how I want to live from now. I want to live as though everyone I used to know has died. And I'd like them to think of me in the same way. Do you think that's possible?'

'Almost anything's possible, Rose, but some things are less desirable or advisable than others. You should try not to cut yourself off so completely. Things may change and one day you may well feel you made an awful mistake by abandoning your family, everyone you know.'

Now she frowned, but only to help her concentrate on making her answer clear. 'I understand what you're saying, but you have to understand that I never felt as though I was *really* a part of the family. I was always excluded from the core, somehow, and that always made me feel unwanted. I think perhaps that's why I used to dream so much. I haven't been doing that since I've been with you and I don't want to do it any more. I can be myself when I'm with you. I don't have to pretend to be anyone else.'

'I'm glad,' he said quietly.

'Joseph, I feel as though my life only really began when I met you.' She meant everything she said but when she heard her words and the silence which followed, she felt embarrassed and knew she was blushing. 'I'm sorry. I shouldn't have said all that. It was silly.'

'No, Rose, I don't think it's silly at all. I've been reluctant to tell you this because it could spoil everything, but . . .' He paused and seemed to take a deep breath before he continued, 'but I'm falling in love with you.'

A sudden surge of emotion and happiness made her tremble, and when she spoke her voice was faint and unsteady. 'I think I feel the same about you.'

He smiled. 'You'll never understand how happy that makes me, Rose. And now I don't know what more to say or do.'

He did not say anything but he held her closer, and she was glad and wrapped her arm about his waist so she could share their closeness properly.

She kept telling herself that she could not be falling in love with him because she hardly knew him and he *was* older than her father, but that did not seem to matter.

She had always hated being touched but she always enjoyed his touch. The first time he had touched her he had changed her and although she did not understand why she did not question it, she simply enjoyed it.

They walked northwards, the only people on the beach, and they walked without speaking. The wind blew in their faces and made their hair and coats flap. When they reached a small promontory they stopped and the wind there seemed to blow all around them. She shivered and he opened his coat and tucked her inside it, close to him, intimate and snug. 'Let's walk back.' He smiled and they walked back the way they had come.

As they came level with the gap which led back to the house he opened his coat and they moved apart and did not even hold hands as they walked along the sand-blown path to the house. What they did, how they behaved when they were alone was their business. It was a secret she guessed they both wanted to keep for their own reasons. They shared something special but he was so much older than her that she sensed Mrs Miller and the rest of the world would not approve.

A special poignancy settled during dinner that night and she was glad when Mrs Miller announced that the change of air had made her tired. 'Then you go up to bed, Mrs Miller, and I'll clear up.'

'Oh, no, Miss Forest. I couldn't do that. Not with you being a guest, and all.'

'There's no reason why I shouldn't help. I'd do it at home and I'd feel more at home here if you'd let me help you occasionally, if Mr Joseph doesn't mind.'

Joseph shrugged his agreement and helped her to persuade Mrs Miller to leave them alone.

They cleared the table and washed and dried everything between them, then went to sit on the settee in front of the big living-room fire.

There were no lamps lit. Indoors the fire flickered and crackled, creaked and settled, and outside the sea sighed against the beach.

She leaned against him, snuggled into his arms, and the warmth and safety and love wafted her asleep.

It was very late when he woke her and suggested they go to bed, and for the first time in her life she wanted to be taken to bed and to be made love to, but he meant they should go to their own beds and even when she kissed him outside her bedroom door it made no difference to him.

She lay awake for a long time, unfamiliar feelings surging through her, and she resented the irony of wanting a man who apparently felt he should not take her. Perhaps that might change. Perhaps she might be able to make him change.

She reached out for her medicine, realised she had taken it earlier, turned over and eventually fell asleep after a long time spent listening to the waves stroking the beach.

Mrs Miller opened the dining-room door, asked if they had finished with breakfast, gave her opinion as to the day's weather and started clearing the table. She loaded up a tray and walked to the door, then stopped. 'And are you able to tell me your plans for today, sir, Miss Forest?'

'I'm not quite sure,' he said, but Lottie smiled at him and suggested it was time to begin clearing all his old files.

'We don't have to,' he argued, then turned sharply as Mrs Miller snorted, giving her unspoken opinion on any further delay and treating him like an errant child even though he was her employer and older than her. Grimacing, he conceded. 'Well, perhaps we should, if you're ready, Rose.'

She was ready, especially now. She loved him and he had said he was falling in love with her, but there was a distance between them that was not yet bridged. He was kind and gentle and could talk about most things but he never talked about himself, about his past.

Perhaps she could learn about him from his files, learn enough to encourage him to talk, to begin to build a bridge.

'Joseph, however did they get into such a jumble?' It seemed to her that the boxes and files and parcels of documents had simply been tipped into the two upstairs rooms where they cluttered the floor from wall to wall.

'It took a lifetime to accrue it all and only a matter of hours to pack it and unpack it,' he explained. 'I never fully understood the system my clerk followed, and when he died everything became too much. Mrs Joseph began to sort things out but—'

'Of course,' she said quickly, sorry to have dragged up emotions better left to lie. 'Tell me what to do and I'll make a start.'

He explained and stayed with her for half an hour but she could see he was unhappy going through the evidence of so many court cases and of his life. He had carried a few files to the window to read them better but his attention had wandered and he had been staring out of the window for several minutes.

'Joseph, would you rather leave me to do this alone?'

'Would you mind?'

'Of course not,' she said softly and took hold of the files he was holding.

'Actually, I do have some business to attend to in Norwich. It's not urgent, but I'd quite like to get away from the house for a while.'

'I can manage here, so why don't you go now?' She touched his arm, urging him to leave. 'How long will you be?'

'I'll be back late tonight. Tell Mrs Miller to leave me just a cold supper because I'll eat a cooked lunch.'

They exchanged a brief, formal kiss, and the moment she was alone she moved to the window so she could watch him drive away. She called goodbye through the glass and waved but he did not hear or see her.

She was still holding the files she had taken from him and before she put them back into the pile which needed sorting she wiped the dust off them.

Edward Forrester.

The name appeared through the dust, the same name as her father. She flicked off more dust so she could read the whole file cover.

Regina versus Edward Forrester 1887.

What had her father's namesake done?

A ribbon bow held the file shut. She undid it easily, opened the file, and scanned the first page. Joseph had defended Edward Forrester against the Crown in a case heard in Durham. Joseph's fees had been paid by Catherine Wyndham.

That was her aunt's name, dead Aunt Catherine.

Her hands trembled. She turned the page and found a letter thanking Joseph for his kindnesses and efforts. The writing was familiar. She glanced at the signature on the second page. Elizabeth Forrester, her Aunt Lizzie's maiden name!

She had come to Norfolk and stumbled on something she was not meant to know about. A family skeleton.

She trembled, so much that she dropped the file and had to scramble about on the floor to gather all the documents together again.

One formal document seemed to leap in front of her.

It said her father had been charged with murder.

Murder!

The word seemed to shout at her.

She read through the charges and thought she might be sick. Her father had been tried for murdering her grandfather, Sebastian John Laybourne. Her mother's father.

She slumped down, too weak to stand or even sit properly, and she turned over another page and then another and another, unable to stop. There were gaps in the file, gaps where documents must have been mislaid or destroyed, but there was enough left for her to piece the story together.

Her father and all his family worked for her mother's father, Sebastian Laybourne, in his mine. There had been a serious accident and when her father learned his family were trapped he had threatened to kill Sebastian Laybourne if any of them died. They had all been killed and her father had broken into the Laybournes' home even though it was guarded by police and had battered Sebastian to death.

He had been sentenced to twenty years imprisonment.

She read the file, stunned by everything she read, staggered by the deceit her parents had woven into their stories about the past. Then she found a note which at first seemed to have nothing to do with the file but had everything to do with her parents.

According to the file her mother had married a man called Hubert Belchester in 1886. The name Belchester did seem vaguely familiar and she associated it with the mission, but she did not know why.

A strong sense of betrayal enveloped her, and she fetched a small table and chair from another room so she could sit and study the file in detail.

Edward sat by Rose, talking to her about all the good things that had happened to them, remembering old dreams and wondering if, even now, they could make them come true.

Then he prayed out loud so she could hear even though he knew she only pretended to have faith in order to please him. Afterwards he sat and stroked her face, and thought how similar she was to the way she looked when he found her again all those autumns ago. They said she was dying then, but he had not let her go, and he would not let her go now.

She had given him all those years, the years he would have been locked away if she had not found the evidence to free him, and now he had to find enough strength to give them back to her, to repay her for everything she had given him.

'Remember the old lodge, Rose? We said we'd like a place like that, one day. Remember?'

He was sure her eyes opened and they were vivid green just as they used to be, but they closed immediately and even talking about the lodge did not seem to work the magic again.

CHAPTER 17

———————

Eve sat on her cot and stared at the door. She had refused to accept their food and now it seemed that they would not allow her to eat.

Nothing had come though the door, neither ordinary nor especially tempting food, and nothing to drink. They had not even supplied water for her to wash herself and now she and the cell stank of soup and sweat and vomit.

She could not move her cracked left arm now, not since the attack to feed her, but she raised her right hand and felt her hair. It was stiff and matted where the soup had congealed. She moved her hand down, over her forehead which had been bruised by the strap used to hold her head still and felt her smashed teeth, then felt the blood clots which had formed where her teeth had been forced through both her lips.

She was not sure how long she had sat like that. Time meant nothing. She could not remember seeing anyone since the attack, but they would come for her when they were ready.

She heard the trolley being brought back.

She did not cling to the door this time, she sat calmly and

listened to the screams and shouts as another woman was forced to submit. And then another.

Then it was her turn.

The door was opened, and as they wheeled the trolley into her cell she sat on her cot and smiled at them, at all of the women she remembered from the last time, and especially at the doctor, even though he was not the same one as before.

And the new doctor was her saviour. 'Good God! Who did this?'

There was a confusion of muffled excuses and feigned shock that she could possibly look so ill so quickly when earlier she was robust and healthy. It was obvious that the doctor did not believe what was said.

'I want her taken to hospital. Now!'

She trembled even before they touched her, and began to cry with relief that it should be over so quickly. Their hands reached out to steady her but she pushed them away. She did not want to give them the satisfaction of being able to claim they had helped her, been at all kind to her. She stared into each woman's eyes in turn, keeping her eyes on theirs until she had embarrassed them into looking away, then, stiff limbed and slow, she walked out through the door and turned along the corridor. As she walked she felt less and less steady and knew she would fall if someone did not help her, but she did not want *their* help. She would only accept help from the doctor who refused to allow her to be tortured any more.

Then, as if he knew, he was alongside her and she felt his arm wrap around her waist. 'Please allow me, Miss Forrester.'

She thought the last two words were the sweetest she had ever heard. He had used her name and her title, and that meant he thought she was a human being.

Lottie was embarrassed because she could not eat, and because it was obvious that Mrs Miller thought she was pining for Joseph.

'I think it's just the accumulation of everything that's

happened, Mrs Miller. That, and reading about some of the cases Mr Joseph's been involved with.'

'Then don't read 'em if they upset you, Miss Forest. That's what I say.'

She smiled and asked Mrs Miller if they could be a little less formal and use each other's first names.

'I'd rather not, miss. I think I could get very fond of you and being familiar'd only make it harder when you go.'

'I don't have any plans to leave, Mrs Miller.'

'Not yet but you will, won't you? You won't want to get stuck with an old man like Mr Joseph, will you, miss?' Mrs Miller obviously suspected she and Joseph had feelings for each other and was trying to draw out an admission by being controversial. 'No, of course you won't.'

Mrs Miller was almost begging her to refute the argument but she could not say anything so she shrugged. She could not tell Mrs Miller that she and Joseph loved each other, and she could not tell her that her father had committed a murder and Joseph had defended him. Or that her parents were not married, or discuss other suspicions that the file raised.

She wanted Joseph to come back quickly, not only because she missed him but also because she wanted to talk about her father, the incomplete file, and about her mother's marriage to Hubert Belchester. Once again she was thankful that Joseph had misheard her name. She was sure that if he had known she was Edward Forrester's daughter he would have avoided her, especially as Fate had also made *her* responsible for a man's death. If she had never stumbled across the file she would never have known the truth.

After the meal she went upstairs again and she was still working on the files when Joseph returned. They exchanged their formal kisses but she noticed he held her waist for several seconds afterwards and there was a softness in his expression which she had not seen before. It was not long before he asked what progress she had made and she admitted having spent a whole day reading just one file.

'Regina versus Edward Forrester. 1887.'

'Oh,' he said irritably.

His reaction puzzled her. 'Have I upset you?'

'I would have preferred you hadn't read it, Rose.'

'Why?'

He hesitated, then said quietly. 'I don't want to talk about it.'

'Tomorrow?' she asked hopefully.

'No, not tomorrow. Not ever. It happened nearly thirty years ago and I don't want to discuss it.'

'It seems a very interesting case.' She tried to hide the forlorn feeling that had crept upon her.

He shrugged and looked unusually strained. 'Interesting? No. It was quite sordid. I had to defend a man who killed his employer. Battered him to death while a mob burned the family's house down.'

'Was he guilty?'

'He was found guilty.'

'Yes, but was he?'

'He confessed. There should be a copy of his signed confession in the file. Didn't you see it?'

She shook her head, and her heart tumbled as her final hope that her father was innocent died, and as if that was not enough Joseph told her something which made the crime seem even worse.

'Not only guilty, which he admitted from the beginning, but he also said he was glad he had killed the old man, a man three times his age.'

'Did he serve his full sentence?' she asked, hoping to draw out more information.

'No. He was released early and rather oddly, his sister married the prison Governor who died shortly afterwards. There was some unpleasant talk about the relationship Edward Forrester shared with his sister, his half sister really, and that's one reason it's all so sordid,' he said distastefully and Lottie shuddered, her thoughts in turmoil. He obviously noticed because he asked her why she wanted to know so much about that particular case.

'It's simply that I stumbled across the file, the name's similar to mine, and I suppose because . . .' she faltered, took a deep breath and said what was on her mind. 'because I killed someone, Joseph, and I'll never forget it.'

'You were protecting yourself, Rose. You didn't mean to kill him.' His arms came around her and he held her tight. 'Now, let's try to forget all about Forrester. There were elements of that case which I found more than distasteful, little touches of madness here and there and...' She shuddered, and still holding her he slackened his grip and smiled into her eyes. 'I'm sorry. I didn't mean to remind you of what your parents tried to do. We've our future to think about now, Rose. It doesn't matter what happened in our pasts. And it especially doesn't matter what happened in the Forresters' lives.'

She wanted to tell him she was Edward Forrester's daughter, but she could not. He was right, they did have their own lives to lead. They loved each other and she was sure they could be happy, but not if she constantly reminded him about something he wanted to forget. Even so, there was one last thing she wanted to know.

'I agree, but there's just one last thing. I found a note which didn't appear to have anything to do with the file. Something about a Mrs Belchester? Where should I file that?'

'Leave it there. She was the murdered man's daughter. She left her husband to live with Forrester when he was released from prison. To live with the man who murdered her father.'

Lottie moved away from him so he would not feel her tremble. 'Rather an odd thing to do?' She tried hard to sound only mildly interested.

'That's what her husband thought.'

'Did you ever meet him?'

He shook his head. 'I know of him. Very wealthy man, rather reclusive and very charitable. Anyway, that's enough, Rose.'

'Did he ever divorce her?'

'Rose?' He sounded exasperated with her. 'I thought we weren't going to discuss this any further?'

'I'm sorry.' She shrugged and forced herself to smile. 'I just wondered.'

'Well, this must be the very last word. He didn't divorce her and I know for a fact that he would take her back even after all she's done. If he could find her.' Now it was his turn to shrug. 'She may not even be alive, Rose, her or Forrester. Now, I don't want to hear any more about the Forresters or the Laybournes or Hubert Belchester. We have our own lives to lead and our new life starts now. Will you marry me?'

'Pardon?' He had asked the question in such a matter-of-fact way that she was not sure she had heard him correctly.

'I asked you to marry me. I'm an old man and it can't be a long marriage I'm afraid. Ten years at the most, I'd say.'

She was stunned, but not so much that she could not see the complications which would pile up if she accepted him, and she began to gabble about her family but he stopped her.

'A few days ago you wanted to forgo your family and forget your past. Now you talk about all those things as though you want to invite them into your future. Which will it be, Rose Forest? Past or future? Only you can choose.'

She hesitated, unsure what she was committing herself to. Joseph did not know who she really was, but if she married him she could never introduce him to her parents, not without showing them she knew of their immense deceit. Then she tried to imagine herself walking out of the house and never seeing Joseph again. 'The future,' she said quietly.

'Good.' He smiled and reached out to hold her but instead he pressed his hands against his temples and screwed up his face.

'What's wrong?' She stepped towards him and held his face in her hands.

'A sudden pain. I've had it a few times over the past few days. I expect it's the excitement.' He smiled and relaxed his face. 'There, it's passed already, but I think I'll sit quietly in my study.'

She watched him leave, then worked on the files for another two hours.

Mrs Miller asked her if she wanted cocoa but she

declined, wished her goodnight and a little later heard her snoring in her sleep.

Joseph had not reappeared so she went to his study and knocked on his door. He did not answer so she placed her ear to the door and listened. No sound.

She opened the door, very quietly so she should not disturb him if he was busy and would not startle him if he was asleep. The curtains were still open but the pitch black outside left the room dark and apparently empty. Perhaps he had gone to bed.

She sighed, disappointed that he had not said goodnight.

'Charlotte?' His voice came out of the darkness and she realised he was sitting back in one of the easy chairs by the unlit fire.

'Joseph, I did knock but I thought you'd gone to bed.'

'Not without saying goodnight, my dear. I've been sitting here, thinking.'

He paused and she was not sure if he was gathering his thoughts or if he expected her to speak, and as the silence lengthened she simply asked why he was sitting in the dark.

'It's easier to face oneself in the dark, my dear.'

'I'm not sure if that's profound or depressing,' she said, hoping he would say what was on his mind.

'Charlotte, please come and sit down for a while.'

She sat in the chair on the opposite side of the fireplace, her back to the window so she could see a faint outline of his face in the darkness.

'Why are you calling me Charlotte when we decided you'd call me Rose,' she asked mildly.

'Several disparate reasons, my dear. The name Rose has connotations concerning our earlier discussion. Rose Laybourne became Rose Belchester, and I've no doubt she called herself Rose Forrester. Rose Forest is too similar to that.' He sighed heavily. 'Also, we've been living a rather unreal life for the past week or so and calling you Rose was a part of that. Reality can be ignored, of course, but it doesn't go away and ignoring it can be dangerous. I think I've been guilty of that, Charlotte, and I'm sorry if I misled you.'

'Misled me?' She had a dreadful feeling that she understood, but she had to be certain.

'You remind me so much of my wife that I've been trying to pretend you are her. You're not, of course. You're a lovely, wonderful girl whom I must not impose myself upon. I shouldn't have asked you to marry me.'

'But could I make you happy, Joseph?'

'My dear, I'm sure you could make me deliriously happy but I've already lived your life-span three times over and it's inevitable that there'll come a time when we'd make each other terribly unhappy.'

'I don't think so, Joseph. I know we haven't known each other for very long, but I do love you. I think I've loved you from the first time you helped me in the underground.'

'Don't Charlotte,' he pleaded softly, 'please don't tempt me.'

'To be happy?'

'To make you unhappy.'

'You won't,' she said.

She lay still, in the dark, and listened to the familiar sound of the waves sweeping the beach, listened to the house groaning and thought it was strange that a house she had lived in for a few days could already seem more like home than the house she had lived in for more than twenty years.

She thought about Joseph, and smiled. She had dreamed of marrying a handsome young prince, but Joseph had come along and she had fallen totally in love with him. She had dreamed of living in a large house in a fashionable London square and, of course, she could, but she would rather live here, settle down in this old house yards from a Norfolk beach, but she would live in London if that was what he wanted. Being with him was all that mattered.

The past few weeks had helped her to see her weaknesses and although she was trying to be strong she still needed someone to support her, and that was what Joseph did. He did not dote on her as Albert had and he did not overwhelm her as her family had, he simply discussed issues and alternatives with her and left her to make up her own mind.

And he was honest. He told her when he thought she was wrong and he had even admitted he had pretended she was his dead wife. Yes, he was honest, she was sure of that, and after all that had happened she needed to be sure there was someone she could believe in.

She stared into the darkness and tears rolled down her face.

Honesty? Her parents had accused *her* of lying when their whole lives were a lie. They had betrayed her time and time again and now, knowing their betrayal, she could not imagine ever returning to them.

Only weeks before she would not have believed some of the things Joseph tried hard not to tell her, but she had seen Aunt Lizzie kissing Mr Crabb, seen the way she kissed him, and her disillusionment had started then. Everything seemed to follow on quite naturally after that, one betrayal after another. Her mother was conducting an affair and even Albert had been drawn into the deceit.

She stopped crying and wiped her eyes with short, angry movements.

Now the crying was over she decided she would not cry for them any more. She would marry Joseph as soon as possible, not as an escape but as something she wanted to do.

She settled against her pillows. Marrying Joseph was more than something she wanted to do, it seemed to be something which Fate itself had ordained. Joseph always seemed to be there when she needed him and he always seemed prepared for the alarms in her life. It was surely more than a coincidence that he should have been the man to defend her father, and only Fate, knowing what was to happen, could have caused him to mishear her name at a crucial moment.

She snuggled down, happy that although it was not the marriage she had expected there was enough evidence to convince her she and Joseph were destined for each other. She had always found it hard to believe in the miracles her father preached about, but she believed in them now. She was about to start an adventure which would last all her life.

The sound of the sea made her drowsy and although she remembered she had not taken her final day's draught of Mrs Miller's tonic she thought she would not bother with it. Then she decided she must. She had to build up the iron in her blood to help sustain her over the next few weeks.

She drank the tonic and settled down again, and just as she slipped into sleep she remembered she must write to Eve, the only tie with her past she would maintain. She would explain why she had to run away from their father and Albert, and tell her she was happy and would soon be married. She would not give Eve her address or tell her any more; Eve had enough to contend with, being in prison for the next two years.

'Come in.' Elizabeth looked up slowly as Bill walked into her office, both hands fumbling with his off-duty cap.

'Good morning, Lizzie,' he said awkwardly, and stood in front of her desk like a schoolboy called forward to talk to his teacher.

'Good morning, Bill. It's been a long time since you called.' She pushed her spectacles up her nose, aware that she looked more than usually formidable when she peered over them.

'I thought I'd better keep away. After . . .' He looked down at the floor.

'After you comforted me when I was upset? Just as a good friend would, Bill?'

'Is that how you saw it, Lizzie?'

'How else could I see it? We were both upset, Bill. We *are* both lonely, in our different ways, but I know how loyal you are to Gladys and I respect you for it. I certainly wouldn't want you to do anything to upset her, or make yourself feel guilty, or spoil *our* friendship. I like your company too much for that.'

'Really?' He sounded brighter. 'I thought you might feel I took advantage of you, Lizzie. Said things I shouldn't have.'

'Of course not. I can't even remember what you did say.' She was lying but it was worth it to see him smile. In truth she thought she had taken advantage of him.

'I'm glad I came now. I was a bit nervous.'

'I'm glad you came, too, because I'm feeling rather nervous myself. I'm going to see Eve this afternoon, in the prison hospital. Can you tell me what it's like, so I know what to expect?'

It was exactly as he described it, but even more depressing. She walked along the ward and thought it smelled exactly like any other hospital, then wondered why she thought it might not. She found her favourite niece, the niece who most took after her, propped up on pillows but fast asleep, so she took the opportunity to look closely at the damage which had been done to Eve's face.

Eve could have been allowed visitors a week ago but she had refused to see anyone, and it was easy to understand why. The injuries must have healed a little in that time, but she still looked awful with weals across her forehead, yellowing bruises over her nose and around both eyes, and a ring of clotted blood around her lips which were swollen and blackened.

She sat by the bed for twenty minutes, waiting for Eve to wake.

Somewhere along the ward someone dropped a tin bowl and Eve opened her eyes.

'Eve, how do you feel?'

'Sore, Aunt Lizzie,' Eve rasped in a dry voice.

'You're being released, Eve. Have they told you?'

'Yes. Only because a few papers caused a fuss.'

'That doesn't matter. You can come home now.'

Eve shook her head. 'No. I'm going to Eastbourne. To the League's nursing home.'

'Well, afterwards then. When you leave there.'

'No.' Eve shook her head. 'They told me Mama's had a bad accident. How is she?'

'We thought she'd die but she didn't, and the doctors reckon she'll live, but that's all they'll say. She's like a baby, Eve, but your father thinks she's getting better. He wants to bring her home and he really does want you to come back, too.'

'To take care of Mama?'

'No, not entirely.' She hesitated and wished she had handled this better. Of course it would be easier if Eve came home, but that was not the main reason why both she and Edward wanted her to come. They missed her, especially since Lottie had left. The house was very quiet, far too quiet. Also Edward had started to brood about things and, as usual, blame himself for most of their problems. 'Come home, Eve. Please!'

'No. I can't. I'm sorry.' A rasping whisper.

'Eve, it's over. Come home.'

'It's not over. They hurt me, badly.' Blood oozed from around the clots and glistened across Eve's lips. Her tongue wiped it away. 'I'm not going to give up. Never.'

'Eve?' She started to plead but Eve had shut her eyes, and that meant she had shut her ears too. It was pointless arguing with her when she had made up her mind because nothing would make her change it. 'Where will you go if you're not coming home?'

'I'll stay in Eastbourne for the time being. I'll probably stay on as a nurse once I've recovered. The WFL Committee have invited me down there because they think I might need to get away from the newspaper reporters.'

'There have been several articles about you, Eve.' She wondered if she should tell Eve that she had saved each one for a scrap-book, but decided that would probably encourage Eve to go out and cause even more trouble. 'Will you see your father before you leave? He's very worried about you.'

'No, I don't want him to see me like this.'

She sensed Eve was not being totally honest. 'Oh, Eve? He's your father. You wouldn't let him see you in prison and now you're going away. Please?'

'No.'

'Please?' She noticed Eve would not look at her. 'Please see him.'

'No.' Eve hesitated and then seemed to want to justify her decision. 'I'll see him when I feel better, but not now. I know what he and Albert tried to do to Lottie.'

She was surprised, and irritated, and immensely relieved. 'Lottie? You've seen her? Is she all right?'

'I had a letter. She says she's going to marry the man on the train. Remember? The missing boot? He exists after all.'

Elizabeth bridled at the scorn in Eve's voice. 'Don't be too critical, Eve. You thought she made it up, too.'

'I know. We were all wrong.'

'Did she say when she's getting married? Where?'

'No. Didn't even tell me his surname. I don't think any of us are invited,' Eve said stolidly.

'Well, it's going to be a strange marriage and maybe a short one if he's as old as she said he was.'

'Just as long as she's happy.' Eve yawned.

'You're tired. I'll leave you to rest. Shall I come back tomorrow?'

'No. I'm leaving tomorrow.'

'You will write?'

Eve nodded, and they parted without touching, just nodding to each other, promising to write. It was almost as if they were about to spend a week apart, not begin to live entirely separate lives, and Elizabeth found it difficult not to cry.

She walked away from Eve's bed and did not look back when she reached the end of the ward, just opened the door and stepped out into the corridor. She felt, in her heart, that Eve was doing what was right for her, and so she turned her mind to Lottie.

Poor Lottie who always seemed to want too much from life now appeared to have settled for too little by marrying so soon and to someone so much older than herself.

Then, because she could not do anything for Lottie, either, she turned her mind to Rose. Poor Rose had enough to contend with at the moment but at least Hubert had stopped writing to her.

On impulse she decided to go and look at the London house Hubert said he had sold, the house Rose ran away from when she found Hubert was drugging her with an opiate medicine meant to help her asthma. She had never been to the house before but she remembered the number and knew it was in Leinster Place.

She thought it was ironic, when she saw it, that the house Rose had run away from was exactly the sort of house Lottie dreamed about living in. She climbed the steps and rang the bell, and trembled a little when a young girl answered and asked if she could help.

'Yes, please.' She swallowed to hide her nerves and the fear that in a few minutes she might come face to face with Hubert Belchester. 'I'm looking for a Mr Hubert Belchester. I understand this is his address?'

The girl shook her head. 'No, madam. This isn't Mr Belchester's home.'

'Oh dear,' she feigned disappointment. 'He did live here. I don't suppose you know Mr Belchester's current address?'

'I don't madam, but if you'd like to come in and wait I'll ask if anyone else knows.'

She accepted the invitation and stepped into the large hall. She glanced at the stairs and saw where Hubert had thrown Rose down a flight, the act which made her run away.

The young girl returned. 'I'm sorry, madam, but no one here knows. The master may know it but he's away in the country and I'm afraid we don't know when Mr Joseph'll be back.'

'Mr Joseph?'

'The master, madam.'

'He's not a barrister, is he?' That would be the full irony if Hubert, who was largely responsible for having Edward imprisoned, had sold his house to the man who tried to keep him out of prison.'

'A barrister? No, madam. Mr Joseph's a gentleman.'

She knew what the girl meant, but she still smiled.

She left, thinking that for once Hubert had told the truth. He had sold the house.

CHAPTER 18

Edward listened as Elizabeth told him what Eve had said. He accepted each piece of news and did not vent his feelings until she had finished.

'So Eve's won her freedom by getting herself smashed up, and now she's going off to fight the world instead of coming home where we could take care of her. And Lottie's gone off to marry a man we don't know and who's three times her age?'

'At least they're both doing what they want to.'

'Perhaps, but it doesn't help Rose, although I suppose I should be grateful that she won't know what a mess I've made of everything.' He thought it would help to say how he felt, but it did not. It made him feel even more stupid.

'Don't say that, Edward,' Elizabeth said in a tired voice. 'We'll get over it. It's just a bad patch. We've had 'em before.'

'Yeah.' He rubbed his face but even that did not help. 'We've had plenty of 'em before and I know exactly when they started. My twenty-second birthday. The first time the mine fell in. When William died.'

'Don't be so ridiculous! That was twenty-eight years ago.

You can't mope about it for the rest of your life. Your friend died that day, but you met Rose the same day. Remember?'

'Tough on her, as it turned out.' He said what he thought.

'She wouldn't see it that way.' Elizabeth slammed a saucepan down on the kitchener. 'You saved her from Hubert. You gave her something to live for, Edward. She would have died if it weren't for you.'

'Perhaps—' He stopped when he saw the shrewd look in Elizabeth's eyes and thought she might have guessed what was frightening him even before she asked the question.

'You're still scared she might die?'

'Of course,' he said, unwilling to admit his real fear that by making Rose suffer God was punishing him for what he had done. 'What d'you expect?'

'She will get better, Edward,' Elizabeth promised. 'I just feel she will. She's overcome everything else that's happened to her and I reckon she'll get through this. You told me that you thought she was getting better, so why are you so down in the dumps now?'

'I don't know how we're going to cope with her.' This was a practical truth which would hide his real feelings for a while longer.

'Well, there's you and me, and Maisie'll help, and there's Helen.'

'But it could go on for years, Lizzie. She might never recover.'

'Perhaps.' She shrugged and then said optimistically, 'Perhaps it'll make a difference, being at home.'

'Just so long as there're no more shocks. That's one thing about the girls going off, life should be a bit calmer.'

Eve thanked Maud Whitton-White for coming to collect her from the hospital to take her to Eastbourne, and for bringing a hat with a heavy veil so she could hide her face from view. She was sure a few newspaper reporters would be waiting for her to leave the prison and she hoped they would have cameras with them. She could take advantage of the veil to shock them.

She was also grateful for the walking stick another

woman had thoughtfully provided, but she still borrowed a second stick so she could make a greater impression.

She practised her walk on the way to the gate and by the time she stepped through to freedom she had it perfected.

'Miss Forrester! Miss Forrester! How does it feel to be released?'

'Do you have a message for the Government?'

'How were you treated while you were in prison?'

'Can you lift your veil, please.'

She leaned on one stick and raised the other to silence the reporters and the small crowd which had assembled to see her leave, but she did not lift the veil, not yet.

'I would answer by saying my release from prison indicates that justice has been done. As for a message for the Government, I would tell them to prepare to see women in Parliament. I would say I was treated inhumanly while I was in prison, and yes, I can lift my veil.'

She did not simply lift her veil, she took her hat off and stood unsteadily on her two sticks as flares flashed and photographs were taken, but the best effect of her dramatic gesture were the gasps of horror as people saw how she had been hurt.

She allowed everyone enough time to see her, and the reporters sufficient time to make their notes, then she placed her hat back on her head. 'I feel too unwell to tell you any more now, but I'll invite you all down to the White House in Eastbourne in exactly one week's time, and by then I should be fit enough to tell you what I propose to do in order to remedy my situation. Thank you all for your support. Without it I would still be languishing in that hell hole, or perhaps I might be dead.'

She knew she was over dramatising the situation, but there would never be another opportunity like this and it was important to make the most of it.

The next opportunity would be in a week's time, but she had time to plan her comments for that meeting and, anyway, whatever she said then would simply be in addition to all the speculation the newspapers would indulge in for the next week.

She shuffled along the pavement, leaning heavily on her two sticks, and smiled at the policeman who helped her clamber into Maud Whitton-White's motor-car.

The following morning six newspapers carried the full story of her imprisonment and release, and gave detailed descriptions of her appearance and frailty when she left Holloway. They speculated that Lady Braithewaite's continued absence from the WFL and public life was a ploy to draw attention to the working-class girl with the upper-class accent who had attracted so much attention over a short period. Several newspapers even suggested the League's Committee might have proposed she take over from Lady Bee as leader, and the Lady's disappearance might have been politically convenient.

Eve decided she had better begin to write her next speech in order to take full advantage of the sympathy which had built up for her, but first she wrote private letters to the editors of all the newspapers, thanking them for leaving her parents alone during her period in prison, and expressing her hope that their kindness would continue.

It was important to keep the newspapers' support.

Lottie always slept with her window open because she liked the invigorating effect of a well-ventilated bedroom and because she enjoyed waking up to the bracing smell of the sea, but this morning she woke up to the smell of a bonfire.

She washed her face in cold water, dressed quickly and made her way downstairs, looked around the kitchen door to say good morning to Mrs Miller and saw Joseph poking a pile of glowing ash with a stick.

'Has Joseph had breakfast, Mrs Miller?'

'No. Mr Joseph said he'd wait to see if you were having any.' Mrs Miller sniffed her disapproval at his behaviour. 'He's been out there for more'n an hour setting fire to things.'

'Good. Yes, I think I will have breakfast, Mrs Miller, thank you.' She went out through the back door into the garden. 'Joseph, good morning. How are you? Any more headaches.'

'I'm feeling well, even better for seeing you, my dear.'

He turned and smiled at her, and she asked him what he had burned.

'Just the old files. We'd finished sorting them out and they were cluttering the place up so I thought I may as well dispose of them. Best to burn them. Wouldn't want them falling into disreputable hands.'

'You are burning the right pile, I hope.' She said it as a joke but the expression which flickered across his face bothered her. 'You did take them from the back room?'

'The front,' he said instantly, obviously confused.

'No! They were the ones you wanted kept! It was the big pile in the back that was—' She stopped as he hunched himself forward, both hands pressed hard against his temples. 'Joseph, you must see a doctor.'

He nodded. 'Yes, but not a country doctor. I want my London doctor.'

'All right, but you can't drive all the way back to London.'

'I'll have a car collect me and take me to Norwich, and I'll take the train from there. I'll let you know how I am after I've seen my doctor.'

'No, Joseph. I'm coming with you.'

'You can't. If the police are still looking for you—'

'It's a chance I'll take. Come indoors and tell me how to make the arrangements.'

After she had telephoned to Norwich and arranged for rail tickets and a motor-car to come out to collect them, she checked the files and found he had burned the wrong pile, the pile in which she had also hidden the Regina versus Forrester file. Another example of Fate taking a hand, she thought. Her last links with her family had been broken by accident.

She and Mrs Miller carried the remaining files downstairs, poured lamp oil over them and burned them, and as the hired car was not expected for another hour she wandered alone down to the beach and the sea she had come to love during the few months she had spent beside it.

She was frightened. She had an awful fear that Joseph

244

was going to die before they could be married, and while she did not want him to die she would rather be his widow than his fianceé. She wanted to marry him, to make him happy, even if it was only for a year or so.

She wondered if she should break the promise she had made to Joseph not to tell Mrs Miller about their plans. It was an element of deceit she found hard to maintain because Mrs Miller had been so kind to her, but she knew she must honour Joseph's wishes.

When she heard a motor-car approaching she turned her back on the sea and wiped away tears that had started. She was ashamed of feeling scared but she was also proud of herself because she was strong enough to conceal her fear, to contain it and stop it spreading to Joseph whom she loved so much.

Lottie locked up the shed where Joseph had left his car and after the man who was driving them to Norwich had carried out their luggage she locked up the house.

She asked Mrs Miller to ride in the front passenger seat so she could sit in the rear with Joseph. As she settled down she found a folded newspaper and pushed it to one side, but after several minutes she noticed a few words of one headline so she opened up the paper and read the story.

The Government had agreed to stop forced feeding. There were comments from all the main suffrage leaders and even one from Eve. She almost showed it to Joseph before she remembered. She was not Eve Forrester's sister, not any more.

Eve sat back and rubbed her fingers, aching from pressing down the keys on the heavy typewriter. She looked at her poor effort which had taken so long to type, and wondered how frail little Lottie could have typed so fast and so accurately.

She also wondered how Lottie was and whether or not she was married yet. It seemed strange to think that indecisive Lottie could have made such a big decision so quickly, and she hoped once again that her pretty twin had made the right decision.

She missed Lottie's company and in particular her inconsequential chatter and half-formed opinions. Everyone at Eastbourne had very considered opinions on everything and there was hardly any general chatter. The intellectual diet was politics and women's rights, and even though Eve was fully committed to the cause it did become boring to talk about nothing else.

'Eve?' Maud Whitton-White looked around the door. 'Can I talk to you? I've a proposition to discuss.'

'Only if you read this and give me your true opinion.' She pulled her article out from the typewriter. 'It's about the so-called Cat and Mouse Act.'

Maud read the article, nodding as she did so. 'Very good, except that you should have emphasised the fact that we still have to hunger strike and make ourselves ill in order to be released on licence and as soon as we're well again the police can re-arrest us and send us back to prison where we starve ourselves all over again.'

'Yes, Maud, you're right, but writing about it doesn't really show how ridiculous the situation is. Now, if we arranged for a number of us to be arrested en masse, and we all starved our way out of prison and promptly got ourselves arrested all over again, and kept doing it . . .' She left the question open, thinking Maud would object, but she did not.

'Yes, and let's find half a dozen of the prettiest girls we can because the newspapers'll feel far more sympathy towards a pretty face than one like yours or mine,' Maud said eagerly.

'Thank you.' She smiled at Maud and reminded her that she had come to discuss a proposition. When Maud told her what was involved she was astounded. 'You want me to take over as leader? Why?'

'Not just me, Eve. The whole committee's voted unanimously for you. You're more stable than Violet, you talk more sense and you're actually here, which she isn't. And the newspapers like you and treat you seriously, the way they would a man.'

'I don't know. It's only a few months since I joined the League.'

'Do it, Eve. We won't accept a refusal.'

'What does Violet say?'

'It doesn't matter. I'll write to her and tell her what we've decided.'

'I'd like to think about it, first.' The newspapers had been kind to her and her parents up until now, but the extra interest she would create by becoming the WFL's leader might become invasive and upset her father now he was looking after her mother at home.

'Are you worried about upsetting your future mother-in-law?' Maud asked lightly.

'Is it that obvious?'

'Doctor Braithewaite does come down here most Sundays, Evelyn.'

'Yes, and I expect he'll arrive later this afternoon. I'd like to discuss this leadership thing with him before I make a decision. Would you mind?'

'Of course not, Evelyn, but I've already told you we won't accept a refusal.'

Eve picked up a novel she was halfway through reading and wandered outside but several people stopped to talk to her and she knew the only way she could be alone was to lose herself in the bushes and trees which grew on top of the cliffs.

She had found a bench which was hidden among dense bushes and offered a rare opportunity of real privacy, and she walked to it and sat staring down at the sunlit sea, the unopened book beside her.

The glinting waves and the sound of the sea and wind relaxed and refreshed her. It was a perfect afternoon, until she heard someone moving along the path which passed behind the bench. She deliberately avoided turning to see who was coming, and she wished she had the book open on her lap; people seemed less inclined to stop and talk if they thought someone was otherwise occupied.

'A beautiful afternoon, and a beautiful view,' Robert growled. 'May I join you?'

'Of course.' Her heart pounded.

He sat down and inspected her face as though he was examining a patient. 'You're healing well, Evelyn. And putting on weight.'

'I feel well. How's your mother. Have you heard from her?'

'I've been to see her, actually.' He sighed. 'I think my mother's condition's best described as ugly.'

'The burns? They've not healed well?'

He shook his head.

'I'm sorry, Robert. She was so beautiful.'

'She could be worse. Anyway, she's no right to complain. A lot of people spend their entire lives looking ugly. At least she enjoyed years of being beautiful.'

'That's hard. Don't you feel any sympathy for her?'

'No, not really.'

'But she's your mother, Robert!' His hardheartedness upset her.

'That's a burden I have to bear. I don't believe I have a duty to be sympathetic.'

She almost screeched at him. 'Duty? She's your mother, Robert!' She folded her arms and turned her face towards the sea, and after a silence which lasted a minute or more she said, 'I don't want to argue with you, Robert, but I do find it incredibly difficult to understand you at times.'

'I didn't come here to argue, either, Evelyn.' There was a short silence and then he said, 'I came to say I may be going away for a while.'

'Where?' she asked sharply.

'To France. Jacques, who runs the hospital that's treating my mother, has offered me a job. It's interesting and more worthwhile than working in General Practice in the East End.'

'What about your patients?'

'There's someone itching to take over from me. A good man, and much keener than I am so the patients won't suffer. I just feel I need to do something new, Evelyn. Face a new challenge. Do you understand that?'

'Yes. I'm in the same position. I've been offered a new job, too.'

'What's that?'

'Leader of the WFL. The Committee wants me to take over from your mother, Robert,' she said warily.

'I think you should.'

His reply surprised her so much she did not know what to say, but he said it for her. 'You shouldn't be too surprised, Evelyn. I am interested in the cause, even support it, but I couldn't condone the way my mother behaved. You're moderate and sensible so I'll support you. I'll even tell my mother I support you.'

She kissed him, something she rarely did because it always seemed to embarrass him even when they were alone, and sure enough she felt him tense.

'You don't like me kissing you, Robert, do you?'

'I'm not used to displays of affection, Evelyn, that's all,' he said a little edgily and because she knew the poor relationship he had with his mother she accepted what he said.

'So, Robert, you're going to France. How long will you be there?'

'A year.'

'And what about us?'

'I thought I'd come back at least once a month, but in the meantime would you like to become engaged?'

'No!' she said firmly, thinking of Lottie and Albert. 'I always think that's like putting down a deposit on something you can't afford just to stop the shop selling it to someone else. Besides that was the most unromantic proposal I've ever heard of.'

He laughed, and agreed. 'But I can't marry you, Evelyn, not yet. Both of us still have to lead our own lives for a while.'

She told him she agreed because she had so much she wanted to do, and she thought he seemed relieved. 'What about Lydia, Robert? What'll happen to her if you go to France?'

'Lydia?' His expression darkened. 'I don't know. I'll have to sort something out but I don't know what.'

His next sentence surprised her. 'I visited your home

yesterday. Your old home. Your mother's doing very well. Sasha Komovsky was there, playing the piano, and your father said he thought she was listening.'

'He always thinks she can understand, Robert. I think it's his way of coping, but I saw her last week and didn't think she was very good. She's like a large baby. She doesn't talk and doesn't seem to know what's going on around her.'

'She's alive, Evelyn, and that's doing well considering how badly she was hurt. Besides, your father's convinced that she does understand some things.'

'Wishful thinking, Robert. He's the only one who believes that.' She looked down into her lap and saw she was pulling her fingers, something she often did when she was unhappy.

'You look sad, Evelyn. I've noticed you've often looked sad, ever since I've known you.'

'And I've often thought the same about you,' she said simply. He reached out and held her hand. He did not look at her but sat quietly holding her hand for several minutes. When he did speak he still looked away to sea and not at her. 'One day, Evelyn, when we've done all the things we think are so important, and when we've finally decided we can stop and have a personal life we must both sit down quietly and tell each other exactly what we have to be sad about.'

'When?'

'When it seems right, I suppose.'

The expression on Joseph's face prepared her before he spoke. 'It's bad news, Charlotte. That ten years I mentioned when I asked you to marry me is more likely to be that number of months. Perhaps even weeks.'

'Can't they do anything?' She tried to cope without breaking down.

'No, it seems not. The doctor believes it's a weakness in the brain. I remember my father died of a similar problem.'

'Is there anything we can do to help, to make it easier.'

'To prolong my days?' He squeezed her hand and laughed gently. 'Help me to avoid excitement, my dear, which is difficult because finding you has been the most exciting thing that's happened to me in years. It does mean we shouldn't marry, of course.'

She tried hard not to cry, and took care to harden herself before they told Mrs Miller how ill Joseph was. Mrs Miller broke down immediately and ran off to her own room.

Lottie was amazed how well she adjusted to days of total idleness, weeks of doing nothing other than reading, playing Joseph's magnificent piano and the violin he bought her. When the weather was fine she and Joseph often walked in Kensington Gardens or Hyde Park and sometimes they visited museums and art galleries and he educated her from his vast knowledge.

She was often idle, but never relaxed. She was constantly alert, watching Joseph, waiting for a tell-tale wince or to see him press his hands against his temples, wondering each time if this would be the last.

The days were a worry but the nights were even worse. She slept in the room she had used when she first came to the house, his wife's room, and he slept in the room next door. They both left their doors open and she found herself sleeping lightly, always listening out for him, waking fully each time she heard him groan or his breath shudder. She told him she would sleep better if they were married because they could share a bed, but he refused to marry her now he knew he was dying, and because she was scared to upset him and cause him more pain, or put him at risk, she did not argue.

The worry, the lack of sleep, and the irritation of never having any real privacy because of Mrs Miller and the other servants combined to make her nervous and fractious; and although she was reluctant to admit it even to herself she had begun to resent Joseph's illness and the way it had ended the future they had glimpsed.

She was surprised that all the strain did not bring on a single asthma attack, and she thought that was due to the tonic Joseph had been buying for her. Unfortunately she had finished a bottle and Joseph said it was not possible to buy any more because the chemist who made it had retired and moved away, but apart from some restlessness and irritability she still had no signs of the asthma which had dogged her for so long.

August lumbered up on her, hot and heavy. She stared out from the drawing-room window and looked across the street to the little enclosed garden where nursemaids sat beneath shady trees and watched over their charges and found herself yearning for Joseph and for his children.

It was ridiculous. In practical terms she had everything she had ever wanted. She lived with a cultured and wealthy man who clearly loved her but made no physical demands on her, she had a sumptuous house, she had occasional visits from neighbours who sometimes brought their polite and clean children for her to enjoy, and she had a perfect summer. It was her dream almost come true, she was in her paradise square, but she was not happy. Joseph was dying, and death was not part of the dream.

Having brought Joseph and her together Fate was now going to pull them apart, and when Joseph died she would be trapped in a perpetual and lonely winter.

As the month wore on and became even hotter, even heavier, she found herself spending more and more time at the piano. The heat increased her resentment of Joseph's illness and provoked other urgent feelings which made her irritable in a way which could only be calmed by playing the piano and remembering the hours she had spent listening to Sasha. She had pushed Sasha Komovsky out of her mind when she tried to forget her old life, but as each day passed she thought of him more and more.

The first days of September were even hotter than August. She prowled restlessly around the house and finally opened up the piano, played badly, and gave up, thumping two hands down on random keys in a dramatic discord.

'Charlotte, why don't you go for a walk? Go to the Gardens and sit by the Italian fountains. You know how soothing you find them, or take a walk by the Long Water or the Serpentine.' Joseph was standing in the doorway.

'Will you come?'

'No, it's far too hot for me but you go, please. You don't have to spend every minute watching me, but just be careful while you're out.'

She knew what he meant. His friend, the police inspector, had told him the police thought Mr Grundley had been killed by a young woman who used to work in his office. They had a very good description and a photograph, and nearly every policeman in London knew what she looked like. The inspector was sure that even though she had disappeared it was only a matter of time before she would come back, and then they would arrest her.

Lottie knew there were very few photographs of her and each of them had belonged to her parents, so it seemed that they had gone as far as betraying her to the police rather than risk too close an investigation into their own lives.

At times she found it hard to believe they could have turned against her in the way they had, and if it had not been for Joseph, and what she had learned about them from his file, she might have risked going home to confront them. As it was she could not afford to risk arrest because Joseph would become implicated, and anyway he always reminded her how they tricked her into meeting Doctor Pryce-Jones and how she had seen her mother betraying her father.

Almost every night she thanked God for making Joseph believe her name was Forest instead of Forrester, and for the fact that he had never met her mother because he would surely have noticed how much like her mother she was.

As usual she dressed in drab clothes to avoid drawing attention to herself, and hid her distinctive hair under a hat which also helped to hide her face. She kept a constant watch for policemen or anyone else who might recognise her and walked to Kensington Gardens.

The Italian fountains did not soothe her so she walked the length of the Long Water and stood on the bridge where the end of that lake joins the Serpentine. She stared towards Westminster and through the hot afternoon haze she could see the outline of Big Ben and a roof she took to be the Houses of Parliament, and they reminded her of Eve.

Eve had effectively taken over the leadership of the WFL and made it less militant, and was even writing newspaper articles now. It seemed almost inevitable that she should be one of the first women elected to Parliament once the law was changed.

Yes, Eve had almost achieved her dream.

'And so have you, Lottie,' she muttered to herself. 'Despite the fact that you killed a man, learned your mother's an adulteress and your father's a murderer. You've got almost everything you ever wanted, and much good'll it do you when Joseph dies.'

'I beg your pardon, young lady?'

She turned and saw a well dressed elderly lady peering at her through a pince-nez. 'I'm sorry. I was talking to myself.'

'That's for old women like me to do, not striplings like you. You shouldn't be standing up here on your own, you should be down there with those other young things.'

She followed the lady's pointing finger and saw three large boats being rowed out to the centre of the lake. The boats were filled with young men and women in summer clothes. Snippets of conversation and guffaws of laughter rippled across the water.

'That's where you should be,' the lady repeated, 'down there enjoying yourself while you're still young enough, not standing alone talking to yourself. Time for that when you get to my age. Plenty of time for that then.'

The lady wished her good day and tottered off towards the Royal Albert Hall, and as she did so the sound of music came up from the lake.

The rowers had brought the boats together, lined abreast, and all but one of those aboard were playing violins, violas, clarinets or flutes. The young man who was not playing was standing up in the middle boat and conducting the others.

The light afternoon breeze brought the music to her and gently blew the three boats nearer. She watched them come closer and closer, slowly turning as they did so, and she recognised something familiar about the conductor, the way he stood and the way he used his hands, just like his mother.

'Sasha!' she whispered. Her heart lurched, and something inside her stirred.

The boats, locked together, revolved until she could see him clearly, and turned further so his face was hidden. He was still too far away to be called, but in just a few minutes he would be closer and facing her and then he must see her.

She would wave to him, perhaps even drop her handkerchief as ladies of old gave their favours to a chosen knight, and then meet him at the boat house. There was so much she had to tell him, so much to discuss.

Then she heard boots crunch, looked away and saw two policemen marching towards her, looking directly at her.

She felt cold. There was nowhere to run, nowhere to hide.

She turned and began to walk away, sensing they were still staring at her, scared to look back, scared that any moment she would feel a hand on her shoulder. She crossed the road and passed through a gate into Kensington Gardens, and kept walking. The music grew fainter and the policemen did not follow.

She turned and would have walked back to the bridge but a crowd had gathered to listen to the music and the two policemen had been joined by several more, so she found an empty bench in the shade of a tree and sat down to think.

She ached to see Sasha but she was too scared, not only of the policemen but what she might find when she met him again. What she might feel when she saw him again.

She sat for an hour or more and eventually, when she stood up, she had convinced herself what she must do. She had responsibilities towards Joseph, so she walked home.

When she arrived Mrs Miller told her that Joseph had gone to bed with a bad headache. 'Might just be this stormy weather, Miss Forest. It brings my bad head on, sometimes.'

'Thank you Mrs Miller. It probably is the weather but I'll go up to see if he wants anything.' She found Joseph fast asleep, but she noticed that he had a bottle of the medicine she used to take beside his bed, the medicine he said he could no longer buy.

She would ask him about it when he woke up, but meanwhile she would play the piano.

The storm broke a few minutes later and she used its drama to accompany her playing. She slipped into her own world of music and nature, and it was not until Joseph spoke that she realised he was watching her from the doorway. 'Your walk appears to have worked wonders, Charlotte.'

'Yes. I'm sorry if I disturbed you,' she apologised, and stood up.

'You didn't disturb me, my dear. God did.' He looked up at the ceiling as thunder crashed directly above the house. 'He often does, unfortunately.'

He suddenly looked so wretched that she wrapped her arms around him and held him tight. 'I love you, Joseph. So much.'

'I know, my dear. I know.' He returned her hug. 'You're the most wonderful thing in my miserable life, Charlotte, and you've changed me more than you'll ever know. I don't think anyone's ever loved me as much as you seem to.'

'Not seem to, Joseph, I really do.' She squeezed him to emphasise what she said but she was puzzled by what he had said. 'Surely your wife loved you as much?'

'No, my dear. Sadly not. I loved her, and I still do which, perhaps, is part of the reason why I should not marry you. Sadly she did not feel as much for me as I did for her.' He sighed and trembled as more thunder crashed. 'I'm sorry I disturbed you, my dear, but I wanted to know you were home safely. Now I think I'll go back to bed.'

She walked upstairs with him and helped him into bed, and noticed that he had put the medicine out of sight, but now was not the time to ask him about it.

She made sure he was comfortable and went to lie down in her own room. As the storm crashed above her she thought about her feelings for Joseph. She had come so close to happiness that not quite achieving it made her miserable.

She did not feel sorry for herself any more, Joseph had

taught her to overcome that, but she did feel frustrated that she was in a situation where she had no choice but accept whatever Fate decided.

She turned over and wept, burying her head in her pillow so Joseph would not hear.

Eve started as the large conservatory suddenly filled with vivid blue light. Seconds later thunder cracked so loud that it rattled the glass. A group of young women sitting around another table all giggled nervously, but she tried to ignore them and settled back to the newspaper she was trying to read.

She was reading a story about how several ministers' homes had been damaged by suffragette bombs. She finished the report and an article telling how Sylvia Pankhurst had been sent to prison again, and then she sat back and listened to the girls she had tried to ignore.

They were nervous because tomorrow they would be at a meeting where they would probably be arrested. Each one of them was free on licence under the Cat and Mouse Act because they had refused food and drink for long enough to embarrass the Authorities into releasing them. They had been warned that they must not indulge in any further suffrage activities and must not incite others to do so, but tomorrow they were going to London to break the terms of their licences, and she was going with them.

She folded her newspaper, put it aside, and opened a folder containing notes she had made, notes for a speech which would ensure she was the first to be arrested. Her hands began to tremble, so much that she could not read her handwriting. She put the notes in her pocket and walked out into the gardens. The lightning flashed and thunder crashed but there was no rain, only a wind which flapped her clothes and sucked in damp air from above the sea.

She walked to the edge of the cliffs, took out her notes and recited her speech into the wind. She imagined staring across a crowd rather than the waves, and before she could control the instant tremble that reached her hands the wind plucked the notes from her fingers and scattered them across the grass.

The rain started before she could collect them up, ruining them, and she wondered if that was an omen.

She still had her doubts when she saw the men and women crowded together in the park. They reminded her of the sea, and within minutes of clambering up onto the temporary staging and being introduced to the audience she recounted what had happened yesterday and told them how she intended to speak without notes. She told them how nervous she was of talking to them and how scared she was of being arrested and sent to prison again. She told them she had not seen such a large crowd since the fourteenth of June, and she listened to the silence which followed.

'You'll remember that day all your lives,' she shouted across the crowd, controlling her hands by holding tight to a rail. 'That was the day we followed Emily Davison's coffin, ten days after she tried to stop the King's horse at the Derby, six days after she died. Thousands of suffragettes followed her body and tens of thousands gathered on the streets to watch us. Bands played funeral music and clergy marched at the procession's head. There were hundreds of wreaths, not only from this country but from all over the world. All that acknowledgement and public support, and our Government still says NO! No, Women cannot have the Vote because it is not in the public interest.'

She stopped as she saw the first two police vans arrive and a column of policemen marching towards the crowd.

'The Government condemned Emily Davison's act as foolish but she wasn't a foolish woman. She was an English graduate, a woman of thirty-eight, a mature woman who had been driven to this final desperate act because everything else she had done and suffered, including imprisonment and forced feeding, had been condemned as foolish acts. Whatever she did, we do, is condemned as foolish by a Government which is scared to give women the vote because it does not have the courage to govern us. It prefers to patronise us and—'

The staging shook and if she had not been holding onto the rail she would have been thrown off. She saw helmets and blue uniforms and heard the roar from the crowd and moments later she was picked up and carried away, then thrown into the back of a van. It rocked as the crowd tried to open it and then it jerked forward and carried her away.

Another woman had already been arrested and was taking off her suffrage sash ready to wave it through the barred windows as the van was driven through the streets. 'Arrest, police station, Court, prison, starve, be told to be a good girl, come out and do it all over again. They know what'll happen as well as we do. I don't know why they bother,' the woman protested indignantly.

Eve looked at her and smiled. 'Perhaps they think we're silly women who'll get bored with it.'

Weeks later, when Eve was released, she did not go back to Eastbourne. She went to her parents, not only to see them but so they could see her and perhaps understand how much she believed in what she was doing. Starving had made her gaunt and weak and she could see her father was shocked by her appearance, but she was even more shocked when she saw her mother.

'Is she no better, Papa?'

He hesitated and then said uncertainly, 'Well, there are signs, I think. Yes, I think she does understand some things, on good days.'

'And bad days?'

'Nothing.'

Guilt swept over her. 'I'm so sorry I can't help, Papa.'

He nodded, neither blaming nor forgiving her, simply accepting things for what they were.

She turned as her aunt came into the room and immediately made it clear she, too, had heard the apology. 'But not sorry enough to come home, Eve, and turn your nursing skills to looking after her?'

'I'll stay and help for a while.' It was one way of easing some of the guilt.

'No,' her aunt said dismissively. 'If she can understand it'll only upset her when you go away again. Either stay or go.'

'Aunt Lizzie, you can see what I look like. You saw me

the last time. This time I haven't been force fed. That's been stopped because of what we all did. We *are* winning and I've got to keep on until we do.'

'Let someone else do it. You're needed here. If it wasn't for you, Eve, your mother wouldn't be in this state.'

'I didn't push her in front of the motor-car, Aunt. She stepped out into the road and you can't blame me for that.'

'So you're saying you don't care?'

'No, I didn't mean that. I'm tired and—'

'We're all tired, Eve!'

'I know.' She could see it was not sensible to stay any longer. 'I do love Mama. I love you all, but I can't help, not yet. Not until after we've won.'

She kissed her mother without evoking any response, watched her aunt walk away into the scullery, and simply squeezed her father's hands because she was too upset to say anything more to him. He followed her to the door and kissed her goodbye and as she reached the front gate he told her to wait.

'I almost forgot, lass. Robert Braithewaite called again. He reckons your last speech was your best yet.'

'I know. He visited me in prison and told me he was at the meeting.'

Her father smiled weakly and nodded. 'Seems he reckons you'd make a good politician, once you've got the vote.'

'Are you sure? He's never said anything like that to me.'

'I reckon he's a bit scared of encouraging you in case you decide you want to be Prime Minister or something similar.' His smile broadened.

'It's a thought, Papa,' she joked thinly, crying because she was upset and sad and because seeing her father smile made her strangely happy. She moved through the gate and pulled it shut, but hesitated as her father walked down the short path.

'Maybe it is, but don't let serving others ruin your life, Eve. If you want this man, then just remember you're using up time which won't come again. And try not to blame Lizzie too much. She's got a lot on her plate at the moment, what with one thing and another.'

260

Elizabeth stood in the back yard where no one could hear her and sobbed.

She had not meant to bully Eve but once she started she could not stop herself. The misery seemed endless. Even good news seemed bad and the fact that Hubert had not made any more demands made her worry more.

And she had an unopened letter from the Trustees in her pocket. The envelope was not typewritten, it was addressed in Mr Buddelscome's own hand and marked confidential and that always meant more trouble. She could even guess the contents.

She wiped her eyes and blew her nose as Edward came through the back door. 'I'm sorry about the way I spoke to Eve, but—'

His raised hand stopped her. 'Don't be. I think she understands, and she didn't help much either. It's all trouble, isn't it?'

'And here's some more.' She showed him the envelope, took out the letter and read it.

'What's Buddelscome bleating about now?' Edward reached for the letter but she held on to it and quickly read it again.

'He's not bleating, Edward, not exactly. The mission's been sold. At least, the building has.'

'Already? I thought that was months away?'

'It seems things have changed, but for the better. Now the building's been sold the Trust has enough money to buy investments which should provide good annual income to support all the missions for the future.'

'Oh yes? Except for Hoxton,' Edward said bitterly.

'No, Edward. Including Hoxton. We've been given a lease, renewable annually. We can stay there, providing we follow the rules.'

'And what's the catch?' he asked sceptically, and she understood why he was suspicious. She was reading the letter yet again, looking for anything she had missed earlier.

'Actually, Edward, there doesn't seem to be one. Apparently the original donor's written to say he's had a change of heart.' She spoke brightly but she still felt there was something not quite right.

'Can I look?'

She handed him the letter and watched him read it, saw him smile and guessed what he was going to say.

'It's wonderful, Lizzie. Let's show Rose, tell her what's happened. She might understand.'

They went to the front room and told Rose, even held the letter for her to read. Elizabeth was sure Rose did not react, but she did not argue with Edward when he said he thought she had.

CHAPTER 19

———————

Lottie looked down into the gardens and saw the November wind tug at the trees and throw their remaining leaves on to the road and paths.

She turned around as Joseph came into the room. 'How are you feeling?'

'Rather well, my dear.'

He looked well, much less strained and more confident. His doctor had recommended a new drug which had reduced the number and severity of his headaches but did not do anything to overcome the vagueness which seemed to have plagued him for months.

'Good. You certainly look well.' She turned to look out of the window again, and felt his hands rest on her shoulders.

'What are you thinking about?'

'Nothing much, just that it'll be Christmas in a few weeks' time.' It would be strange not to be with the family for Christmas.

'What would you like as a present?' His chin brushed the top of her head.

'A husband?' She felt him move away and knew she had upset him, but upsetting him was a risk she had to take now he was stronger. He had changed over the past few months, become quite distant from her. Now she found herself not only resenting his illness but also the fact that he was using it both as a reason not to marry her and also as a reason to assume she was committed to him. She felt as though Joseph had trapped her, and that, in turn, made her feel guilty because she owed him so much.

His hands rested on her shoulders again.

'Charlotte, I love you more than life itself and nothing would please me more than to marry you. In fact I already think of us as being married, which we are, virtually. We live in the same house, share the same food, spend our time together and sleep in adjacent rooms with the doors open so we can hear each other.'

'Yes, we have a platonic friendship, almost a platonic affair Joseph. We don't have to change that if you don't want to but I want to sleep beside you, Joseph. I love you and I want to wake up next to you every morning.'

'Charlotte, if it was that simple I'd marry you tomorrow, but it isn't!'

'But it *is*, Joseph!'

'But why, Charlotte? Why is it so important to marry me?'

She tried to explain but she realised she could not, not without hurting him terribly, and she could not do that. She could not explain that every time she left the house his entreaty to 'be careful' unnerved her and made her go out less and less because that would not change with marriage. She could not explain that she could not relax in his house because she still thought of it as *his* house, not their home because he would feel he had failed to make her welcome.

Worst of all, she could not explain to him that she hoped marrying him would help to stop the thoughts of Sasha Komovsky creeping into her mind every day and every night. She had not been able to stop thinking about him and his music since she had seen him in the park.

'Anyway, Charlotte,' Joseph interrupted her thoughts, 'one morning soon I simply won't wake up, and I couldn't abide the thought of you waking up next to a corpse.'

'A corpse?' She trembled and turned to face him. 'I thought you were getting better?'

He held her and stroked her hair. 'The pain is less but the condition is the same. I'm not going to make old bones, Charlotte. You know that.'

'I can't believe it. Not looking at you now.'

'Well, it's a fact, I'm afraid. I could ask the doctor to explain everything to you if you'd like me to?'

She nodded, her mouth closed tight because she was already crying into his shoulder and she did not want him to know.

The doctor came at eleven o'clock the following morning. He examined Joseph in his study and after half an hour's anxious wait she was invited to join them. The doctor looked extremely uneasy as they all sat down to talk, and she soon realised why.

He sounded uneasy as he spoke to her. 'I'm afraid I've had to advise this young man to put all his affairs in order. Immediately. There's evidence to suggest he has several damaged and weakened blood vessels in his brain and any of these could rupture at any time. I'm afraid, Miss Forest, that his next head pain could be his last. He might live for a while, but he might become an invalid and he might even lose his mind. I understand you wish to marry him but marriage would be a death sentence, Miss Forest. For both of you.'

Lottie sat with Joseph after the doctor had left and he told her she would inherit most of his estate but she told him she did not want it. She said she only wanted him, and without him there was nothing.

'It's a sunny afternoon, Charlotte, so why don't you wrap yourself up and go for a walk? You spend far too much time moping around here with me.'

'I'll go if you'll come with me.'

He hesitated but she bullied him gently and he relented, and joked that it was the fear of her nagging which really stopped him marrying her.

They walked slowly through Kensington Gardens and Hyde Park, arm in arm and without talking. The grass and the paths were littered with leaves, the late autumn colours contrasting and blending to add mellowness to the slightly misty afternoon light. London seemed slow and that suited her mood. They walked all around the Serpentine and stood together on the bridge where she had watched Sasha conducting his small waterborne orchestra.

'It's strange,' Joseph said quietly, 'but I've just remembered something I haven't recalled before. Something I remember seeing as a child. I lived at a school in Dorset and my parents had a large house on the Dorset coast but we always came to the London house for the Christmas season. I remember seeing all this frozen over one year, and people skating on it. They carried lanterns. It seemed to be fun and I wanted to join them but my mother wouldn't allow me to.'

'Was she very strict?'

'Strict? I certainly don't remember much laughter, Charlotte.' As he spoke there was a tremendous burst of laughter from a group of young people chattering excitedly and laughing at a story a young man was telling. 'I don't remember doing anything like that, for example.'

'Nor do I,' she said sympathetically.

'Then you should have, Charlotte. In fact, you still should. How old are you? Twenty? You're the same age as them and you should be enjoying yourself as they are.'

She stared at him and sensed that an even greater distance had opened between them. He still thought of her as being twenty but she felt so much older and his comment reminded her of the lady who had talked to her the day she saw Sasha. 'It's strange you should say that. A lady told me the same thing on this very spot a few months ago, during the summer.' She spoke without thinking, then looked up at him, her guilt at her thoughtlessness vying with her fear of upsetting him; but he was smiling.

'You should listen to your elders, Charlotte, and make friends with some people of your own age.'

'I'm happy just being with you.' She squeezed his arm and rubbed her head against him.

'Then why did you remember an insignificant conversation with a stranger, my dear?' he asked gently.

It was easier to explain the significance of what had happened that afternoon than give him a direct answer to his question. He listened to her brief recollection of seeing Sasha and his orchestra then smiled and looked away quickly, leaning over the parapet of the bridge so she could not see his face.

'Joseph? Are you in pain?'

He sighed. 'No, my dear. At least, not the pain you imagine.'

The noisy crowd passed behind her as she placed an arm around Joseph's waist and hugged him. 'I do love you, Joseph.'

'I know you do, my dear. I know.'

She became aware of a young man standing beside her. 'Excuse me, miss, but is your father ill? Can I help at all?'

'He's not my father . . . No, thank you. He's quite well.' She recovered, strangely annoyed that the man should have mistaken Joseph for her father even though she knew it was a perfectly reasonable assumption.

Then she noticed the man was carrying a violin case. She glanced at the rest of his group, saw they were all musicians, and trembled.

The young man was smiling at her, moving away. 'If you're quite sure there's nothing I can do to help?'

Her trembling meant she had to ask if any of them knew Sasha, but she was scared. She hesitated for too long and the opportunity passed.

'Excuse me, but you weren't one of the people who played from a boat on the lake, during the summer?'

Joseph had asked the question for her.

'Yes.' The man smiled. 'We did it several times, between rehearsals at the Royal Albert. For fun.'

She knew Joseph approved, and found her own voice. 'Then you know Sasha Komovsky?' Her trembling made her breathless.

'Know him? We all live in his house. Well, his brother's house. Sasha and Peter live in isolated splendour in an apartment on the top floor and we all live in communal chaos in all the other rooms. It's fun. If you know him you should come, some time. It's only five minutes away.'

'Thank you, but we couldn't impose ourselves on you.'

'Of course you could. We've people coming and going all the time and I'm sure Sasha'd like to see you. I'll give you the address.' The young man took out a small notepad and scribbled an address in pencil. 'Here. Come any time, but not too early in the mornings. We're not at our best in the mornings.'

'I couldn't,' she argued but the man still offered her the note, and Joseph took it and thanked him for his help.

She watched Joseph read the address then fold the note and slip it into his pocket as if he did not want her to see it, and a small sense of resentment pricked her. Why had he made a point of asking about Sasha if he was not going to allow her to know where Sasha lived? It seemed pointless, even a little cruel, but she did not say anything, simply agreed with him when he said it was turning cold, allowed him to take her arm, and walked home with him, in silence.

The moment they arrived home Mrs Miller offered to make them tea. 'It'll warm you both up, Miss Forest, and if you go up to the drawing room you'll find we've just banked the fire up for you.'

'Thank you, Mrs Miller. That's very thoughtful of you.' She smiled at her, and was embarrassed as Joseph simply grunted and announced that he would go to his study and he trusted they had made up a fire for him in there.

'Yes, sir.' Mrs Miller sounded cautious. 'Would you like some tea brought up to you, sir?'

'Tea? Would I like tea?' Joseph asked irritably.

'Yes, sir.' Mrs Miller glanced at Lottie, then looked back at Joseph. 'Tea to warm you up after your walk, Mr Joseph.'

'No. We stayed out too long and I'm chilled. I'll take some brandy.'

Lottie waited until Mrs Miller had walked away before

268

she reminded Joseph that the doctor had advised him not to drink too much.

'I don't intend to drink too much, Charlotte. I intend to drink enough to warm me through.' He scowled and walked away from her, muttering something she could not hear.

She thought it was best not to ask what he was saying.

She sat alone in the drawing room for two hours and then went to his study, knocked on the closed door and waited for him to call her in. She knocked again, heard a grunt, opened the door and found the room in darkness.

'Joseph, are you all right?'

Glass chinked against a glass and she heard two words, short and slurred. 'Yes. Why?'

'You've been gone a long time.' She walked towards his fireside chair and smelled brandy fumes from halfway across the room.

'Keeping watch on me?'

'Trying to take care of you, and drinking that much won't do you any good at all.'

'I'm going to die anyway. I might as well enjoy the time that's left.'

'By getting drunk?' She leaned over him and tried to take his glass away but his free hand suddenly clamped over her wrist and pulled her down to her knees. She looked up at him, his face shadowed and red in the firelight. 'You're hurting me, Joseph.'

He did not not seem to hear her and his grip tightened, hurting her even more.

'Joseph, you're hurting me!'

He stared at her, still holding her painfully tight, then he suddenly dropped his glass and simultaneously released her. She fell backwards, tried to steady herself, knocked his brandy bottle off the small table he had been using and just failed to catch it as it fell on top of her. She lay on her back, soaked with liquor, and saw him pressing his thumbs hard against his temples.

'Joseph!' She sat up, and without thinking placed the brandy bottle in the hearth. 'Joseph!'

269

She leaned towards him, her hands holding his head. He moaned and she held him tighter, her arms around him, his head cradled against her breasts, his arms around her and pulling her tight to him.

'Joseph, don't die. Please don't die!' She rocked him as he moaned and held her tighter, and suddenly there was a flash, searing heat and she found herself on the floor, Joseph lying on top of her.

'Charlotte, are you hurt? Burned?'

She was not sure. She could not feel any pain but she had other feelings which overpowered everything. 'Joseph, I love you.'

He did not reply, but he clambered off her and stood up unsteadily, his pain seemingly forgotten, and switched on the electric light.

She saw the brandy bottle still standing in the hearth where she had placed it but its neck had shattered and the fireplace and chimney breast were blackened by the fumes which had ignited. Joseph looked as black as a chimney sweep and she realised she must look the same. She wiped her face and felt the soot even before she saw the black on her fingers and realised her dress was singed.

'I think we should both bathe before dinner,' Joseph said in a strained voice.

She stared at him, shocked by how ill he looked, and agreed.

When she stood in front of the full-length mirror in her dressing room and saw how badly singed her dress was she realised how she was lucky not to have been injured by the igniting fumes. All her clothes seemed to *smell* of brandy or soot and as she took them off she dropped them into a laundry chest, and because her hands were still dirty she did not prepare fresh clothes to put on after her bath.

Of all the advantages living with Joseph provided, ample hot water on tap in a private bathroom was the luxury she appreciated most. She soaked for a long time, hot water and scented oils relaxing her, softening her anger with Joseph until she thought she could understand why he had suddenly changed. He depended upon her and although he had told her she should meet younger people he did not want her to. Perhaps he had said it as a test of her feelings for him? Perhaps he became scared she might leave him when she mentioned Sasha, and when the young man offered her Sasha's address.

It would be fruitless to ask him outright, but there were ways to discover what was on his mind. She would simply be even more loving towards him, to prove she had no intention of leaving.

She dried herself and walked into the dressing room to choose something to wear for the evening at home. She did not bother to cover herself because her dressing room was sandwiched between her bathroom and bedroom, but as she reached into a clothes cupboard she sensed she was not alone.

She turned quickly and saw Joseph, embarrassed and dressed, staring at her nudity. 'I'm sorry, Charlotte. You were so long I came to see if you were all right. And to apologise.' He turned to leave.

'Don't go,' she said eagerly.

'But—' He turned back and looked into her eyes.

'I don't mind. Really,' she reassured him.

Not only did she not mind, she enjoyed him seeing her body. Enjoyed watching his eyes travel over her, seeing what no other man on earth had seen. *She enjoyed it!*

She would never have thought it was possible, but not only was she enjoying having him look at her but she wanted him to touch her, hold her, kiss her and make love to her. She wanted him, wanted to feel him inside her when only months ago she could not bear the thought of anyone even touching her.

'You're beautiful, Rose.' He moved towards her.

'You haven't called me Rose since we left Norfolk.' She spoke without thinking it mattered what he called her, but it clearly did matter to him.

He stopped where he was. 'Charlotte?'

'Yes?'

He looked unsteady, unsure of himself. The worrying

vagueness had returned. She stepped close to him and felt the rough material of his jacket prickly against her breasts. She hugged him and trembled as his hands rested on her hips. And she noticed his breath smelled of the medicine he had been taking secretly.

'Make love to me, Joseph.'

She tried to kiss him but he stepped away. 'Later, Charlotte, later.'

'Joseph?'

'Yes?' He turned around as he reached the door.

'You do love me, don't you?'

'Very much, Charlotte. Very much, and that's why it would be wrong to do anything . . .' he paused and she felt her heart beat several times, 'too hastily.'

He apologised again over dinner, both for his behaviour that afternoon and for walking into her dressing room.

'I asked you not to apologise for coming into my room, Joseph. You're welcome any time, but what upset you this afternoon? Why did you drink so much?'

'I suddenly saw my own mortality, my dear. Worse, I realised how I've wasted what life I had. I've become accustomed to the thought of not living for much longer, but now it's too late to do anything about it I've suddenly realised that I've hardly lived at all.'

She walked around the table and hugged him as he sat. 'I'm sorry I made you unhappy.'

'It's a conundrum, my dear. I was unhappy until I met you and you made me happy but it cannot last. It's inevitable that my new happiness should make me unhappy. Don't waste your life the way I've wasted mine.' He took out the note containing Sasha's address. 'There was a light in your eyes when you told me about this young man, Charlotte, a light I'm sure I can't inspire. Go to see him. Please?'

His brow crinkled as he spoke and she knew the emotion he felt had brought on his pains again, so she said the first thing that came into her head. 'You're mistaken, Joseph. Sasha's a nice young man and a friend whose company I enjoy, but that's all. I told you I love you. I'll never go to see Sasha if there's the slightest possibility it might make you unhappy.'

He smiled and she saw the pain had left him.

They talked throughout a dinner during which Joseph uncharacteristically drank only water and at the end of which he stood up and excused himself, rather pointedly saying he felt extremely tired and must go to bed.

He kissed her on her forehead, walked to the door, and suddenly turned back to the table. 'I almost forgot this, Charlotte.' He picked up the note of Sasha's address. 'I'll leave it up here for you.'

She watched him tuck it behind the clock on the mantelpiece. 'There's no need, Joseph. I won't go.'

He smiled at her, wished her goodnight, and left.

She sat alone in the dining room for a long time after the table had been cleared, her eyes on the note Joseph had quietly tucked behind the clock.

He had told her she should go to see Sasha but he had not given her the note with his address, he had simply put it where she could see it. He had challenged her to decide what was most important to her, who was most important to her, and every time she came into this room the note would be there, testing her resolve, the emotional promise she had made not to go to Sasha.

Lottie left the note unread and went to bed, but she could not sleep.

She could hear Joseph sleeping soundly and that simply made her more restless. It was his fault she could not sleep. He had stirred up strong feelings. Feelings that excited her and frightened her, feelings she could not calm.

She felt hot and went to the bathroom, stripped off her nightdress and tried to cool herself with a cold flannel but if anything it made her feel even worse. She stood in her dressing room and recaptured the feelings she had when Joseph saw her, tried to imagine him watching her again, but it was not Joseph she saw in her mind.

It was Sasha, and her feelings for him were different now.

273

Now she wanted him the way she thought she wanted Joseph earlier. She could not have Joseph that way, it might kill him, but Sasha was less than a mile away and suddenly the memories of kissing him made her even hotter. She remembered how she felt when she saw him again months ago, and she remembered everything Joseph said about her and Sasha, the way her face lit up when she mentioned him, that she should go to him and not waste her life.

And then she remembered the pained look on Joseph's face when he thought she might leave him. She pulled on her nightgown, slipped back into her own bed, determined not to do anything that might hurt Joseph.

But Joseph could not be hurt by what he did not know.

She debated with herself for nearly an hour before she climbed out of bed and crept down to the dining room.

Her fingers trembled as she plucked the note from behind the clock and opened it up. She half expected it to be a blank sheet of paper, but there, written in perfect script, was Sasha's address. She read it once. That was enough. It was too important for her to forget.

Guilt welled up as she replaced the note exactly as Joseph had left it. It was four o'clock in the morning and she felt exhausted.

The floor creaked behind her.

She spun around, heart thumping, guilt gushing out of her like sweat, not sure what to say, how to explain, but the room was empty.

The floor creaked again as the house cooled with the night.

She was thankful Joseph had not seen her but as she stepped away from the fireplace she sensed she had done something that would change everything.

Joseph was the only person she had ever really loved and trusted and he had returned her trust, and in his way, her love.

Now she was planning to deceive him, her instincts told her that her life would never be the same again.

CHAPTER 20

———————

Eve pulled her coat tighter around her and looked up at the white sky above Buckingham Palace. Only a week until Christmas, but just enough time to arrange one last sympathy-winning protest.

She studied the crowd outside the railings to satisfy herself that everything was in place, then turned her back on the palace and looked out across St James's Park. Her mother had brought Lottie and her to see where the Queen lived when they were little and although Lottie stood still and stared at the building and tried to guess how the rooms were decorated and furnished, Eve remembered being more interested in running free on the endless grass across the road.

Now she could run free, perhaps a little too free and with too few commitments except to the suffrage movement, and she wondered how Lottie was. Eve had received two letters from Lottie since she left prison, both addressed to the White House in Eastbourne, both proving Lottie knew about her suffrage activities, and neither mentioning their parents or saying much about Lottie's own life. Lottie had said she was quite happy, but nothing more.

It was nearly time to start. Eve turned around and gazed at the palace, pretending to be just another visitor who had come to see where the royal family lived, but the moment she heard Big Ben begin to strike noon she moved towards the palace. She did not rush because she did not want to attract attention, and because she had to give the twenty women with her enough time to fasten themselves to the railings. The women wore chains under their coats and each one had to open her coat, work a loop of chain around the railings, snap a padlock shut and remove a key for Eve to collect. All without being noticed by the scarlet-uniformed soldiers acting as sentries or by the watching policemen.

She waited for the small hand signals which told her each woman was ready, and then walked passed every one, took her key, dropped it into a wide-necked shopping bag she carried and simply walked away to join a crowd of men and women who were completely unaware of what was about to happen.

Big Ben's chimes had drowned the sounds made by the chains and padlocks, and seconds after the clock stopped striking the first woman turned towards the crowd, took off her hat and pulled her cloak over her head to reveal its lining. The cloak, strongly stitched to the arms and shoulders of her coat, bore three words in lilac on a green background: Votes for Women.

Neither the police nor the soldiers seemed to have noticed, until the woman began to shout.

'Votes for Women! Votes for Women! Votes for Women!'

The effect was startling. The woman managed three clear shouts before three policemen fell on her and then her voice disappeared under the welter of grunts and curses which came from the policemen as she punched and kicked out.

Eve watched the faces of the crowd. They had showed surprise at first, and then tolerant amusement as the woman began to shout, and then they looked embarrassed as the policemen tackled her. Finally they looked angry and several of the men as well as women yelled at the police not to hurt her, but no one went to help.

'Votes for Women! Votes for Women!' The cry went up

again at the far end of the railings and another woman turned her coat into a banner bearing the same words. Another detachment of police rushed at her. Seconds later another woman turned and showed her banner and again chanted the words.

A few onlookers cheered and a very few joined in the chant but they stopped as soon as a police sergeant glared at them and unhitched his truncheon.

Then another woman at the railings began to shout and then another and another. The policemen raced about achieving very little and as they lost control men and women in the crowd became bolder and shouted their support. Ominously, other voices tried to shout them down, but other than the shouts there was no sign of trouble starting within the crowd.

'Evelyn?' She turned and saw Robert Braithewaite. He was smiling. 'I was told you'd be here. Naughty but very impressive. No wonder you've taken over from my mother.' He kissed her cheek and held her hand.

'I didn't mean to,' she reminded him, 'but you know what happened.'

'Yes,' he said, his smile gone. 'Well, she's under no illusion that she won't be invited back. The newspapers used to write about her but now it's your name and not my mother's that's synonymous with the WFL, and she wants to offer you her support and help. That's why she would like to see you. Can you come?'

'To France?'

'No, she's at home.'

'Of course.' She did not hesitate. There was nothing more she could do to support the women who were chained to the railing and it was probably better if she left before she was recognised and the police found the keys which would make their job easier.

'Is your mother home to stay?' she asked as Perkins drove them through the early afternoon traffic.

Robert nodded, so she asked what his intentions were.

'I'm staying in France for a while longer.' He shifted as

though he was feeling uncomfortable. 'I've learned a lot from Jacques, enough to be let loose with some of the patients, and—'

He did not finish so she prompted him. 'And?'

'And it's sort of built up a personal commitment. I can't just leave, not now. I have to stay on for a while.'

'Of course,' she said, secretly glad that he found it difficult to admit that he was not coming home yet – it suggested he felt he owed her some commitment still. They had not been looking at each other but she made sure she had his full attention before she asked her next question. 'What are your future plans?'

He looked uneasy, embarrassed, but he kept his eyes on hers. 'Future? That depends, on a number of things, Evelyn.'

'Such as?'

He shrugged and waited a long time before he spoke, very quietly, his hand on the seat beside hers, his fingers idly brushing hers. 'What are your plans?'

Now she hesitated, aware this was an important moment but she was unrehearsed, not sure exactly what to say. 'I must see this through, get the vote, and then I think I'd like to go into politics properly, but I don't want to sacrifice my personal life to it. Does that sound selfish?'

'No, I don't think so, but just how ambitious are you?'

She sighed, unhappy about giving him an answer. 'I know this sounds ridiculous when we don't even have the vote but I'd like to be a Member of Parliament.'

'A socialist?' It was a statement more than a question.

'Of course, but I also want, well, a normal life , I suppose.' She saw him nod. He seemed to be thinking but he did not say anything. His slowness irritated her. 'Well, Robert, I've told you what I want. What about you?'

'I'd like to live a normal life too I suppose,' he said as Perkins pulled the car into the kerb and stopped. 'Come on, we're here.'

'No!' She refused to move even though Perkins was standing outside the car and was obviously waiting for her signal to open the door for her. 'We need to talk, Robert.

278

Properly, and not another of our "almost but not quite committed" conversations. I've told you exactly what I want and I need to know how you feel. You've implied that you want to marry me, but never really said so—'

'I do want to marry you, Evelyn, but not yet.'

'And I don't want to marry you yet, either, but I've told you why I want to wait and I'd like to know your reason.'

He looked very uncomfortable and she stared at him, unblinking, trying hard to make him even more uncomfortable so he would give her an answer, but he looked away before he spoke. 'Evelyn, now isn't the time to talk about it. I will tell you, I promise, but not right now.'

'Is it something to do with Lydia?' She was suspicious of his true feelings for his brother's wife, and when he looked at her and she saw his eyes she was even more suspicious.

'It's more to do with unhappy marriages, Evelyn. Our family doesn't make happy marriages.'

There was a desperate look in his eyes and she knew he was right – this was not the time to pursue the question so she took his hand and let him help her out of the car.

They walked upstairs to the drawing room and she noticed immediately that the curtains had been altered subtly to make them drape differently, darkening the room a little. Lady Braithewaite was sitting in a winged chair, half hidden, but she stood up to greet them

'Good afternoon, Evelyn. It's so nice of you to come.' Violet extended her left hand, not her right.

She accepted it awkwardly, squeezed it gently and noticed that Lady Braithewaite kept her head half turned so only the left side of her face was revealed. When they sat down her hostess sat back in the depths of the winged chair.

'How are you, Violet?' she asked softly.

The response was typically brisk. 'I'm well, thank you. I understand you've recovered from all your trials and you've been making quite a name for yourself. Well, I've had rather a lot of time to think about things and develop arguments which I believe will help us achieve what we demand, but these need to be broadcast. Now, I've made all the necessary arrangements but I'm simply not up to making an extended speaking tour all around the country, not yet. I'd like you to make it on my behalf.'

'I beg your pardon?'

'A tour. A grand speaking tour. I thought I'd made myself quite plain?'

'When? I do have other commitments.' She had promised to spend Christmas at home so she could help her father and Aunt Lizzie by looking after her mother.

'Now. You'd need to leave London tomorrow morning.'

'I can't.'

'Evelyn this is an opportunity to make your name known throughout the country, to associate with the most prominent people in the movement. It is not an opportunity to decline if you still wish to make a career of politics and it is certainly not one to decline if you wish to maintain faith with your sisters who've sacrificed so much more than their time.' Lady Braithewaite leaned forwards and Eve saw her face fully.

She tried not to stare but she could not help it. There was not a scar to be seen.

'Impressive, isn't it, my dear?' Lady Braithewaite said coldly. 'But not quite so good when I take it off.'

She was confused. 'I'm sorry, I don't understand.'

'Then watch.' Lady Braithewaite raised both hands.

'Mother! No!' Robert rose but he was too late, his mother had already hooked her fingers around the mask she was wearing.

Eve gasped. Nothing she had seen as a nurse had been as bad as this.

'Mother was doing well until an infection set in,' Robert said quietly. 'The only way we could save her life was by cutting away most of the right side of her face.'

'I hope now that you understand why I cannot undertake this tour. I would turn it into a freak show, and besides, it's too painful for me to talk for more than a few minutes. Now, my dear, can I rely upon you, or not?'

Eve could not refuse, but she did place conditions. 'I'll do what I can but I must spend Christmas and the following week with my family. It's my birthday on New Year's Eve.'

Lady Braithewaite seemed surprised. 'Really? How old are you?'

'I'll be twenty-one.'

'Twenty-one? I thought you were much older than that. Nearer thirty, I'd have said, looking at you.' Lady Braithewaite's bluntness did not bother her. She took her comments as compliments, and anyway she felt much older than twenty-one. So many things had happened during the past twelve months that it seemed much longer than a year since her twentieth birthday. She reached out as Lady Braithewaite passed her a bulging envelope. 'Anyway, Evelyn, I'm sure we can rearrange matters so you can be at home during that period but meanwhile read what I've written and acquaint yourself with the timetable. I must rearrange my new face but I assume you'll stay for luncheon?'

'Yes. Thank you.' She rose, as did Robert, and watched Lady Braithewaite leave, the mask already held loosely over her face.

'I had no idea she was that damaged, Robert.'

'She's still alive, unlike some others.'

'You still have no sympathy for her, do you?' She was stunned that he could be so callous.

'Evelyn, she's led other women into situations where they've been injured or suffered. Polly Dobbs. Lou Dobbs. You, for example, the scars around your mouth.'

'They're minor, Robert.' The forced feeding had left little silvery scars around her lips where her teeth had bitten through but she hardly ever noticed them now. 'Do they bother you?'

'No, but that's not the point I'm making. She made other women take risks so she can't complain if she's been hurt.'

'I don't agree, but what do you think of me? I encourage other women to take risks, too.'

'But, Evelyn, that's different. Don't ask me to explain why, but it is.'

She looked at him for several seconds and thought that

perhaps now was the right moment to ask him to commit himself. 'Because you love me?'

'Yes. Perhaps that is the reason I think it's different. I don't know.'

'But how much, Robert?'

'More than I can tell you, Evelyn.' His arms reached for her.

She put her arms around him and closed her eyes as his lips covered hers. The kiss seemed endless. She pulled away reluctantly when the door opened but by the time she looked it had been closed again. 'Who was that?'

Robert shrugged. 'I didn't see, but our secret's out, Evelyn.'

'Does that make any difference?' she asked, not aware that it had been a secret as such.

'That rather depends on who knows.'

'You look sad again.' She trailed her fingers across his face and kissed him lightly.

'Just tired,' he said and smiled.

She smiled back and chose to believe him. For once he had not tensed when she kissed him.

Lottie had gone to the house twice before, but her nerve had failed both times and she walked past. It was a large house, four storeys high and with a half basement closed in behind railings. Four steps rose over the sunken front area and led to a front door which needed a fresh coat of black paint and someone to clean its brasswork. The whole house looked rather neglected with patches of rendering which needed repair and with peeling paintwork, but neglected or not it did exude a quiet charm which she thought reflected Sasha very well, especially now with the late afternoon sunshine washing it with pale pink light.

She looked at it for the third time and told herself to be brave and knock on the door. Third time lucky.

Besides, it was the ideal opportunity to meet Sasha without hurting Joseph because he was dining at his club. He had said it might be his very last opportunity to enjoy a formal dinner with all his friends, and she had encouraged him to go, and to stay the night rather than come home in the cold.

Two violins played in unison. Someone was at home. She took a deep breath and walked across the road, but as she reached the steps her nerve failed yet again and she turned and walked away, quickly, eager to put the shameful temptation behind her.

She half saw a couple walk around the corner as she turned away, but she took no notice until she heard the call, 'Lottie? Is it you?'

She stopped. She did not have to turn around to see who had called, she recognised his voice. 'Yes, Sasha, it is.'

When she did turn she was surprised by how much he had changed. He looked much older and he had grown a beard since she saw him conducting on the lake. And he had a pretty girl with him, a girl carrying a violin case.

'Annie plays the violin, like you,' Sasha smiled, 'and she is very good but she cannot make Peter want to dance.'

'Oh, Peter. How is he, and you, and your mother and Paul?'

'We are all very well, and much has happened to tell you about, but how are you, Lottie? I assume you are married now?'

'No, I'm not married, Sasha.' She saw a flash of light in his eyes but her attention was drawn to Annie who linked her arm to Sasha's, then smiled at her.

'Will you come indoors for something to eat and drink? We've just come home from rehearsals,' Annie asked pleasantly, and staked her claim on Sasha by rubbing her shoulder against his arm.

Just come home? She glanced down at the girl's hand, desperate not to see a wedding ring, frustrated because Annie was wearing gloves.

'Yes. Thank you. I'd like that, but I don't want to cause you any trouble.'

'You won't.' Sasha laughed and led her up the front steps. 'If you stay long enough you can help to prepare dinner.'

Annie led the way up to the top floor and walked through

283

an unlocked door into a large and well furnished room. 'I'll make tea.'

'My usual,' Sasha called out, and turned to her, 'Sit down, Lottie, and tell me what has been happening to you.'

They sat at opposite ends of a long settee.

'No, Sasha, you tell me what you've been doing, first. Your story seems much more interesting.' She wanted to understand his circumstances before she told him anything about herself.

'I'm a musician again, Lottie. I have left the hotel and I play the piano once more, but now I am paid for doing so. I live here with Peter, except that he is not often here. He works very hard and travels all over the continent.' He paused momentarily. 'He helps Russian firms find foreign customers.'

'He must be very successful to be able to afford a beautiful house like this.'

'Yes. Peter says I have a way with dreams and he has a way with money.' He spoke quietly, in a tone which suggested he was embarrassed by Peter's generosity.

'Your mother and Paul, Sasha?'

'They still live with your parents although Peter hopes that next year he can afford to give mother the money to buy an apartment for herself. I would like her to come and live here but Peter says that is not sensible as we must both lead our own lives. I suppose he's right, and anyway I believe she would rather remain with your parents and aunt. They are supposed to be coming here over the Christmas holiday. Peter has a motor-car and he's arranged to bring them here on Christmas morning.'

He stopped as Annie suddenly reappeared and said in a concerned tone, 'Lottie. I've just realised, you must be Charlotte. Charlotte of the Charlotte Sonata.'

'I beg your pardon?'

Sasha glanced towards Annie and explained for her. 'I've written a sonata, Lottie, which I named after you. I would like to play it for you, one day.'

'I'd like that, too.' She felt awkward, embarrassed to be there with him and Annie, especially as Annie was standing behind Sasha with her hands on his shoulders. It was something intimate, something she used to do, something which made her feel intensely jealous.

Annie smiled at her, clearly aware of the feelings she had stirred up. 'It's beautiful, Lottie. I'm sure you'll like it when you hear it and I'm glad you're here because Sasha's written three different endings and he won't decide which one to use. He always says you're the only one who can decide.' Annie's voice seemed to harden before she finished speaking.

'Three endings?' She looked at Sasha.

He smiled and she thought he seemed embarrassed at being asked to explain. 'I'm afraid so, Lottie. I'll explain later but, first, please tell me what's been happening to you.'

She watched Annie leave to bring the tea she had made, and as she still had not seen Annie's hand she asked quietly. 'You and Annie? Are you married?'

'Not quite. Annie would like to be married.'

She was shocked by how relieved she felt. He was not married.

Before she could begin her story Annie came back with the tea and curled up, kitten-like, on the floor by Sasha's feet. It was disconcerting to see this pretty, wide-eyed stranger smiling up at her, and she sipped her tea slowly, using it as an excuse not to talk until she had decided what to say.

She had come prepared with a neat little speech which she expected to deliver to Sasha alone. She had not anticipated having an audience, especially a very pretty young girl who obviously adored Sasha and would probably fight to keep him.

'Well?' Sasha prompted her, and as he did so the door opened and the room quickly filled up with young men and women who slumped down on chairs or on the floor and began to talk among themselves.

She saw Sasha grimace an apology but she was glad they had arrived. He introduced her as an old friend and apart from remembering Ian as the man who had written down Sasha's address she forgot their names immediately, but it did not matter. They were all musicians or artists and several seemed to be poets, too, and once she had adjusted to the speed and variety of their conversations she began to enjoy herself.

They were fun, joking about each other and laughing all the time, a mass of grinning faces and careless noise. Someone passed her a glass of wine. It was obviously cheap and not the sort Joseph would have allowed in the house. It tasted awful but she drank it and the second and third glasses seemed to taste much better.

She glanced at the window and saw the rose-coloured light had faded and the sky was dark. It was growing late but that did not matter. She had warned Mrs Miller that she might not be home until quite late and Joseph had left for an appointment with his solicitors even before she left the house. No one would miss her. For once she was free with no obligations, no responsibilities and able to enjoy herself.

The final contents of another bottle were emptied into her glass and she was aware of everyone preparing to leave.

'We're all going on somewhere else to eat and have some fun.' Ian smiled at her. 'Would you care to come?'

She shrugged, not sure what she wanted to do, and glanced towards Sasha.

Ian laughed. 'Oh, he won't come, not the old man.'

She smiled and thought Sasha may have changed but he still had the reputation he had brought with him from St Petersburg, then she declined Ian's offer. 'Thank you, but I don't think I will either. I'd better go home.'

She added the last words defensively, hoping they would all assume she would leave, hoping Annie would assume she would leave, and give her some time to spend alone with Sasha.

'Ah, well,' Ian spread his arms in a philosophical gesture, 'once again I'm denied the company of a beautiful young woman. Well, Annie, will you come with me, to give me the solace I need so much?'

'Would you mind?' She saw how Annie asked Sasha before she answered Ian, and noticed how sad she looked when Sasha told her to go and enjoy herself.

The room emptied quickly, Ian kissing her hand with slightly drunken formality and everyone else simply calling out their goodbyes as they left.

Only Annie remained, and she had stopped only to say goodbye in a more formal way.

They shook hands, then she watched as Annie kissed Sasha on his cheek before she left, the girl's face set so as not to show how emotional she felt.

After Annie closed the door Lottie turned to Sasha and watched his face as she said, 'Very pretty girl, Annie. And she's very much in love with you.'

He blushed. 'I know, but I'm not in love with her. I love only my music, now.'

'Only your music?'

'The music is constant, Lottie. I know what the music wants, and what it will give me in return.' His voice was low, full of the Russian emotion she remembered, and his eyes looked directly into hers.

She did not look away. 'I can explain, Sasha, but will you play your sonata for me?'

'Of course. When must you leave?'

'Whenever you want me to.'

'And if I don't want you to leave?'

'That's what we must talk about, Sasha. I didn't want to leave at all, earlier this year, but things happened and I had to. Then I saw you during the summer, conducting your friends on boats on the Serpentine. I haven't been able to forget you since then.'

'Then it *was* you! I thought I was dreaming! Where did you go? Why did you go?'

She told him everything she had planned to tell him, hesitantly at first and then as she gained confidence faster and faster, so fast that sometimes he asked her to repeat herself or clarify certain things. She told him all about being followed and about Mr Grundley during the last day in the office, about how he tried to attack her in the alley and how she had accidentally forced him down the steps where he died. She told him that the police were going to arrest her if they found her, and she told him how she would almost certainly be committed to an asylum.

She told him about Joseph and how he had helped her, asked her to marry him and then changed his mind when he knew he was dying, and finally how Joseph had helped her to find him.

Then, with nothing more to tell him she felt hollow, as though she had poured out all her emotions and left herself empty of every feeling, and she began to cry.

They were sitting on the settee and Sasha reached for her and pulled her towards him. She did not resist, not even when his hand turned her face up to his and she felt his lips on hers.

The feeling was as pleasant as she remembered and she moaned with the pleasure of it. Moments later another feeling stirred. She pressed herself against him, enjoyed the feeling of his body hard against hers, recalled how she felt when she wanted Joseph to make love to her. But now she wanted Sasha to see her, wanted him to hold her and feel her and be the first man to make love to her, the only man to make love to her.

She felt his lips move from hers and press soft and warm against her throat. 'When did you say you had to leave, Krasnaya?'

'Whenever you want me to.' She stretched her neck as he nuzzled into her.

'And if I don't want you to leave?'

'Then I won't,' she committed herself, and because her blouse collar was cutting into her she loosened it.

Sasha nuzzled deeper and deeper and she undid more and more buttons until she could feel his lips on the tops of her breasts. She was trembling, physically shaking with pleasure and excitement and from the sense of danger she felt now that she believed she had moved beyond the point where she could expect Sasha to stop.

The settee cushions tipped up and she slipped off, slowly, half falling and half being lowered by Sasha as he followed her down onto the floor. He laid on top of her, his weight pressing her down.

'Come on, Krasnaya.' He stood up and pulled her to her

feet. 'The bed is softer, and the door can be locked.'

Sasha was amazed when she held his hand and followed him into the bedroom. Surely this exotic, erotic, dream would end and he would wake up? Surely none of this could be true?

He had fallen in love with her the moment he saw her and heard her quiet voice but it was a safe love, a forlorn love because she was out of reach, the glittering prize that could never be his.

But she was here with him now, smiling at him, flushed and soft and his for the taking. His heart pounded, he wished he had not drunk so much wine, and wondered if she would still be there if she had not drunk quite so much.

He turned the key in the lock and pulled her into him. They fell against the door and still locked in each other's arms staggered across to the bed. He lowered her, lay down beside her and saw her eyes dilate as he felt her breasts.

Then, urgently, he wanted more. He wanted to see her and claim her as his but women's clothes were strange to him and he prayed that his fumbling attempts to undress her would not ruin the mood. Prayed that she would not change her mind. Prayed, that if he was to wake up he could enjoy her first.

She rolled away from him and he followed her across the bed, stood beside her as she stood up, then stood back as she began to undress herself.

The room was dark but the moon was shining and he could see her body as she revealed it. She stood with her back to him but as soon as she was completely naked she turned to him and moved into his arms.

She was crying.

'What's wrong, Krasnaya?' He stroked her hair and kissed her tears.

'I'm happy, Sasha. So happy I can't help crying.'

He laid her on the bed and looked at her, felt her, touched her, whispered to her and told her he loved her.

And then he claimed her.

It was the most intense feeling he had known, and the

most exhausting, and afterwards he lay beside her, tucked her into his arms, tried to wrap her up in all the love he felt for her, and fell asleep with his face buried in her long, reddish, copper-coloured hair.

Lottie was astounded by the way she felt. Making love was the most incredibly consummate feeling she had ever had. It was perfection, the only way she could ever have expressed the love she felt for this man, the love she had tried to ignore for so long.

She lay in his arms and all her confusions were clear. She had never loved Albert. He was safe because he would never have made the demands Sasha would make, and of course Albert could give her the safe life she thought she wanted.

Joseph was similar to Albert, but older, almost a mix of how she would have liked her father to have been and the sort of husband she dreamed of, and she felt safe with him because he loved her so much he would never harm her, not wittingly. The only time he had ever frightened her was when he was drunk, and she had to accept much of the blame for the way he felt that day.

But Sasha was different. He was as kind as Joseph, as protective, but he was a dreamer like her and with him beside her she would dare to take risks, dare to travel to all the places she wanted to see, dare to do all the things she secretly wanted to do but was too scared even to think about. She would try to have her dreams if she had him beside her.

And with those happy thoughts lulling her, she slipped into sleep.

She awoke alone, but with the sound of a piano coming from another room. It was still dark so she did not bother to look for her clothes to dress, she simply pulled the quilted eiderdown off the bed, wrapped it around her and went to find Sasha.

She found him in a large room at the rear of the apartment, a room with a wall made up entirely of french windows which led out onto a roof-garden. Moonlight flooded across the floor and she saw Sasha sitting at a concert-sized grand piano. He smiled when he saw her but he did not stop playing.

He was wearing trousers and a dressing-gown and as she moved behind him she could see his feet were bare, like hers. She stood behind him and placed her hands on his shoulders as she had before in their other life, and as Annie had hours earlier, and she silently thanked Annie for making her jealous enough to be frightened of losing him. He felt cold to her so she opened the eiderdown and then wrapped it around both of them, keeping him warm with her body but not restricting his arms so much he could not continue to play.

'I think it's beautiful, Sasha.' It had to be the sonata he had written for her.

'Good. It's meant to reflect my feelings for you. You must listen to the three final passages and tell me which is the one I should use.'

'I couldn't do that! I know nothing about music, Sasha.'

'You don't need to know about music, Krasnaya, only about love.'

He played on and she floated on the gentle emotions his music evoked, until he told her he would play each of his three endings. The first was wistfully lyrical and dreamlike. The second was dramatic and ended with an almost savage chord and the third was lyrical again, strongly and romantically lyrical.

When he finished he asked her first to tell him which ones she had not chosen, and as she did so she understood why.

'The second one is beautiful, Sasha, and very dramatic but too sad.'

'And also my least favourite. It depicts suicide.' He struck the final chord again and she understood its significance.

'It's very difficult to choose between the next two, but I don't think you should use the first ending.'

'We agree again, Krasnaya. It is meant to show how an affair of the mind will end.'

'An affair of the mind?'

'An unrequited love, Lottie, is an affair of the mind.'

'Of course.' She fumbled with her fingers, unable to look him in the eyes as he stood up and pushed the eiderdown off her so he could look at her again.

'The third ending is my favourite, too.' He held her close. 'It depicts a wedding and the joy of the wedding night and a future together. I wrote the piece in the hope that one day I might be able to play this to you on our wedding night.'

'You have, in a sense.' Reality was already beginning to impinge on the romance.

'Will you marry me, Krasnaya?'

She felt cold and stepped away from him then picked up the eiderdown, wrapped it around her and stared out at the moonlit roof-garden. 'What does that word mean? Krasnaya?'

'It means red, like your hair.'

'It's hardly red.'

'In certain lights it is. Like sparks in a fire.' He came up behind her and placed his hands on her shoulders. 'It also means beautiful. You are *krasnaya devitsa*, a beautiful girl.'

They stood still for several minutes, both of them silent and looking out at the silver light. His hands squeezed her shoulders and his voice sounded gruff when he spoke again. 'I asked you to marry me.'

'I know.'

'Will you?'

She hesitated. Joseph! What was she going to do about Joseph?

'Will you?' He asked again.

'Sasha, you have to understand—'

'When?' He did not let her finish.

'Listen to me! Your first ending, the suicide, reminded me of Joseph. He's dying and if I leave him now it'll kill him.'

She felt Sasha pull the eiderdown off her and reach around her to feel her breasts. 'And if you leave me it'll kill me.'

'I don't think so, Sasha. Not really. Not outside your music. Anyway, I'll come back, as often as I can.'

'But I don't want you to come to me as often as you can. I want you all the time and I don't want you to go back to him. Not to live in the same house as him, to sleep in the next bedroom. He's already asked you to marry him. What if he decides he still wants to? What'll you say to him then?'

'He won't, and he won't touch me, either. He's had plenty of opportunity, Sasha, and he's not once taken the slightest advantage.' She heard Sasha's breathing deepen and his grip become firmer, and she knew that if she did not leave now she would spend the whole night with him and that could be difficult to explain to Mrs Miller. 'It's late, Sasha. I must go.'

'You said you didn't have to.'

'I think I was wrong.'

'But I don't want you to go home to him,' he said hotly.

Her temper flared. 'I know, but I have to. The poor man's dying, Sasha, and I'm not prepared to abandon him. Besides, you've got Annie. I assume you're not going to throw her out on the streets?'

The emotion spent she burst into tears again and ran back to the bedroom.

He ran after her and switched on the electric light so she could find her clothes. 'I'm sorry. I always seem to make you cry.'

'That isn't difficult at the moment,' she said over her shoulder.

'Are you that unhappy?'

She shrugged. 'Please don't tell anyone you've seen me, Sasha.'

'Of course not.' He shrugged, picked up his own clothes and began to dress properly. 'You haven't asked about your family, Lottie. Aren't you interested in them?'

'Of course I am, but things have changed, Sasha, you can see that.' She did not want to tell him about her family's secrets, not yet. 'I can't go to them and anyway I'm not sure they'd really want to see me. Besides I've enough to think about with Joseph. I can't cope with anything more.'

'Not even me?'

She grimaced. 'I wanted to talk to you, Sasha. I didn't expect all this to happen.'

'When will I see you again?'

'I told you, I don't know. And now I must go. May I have my coat, please.'

He fetched both her coat and his. 'I'll walk home with you, Lottie.'

'There's no need to do that.'

'I want to. I want to see you're safe.'

'I will be, don't worry.' She did not want him to know where she lived because she knew she could not trust him to stay away. 'I need time alone, Sasha. To think. I'll be all right, don't worry.'

He walked down to the street with her. The moon shone down from a clear sky. He shivered.

'It's cold, Krasnaya.' He reached out and turned her collar up. 'I'm sorry I behaved badly, but I'm scared of losing you.'

'You won't. I'll see you next Wednesday night. Christmas Eve.' She hugged him tight. 'And thank you for the music. It's wonderful.'

'The next time you hear it will be at our wedding.'

'I'll look forward to it.'

'And you are sure about the ending?' He looked deeply into her eyes. 'You're sure you've chosen the right one?'

Lottie knew he was asking her about something far more important than the Sonata. 'There's no doubt, Sasha. No doubt at all in my mind.'

She turned and left quickly and without looking back, but she knew he was watching her as she walked down the empty moonlit street. She could feel his eyes on her, and she felt wanted.

Joseph returned home late the following morning and she found it difficult to behave naturally, so difficult that he noticed and commented on it over lunch.

'You appear very ill at ease, Charlotte.'

'I'm sorry, Joseph. It's just a mood.'

He inclined his head towards the note still tucked behind the clock. 'You haven't visited your friend, yet?'

'No,' she answered sharply and stared down at her plate to hide the lie.

'Oh. I simply wondered.'

'I did say I wouldn't, Joseph.'

'Yes, I know you did. But perhaps we should make an arrangement and visit him together. Would you like that?'

'No.' She could not think of anything worse, or more dangerous for Joseph. 'I think perhaps we shouldn't bother at all.'

'If you say so, my dear.'

His acceptance of her lies made her feel worse, and at every meal time she sat down opposite the clock and saw the little scrap of paper accusing her of lying. Her nerves became more and more brittle, and in response Joseph became more irritably polite and charming.

She wished she had told him she had taken his advice and gone to visit Sasha, and reassured him by telling him that she still loved him and would stay with him until . . .

Until he died. But she could not tell him that. It would be too cruel.

Instead she had to endure the guilt she felt every time she saw the note which she dare not remove for fear of rousing Joseph's suspicions, and she had to endure every meal time because she could not help glancing up at the note without being afraid that Joseph would notice and jump to the wrong conclusion.

Except that it was not the wrong conclusion.

She had already been sleeping badly but now she could not sleep at all. She spent whole nights awake, then fell asleep for minutes at a time during the day only to spend the night awake. Joseph asked her to allow his doctor to examine her but she refused and told him it was nothing more than a reaction to everything that had happened over the past year and she would soon settle down again.

Eve accepted Perkins' steadying hand as she stepped down from the car.

'Forgive me for saying so, Miss Forrester, but you look awful tired.'

She smiled at him and said lightly, 'I forgive you, Mr Perkins.'

Months of work and worry, and weeks of starving, had made her tired before she started the week's tour and now she was exhausted.

'You make sure you get a good rest over Christmas, miss,' Perkins advised kindly and slipped his arm under hers to help her climb the steps up to Lady Braithewaite's front door.

'I'll try. Thank you.' Her feet were heavy, her whole body felt heavy, and all she wanted to do was lie down somewhere and sleep until she felt better, but first she had to tell Lady Braithewaite how successful the tour had been and then go home and be bright and full of Christmas spirit and take care of her mother and Aunt Lizzie and her father. Perkins was kind, but sometimes he could be unutterably simple.

The single consolation of this particular diversion was that she would probably see Robert.

'Evelyn! How nice to see you again. Sit down here and I'll have some tea brought up.' Lady Braithewaite's voice smiled, but her painted mask did not. 'Now, tell me everything that happened.'

Everything? That would take another week. Her eyelids slipped and her brain would not think.

'Evelyn! Are you ill?'

'Tired, Violet. Just very tired.'

'You young girls! No stamina. No stamina at all!' The mask sounded tetchy now the woman behind it was disappointed. 'Now, pull yourself together.'

She tried but she could not. A week of almost constant travel, studying Lady Braithewaite's handwritten notes, thinking about speeches, writing speeches, making speeches, three and sometimes four a day, answering questions, meeting strangers – it had all merged together in her mind and she did not know where to start.

She wanted to tell Lady Braithewaite that *she* could not have done it, even when she was fit. *She* could not have stood in the cold and rain outside factory gates and lectured the factory women during their lunchtimes; *she* could not have persuaded the trade union workers to encourage people to come along to evening meetings; *she* could not have attracted audiences from all classes and professions.

Suddenly a doubt which had been gnawing her all week resolved itself. Lady Braithewaite *could not* have done it. Despite what she had said Lady Braithewaite never even intended to do it. Lady Braithewaite was experienced enough to know the schedule was too tiring, and moments later her suspicion was confirmed.

'Not quite as easy as you thought it would be, Evelyn? Taking over my position? Taking over my League? Thought you could just slide in, did you, a little working girl snake in the grass, and steal everything I'd built up? My life? My future?' The mask was impassive but the voice was almost hysterical.

Eve wanted to argue but she could not, she was too tired to think any more. All she could manage was a weary denial. 'No, you're wrong, Violet.'

'Violet? You dare to call me Violet? After everything you've done?'

Eve stood up. 'I'm going home.'

She had reached the door when Lady Braithewaite screeched at her. 'And don't think you can steal my son, either. He won't marry you. Ever. He can't, no matter what he says.'

She turned to face the harridan who was standing, crouched and trembling, and flapping her arms like a big, distressed bird. 'I'm not trying to steal Robert from you. He wants to marry me. He suggested marriage, not me.'

Lady Braithewaite laughed, a low, false laugh. 'I found you for him. The greedy working girl that'll marry him then keep quiet when she finds out.'

She did not want to ask, but she had to. 'Finds out what?'

'That he can't satisfy women, Miss Forrester. Women. Do you understand? That's why he's gone back to spend Christmas with his friend in France.'

Even through her tiredness she understood what his mother meant, and she turned away so that Lady Braithewaite would not see her cry.

* * *

Lottie kissed Joseph goodnight and stepped out into the night. It was Christmas Eve and she was dressed to go to the midnight service, or more truthfully, she thought, dressed to make Joseph believe she was going to the midnight service.

She walked towards Sasha's home, thinking she should be happy at the prospect of seeing him, not feeling guilty that she had used God as an excuse to deceive Joseph.

The front door was unlocked so she climbed the stairs to the top apartment and knocked. Sasha opened the door.

'Lottie! You look awful. What's wrong with you?' He pulled her into the room, took her coat and hat and sat her down on the settee. 'Are you ill?'

'I'm better for seeing you, Sasha, but I am tired. Very tired.'

'Tired? You look exhausted. You're working too hard, Lottie.'

She laughed at him. 'Working too hard? I don't do anything from one day to the next, Sasha. I'm the lady of leisure I always wanted to be. I'm tired because I'm not sleeping, and I'm not sleeping because I feel guilty about what I've done to Joseph.'

'But you haven't done anything to him, Lottie. Nothing's changed.' Sasha was kneeling in front of her, squeezing her hands to emphasise his words.

'It has, in my mind. I've let him down, lied to him, and I shouldn't have. He's a nice man, Sasha, an honest and caring man and he's dying. I'm all he has and he needs to be sure I'll be there for him whenever he needs me, night or day. I love you, but I love him too, in an entirely different way, and I can't risk him finding out about you because it would hurt him and might even kill him. I'm already responsible for one man's death. I can't carry another in my conscience.'

'What are you trying to say, Lottie?' Sasha sounded desperate.

'She's telling you she doesn't want to see you any more, little brother.'

Lottie turned and saw Peter standing in the doorway, his face bent over his hands as he lit one of the dark cigarettes he smoked. 'Get up off your knees, she's not worth it.'

There was a furious exchange in Russian and she understood only one word which Peter repeated over and over again, the only word they used which was not Russian.

America.

The row stopped, the door slammed, and Peter had gone, leaving behind the smell of burning tobacco.

'What was all that about, Sasha?'

'Peter says you don't want to see me until after Joseph has died. Is that true?'

'It's not that I don't *want* to see you, but—'

'So he is correct.' Sasha nodded and seemed to be thinking. 'Well then, perhaps he is also correct about another thing.'

She could hear the angry tremble in Sasha's voice and it frightened her. 'About what?'

'He has arranged for me to go to America for four months, to tour with an orchestra. It is not a very grand orchestra but it is work and experience. I am supposed to leave in the middle of January but I told him I would not go because I wanted to be with you.'

She bit her lip. 'You must go, Sasha, and perhaps when you come back things will be different.'

'Your Joseph will have died?'

'Perhaps, but I don't want to think about that.'

They sat together on the settee, neither of them in the mood for passion or even conversation. A few minutes after midnight she kissed him. 'Merry Christmas, Sasha.'

'Merry Christmas when we won't see each other for months?' He scoffed ironically and went to his room, reappearing a few moments later with a tiny parcel wrapped in red paper. 'A present for Krasnaya.'

'I didn't think to bring you anything,' she admitted.

'You brought yourself. I couldn't ask for anything more.' He smiled and watched her unwrap the tiny parcel.

'Oh, Sasha, it's beautiful.' She held it up from its chain, a tiny enamel pendant, a grand piano and a violin.

'You will find it will hang close to your heart, Krasnaya, and remind you of the beautiful music which will come from us when we are together. Wear it always, my love.' He kissed it and hung it around her neck and she pressed it against her heart.

She told him she had to leave and that she would see him again after Christmas. He told her he would give her an address where she could send letters to him while he was in America.

Then she cried and he cried with her.

'Goodbye, Sasha. Take care of yourself.'

'I will, and you. I'll come downstairs with you.'

'No. Stay here. Please. Goodbye.' She kissed him again and ran.

She ran, sobbing, all the way down the street, silently waving back at the few people who wished her a Merry Christmas as they returned from church, her only comfort knowing that Sasha was crying too, and watching her from his window.

The following morning she hid her misery and tried to smile as each of the servants came into the breakfast room in turn. Every one bowed or bobbed nervously before wishing her and Joseph a Happy Christmas and thanked Joseph for the Christmas box he had given them. She was glad when the ordeal was over, but there was worse to come.

'And now for you, my dear.' He gave her a small parcel, obviously a box, wrapped in bright paper. 'Please open it.'

She pulled off the wrapping, carefully so as not to ruin it, and opened the black legal tin it contained. The box was full of documents, deeds, share certificates and a host of other papers. She lifted a few until she realised what they were and then she put them all back, quickly without looking at them. 'No, Joseph. I don't want all this. I told you.'

'Perhaps you don't, my dear, but I want you to have them and there's nothing you can do to stop me giving them to you. You can give everything away afterwards, if you wish, but I want you to make me happy by accepting them now.'

'Joseph, I can't. Really. It's not right.'

'It would be if . . .' He paused and pointed to the tin. 'Look in there again. The bottom document, if that's what it can be called.'

She did as he asked, lifted everything else out until she found a white envelope. She lifted the flap, pulled out a folded invitation card and opened it.

It was an invitation to her own wedding.

'You kept asking when we could marry, Charlotte, and I've decided that we should, no matter what the doctors say. My solicitors say it'll also make the transfer of all my property much simpler. Are you happy now?'

She did not move. She looked at him, tears running down her face.

CHAPTER 21

———————

Eve sat at one end of the kitchener and Helen sat at the other, both lounged back in the easy chairs that had always been a familiar part of the furniture. Christmas Day was almost over, the chores, and the fun, completed.

'Strange sort of Christmas,' Eve said quietly, and through her half-closed eyes she saw Helen nod.

'Children enjoyed it.'

'Children do, though, don't they? It's part of the magic. I can't remember much about any particular Christmas but I can remember the excitement and the special feeling when we were all together on Christmas Day. There's no other day like it.'

The wind lashed rain against the window, emphasising the kitchen's cosiness.

'I'm glad you came home, Eve. I just wish Lottie had, too. Not that I think Mama noticed who was or wasn't here. D'you think she'll ever get better?'

'I don't know. I was a nurse, not a doctor but . . .' She hesitated, unsure if she should give a personal opinion when the medical facts seemed to prove she was wrong.

'But what?' Helen prompted her.

'But I've seen a few patients who had similar accidents to Mama and they were different, somehow. I know this is a stupid thing to say, so please don't mention it to Papa or anyone else, but I have the feeling that Mama wants to be the way she is.'

'That's not stupid, Eve. Jamie and I have both said the same. I know this is a silly analogy but last summer Jamie stopped a cat playing with a mouse. He thought the mouse was dead and threw it in the dustbin. Two days later it jumped out when Maisie put some more rubbish in the bin. The mouse wasn't dead, it was terrified, literally petrified.'

'But why should Mama be petrified, Helen?'

'I've no idea, Eve. I blamed you at first because I thought she was worried about you, then I blamed Lottie, and still do to some extent, but I don't think it's your or Lottie's fault. After all, from what Papa's told me, they did treat Lottie badly, having her examined secretly.'

'Misunderstandings, I think, Helen. Anyway, it was rather silly of Lottie to run off like that, although she seems to be happy enough.'

'And you, Eve? I'm proud of you, we all are, but what about you and Robert? Any news yet, or are you too busy trying to reorganise the country?'

'Robert? He's still a mystery to me, but maybe I'm beginning to understand him a little better. At least, I can understand why he dislikes his mother so much, and even agree with him.' She told Helen how Lady Braithewaite had behaved, and what she had said about Robert.

Helen looked shocked. 'Do you think there's any truth in it?'

'I don't know. It could explain several things, but it doesn't stop him being a nice man, Helen, or immediately change my feelings for him. Perhaps it's as well we didn't rush off and get married. He actually said one of his reasons for not getting married was that his family didn't make good marriages, but it's ironic that his brother seemed to be happily married until he was killed in a car crash.' She told Helen all she knew about Lydia.

'Robert comes over from France to see her every other week.'

303

'So he sees more of his mad sister-in-law than he does of you?' Eve saw the sceptical look in Helen's eyes and had to agree with her sister's suspicions. 'I know. It does seem to suggest his mother's telling the truth, but I want to hear it from him before I believe it.'

'And how are you going to ask him?'

She shrugged. She did not know how, and as another rainy squall hit the window she closed the matter by remarking to Helen that she, Joe, and Josephine were going to get wet when they walked home.

Lottie sighed with relief. It had finally stopped raining.

The rain had started on Christmas Day and had not stopped once in three days. Three days when she was forced to sit around indoors growing more and more agitated because she could not find an excuse to slip out and tell Sasha what she wanted him to do now that Joseph wanted to marry her.

She had devised a plan which should persuade Joseph not to marry her without causing him too much pain. It simply involved Sasha taking a walk along a particular route at the same time every day, and her persuading Joseph to walk with her. They would all meet, apparently quite by chance, and she and Sasha would then have to create an impression that would persuade Joseph to change his mind about marrying her.

The plan was deceitful but it should avoid Joseph being hurt too much, and it was so simple it could not go wrong.

Joseph had been noticeably free from head pains since he had told Lottie he planned to marry her and when she made an excuse to go out for a walk she was glad that he did not decide to exercise his new vitality and come with her.

The streets were Sunday quiet and she was so eager to talk to Sasha that she did not remember that his mother might still be in the house until she had reached the front door. She pushed it and found that, unusually, it was locked, so she rapped the brass door-knocker and waited. It was several minutes before someone moved into the hall and pulled the door open.

'Good morning, Ian.' She returned his smile, and asked conspiratorially, 'Sasha's mother and young brother aren't here, are they?'

'No. They left yesterday.'

'Good. May I come in? I must see Sasha, urgently.'

'That's difficult, Lottie,' he said defensively, and her hackles rose as she suspected Sasha might be with Annie.

'Why? Is he out?'

'Rather. He's on his way to America. I thought you knew?'

She slumped against the door jamb. 'He was not supposed to go so soon.'

'It was rather a rush at the last minute. He left yesterday, and Peter's gone off on another of his trips.'

'Do you know if Sasha left a letter for me?'

'No. I actually asked him if he wanted me to pass a message to you and he said there was no need.'

No need? She was too numb to say anything more. Then an awful thought struck her. 'Annie. Did she go with him?'

'No. She and Sasha had a row and she's stayed here.'

'Thank you.' She patted Ian's arm, turned around and walked away.

This time she could not feel Sasha's eyes on her, and she felt confused, disappointed and incredibly lonely.

Her mind kept repeating two thoughts and no matter what she did she could not stop the repetition going on and on and on. Peter had made Sasha leave and Sasha had not stood up to him. And she would have to marry Joseph even though she did not want to any more.

She walked for a long time, and even stood on the bridge at the end of the Serpentine in the hope that by some magic she would wake up and find it was still the summer afternoon when she saw Sasha conducting his friends. She even hoped the lady who had talked to her that day might come by and talk again, but the lady did not come, so she turned around and walked home.

'Lottie! You look awful. What's wrong with you?' Joseph pulled her into his study, took her coat and hat and sat her down in one of the fireside chairs. 'Are you ill?'

He knelt down in front of her and squeezed her hands, making it a complete parody of the last time Sasha had seen her. 'I feel tired, Joseph. So tired.'

He kissed her on her forehead, but as his mouth passed her nose she noticed a smell she only half recognised. 'What's that smell?'

'Probably something used to clean up the room after our little fire,' he said softly and glanced towards the newly cleaned fireplace, and she did not question what he said because she was still trying to remember what the smell reminded her of.

Eve was pleased to see Mr Perkins when he arrived to collect her early on the first Monday in the new year, just as he said he would in his telegram.

'Have you had a good rest like I said you should, Miss Forrester?'

'Yes, thank you, Mr Perkins. Eleven days of idleness has done me the world of good.' It had actually been eleven days of almost non-stop chores and nursing, but she did feel better for it, refreshed in both her body and her mind. 'I'm fighting fit now, and eager to get on with things.'

'I'm very pleased to hear it, miss. Lady Braithewaite's gone back to France but Doctor Braithewaite's told me to do everything I can for you, Miss Forrester. By telegram. Long and detailed it was, too. He said he understood you and his mother had a disagreement but he was sure you'd want to continue with the tour to prove you could do it. But he also said I was to keep an eye on you and stop you from overdoing things, sort of.'

'That's very understanding of him.' Eve wondered why Robert did not have the decency to send her a telegram herself as she was the injured party, and the woman he was supposed to marry. And she thought again that he was the most bizarre and irritating man she had ever known, and wondered why she loved him and hoped so much that his mother had lied about him.

She invited Mr Perkins into the house and told him she

was already packed and only needed ten minutes or so to say goodbye to everyone, especially her mother.

'That's all right, miss. You take your time. We've got to stop off on our way, to collect some posters from a Mr Henry, Mr Hubert Henry the Hammersmith printer, but he'll wait for us.'

She laughed. 'Mr Hubert Henry, the Hammersmith printer? He sounds like a circus act or a master forger.'

Perkins laughed, too. 'His son's called Harold, Miss Forrester.'

She was still laughing when she walked into her parents' bedroom, but the smell of incontinence stopped her. She sat on the side of her mother's bed, one of the two singles that had replaced the double bed, and stroked her mother's face and hands. 'Bye, Mama. Thanks for inviting me for Christmas. It was good to be home for a while but I must go and put the world to rights, or at least try to. I'll be back again in two weeks and we'll have another chat then.'

She was still looking at her mother when her father walked into the room and jovially asked what had made her laugh so much.

'Mr Perkins told me we had to collect some posters from a printer, Papa.'

'Well, what's so funny about that?'

'The name, that's all, and I know it's rude to laugh but I just thought it was funny.'

'Well, come on then, let us all in on the joke.'

'Mr Perkins called the man Mr Hubert Henry, the Hamersmith printer.'

'Hubert!' her mother said clearly and jerked her hand away.

'Rose!' Her father lunged and Eve stood up as he shoved past. 'Rose. Can you hear me?'

Her mother stared back, her throat working hard and her lips moving but not speaking. It was half an hour before she settled, and even then her lips still trembled.

Downstairs, Mr Perkins had volunteered to make tea and when Eve and her father felt it was better to leave Rose alone Mr Perkins poured them cups of strong brew. 'It must be a good sign, eh, Miss Forrester?'

'I suppose so, Mr Perkins, but she looked terrified and I'm not sure being that scared'll do her any good at all.' She looked at her father and noticed how much his hands were trembling. 'Why should the name Hubert scare her so much, Papa?'

Her father shook his head to show he did not know, and because she could see he was close to tears she did not press him. Then she looked at Mr Perkins. 'Can we delay our tour by a day?'

'Difficult to delay it, but we could abandon the first day.'

Her father stood up quickly. 'No, don't change anything. You can't do any more so carry on with your plans. Just give me a list of places where I can find you if I need to.'

Eve tried to argue but he would not listen. Before she left she went back to her mother but found she was asleep. She kissed her father goodbye, said a formal goodbye to Katarina who had just returned with the day's shopping, and promised to tell Helen what had happened.

'So Papa was right, after all?' Helen nodded when she heard about the incident. 'And perhaps you were, too.'

'Possibly, Helen, but I'm not sure it didn't do more harm than good. Mama looked terrified, absolutely terrified, and I'm sure Papa knows more than he's admitting. The only other one who might know something is Aunt Lizzie. Now, I know it's a lot to ask, especially as I'm ducking out by going away for a few weeks, but d'you think you and Jamie could try to weasel something out of her? Anything she can remember about someone called Hubert.'

Elizabeth sat back as Bill Crabb came into her office.

'Your Evelyn's wonderful, Lizzie.' He beamed at her.

'I wouldn't go quite that far, Bill,' she said, trying not to look too proud and wondering what Eve had done to inspire his praise. 'Well, aren't you going to tell me why she's so wonderful?'

'She's arranged for Gladys and me to go on holiday. From tomorrow until next Monday. Down in Eastbourne.

In a hotel. Even arranged for one of her suffragette friends to take us down and bring us back in a motor-car.'

'This hotel's not called the White House, by any chance? You'll both come back as confirmed suffragettes if it is.' She laughed at him and his obvious embarrassment at being teased.

'No, it's the White Cliffs. I think it's just down the road from her place because she's promised to make sure there'll always be a nurse ready to help Gladys if necessary.'

'Eve did not say anything. How did it all come about?'

'Well, Lizzie, last year Gladys wanted to go into a home for a bit so I could have a rest, and she asked Evelyn to help. Miss Evelyn couldn't find anywhere, and Gladys thought she'd forgotten, what with everything else she's been doing, but it turns out she's arranged this for us, all paid. This way we both get a change and a rest. We've never had a holiday before, not away from home. She told us yesterday and we're off tomorrow.'

'Not much warning?'

'No, but that doesn't matter. My governor's let me have the time off and it's a nice surprise. I'll miss not talking to you though.'

'Well, you can tell me all about it when you get back. Give Gladys my love.'

'I will.' He suddenly leaned forward and kissed her on the cheek. 'Thanks, Lizzie. You're a treasure.'

She smiled, unable to speak because she knew she would cry. She did not know why, but she knew she would. Then, thankfully, he was gone.

When Elizabeth arrived home that evening she was keen to tell Edward what his youngest daughter had done for Bill and Gladys, but the moment she saw his face she knew he had something more important to tell her.

'Rose spoke.'

She was stunned, then excited. 'What did she say? Very much? How is she now?'

His dour expression killed her enthusiasm and somehow she guessed even before he told her.

309

'Hubert. She said Hubert, Lizzie. And went into a sort of fit, but she's all right now.'

She listened as he told her exactly what had happened, and she realised the connotations immediately.

'Eve told Helen and I've had both Helen and Jamie pressing me to find out why the name upset Rose so much. We'll have to be careful, Lizzie, because they'll start badgering you next.'

'Perhaps it's time to tell them, Edward. After all, it was a long time ago and if he is behind what's been happening—'

'No,' he said dismissively before she could finish. 'Look, we had the crisis over the mission and we half thought Hubert was behind that, but it was sorted out. We sort of thought he might be responsible for some of what happened to Eve, but she reckons she didn't suffer anything more than any of the other women. We can't blame him for what happened to Rose because I was there and saw exactly what happened. And as for Lottie, well we know she made up the stories about being followed and according to the letters she sent Eve she's quite happy.'

'I still think—'

'No!' He interrupted her again. 'I know you and Rose reckon he's manipulative and evil but I reckon you've got it all out of proportion. It's all been going on for over a year now and I don't believe any man's so patient he'd play around all that time without doing something concrete, Lizzie, and you haven't got any evidence at all. If you had I'd go and look for him myself.'

His last sentence frightened her. Rose had burned Hubert's letters so Edward would not find them, because they both knew the risks if he did. The only way Elizabeth could convince him that Hubert was playing one of his evil games was to tell him about the letters, but that would betray Rose's trust in her and play into Hubert's hands.

The family had come close to pulling itself apart some months before when everyone was arguing with everyone else, but they had struggled through that, somehow. She had to make sure that did not happen again, and if Hubert was manipulating them she had to find him. But how?

'What are you thinking about, Lizzie?' she heard Edward ask.

'Just trying to think things through, that's all.'

'Don't bother, lass. As I said, no man's that patient.'

She looked at him and knew he was wrong. Hubert was that patient. He had already waited twenty-four years. Another year or two would not worry him, but she had to admit that she was confused. Both she and Rose believed Hubert was behind last year's threat to the mission, but why had he suddenly changed his plans and secured her, Rose's and the mission's future?

It had worried her for a long time, as did the fact that he had stopped writing to Rose, and she wondered if that was his plan. To worry them by doing nothing. To let them frighten themselves.

She lay awake worrying for most of the night. Worrying about how to find Hubert, worrying about what to do if she could find him, and worrying about what might happen if she did not find him.

Most of all she worried about what was happening deep in Rose's mind and if Rose was re-living the misery and terror of her life with Hubert.

She climbed out of bed, walked to the window and pulled the sash down so cold air could clear out the room. Rain poured down the roof and gurgled in the gutters and pipes and a train hooted in the distance, long siren-like sounds – and she had an awful feeling this had all happened before, in this room.

She stood and thought. Paul had moved into Lottie's old room after she had gone, Katarina had moved into the room above her son, and Lizzie had returned to her old room at the front. She sensed there was some significance in all that, but she could not think what it was.

She leaned against the window, put her hand outside, palm upwards to gather rain, then licked up the cold water that had gathered. It tasted of soot. Another train hooted and a memory came back, something from years ago.

She leaned out of the window and looked along the street. She could barely see the corner where the little angel

311

sat in its niche outside the Angel Inn, but she knew it was there. She often talked to it when no one could hear her.

'Tell me where she is. Please.' She shut the window and shook the rain out of her hair.

Edward had his beliefs and she had hers.

She went to sleep, and when she woke up she knew she had to find Lottie. Lottie was the key.

She would start by asking everyone at Lottie's old office if they had ever heard of Hubert Belchester.

Lottie woke from a fitful sleep and knew that the moment she moved she would feel sick. It was nearly four weeks since Sasha had made love to her and morning sickness was not the only sign that she was pregnant.

She eased herself off the bed and sprinted to the bathroom, her hand clutched over her mouth to contain her vomit, and once she had released it she tried to be sick as quietly as possible. Joseph had been sleeping very soundly over the past weeks and he had not heard her, but she had noticed the way Mrs Miller sometimes looked at her and thought she might be suspicious.

She flushed the toilet, rinsed her mouth and face, and turned as she heard a quiet knock on her bedroom door.

'Who is it?'

She heard the door open, and a moment later Mrs Miller peered into the bathroom. 'Are you all right, my dear?'

'Yes, thank you, Mrs Miller.' She tried to sound as though she did not understand the reason for the question but moments later her stomach heaved and she had to turn back to the lavatory pan.

'There, there, my dear. Worse things happen at sea and at least you'll be married in a few weeks. No one'll need to know. You can just say it's an early baby. Nothing unusual in that.'

She stayed on her knees as her stomach heaved again and she clung onto the bowl, sweating and chilled at the same time. 'I'm sorry to embarrass you, Mrs Miller.'

'You haven't, my dear,' Mrs Miller said kindly, 'and I hope I haven't embarrassed you but I had my suspicions

312

and I thought you might want someone to help you and to talk to. Have you told Mr Joseph yet?'

'No.' She spluttered some more bile into the pan.

'Don't you think you ought to?'

'I'd rather not. It's not his.'

'Oh my God!'

'And it's not a virgin birth either, I'm afraid.'

'Miss Forest!'

She stood up and wiped her face again. 'I'm sorry, Mrs Miller, but joking is the only way I can cope with this. I daren't tell Mr Joseph in case the shock kills him. I don't know what to do.'

'Where is the, um, baby's father?' Mrs Miller whispered as though she did not want the baby to know it was being talked about.

'In America at the moment. He doesn't know, and he's not due back until after my wedding to Mr Joseph.'

'Are you sure he doesn't know?'

'Positive. I didn't know myself until after he'd left.'

'Well, if I were you I'd tell Mr Joseph as soon as you can, Miss Forest. I know you're worried about his head pains and all that, but he has not had any since you two agreed to get married.'

She knew Mrs Miller was right: she would have to tell Joseph, whatever the consequences, and hope that he would not be too hurt. Hopefully he would allow her to stay with him, at least until Sasha returned, but if he threw her out she would stay in Sasha's apartment until she could decide what to do. She was sure Ian and the others would understand and help her in the meantime.

'Good morning, my dear.' Joseph was leaving the breakfast room as she came downstairs. 'I'm afraid I had everything cleared away as I didn't think you were coming down to breakfast. You'll have to ask Cook for something.'

'No, thank you, Joseph. I don't feel particularly well. How are you?'

'I'm feeling very well, but I'm worried about you and I do think you need to see a doctor. You've looked ill for weeks.'

'I'll soon be all right. Don't worry about me because you'll just make yourself ill.'

'I'd worry less if you'd see my doctor, Charlotte.'

She hesitated, inclined to refuse again but aware that not only would he worry less but that she ought to see a doctor for her baby's sake. 'All right, but not today. Tomorrow. I can't face being prodded about today.'

He led her into the drawing room and made her sit down. 'Charlotte, would you like to go to Norfolk for a few days? You seemed so much more at ease up there.'

'No, thank you, Joseph. I'm too tired even to enjoy the peace and quiet of the place.'

He looked into her eyes and played with the hair over her forehead. 'Are you worried about marrying me, Charlotte? What might happen?'

'Yes.' It was such a relief to say so.

'And is that making you ill?'

'It's not helping, Joseph.'

'Then we'll postpone it. Indefinitely,' he said in a gentle voice and relief flooded through her, calming her body and her mind. 'But you were so eager, Joseph? What's happened?'

'Perhaps I've come to my senses, Charlotte. I wanted to know that you *would* marry me, that you loved me enough to do so.' He stood up and walked to the window, leaned against the sash and stared down into the gardens. 'You made me jealous a few weeks ago. Jealous of this Russian boy. I needed reassurance that you wouldn't leave me. That you wouldn't fall in love with someone else. I don't know what I'd do if that happened.'

She walked over to him, put her arms around him and hugged him from behind. She was conscious of the baby inside her, the fact that she did not know how Sasha would react when she told him it was his, and she was very aware that she had to tell Joseph the truth before she saw the doctor tomorrow.

He turned around, wrapped his arms around her and sighed deeply.

And she smelled the odour which had puzzled her

314

before. 'What is that smell, Joseph? I half recognise it—'

He sounded defensive when he answered, and his voice grew progressively sharper. 'It's my medicine, probably. I understand it's made from a similar drug to the medicine you took to calm your asthma, but it's much stronger. You can see that it works. I've had no pain for weeks. None at all.'

She watched his eyes as she asked, gently, 'How much are you taking, Joseph?'

'I take it when I need to.' His eyes flickered.

'And how often is that? Truthfully?'

He looked her directly in the eyes. 'Quite often, Charlotte. Too often, probably, but does it matter so long as the pain goes away?'

She held both his hands. 'No, Joseph. Nothing else matters.'

She realised that they had been spending less and less time together so she sat with him in the drawing room, and when he moved into his study she followed, and watched him. His right hand went to his head in what seemed to be an ordinary way, as a prop or an act of concentration, but she noticed how his fingers pressed hard on a particular place and how the muscles in his jaw worked as he fought the pain he was trying to hide. He went to his bedroom and returned minutes later, smiling and relaxed.

In less than an hour his hand reached up to his head and she knew he was suffering again. She watched him all morning and afternoon. The pains came every half hour.

She would talk to his doctor tomorrow. Perhaps there was no need for Joseph to know about the baby. Perhaps, during his final few days, she could spare him that pain at least.

Elizabeth noticed that although Bill was joking he was not smiling. 'Perhaps you should join the police force, Lizzie.'

'It wasn't difficult, Bill. I simply called at the shipping office where Lottie used to work, told them I was Hubert Belchester's personal secretary and asked them to confirm that his accounts had all been paid up to date. They told me they had, so I knew he had dealt with the company. Then I told them he might be calling there in a day or so and they said they thought perhaps he had moved back to Spain because they hadn't seen him since Christmas Eve. Not the last one, the one before. Lottie was working there then, Bill. I just wish I'd thought about doing it before, but what with everything else and the letters Lottie sent Eve—'

'You can't blame yourself, Lizzie. Now, you say this Hubert Belchester's got a grudge against Rose's family and he once abducted her and knocked her about a lot?'

She nodded, confirming the story she had made up so she could ask for Bill's help without telling him Rose's real secret.

'Quite frankly, Lizzie, I'd be a lot happier if we could tell Edward, but if you don't want him to know, well . . .' He shrugged, then leaned forward on her desk. 'You'd better tell me all you know and then we'll work out what to do.'

Lottie had a difficult evening, watching Joseph pretend he was not in pain and was not scared, while trying to hide her own worries and find excuses not to drink the wine and cognac he tried to press on her. She gave up the struggle and went to bed early.

She went to bed but she did not sleep, and even long after midnight when Joseph stopped by on his way to his own bed she was still awake.

'Perhaps you should take some of my medicine, Charlotte. It makes me sleep.' His voice was slurred and his breath stank of so much alcohol that she had to turn her face away.

'No, Joseph, I'll be all right.'

'I'll get you some. It won't do you any harm.'

'No, I'd rather not.' She searched for an excuse that did not involve telling him she was pregnant. 'The doctor'll be here in a few hours. I'll be all right.'

He slumped down on the side of the bed and took her face in both his hands. 'You do look lovely, Charlotte.'

'Thank you.'

'I've been thinking, Charlotte. About us. About you.'

His fingers trailed from her face and ran over her throat and shoulders, one shoulder bare where her nightdress had slipped. 'Yes?'

'Since the other week, when I saw you in your dressing room.' His fingers were shaking slightly and she found herself trembling as she thought about the way she had tried to seduce him. 'You're young and very beautiful, and I can understand that you need, certain affections.'

His fingers had slipped down inside the lacy collar of her nightdress and as he ran his fingers along the lace edging his knuckles rippled against the top of her breast. She looked into his eyes, and saw a sorry old man who was older than her father. Her mind went blank.

'So, Charlotte, I think, perhaps, we *should* go to see your young Russian. Tomorrow.'

The relief was immense, so immense that she spoke without thinking. 'We can't, Joseph. He's in America for four months.'

Then she realised what she had done.

'How do you know that?'

'I've been to see him, Joseph,' she said quietly, knowing she had to tell him she was expecting Sasha's child.

'What!' He stood up fast, pulling the covers down and ripping the buttons off her nightdress as he did so.

She lay there, both breasts exposed, shocked and too scared to move.

'You said you hadn't been there. That you wouldn't go without me. How did you know where to go?'

'You left his address behind the clock, Joseph.' She gasped out the explanation, trying to shift some of the blame back on to him.

'But you said you hadn't read it. And the note hadn't been moved?'

'I put it back exactly as you left it.'

'God, Charlotte! It was a test of trust! Didn't you know that? I was testing you and I thought you loved me. You said you did!'

'And I do, Joseph, but not in the way I thought I did. Not in the way I love Sasha.'

'And did you throw yourself at him the way you did at me?' His voice turned bitter.

'Oh, Joseph, please don't!'

'Did you, you whoring cow!'

'Joseph!'

His punch silenced her and suddenly her nightdress was ripped fully open and he was on top of her, her hands held above her head, his teeth biting her breast.

'Joseph! Please!' she screamed.

He lifted himself and she saw a strange look in his eyes. Then he fell off the bed.

She jumped up, grabbed her dressing-gown from the foot of the bed and wrapped it around herself. Moments later Mrs Miller was there.

'Oh, my God, Miss Forest. Did you tell him? About your baby?'

'No. He came in and,' – her mind was in a muddle and she tried to think of the best way to handle matters – 'he collapsed on top of me.'

'Oh, my God. We'd better get him to bed and call the doctor, Miss Forest.'

'He's breathing normally, Miss Forest, but he's deeply unconscious and very ill so I daren't move him. Can you cope with him here, until I can have a qualified nurse sent over?' the doctor asked her.

'Of course.'

'I can quite see why he doted on you so much, Miss Forest. He told me he sometimes thought of you as his special daughter.'

'His daughter? He wanted to marry me.'

'Only so you'd stay with him. He was a very lonely man until you came along.'

'What was his wife like?' she asked stiffly, trying hard not to cry.

'I don't know. I didn't start treating him until a little over a year ago and he was already a widower by then.'

Lottie sat by Joseph's bed until dawn and then felt so tired she had to go to her own bed. Mrs Miller woke her a few minutes after nine.

'Your folks, Miss Forest? Do you mind me asking if they approve of your marrying Mr Joseph?'

The question confused her for a moment until she remembered her father was supposed to be one of Joseph's friends. 'Yes, of course. Why?'

'You're sure?'

'Yes. Why?'

'Come with me, miss.' Mrs Miller led her to the bedroom window. 'You see that man standing under what's left of that tree? Well, he's been there before, twice yesterday, and two other men. They don't stop long and they keep walking past all innocently, but they look like policemen to me and I thought, perhaps, your folks had—'

She ran into the bathroom and was sick before Mrs Miller had finished talking.

'Oh dear, Miss Forest. You feeling bad again?'

'Yes. Would you mind leaving me alone, Mrs Miller? And don't worry about the men outside. My parents are very happy for me to marry Mr Joseph and I don't think those men look like policemen at all. Now, it's late and I must get myself ready before the nurse comes.'

She saw how reluctant Mrs Miller was to leave her so she ushered her out and shut the bedroom door. She was sick several more times before she could return to the window and look down into the street. There were two men now, and the one that had been there earlier was pointing to the house. She thought Mrs Miller was right. They did look like policemen and she was the reason they were there.

She waited, her heart beating fast, thinking that if they arrested her now her baby would be born in prison, then taken away from her and she would never see it again. And she would never see Sasha again, not when they sent her to prison or an asylum.

She watched the first man walk away and the second man saunter off and wander behind some bushes in the garden square.

She knew she did not have much time, certainly not

enough for a bath. She washed quickly, and dressed in several sets of clothes, both as a disguise and as a means of taking clothes with her without carrying too much luggage. A few extra clothes and the personal items she had taken from her old home fitted into a very large handbag. Her biggest and warmest overcoat buttoned tight over all the other clothes, and a wide-brimmed hat with a half veil completed an ensemble which made her look heavier and twenty years older than she was.

Joseph was asleep, or unconscious, so she simply kissed him and went back into her own room to write him a short note which, she hoped, would explain why she had left so quickly, but would not incriminate him if it was found by the police.

She went back to his room and tucked the note under the covers where it was sure to be found, and on impulse, kissed him again.

His eyes popped open as she pulled away.

'Charlotte! Charlotte.' He sounded pitiful and suddenly shocked. 'You're leaving?'

'I have to, Joseph. I must. The police.'

His face twitched and a spasm ran through him. 'It wasn't meant to happen like this,' he said, suddenly clear and agitated but then his breath seemed to fail and he crumpled. His eyes called her closer and as he mumbled incoherently she knelt down close to him and concentrated very hard in order to understand his slurred and broken words. 'Didn't think . . . could love anyone again. But you . . . Sorry what I've done to you. Went too far. Didn't mean . . .' He gasped and slumped back, his head down, his chin against his chest so he could not say more.

She knelt beside him, crying hot tears. She wanted to stay to comfort him but knew she could not. She reached out to make him more comfortable, moved his head so he could breathe more easily and saw his lips move. She placed her ear so close to his mouth she could feel his faint breath.

'Charlotte. Don't leave me . . .'

She looked into his eyes and knew he had not intended to harm her, but she had to leave him. She saw him mouth her name, and noticed his eyes change as though he were asking a question.

She did not hesitate to answer it. 'And I love you, Joseph. Oh, so much. And I won't leave you.'

'Never?'

'Never, Joseph.' She saw him smile and shut his eyes, and then she kissed his lips for the last time.

Then she stood up, gulped back her tears, and ran away.

PART 3

CHAPTER 22

London, January 1914

Lottie felt the door open as she pushed it. She shivered with relief, stepped into the hall and shut the door behind her, glad to be off the streets and safe for the moment. She paused in the hall, unsure what formalities she should follow, decided there probably were not any and ran up the stairs to Sasha's apartment.

Her stamina drained before she climbed the final flight. She paused again, took deep breaths to revive herself, and recognised the smell of Peter's cigarettes. Her heart stumbled, then lifted immediately. Sasha was in America and he could not help her, but even though Peter disapproved of her he could probably help. He gave her the impression he was the sort of man who would know exactly how to help someone who was running away from the police – which was precisely why she did not like him.

She walked up the last few steps and stood outside the apartment while she tried to think of the best way to explain why she had come there, and tried to imagine Peter's response. She could not manage either so she knocked on the door and hoped she could improvise when Peter opened it.

The door did not open. She knocked again. Still no answer but she noticed the door moved slightly when she pressed it. She pressed harder. The door opened further but the increased stench of tobacco smoke made her step back.

'Peter? Annie? Anyone home?'

No reply. She pushed the door fully open, stepped into the room and stopped.

The room had been wrecked. The fine furniture had been smashed or slashed and everything had been turned on its side or thrown on the floor. It was exactly how Sasha had described their St Petersburg apartment after the Secret Police had tried to arrest them.

She stepped back onto the landing. She had enough problems and did not want any more, but it occurred to her that Peter might need her help. He might have been hurt by whoever wrecked the apartment.

She stepped back into the apartment and searched every room but all she saw were opened drawers, scattered clothes and smashed furniture, but although there was no sign of Peter the cigarette smell was still strong so he must have left only minutes before the apartment was attacked. Unless he was in the bathroom?

She ran to the final door and pushed it open, scared she might find him lying with his throat cut, but the bathroom was empty, untouched by whoever had smashed the place.

She turned around and looked back at the wreckage that surrounded her and it occurred to her that it symbolised her life, but whereas someone else had wrecked the apartment she had wrecked her life all on her own.

'Oh, Lottie,' she sighed quietly. There was only one option left. She would have to go to Eastbourne and ask Eve for help.

Then a hand grabbed her.

Another hand clamped over her mouth. 'Shush! I won't hurt you if you keep quiet. If you don't I'll kill you. Nod if you understand.'

She nodded, heart hammering in her throat and almost drowning out the man's whisper. He did not release her immediately. He eased her backwards into the bathroom and pushed the door almost closed with his foot.

He released her but she was too scared to turn around until he told he to, and she recognised him instantly.

'Peter? Where did you come from?'

He did not answer until he had reached out and removed her half-veiled hat. 'You? What's happened to you? You look—'

'I'm wearing a lot of clothes,' she said lamely.

He frowned. 'Why are you here?'

'I need somewhere to stay. Until Sasha comes back from America.'

'I don't suggest you stay here. I'm going and I think you should, too.' He jumped up on to the edge of the bath, reached up through a trap-door in the ceiling and pulled down a large leather valise.

'You were hiding, up there?' She understood now. He had climbed into the loft.

'Yes. Fortunately I had time. They knocked on the door and told me to open it before they kicked it open. I was lucky. I may not be so lucky again.' He pulled the bathroom door open and tried to push past. 'That's why I'm leaving, and I suggest you leave too.'

'Could I stay here?' she asked, and held onto him.

'You can if you want to but they'll be back and I don't know what they'd do to you.'

'They?'

'Yes. They,' he said uninformatively. 'Now I must go.'

'Can I come with you?' She saw him hesitate. 'Please? I'm in trouble and I'm desperate.'

'What sort of trouble?'

'The police are looking for me?'

He looked surprised. 'You kill your rich man friend or something?'

'Not exactly, but it is serious.'

'No, no.' He backed through the door and halfway across the room. 'I've got enough trouble of my own without having the English police chasing me.'

'I'm pregnant with Sasha's child.'

She saw his eyes constrict, then he asked suspiciously, 'When?'

'The Wednesday before Christmas Eve.' She was precise because she thought he wanted her to be precise, and then because she thought it would make her sound more plausible she added, 'He played his sonata for me and asked me to choose an ending.'

'Yes, he would.' Peter seemed to be considering the situation. 'And which one—'

'The last one. The happy one.'

He nodded curtly and held out his hand. 'Come on. They may not come back for days, but it might be only minutes.'

He led her around the block and helped her into a small motor-car with a cover like a pram-hood.

'It's fortunate you wore a big hat and extra clothes,' he smiled, as he sat down in the driving seat. 'Once we're on the road outside London you'll need them to keep warm.'

'Outside London? Where're we going?'

'Dover.' They drove across the bridge she had stood on when she saw Sasha on the Serpentine. 'And then Paris.'

'Paris! Why Paris?' She suddenly felt trapped in his car and longed to get out, no matter what the consequences were.

'I would like to say it's because you are a beautiful young woman and I'm taking you there to romance you, but I'm not. I'm going there first to save my life, second to maybe save yours, third because I have money there and fourth because I have contacts there. My contacts can find me some business and maybe take care of you until Sasha can collect you. You speak French well. You'll speak it even better once you've lived there for a while.'

'But I've never been abroad before!'

'I don't suppose you've ever run away from the police before. It must be quite an exciting day for you,' he said laconically.

She laughed because his understatement amused her and because he seemed able to cope with whatever happened, and that suddenly made her feel safe. She sensed that even though he did not like her he would take care of her simply because she was carrying Sasha's child.

Sasha? Should she ask Peter why Sasha left London so suddenly? She was not sure whether or not she should risk upsetting him, but he was far more astute than she realised.

'I suppose you're wondering why Sasha left so suddenly?' he asked without any preamble.

'No, not really. I assume he has his reasons,' she lied, and looked out through the side screen.

'He did,' Peter said, and fell silent.

Several minutes passed before she surrendered her pride. 'You were talking about Sasha,' she reminded him.

'Yes, but I did not think you were interested, so I stopped,' he then conceded, 'but I'll tell you anyway. I lied to him. I told him that I had made a mistake and the orchestra needed him earlier than I had said and he had to leave immediately.'

'Why? To get him away from me?'

'Yes. He gave me a letter for you but I threw it away.'

She was furious, so angry she could not speak.

'There was another reason. I made him go because the men who came today came once before and threatened to smash his hands.'

She was horrified, and frightened again. 'Why? Why would they do that?'

'You don't need to know why, only that they would. I have to look after my little brother. He's very precious to me.'

She did not ask any more questions and Peter said very little during the drive to Dover, even when they stopped for petrol and for food. She was grateful for the extra clothes she was wearing because the car cover allowed in draughts, although she was grateful for the draughts because they cleared the smell and smoke from Peter's cigarettes.

The motion, the cold, the smells from tobacco and petrol, and the fear for what the future might hold made her feel ill and miserable. They reached Dover a little before dark and left the tiny car in a hostelry which had been adapted to offer that service, and then they boarded a paddle-steamer which left Dover an hour or so after nightfall.

Peter paid for a single cabin in his name and claimed they had just married and were beginning a Continental tour. She tried to sleep in a narrow bunk but the steamer wallowed constantly and the paddles made such a noise it was impossible to relax. Her morning sickness started at three o'clock and did not stop until they disembarked in grey Boulogne during a dismal dawn.

After a short walk along the quayside Peter helped her up into an almost empty railway carriage. She did not know it was possible to feel so ill and still live.

'Peter, when do we reach Paris?'

'A few hours, that's all.'

It was a lot longer than a few hours but Peter sat with his arm around her all the way to Paris, softening the train's buffeting and reassuring her in a way she was warily grateful for. He said very little and she was grateful for that too.

They had been on the train for hours before she noticed that he was not smoking his cigarettes, so she asked him why not.

'I've stopped because I think they may make you feel more ill.'

'That's very considerate of you, Peter. Thank you.'

He shrugged off her thanks. 'It's better for me if you're not ill. And for the baby.'

Lottie could not sleep and she did not want to eat or drink. She simply wanted it to be over, even if that meant returning to England and prison. Nothing could make her feel as miserable as she did now.

She knew she had been verging on physical exhaustion for weeks, but now her emotional reserves were also drained and although she could not fall to sleep properly she was also not fully aware of what was happening around her as the daylight faded and sheeting rain hid everything outside the carriage windows. After a while she sensed the train had stopped and she heard whistles and shouts and much coming and going but she did not realise they had finally reached Paris until Peter told her.

Paris was one of the many places she had always wanted to visit but she hardly bothered to look out of the taxi's windows as the driver raced the little motor through torrential rain, speeding through squares and streets, along wide boulevards and down narrow alleyways.

It was dark when he stopped the taxi in a small square stuck with leafless lime trees. She was aware of high grey buildings with shuttered windows, deserted tables set out on pavements, and a bar packed tight with people drinking strong-smelling coffee and red wine from tumblers, and smoking cigarettes which burned with a pungent farmyard stench. She saw flickering candles stuck in saucers and heard a babble of conversation spoken so fast and sounding so foreign it might well have been Chinese or Zulu.

She felt lost.

Peter paid some money to an ancient clerk sitting in something like a large sentry-box, took a key and swung her across his shoulder so he could carry her up the stairs. He took her into a room, laid her on a bed, pulled off her shoes and covered her with several blankets.

She woke up, still dressed, still covered by the blankets, with the sun streaming onto her face. Peter was sitting smoking in a sort of shuttered doorway which led out onto a balcony. His feet were resting on the balcony's rail.

'Good afternoon,' he said affably.

'Afternoon?'

'Three o'clock. Hungry?'

'Yes. And dirty.'

He nodded to a round bath plumbed into the corner of the large room. 'Wash in there. Water's cold. I'll move right outside. Shout when you're finished.'

He shifted his chair and pulled the door shut.

She stripped off each layer of clothes and prayed Peter was honourable if not a gentleman and that he would not come into the room while she was undressed. She half filled the bath with water which was clean if slow running, and gradually lowered herself into it.

The water chilled her, then numbed her, and it was not until she ran enough into the bath to sit with only her head above the surface that she stopped shivering. She had brought soap and a flannel, a soft brush, a medium-sized towel, and a bottle of perfume, and half an hour later, wearing a change of clothes and with her hair brushed she felt clean, refreshed and fragrant again.

She had forgotten to let Peter know that she had finished bathing and dressing so she opened the shutters to tell him he could come back inside. She found him asleep, his chair propped back and leaning against the rail at one end of the balcony, his feet on the rail at the other end, and a neat little hole burned in his jacket where his cigarette had slipped from his mouth when he fell asleep.

He was oblivious to the tremendous noise echoing up from the street and to the cold wind which whipped along under the sunlight. He must be exhausted. She knew he had not slept while they were on the paddle-steamer and she guessed he had probably sat up all the previous night so she could sleep comfortably on the bed.

Now it was his turn to sleep. She woke him gently, led him to the bed without allowing him to wake fully, laid him down and covered him with the blankets. He muttered something in Russian and began to snore.

She wrapped herself in a spare blanket and sat out on the balcony. The darkness came earlier than she expected but not before she had a better understanding of what *foreign* meant. The buildings were different, the air was full of strange smells and sounds, the people spoke a language which was coarser and faster than the French she knew and they dressed differently, behaved differently, and were even different shapes to English people. She would have been scared if she were here on her own but she knew she was safe with Peter. Just as safe as she would have been with Joseph.

Poor Joseph. He did not deserve what had happened to him. God could be so unfair sometimes.

And then the guilt welled up again. Joseph had helped

her when she needed him but she had run away when he needed her. She recalled the awful moment when she told him she would stay even though she knew she had to leave, and wondered what the effect was on him when he knew she had abandoned him.

She could not change what had happened, all she could try to do was come to terms with it. Joseph was dying anyway, and she was carrying a new life. He had been unlucky to fall ill, but she had been unlucky to be accused of killing a man who had attacked her, and she was unlucky to have parents who never really wanted her and would have her committed to an insane asylum.

She tried hard to come to terms with what she had done to Joseph, but it was very hard to justify running away. Then she fell asleep again and did not wake up until Peter touched her shoulder.

'Strange,' he said mildly, 'I thought I was out here and you were in there. Still hungry?'

'Ravenous. I could eat the proverbial horse.'

'You may well do so, or at least a little part of it.'

He took her to a dingy restaurant ten minutes' walk from the rooming house and told her not to expect too much as the food was cooked by a woman who had only ever cooked for her family before her husband died and she was forced to open up the ground floor of their rented house to guests. He said the food may not be up to the standard she was used to but it was filling, wholesome, and cheap.

The meal was one of the most memorable she had ever eaten. Soup which tasted of tomatoes and spice, shell fish which tasted of the sea, stewed meat which melted and vegetables that crunched with flavour, and cheese which looked mouldy but provided flavours and scents she had never known before.

Peter drank red wine and a cloudy drink which smelled of aniseed, and she drank red wine and water. She told him the wine reminded her of the first time she went to Sasha's apartment; the first glass being awful but all subsequent glasses becoming better and better, and he laughed at her and accused her of being bourgeois, middle class and protected from the realities of life.

'I grew up in Angel Street, Peter. My mother and aunt ran a mission for the destitute and visited the slums,' she said defensively, even though she knew he was right.

'Your mother and aunt? What about you? Did you spend time in your London slums? Get to know how the people lived?'

'No. They didn't let me.'

'Then they were protecting you, Lottie, and there are millions of people all over the world who have been protected from real life, and they're the ones who make the laws the rest of us have to live by.'

'That sounds like politics and I don't know anything about politics.' She still tried to defend herself but she sensed he was not really listening to what she said.

'It's no wonder you get on so well with Sasha. You can't live and know nothing about politics. It's the reason you do what you do, eat what you eat. The reason some people live in houses and some in palaces, and even more on the streets. It's the reason some people grow rich sitting on their backsides while others work fourteen hours a day and starve. Why rich children grow fat and poor children die starving. Politics is life. You can't live and say you don't know anything about politics!'

'I can.'

'Coffee, please,' he called in rough French which madame clearly understood, and then turned to her and looked her in the eyes. 'Well then, petite bourgeois, I'll show you you're wrong.'

When they had finished their coffee, sluggish and strong, he paid the bill with a bandit's flourish, thrust Lottie into her coat and almost pulled her out onto the street. 'Now I'll show you some Paris night-life. Come on, Krasnaya.'

'That's what Sasha calls me,' she said sharply, jealous of the few memories she and Sasha might so far share.

'Do you know what it means?' he asked, smiling in his arrogant way.

'Yes. Red,' she paused and stared challengingly into his

eyes, then her courage failed and she felt a little foolish and immodest, 'and beautiful.'

'Very fitting, in my opinion, Krasnaya.' He had drunk far too much and although he was amiable and talkative she thought it would be easier to humour him than to argue. Besides, it was long after midnight and she had never been out this late and wondered what life was like in the early hours of the morning.

They walked until they reached a bridge spanning a wide river which seemed to divide into two.

'Ile de la cité. Most visitors come here to look at the churches and don't realise this is the place where Paris was born when some Celtic fishermen of the Parisii settled here two hundred years before Christ was born. They called it Lutetia, a much prettier name than Paris.'

She was impressed, but not so much by what he knew as by his carelessly expressed opinion that the Celtic name was prettier. Prettier was not a word she expected to find in his vocabulary.

She looked at the river, banks of lights reflecting in the black waters, and wished she were there with Sasha. 'Paris, Peter. They say it's the most romantic city in the world.'

'The Parisians do. It's no more beautiful than London, not as striking as Moscow and the people aren't as friendly as in Dublin.'

'And St Petersburg?' she asked quickly.

'Something out of hell. It stinks in the summer when it's hot, freezes you to death in the winter and in the autumn the days are so short and dark half the population gets drunk to preserve its sanity. Fogs come down from Finland and typhus and cholera are endemic. In the summer the streets are so rutted and hard you can break an ankle crossing them and in the winter you sink up to your ankles in mud.'

She was shocked. 'But Sasha said is was the most beautiful city in the world.'

'Sasha boasts he can hold a whole orchestra in his head, which he can. The trouble is, that doesn't leave much room for anything else. The only thing St Petersburg is good for is giving birth.' He stopped suddenly, as if he realised he was talking too much.

He took her away from the river and led her along some cobbled streets and into an area which looked shabby and run down. He pointed to where people slept in doorways and among rubbish in alleyways. 'Paris is no different to London, Krasnaya, except it's colder and the winter's usually longer.'

'It's awful, but why do they have to live like this?'

'Some of them are drunks, others are just unlucky or unwanted or ill. Various reasons but not many choose to live this way.'

'Can't someone do something for them?'

'Missions like your mother's and aunt's? Maybe they can help a few, but not everyone, and there's an argument that while they're helping a few the Government won't do anything to help the many?'

'But why won't they?' She could not understand.

'Because they're bourgeois and they don't understand the real problem.'

She did understand the point he made, although she was sure he had deliberately made the lesson simple for her, but there was something she did not understand. 'If you feel so strongly about all this, why don't you do something to help?'

'In France? There's enough to do in Russia, and in England and in many countries.'

'But someone has to start.'

'It's a big job, Lottie.'

'Perhaps, but someone has to start it, and if you're so sure it's all so wrong, why don't you do something about it?'

He did not reply, simply looked ahead and led her back to where they were staying.

He bought a half candle in a saucer from the ancient clerk in the sentry-box and lit it as soon as he unlocked their room. 'I'll stand outside while you undress and get into bed. Shout when you're ready. I'll sleep on the floor.'

'Thank you, Peter.' It seemed the friendliness which had

been building up had been demolished. 'I'm sorry if I upset you. I wasn't criticising you, simply trying to understand how you could feel so strongly and not do anything.'

He spun around, grabbed her hands and forced her to sit down on the bed. 'I'll try to find you somewhere to stay tomorrow, and once I've left you it's better you don't admit to anyone that you know me. I'll let Sasha know where to find you, but then you must both move away, quickly.'

His attitude frightened her and made her curious. 'Why? I need to know more so I don't say anything which might cause you trouble.'

'No, Lottie, you don't need to know. I am whatever I want people to believe I am, an honest businessman or a thief and a cheat.'

She smiled at him. 'I thought you looked like a bandit the first time I saw you.'

He smiled back. 'You're very beautiful and very honest, Lottie, and you're not the sort of person I thought you were. Maybe, if you weren't carrying my brother's baby . . .' He leaned towards her and kissed her forehead. 'I'll wait outside until you say it is all right for me to come back in.'

Lottie slept heavily for a while, then woke up suddenly, listening in the way she used to listen for any change in Joseph's breathing.

She lifted herself onto one elbow, concentrated hard, holding her breath.

There it was again. Mice? A rat?

The doorknob creaked.

There was someone at the door.

She sat up and stared into the dark, trying hard to see, then swung out of bed to investigate.

A hand pushed her back. 'Shush!'

The doorknob creaked again. Peter pushed her away gently and kept on pushing her until she reached the far side of the bed and rolled over, soundlessly, to lie on the floor. 'Shush!'

He left her, there was a quiet rustle and the door opened suddenly.

'What do you want?' Peter asked in rough French.

A man's voice slurred an answer. Peter asked him which room he wanted, and demanded to see his key. The man was on the wrong floor.

'It's downstairs, you fool!' He almost dragged the man to the stairs and must have half pushed him down because there was a series of bumps and curses, then Peter came back.

She had already slipped back into bed.

'Get up! Get dressed. We're leaving.'

'Why?'

'Because he didn't smell drunk enough and he didn't fall all the way down the stairs. Get up. Quickly.'

She remembered what had happened in Peter's apartment and did not argue with the need to leave, but she did expect him to leave the room while she dressed and she told him so.

'It won't do you any harm to dress with me in the room. It might do me harm to stand outside and be shot. So get on with it and I promise I won't look. But carry your shoes until we're outside.'

He turned his back to her. She dressed as fast as she could and threw everything into a bag he had bought her. She worked in the dark but she noticed it must be after dawn because grey light was filtering through the cracks in the window shutters.

'I'm ready,' she said and moved to the door.

'Careful!' he whispered, and listened before opening it. 'Come on. The corridor is very dark. Be silent!'

She slipped out and turned towards the stairs.

'Not that way. This way.' He pulled the door but did not shut it completely, gripped her hand and led her along the passage and through another door to a fire escape which led down into a dark alley.

They crept down it and walked the full length of the alley before putting on their shoes. It was obvious that he had known about the fire escape before they needed to use it, and she wondered why he was so well prepared to run away.

'Why are you so unpopular?' she asked as mildly as her thumping heart would allow.

'I'm only unpopular with some people. Others like me quite a lot.'

'Can we try to meet some of them, for a change?'

'That's where we're going now.'

They walked for an hour or so, until it was almost full daylight and the city was bustling with people going about their ordinary and legal business. Peter had hardly spoken during that time and Lottie was about to ask him some questions when he pulled her into a small café for breakfast.

'You realise you haven't been sick for over a day now?'

'That's because I'm too scared to be anything but frightened.' She tasted the coffee and winced. 'What's in here, apart from coffee?'

'A little reviving spirit. It helps overcome fear.'

'Peter! Don't forget I'm expecting a baby.'

'I won't. Believe me, Krasnaya, I keep reminding myself that soon you'll be a mother.' He grinned and swallowed some coffee. 'Don't worry about what's in this. It's *eau-de-vie*, the water of life, and the amount you're drinking will do you and Sasha's baby nothing but good. Now eat.'

She nibbled at the cake-like bread he had ordered and studied him. Everything about him, his looks, his clothes, his swaggering manner, were meant to portray a vagabond, but his dark eyes did not always twinkle as a bandit's eyes were supposed to and she realised that his laconic talk and attitude were meant to disguise that weakness. Her earlier impression of him had changed enough for her to start liking him and she realised that almost without thinking she had even begun to adopt his way of speaking. She smiled at him when he looked up at her.

'You ought to know, Krasnaya, that I didn't like you at first.'

'It was quite mutual.' She grinned when she saw the surprise on his face.

He shrugged and grinned back. 'Now, I think you're quite a lady. You've got more guts than I'd have thought and I reckon you're just what little Sasha needs. He's a dreamer and he needs someone like you who can cope with anything to keep his feet on the ground.'

'I'll try,' she said simply, surprised and more pleased than she could ever tell him that he had changed from thinking she was bad for Sasha to thinking she could actually be good for him. All her life people had told her *she* was a dreamer and needed someone to keep her feet on the ground, and now, in these circumstances, the bandit Peter was telling her that he admired her and precisely for the qualities she was supposed to lack.

She suddenly felt bold enough to ask why he was always running away from people who wanted to hurt him, what he had done to attract so much attention, and when he tried to tell her she did not need to know she argued so loudly that he gave in.

'All right, I'll tell you, but don't attract so much attention, and hold my hands so it looks as if we're making up after a lover's argument.' He held her hands and smiled at her, and she smiled back and tried hard not to laugh at the play-acting. 'We left Russia with no more than we could carry, Lottie. I even had to make my mother sell her rings so we could live, so how do you think I can afford to buy big houses and motor-cars and get enough influence to have Sasha invited to join an American orchestra?'

'I thought you were in business?'

He laughed. 'Your father's been in business nearly all his life. Why can't he buy what I can?'

'That's a different kind of business, Peter. You deal in international trade. I know a little about that from the office I used to work in and from listening to Albert and his family, so I know it's possible to make a lot of money from it.'

'Only if you're lucky or a banker or you have a lot to start with. I trade, Lottie, but I trade with things people don't want to admit to.'

'I don't understand.'

'I realised when I tried to sell my mother's rings that I could only get a tenth of what they were worth. Now, there are a lot of wealthy people all over the world who have money to buy almost anything they want, and there are a lot of other people who are scared they're soon going to lose most of what they have and would rather have cash or gold instead. Especially in Russia and in the Balkan countries. I help one sort of person deal with the other.'

'You introduce them to each other for a commission?'

'No, I buy from one and sell to the other.'

'Then why are all these people trying to stop you?'

'Because although they've been doing it for longer, I'm better at it than they are. They don't like my competition.'

'Can't you simply tell the police?'

He laughed again, and reached out to finger her hair. 'No. Let's say I sometimes don't complete all the formalities I should.'

'You smuggle?'

'The Tsar, and others, wouldn't appreciate some of the items I export for him.'

'I don't understand.' She was sure he was not telling her everything

'Good. I'll explain it all one day, when it's safer for you to know.' He stood up, grabbed both bags in one hand and still held her hand in the other. 'Come on, protect me by pretending you're my lover. I told the last place you were a prostitute I'd picked up so no one'll be expecting me still to be with a woman.'

'Thank you,' she said stiffly.

'There are worse things to be called, Krasnaya. Anyway, it's not much further and I'm sure my friend will give you a home for a few months, until Sasha comes for you. With luck you shouldn't have to put up with me dragging you around for more than another hour or so.' She nodded, not sure yet whether or not she wanted to be left alone in this strange country. She had only ever met three men who treated her like a real adult and one was on the other side of the world, one was dying and might already be dead for all she knew, and the third was standing beside her. If she allowed Peter to go she would lose her only contact with Sasha, the father of the child she was carrying. Frighteningly, Peter Igorovitch Komovsky was the key to her future.

'Who is this friend, Peter?'

'Marguerite, more a friend of my mother's really. Don't worry, she'll take care of you and she knows nothing about my business. I don't know where Sasha will be as he moves around America but we can write to an address where someone will forward letters on to him. I'll make sure he knows where you are.'

She thought it all sounded a little vague and when Peter led her towards a large house half hidden behind an overgrown garden and she knew he would soon leave her she began to panic.

'Calm down, Lottie.' He stemmed her barrage of questions. 'Let's see what Marguerite has to say before you start worrying.'

He pulled a long bell-handle. The bell jangled far off inside the house, and they waited. And waited. He rang again and she stepped back and quickly inspected the drawn wooden shutters, paint peeling off and fastenings looking quite rusty.

'I think the house is empty, Peter.'

'Yes.' He sounded terse and irritable.

They walked all around the house and saw no one, no sign of life, and as they returned to the front garden an elderly woman told them that the owner had moved away the previous summer and was not expected back.

'Hell!' Peter sat down on the front step.

'I'm sorry, Peter. Perhaps you should just leave me here and I'll try to find work for myself.' She smiled down at him and hoped he would not agree, and he did not.

'No. Unless you were lucky you'd end up on the streets, one way or another. You speak the language, sort of, but you don't know how to live over here.'

'Well, what were you planning to do next? If your friend had been able to help?'

'Most immediately go to a bank, then to see a couple of men, and then leave Paris and go on to somewhere else.'

'Where?' She thought he looked uncomfortable but she pressed him for an answer. 'Where, exactly?'

'St Petersburg.'

'Russia? I thought you'd left Russia because the Secret Police were looking for you?'

'We did.'

'And you're going back? Why?'

'I told you earlier. For business, and for other reasons.'

'But isn't it dangerous for you to go back?'

'Only if I'm recognised by the wrong people, and if I get caught,' he said wryly.

She sat down beside him and smiled at him. She had a plan. A plan which might help him and would help her understand Sasha better.

All she had to do was convince Peter, and she sensed that might not be too difficult. 'Remember that earlier you told me to pretend we were together because the people who were looking for you expected you to be alone?'

He stared at her, obviously puzzled, and then his face cleared. 'Oh no Krasnaya, Lottie. That's not possible. I'm not taking you to St Petersburg. Not in your condition. It'd be madness.'

CHAPTER 23

Elizabeth tried to remain calm as Bill told her all that he had discovered.

'I went to the underground station Charlotte used, Lizzie, and found a young ticket collector who remembered her well, not only because she was very pretty but because the last time he saw her she had blood on her hair and coat. When he asked Charlotte if she was all right she insisted she was, and told him an elaborate story about how she'd helped a man who'd been hurt and must've got his blood on her clothes.' Bill leaned forward. 'This young fellow thought that was rather strange, and he thought it was even more strange some minutes later when Charlotte came back up from the platform accompanied by a well dressed elderly gentleman she appeared to know and who seemed to be taking care of her.'

Elizabeth frowned. 'Did he remember what this man looked like, Bill?'

'Oh yes,' Bill nodded. 'He remembered him well. As well as the girl at the shipping office remembered Hubert Belchester. They both described the same man, Lizzie.'

'Oh God!'

'I'm afraid there's more. I went to see Stan Butcher and scared him into admitting that he had been passing on information about the mission, until he was told it was no longer necessary.'

'And who did he tell, Bill?' Elizabeth asked, already guessing the answer.

'A Mr Joseph. His description was the same as the others.'

'So Hubert Belchester's calling himself Mr Joseph? Why?' she asked, and wondered silently if it was just coincidence that he had used the name Joseph or whether there was a more sinister reason behind the choice. She jumped to her feet and was halfway across her office before Bill could even stand up. 'Come on, Bill. We'd better get over there now. God knows what he might have done to Lottie but if she's there we've got to find her.'

'I'll come with you, Lizzie, and there's already someone close by, but I'd like to make it official just in case anything goes wrong.'

'Do we have to? Rose and Edward?' Her mind whirled with the implications and the difficulties of sorting out priorities.

Bill seemed to hover between her and the door, hands outstretched, obviously unsure what to do. 'All right, come on. But I've got my whistle with me and if there's any sign of trouble I'm blowing it and we'll call everyone in.'

Elizabeth listened as Bill told his colleague what they were about to do then she ran up the steps to the front door. Bill stepped aside so he could not be seen and she pulled on the bell. It was answered by a large, homely woman who spoke with a West Country accent.

'Excuse me, may I speak to Mr Joseph, please?'

'I'm afraid he's not accepting visitors, madam. He's very ill, you see.'

'May I ask if you have a young woman staying here. Twenty-one, very pretty, curly auburn hair?'

'Why?'

Bill suddenly stepped forward, his foot planted between the door jamb and the door. 'We're police, madam. We're looking for a Miss Charlotte Forrester and we've been told she was seen coming into this house but hasn't left it.'

'You'd better both come in.' The woman did not hesitate to wave them into the hall. 'Miss Charlotte was here but she left on Monday. Called herself Forest though, not Forrester.'

Lizzie thought names were irrelevant. She wanted to know where Lottie had gone, but the homely woman could not tell her.

'She just left without saying goodbye to any of us, but she did take a few clothes and plenty of money so she should be all right for a while, poor thing. She was running away from the police, though, I do know that. We saw you watching the house.'

Elizabeth glanced at Bill. It was their fault that Lottie had run away again. But why would she run away from the police?

'How was she, when she left?' Bill asked the question before she could ask hers.

'All right, apart from being tired from worrying so much about Mr Joseph, and apart from expecting, of course.'

'What?' Elizabeth felt her legs give way. She clutched at Bill as she fell and he hauled her into an upright chair.

A nurse appeared at the top of the stairs. 'Mrs Miller? Do you need any help?'

'This lady just feels a bit faint, that's all. I'll give her some water. She'll be all right.'

The way Mrs Miller reacted suggested that she could be trusted, so Elizabeth thought they ought to be honest with her. She told her who they really were and explained that Lottie had disappeared from home a year ago and no one had heard anything from her.

Mrs Miller listened, then scratched her head. 'Well, I don't know, Mrs Hampton. Mr Joseph told me Charlotte was one of his friend's daughters who had been in a bit of an accident. When she came here she had blood all over her hair and clothes, but apart from being a bit shaky she wasn't hurt at all.'

Elizabeth asked Mrs Miller if she thought that whatever

had happened then might account for Lottie thinking the police were looking for her.

'I don't know, Mrs Hampton. I suppose Mr Joseph might know but he's been so ill I haven't liked to ask him.' Mrs Miller shrugged. 'I don't even know if that's why she ran away. She told me she didn't think the men were policemen. I don't understand any of it any more.'

She listened to Mrs Miller, and steadied herself to ask another unpalatable question. 'You said she was expecting a baby? Whose baby? Mr Joseph's?'

'Good Lord no, madam. Mr Joseph doesn't even know about it and I don't want him to either. It'd hurt him terrible.' Mrs Miller shook her head and added quietly, 'Miss Charlotte didn't say who the father is, but she did say he's in America. She told me that before she left, and I wondered if that's where she's gone.'

'Sasha Komovsky's gone to America, Bill?' Elizabeth said, her mind working on the coincidence. Then she felt she needed reassurance that it wasn't Hubert's child. 'Are you sure Mr Joseph isn't the father, Mrs Miller?'

'Oh yes. Miss Forest, sorry Forrester, said he wasn't and insisted she didn't want him to know. She wasn't a prisoner here, madam. She came and went as she pleased. Mr Joseph went with her sometimes but once he became ill she used to go out by herself most of the time. To be honest he had to insist on her going out sometimes because she wanted to stay in and take care of him, she was so fond of him. You'd have thought they were father and daughter, to see them. They did have some silly idea about getting married but whatever they said I don't think they would ever have gone through with it. She sometimes said she thought of him as a sort of father, and he only ever thought of her as his daughter. He told me so.'

She listened to Mrs Miller then turned to Bill. 'I'm confused, Bill. Mr Joseph can't be Hubert. He sounds too nice.'

Bill grimaced, and asked Mrs Miller if it was possible for them to see Mr Joseph and Mrs Miller went off to ask the nurse.

The nurse appeared on the landing and called down, promising they could see him if he agreed. 'What name should I give Mr Joseph?'

'I'm Mrs Hampton but he won't recognise that. Please give him my maiden name. Forrester. Elizabeth Forrester.'

The nurse nodded, walked back into a room and shut the door behind her. Five minutes later she reappeared. 'He'll see you now, Mrs Hampton, but please don't excite or tire him. He has a few problems and he's also had quite a bad seizure so he's very slow to respond and his speech is quite slurred. He's also partially paralysed.'

'Just how ill is he, Nurse? I mean, is he in danger of dying?'

'There's always a possibility, of course, but he's already recovered some of his faculties so well that the doctor's hopeful he might live for years.'

'I see,' she said quietly, and hoped she did not sound too disappointed.

Elizabeth followed the nurse into what was obviously a man's study converted into a temporary bedroom. Mrs Miller stood beside the bed and her worried expression showed she was very concerned about her employer. Elizabeth had only seen Hubert two or three times before, and twenty-seven years ago at that, but she recognised him instantly. Rose had always said he was beautiful and he still was, in a rather haggard way, but she found it difficult to reconcile the sadistic bully who was Hubert Belchester with the supposedly gentle Mr Joseph.

'You've come about Charlotte?' He slurred the words slowly, dribbling as he did so.

'Yes. Do you know where she is?'

His answer came very slowly. 'No.' He sank back and his eyes closed.

The nurse swooped in to protect him, but she smiled as she did so.

'Thank you, Nurse,' Elizabeth said, and looked at Hubert as his eyes flickered open. 'And thank you for seeing me, Hubert.'

He grimaced and then said, very slowly and quietly, 'I'm sorry for what I've done. Please ask Rose to forgive me, and to come.'

'She's also very ill, Hubert, and won't be able to come here.'

'Serious?' he croaked.

'Her brain.'

'I hope she recovers.' His eyes closed again and he settled deeper into his pillow.

The nurse indicated they should leave so they thanked her and walked back down to the hall, followed by Mrs Miller.

'Excuse me, Mrs Hampton, but Mr Joseph asked me to give this to you!' Mrs Miller handed her a brown paper parcel which was addressed to Rose Forrester.

'Thank you, Mrs Miller.' Elizabeth accepted the parcel, and it occurred to her that by addressing it to Rose Forrester and not Belchester, Hubert had shown that he accepted what she had done.

They were just leaving when the nurse came running down the stairs. 'Wait! Don't go. Mr Joseph's just asked me to tell you something else. You too, Mrs Miller.'

Elizabeth was stunned by what the nurse said. 'He actually convinced Lottie she'd killed someone? That was why she ran away?'

'That's what he told me,' the nurse shrugged.

Mrs Miller slumped down into a chair. 'Oh my God. That's wicked, but he must have had his reasons. He's not a bad man, not really.'

'That's a matter of opinion,' Bill Crabb said quietly. 'Our only hope is that as Lottie was so fond of him she'll probably contact him, somehow.'

Elizabeth nodded and suggested they should leave. They thanked Mrs Miller and the nurse as they left, and hardly took any notice of the telegram boy who walked past them as they reached the corner of the road.

They had walked several hundred yards before they heard Mrs Miller shout after them.

'She's done what you said, Mr Crabb. Miss Charlotte! She's sent a telegram.'

They rushed back and read the paper Mrs Miller showed them. Lottie was well, and in Paris.

Edward stared at Elizabeth, not really understanding what she had just said, then he roared, 'WHAT?'

'Lottie's been living with Hubert Belchester, but she doesn't know that's who he is, or anything about him.'

'Lizzie? Lizzie? Why?'

'He tricked her, somehow. We don't know exactly how, not for sure, but he didn't hurt her, Edward.'

'Well, where is she? Can I see her? How is she?'

'We're not sure where she is, Edward. She disappeared a few days ago, but we do know she's well, and being looked after.'

'How d'you know that?'

'Because she sent Hubert a telegram, Edward. Today. She's very fond of him, so you can see he didn't mistreat her.'

'I don't understand. Tell me—' His mouth dried up and he could not finish the sentence.

'I will, in a moment, but there's something else, first.'

He nodded for her to continue, his heart thumping and his hands sweating with worry and fear.

'Firstly, she's pregnant.'

He was horrified. 'Hubert?'

'No. He's very ill and he doesn't even know, but according to his nurse Hubert thinks she may have run off with Sasha. She hasn't because, as you know, Sasha left for America several weeks ago, but a young man who lives in Sasha's house told me she was alone with Sasha before he left.'

Edward's mind whirled as he tried to make sense of everything. 'She's pregnant but we don't know where she is. How pregnant? Where could she have gone?'

'Only a month or so, and we don't know exactly where she might have gone, but Peter Komovsky's disappeared, too, so they might be together.'

'I'm confused, Lizzie,' he admitted. 'Why did she run off if she was happy?'

Elizabeth did not answer so he asked her again, and when she did speak she burst into tears. 'Edward, I'm sorry, but I asked Bill if he could have the house watched and Lottie thought his friends had come to arrest her. That's why she ran away.'

'Arrest her for what, Lizzie? Arrest her for what?'

'Murder, Edward! She thinks she's killed someone.'

'What?' He felt his shaky world collapse around him. 'Murder? Murder? Lottie couldn't kill anyone!'

'She didn't, Edward, but Hubert tricked her into thinking she did. He tricked her so she would go with him and stay with him, but in the end it made her run away.'

'So she's hiding from the police, Lizzie. Just like I did, and for the same reason?' The shock had cleared his mind and sharpened his concentration. 'So Hubert's getting his revenge after all?'

'Yes, Edward,' Elizabeth said, wiping her eyes, 'but the irony is that he no longer wants it.'

He watched as she took a parcel out of her bag and placed it on the table.

'He sent this, addressed to Rose *Forrester*, Edward. Rose *Forrester*, and he's asked to see Rose when she's well enough, so he can apologise properly and explain.'

'Oh yes?' he said, suspiciously.

'I think he means it, Edward. He is very ill, perhaps dying.'

He looked at Elizabeth but did not answer. He could not commit Rose to doing that, even if she recovered before Hubert died, but it *would* put an end to it. They would not have to hide any more.

Meanwhile he would have to wait; for Rose to recover and Lottie to come home.

Edward was furious with Sasha for not indicating that Lottie was safe and well, but he did not wish to create a bad relationship with Katarina so he approached her very carefully.

'Did Sasha mention Lottie when you saw him at Christmas?'

'Not really, but he sat and played the music he wrote for her over and over. What makes you ask, Edward?'

'Lizzie's met someone who says they've been seeing each other. So much of each other that Lottie's expecting a baby.' Once he had started he could not keep his concerns to himself.

Katarina stared at him, not angrily but with a quiet, resigned, almost enlightened expression. 'Yes, I can see that would make sense. *Now.*'

'Only now? Why?'

'You may remember he wrote three endings for his piece and he said only Lottie could really choose how it should end. Each time he played it over Christmas he played the same ending. The happy one, Edward. The happy one.'

'Well, forgive me, Katarina, but I'll give him a happy ending when I get hold of him. We've been worried enough about Lottie for almost a year and now we find that Sasha's been seeing her but didn't tell us.'

'Please, Edward, I can understand why you're angry and I'm also annoyed with Sasha that he should repay your kindness in this way, but remember that we don't know for certain if we are correct, and if Lottie could go to see Sasha she could also have come to see you. Perhaps she told Sasha not to tell you about her?'

Katarina was right, of course, but that did not help his mood. 'I suppose you're right, but now it seems she's expecting a baby and instead of being somewhere safe she's in a foreign country.'

'She's gone to meet Sasha?'

'Well, she hadn't left for America this morning because she sent a telegram from Paris. Can you write to Sasha, let him know the situation and ask him to watch out for her?'

'Yes, I have an address to write to and a letter will be passed on to him but it will take some time because I don't know exactly where he is. Anyway, Edward, we are assuming it is his baby, but it might not be.'

'I'm sure it is, Katarina. I wondered months ago, even

352

before she left, if she was expecting his baby. It seemed inevitable that those two would come together one day.'

'So you don't mind, Edward?'

He sighed. 'No, I don't mind, Katarina. I don't mind at all. I just want her back. I've always wanted her back, ever since she drifted away when she was little. And I want Rose back, too.' He stood up quickly and walked to the window, his eyes burning with tears he had so far managed to keep to himself.

Edward still had not opened the parcel Lizzie had given him and now it was late, very late, and the house was quiet, he decided it was time he did so. His fingers trembled as he tore the brown paper open.

The first thing he found was Lottie's missing boot, the one he had accused her of throwing away. A folded razor and pieces of shoelace were tucked inside, and he could see how easy it had been to slice through the lace and remove the boot while Lottie was unconscious. A small bottle of chloroform showed why she had gone into what appeared to be such a deep faint.

Edward put those items aside, looked at a page from a newspaper printed in July 1912, and studied an article about the Hoxton Mission and the efforts made by Elizabeth Hampton and her sister-in-law, Rose Forrester, to help homeless women in the East End. Several reports from a firm of private detectives showed how Hubert had the family watched after he had read the report, and a copy of a letter to the shipping firm Lottie had joined proved he had given that company a contract to carry all his wine cargoes.

There were written records of information about Lottie which Mr Grundley had passed on to Hubert, and copies of detailed instructions telling two anonymous men exactly how they should work together to follow and intimidate Lottie, and ensure no one saw them.

Edward's hands shook as he picked up and read the final item, a receipt for the entire contents of Mr Joseph's offices; his furniture and his files.

'Oh, no.'

Now he understood why Hubert had called himself Mr Joseph. It had not only made it so much easier to tell Lottie what had happened in Pincote all those years ago, it also implied, as the defending barrister, that he was sympathetic, an ally, even a friend. No wonder Lottie was taken in.

This, after everything else Hubert seemed have done for her, must have made Lottie feel he was the only person in the world she could trust. And, Edward thought, it must have destroyed any remaining trust Lottie had in him or Rose.

He stared at the items on the table, some things quite insignificant in themselves, but together they were an indictment of his own stupidity and Hubert's cunning and cruelty.

But Lizzie said he had not been cruel. Lottie had telegraphed from abroad to tell him how she was.

It occurred to Edward that Lottie thought more of Hubert than she did of him or her own mother. He yearned to talk to her, explain everything, and then he began to sob. Enormous sobs that shook his body and made him ache.

When the tour ended Eve spent a week at home.

Both her father and Aunt Lizzie seemed to be very quiet. Neither would tell her what was wrong, and she assumed they were upset because her mother was not improving as they all hoped she would after reacting so strongly to hearing the name Hubert. At least they now realised why the name had caused such a reaction. Her mother had had an uncle Hubert who had killed himself.

After the week at home she returned to Eastbourne where Maud Whitton-White handed her a letter from an American suffrage organisation asking if she would like to speak in the United States in March. A broad smile spread across her face. America!

'You look happy,' a deep voice said and she looked up and saw Robert standing in the doorway. 'I thought I'd come and congratulate you on a splendid tour. You've certainly proved my mother totally wrong.'

'Thank you, Robert but that wasn't really the object of the exercise. Still, as we're on the subject of proving your mother wrong, how would you like to do the same?'

'I beg your pardon?'

'I've decided I'd like us to get married. Now. At once.'

'I beg your pardon?'

'Don't keep saying that. The last time we met you told me you loved me more than you could say. I assume that means you still want to marry me?'

'Of course it does. What's all this about, Evelyn?'

'It's largely about what your mother told me the last time I met her, and perhaps what you haven't actually told me.' Several weeks of thinking about this moment had not prepared her for it and she launched herself into an ill-prepared attack even when she knew that fighting with him was falling for his mother's ploy. 'Your mother doesn't approve of us, or perhaps she does. I'm not sure.'

'What are you talking about, Evelyn? You're not making sense.'

'Your mother told me she found me for you because I'm a greedy working girl who'll marry you then keep quiet when I find out.'

'Find out what?'

'That's what I asked her, Robert. She told me you can't satisfy women. She said that's why you'd gone back to spend Christmas with your boyfriend in France.'

'And you believed her?'

'What am I supposed to do? I don't feel you're being completely honest with me, Robert. I think you're holding something back and it worries me, especially in view of what your mother's said about you.'

'You're saying you don't trust me? Is that it? You don't trust me and you think I've been lying to you?'

She hesitated. She had pushed him to the brink and she did not want to push him any further but she could not stop now. He continually prevaricated and had not done one single thing to inspire any trust. 'No, Robert, I'm afraid I don't.'

'Fine.' He shrugged, turned around and walked away,

and before she had recovered from the shock she heard an engine burst into life and a motor-car drive down the gravelled yard. She reached the front door in time to see him turn through the gates.

So that was it. She had confronted him and he had not answered – not in the way she had hoped. The non-romance was over.

She turned, glad she still had much to occupy her, walked back to her office and composed an answer to the Americans accepting their invitation.

Then she wrote to Aunt Lizzie and told her that she was going to the United States, and that her non-affair with Robert Braithewaite had ended.

Elizabeth read Eve's letter, tactfully addressed to the mission and not to home, and read as much between the lines as she read on them.

She guessed Eve had been hot-headed when she dealt with Robert and that sooner or later she would regret it, a tendency they shared when dealing with men. She also guessed that the wish to go to America was as much to do with Eve's adventurous spirit as the belief that the movement would benefit from the tour.

She sat back, arms folded behind her head, and thought about how much Eve had achieved, and how ambitious her niece was compared to herself at the same age.

Elizabeth remembered how when she was twenty she was a village school teacher, and her most demonstrative act was to break off her engagement by publicly throwing a bucket of water over her fiancé because he had told her he wanted her to keep the fact she came from a mining family secret. The extent of her own political ambitions at that age was to write pamphlets explaining the advantages of education for all and better health care and housing. She had never even thought about having the right to vote, let alone hope to be elected to sit in the House of Commons.

Now she was fifty years old, living in a different world she did not quite understand. She went downstairs and put the kettle on for her evening tea, and heard Edward arrive.

'Lizzie, do you think you could talk to Belchester for me?'

'You can do it yourself, lad.'

'No, I couldn't trust myself to be civil, but I want to know when he might be fit enough to see Rose, if I can get her over to him.'

'Are you sure?'

'Yes,' he nodded. 'I reckon the time's come to put an end to all the arguments. They've already hurt Lottie and I've a feeling they'll destroy the family if we're not careful.'

She nodded. She was sure he was right, but she had an uneasy feeling he might already be too late.

CHAPTER 24

Edward looked out of the window at the early daffodils which were just opening in a sheltered part of the back garden, and thought that was how he would try to interest Rose.

He had spent hours trying to think how to tell her he wanted her to meet Hubert and he hoped he finally had it right. Hours spent thinking about it and hours more spent rehearsing; rehearsing and relearning a little speech old George Willis had taught him a long time ago. He guessed it must be around forty years since he learned it and probably thirty since he had last performed it. He just hoped Rose would remember its significance and react to it. His faith had failed him when Elizabeth told him what had happened to Lottie and he had stopped praying for Rose to recover because he thought God had abandoned him.

He went upstairs and talked to Rose just as he usually did every day.

'How're you feeling, sweetheart?' She did not respond, just as she never did, but he studied her face for the slightest sign of any movement, just as *he* always did. 'Just been looking out of the back window and the daffs're coming up again. Remember the daffodils around the old lodge at Pincote? Never saw 'em but you've told me about them so much I reckon I can see 'em as well as you. See 'em and smell 'em, just like this.'

He produced a bunch he had picked especially for her and wafted them in front of her, slowly so she could see them, and so she could smell them if she still had any sense of smell.

Her nostrils twitched. His heart thumped. He was on the brink. If he could not help Rose now, she was lost for ever.

'Rose! Remember that day I brought Lizzie up to the manor and you were trying to learn Portia's mercy speech from the *Merchant of Venice*, and we made Lizzie do it. Then I did King Henry at Harfleur. Remember?' He left the daffodils on the blanket right under her chin and threw himself into the speech.

'Once more unto the breach, dear friends, once more; or close the wall up with our English dead.' He worked through the speech, throwing himself at it, his face, his body and most of all his voice portraying the English king, until he reached the grand finale which he roared at the top of his voice. 'Cry "God for Harry, England and Saint George!" ' He looked down and saw tears streaming from Rose's eyes.

'Rose, come back to me, please! I need you now more than ever before. Don't slip away, not now. Please reach out and touch me, Rose, I'm desperate for you and I can't go on without you.'

'Edward?' she said weakly and he hugged her to him and cried so she could see how happy he was. 'Edward?'

'Yes, yes. Come on Rose, tell me what you want. Anything. Anything in the world, Rose, just tell me.'

'Cuddle me?' she cried quietly. 'Hold me so I don't fall again.'

He yanked the sheets back and lay beside her, holding her and cuddling her and telling her how much he loved her so she would not slip back again, and in his mind he was happy even if she never went to see Hubert Belchester. He had all he wanted in his arms and he didn't care what happened to the rest of the world.

Lottie always accompanied Peter on his business trips into the centre of Paris, and they always stayed at a different hotel, always booked in under false names and always pretended they were married. He insisted that was safer for both of them and she enjoyed the diversion of seeing different parts of the city because she had little to occupy herself with and the time often seemed to drag.

She had written several letters to Sasha, and Peter had suggested she ought to write to her parents and explain her situation. She had resisted at first, until he had reminded her that her future mother-in-law lived with her parents and that by continuing the rift between them she would prevent Sasha from seeing his mother, and prevent her child from meeting its grandparents.

It was during one seemingly endless afternoon that she decided Peter was right. Whatever her parents had done was in the past and she should not allow that to spoil her future. Having decided to write she took out her paper, prepared her pen, and tried to think what to say.

It was not easy but she was writing the letter when Peter came back to their room.

'Another letter to Sasha? I can't imagine what you find to say.'

'No, this one's to my parents. Shall I ask them to pass your love on to your mother?' She smiled at the surprise he could not conceal.

'Yes, please do, and ask them to tell her I've bought her rings back. I'll give them to her when I see her.'

'That's wonderful, Peter. How did you manage to do that?'

'I did it, Krasnaya, and that's all that matters.'

'When do you expect to see her?' she asked, carefully avoiding the expression *go home* because he always insisted he no longer had a home.

'When little Sasha comes to claim you, not before, so don't argue.'

'You make me sound like something in a pawn shop, Peter,' she said lightly.

He shrugged, grinned, placed his hands on her shoulders

and kissed her forehead. 'Krasnaya, if I had the ticket to redeem you I'd do it today.'

She smiled, and felt safe. She had misjudged him when she first met him. They had grown close during the weeks they had been together, sharing hotel rooms as though they were lovers or married, and living alone in Marguerite's house since they had obtained her keys and permission to stay there, but he had never once attempted to do anything more than kiss her hand or forehead.

She watched him walk back across the room, pick up the thin leather satchel he often carried and push it under the mattress. 'I've done all I can here, for the moment, Lottie, so I've told the hotel we'll leave in the morning.'

'Back to Marguerite's?'

'Yes. That is where you told Sasha to meet you?'

'Yes, but he may not even have received my letter yet and it could be weeks before he comes. Months even, if he can't reduce his contract. Are you sure you want to wait there all that time? I thought you had business in St Petersburg?'

'Not business, exactly, and it can wait.'

'Peter, why don't you go? I'll be all right in the house. Now I have somewhere to stay I'm not likely to be forced into earning a living from the streets as you said a few weeks ago.' She laughed to make herself sound more confident and capable of looking after herself, but she did not relish the thought of spending weeks on her own.

'No, I can't leave you, Lottie. You saw what happened the second night we came to Paris. I know we've always taken hotel rooms when I've come into the city to do business but I can't be sure no one knows about the house and I cannot put you at risk by leaving you alone there.'

They had seen no trouble since they had left London and she was beginning to believe he was exaggerating the dangers he lived with. She wondered if he had arranged their escape from the first Paris hotel purely to impress her or even to avoid paying the bill, but she could not really understand why he would want to do either.

'Well, Peter, if you remember I did suggest I go to St Petersburg with you?'

'And you may remember I said no because it's a hellhole and certainly no place for a woman in your condition.'

'Ah, but you once said it was a good place to give birth.'

'Not to babies, Krasnaya. I wasn't talking about giving birth to babies.' His voice deepened as it sometimes did. A brooding expression masked his face, and she knew better than to ask him to explain.

Rose sat and looked out of the window at the rain which had not stopped once during the three days since they came to Eastbourne. After all the weeks travelling backwards and forwards to hospital, and having the family crowding around her, always asking if she was all right when she was quiet, always trying to jolly her along, she was glad to get away and be alone with Edward, and also very grateful to Eve for arranging this holiday.

She did not mind not being able to leave the hotel. She was happy just to be there, watching all the everyday activities or simply sitting and reading until her eyes and head began to ache, but she could see Edward was becoming restless. 'Go for a walk, Darling. You don't have to stay with me all day.'

'I know, but I want to stay with you. I want to spend every minute with you now I've got you back and I don't ever want to be separated from you again.'

She smiled and squeezed his hand. 'I love you, Edward. I always have.'

She had, ever since she was six years old and her brother John had lost her in a fairground. Edward, an eight-year-old stranger, had looked after her until he found her parents and it seemed he had been looking after her ever since.

She saw him smile, and heard him say quietly so no one else could hear, 'And I love you, sweetheart. Much more than I can ever tell you.'

'I know,' she said, and squeezed his hand again.

Helen and Lizzie had told her how much time he had spent talking to her over the past year, talking to her and encouraging her month after month even though she gave no response and everyone else thought he should learn to

362

accept that she was never going to get better.

It was strange because she could half remember him being there, talking to her, but it seemed like minutes, not months. There were several times when she seemed to wake up but the deep sleep always came over her before she could pull herself together and shake off the comfortable slumber that made her feel so cosy and safe. It was the speech from Henry V which had roused her, taken her back to another time, although she could not admit to Edward that it was not a time when she was with him. In fact, at that time she thought he was dead.

She was with Hubert then, but she dare not tell Edward that. Strangely, when she was ill she dreamed she had gone off to the Savoy to meet Hubert without telling Edward, but she could not remember ever actually seeing Hubert in her dream. Just as well, probably. She might never have recovered if she had seen him again.

She stopped trying to think when her head began to hurt, and minutes later a gong sounded and they went into the dining room for luncheon. By the time they had finished the meal the rain had petered out and someone sitting near a window said the sun was trying to shine.

The sun shone on her face and the fresh air carried the smell of the sea.

'Into town or up along the cliffs?' Edward asked, leaving the choice to her.

'Can you manage the cliffs?'

'I reckon so, lass. I reckon so.' He shoved her wheelchair forward, negotiated two small steps without jarring her too much, and set off along a path which seemed to lead towards the sea, invisible below the high, sheer cliff.

She felt guilty about having to be pushed everywhere, and resentful that a single moment's carelessness could cripple her for life, but she was grateful she had come back to that life and that the rain had stopped because that meant Edward could take some exercise which might make him a little less restless. He was in a strange mood, as though he had something on his mind. Hopefully, out in the fresh air and with no one around, he might tell her what it was.

They climbed quite high and he pushed her out onto a slight promontory to a seat which faced the sea, latched the brake on her wheelchair and sat down beside her on the seat. The air was clear and all she could hear were screeching gulls and the rush of the sea.

Edward's arm suddenly went out. 'Look over there, by those stones,' and he was off, returning moments later with a small bunch of wild primroses. 'Remember, King's Crag at Pincote all those years ago, when we found some of these?'

She nodded and smiled, and brushed the flowers against her nose. 'Yes, I remember.'

He reached out and took her hand and they sat still, watching the sea move below them. She knew he was thinking about King's Crag and what had happened in Pincote all those years ago, but she was thinking about what had almost happened to her a year later, on a similar cliff-top overlooking the English Channel.

'Penny for them?' she heard him ask.

'Oh, it's nothing. Just something I remembered.'

'Pincote?'

'No, later,' she admitted, and when she saw him frown she knew she had to tell him even though it might upset him. 'I nearly killed myself once, you know. It was a year after I thought you'd died and I was standing on a cliff similar to this one thinking, I remember, that it was better to die young and tragically than old and lonely. I was very unhappy at the time and it was made worse because I'd also just found a bunch of primroses and, of course, they'd reminded me of the times up on King's Crag. Anyway, I was on the point of jumping off the cliff when Hubert's Grandpa grabbed me and pulled me back.'

She looked at him when she felt his hand tighten on hers. His face was creased as if he was in pain. 'Are you all right, Darling?'

'Yes. It's just when you talk about Hubert I—'

She knew he was hurt because he did not finish what he was saying, so she spoke gently when she said what she wanted to. 'He's a part of my life, of our lives, whether we like it or not, and we can't just cut that part out. Have you ever thought that if it hadn't been for Hubert we wouldn't have found each other again?'

He did not answer her question, but he did ask one of his own. 'Doesn't it hurt to think about him?'

'I don't do it very often, Darling, but no, not really. I've gone beyond that now. After all, it's what, twenty-five years since I left him? And I haven't seen him since.'

'Would you like to?'

She shrugged. 'He may not even be alive, Edward.' A seagull distracted her and she watched it cavort across the grass near her chair.

'But would you want to see him if you knew he was still alive? Or do you think it might bring back too many memories, be too frightening?'

'Too frightening? I don't think so, not now,' she said. She glanced back at him and guessed she had stumbled upon what was on his mind. 'You can't hide anything from me, my Darling, so tell me what's troubling you.'

'I know where Hubert is. He's very ill and dying—'

'But he wants to see me again?' she interrupted to save him any more pain.

'Yes.'

'I see,' she said quietly and now, faced with the reality, her confidence began to fade and the cosy, safe, sleepy world she had lived in for so long seemed to invite her back.

'You don't have to see him, sweetheart, and even if you want to see him you certainly don't have to do it until you feel you're ready.'

'And when might that be, Edward?'

'Only you can say, but from what Lizzie tells me I think—'

'Lizzie? Has she seen him?'

'Yes. Some weeks ago.'

'Oh, but you didn't tell me because you thought I might not be able to cope?' she asked sharply.

'Something like that,' he admitted quietly.

She thought for a moment, a little irritated by the way they had protected her, but then she realised she could not blame them and they were only doing what they thought was best for her. 'And how was he?'

'He's had a seizure and he's partly paralysed, he's very slow and he can't talk properly.'

'Is he going to die?'

'Possibly.' Edward nodded, and she heard a slightly optimistic tone in his voice as he added, 'Quite frankly I'd half hoped he might die before you had a chance to see him.'

'Oh, don't think like that, Darling,' she said softly and saw the astonishment on his face, so she thought she should explain quickly. 'After all this time I've nothing to fear but fear itself, and not seeing him would be like running away all over again – admitting I'm scared of him and what he could do to me, or you or the children. I need to face up to him before he dies or I'll never know how it feels to prove to him that he can't bully me any more. I'll never know how strong I really am.'

Edward looked at her and he wondered how strong she really was, whether the strain of seeing Hubert or even telling her the truth about Lottie might push her back down into the labyrinth she had only just escaped from. Unfortunately there was only one way to find out, and he could see from the expression on her face that she was determined to put herself to the test.

'You still want to tell me something else, don't you?' she asked. 'About Lottie?'

He nodded. 'She's quite well and she wrote to us a few days ago. I've written back explaining everything so I'm hoping she'll forgive me and might come home.'

'Why didn't you show me her letter, Edward?' Rose asked astutely.

He sighed, walked a few feet away and looked out to sea, the only way he could hide the tears which were streaming down his face, and gently told her as much of the truth as he knew.

Rose did not speak for a long while. When she did speak she simply said, 'Come here, Darling. I want to hold you. You sound as though you need someone to hold you.'

CHAPTER 25

Rose looked up at the house in Leinster Place and thought Lottie should have enjoyed living there because it was exactly the sort of house she wanted, and with that in mind she asked Bill Crabb to carry her to the front door while Lizzie wrestled the wheelchair up the steps.

She had insisted Edward did not come. It would have been too much to expect Edward to be civil to the man who had tortured her and intimidated their daughter into running away from home. Besides, Hubert wanted to see her alone and it would have seemed almost cowardly not to meet him on his terms. Also she wanted to ask questions she could not ask with Edward present. She wanted to know what Hubert did to become closer to Lottie than Edward ever had, and whether his relationship with Lottie had ever gone beyond the father and daughter relationship Mrs Miller had described to Lizzie.

She had found it difficult to decide what clothes to wear because she did not want to appear either too dowdy or too attractive, but suddenly, for the first time in her life, she had sensed that it did not matter how she dressed. She was not attractive any more. She was drawn and scrawny and grey, so she chose a loose-fitting high-necked woollen dress in warm maroon, and added a little elegance with a long looped pearl necklace. Edward had kissed her and gazed at her just as he always had, and although she knew she did not look beautiful it did not matter. He made her *feel* beautiful, and that had boosted her confidence.

She thanked Bill as he placed her back in the wheelchair and draped her cape around her, and she nodded to Lizzie for her to pull the bell. Her heart thumped noisily as she waited for the door to be opened for her to enter the house she had run away from five years before Lottie was born.

She noted ironically that she had run away from this house with two babies in her arms, and now she was being carried back in someone else's arms.

'Mrs Forrester?' the woman who opened the door asked in a kind voice. 'I'm Mrs Miller, Mr Joseph's housekeeper. Please come in.'

'Thank you, Mrs Miller.' She shook hands with the kindly-looking lady. 'I'd like to thank you for taking care of Charlotte for so long. I wouldn't have been half so worried if I'd known she was in such friendly hands.'

'She was nothing but a pleasure, Mrs Forrester. I enjoyed every minute I spent with her, and that's credit to the way you brought her up.'

Rose smiled her appreciation to Mrs Miller and then turned to Lizzie and Bill, assured them she could be left alone, asked them to collect her by taxi at eleven o'clock so they could all be home by midnight, and watched them leave.

She asked Mrs Miller to take her cape and then wheeled herself through an open door and into a large room off the hall. She gasped, 'Mrs Miller, I first came into this room almost exactly twenty-eight years ago. I wasn't quite nineteen years old then and it hasn't changed at all.'

'Unlike us, Rose. Good evening. It's so nice to see you,' Hubert said from somewhere behind her.

She turned her chair and tried to hide the shock she felt when she saw him. She could see he was trying not to react to the shock of seeing her.

368

His nurse had pushed him in and he sat lopsided in his wheelchair, his drawn and twisted face emphasising his ungainliness, and although she could still see some of his youthful beauty it was nothing other than an impression of what he had been. The slim, graceful cat that he had once reminded her of was squashed now, broken and dishevelled.

She knew she looked only a little better. She was skeleton thin, her head was skull-like and her hair was brittle and grey.

Mrs Miller broke the silence which developed as neither of them spoke. 'Would you like us to leave you alone?'

Hubert's mouth twitched and his forehead and eyes showed he was trying to smile. He slurred his answer. 'Yes, but push me to the table please, Nurse. I'm not as agile as Rose.'

The nurse obligingly pushed him to a small table which had been set for two, a table which had been lowered so they could eat without leaving their wheelchairs. Rose followed, manoeuvring herself to sit opposite him.

'It's a long time since we sat at the same table, Hubert,' she said, careful not to concede too much reserve too quickly.

'Yes, and I apologise for that, Rose. I should have come to meet you. It was inexcusable of me – almost.'

His answer confused her. It did not make sense. 'Pardon? I don't understand.'

'The Savoy. I should have come.'

'The Savoy?'

'You came twice, at my invitation. I watched you, and thought you looked very beautiful, and I used one of their telephones to telephone another of their numbers to make my apologies. It was wrong. I should have joined you. But I cannot regret what followed.'

'I thought I'd dreamed all that,' she admitted without feeling any embarrassment. It was not the first time she had admitted to being confused by something forgotten or only half-remembered and Edward and the others were quite used to it by now.

'Oh, my dear Rose, you really are in a poor state.'

She thought he sounded genuinely sorry, but although she did not lower her defences she did give him a sympathetic smile. 'And you. What caused this?'

'Inherited from my father, Rose.'

She laughed a little ironically. 'Ah, yes. Edward often complains he can see himself turning into his father.'

'Edward? You're very happy with him, aren't you?'

'Yes,' she said quickly and firmly and without even trying to hide her objection to his making such a comment. 'We're still happy even after all these years, Hubert.'

She saw him wince and knew she had hurt him but it did not give her any satisfaction. Surprisingly, it left her feeling uncomfortable and a little guilty, but she knew how to redress that. 'I've been told what you did, Hubert.'

'So you know?'

'Everything. The way you had Lottie followed and abducted, the way you manipulated events at the mission, the way—'

'Please, Rose,' he interrupted her, his voice mild but laboured as he struggled to speak clearly. 'I've admitted I was wrong. I gave you my "confession box" because I was too ill to explain in any other way. I had intended you to have it when I died, but events rather overtook me. I asked you here so I could apologise personally for all I've ever done to you, to try to make amends and, perhaps most importantly, to explain what made me change.'

His response stunned her, but she asked him to continue, and not to spare her feelings.

'Very well, Rose. You married me, Rose, but you still loved Edward Forrester even though you thought he was dead. Did you ever wonder how that made me feel? Then you ran away, and when I found you with him the only reason you came back to me was to save him and his children. I grew to hate you, Rose, and Edward Forrester, and even your children. Especially later when both my parents were dead and I was alone. I hated you even though I supposed you were dead, but then I learned that you weren't only alive but were happy and surrounded by a family. It seemed very unfair to me, Rose, that you and Edward Forrester should be so happy when you were the reason for my loneliness and misery.' He paused for several seconds. 'For a while I wanted to destroy everything you had and make you miserable too. And I would have done so, if Charlotte, your own daughter, Rose, hadn't taught me what it was like to be loved. *Really* loved.'

'Mrs Miller told Lizzie that Charlotte loved you like a father. Was it ever any more than that?' She was haunted by the thought that innocent Lottie could have been tainted by him.

'Please don't worry, Rose. I was very proper with her and did little more than a father might, except that I had her dress in your clothes and sleep in your bed, and for a short while I pretended she *was* you. I stole her from you, to hurt you, but then I fell in love with you all over again. Through Charlotte you filled my life with your love and warmth, and for a while I believed you had never left me.'

He paused while Mrs Miller served their first course, a mixture of cold meats, and Rose noticed that Hubert's had been cut into small pieces. After Mrs Miller left he forked the food into his mouth and Rose realised, now he had stopped talking, that for a while he had spoken without slurring a word. She ate her own food and waited for him to talk again.

'But it wasn't you, Rose. I'd fallen in love with Charlotte and I believe she loved me in return. I convinced her she needed my protection, and I found I needed her trust. Rose, you don't know how terribly sorry I am now. It was a trick which brought Charlotte to me, but the same trick drove her away in the end. Drove her away from both of us.' He suddenly burst into tears, something she had never seen him do before, and she began to feel sorry for him and even feel guilty that she was partly to blame for the miserable life he had led.

She should never have married him. She had loved him for a little while, or thought she did, but Edward was the only man she had ever really loved, or would ever love.

She nodded reassurance to Mrs Miller who looked very

agitated when she came in with the next course, then she wheeled herself around to Hubert's side and put her arm around his shoulders until he stopped crying.

'Hubert, how did she meet Sasha Komovsky?'

He told her what had happened in Hyde Park and how he had tested Lottie with the note of Sasha's address. 'I was wrong to test her. She trusted me and I should've trusted her.'

'Fragile thing, trust, Hubert. Edward and I find it hard to trust anyone.'

'I know,' he said. 'That was why I knew I could hurt you both so easily, just by revealing your secrets.'

'And now you wish you hadn't?' she asked, and believed him when he nodded. 'Well, despite everything you've done, no one except Lottie knows anything more than we do.'

'I won't tell anyone else, Rose.'

'Thank you.' The relief was short lived.

'But I think *you should*, Rose, or you'll always be scared they'll find out.'

She nodded, not committing herself. He was right, of course, but she did not have the courage, not yet.

There was a long silence while they both picked at their food, and then, after they pushed their plates aside, they talked about Helen and Jamie, not the names Hubert had insisted upon giving them when they were born, and their children, and about Eve who was at sea and bound for America.

They refused the other dishes Mrs Miller brought in and sat and drank weak tea until ten o'clock when Hubert suddenly sighed very deeply. 'Rose, I feel very tired. Would you mind if I retired early?'

'No, of course not.'

'Will you come again?' he asked eagerly.

'Perhaps, but I'm not sure if that would be wise,' she said, aware that Edward might feel hurt if she suggested future visits.

'I understand, and I have a present for you,' he said quietly and rang a hand-bell.

Mrs Miller came in, handed her a large envelope, and left after a long look at Hubert.

He nodded towards the envelope she held, his eyes heavy, and when he spoke his words were badly slurred. 'The mission's title deeds are in the envelope, and stock and share certificates which should provide an income to support it.'

'There's really no need, Hubert—'

'There is. For me. To make amends. I'm ashamed, Rose, for now and before.' He rang the hand-bell to call Mrs Miller back. 'I didn't want to die without you knowing, Rose, or without seeing you again. And I wanted to tell you I've forgiven you for all you did. I understand, now, what it's like to love someone the way you love Edward, and to be loved in return, and how that feeling overpowers everything else. Charlotte taught me that.'

Mrs Miller appeared and he told her he wanted to be taken to his room, then he tried to smile once more. 'Goodnight, Rose. Thank you for coming. I hope Charlotte finds the right young man, someone who'll love her as much as I do.'

She wheeled herself close enough to take his hand and squeeze it. 'Goodnight, Hubert. I'm sure she will.'

Rose deliberately did not tell him Lottie was expecting Sasha's child. It would have hurt him too much and, significantly, she wanted to protect him from any more pain.

The past was done with and he had forgiven her even though he had not asked her to forgive him. That was just as well because she never would.

She suddenly felt very old and haggard, sitting in a room she remembered from a time when she was young and beautiful.

She began to cry, not for herself as much as for the years everyone had wasted hating and being afraid. After several minutes she felt someone's hands resting on her shoulders. Mrs Miller smiled at her and asked if she would object to company.

'No, Mrs Miller. I'd love some company. It'll remind me of the few good days I spent in this house, not the worst.'

They did not know anyone was in the hotel room until Peter had closed the door and switched on the electric light, and then it was too late. Two men grabbed Peter's arms and a third came from behind. He slipped a garrote around Peter's neck and pulled it so tight the wire cut into Peter's skin and made it bleed.

Another man, who stood back in shadow, was the only one to speak. 'Komovsky?' he asked gruffly.

'No,' Peter snorted.

Lottie saw a fifth man edge towards her and she backed away until she felt the wall behind her. She stood very still and did not know what to do with her hands or eyes as the man looked her over closely, and unconsciously licked back the saliva which had formed in his mouth and spilled onto his lips.

'Mademoiselle,' he said very properly, but his eyes were not on hers, they were ranged somewhere between her breasts and her thighs and she felt as though he was looking through her clothes at her naked body.

The man in the shadows growled again. 'This is Komovsky's room and that is Komovsky's woman.'

'This is Komovsky's room,' Peter agreed, 'but she is anyone's woman. Anyone who can afford her.'

The answer obviously confused the man in the shadows. 'If you are not Komovsky, who are you?'

'You don't recognise me?'

'No. Not in this light.'

'Then turn the light onto my face so you can see me better. And loosen that cable. It's cutting me.' The wire noose was loosened and the man stepped out from the shadows, reached up to tilt the green wigwam lampshade so the bulb spilled light onto Peter's face. Peter blinked in the light, then asked, 'Well?'

No one spoke and she heard exasperation in Peter's voice as he said, 'Grinevetsky. I am Grinevetsky.'

She could see the name frightened the men holding

Peter's arms, and the slight tremble in the other man's voice showed that he, too, was nervous.

'You are Pavlo Grinevetsky?'

'No, you fool, I'm his cousin, but if you've been clumsy enough to frighten off Komovsky I think you may well get to see Pavlo for yourselves. Now let me go and you can all get out of here the way you came in. I don't want Komovsky warned that there's anyone here but her. I want to kill him in the act, if you understand. When he is defenceless.'

The men crowded towards the door but Peter stopped them. 'Not that way! He's due now and he'll see you. The window!'

The only man who had spoken opened the window and leaned out. 'We're two floors high!'

Peter shoved all the men towards the window. 'Yes, and dropping onto bushes. Pavlo'll throw you off a high roof if Komovsky gets away.' Moments later they heard a door bang at the end of the corridor.

'Jump!'

She could see the men were not going to jump and that Peter had pushed his bluff too far, but there was another way out, the escape route Peter always insisted every room should have. She ran across the room, opened the washroom door, and said to them in French, 'This way. Through this window. There're steps down to the street.'

She opened the window for them and watched them leave then shut the window and fastened the catch. In the few seconds it took her to return to the bedroom Peter had already started packing.

'Thank you, Krasnaya. They wouldn't have jumped.'

'No. Why did you want them to?'

'This is supposed to be my first time here, remember? Besides, they would have hurt themselves a little and that might have slowed them if they followed us.'

'Who were they, Peter?'

'I don't know. They obviously didn't know who I was or they'd have beaten me senseless and raped you.'

'They weren't here to kill you?'

'No, Lottie. They were cheap thugs, not killers. But they did what they were meant to.'

'What's that.

He had already finished packing both his clothes and hers. 'Frighten me out of Paris.'

He opened the door and pulled her towards him, and when her hand went up to turn off the light he stopped her. 'Leave it on. If they're watching they'll assume we're still here.'

He took the bags and told her to leave the hotel, cross over the road, turn right and walk close to the kerb, and then he stepped backwards into a service corridor and left her alone. She did as he said and after a little more than one block a taxi-cab pulled up in front of her and the door swung open. She stepped in and the taxi drove smoothly out into the traffic.

'And who is Grinevetsky?' she asked Peter as he leaned across her lap and pulled the door shut.

'Probably the biggest man in our business. Quite ruthless.'

'And is he trying to have you killed?'

'I shouldn't think so,' he said calmly. 'I'm only in trouble in England because I was trying to help him, and in return he helped me recover my mother's rings.'

'So everything you said to those men was bluff?'

'Of course, Krasnaya. That's how most people lead most of their lives. But I'm afraid I have used up my entire supply of bluff and now it'll be safer for both of us if we leave Paris.'

She remembered the way the man who guarded her had looked at her, and Peter's comment that if they had known who he was they would have beaten him and raped her. 'St Petersburg?'

'Yes. I have things to do and I have friends who will offer us beds and food until Sasha comes.'

'But he'll come to Paris!'

'Yes, and I'll leave something to help him guess where we are. Don't worry.'

But she was worried. Once again she had been wrong

about Peter. He did live dangerously. It was not simply a game he played, and if he was in danger then she was, too, and Russia was a strange country whose language she did not speak. And he had said St Petersburg was not a good place to have children.

'Peter, will I have time to write to Sasha before we leave?'

'No, but you'll have plenty of time once we're on a train, and then you should write to your parents also, in case Sasha doesn't receive his letter before he leaves America. You can post the letters at a railway station before we leave France.'

She could see he intended to leave immediately because he asked the taxi driver to wait for them. It took very little time to gather up their belongings and load them into the taxi and the last thing Peter did was place something in a dovecote in the front garden.

'For Sasha,' he said without being asked.

As they drove away they passed the man who delivered post along the street, and seeing him reminded her that her parents had not yet replied to her original letter. Then she forgot about that and asked Peter what St Petersburg was really like.

Eve stood on deck and watched America come towards her.

New York. It was so overwhelming she could not believe it actually existed – it must be part of a dream and before long she would wake up and find she was back in Angel Street, an ordinary young woman training to be a nurse and with no particular ambition in life.

Everything had happened so fast. In little more than a year she had won a political voice, albeit a small one compared to the Pankhursts and many other women who were making themselves heard, but it was a voice, and one which most English newspapers seemed to like.

There were exceptions, the most surprising being the *London and National Cryer* whose printers she had tried to save from Violet Braithewaite's bomb. Its Political Editor, Cedric Rathbone, sniped at her at every opportunity and she assumed that was because he resented the newspaper's owner insisting that he suppress the story about her earliest suffrage activities.

She would soon learn whether or not the American newspapers liked to hear what she had to say, and she was grateful for the advice Mrs Pankhurst had personally given her about how to respond to the Americans and the American press – be clear-minded, commonplace and enthusiastic.

When Mrs Pankhurst had last arrived in America she had promptly been held for deportation on the dubious grounds of 'Moral Turpitude' and President Wilson had personally intervened to reverse the deportation order. Eve had been guaranteed that would not be the case when she arrived because her leadership of the WFL had changed it from a militant suffrage movement to a passive movement which attempted to advance not only the political but the social and economic needs of women.

She had smiled when she read the guarantee in the letter which confirmed details of the tour and thought it more probable that she was being allowed to travel freely because no one outside Great Britain knew who she was. She did not have the Pankhurst reputation or charisma.

Three fashionable young women met her as the ship docked and confidently whisked her away to her hotel. Their combination of friendliness and composure was overpowering, as was the size of the comfortable car, and the fact that while they were driving through the bustling streets she could not see the tops of any buildings – they just seemed to go on up for ever.

Eve had nearly exhausted herself on her English tour and she was daunted to find the Americans had prepared a programme which was even more intense. However, she found that much of the travel was at night and on trains where she could sleep, and everything was so well-organised that the effect was more leisurely. The Americans also had a greater sense of fun than their English counterparts and she found herself speaking at baby shows, arranged to prove that suffragettes could also be good and loving mothers, at needlework parties where the women made and repaired clothes for the needy and at shelters where they helped to care for the homeless. The whole thrust of the American suffragettes was to prove themselves to be ordinary, caring women who wanted to have the same rights as their menfolk to say how their country should be run.

A month passed quickly and suddenly Eve was taking the final overnight train journey back to New York with the three women who had taken care of her since she arrived in their enormous country. They were all relaxed and had just started toasting each other with their second bottle of champagne when a young newspaperman whom she had already met several times paused at their table.

'Miss Forrester, you certainly have a way with the press. I've never seen anyone so at ease and open with us.'

'Thank you.' She smiled at him, grateful the advice she had been given by Mrs Pankhurst had helped her so much. 'I've had some disagreements with a few English newspapers about the way they've reported my activities and speeches, but I've only ever had real trouble with one newspaper, the *London and National Cryer*.'

'Of course you did.' He slapped his hands together. 'What actually happened? Somehow I can't imagine you exploding bombs.'

'Well, it wasn't that much of an exaggeration, except that I was actually trying to stop someone else exploding a bomb and I was too late arriving. The poor girl killed herself. I was injured, and blamed for the explosion,' she said, aware that the champagne was making her talk more openly than she should have.

'Totally circumstantial, huh? Surely your lawyers could've made a better case, Miss Forrester?'

'Maybe, but it might have hurt a lot of people if I'd defended myself better. Anyway, it projected me into politics in a way I could never have achieved without the notoriety those few weeks in prison gave me. Within months I found myself elected leader of the WFL and in a position to change its policies, so from that point of view it helped me. I'd have preferred it if Lou Dobbs hadn't been killed, of course, especially as I'd seen her sister, Polly, die from the effects of forced feeding only a few weeks earlier.'

Then, because the other women said they should not allow the conversation to dwell on such gloomy matters they talked about other things – fashion, art, literature and music. She had already told them Sasha was also somewhere in America and now they asked a number of questions about Sasha and her life at home. She talked for as long as she could but the effect of the long tour, the relaxing company and the champagne took their toll and she excused herself and went to her bunk.

They left the train the following morning and a porter wheeled their baggage to a motor-car which was waiting outside the station. The other women sent Eve ahead with the luggage while they completed some formalities, and as she slid into the car's rear seat she heard a man say, 'Good morning, Evelyn. I trust you had an enjoyable tour.'

She was stunned. 'Sasha!'

They hugged each other and it was several moments before she was composed enough to ask him why he was there.

'Your friends have arranged for us to sail together, Evelyn.'

'But how did they find you? Anyway, you're not due to go home yet.'

'Things have changed. You do not know?'

Her heart fell. 'Know what?'

'About Lottie? I met her again before I came to America. More than simply met her,' he admitted sheepishly, and quickly told her he was going to France to marry Lottie who was expecting his baby.

'That's wonderful,' she said, and smiled to hide the pin-prick of jealousy she suddenly felt.

When they reached the dock Eve suddenly realised her adventure was almost over and it was time to go home. She thanked the American ladies for their care and help, and they cried as they said goodbye. She cried too, but she was glad to be leaving. She had enjoyed America, and thought the people she met were wonderful and energetic and extremely polite, but now she was leaving she yearned for England and peace and quiet. Most of all she wanted privacy.

She was still a very minor figure in British politics but she had already sacrificed her personal life to pursue her political ambitions, and she was no longer sure she wanted to continue doing that, because now the American adventure was over she realised that she was going back to nothing.

She had left her home in Angel Street a year ago and had become so used to her independence that she could never go back to living with her parents, but she had no proper home of her own, no real job other than the virtually honorary position of running the WFL, and she had no one to share her life with. She looked at Sasha and thought about him and Lottie, and realised how much she envied them their futures, domestic and otherwise.

After the first day at sea she managed to put her worries aside and the return voyage became a total pleasure. Sasha was wonderful company. He talked when she felt like talking and he was quiet when she wanted to be quiet. They ate together and danced together, and stood together on deck and watched the stars and the sea's phosphorescence.

Sasha was such good company that she had to keep reminding herself that her sister was expecting his baby.

Suddenly the ship had docked in Cherbourg for its last night before Southampton and she knew it would soon be time to face the future. She sat down for her final dinner on board, amid the bunting and noise and gaiety that combined to create a party atmosphere, and she felt sad. To make matters worse Sasha told her he was leaving the ship in the morning and travelling directly to Paris to find Lottie.

The crew did all they could to make all the passengers enjoy the final night's party and when she could not stand the merriment any longer she walked out on deck and stared at the moon trailing its light across the black, mirror-calm sea.

The sound of singing came from somewhere on the ship, rousing choruses of the last year's and the previous year's popular tunes.

The wind rustled her hair and shawl and she gripped the rail hard as the words floated past her. 'You made me love you, I didn't want to do it, I didn't want to do it, you made me . . .'

Tears flowed from her eyes and her heart ached, not especially for Sasha but for someone who would stand by her, someone she could turn to for comfort, someone to hold her when she felt scared and lonely, as she did now.

She gulped and let the warm breeze dry her face, and as bells told her it was midnight a door opened and she heard the swell of another song from a year or more ago.

'It's a long way to Tipperary, It's a long way . . .' The door shut off the sound, she dried her face properly, retouched the make-up she rarely used, put on a bright smile and went back to join the party.

The following morning Sasha gave her a letter to pass on to his mother. She kissed him goodbye, told him to give Lottie her love and to bring her to Eastbourne as soon as he could.

She stood on deck and watched him walk along the quayside, soft-brimmed hat on the back of his head, raincoat thrown over his shoulder, and carrying a large leather valise which held all his possessions.

She thought he looked like a man with very little but knew he actually had so much more than her.

She watched him until he turned and waved, then disappeared into a building, and then she set her thoughts on arriving at Southampton.

Eve's sense of loneliness increased as the ship ploughed across the Channel towards England, towards her comfortless and institutionalised life in the White House which was her headquarters rather than her home. Her mood was made worse because there was an anti-climactic atmosphere on board the ship and she was pleased when a pair of ugly-looking tugs came out to tow the sleek ocean-crossing ship into a dock.

She was even more pleased when she had collected her cases and stood outside the shipping offices on an ordinary English pavement and felt normality soaking into her, but the sensation did not last for more than a few moments.

'Miss Forrester?'

She turned and saw a man with a notebook held ready, and knew the privacy she had enjoyed on board ship had ended.

'Good evening,' she smiled, then frowned as he handed her a newspaper.

'What comment do you have to make about this story, Miss Forrester?' She glanced at the newspaper, opened and folded with one story outlined with heavy pencil lines, read the headline and continued on through the report.

SUFFRAGE LEADER LIED TO COURT

An American newspaper has reported that Miss Evelyn Forrester, the new leader of the Women's Freedom League, has admitted that she misled the English Court when she was charged with exploding a bomb at premises owned by this newspaper's printers.

Miss Forrester pleaded Not Guilty to the charge and offered no defence because she claimed the bombing was a political act committed in the interest of women's suffrage and she should not be tried as a common criminal. She was sentenced to two years imprisonment but was released in a matter of weeks because of public concerns which were voiced following her hunger strike.

According to the latest report it appears that Miss Forrester has now claimed that she had no part in the plan to bomb the printers. She became involved when she attempted to prevent the bomb being exploded but having arrived too late and sustained minor injuries she realised there was a political advantage to be gained from suppressing the truth in order to obtain public sympathy for her cause.

Many British newspapers and politicians who have

*supported what they believed were Miss Forrester's moderate
and honest policies now have reason to cast doubt upon her
future as leader of the WFL.*

'Well, Miss Forrester? Do you have anything to say?'

'What would you like me to say?' she asked him quietly.

'Would you deny the report's accuracy, Miss Forrester?'

'I can't see the value of my making any comment to your
newspaper because you'll probably misrepresent anything
I say. Good day.' She turned away and then turned back.
'I'm surprised Cedric Rathbone wasn't sent here to meet
me?'

'He's been given a special assignment and been sent out
to the Balkans, miss. The Serbians are attacking the
Albanian Moslems and it looks like there could be another
war out there.'

'Not another one. It's less than a year since the last one
ended,' she said wearily and waved down a taxi-cab. She
guessed the article was Rathbone's parting shot at her, and
she knew it could be his most damaging.

She went to the railway station and asked for a ticket to
Eastbourne, then on impulse changed her mind.

'No, I'm sorry, but can you please change that. I think I'd
like to go to London, instead.' Maud Whitton-White could
continue deputising for her until she felt ready to return. If
she ever felt ready to return.

The taxi driver heaved her cases out of the cab and carried
them to the front door, thanked her when she paid him, and
drove off into the late evening gloom. She did not knock
immediately because she needed a few moments to think,
to adjust to a different life, and to prepare herself before she
saw her parents.

She had assumed her father would be relieved when her
mother came back to life but he had been very quiet, even
worse after their short holiday in Eastbourne, and her
mother had also changed. She wondered what they would
be like now, a month after she had last seen them. She had
written home every week but because she was moving

nearly every day and it was impossible to predict how long post would take to arrive from England her parents had not written to her and so she had no idea how they felt about Lottie expecting Sasha's child.

She took a deep breath, knocked on the door, and gasped when her father opened it and immediately threw his arms around her.

'Eve! You look wonderful.'

'So do you, Papa.' She was astounded by how much fitter and happier he looked.

'Come in. Come in.' He bustled her inside and told her to go and see her mother in the kitchen while he carted her cases into the hall.

'Mama, you've put on weight and you look wonderful.' She hugged her mother and noticed she was well covered now, not half as boney as she had been, and that her green eyes were beginning to sparkle again.

'It's your father and Aunt Lizzie, and Katarina. They take very good care of me. And your letters helped. Anyway how are you?'

They talked and drank the inevitable tea, and she told them that she had met Sasha in New York and he had explained about Lottie and sailed home with her but left the ship at Cherbourg.

'Well, he won't find her in Paris with Peter,' her mother said quietly. 'She's with Peter but they've gone to Russia.'

'Russia? Why? I thought Peter had run away from Russia?'

Her father shrugged. 'I've a feeling that you and Peter have something in common. Politics.'

Politics? She was too tired to think any more about politics, even her own, and when her father asked her if she had read the latest story about herself she simply told him she had.

'D'you think it could harm you, Eve?' He was clearly concerned enough to have thought about the consequences.

'Politically? Yes, it probably will. Personally? No, because there's nothing left to harm. I don't have a proper personal life any more, Papa.'

Her mother reached out and squeezed her hand. 'You sound bitter, Eve? Are you?'

'Not bitter, Mama, just sad. I'm well on the way to achieving nearly everything I hoped to, and I don't know if I want it any more.'

Rose looked at her daughter, saw the way her lips were drawn tight across her mouth and sensed her disappointment. Eve almost had what she wanted and yet she was unhappy.

Lottie had also found what she once had wanted, and that had made her unhappy.

Perhaps there was a lesson to be learned from these two, and perhaps she and Edward should not try to achieve all their dreams because with nothing left to dream for, they too might be unhappy.

She searched desperately for something to make Eve feel better or at least distract her, and only one thing came to mind.

'Tom Dobbs has called here twice since that story was printed about you.'

'Oh yes?' Eve sounded wary.

'He says he knows the story isn't true and he's not sure about your personal circumstances now, but if you'd like to see him he'd still be very happy to meet you.'

She was surprised to see the change in Eve.

Suddenly the sadness seemed to pass and Eve smiled, but it was only momentary.

CHAPTER 26

There were several reasons why Eve did not rush to see Tom Dobbs. The unguarded comments she had made during her last night in America had diminished her reputation and that had reflected on the WFL so she felt she had to spend time repairing the harm she had done.

Also, several WFL members told her that Lady Braithewaite was covertly criticising her non-militant stand when the WSPU and other suffrage organisations were generally causing mayhem in the name of the cause. Finally she learned by accident that Lady Braithewaite was also developing her greedy working girl campaign in the hope of discrediting Eve on the basis of too much personal ambition.

Lady Braithewaite's secretive campaigns actually renewed Eve's energy to fight for what she believed in, particularly when the London and National Cryer appeared to give her indirect support by reporting in its Social Column that the editor of the American newspaper which first reported the 'Suffrage Leader Lied to Court' story had been entertained at Lady Braithewaite's home for seven nights.

But the main reason she did not rush to see Tom Dobbs

was that she did not want him to think she was too eager to see him. Even when she did call on him some weeks later she felt uneasy talking with him in the Jacksons' front room, especially when he told her he had joined the suffrage movement.

'Why, Tom?'

He looked uncomfortable. 'I'm not the only man to support your cause. Anyway, I've lost two sisters because of it and I think I owe it to them to do something to help.'

'What do you do, exactly?'

'March, protest, sign petitions. Anything, really. We've got a demonstration tomorrow, at Buckingham Palace. Why don't you come as you're in London?'

'All right, but only to watch and build up the numbers.' She did know about it but had not intended to go. 'At least we'll be well chaperoned, Tom, surrounded by a few thousand women and, no doubt, a good number of policemen.'

He smiled softly. 'Yeah. Perhaps, afterwards, we could go on somewhere, for a proper rendezvous.' His smile brightened. 'See, I've even been learning French just to impress you a bit more.'

She was not very enthusiastic about going out with him but she thought that after all that had happened to Polly and Lou she did owe him some of her time. 'Yes, if you'd like to.'

'Really?'

'Yes,' she said, but when she saw him grin she tried to find a way to caution him that she was offering friendship, nothing more. There was a way, a way he would appreciate because it meant she was turning his joke back on him. 'But that doesn't mean you have to marry me, Tom.'

He laughed and she felt happier now she had made her position clearer.

She did not laugh the following day when she saw how many policemen were massed outside the Palace gates, and saw the way they drew their sticks and prepared themselves as the column of suffragettes marched towards them.

'The women only want to present a petition to the King,' Tom said, standing by her side.

'They won't even get near the gates, Tom,' she said and as she looked across the heads in the crowd she saw four or five policemen already grappling with two women who had pulled them to the ground.

A moment later Tom was shouting and running towards the scuffle.

'Tom!' She tried to grab him and missed, lost her footing and fell.

As she scrambled upright she saw Tom pull two of the policemen off the women and reach for another. A sharp crack with a police truncheon stopped him and pushed him onto his knees. She saw Tom clutch the policeman's legs and the policeman raise his truncheon to hit Tom's head again.

'Don't!' she screamed and dived to protect Tom. 'He's already had one bad bang on the head—' Everything went blank.

Eve recovered consciousness as she was lifted into a police van, and above the roar of blood in her brain she could hear an incredible amount of noise outside the van. Women were screaming, whistles were being blown, horses were scuffing their hooves and fists were hammering the sides of the van as the driver tried to move away.

She lay in the van and searched the shocked faces which stared back at her. 'Did any of you see what happened to the man I was with?' There were a few murmurs but the rest of the women either ignored her or shook their heads.

She and the other prisoners were unloaded at the police station and the van left to collect another load. She watched it go, prayed that Tom was all right, and joined the queue of women waiting to be formally charged and locked up until they could be taken to Court the following day.

The routine was familiar to her. She accepted the charge that was read out and allowed herself to be shoved into a cell with three other women. They had all been to prison before and some pretended to be quite cheerful at the prospect of going back again.

'No cooking or cleaning or putting up with the old man,' one of them joked, but Eve did not think it was anything to laugh about and she told her.

'Who're you then?'

'Eve Forrester. I'm leader of the WFL.'

'You're the one who lied about the bombing, aincha?'

'No, not exactly,' she said, suddenly aware that it was not only some newspapers who were delighting in her possible downfall; so were some of the women she was trying to help.

Eve did not say any more. Her head ached, her brain felt as though it was loose inside her skull, and her eyes hurt every time she moved.

In the morning she and the others were taken to Court. While she was waiting for her case to be heard she asked about Tom and learned he was all right but had been sentenced to one month in prison for assaulting three policemen.

When Eve was called into the court room she defended herself by saying that she was not at the Palace to take part in the demonstration. She said she had only become involved when she tried to stop Tom Dobbs being hit on the head, and she had tried to stop the policeman because, in her opinion as a nurse, the second blow could have had severe medical consequences which were far beyond those the policeman would have intended to inflict.

The Court listened to her but accepted the police argument that her previous activities made it difficult to believe she was at the Palace for anything other than active reasons. She was sentenced to three months' imprisonment.

Aunt Lizzie visited Eve a week later. 'You seem to get yourself into trouble even when you *don't* mean to, Eve.'

'I know. I heard there were fifty-seven arrests, Aunt Lizzie. The numbers go up each time. They've got to give us the vote soon or the prisons'll be full of suffragettes.'

'So you're still fighting? You're not going to settle down and be a quiet little housewife?'

'I've got no one to settle down with, Aunt.'

'Tom Dobbs?'

'Lord, no! He's a decent man but I wouldn't marry him.'

'I think he'd marry you, Eve. I've been to see him and he's very sweet on you. I reckon he'd do anything for you.'

'Perhaps he would, but he's not the one for me. I don't think there is anyone for me. I'm too much trouble for most men. Robert was the only one who really understood me and that was only because he never had any intention of getting too involved.'

'Don't give up, Eve. It took me years to find Richard, but I did, and I'm sure we'd still have been happy if he hadn't been killed.'

'Don't you ever get lonely, though, Aunt?'

'Of course, but I've got you and your parents, and the others. It could be a lot worse for me, and for you.'

'How are Mama and Papa?'

'Very well, although they're both worried about you. You won't risk another hunger strike will you? It'd worry your mother to death.'

'No. I'll serve my sentence this time, and please tell Mama that it's not too bad in here. I'm quite used to it by now and I've probably got more friends here than I have outside. Maud Whitton-White's promised to visit regularly and keep me informed of what's happening, and no doubt Tom will come once he's been released. They'll let me out before the end of August and then, perhaps, we can arrange a short holiday together.'

'I'm sure your mother would like that, Eve. She won't come and see you in here but she'll miss you, especially after your month in America.'

The train arrived in St Petersburg late at night. Thick fog made everything cold and wet and all Lottie could smell was sewage.

She shivered as Peter helped her down from the carriage but she was not cold, she was sweating.

'Wait here, Lottie. I'll find someone to take us to the lodgings.'

'No! Don't leave me!'

'I won't be gone for more than five or ten minutes.'

'No!' She felt faint and was frightened she might pass out and be taken away. Frightened that because she could not make herself understood she might be given treatment which would harm the baby. 'Let's both go to find a taxi.'

'Taxi?' Peter said sharply. 'Lottie, when we changed trains at the border we didn't simply change trains. We changed centuries, too. We could walk all the way to Moscow before we found a taxi.'

'How far away is your friend's house?'

'Half an hour?' Peter shrugged.

'I think I can manage that, if I have some tea first.'

He took her to a steaming samovar and bought two teas, a cup for her and a glass for him. She drank hers quickly, grateful that it had no milk because milk made her sick.

She had hardly suffered any sickness in Paris but within minutes of being on the train she had begun to feel ill, and the feeling had persisted throughout the long journey. Then, when they changed to the wider gauge Russian train and waited around in the cold while Peter processed the seemingly endless paperwork she had begun to shiver. That and Peter's announcement that she was pregnant had speeded up the bureaucracy but had not made her feel any better. Now she simply wanted to lie down in a proper bed which was soft and warm, and did not move.

Lottie fainted minutes after leaving the railway station and later she was only half aware of Peter holding her upright on a seat which jerked her about. Then she had the impression of a young woman with soft fingers looking down at her and stroking her face, then she was back on the seat and it was juddering again. At some point a gentle old man with a pointed beard and pince-nez, and smelling strongly of carbolic, tutted over her.

When she woke properly she smelled fish, then lamp oil, then sweat. When she opened her eyes she saw Peter and behind him a drab room with bare walls and a small window covered with a thin curtain which filtered dull grey light.

'Welcome to Russia,' Peter said dryly, sitting on the side of the bed she lay in.

'What time is it?' Her mouth tasted foul and her voice croaked.

'Noon. Why? It's thick, freezing fog out there so you can't go anywhere and you've got nothing to do but get better. Drink this. It's a fever mixture and it won't hurt the baby.' He slipped his arm around her and half lifted her so she could sip the medicine which tasted worse than her mouth, and as he did so she realised she was naked. 'I'm sorry, Lottie, but I had to keep sponging you – doctor's orders.'

'You nursed me?' She was surprised and embarrassed but nothing more than that. It was obvious that he had no choice but to undress and wash her and she was grateful for his care.

'There isn't anyone else, not here. I took the first place I could just to get you off the street.' He paused, and then added, 'Well, it was the second. We couldn't stay at my friends'. They said it would be too dangerous for us and them.'

She didn't ask why it could be dangerous, and simply accepted what he said. 'Thank you. I'm sorry to be such a nuisance.'

He smiled and shrugged, then nodded towards her stomach. 'I think, perhaps, you've started to look pregnant. I didn't notice it before.'

She felt herself and then lifted the covers to look. 'Yes, you're right.'

'Excited? Or scared?' he asked gently.

'Both,' she said, and began to cry.

His arms were around her in a moment and he held her tight, stroked her hair and rocked her, all the time making soft, soothing sounds until she stopped sobbing, and then kissed her forehead, the way he sometimes did.

She lifted her face to him and felt the bedcover fall down to her hips. His mouth came close to hers and she felt his hand brush her breast, but then his lips settled briefly on the end of her nose and his hand toyed with the pendant Sasha had given her and which still hung around her neck, close to her heart. A moment later he stood up.

'Here,' he pulled a flannel shirt down from the iron bedhead. 'Put this on. It'll keep you warm now the fever's going.'

He took her arms and slipped them into the sleeves, closed the shirt and buttoned it up from bottom to top, lowered her gently back onto the mattress and pulled the covers close around her neck, tucking her up tightly. He looked at her, smiled, kissed her forehead again and hugged her through the covers.

She felt safe and as though she was the most precious thing in the world.

'Hungry?'

She nodded. She was hungry in spite of the awful smell of both fresh and rotting fish.

He stood up. 'I'll be half an hour. Don't go anywhere.'

She smiled at him and felt a little better.

He brought back steaming soup made from red cabbage and meat, and bowls of rice with meat and fish stirred into it. It was not until they had eaten everything that he told her she had been ill for four days and that he had not eaten during that time because he would not leave her alone. He said he had sustained himself on tea and vodka.

'We must feed you, Krasnaya, so we can move from here. We're above a fish seller's shop and this room's only available for a short while until the owner's son returns. I know of other places and I'll make arrangements as soon as you feel well enough to be left alone for a few hours.'

She ate and rested, and over the next few days he went out for several hours at a time to organise better lodgings, but she noticed that he seemed more concerned each time he returned to the bleak and smelly room.

'It's difficult to find somewhere to stay, Krasnaya. There isn't much free accommodation in the city – many of the factory workers even have to sleep on the factory floor at night, and what is available is perhaps unsafe because of the police. The Third Department, the Okhrana, are everywhere because of the strikes and protests which are happening each week. If I had known it was this bad I would not have brought you here, Lottie.'

'But you have found somewhere? Or can we stay here?'

'We can't stay in this room for much longer and I can't leave Russia because there are things I must do. We could both be in danger if I avoid these duties, Lottie. Also, as you have no proper papers it would be very unwise for you to try leaving Russia on your own.' He paused, sighed and added, 'I have found somewhere which is safe but it's very poor and not somewhere I would choose to take you. We have no choice but to stay there until I can find something better or until Sasha comes.'

'I'm sure it'll be perfect, Peter,' she said, and thought it had to be better than this room with its depressing walls and constant stench.

He grimaced. 'I don't think it is.'

Even though the landlord seemed to want them to go Peter would not allow her to leave the room for five more days. When they did leave he insisted on her wearing a fur hat and a ragged old tulup, a rough overcoat made from uncured skin with the fur worn inside. It was stiff and uncomfortable, and it still stank even though the animal it had come from had been dead for years, but it was warm, and she was grateful for it as the little cart he had hired juddered through the heavy freezing mist which was thickest by the rivers and the poor districts.

The juddering stopped as they turned into a narrow alley between high wooden buildings. She realised they had moved from cobbles to mud. Peter touched the driver's shoulder and the cart stopped.

Moments later he lifted Lottie down and carried her to a flight of wooden steps, paid off the cart driver and came back with their bags. She noticed the mud from the alley had covered his boots and reached up above his ankles.

'Krasnaya, this house belongs to Maxim Suvarin. I trust him with my freedom but he is not a kind man. He believes women are good for two things only, to please him in bed or the kitchen. In your case he would not expect you to cook. I'll tell him you're mine, which should protect you, and I won't leave you alone with him when he is drinking.'

Lottie wondered what he was leading her into. 'Thank you. We'll share a room again?'

'We will share a room, yes,' he said in a tone which made her suspicious. 'We'll also share a bed. You'll understand why when you come inside. Anyway, sharing with me will keep you warmer, and safer.'

She did not like Maxim Suvarin and she did not like his house. They were both big, ugly, ill cared for and smelled of tobacco, damp and cabbage.

Suvarin was very tall but he had enough flesh for two men of his height and much of it hung around his neck and waist. His greasy black hair ran into a shaggy beard which flopped against his chest, and his large eyes were as black and rambling as his beard. He grinned constantly, showing what remained of his broken yellow teeth. Peculiarly, he had a delicate nose, which he repeatedly picked at with the little finger of his fat right hand.

The house creaked as badly as it smelled, and it leaned so that all the floors ran in the same direction. All the internal doors had been removed or had jammed open against the floor. She realised, nervously, that the wooden house was built on piles which kept it and all the others in the row just a few feet above the river's surface. The floors sloped because the house was slowly toppling into the river.

Suvarin's house was three storeys high and the steps which led to the upper floors resembled ladders more than stairs.

Peter explained, 'It was one of the first houses built when the city was founded.'

'I don't care about its pedigree, Peter, it's awful.'

'It's all I could find, for the moment.'

'Hotels?'

'Not without the correct papers, and we don't have those. We'd end up in prison.'

She shrugged, then nodded. They had no choice.

'Lottie, I'm sorry I can't find anywhere better than this for you.' She could see he was upset and she felt guilty for making him feel like that. She had imposed herself on him from the beginning, given him problems which he had overcome without complaining, and he had taken very good care of her. It was not his fault that they were reduced to this shabby lodging house, so she told him so and clutched his arm to emphasise how she felt.

Suvarin said they could sleep on the top floor. What he meant was in the attic, under the roof, in a space lit by a filthy skylight.

The house was so dark it did not take her eyes long to adjust to the dim attic light and when she saw two beds she was relieved. She and Peter would not have to share after all. Then as she turned around she saw another two, and then another two. And she realised each bed was meant for a couple.

This was not a bedroom it was a dormitory for twelve people!

'Oh, Peter!' The words came before she could stop them.

'We'll have to for tonight,' he said, shaking his head. 'There *is* nowhere else for *us*, Lottie, but I'll try to find you somewhere better tomorrow.'

She shook her head. 'No, Komovsky, I'll stay with you.'

'Why did you call me Komovsky?'

'Because it's a name I'm going to grow very proud of and I might as well start enjoying it now.'

She felt very tired so she lay down on the bed, which she found surprisingly clean and dry, and Peter covered her with the tulup. She did not undress and she wondered if she ever would while she stayed in that house. As she laid back she prayed that Sasha would be able to find them. Soon.

Peter stayed with her for several hours, either sitting on the bed or lying down beside her while she dozed. As she slipped into and out of sleep she heard a number of people shuffling about the attic, but none of them spoke anything but short and sullen greetings. When she woke fully Peter said he was going downstairs for a while but would not leave the house and if she needed him she should call, but before he left he reached inside his jacket and pulled something out from behind his back.

'Take this, and if anyone gives you any trouble and I don't get here quick enough just flash this in their face.' He pulled a small cutlass out of a leather scabbard. 'Be careful, it's very sharp. Like a razor.'

He pushed it back in its scabbard and hid it under the mattress where she could reach it easily.

Like the bedrooms, life in the rest of the house was communal. The only place which offered any privacy was the basic lavatory and even that had no door, simply a thin curtain which left a gap of a foot or so above the floor.

There was one daily meal eaten in the steamy, cabbage-smelling room where she first met Suvarin, and that always consisted of a gruel they called kasha, or a sour cabbage soup, and then various forms of the kulibyaki Peter had brought her in the fish seller's room, either fish or meat or sometimes even just cabbage mixed with rice. He encouraged her to drink her fill of vodka or kvass because he said it would warm her and protect her digestion, and she did so even though she disliked both spirits. She drank it because he said she should, but more because it numbed her mind for a while and things did not seem so bad.

She lost count of the number of people who lived in the house or passed through during the days and nights, each of them furtive, each wearing deep and dark expressions and talking only Russian, which she did not understand.

She spoke to no one except Peter, and she only felt safe when he was with her. She dared not leave the house because she still felt weak from the fever and the wet and freezing fog would have made her ill again. Torrential rain cleared the fog after four days, but it turned the roadway into a muddy stream which she could not have crossed even if she had felt fit enough to venture out.

The days were long and boring, lying on her bed in the attic and doing nothing at all because she had nothing to do. She learned to sleep more than she would have done, but that sometimes meant she would lie awake most of the night, and in one sense the nights were even worse than the days.

At night she had to listen to what was happening in the beds around her, and she had to listen to the men who had enjoyed their own women taunting Peter for not taking her. She could not understand the words used and Peter never complained to her, but she could tell what was being said and she noticed how the other men began to treat him during the day. And the way they grouped together and looked at her.

An atmosphere was building up in the house, things she did not understand were being whispered, and she was scared.

A wind came up and thrashed rain across the roof and the skylight, drumming loudly in the darkness but not loud enough to drown out the noise of the bed alongside her creaking, or overcome the groaning sounds coming from the couple in it.

She buried her head against Peter's shoulder as he cuddled her in the innocent way he always did. 'Peter, isn't there anywhere else we could go?'

'I've been thinking I could take you to the British Embassy.'

'No. I told you, Komovsky, I want to stay with you. Anyway, if they sent me home the police would arrest me.'

'I forgot,' he said quietly. 'I still can't see you as a killer.'

'Well, I am.' She paused as sounds of ecstasy came from the next bed and then heard the couple opposite start their performance. 'What are you doing about the things you said you have to do? You haven't left this house since we came here.'

'I don't need to. People come to me. I've been working since we arrived here,' he said quietly.

'I didn't realise.'

'You weren't meant to. No one is. Except Maxim.'

She knew better than to ask any questions and they lay still, holding each other for warmth and comfort and trying to ignore the exaggerated sounds coming from the man and woman in the opposite bed. Sometimes it was quite farcical to hear the couples pretending they were enjoying themselves more than the couple before them, but most of the time it was embarrassing and degrading, and it reminded her of the almost forgotten wasteland dogs.

As the groans of ecstasy faded the jibes began and she felt Peter tense himself, but all he did was answer them in a dismissive tone.

'Peter, I can guess what they're all saying. Do you want to? You know what I mean?' Perhaps that was the safest way to release the tension which was building up. Better for Peter and, perhaps, for her. Better that Peter used her gently than some of the other men took her by force. 'Peter? It might be for the best?'

'Do you want me to?' he asked.

She hesitated. 'Do *you* want to?'

'My body says yes, but my heart and my brain say no, Krasnaya, and you also think no, or you wouldn't have hesitated. So go to sleep and try to dream of good things. Tomorrow will be better.'

Tomorrow was worse. A freezing wind hit the house and shook it so much she thought it must either fall into the river or be lifted off its stilts and be blown across the city. Then, in the late afternoon when it was already dark, Peter came up into the attic and told her he had to leave her alone for several hours.

'Stay up here. I'll be back as soon as I can, but meanwhile Maxim'll take care of you. I've told him I'll cut his nose off if you're harmed.'

His words did not make her feel any safer.

She sat alone in the attic, listening to the whining wind and the hail as it rattled against the walls and roof, and to raucous sounds coming from the men and women gathered in the smelly room on the bottom floor.

After a while she crept downstairs to the lavatory, unnoticed until she had finished and was about to return.

A rough-looking man blocked her path to the stairs and said something she did not understand. She shrugged. He spoke again so she tried to show him she did not understand by shrugging and shaking her head, but he simply spoke louder.

'I'm sorry, I don't understand you,' she said in English and French, and waited for him to move aside.

Suddenly he grabbed her waist and hauled her into the room where everyone else was gathered on chairs or on the floor, each with glasses or bottles in their hands. A huge cheer went up as she was carried in and moments later the men, and the women, started making obscene gestures and joking exchanges in their own language.

'Please don't! Please don't!' She looked around for Maxim Suvarin, and saw him on the floor and sprawled against a wall, eyes closed, sleeping drunk.

She felt a hand on her back and stiffened with fear. The hand pushed her, other hands caught her and pushed her back until more hands clutched at her and pushed her again. She was shoved around the room, hands feeling her and pushing her onto someone else, and she let them because she did not know what else to do. She stumbled but somehow kept on her feet because she guessed what would happen if she fell. This was bad enough but the alternative was worse.

The motion grew faster and the groping harder until they were all acting like savages. She was pushed round and round the room and suddenly she found herself facing the door opening. She rushed through it, ran for the steps and scrambled up, the hem of her skirt catching and ripping as she went. There was a trap-door in the attic and if she could drop that over the opening and pull something heavy on to it she might be safe until Peter came back or Maxim woke up.

A hand grabbed her skirt but she tugged herself free and climbed as fast as she could, until someone caught hold of her boot. She stamped on their hand with her other boot, came free and lunged upwards.

Suddenly she was in the attic, heaving the flap shut. Fingers came over the edge of the opening. She slammed the trap down on them and heard a howl of pain but did not care.

She sat on the trap and looked for something, anything, to weight it down, but there wasn't anything within reach. She turned and crouched with her feet over the opening edge of the trap, using her light weight to the best advantage, and wondered how long she could stay like that as the men below tried to push the trap-door open.

The house rattled as the wind slammed against it. Her legs went numb and she worried what harm might have been done to her baby. She prayed Peter would come back, or Sasha, or even Maxim would come to help her.

She felt the trap lift, lift further, and further. She stamped on it to force it down but it opened more and more. A hand reached through the gap, grabbed her ankle, and pulled.

She broke free, jumped off the trap and ran to the bed. She had the unsheathed knife in her hand as the first men scrambled into the attic. She waved it in front of her and the first man wavered and moved back and warned the others as they climbed into the attic. She counted eight men, and then two more came with oil lamps. Ten in all!

The last man closed the trap and two others dragged a bed across it to stop it being forced open, and five of the men sat on the bed to watch what the others did to her.

They approached her one by one and at first she frightened them off with the knife. Then two or three of them tormented her by coming from different directions, touching her and pulling away before she could turn on them. She caught one man's fingers which spouted blood and made him scream but that simply excited those who were watching and made the others more careful.

Then two of them picked up a bed cover and used it as a net.

They threw it over her head and pulled it down tight around her arms. She could not see or move but she held onto the knife, until a hand gripped her wrist and forced her fingers open. The knife fell away, and she was defenceless.

The cover was pulled off and two men pushed her onto the bed and held her arms while two more held her feet. A fifth came at her with the knife, hooked it into her skirt and used its razor-sharp blade to cut her clothing open.

She dared not move as she felt the blunt side of the knife pressing against her. The man cut away one layer of her clothes at a time, prolonging his pleasure and her terror.

She thought about her baby, and then the dogs on the wasteland, and then she listened to the giant wind slam its shoulder against the house, again and again, and wished it would blow the house down. Better to die in the freezing river than this.

Then the cold edge of the knife pressed against her bare stomach and slid upwards, and she saw the men all grouping around her, both oil lamps held high, ready for her final unveiling, and what would happen afterwards.

She heard hail scatter down the roof and the skylight rattle as the wind whined underneath it and lifted it slightly.

The knife passed between her breasts and over her chest. She prayed. The house shuddered as the wind hit it, settled, shuddered again.

She suddenly felt cold air rush over her body and saw the men's eyes open wide, and beyond them the skylight lift high in the wind. Then it slammed back down and smashed. Glass scattered across the bed. A man screamed and dropped his oil lamp as a foot-long shard of glass sliced his forearm.

Numbed, she was vaguely aware of the men panicking. They were fighting each other to get to the trap-door, yanking the bed off it and falling down the steps. She turned on her side, and saw part of the floor was ablaze.

Her clothes hung off her, neatly sliced open and useless, but she was too stunned to panic. She crouched on the bed, pulled off the ruined clothes, grabbed her bag from under her bed and quickly dressed in whatever she could find. Then she calmly retrieved Peter's knife and its scabbard from the floor, grabbed his bag as well as hers, and the tulup, and stepped towards the opening which led downstairs.

Two of the beds were smouldering and half the floor was alight but after the initial flare the fire had followed the spilled oil which had run towards the far end of the attic.

Nevertheless, she was grateful for the panic it caused, and she was glad the man with the second lamp had left it beside the trap as he escaped. She threw the bags and the tulup down to the floor below, grabbed the lamp and climbed down the steps. Then she threw the bags and coat down the next flight, calmly smashed the lamp against a far wall and watched the flames lick at the ceiling. For good measure she hurled a chair through the landing window and saw the draught fan the flames even more.

It was small revenge for what they had put her through, but knowing the men would lose everything they owned gave her at least a little satisfaction.

She turned and clambered down the steps to the ground floor. It did not occur to her that anyone might still be left in the house until after she had reached the street and mingled with the residents of that and the other wooden houses on either side.

There was so much panic in the alley that no one seemed to notice her so she trudged through the thick mud until she reached the end of the alley, crossed the cobbled street and stood in a shop's recessed doorway. She watched the roaring flames reach into the black night. The wind caught them, flattening them and twisting them but not blowing them out, and as they lit the area with a strange orange light she heard the wooden building crack and begin to collapse.

She pulled the tulup tight around her, hoping Peter would come before too long, but her fear and shock had helped her to decide what to do if he did not find her. She would find the British Embassy and give herself up.

Peter arrived a few minutes after the fire service. She did not notice him at first because he was with a woman, and even when she stepped out of the shadows he did not see her because he was staring, horrified, at the burning house.

When he did see her he hugged her so tight he hurt her. 'What happened?'

She told him, briefly, and saw the fury in his face, but before he could say anything the woman with him stepped forward, touched her arm, and said in very good English,

404

'Welcome to St Petersburg, Charlotte. My name's Olga. You're coming to stay in my apartment for a few days.'

After four days in Olga's apartment the shock of the men's attempt to rape her and the nightmare of living in Maxim Suvarin's lodging house began to fade. She did not see Peter during those days but she felt completely safe with the self-assured Olga who was probably about the same age as her, dark, small and plain, and wore her hair in plaits formed into a horse shoe.

Olga took her shopping to buy essentials and a few extras that she said Peter insisted she have, but avoided explaining how she had come to meet Peter although she did say she had been in Moscow and only returned to the capital, St Petersburg, the day Suvarin's house was burned.

The only other things Olga said about herself were that she was employed in the Ministry of Information and that she worked for a very respectable man, Valerie Vassilievitch Zubov, whose wife Tatiana was a friend of her own mother, and whose daughter, Natasha, she had gone to school with in Zürich and near Bath, in England.

'It sounds very cosy, Olga,' Lottie said enviously.

'It is. The Zubovs own an enormous estate in the wheat fields. It's called Irina, after Mr Zubov's grandmother. When I was little, Aunt Tass, that's what I call Mrs Zubova, used to take Natasha and me there for the summer. Sometimes we would go to Biarritz where the Zubovs have another house.'

Lottie was stunned by the level of wealth, having seen the appalling poverty that was evident in St Petersburg, and she said so.

Olga put her finger up to her lips as if to silence her. 'While you are here you must learn to be reticent, Charlotte, or you'll find yourself in serious trouble. Now, I understand you have no proper papers, you are expecting a baby in late August or September, you cannot go back to England and you are waiting for Peter's brother to come for you? Also you speak fluent French and play the violin?'

She nodded.

'I'm very concerned that you're pregnant and you've already had one fever so you are weakened. You shouldn't wait in the capital, particularly at the moment. The weather's poor, there are outbreaks of typhus, and there are various strikes which make the city dangerous. Also, with no papers and considering the current political situation, you'll find it difficult to leave Russia because officials will check everything as only Russian officials can. I think we must get you away to somewhere healthier but where Sasha can still find you.'

'But Sasha could arrive at any time.' She did not want to leave St Petersburg. She had moved about quite enough.

'But your baby won't wait if Sasha doesn't come, and it'll be very difficult to take care of you here. Besides, even when Sasha does come you'll still need somewhere to live until you and the baby can travel. I think you should go to Estate Irina. Tass will take you when she leaves in two days. Don't worry, she doesn't speak English but she does speak very good French. Many people of her position speak better French than they do true Russian.'

'But why should she help me?'

Olga smiled brightly. 'Because, perhaps, she still feels a little sorry for Katarina Komovskaya. And because I will ask her as a special favour to me.'

'She knows Katarina? Sasha's mother?'

'Oh, yes, Charlotte, but that is for her to discuss with you, when she is ready.'

The Zubovs' St Petersburg house was a small mansion, three times the size of Joseph's house, set back behind high iron gates and with a fountain in the front courtyard. It was in a turning off Fourstatskaya Street, near the Tauride Palace where the non-elected government body, the Duma, held its meetings.

Olga led her to an extravagantly furnished reception room, introduced her to Mrs Zubova, and left.

Tatiana Zubova was probably forty-five, or perhaps fifty years old. She was dressed in a simple peach-coloured silk dress which was yoked across her shoulders, had no collar, a round neck, hung in folds to within an inch of the floor and had no adornments at all. She wore no jewellery, was tall, slim, blue eyed, silver-grey haired and beautiful. And very kind.

'Charlotte, you speak English and you play the violin. Could you bear to teach a little of each to both Leo and Sergei, my late additions?'

As she spoke two little boys, aged perhaps four and six, and dressed in blue velvet breeches and white silk blouses appeared from behind a large, brocaded sofa. They approached Lottie solemnly, looking down at the floor so she could not see their faces which were half covered by dark curls.

'Good morning, young gentlemen,' Lottie said in French.

The older boy looked up at her and replied in very formal French. 'Good morning, miss, but I regret that we are not yet gentlemen. We are still quite little boys.'

She smothered a giggle and bit her lip as the younger boy looked up, studied her, and said seriously, 'You are very beautiful, miss. Are you going to play with us?'

She crouched down and pushed the curls back off his forehead. 'Yes, Sergei, if you want me to.'

He took hold of her hand and led her to the nursery. Tatiana Zubova laughed and said they would leave for Irina the following day.

They travelled in style. Lottie had her own small suite on a train which swept them across a vast flat plain, but the motion still made her sick. Natasha, who seemed to be about her age and was small, neat and had deep brown hair and eyes, took turns with Tatiana to sit with her and quite unselfconsciously act as her maid and nurse. A nanny looked after the two boys and a number of other servants who travelled with them saw to whatever chores needed attention. When Lottie did venture from her bedroom she found the Zubovs' carriage resembled Joseph's house, but on wheels.

Outside, endless fields and countless telegraph poles flashed past. The train stopped at stations which were usually remote, neither in nor near a town, and the small but complete station where they finally left the train was the only building she could see. She wondered if it had been built entirely for the Zubov family's benefit, especially as the old man who greeted them was wearing a splendid red and blue uniform with the Zubov crest on his buttons.

'Yes, Charlotte,' Natasha spoke quietly and seemed embarrassed, 'that was precisely why it was built, but it also has another use. There is a telegraph installed here, and Igor, with his lovely uniform, lives here all year not only to drive us to and from the house but to supply a service to the local village. When we are here this station is our only connection with the outside world. There is a telegraph in Papa's office and that is how we talk to each other when we are apart.'

Igor abandoned the railway station and telegraph and drove them to the Zubovs' country house, and on the way Tatiana and Natasha explained how the Estate Irina was a fantasy brought to life.

Valerie Vassilievitch Zubov's great grandfather had visited the cotton-growing states of America before the Civil War and stayed at a grand house which he liked so much he had architects copy the plans. He employed artists who were skilled in copying detail to paint intricate pictures of each room and the various external elevations, and landscape artists to paint pictures of the surroundings. He then had simple outline sketches made of the landscapes and employed gardeners to identify the various plants and trees on those sketches.

When he returned to his estate he employed men to build his dream home, and even had the land sculptured and where possible the trees and plants duplicated.

Work began two weeks after Irina, his first child was born, and the house and gardens were completed in time for her sixth birthday. By her seventh birthday the Zubov family's old house had been demolished and its foundations grassed over. All that remained were the enormous cellars which were used for storing food and wine and were approached through a concealed entrance hidden in a wisteria-covered folly.

It seemed Grandfather Zubov was heartbroken when he heard that the house he had visited in America had virtually been destroyed during the Civil War, and he twice offered to have it rebuilt at his expense. His offers received no response and he carried the grievance for what he thought was a snub until he died.

Lottie believed every word of the story. It was obvious that the Zubovs were accustomed to having what they wanted at any cost, and various small happenings which had occurred on the train showed that they were also generous towards others.

Within weeks Lottie had formed a strong loyalty towards the family and fallen in love with Irina, both the estate and the house. The building had classic façades with columns and pelmets in clean, white stone, and a green copper roof.

She sighed every time she saw the almost palatial reception hall with its white marble floors and walls, and the twin staircases which swept down in semi-circles like two welcoming arms, and she wondered at the brilliance of a large crystal candelabra which hung twenty feet above the floor.

The discreetly decorated rooms in which the sun seemed to shine all the time entranced her. Large and airy, they were a delight to escape into when it became too hot to sit on the shaded veranda which ran along the back and one side wall, but for all their grandness they were comfortable and homely.

Outside, the lawns were soft to look at and to walk on and the gardens were an excitement of colour and scents as a hot spring transformed her world and her mood.

The food cooked at Irina was what she had already come to think of as typically French and she accepted Tatiana's advice on what food, drink, rest and exercise would best equip her to deliver a healthy and bright baby.

Her only concerns were that Sasha did not arrive, that apart from letters she had no means of contacting Peter, Joseph or her parents, and that she felt remote from the outside world which she had begun to think of as the real world.

May slipped into June and June drifted by quite blissfully. Although the weather was very hot and she was getting very large, she simply did nothing except stare at the clear skies or cool lawns, and read English novels which Tatiana had delivered for her. There were few formalities at Irina and no guests who needed to be impressed so they all wore cool cotton dresses in calm pastel shades, and pinned their hair loosely so it was comfortable but did not make their necks hot.

She improved Leo's and Sergei's English for an hour each day but they were far more interested in measuring her increasing girth and watching her closely with the mystification of small children who have been told she is expecting a baby but cannot relate her growth to something they think will come with a parcel of books.

Mr Zubov and Olga were due to visit Irina for ten days from the first of July but they did not arrive. Then someone came from the village to deliver a telegram which said Olga would come alone and explain why plans had been changed.

It was an especially hot day when she arrived.

'Mama, Charlotte! Olga's here! Olga's here!' Natasha rushed through the house and they all gathered outside the front door as the pony cart, dragging a column of dust behind it, brought Olga and her surprisingly small amount of luggage up the long front drive.

'Aunt Tass, Natasha, Charlotte.' Olga kissed them all and left the cart driver and the luggage to be cared for by the servants.

'Why isn't Valerie coming?' Tatiana asked as they walked through the front door and into the cool hall.

'He's very busy. I'll explain, but please may I have some tea? The dust has parched my throat.'

Tatiana nodded to a waiting maid, who ran off, and they wandered into the drawing room.

410

'Charlotte,' Olga turned to her. 'How are you?'

'Very well, but I wish I knew where Sasha was. I'd hoped he'd be here by now, if he *is* coming.' It was the first time she had admitted the fear that had been increasing every day, and even as she spoke she wished she had not doubted him.

'He's coming, Charlotte. Peter told me he's been seen in St Petersburg but not by anyone that Peter's left messages with. I can't think what he's doing. It's very frustrating.'

'You've seen Peter?'

'Three days ago. He's sent you a present. I'll give it to you later.'

'Olga! What about Valerie?' Tatiana said impatiently and at that moment a trolley loaded with a samovar, tea and cups was wheeled in so she attended to that but nodded for Olga to continue.

'You haven't heard what happened in Bosnia last Sunday? Sarajevo?' Olga asked, and looked surprised when she realised they had not heard the news. 'Archduke Franz Ferdinand and the Duchess were shot and killed by a Serbian agitator.'

Lottie saw the concerned looks on Olga's and Tatiana's faces and assumed the Austrian Archduke must be a personal friend, or even a relation.

Then Natasha spoke. 'Why do you both look so worried?'

Her mother held her hand up for silence and turned to Olga. 'And what's happening in Vienna? And Berlin? Do we know?'

'They're muttering about making an example of Serbia.'

'Oh God!' Tatiana's hand went to her mouth.

Natasha stood up. 'What's happening, Mama? Why *are* you so worried?'

'Russia, together with Britain and France has a treaty with Serbia to defend each other if any country is attacked. Austria-Hungary, Germany and Bosnia have a similar treaty. If Austria attacks Serbia we should go to war to support the alliance, and that would mean not simply with the Austro-Hungarians but with Bosnia. And, more importantly, with Germany.'

'Oh, Mama!' Natasha said in a dismissive tone. 'You

411

don't honestly think we'd go to war with Austria-Hungary and Germany because two people have been shot by an agitator?'

Her mother looked contrite. 'No, I suppose it does seem silly. But why has your father stayed in the capital?'

Olga stood up as she answered. 'Because he feels the same as you, Aunt Tass. It may seem silly, but . . .' She shrugged and fell silent, and went to look out of the window.

They ate dinner late because of the heat and then sat outside in the cooling evening air. First Tatiana and then Natasha excused themselves and went to bed.

'Now we're alone I'll bring Peter's present to you, Charlotte.' Olga went indoors and returned a few minutes later with what looked like a cigar box. 'Here, but please keep quiet when you see it.'

'Thank you,' she said, and accepted the box which was well finished and inlaid with coloured woods and mother of pearl. She lifted the lid and found a miniature pistol, packed neatly into a shaped satin cushion. 'What is it? Exactly?'

'It's an American pistol called a Derringer. As you can see it has two barrels so you can fire twice in quick succession. It's small so you can easily conceal it. It's meant to be a lady's gun. It's very small but very effective, especially if it's fired into a man's face or chest, or his more private parts. Peter thought you should have it after what happened at Maxim's.'

'Why? I'm safe enough here. This isn't like Suvarin's house.'

'Not yet, Charlotte. But maybe things will change if there's a war, and then dangers will come not only from Austria and Germany. Both Mr Zubov and Peter believe so. Please allow me to show you how to load and use the gun.'

The Derringer and the talk of war frightened Lottie and when she went to bed she lay awake for hours.

A hot and surprisingly uneventful July unrolled slowly, and she felt bigger and heavier than ever.

Also, now she knew Sasha had come to Russia but not to her, and the talk of war had made her uncertain about even the immediate future, the pleasant languor that Irina had induced in her became irritating and frustrating. She wanted to know what was going to happen, however bad it was. The waiting, the lack of news, the very remoteness of the estate unsettled her.

The peasants went about their work in their usual unrushed way. In late July they took their long-handled scythes out into the shoulder-high grass beyond the lawns. She stood on the balcony outside her room and watched them work in line, scything in unison to within inches of each others' legs, their children following on behind, gathering the cut grass into stooks to dry and provide hay, winter food for the cattle and bedding for both the livestock and the gatherers. Even at their slow pace they worked their way steadily through the high grass, cutting the stubble low to avoid waste.

She watched them and thought this had been happening for hundreds of years. Surely it was not going to change now, and if it was going to change then why had it happened just when she finally found peace of mind and had so much happiness to look forward to?

She looked up and saw a low dustcloud coming from the direction of a village beyond the station. A horseman. Irina had a visitor.

Her mouth dried. They were not expecting anybody so it must be bad news, a messenger sent from St Petersburg.

The baby seemed to sense her mood and shifted itself. She winced with pain, concerned because she had felt a few pains lately and because she was enormous now and still had six weeks to wait.

She went back into her room and sat down, stretching to ease the ache in her back, and wishing she could give birth tonight, when it was dark and cool.

She heard someone hurry to the front door, and then her heart leapt.

'Sasha?' Tatiana called in a surprised voice. Then louder, 'Sasha!'

413

She struggled to her feet and waddled towards the door but stopped when she heard Tatiana tell Sasha where to find her. She did not have time to tidy her hair or make herself look better before the marble stairs rang under his feet and the door burst open.

He hesitated in the doorway, studied her round body, and frowned.

'How can you look so beautiful when you're that big?' He hugged her so hard she pleaded with him to let go, and only then did he kiss her. Suddenly the past seven months became worthwhile.

Chapter 27

Eve guessed her aunt would visit her again and bring real news of what was happening. The prison was buzzing with gossip but it was impossible to confirm any of the fantastic stories which were going around, impossible to decide which were true and which were embellishments of the truth or perhaps no more than rumours.

The most popular story claimed Britain was already at war, the Germans had overrun the French Army and were approaching the French coast, and orders had been given that unless the Royal Navy could defend the Channel the prison staff would open the doors and allow everyone to go free rather than have hundreds of women locked up and left at the mercy of rampaging German hordes.

Eve thought that everyone was exaggerating everything. Why should Europe go to war because an unpopular Austrian Royal had been murdered in a country which was always at war with its neighbours or itself? Apart from anything else most of the European royal families were related to each other and in spite of all she had heard to the contrary it seemed most unlikely to her that cousins and uncles would commit their armies and navies to fighting each other. It was something which might almost happen in a Gilbert and Sullivan opera, but even there it would not actually occur. Something or someone would intervene and stop it all before anyone was hurt, both in the opera and in real life.

'It's happened,' Aunt Lizzie said, white-faced. 'The Kaiser's declared war on his cousin, the Tsar, and the German and Russian armies are already fighting.'

Eve's heart fell. 'Have you heard from Lottie? Will she be in danger?'

'We haven't heard, Eve, but she'll be safer in Russia than in Germany because if Britain does get dragged in we'll be fighting with the Russians and not against them so she won't be seen as an enemy.'

'But how can we all suddenly go to war just because one man's been killed? It's ridiculous, Aunt?'

'Well, I don't suppose it'll last for long, Eve, these things never do. It's all about treaties and alliances, and if that's really the case they'll fight for a while and then redraw the agreements and that'll be an end to it.'

'*If* that's the case? What do you mean? *If* that's the case?'

'Just think, Eve. There's political unrest all over the Continent, over half the world. Even in our own country we've got your suffragettes bombing and burning, and two million people on strike for better wages and conditions. We've got near civil war in Ireland and English people are going onto the streets to show they don't want our troops sent over there. All over the world ordinary people like you have found the courage to stand up for themselves even when they're sent to prison. I simply wonder if the various governments see a war as a diversion or a way to make everyone toe the line again, and I'm against us getting involved.'

'I don't have much confidence in our Government, Aunt, but I don't think they'd go to war unless they had to.'

'No?' her aunt asked, and the simple question had a chill in it. 'Listen, Eve. I've heard that suffragettes and strikers might be released if we go to war, and only real *criminals* would be detained. That'd mean the Government recognises you all as political prisoners. It's only a proposal at the moment, and I reckon Parliament would try to overcome the political significance by getting the King to grant an amnesty, but in the long run it *would* strengthen your argument.'

'Let's wait and see, Aunt.' She sighed. 'I don't want to see us go to war, either, even if it does help us get the vote.'

'Well, perhaps it won't come to that after all,' her aunt said, and smiled a little too thinly.

The next day word spread fast.

'War! We're at war with Germany!'

Eve felt ill with fear, and wished she and Lottie were both at home. Safe.

Irina was quiet. The sky was full of fleecy clouds which reflected the golden sunset back to earth and somehow made the lawns look even softer and greener than usual. The sun was setting directly behind the house, framing it inside an aura of shining gold.

Lottie turned on the garden seat and looked the other way, into the coming night, and in the middle distance saw a single line of mowers wearing brightly-coloured shirts, and heard their low voices singing as they worked their way into the evening, scything down the wheat they had helped to grow.

August had been a stormy month, thunder coming most nights but not bringing rain. Now, however, beyond the mowers where the skies were already dark grey with night, brilliant forks stabbed at the ground.

'I hope it rains and freshens the air,' she said.

Sasha reached across and squeezed her hand. 'Not much longer.'

'What's it like here in the winter?' she asked, and closed her eyes.

'I don't know. Cold, probably. Very cold. Wet anyway. Why?'

'I like it here.' She knew he would understand she was not simply saying that she liked Irina, she was saying she wanted to stay there. For ever, if the Zubovs agreed. He could write music anywhere he could take the orchestra in his head. He did not answer. 'Sasha?'

'I was thinking of America, Lottie. Thinking we might live there. It has huge skies, like Russia. They help the soul to expand, big skies. And you're *allowed* to let your soul expand in America. There's no Tsar in America.'

'Yes, we'll do that,' she said easily, happy to do whatever he wanted when he spoke like that, and because down here she had forgotten about the politics which made her uncomfortable. 'How soon could we go?'

'God knows, Lottie. We're at war, remember?' he said in a resigned voice.

'No, Russia's at war. We're not.'

'Well, we're assumed to be at war,' he said calmly, 'and I don't expect the Germans and the French and British would stop fighting each other just so we could take a train out of Russia and across Poland, Germany and France to reach Cherbourg and an American ship.'

Poland, Germany and France? She realised, for the first time, how far from England she was. 'Do you think the war means we won't be able to write to England? Since I've been here I've written two letters to Mama and Papa but not received a reply to either.'

'I don't know what you said in them but they may not have received them, Lottie. Perhaps, even, Mr Zubov has them.'

'I beg your pardon? I don't understand.' She sat up and opened her eyes.

'The Third Department, the Okhrana, Lottie. The Secret Police. Some people say it's necessary in order to maintain peace in a violent nation. Others disagree, but it's there, anyway.'

'But what does that have to do with Mr Zubov?'

'He's the Head of one of its information gathering sections. Didn't you know? His department reads letters and if they find anything they don't like they investigate or lose the letter. Maybe they also arrange to lose the writer.'

Her stomach churned and upset the baby. 'I did say some

418

things against the Government, Sasha. What d'you think will happen?'

'Nothing. If you left the letters to be posted from here they almost certainly went directly to Mr Zubov, and he'll probably have burned them. He knows you're not a national threat, Lottie, so don't worry about it. Anyway, he's a very kind man. It's simply that he's loyal to the Tsar, and the traditional ways. And if those traditions had given your family all this, wouldn't you be grateful and loyal to them?' Sasha waved towards the house and the ground that surrounded them.

'Of course.' What he said reflected her own feelings towards the Zubovs, but she was angry at the thought of her letters not being forwarded so her parents might know she was well.

Sasha suddenly sat up and peered towards the folly. 'I can see something flashing.'

'It's probably lightning.'

'No,' he said and stood up. 'I'm going to see what it is.'

She saw him reach the folly then turn and wave to her to join him.

She waddled over to him as fast as she could, and heard thunder rolling against the distant grey skies.

'Krasnaya!' Peter grinned at her.

'Komovsky!' She threw her arms around him and cried with pleasure and relief that he was safe.

They sat in the pretend tower, looking out through the wisteria as the sky turned black and the mowers shouldered their long-handled scythes and ran off, abandoning what was left of the wheat to the rain which charged across the plain. Minutes later the wind flayed the wheat about and the rain flattened it.

'Like a cavalry charge,' Peter said.

'I wouldn't know,' Sasha answered, and she saw the way he flicked his hand as a warning to Peter not to talk about the war in front of her.

'Don't worry about Lottie,' Peter told him. 'Until you finally got here I'd spent more time with her than you had, and I can assure you she's tougher than you think. Why did you take so long getting here, anyway?'

'I lost your trail when I couldn't find Suvarin, and then had all my money stolen so I had to find work playing the piano in a restaurant. That was where Olga and Mr Zubov found me.'

'I heard about that part,' Peter said. 'Anyway, it would have been better if you'd come in time to meet us in Paris, or even two months ago. I'd like to get you both away from Russia but I can't smuggle you out now, not with Lottie so close to delivering. I think it's safer for you to stay here, for the moment, and I'll see what I can do later. Meanwhile you, Sasha, must keep out of sight and avoid being conscripted into the army.'

Lottie was shocked. That was something she had not thought about. 'But he's not a soldier.'

'And neither are those reapers we watched cutting wheat, but they'll have changed their scythes for rifles within a year.' Peter scowled. 'Try not to get caught up in it, Sasha. It's not your fight and you'll get no thanks for having your hands blown off.'

She felt the baby lurch. Lightning flashed around the folly and the tower caught the heavy thunder and made it seem louder.

'What about you, Peter? What will you do?' Sasha asked.

'I've got other things to do, Sasha, more important than fighting *nemets*. Just take care of yourself, and take care of Lottie. She's very special, so don't you let her out of your sight.' Peter kissed her on the lips. 'Now, Krasnaya, go indoors before you get too cold. Kiss your baby for me and tell him nice things about Uncle Peter.'

'Aren't you coming into the house?' She had assumed he would stay for a while, a night at least.

'No, Krasnaya. The Zubova ladies don't approve of me. Besides I have things to do in Petrograd.'

'Petrograd?' Sasha asked sharply.

'Oh you are in your own little world, dear brother! Your beloved city has been renamed Petrograd to make it sound less German. If that's the finest war strategy our leaders can evolve I think we need peace or new leaders.' He shook hands with Sasha and smiled at Lottie. 'Take care, and don't forget to carry your little American guardian wherever you go.'

He turned to leave and then turned back and grabbed her. 'I love you, Krasnaya.'

'And I love you, Komovsky.' She tried to smile but she could not, and she was not sure whether it was rain or tears she saw on his face. The lightning flashed again, vivid, dazzling, blue and green, and when her sight cleared Peter was gone.

Eve smiled when she heard her aunt's prophesy had come true. All suffragettes and strikers imprisoned for assault were released under the King's amnesty.

She stood outside the gates where last year she had been collected and taken off to Eastbourne to begin an adventure, and sensed that an ever greater adventure was about to begin. There seemed to be an oddly euphoric atmosphere about, a sense of urgency and shared danger that charged the sunny afternoon air.

'Eve?' She turned and saw her father, seemingly even smaller than she remembered him, jacket open, collar and tie fastened despite the early afternoon heat, but wearing a straw boater instead of his usual cloth cap. 'Are you coming home?'

'May I?'

'Of course you can,' he said, grabbing her and hugging her quite shamelessly in the street, something he would not have done a year ago.

'How's Mama?'

'Well, under the circumstances. Worried about the war, of course, like we all are.'

'And Lottie?' she asked and noted his brief nod. 'Have you heard from her?'

'No. We're worried, obviously, and so's Katarina. As far as we know both Sasha and Peter are out there. It's madness, Eve. The whole world's gone mad.'

'I'm sure it won't last long, Papa.' She took his arm and they walked home.

She had been home for an hour when Maud Whitton-White arrived, reminded her that there was a war going on and asked her if they could leave for Eastbourne as soon as possible because there were urgent matters which needed attention.

'I really think that right now some things are more important than the vote, Maud,' she protested, but not too violently because she knew she had imposed far too much on the loyal Maud.

'Of course, Evelyn, but there's a general agreement being reached among the suffrage leaders that the movement should throw its weight behind the Government because our King and Country need our support and because we don't want to be seen as disloyal. Violet Braithewaite's actually at the White House now and I believe it'd be good for both the WFL and you if you and she were seen to support the general mood.'

Eve turned to her parents and shrugged.

'Go on, dear,' her mother responded immediately. 'There's a lot happening and I think you should do whatever's needed of you.'

Lady Braithewaite greeted her quite affably in public but the moment they were alone she returned to her sour character. 'So, Miss Forrester, the newspapers finally caught up with you and I see you didn't deny their charges concerning the way you virtually perjured yourself to take over the WFL?'

'That's a ridiculous statement, Lady Braithewaite. Anyway I've been in prison for the past three months and could hardly do anything about it. How's Robert?' she asked quickly and saw she had caught Lady Braithewaite offguard.

'He's well.' Lady Braithewaite had paused before answering, and Eve wondered what else had happened in the uneasy relationship between the woman and her son.

'Is he still with Jacques?'

'Yes, but not in the way you may think, Miss Forrester. In fact I believe you may have completely misinterpreted what

I said to you the last time we discussed Robert. You appear to have assumed that Robert is of,' she fumbled, obviously trying to find an expression which would not offend her own sensibilities, 'a certain persuasion. That isn't the case.'

Before she could respond Maud came into the room. 'Excuse me, Evelyn, but I've Cedric Rathbone asking to see you. He's now War Correspondent for the *London and National Cryer* and he wants to ask your views on military recruitment. You might like to know that Mrs Pankhurst is urging men to join the ranks.' Maud paused. 'Shall I show him in?'

Eve's reaction was to tell Cedric Rathbone to wait until she had time to think about her reply but Lady Braithewaite took the initiative and bellowed out to him to enter. Maud was almost pushed aside as Rathbone rushed in and greeted Lady Braithewaite in an overly servile way.

'Lady Braithewaite, it's wonderful to see you, especially here with Miss Forrester. Can I report that any differences you may have once had are now resolved?'

'Of course, young man,' Lady Braithewaite said imperiously. 'And you can also report that I'm in full support of the movement to encourage men to do their duty for King and Country. It's an inherent obligation bred into the English yeomen and ruling classes, but of course I can't speak for Miss Forrester as she represents the working classes who may not have the same ideals.'

'Your views, Miss Forrester?' Rathbone turned to her.

'I'm sure the working classes which support this country in so many ways will continue to support it in time of war, Mr Rathbone.'

'So you feel all young men should march to the recruiting office, Miss Forrester?'

'Yes, I suppose so, if they're free to do so, but let's hope it won't come to that because the fighting'll be over quickly.'

Elizabeth was furious when she read what the newspapers reported was the official WFL statement on Forces recruitment. 'Eve doesn't even believe in the war and yet she's encouraging men to join the forces! What's she thinking of, stirring up war fever like that? Or is she just doing what she thinks'll look right and benefit her career in the long run?'

Rose grimaced. 'I don't know what made her say those things, Lizzie, but Helen and Maisie are both furious with her. They're saying she's as good as telling Jamie and Joe to volunteer. And it seems that some of the suffrage women are already handing out white feathers of cowardice to men who haven't volunteered yet. Poor Tom's totally confused by it all. The women he's marched with and supported for the past year know he's a pacifist and yet they've turned against him and are calling him a coward. He's desperate to talk to Eve to see how she feels about the situation and about him. He reckons she was very friendly and encouraging to him when he visited her in prison, but he doesn't know how she'll take to his pacifist stand now she's allied herself to the other side.'

'Well, I don't think he should build up his hopes too much,' Elizabeth said and told Rose what Eve had told her. 'I really don't think Eve's interested in Tom other than as a friend.'

Eve walked around the White House, going from room to room, checking the windows were shut tight and all the furniture was covered with white dust sheets. The house had been the centre of her life for over a year, but it seemed as though the life blood had been drained out of it now the women had all left. Now it was just a building, a large empty building.

'Come on, Evelyn,' Maud said gently. 'It's over. We didn't get what we wanted but it's only a matter of time, now. If we don't get the vote we'll be back, and if we do get it then this place will have served its purpose, so you should really be hoping we never see it again.'

'I know, Maud, but I learned so much here. I came almost to hate the place, and the movement and the demands it made, but I'll never forget any of it and I know I'll miss it.'

'Of course you'll miss it. We all will. Now come on. Lock up and let's get going. I'll see you at the car.'

'Yes,' she said, paused for one final look at the hall, then pulled the front door shut and locked it.

'Good afternoon, Eve,' a man said.

'Tom! You frightened me. Didn't Maud see you?'

'A lady walked away as I came the opposite way around the house. Can we talk? Alone? It's important.'

'It must be if you've come all the way from London.' She hesitated, then added, 'Look, Maud's waiting for me. Give me a few minutes to explain to her and then I'll meet you on the cliff-top, I'd quite like one last look at the sea.'

He wandered off as she walked over to Maud and explained what was happening. 'The man you went to prison for, Evelyn? Take your time, and ask him if he wants to ride back to London with us.'

'Thank you.' She walked away and found Tom standing on the edge of the cliffs, staring down at a sea which seemed as restless as everything else in and around the country. 'It's nice to see you, Tom, but what's on your mind?'

'Just thinking.'

'You've come a long way just to think,' she said a little impatiently, and then her eyes looked across the sea to the horizon, smudged by the afternoon heat. 'Mind you, I've been standing here and thinking that just over there, just a few miles further than we can see, men are lining up to kill each other.'

'They're already killing each other, Eve. Do you think they should? I know you told the papers that men should join up but do you really believe it?'

'When you hear what the Germans are doing to the people in the towns and villages they overrun you realise that someone has to stop them, Tom. They're burning and murdering, raping women and girls. Someone has to stop them.'

'Yes, I suppose you're right. Will you marry me?'

He spoke so quietly and so without emphasis that his words did not register for several moments, and when they did she was stunned. 'I don't know.'

'Why don't you?'

'Because I hardly know you, really. We still haven't been

425

out together even after all our attempts, and anyway, there's a war on.'

'I know there's a bloody war on! That's why I'm asking you,' he said hotly and immediately calmed down. 'Well, it's one reason anyway. I'd like to marry you before I join up and go away, just to stop some other bloke creeping in and taking my place before I can get back.'

'You're joining up? You're a pacifist!'

'Well, you've just convinced me I'm wrong. Will you marry me before I go?'

'No. Let's talk about it when you get back, or some other time, but not now. We're both emotional and you don't really know what I'm like.'

'All right, but can I at least kiss you? Properly?'

'Of course you can.'

His arms slipped around her and his lips came down on hers and for once she felt wanted for herself, for what she was rather than who she was, and it took all her effort to maintain her common sense and not agree to marry him after all.

Lightning hit a pine tree and exploded it like a firework against the night sky. The little Cossack horse reared high and stayed up. Sasha stood in his stirrups and leaned his head against the horse's head to calm the animal and bring it down.

'Easy, easy, boy,' he said in Russian, his lips brushing the horse's ear.

The horse came down at once and he turned it, took it downwind of the smouldering tree and urged it on. Thunder rolled and lightning struck something behind him but all he could hear, in his mind, was Lottie screaming.

The horse almost flew, suddenly enjoying its freedom or sensing the drama of the night, and Sasha thanked whatever Gods were still left in heaven that when he first started playing the piano someone suggested he take up horse riding to improve his back strength and balance.

They broke out from the trees and pounded over the plain which was curved like the earth so they always

426

seemed to be on the crest of a hill, and around them the lightning cracked like whips and drove the Cossack on. The horse was wiry and strong and now raced without any signs of effort or fear. There were bushes and a few trees, no hedges or ditches or fences or obvious landmarks but Sasha knew he had only to follow the railway and go beyond the station to reach the village twenty minutes' fast ride away.

There he reined in outside the doctor's door and shouted from the saddle. 'Doctor! Doctor! Doctor Sytin.'

An upstairs window flew open and a bearded head poked out. 'Who is it?'

'Komovsky. Tatiana Zubova's English guest is giving birth but the baby won't come out.'

'Wait!' The window slammed shut.

Sasha turned his coat collar up against the rain. The horse was eager to run again. It stamped and breathed steam so he kept it warm and its muscles loose by riding up and down the village street several times, always stopping by the doctor's house, and calling 'Doctor!'

Finally the doctor appeared, a tall slim figure silhouetted in his doorway, grappling with a long coat and wide-brimmed hat. 'I'm ready, Komovsky. Catch this and give me a stirrup.'

Sasha caught the bag and wedged it on the saddle as he steadied the horse and kicked his left foot free of the stirrup. He bent and grabbed the doctor's wrist and suddenly the man was seated behind him. The doctor's arms wrapped around him and his hands held onto the bag. The Cossack broke into a canter and even before Sasha caught the stirrup he felt the horse lengthen its stride into a gallop.

He rode towards the storm and Irina, the gleaming railway lines on his left. He turned away the moment he saw the outline of the house and thundered across the smooth lawns and onto the mud by the front steps. As the horse stopped the doctor jumped down, ran up the steps and through the open door.

Sasha patted the horse and thanked it, then swung off and handed the reins to an old groom.

'How is she?' Sasha asked as he ran into the bedroom.

'Bad. She's split and bleeding,' Sytin said quietly. 'Now get out. I don't need you. I've got the women.'

Tatiana, Natasha and the children's nurse, Maria, all shrugged. Lottie screamed in agony.

'Go, man. Get out! You're in my way!' Doctor Sytin shouldered him aside and he left, running downstairs and outside into the storm to get some air and to ensure the horse was being looked after.

'Please God, please let her be all right.' He knelt in the rain and prayed, and heard Lottie scream again.

'Come inside, sir, please,' one of the old men who did odd chores implored him. 'And you give God a present by playing the piano.'

'I couldn't, Nikolas. I couldn't.'

'Then just come and sit and talk, sir.'

'Talk with a Russian on a night like this? I'd rather play the piano,' he tried to joke and the old man came and put his arm around him and took him back indoors.

Nikolas took him into the room where the piano was kept. A big fire had been lit and hot tea and good vodka prepared. Nikolas led him to the piano and sat himself on another stool which was within reach of both tea and vodka. 'Now, sir, you sit there and I'll sit here, and I'll talk to you. And when you get bored or I get too drunk to talk any more you can play the piano.'

'You're a good man, Nikolas.'

The old man smiled, poured them both tea, talked non-stop for ten minutes then fell asleep leaning against the piano. Sasha played with the keys, could not settle to anything he knew, and played the introduction to a new piece he had started to compose in America.

It was light, and very quiet. All she could hear was the memory of her screams and the intermittent sound of Sasha composing.

'Charlotte?' Tatiana looked drawn, washed out, and her uncombed silver-grey hair made her look old. 'I didn't realise you were awake. How do you feel?'

She felt as though she had given birth to a tree trunk but that did not matter so she ignored the question. 'The baby?'

Tatiana looked grim and could not hide her tears, could not speak.

'Dead?' Lottie asked, and knew the answer even without hearing it.

Tatiana nodded. 'One of them.'

One of them? 'How many?'

'Two. Your little girl's beautiful. Just like you.'

'Can I see her?'

Tatiana nodded and rustled to the door. 'Maria! Maria! Please bring the baby. Sasha! Sasha! Come up here. Charlotte's awake.' Lottie lay back, heard all the activity and excitement she had caused simply by waking up, and then heard Sasha just outside the door.

'Thank you, Maria,' he said softly, 'I'll take her in to see her mother.'

He walked in, dishevelled, red eyed, dried mud specks stuck to his face, and presented her with her tiny pink daughter who had rust-coloured down on the top of her head, a sign of things to come.

'Good morning, Irina,' she said, and was glad he smiled and nodded his acceptance of their daughter's name.

CHAPTER 28

'Evelyn! Come in.'

'Thank you, Sister Brewer. I hope you don't mind me disturbing you at home.'

'Not at all. Come on, come through to the kitchen, and my name's Ada, not Sister.' They walked through to a small kitchen and seconds later tea was being poured. 'I'm pleased to see you, Eve, but what brings you here?'

'Two things really. First, I need a job and I wondered if there was a possibility of finishing my training. I should think that with the war on the country'll be crying out for nurses and I thought perhaps some of the regular staff might have joined up.'

'Try the London Hospital. I've a friend who nurses there and I'll give you a reference. I shouldn't think you'll have any trouble if you apply there. Do it tomorrow,' Ada said briskly. 'The second thing?'

'I remember you used to take in lodgers and I wondered if you still did. I'm living at home again, in my aunt's house, but it's not easy because we don't see eye to eye on the war.'

'Oh, dear. What happened?'

She explained about a row which erupted when her aunt

accused her of encouraging Tom to volunteer, and also about the way Helen and Maisie were very short with her because of the report in the *London and National Cryer* on what she had said about recruitment.'

'Why don't you just tell them you were inaccurately reported?'

'Because it was a bit late to do that by the time I knew how they felt, and anyway, it would have made me look unpatriotic and that would have caused even more of a fuss. Besides, knowing Jamie and Joe they would have joined up just to prove our family's as patriotic as any other. I was going to be seen as being in the wrong whatever I did or didn't do, so I reckoned it's best left as it is. I'll have to put up with whatever people think of me.'

'Well, I'm sorry, Eve, and I'm sorry we don't have a spare room at the moment but try not to worry. I'm sure things'll get better at home. And I'm sure you'll get back into the hospital.'

Eve was back on a ward within the week.

It seemed strange to return to her old life, and the fact that she was working in a different hospital made very little difference.

The atmosphere at home did improve slightly when everyone saw she was doing all she could to make amends for supporting the war. Also, Helen and Maisie became less hostile towards her as the Germans were thrown back and Paris was saved and people began to tell each other it would all be over by Christmas.

September rolled into October. The Germans moved through Flanders, and then pounded Belgium.

Until then the war had very little impact on the hospital, and apart from the family situation and news in the papers it had little impact on her life. That changed suddenly in the early hours of an October morning.

She was asleep when the front door was hammered so loudly she thought it would break down. Her father ran down the stairs ahead of her and opened it to a policeman.

431

'Sorry, sir, but I've been sent to collect Miss Evelyn Forrester.'

She panicked for a moment, mind and heart lurching as she tried to remember whether or not she was free on licence, and it was several moments before her mind cleared enough to remember all that was over.

'What for?' she heard her father try to protect her.

'Belgium's falling fast and we've got shiploads of wounded soldiers coming in. We're knocking up 'alf the country, sir, making hospitals out of schools and halls and using anything to carry the wounded. We need nurses urgently. We got train loads of wounded coming into Charing Cross and half of 'em don't speak English, only French, so I've been sent to get Miss Forrester 'cos she speaks their lingo.'

'I'm dressing now,' she yelled down the stairs, and ten minutes later she was in a car being driven fast towards the station.

The scene was desperate. The walking wounded had been cleared by the time she arrived but powerful electric lights had been rigged and she saw the platform was littered with men on stretchers, or what passed for stretchers, or simply lying in greatcoats or blankets on the ground. VADs, the Voluntary Aid Detachments were everywhere, cleaning, helping, soothing, feeding or just sitting, holding a man's hand while he whimpered in a foreign language.

Red Cross nurses worked their way along the lines of men, trying hard to assess the degree of injury, calling doctors when they thought they were needed or sometimes simply shaking their heads and calling a VAD over to sit with a man who would soon be dead.

She had seen bad wounds before but never seen such carnage on such a scale. She watched experienced policemen fix their faces as they became voluntary stretcher-bearers, but she saw no one shirk any duty no matter how much they might have wanted to

She talked to the men for hours, trying hard to understand their odd dialect and improving all the time,

432

helping them and translating for the doctors who were trying to treat them.

The station cleared slowly and she realised it was light, and that her apron was red with blood and green with the slime most of the men seemed to have stuck to their clothes. She leaned against a wall and sipped a cup of hot Bovril one of the VADs gave her.

'If you think that was bad you should see it on the other side, lassy,' a gravel-voiced, scrawny Scotsman growled at her. He was wearing a Medical Officer's uniform, which somehow did not seem to suit him, and she thought he could have been any age from thirty to sixty. 'We're fitting out trains to carry the wounded away from the line but half the time we're having to shift 'em back in trucks I reckon carried cattle three days ago. I'm amputating on the wagon floor as we go. This is Heaven, girlie. Sheer bloody Heaven.'

'Is it really that bad?'

'Aye, it is. And worse. The ones you've seen are the lucky ones. The other poor bastards are still stuck over there or are dying so fast there's no point in taking space by sending 'em here.'

'I'm surprised they let you come away, sir.'

The army doctor rubbed his eyes. 'I speak their language and someone had to come along. Besides, as the army says, I've got duties to perform over here. Frankly, I'll be glad when I get back there next week.'

'Can I come with you?'

She straightened herself as he looked her up and down. 'You fully trained?'

'Yes, of course,' she lied without showing any sign, sure she knew enough to be safely let loose.

'You'd have to join up. You prepared to do that?'

'Of course. How do I go about it – without wasting time with stacks of formalities.'

He scratched his chin. 'You sure about this? It's bloody hell, you know? Cold, wet, dangerous and filthy. And you work until you drop.'

'I'm sure. I've been trying to find something I can get my teeth into.'

Aye? Well then, come and see me at my hotel this evening. We'll find a way to get around the system.' He started to walk away, then turned. 'Oh, my name's Alistair MacKenzie, Captain. Don't worry if you change your mind and decide not to come. I'll understand.'

Six days later Eve told her mother she had been accepted as an army nurse.

'You're going to France? Tomorrow?' Her mother looked shocked.

'The hospital and everyone've been wonderful in getting things organised so fast. I want to go because I can do more over there than I can here, Mama. Men're dying because there aren't enough nurses, Mama, and I can't stay here when I know that's happening. Not when I know a lot of them might not even be over there if I hadn't told them they should go and fight.'

'Why did you do that, Eve? I've never understood but I couldn't ask you before, not when Lizzie and the girls were already so critical of you.'

She explained how Cedric Rathbone and Lady Braithewaite had bludgeoned her into making the statement which the *London and National Cryer* had printed, and that once it had been made she did not think she had the right to retract.

'I think you're too honest for public life, Eve. Far too honest.'

'No, Mama, but I am too trusting.'

'Perhaps, but don't ever be ashamed of that, Eve. You won't mind, when you've gone, if I tell the others what you've just told me?'

'Of course not, Mama, if it makes you happy.'

'It won't make me happy, my dear, knowing you're over there. Be careful, won't you, and write whenever you can.'

'I'll try.'

Eve wrote a letter on the night she arrived, telling how the French coast either side of Boulogne seemed to have a lace-edging sewn to the cliff tops, and how when the ship sailed closer she could see it was a vast tented encampment. Canvas hospitals.

It was a short letter, one page written with a pencil stub. A page was all she could manage without telling the family about things she did not want them to know. She did not want them to know she was living in an unheated tent with seven other nurses, that the sanitary arrangements were insanitary, that the hospitals looked much as they must have during the Crimean War, that the canvas wards stank of enteric illnesses and rotting gangrenous flesh and that shattered men were being brought in by the train load.

Later, as each day rolled into the next so she was never sure what day it was unless she looked at a calendar, when she was too tired even to sleep properly, she forgot to write. Later still, when she developed chilblains on her feet and fingers, boils, sties and numerous aches and pains from being wet and cold, and she was over-tired from being on her feet for too long, she could not be bothered to write.

Two months after her arrival she did not even write to tell her mother that a sudden shortage of nursing Sisters had resulted in her unofficial promotion to Sister.

It seemed to her that life on Angel Street was akin to life on a different planet. It had nothing to do with the reality she knew every day as she saw men with limbs blown half off, intestines hanging out, holes and cuts which excreted foul-smelling pus, or wounds which disfigured them into something almost sub-human. She learned to deal with it all, smiling when she remembered, being briskly friendly when possible, and always being cheerful because that helped her as much as it helped the men she was nursing.

Eve stood by the entrance of a large marquee bearing the red cross of a hospital tent, stared out into the pitch black night and watched the rain sheet down off the tent roof and dilute the muddy ground even more. Light from a hurricane lamp showed that the duck-board path which was meant to keep everyone out of the mud was already half submerged and was about to disappear altogether. She pulled her cape over her head, stepped onto the slippery

435

board and was about to run when she heard someone pounding towards her through the dark.

The duck-board was not wide enough for two people to pass so she stepped off it and moved back under cover, holding the tent flap up so whoever was approaching could rush in without stopping.

'That's kind of you, Nurse.' The greatcoated doctor brushed past her and turned as he recognised her. 'Oh, it's you. Our French-speaking acquisition and just the lady I was hoping to see. How're you enjoying yourself?'

'I'm managing, sir.'

He flicked water off his cap and coat. 'Aye? More than just managing from what I've heard. You're acting as Sister, aren't you?'

'Yes, sir.'

'How'd you like to come and work with me – trying to help these poor devils before they're brought here?'

'Where?'

'On one of the hospital trains. We run up as far as Ypres and down as far as Le Havre if we can't offload here or somewhere nearer. It's bloody hard but no worse than here. We just have different problems, that's all.' He paused, peered at her, and asked impatiently, 'Well?'

'How long do I have to make up my mind?'

'I've just lost one of my Sisters and I've already got permission from your boss to poach you if you want to do it. The train leaves in fifteen minutes.'

'You don't waste much time, sir.'

'I don't have it to waste. I'll see you on the train, if you're coming.' He slapped his cap back on his head, turned up his greatcoat collar and ducked through the canvas opening out into the rain.

Eve followed minutes later, ran to her tent, threw all her possessions into a kitbag, tied canvas overboots over her shoes, said goodbye to the three off-duty friends she was leaving behind, and rushed out into the rain.

There was very little light and the duck-boards were nearly all submerged so she slithered and slipped her way through sticky mud and puddles as she made her way through the canvas village, carefully avoiding the tent ropes which could have tripped her. She reached the makeshift station and ran through the steam and smoke as the locomotive coughed and spun its wheels on the wet rails.

'Sister!' The doctor was leaning out from a carriage door. 'Over here!'

She ran to him as the train started to move. He took her kitbag from her as she trotted beside the carriage and gripped her arm to steady her as she skipped up onto the step. He helped her into the carriage and slammed the door shut.

'Your name's Eve, isn't it? I'll introduce you to the others and show you your quarters, Sister. I'm Captain Alistair MacKenzie, but everyone calls me Mac. I'm in charge and I've two more Medical Officers to help. They're Scots, like me, and they're called Ian and Gordon. I used to be a ship's surgeon and we treat this train a bit like a ship. It's run very informally and we're too busy to stand on ceremony. There're three more Sisters, Beattie, Winnie and Ann, and thirty-odd orderlies.' He carried her kitbag along the corridor. 'I'm not sure where we're going tonight, but it's probably up around Ypres.'

The train shuddered and gathered speed. She looked through a slit in one of the shutters which all but covered the windows and saw the hospital camp slide past, the glow from the lamp-lit tents ephemeral in the black night.

She was scared. They were going to Ypres! Large numbers of the wounded men came from Ypres and she had heard the orderlies who carried the men off the train say they went close enough to the line to feel the percussion of shells exploding. They said they were close enough to hear small arms firing quite clearly.

Mac led her along the swaying corridor until he opened a door into a first-class sleeping compartment. 'Here's your bunk, your home until we lay off in our base in Rouen. Excuse the junk. It's comforts for the men. We get around so we get the job of distributing them. It cheers 'em up so it's well worth it. You'll find we're a bit short of space.'

She peered into the compartment, about six feet square, and saw the floor was littered with bales of gloves and socks, scarfs, boxes of soap and cigarettes, parcels of magazines, anything the men might like to ease their misery and fear for a few minutes.

'Well, it's luxury compared to the tent, sir.'

'Maybe, but you'll still get sick of it. And it's Mac, not sir.'

'Yes, Mac.' She dumped her kitbag into the compartment and followed him to meet the other Sisters.

Winnie and Ann were small and slim and blonde and looked so alike they could have been sisters, and she guessed they were about the same age as her. Beattie was probably in her early thirties, tall and slim with dark brown hair. They all had their hair cut fairly short and they told her that made it easier for them to get rid of the trench lice the men inevitably brought on board the train.

She drank some cocoa with them, returned to her own quarters, lay down on her bunk, and wondered what she had let herself in for.

She woke up, feeling drugged, realised the train was not moving and peered through the slit in her window-shutter into a grey dawn. She could see trees and cattle grazing in fields, and a man and woman with a bucket throwing down grain for chickens to eat. It all seemed strangely unwarlike. She looked at the scene for a long time, then washed herself with warm water in the compartment's canvas bowl, then took the opportunity to wash her dirty clothes and hang them up to dry on an improvised washing line. Beattie, the natural leader, had given her two fresh uniforms to wear, and having washed herself properly and dressed in crisp clothes for the first time in weeks she felt ready for anything.

In the distance she heard the familiar chugging sound of a steam engine pulling a heavy train and she moved into the corridor and looked through another shutter. A long troop train rolled past, carriages first then flat wagons carrying artillery pieces, and finally closed wagons painted with signs that warned explosives were being carried.

She wondered how the men who were going to war felt when they saw the hospital train waiting to take them away again. Did it give them comfort or make them think there were German trains loaded just like theirs not far away?

The troop train rumbled off into the distance but the hospital train still waited on the little piece of track laid to form a passing place. Ten minutes later she heard a steam whistle and the roar of a train approaching fast from the opposite direction. The carriage shuddered as the empty train flashed past, its flat wagons empty of weapons and its closed wagons probably empty of ammunition.

She turned as Beattie made her way along the narrow corridor. 'Good morning, Eve. We're likely to be stuck here for a few hours while they move stuff up to the Front, so Mac's suggested we might like to go for a walk. There's a village about a mile up the track, and Ann and Winnie are game so what about you?'

'Yes,' she said immediately. She had been in France for two months and had spent every minute of the time in the hospital camp. This would be her first glimpse of the locals.

They helped each other down from the train's high step and walked past the engine and along the railway track which was straight and raised several feet above the flat green fields that spread for miles. Unlike English fields these merged with one another or were separated by small ditches rather than hedges. There were small clusters of remote buildings half-hidden in the grey light and early mist, and in the distance she could just see a village entangled in a long fringe of poplar trees.

The air was damp and smelled fresh, and apart from the noise they made walking on the clinker railway bed or the wooden sleepers there was total silence. The world seemed to be holding its breath.

They walked for five minutes until they reached an ungated level-crossing which allowed a cart track to cross the railway line, and they followed the track which led towards the village.

Minutes after they stepped off the line they heard the whistle of another train moving towards the Front, two locomotives coupled together to pull a long train of carriages and wagons full of men and weapons. Eve noticed how quiet the other women were, how resigned they seemed when they turned away after standing and waving to the troops who were going forward.

Beattie broke a long silence as two trains passed with less than a minute separating them. 'Looks like they're getting a whole new lot of customers ready for us, girls. We'll be shuttling backwards and forwards between here and the BHs without stopping.'

'BHs?' she asked.

'Base hospitals,' Ann explained. 'Should be PHs for pretend hospitals. We've taken over the casinos in Boulogne and Le Touquet, a lot of half-suitable buildings in Rouen, and right down in Le Havre they've even converted the Ocean Terminal's First Class waiting rooms into what we call hospitals. They can't cater for the numbers, though, which is why we've got all the hospital camps too.'

'I see,' she said, remembering the rumours she had heard about warehouses and breweries being used as hospitals because they were big buildings which always had easy access for trains or lorries. Obviously the rumours which she and the other new arrivals had thought were exaggerations were the truth. The war was four and a half months old and although she had been out here for two of those months she still felt like a newcomer, particularly among these women who, as yet, saw her as an outsider.

They reached the village and she was struck by the fact that all the buildings were covered with unpainted concrete rendering and all the windows had shutters which needed paint. Moss and thin blades of grass grew among roof-tiles. The village was shabby and astonishingly quiet. It was empty. There was no one about.

Then she heard one voice, muffled and indistinct. Moments later a chorus of voices burst into song. A hymn.

'Good God, it must be Sunday,' Winnie said inappropriately.

They walked towards the sound, found themselves in a

small village square, saw a square concrete church with its door half open and entered.

She smelled incense and realised these people worshipped in a different way to her but it did not seem to matter. She sat in one of the rear pews and the others followed. They seemed to understand the order of service better than her but she could understand enough of the service to feel some benefit from it, and even understood the welcome and the prayer of thanks which was directed at her and the others when their presence was noticed.

The whole congregation, except her, moved forward to take communion. She sat still and closed her eyes and allowed the feeling of the church to shroud her. It was not difficult to pretend she was in the Methodist chapel in Angel Street, and in spite of the incense and the foreign language and the strange land outside she felt close enough to her family at home to think they might hear her praying for them. She knew they would pray for her and Lottie and that seemed to bring her even closer to her sister who, like her, was in a foreign land.

When the service ended she stood outside talking to several local women who were surprised that she could speak their language and who invited her and the others back to their homes for food and coffee.

She asked Beattie if there was time but there was not, and minutes later they shook hands with the villagers, exchanged wishes for each other's safety and a quick end to the war and walked back towards the train. Even when they were some distance from the village they could still hear the villagers singing hymns for their benefit. The voices died away and the earlier silence bore down again.

Eve was sorry to leave the village and its feeling of homeliness, and for the first time since she had left England she felt homesick. A disc of white sun hung above thin cloud and threw a strange light over the fields and the raised railway and emphasised the foreignness of the land she was in. It was strange because she had not felt homesick when she was in America, thousands of miles from home, yet here, where she was probably less than a hundred miles from London, she felt completely out of place.

'D'you have a young man, Eve?' Beattie asked.

'No, not really. There is a young man, Tom Dobbs, who asked me to marry him before he joined up but I don't know if we ever will. And there was another man, a doctor who might even be out here because he was already working in a hospital near Le Havre, but we broke up months ago.' It suddenly seemed important to form something like a friendship with Beattie and the others because they were all she had now. 'Do you, or the others have anyone?'

Beattie glanced back at Winnie and Ann who were following them along the cart track. 'Winnie's young man's out here somewhere, and Ann has three brothers in the line although she doesn't know where, exactly. She had four brothers but one was killed in the retreat from Mons. That was in the early days. Anyway, what's your doctor's name, Eve? One of us might know him.'

'It's Robert Braithewaite.'

'Is that Lady Braithewaite's son?'

'Yes!' Her mood suddenly felt lighter. 'Do you know him?'

'I don't *know* him, exactly, but I do know *of* him and if he's somewhere in this sector you might come across him. I'll tell the others to keep their ears open and we'll let you know if we hear of anything. That's if you want us to?'

'Yes, please.' She noticed the way her heart beat faster and realised that ever since Lady Braithewaite had suggested she may have misled her she had wanted to meet Robert again. It would be good to clear the air even if it did not change things between them. With all that was happening around her she felt she needed to settle all unfinished business, and that was how she thought of her relationship with Robert. They had parted on bad terms and their parting would not be complete until they had resolved the misunderstandings which had caused their final argument.

The train, still standing in the short siding, blew its whistle three times, the signal that it was time to leave, but although the others lifted their coats and long white skirts and started to hurry she stopped and listened to a distant rumble. 'I can hear thunder,' she called out.

'It's not thunder, Eve,' Ann called back to her.

'It sounds like it.'

'It's *not* thunder, Eve,' Beattie said. 'The Hun're shelling our trenches.'

All the familiarity with home dissipated at once. Winnie and Ann were white-faced and Beattie looked stern as she told them to double up. They ran the remaining distance to the train and found a couple of RAMC orderlies were standing ready to help them back up onto the train's high step.

The engine chuffed, wheels screamed, and the train jolted forwards, towards the artillery barrage.

'Scared?' Winnie asked as they wedged themselves in a corner of the corridor.

'Yes,' she admitted.

'Well, we don't go right up to the line. Not quite.' Winnie grinned. 'They've got Regimental Aid posts in the trenches, close enough for the men to crawl to if need be. They get their wounds dressed there and then they're taken back to a Field Dressing Station which is just behind the lines. They're set up in anything that's got three walls and something that keeps most of the rain and shrapnel out, although sometimes they're in tents. They shove antitetanus into the wounded and put 'em in ambulances that carry 'em back to Casualty Clearing Stations about eight miles behind the line. We collect 'em from there.'

Eve thought it sounded well organised and said so.

Ann scoffed. 'It is, in a sense, but there're so many men hurt and falling ill that the system can't cope. You'll see when we get there, and realise why *we* have to be so well-organised.'

The train gathered speed.

Eve saw they had reached a town, and clung to a door handle as the train swung off the main line, rattled across points and slowed alongside a makeshift platform built along a goods yard stacked with piles of stone blocks, sand and coal, and littered with stands of timber. Whistles blew and she threw open the door as the train stopped. Mac had already leapt down onto the platform and was talking to an officer who held a sheaf of papers.

Shells exploded a few miles away and a blackish haze hung above the town's buildings, obliterating the weak, round sun she had noticed earlier. Mac saw her watching and called her down, and as she clambered off the train Beattie dropped from the next carriage and joined her. Mac addressed them both. 'Four hundred cases, mostly enterics and pneumonia but about forty with trench foot. No casualties, as such, but we must load fast because there's another hospital train on its way and we need to clear the dock. The Clearing Station's over the road and as most men can walk across you'd better get 'em loaded the way you want or they'll just jump on anywhere.'

Winnie and Ann had joined them and Beattie issued her orders fast. She told them to load the enteric cases at the rear, the pneumonia cases next and the men with trench foot at the front. 'You come with me, Eve. We'll try to organise the way they leave and we'll ask about your Doctor Braithewaite.'

She followed Beattie off the platform, through high wooden gates which could be opened to allow lorries into the yard, and across a road lined on one side by ambulances with red crosses painted on their canvas bodies.

She was shocked to find that the Casualty Clearing Station, really a temporary hospital, had been set up in an abattoir, but Beattie explained that it made an ideal hospital because it was easy to keep clean. 'Cleanliness and speed are what we try to achieve. We need to make the men as comfortable as possible and get them to hospital as fast as possible.'

Everyone flinched as a shell screamed overhead and flinched again as it exploded on the far side of the town. The men who knew they were to be taken away started to move, warily looking about them as another shell screamed over and exploded out of sight, leaving a column of thick black

444

smoke beyond the town's buildings.

'Right, Eve, you get the enterics loaded and help Winnie with them. Ann'll take care of the pneumonia cases and I'll help her and look after the men with rotten feet.' Beattie started to organise the loading and two columns of men walked across the road, the stronger ones helping their weaker mates.

Eve helped those who seemed to need urgent help and felt sorry for the men's embarrassment as their enteritis got the better of them.

'What's made so many of them so ill?' she asked one of the orderlies.

'The trenches, Sister. They spend half their lives up to their waist in water when it rains like this. There ain't no nice lavatories out there, so they do what they have to wherever they are. Then if the water carriers can't get through they drink whatever water looks clean, but none of it is. They might try and boil it but it's got everything in it from drowned rats to dead men. Enteritis is rife, Sister, and dysentery in some parts.'

'I see,' she said quietly, and remembered the summer afternoon when she had followed Lady Braithewaite's lead in encouraging men to join this noble war. And once again she thought it was incredible that she was little more than a hundred miles from her home and that no one back there had any concept of what this war was really like.

More shells came over but the men were too busy trying to get to the train to stop and cower, so she followed their example.

One and a half hours later, a little after noon, the loaded train pulled away from the station and proper nursing began. All the men were suffering, whether from painful feet, congested lungs or various forms of enteritis. Nursing in the cramped and swaying train was difficult and hard work and she lost count of the number of times she walked along the corridors, catching her long cotton dress on one of the hundred obstructions there seemed to be, forgetting which carriage she had left earlier, and banging her elbows as the carriage jolted her against a wall or door or window.

The journey back to the coast was made long and erratic because it seemed that the train was for ever pulling into sidings to allow more important trains to pass. Night came. She did not think about eating and even if she had felt hungry the smell coming from the enteric cases would have stopped her. The only drinks she had in ten hours were a single mug of stewed and lukewarm tea which Mac pressed on her and a glass of water which Ann passed to her.

Eve did not sit down once but although she was relieved when Beattie said they were finally pulling into Boulogne she also felt that this very active form of nursing suited her better than staying in one place.

'Back where you started,' Mac said to her. 'That was an easy run because we can offload everyone here but it gave you an idea of what's involved. Do you want to stay with us or stop here in Boulogne?'

'I'd like to stay with you,' she said without hesitating.

'Good.' Beattie smiled. 'We've all said we'd like you to stay, but you don't have to try to do it all yourself, Eve. There's hard work, and there's stupidity. There's no point in wearing yourself out.'

'I'm sorry, but I just feel so sorry for them. All of them.'

'And guilty?' Mac asked. 'If I'd known who you were before we brought you aboard I mightn't have asked you. I didn't realise you were *the* Evelyn Forrester, the WFL leader, until Beattie asked me if I knew anything about Robert Braithewaite, and then I guessed. Look, lassie, I know you were one of those who said these poor buggers should join up and fight, and I admire you for coming over here and doing what you can, but Beattie's right. Don't wear yourself out, Eve, or you'll be no use to us.'

'I'll try to remember,' she promised and was grateful that he had not criticised her for encouraging men to join up.

'Good.' Mac nodded, then turned away as someone called him. 'Sorry, ladies, I'm needed, but Eve, if you find Robert Braithewaite give him my best wishes, will you.'

'You know him?'

'Aye. I bumped into him a few times. Good doctor. Very good. The last time I saw him he was being shelled to hell in an advance Casualty Clearing Station, but I don't know where he is now. Total waste of a good man, I reckon, but he seemed to be keen to risk his neck to prove something. What or who to, I don't know.'

She watched him stride away and her spirits fell as she wondered if he was right about Robert. Was he risking his life to prove something? And if so what was it? And who was he trying to impress?

Eve helped with various chores as the train was offloaded, cleaned with disinfectant, restocked with supplies and refuelled, and she was glad she had something to concentrate on. At one o'clock in the morning Beattie took her and the others off to a canteen where they ate their first and last meal of that working day and were finally able to sit down. The canteen's food and warmth held them until Ian, one of the other doctors, came for them and told them the train was leaving in ten minutes.

They walked back through rain which had started to fall, clambered back aboard the train, and as it left the station she climbed into her bunk and fell asleep thinking that tomorrow she would ask Mac to tell her more about Robert.

She woke up late and was only just dressed and ready as the train pulled into a shattered railway station in a town which had been flattened by shelling. Eve opened the carriage door and was stunned by the destruction. There was no Casualty Clearing Station here, just a long line of ambulances and lorries, and unbelievably, five two-decked London buses complete with advertisements for familiar products. They looked incongruous so close to the battlefield.

It took four hours to load the men. This loading was not organised like yesterday's but that did not matter because all the men were battle casualties and there was no real advantage to be gained by separating them for different types of treatment. Also, halfway through the loading a

German scout had flown overhead and the Captain in charge of the ambulances thought it was important to get the men on board the train before the aeroplane could fly back and report their position for the German artillery to bring down a barrage.

The barrage did not come. Whether that was because the Germans refrained from shelling wounded men, or the scout had not reported back or had been shot down somewhere no one knew. All that concerned them was that the barrage did not come.

The train ran down to Le Touquet, unloaded, was cleaned and restocked in record time and returned to load another four hundred men further along the line by three o'clock the following morning.

Eve snatched whatever sleep she could during the four-hour return journey and was surprised how alert she felt as she helped to load the men by the light of hurricane lamps and the flares the Germans fired over the trenches a few miles ahead. They loaded the men very quickly, in less than an hour, and when she walked along the corridor she realised why. The train was less than half full.

When it jolted into life it went forwards, not back. They were going closer to the Front. The train moved forwards into a cutting and stopped.

She concentrated on whatever she had to do, putting drainage tubes into suppurating wounds, washing out puss, stitching wounds which were clean enough to be stitched and trying to cool and calm men who were burning up with fever caused by wound infections. She helped drug one man who had already gone mad with gangrene infection so he would be oblivious of his own misery and could not inflict it on others, and she called the orderlies to remove several men who had died since being loaded on to the train they thought might take them back to England and home.

One very young lieutenant, still alive with half his brain shot away, kept asking if his men had been fed.

She was exhausted when dawn crept up, and very aware of one thing in particular.

No matter how old the men were, and whether or not they were married, when they were in the deepest depths of pain and misery they each called out for their mothers.

The same rule seemed to apply to all the men, no matter what their background or their circumstances. The power their mothers had over them even extended to hell.

The train inched forward again as the dawn expanded, and when she looked out of an unshuttered window she saw a landscape which almost convinced her she *was* in hell. What she saw did not look real. There were no trees, only charcoal stumps, but worse than that, there was no flat land.

The earth had been blown apart. Houses could have been hidden in the holes the shells had created, streets could have been lost in some of them. She had heard stories about whole companies, two hundred and fifty men, disappearing without trace, and now she knew it was possible.

The train stopped.

'What's happening?' she saw Ian and hoped he might know.

'We had to pull forwards so they could offload more troops but we can't go too far because the line's torn up.'

'Thank Christ for that.' As she spoke she heard a loud screech and a thud and seconds later the carriage rocked and the window she had looked out of was plastered with mud. The train shifted backwards and seconds later Mac raced past her, going to the rear of the train.

Another shell ripped into the earth on the far side of the train and a sound like heavy rain hammered the carriages as mud hit them. Wheels screamed against the rails and the train slowed. She looked through a slit in one of the shutters and saw they were back in the cover of the cutting but she did not feel any safer. She had seen the damage the shells could inflict and they came from above. There *was* no protection from the German artillery.

Mac raced back, opened a door and jumped down onto the track. She reached the door and leaned out. A long queue of men rose up from the mud where they had been waiting and the familiar whistles blew to call men to order and get them loaded on board the train. These men were all medical cases, the usual enteritis and pneumonia or bronchitis. She thought at first that almost all of them had been dressed for head wounds but she then saw they were Indians wearing Sikh turbans. They were very polite and uncomplaining as the orderlies yanked them on board, and they organised themselves into coteries she realised related to their various castes.

She saw Mac run back past the train, already shouting and waving his arms at the officers who were offloading fresh troops behind them and blocking the track. More shells screamed down as she busied herself with the latest intake and she hardly heard Ann when she came to explain that a German spotter balloon had been seen and that it must have seen the trains and brought down the barrage on them.

Suddenly the train was moving steadily backwards and gaining speed and the noise it made overcame the screams and explosions from the shells.

They ran to Le Touquet without stopping and once again they offloaded all the men, cleaned, restocked, and headed north once more.

They were well on their way before they learned Mac was not with them. He had gone off to protest about the hospital train being put at such risk by bringing troop trains too close when the wounded were being loaded.

The next morning they stopped at the station they had used before and collected four hundred more men, half of them battle casualties. The Germans had put down a heavy barrage and launched an infantry attack. There were too many casualties for the clearing station to process and many of the men had received little or no treatment.

She and the others did whatever they could for the men as the train carried them back towards Boulogne, constantly pulling off the main line so reinforcements and supplies could be carried north.

This time there were not enough beds for them to offload at Boulogne or Le Touquet and they were forced to go on to Rouen. It took two more days.

Eve was numb with fatigue when she stepped off the train in Rouen and once she was shown her room at base it took all her effort to undress and run a bath. She shoved her clothes into a bin with a lid which was tight enough to stop any lice from escaping and plunged into the lukewarm water, washed herself with Lysol and attended to the damage the lice had done to her.

Then she slept. It seemed a long time before she woke up.

When Eve woke she found a note from Beattie inviting her to breakfast at the Jeanne d'Arque Café and telling her how to find her way there. The note ended with the promise that it would be worth her while.

She found the café without any difficulty and was surprised to see Beattie and Ann looking completely refreshed and accompanied by a Medical Officer she guessed was aged around thirty-five.

He rose as she approached, held his hand out and said, 'You must be Evelyn Forrester. You're exactly as Robert described you.'

She was stunned. 'He described me to you? Why?'

'Because you came up in conversation.'

'In what context?'

'I was staying with him, at his mother's house, and we were discussing the Women's Freedom League. I asked what sort of woman could take Lady Braithewaite's place and there seemed to be rather a difference of opinion. Lady Braithewaite wasn't exactly complimentary but Robert gave a much more accurate description, although, if you don't mind me saying so, I don't think even he did you justice.'

'Thank you,' she said and knew she was blushing. 'I assume you know Robert well?'

'Rather! We were at school together, learned to be doctors together, and actually shared lodgings until Lydia came along and they got themselves married.' He stopped suddenly and frowned at her. 'You look puzzled, Miss Forrester?'

She was puzzled. Robert had said Lydia was his brother's wife, but she did not admit that. 'No, I'm still tired, that's all. Were you at their wedding?'

'Yes, I was his best man. Even though I told him I didn't think he should marry the woman I agreed to support his decision. I wished I hadn't afterwards, of course.'

She took a chance in order to find out more about Robert and Lydia. 'What exactly did happen? He told me something about the accident and Lydia losing the baby, and going into the home, of course, but then his mother came into the room and he never got around to finishing the story. I didn't like to ask him because it seemed so painful.'

He shrugged, obviously accepting her lie. 'Lydia was quite beautiful but immensely selfish. She'd always been sweet on Robert's brother and when he refused to play her matrimonial game she suddenly turned her full attention on Robert. I'm sure she only married him out of pique and when she announced she was pregnant I was never sure whose baby it was. Robert, of course, did not know what was happening and assumed it was his, even when dear Lydia and older brother ran away. I'm sure you know the rest. Almighty car crash, brother dies, Lydia loses baby, and full of remorse loses her mind. Robert, honest chap that he is, allows mother to make up a story to avoid family scandal and lands himself with a wife who'll never be a wife to him.'

'Surely he could divorce her, under the circumstances?'

'Of course, but mother wouldn't like it, and anyway I think he still hankers after the little beauty, even if she has ruined his life. Besides, what's the point of divorcing her? He's so scared of making another mistake he won't do anything worthwhile with his life, which is why he dabbles in a dozen things but never commits himself to anything. It would take an incredibly stupid woman to marry Robert, and I say that as his friend. His mother's ruined him, Evelyn, but he doesn't have the guts to leave her. That's probably why he's gone back home now. I imagine she wangled him a home posting and he took it just to keep her quiet.'

Beattie had told her it would be worth her while to come, but she was not sure it had been. One short conversation had made sense of several mysteries and had ended a part of her life.

Well, Robert's friend had concentrated her mind and she had to agree with his opinion of Robert. It was one she had formed herself but had not really wanted to admit to.

A week later, Christmas Eve, the train stopped at Boulogne and Eve took the opportunity to visit the nurses she had once shared a tent with.

They handed her a Christmas postcard from Tom Dobbs and some letters from England. All except one were from her family. The other one was from Sister Brewer who hoped she was safe and felt she was at last doing something worthwhile.

Yes. When she had time she would write back and say she was doing something worthwhile. Nursing was the most important thing in her life.

CHAPTER 29

It was exactly two months since Irina had been born and John had been buried. They named him because they wanted to have a name to call him by when they talked about him in years to come, and they held him and kissed him because though he was born dead they did not want him to think he was not loved or wanted, but they buried him quickly because he *was* dead and it was better to put him in the past.

Irina was the future and they both thought she grew more beautiful each day. Leo and Sergei were besotted and already arguing over which one of them would marry her. They compromised by agreeing that, as they did with most things, they would share her.

Lottie took six weeks to recover and when Doctor Sytin removed the stitches he said there was no reason why she should not have a dozen more children if she wanted them, but he asked her not to have them in the middle of a stormy night. He also said he was impressed by Sasha's horsemanship and wondered if Sasha had thought of applying to the cavalry when he undertook his patriotic duty.

It was a pointed comment.

She told Sasha what the doctor had said and realised he had already thought about his situation.

'The war's not going well, Lottie, and I'm sure he and a lot of others think I should be doing my duty, especially now we have a little Russian daughter who I should be protecting from the *nemets*.'

'I keep hearing this word, *nemets*. What does it mean?'

'Both foreigners and Germans. Russia has the same word for both. We have never lived easily with the Germans.'

'Do you want to go and fight?' She had to ask the question but she dreaded his answer.

'No, I don't *want* to fight because I don't want to leave you and Irina and I don't want to get hurt or killed, but I think I may have to. Tatiana says I could avoid conscription by saying I was the estate manager and arguing that I would be more use running the estate than carrying a rifle, but I don't want to. I owe Zubov enough and I wouldn't like to be seen as his sop. It's also complicated because of the family situation.'

'The reason why Peter isn't welcome here?'

'Yes. It was thought he would marry Natasha, but then he fell in love with Olga,' Sasha said briefly.

'But these things happen and he hasn't married either. Anyway, Natasha and Olga are friends.'

'At Peter's expense. You see, my mother was to have married Valerie Vassilievitch but Tatiana stole him. That's what's always been said to protect his reputation but in fact my mother found out that he was visiting a number of women and refused to marry him. She even warned Tatiana but she would not hear anything bad said against the man. This was all years ago, but later there was a suggestion that by courting both Natasha and Olga, Peter was simply taking revenge on Tatiana. He still sees Olga but she pretends he doesn't in order to keep the family happy.'

'It seems very complicated, Sasha.'

'No, simply very Russian!' Sasha grunted. 'Russians love intrigue. Haven't you noticed?'

'What's Mr Zubov like? I've never met him.'

Sasha smiled. 'He's handsome, charming, very rich, very generous and he likes women. Too much. Tatiana cannot satisfy him on her own, so Olga helps. Olga's also very strong and can ensure he doesn't go to the cafés to find women, but you can see the complication. Anyway, Krasnaya, they will try to keep him away from you, but if I have to go away and he comes here, you sleep with your gun, or a very clear head. He would never force you, but he would try to persuade you.'

She laughed and said Sasha was the only man who could persuade her, and she turned as the door opened. Tatiana walked into the room. She looked ill.

'Charlotte. They've come to take the working men away to war. They say the harvesting is done and women can do whatever else is needed. I have to give them a list of every man on the estate. Even guests.'

She went numb.

A fat, fur-hatted, bearded man who wore a nondescript uniform and called himself a Marshal strode into the room and she heard an argument break out between him and Sasha and Tatiana.

'What's happening?' she asked as Natasha rushed in to ask what all the fuss was about.

Natasha listened. 'He says he wants to take Nikolas off to war.'

'That's ridiculous. He's far too old,' Lottie said.

'Yes, that's what Sasha told him, so the Marshal's said he'll take Sasha instead.'

A chill settled on her. Sasha was red-faced and shouting, his arms thrusting at the air, but the Marshal simply smiled and shook his head. Finally he shouted an order and two equally nondescript characters stepped into the room, snapped the bolts on the rifles, pushed them to their shoulders and pointed them at Sasha. They looked very amateurish, but that simply made them seem more dangerous.

Sasha turned to her. 'I'll have to go with them to sort this out. I'll explain it all when I get back.'

'You will be back?'

'Oh yes, don't worry, yet. I'll have to go sooner or later but not today. They've agreed to that. And they're not taking Nikolas although they do want all the other male servants and the men from the estate.'

She kissed him even though the Marshal was already trying to drag him away. 'I love you, Sasha.'

'And I love you, Krasnaya. Kiss Irina for me. I'll see you this evening and we'll talk.' He walked away and she could see he was crying.

He did not come back. She did not hear from him and she could not find anyone who would tell her where he had been sent.

The winter came quickly and proved Sasha's prediction was right. The winter was cold. Colder than she could have imagined.

The first frost killed the leaves, but left them hanging from the trees, and standing stark against the huge white skies the trees which had once looked so proud now looked like a ragged and defeated army. She hoped that was not an omen.

Days later a wind came from the east and ripped the limp leaves off the branches. Lottie sat for hours, looking at the bare trees, dark skeletons hanging from an unforgiving sky. She thought of Sasha, somewhere under that sky, alone and probably frightened.

She opened a window and whispered, 'I love you, Sasha,' hoping the wind would carry the words to him, but when she shut the window she saw her breath frozen on the glass.

She stared at it, transfixed, scared, and then Irina cried and she went to her. Irina was all that she had left of Sasha apart from the piano and violin pendant she still wore next to her heart, a bag full of clothes which she occasionally took out, hugged and smelled, and a few sheets of handwritten music.

Irina was a summer estate, not meant for winters which were always spent in the capital, but this winter they all stayed at Irina.

Lottie concentrated on her daughter, on improving her own piano skills enough to play Sasha's music competently if not well, on teaching Leo and Sergei what she could, and on learning Russian. Her instincts told her she might remain in Russia for a long time. Perhaps for ever.

She had made herself believe Sasha would survive but she knew the war was not going to end as quickly as so many had predicted during the early weeks. The fast advances the Russians had made in the first month had been halted by the better-equipped and organised Germans and she was sure this war was going to drag on. From what Tatiana and Natasha said, in low voices so the servants would not hear, she gathered they agreed with Mr Zubov and Peter that there was also going to be another war, of sorts.

She listened as they explained how the people would not forgive the Tsarists if Russia lost the war but if Russia won, those same people would see both the sacrifices and the victory as theirs. In either case, defeated or triumphant, when the war ended there would be a mass of ordinary Russian people who were armed and trained to use those arms, and they had a surfeit of leaders who would excite their grievances and show them how to use their power to take whatever they wanted.

'The Tsar murdered Tsarism when he declared war on the Kaiser,' Tatiana said, and added coldly, 'And he may have murdered loyal Tsarists like us. And even our children, who have no cause to suffer.'

Lottie thought about the house and estate, copied from an American estate which was later destroyed in the American Civil War, and she shivered with a sense of what might come. 'Do you really believe that's the future, Tatiana?'

'I do, and Valerie does, as do many of our friends. The people have genuine grievances, and here, at Irina, we have tried to be just. But Russia isn't like Irina, Lottie, and when the storm comes it will sweep away Irina as it sweeps away less happy estates. You must never forget that you are English and you must try, if possible, to get away before that storm breaks. And take little Irina with you.'

458

'But she is Russian, Tatiana. Just as Russian as Leo and Sergei.'

Tatiana looked at her and tears formed and flowed over her cheeks. 'Lottie, if it happens, as we think it will, will you take them too?'

'Of course, but surely it'll never come to that.'

Tatiana held her hands up in a sign of prayer. 'I pray it won't but there are others who pray it will, and I think there are more of them, Lottie.'

It was a frightening and depressing thought, and one which they lived with as the winter aged and gloom settled like dust inside the cold, iced-up house. Even Nikolas became morose as, with only women to talk to, he shuffled about doing light chores and carrying in logs for the fires, always first shaking the ice off his long beard.

He said it was the coldest winter he had ever known, then added that maybe it just seemed like that because he was becoming ancient.

One morning Lottie woke up and noticed the frost had started melting from the inside of her bedroom windows, and when she looked through a small circle of clear glass she saw green shoots and buds reaching for a thin, white sun. Spring was coming.

Within a week she and the others were all too busy to be gloomy. Spring had come, the sun was already warming the soil and there was estate work to do. Work only old Nikolas really knew how to do, so they called him President, which he preferred to Tsar, and while they worked in the fields or gardens they became his servants.

She found he was a kind and patient man to work for.

She worked alongside the peasant women, and little Irina, like their babies, was left in a basket at the side of the field. The women laughed at her Russian and taught her to speak *real* Russian; not, they said, the rubbish the Frenchies spoke in the cities.

Her hands turned to leather, her face turned brown, her body slimmed and developed muscles, and she felt fitter than ever before.

She sang Russian songs and even found baby Irina seemed happier and slept better if she sang Russian rather than English nursery songs to her. She felt truly Russified, and knew Sasha and Peter would be proud of her.

Then she received her first letter from Sasha. A single page of thin paper written in pencil on one side only.

He was an infantryman. He was strong, well and unharmed despite having fought in several battles. He was with a good crowd of men who knew what they were about so he felt as safe as he could be. The food varied according to what they could find to eat and if they could find some way to cook it. He was optimistic and he missed her and little Irina and loved them both very much and he hoped she had a peaceful Christmas and enjoyed her birthday.

She looked desperately for a date and saw it scrawled right at the bottom of the letter. The twentieth of December! Months ago. Anything could have happened since then.

She received another letter in June and another in August, both delivered months after they were written.

The harvest ripened late and the rain came early, and she, Tatiana and Natasha sat in the house and watched much of their season's work ruined. A letter from Valerie Vassilievitch told them conditions were bad in Petrograd and they should stay away for the children's sake as well as their own, so they decided they would spend another winter at Irina.

The winter gloom settled and she read Sasha's three letters over and over, carefully so she did not erase the faint pencilled words. She did not receive any more letters, and she did not hear from Peter, and it seemed that the war had rubbed out her previous life.

She watched little Irina grow bigger, and in the grey eyes and the rust hair she saw the rebirth of herself. She worried when Irina sat quietly for hours that perhaps she was already dreaming of things beyond her understanding, and she prayed that her daughter would not grow up to believe she might one day live in an earthly paradise where the sun always shines.

They were careful not to be extravagant with food but she applauded Tatiana's suggestion that they have a special dinner on the last day of 1915. The intention was to celebrate having survived another year, and she chose not to tell the others that the New Year also coincided with her birthday, particularly as the previous year she had forgotten all about it until halfway through January. They invited Maria and Nikolas to join them, and Nikolas tactfully reminded Tatiana that below the folly there was a cellar full of good wines.

'Charlotte? You've never been to the cellars, have you? Put a heavy coat on and go with Nikolas to choose some wine. I think you'll find it interesting.'

It was interesting, especially when Nikolas showed her how well the cellar entrance was concealed.

'Sit down on the bench seat, Miss Charlotte, and push it backwards.'

She sat where she often sat on summer evenings, pushed as Nikolas showed her, and the seat moved, pivoting at one end. As it moved a counter-weighted paving-slab lifted, revealing steps leading down to the cellar. 'It's wonderful, Nikolas. So simple.'

'Come down and I'll show you something better,' he said, picked up his lamp, helped her down the steps, and turned. 'Look, you take this pole, shove it in that hole, lever it against that stone, and the trap closes and no one knows you're down here. There're cooked meats and cheeses, fruit, wine and even the old well down here, Miss Charlotte, so if you could manage the cold you could live down here for weeks and no one need know.'

She saw the serious look on his face and knew he was telling her for a reason, and when he showed her how the cellars were arranged she took special note. Nikolas obviously thought there was going to be trouble, too, and she guessed that was why Tatiana wanted him to show her around.

They had their meal on the final day of 1915 and they repeated it a year later. 1916 had been similar to the previous year except that they had a better harvest. But she still had not heard from Sasha and now she had adjusted herself to the fact that she never would.

By now the Military was counting its dead in millions and its Staff Officers could not account for what had happened to whole armies, never mind individual soldiers. Olga had made enquiries for her and learned nothing, and when Olga asked Valerie Vassilievitch Zubov for help even he had admitted that the inept records had been thrown away. Olga told her she had to accept that no official confirmation of Sasha's death was not evidence that he was alive.

In Lottie's own mind the fact that he had stopped writing to her was a clear indication that he was dead.

She was not shocked by the realisation, just worn down by it because it dawned so slowly. And she was very grateful that she had little Irina to remember him by.

CHAPTER 30

July 1916

Eve read the letter she had received from her mother then stared out of the carriage window at the scarlet sunset. The colours deepened and she looked down from the sky to the ground, a carpet of red poppies which fluttered in the evening breeze. The poppies became darker as the light faded, and the ground looked as if it was soaked with blood.

'Bad news, Eve?' Beattie asked softly.

'Yes,' she sighed, 'An old friend, Tom Dobbs. Wounded. Badly.' Her eyes stung. It was her fault. He had only come out here because he thought she might marry him if he did.

She concentrated on the poppies and was only half aware that Beattie had taken the letter from her and rustled out of the compartment and into Mac's office, next door.

'He wants to marry her and they've been writing to each other ever since she joined us. I think you should send her home to see him.' Beattie's quiet voice penetrated the screen that separated the compartments.

She heard Mac's muffled reply, 'Well, she's certainly overdue for some leave,' and moments later she felt his hand on her shoulder and heard him order her to go home.

'I can't. Not while this offensive's on.' The distant rumble of artillery increased for a moment, emphasising her answer.

'I'm sure the army can manage without you, Eve. It's nearly two years since you came out here and over eighteen months since you joined us. You haven't taken any home leave in that time. You're as worn out and battle-weary as the men you're nursing. I insist you go home for a couple of weeks.'

'I can't. My brother and brother-in-law are out here somewhere. I'd feel as though I was abandoning them if I went home.'

Beattie intervened. 'You won't be, Eve. Go home, and come back refreshed.'

She shook her head and promptly burst into tears because she knew they were right. She was tired, nearly exhausted physically and mentally, and she needed a rest, but she was scared to go home. She did not want to face Tom, and she was worried that having gone home she might be too frightened to come back.

Mac gently squeezed her shoulder. 'We'll be moving shortly but this'll be your last trip for a while. I think we're probably picking up somewhere around Albert, but once we get the men off I'll make sure you get a boat home. Go and see your family and your young man. They deserve attention just as much as the men out here.'

She nodded, dried her eyes, and did not bother to tell Mac that Tom was not her young man. She could not make Tom understand that, so she knew Mac would not.

At dawn the next morning they stopped in flat country, in front of a section of British artillery which was dug into huge earthworks half a mile away, the heavy guns firing over the train. She could hear each enormous shell make a sucking noise as it went over and as she heard a disconnected crump in the far distance she imagined more men being ripped apart by high explosives and hot steel.

All around her, smaller guns fired up at a German scout, and then three British aeroplanes joined the fight to knock the German down before he could fly back and report the artillery's position. She watched the fight for several minutes and then began to cry, very quietly and without any emotion.

She had seen hundreds of soldiers do this when they were told their wounds were bad enough for them to be sent home and discharged as unfit for further service. The Blessed Blighty one, the men called the wounds which took them away from hell.

Now she was going home courtesy of Tom Dobbs's wound. It did not seem fair, and the circumstances of her leaving suddenly made her feel ashamed.

But she would be glad to go. Glad to leave the noise and fear, the air which vibrated with explosions and smelled of sickness and death. She would be glad not to spend each day knowing that however much she did it would never be enough. That no matter how many men she helped thousands more were queuing up to throw themselves at bullets and bayonets or to be blown apart by mines and the never-ending shells.

Suddenly she heard the familiar whistles blowing and saw a line of ambulances and covered lorries racing across fields which must have been churned up by a million footsteps and thousands of hooves and tyres because they were awash with the poppies which flourish in newly turned earth.

The Somme offensive had created far more casualties than the Generals had planned for and the ambulances which carried the men away from the Field Dressing Stations sometimes did not stop to offload at the swamped Casualty Clearing Stations but simply met the hospital trains in open country to pass over their charges.

She stopped crying, wiped her eyes and prepared herself for the inrush of men who would have received only basic attention in a frontline aid post or lying on a stretcher outside a Field Dressing Station.

Beattie handed her a steel helmet and said she wished they did not have to load the men under the barrels of an artillery battery, especially one which had been spotted by a German scout. Mac had obviously realised the danger because he had ordered all the carriage doors open and as the vehicles pulled up alongside the train the orderlies climbed down to help load the men who were strapped to their stretchers, or reached down and hauled the walking wounded aboard the train. Everyone hurried as best they could but there were numerous stretcher cases and after an hour they still had a long column of vehicles waiting.

She was on the back of an open lorry, dressing a serious stomach wound when she heard the German's first retaliatory shell hit the earthworks half a mile away. Like everyone who could do so she dived for cover as a torrent of mud and stones rained down. Moments later she was back on the lorry to complete her patient's dressing. The next sally of German shells overshot and she prayed they had not trapped the train by destroying the railway line where it passed behind the big guns.

Beattie called her back inside the train and another explosion rocked the carriage as she swung into a compartment filled with wounded men. She stooped to help a man whose dressing had fallen from his head wound and a further shell exploded close by and blew her onto her knees. She stood up again as another explosion shook the train, and then another and another.

'Bumpy ol' ride, this is, Sister. And we ain't even moving!' the man with the head wound joked and she held his shoulders to steady herself and him.

'Square wheels,' she joked. 'The army's used up all its round ones.'

She was halfway through redressing his wound as another shell screamed down. The soldier looked up and she felt him tense.

'Jesus!' He yelled as the shell exploded, and suddenly threw himself at her.

She fell backwards onto the floor and lay still, the man on top of her.

'Get off!'

He grinned at her but he did not move.

'Come on 'arry, don't sod about,' a man with a splinted

leg complained, but Harry still lay on her, grinning but not speaking. She realised he was dead.

She screamed, immediately felt a sharp pain in her chest and back and thought she must have broken some ribs when she fell.

The man who had told Harry to get up lurched onto his one good leg and edged his way around her and out into the corridor. 'Nurse! Nurse! Someone! Help! QUICK!'

Two more shells screamed down and the carriage rocked again but Harry still lay on top of her. She tried to push him away but her chest hurt too much so she stopped.

Then she passed out.

She saw Mac and Winnie looking down at her. The train was moving quite fast and everything was rattling and shaking about.

'Try not to move, Eve.' Mac pressed her down as she tried to sit up. 'You've got a nice little chest wound and a collapsed lung, but we've put a tube in you and you'll be all right. You'll have to go home now.'

'Chest wound?' It was hard to speak and the pain was incredible.

Mac smiled and explained. 'The shelling. A big piece of metal penetrated the carriage, and the man you were nursing, and stabbed you in your chest. It was very neat. It went between your ribs, missed your heart but caught your left lung. You'll live. Winnie'll keep an eye on you.'

'What about the soldier?'

'He's dead. Right through his heart.'

'Oh. Sorry to be a nuisance,' she apologised, then passed out again.

Beattie had found her a wheelchair and wheeled her into the waiting room, once a large and elegant restaurant, where the soldiers who were going home for treatment or for leave were being assembled. Ann and Winnie had also insisted on coming to see her off and the injured soldiers thought it was great fun to have four Sisters with them, especially as one of them was wounded. They joked all the

467

time and it was difficult not to laugh and make her chest hurt more.

Boulogne was in darkness because of the Zeppelin threat but the moon shone and made the sea look especially lovely. She was sad to leave in a wheelchair because, even though everyone said she would be back when she was better, she knew her wound would not allow her to go back on the trains even if she was allowed to return to France.

Several VADs served tea and one young girl was quietly playing some Lizt and Chopin on a grand piano. The girl reminded her of Lottie, and for the first time in weeks she wondered how Lottie was, and how the war was treating her. The newspapers said Russia was in a bad way, living on starvation rations and in the throes of political upheaval.

She forgot about Lottie as she heard the rhythmic crunch of men marching past the waiting room. She looked out of the large windows and saw the men in the moonlight – young men with straight backs and clean uniforms, correctly ordered backpacks and bellypacks, virgin rifles slung correctly on shoulders that had not yet carried dead and mutilated friends through shell holes and across barbed-wire entanglements.

The sound of their marching feet faded as the long column of smart new soldiers passed on the way to war. She watched them go, then turned to look towards the docks, and saw orderlies bring mutilated soldiers out from the place where they had been hidden, and carry or push them onto the ship which would take them home.

The men around her stopped laughing and joking as their replacements marched past, and the VAD at the piano caught the men's mood and began to play a tune which everyone knew well. Each of the men began to hum or sing quietly, as if he was on his own and singing to himself, but the combined sounds were beautiful, if mournful.

There's a long, long trail a winding,
Into the land of my dreams,
Where the nightingales are singing,
And a white moon beams . . .

She sensed that each man's thoughts were with the man who had come to take his place and would stand where he had stood, take the risks he had taken, see what he had seen.

She cried, and looked around her, and every man she saw was crying too.

She said goodbye to the three women she had shared her life with for a year and a half, and a seaman took control of her chair, pushed her up the gangplank and offered to find her a cabin. She declined. She preferred to sit on deck with men she had, perhaps, nursed, and with whom she shared a rare camaraderie.

The ship nosed out into the moonlit sea and a soldier with his eyes bandaged, told her he had heard a comrade warn about 'language' because there was a woman on board, and offered to play her a tune on his mouth organ.

'Anything, miss. I can play anything.'

'You made me love you?' she asked, smiling.

He played it beautifully and a chorus of voices joined in. She sang with them, to stop herself crying, but as she sang the words and watched the moonlit sea she had a strong sensation of *déjà vu*.

It was more than two years since she had heard the same song and looked at the same sea and the same moon. Everything else had changed except for one thing.

She was still going home to nothing and no one.

The taxi driver who took Eve to Angel Street refused to accept her fair. 'If you don't mind me saying, miss, you've still got the smell of the war on you. I got three boys out there so I won't take your money. It's a privilege to serve you, miss.'

She thanked him and he carried her kitbag to the door, knocked, and waited to see if there was someone at home before he left her.

'Eve?' Her father looked surprised. 'We didn't expect you this soon.'

'They put me on an earlier ship. It's good to see you, Papa.'

'Thank God you're home. How are you? Is the pain bad?'

'It doesn't hurt any more, Papa, and my lung's all right now. Where's Mama?' She kissed him, careful not to let him hug her because her chest did hurt, and then she went into the kitchen to see her mother, who cried.

Eve was pleased to see that both her mother and father looked well, better than she had expected they might, but it seemed strange to be home, almost like stepping back in time. Aunt Lizzie and Helen and Maisie all came to welcome her home, but a certain look in their eyes told her they still had not forgiven her, and warned her that the old arguments would be renewed if anything happened to Jamie or Joe. Eve promised to see the children the next day. Helen now had a son as well as a daughter and the existence of a nephew she had not seen helped bring her long absence into perspective.

Katarina Komovskaya and Paul greeted her warmly but soon made excuses to go to their own rooms, and she guessed they must have found the family reunion difficult to watch as they had not heard from Sasha or Peter for two years.

She found it impossible to answer her parents constant questions about conditions across the Channel. They were obviously worried about Jamie and Joe and she knew that if she told them the truth they would worry even more, and perhaps she would even drive her mother back into the half world she had lived in for so long, but she did not want to give them false hope. She compromised by persuading them to tell her what they thought it was like, and then correcting their ideas without giving them too much detail.

She noticed how much her parents had changed. They seemed less sure of themselves, but more settled in other ways. She assumed it was all a part of growing older.

The house was strangely claustrophobic so she strolled out into the back garden, and was joined by Aunt Lizzie.

'Eve, I ought to tell you that I've been to see Tom. He's got no one else so I thought he deserved some attention.'

'That was nice of you, Aunt. How is he?'

'He talked about you all the time, Eve. You and his plans for your future.'

470

'We don't have a future, Aunt. At least, not a future together. We never have.'

She saw her aunt's chin go out and her face become stern, and she knew that a lecture was being prepared.

'He only went out because of you, Eve. He said you promised to marry him if he joined up.'

'I didn't say that at all. I said we'd have to talk about it. I do feel partly responsible for what happened to him, but only partly responsible. What did happen, anyway, and how bad is he?'

'A shell. He's lost his legs, and his manhood, and he's burned.'

'Oh God!'

'He wouldn't have gone if you hadn't told him to, Eve.'

'They would have conscripted him anyway, Aunt.'

'Perhaps, perhaps not, but this is a most stupid war. There's no sense to it, all the killing and maiming.'

'I won't argue with that, but someone thinks there's sense in it or we wouldn't still be fighting.'

She was tired and did not want to argue so she made her excuses and went to bed early, but she did not sleep well because the silence worried her.

Tom was at a hospital in south London and she wrote to him the next day to explain that she was home but would not visit him until she was strong enough to manage the journey. She felt guilty about using her own injuries as an excuse, particularly as she had made her way from Folkestone without any trouble, but she needed to adjust to being home from France before she exposed her still raw feelings to him.

After a week she still had not settled and decided that perhaps she would not be able to until she had squared matters with Tom.

She wrote to make arrangements to visit outside normal hours and when she arrived at the hospital she introduced herself to the Sister in charge of Tom's ward. She was relieved when the Sister not only appeared to be expecting her but agreed they go into a more private office and discuss Tom's injuries before they disturbed him.

'He's very badly hurt, Miss Forrester,' the Sister warned her.

'I've only been back from France for a week or so, Sister. I don't think anything could shock me ever again.'

'Perhaps not, but this is your fiancé, Miss Forrester.'

'No, he isn't. I've never said I'd marry him.'

'That's not what he says.'

'Well, that's something else. Anyway, what treatment has he had.'

'Too much, in my honest view. He is in incredible pain and I think it would have been merciful to have left him to die in the trench. I don't know why Corporal Dobbs's mates brought him out, Miss Forrester.'

'You have to be there to understand that, Sister. What have you done to him?'

'Removed everything that could not be saved. His legs from just below the rump and everything else. A silver tube's been inserted into his bladder but we have to clean and repack the wound every day. It's sheer agony for him but there's nothing for it.'

'Good God!'

'And we're trying to get the skin to grow back on his stomach but it keeps festering.'

'Will he live?'

'He should have died already, but something seems to be keeping him alive. Perhaps that's thinking of you, Miss Forrester?'

God, she hoped not.

She heard the door open behind her but did not take any notice until she heard her name spoken. 'Evelyn?'

Her heart leapt and she turned quickly. 'Robert? What are you doing here?'

He did not answer so the Ward Sister answered for him in a very stiff voice. 'Doctor Braithewaite comes three times each week to supervise our burns patients, and he asked me to inform him if you visited Corporal Dobbs.'

'You're looking after Tom Dobbs?' she asked quickly

'Yes, among others, and I hoped his being here might

472

attract you, sooner or later. You won't believe how pleased I am to see you, Evelyn, or how much I've to tell you. To ask you.' She saw the glance he gave the Sister, almost ordering her to leave, and then she noticed the awkward way he moved away from the door.

'Hurt your leg?' she asked.

'No, my back. A bit like you, I caught some stuff over in France. Nothing too bad but I had to come back.'

'Oh, I'm sorry,' she softened, until she saw him nod towards the Sister, clearly telling her to leave the office.

'Perhaps you'd like to be left alone, Doctor? Miss Forrester?' the Ward Sister asked pointedly and moved towards the office door.

'No,' she said, embarrassed by the position Robert had put her in, and moved to follow the Sister.

'Yes, we would,' Robert contradicted her, and grabbed her arm to stop her leaving. As soon as the Sister shut the door he repeated himself. 'Yes, we would like to be alone. At least, Evelyn, I would like to be alone with you.'

'You're hurting my arm, Robert,' she said.

'Only because I have to stop you running out on me again.'

'*I* didn't run out on you, Robert. *You* ran out on me,' she said sharply, eager to make the point but just as eager to hear what he had to say.

'All right, I'm not going to argue with you again. I did run out on you and it was the most stupid thing I've ever done in my life. No, it was the second most stupid thing I've done in my life. The first was . . .' he paused, shrugged, and added simply, 'something far worse. Now, Evelyn, before I let you out of this room I want to ask you something.'

'What?' Her heart thumped and her head swam, and she cursed herself for feeling that way. The moment she learned he was married she had decided to forget him but although she thought about him less and less she could not forget him entirely, or the way she had felt about him, and his sudden reappearance had evoked the best of all her old feelings. 'What do you want to ask me?'

'Evelyn, will you marry me?'

The proposal astonished her, and she gave the only answer she could. 'But you're already married.'

'You know?'

'Yes, fortunately. I met your best man out in France and he had the decency to tell me even if you didn't.' She tried to sound distant but not too offhand with him.

'I *was* going to tell you, Evelyn, I promise. I just wanted to get the divorce arranged first. To protect you. Your reputation, anyway.' He spoke with an insistent, almost desperate tone which convinced her he was telling the truth, and her pulse raced as he explained further. 'Quite simply, Evelyn, I didn't want to drag you into a scandal that'd destroy any chance you had of building the career you wanted, so I tried to do things quietly and in a way which wouldn't be noticed. It was obvious that if the newspapers learned that Braithewaite's son was divorcing his mad wife they'd want to know all about it and someone would dig up the whole, sordid story. The newspapers have already harassed you enough not least because of your relationship with my mother. If they connected my divorce with my intention to marry you, the very woman they claim usurped my mother from the WFL, you'd be portrayed as a scarlet women and that'd destroy any hope you may have of ever pursuing public life.'

'Oh, Robert!' If only he had told her all this before he could have saved them both a lot of heartache and wasted time, but she could understand why he had not. 'Well?' He asked.

'Yes,' she said simply.

'Are you saying you understand?' he asked, frowning with concern.

'Yes, Robert, I do understand, now you've explained everything, but I was actually answering your earlier question.' She saw he was trying to remember what he had asked, so she reminded him. 'You asked me if I'd marry you, Robert. The answer is, yes, I will.'

He pulled her against him, seemed to tuck her up in his arms, and kissed her gently but firmly. They parted when the door opened, and she heard him utter in a slightly unbelieving tone, 'Sister! You can be the first to congratulate us. We're getting married.'

'I see,' Sister sniffed, 'and which of you'll be the one to tell Corporal Dobbs? He seems to think Miss Forrester's going to marry him.' Eve slumped as her sudden elation drained away. The earlier sense of horror returned. 'Robert, Sister and I were discussing Tom when you arrived. How bad do you think he is?'

'Staying alive against all the odds, Evelyn,' he answered evenly.

Tom was awake when she approached his bed. He saw her coming and before she could speak he asked her how she was.

'I'm all right, Tom. Lungs's working again and the wound's healing,' she said quietly, and smiled. 'But how do you feel?'

'Better for seeing you, Evelyn.' He grinned. She saw how thin his face was and how deep-set and frightened his eyes were. She leaned over him to kiss him on his cheek but his hand came up and held her mouth against his for several seconds. 'By God, Evelyn, you taste good.'

'Is there anything I can do for you?' she asked awkwardly as she pulled away and his other hand caught hold of hers.

'They've told you what's happened to me?'

'Yes. I'm sorry.'

'Well, at least I'm still alive, and where there's life there's hope, eh?'

'Yes,' she said, trying to agree without sounding too reassuring or at all patronising.

'I don't look very pretty, Evelyn, but I reckon you've probably seen a lot worse so I hope it doesn't shock you too much,' he said, and she gave a weak smile and shook her head. 'Anyway, I've got plans. I reckon I've thought of a way I can make a fair living when I get out of here. I know I haven't got any legs, and I can never be a proper husband to you, but I reckon we'll be all right.' He stared at her and she found herself trying hard not to react and show her feelings.

He really did expect her to marry him! She could not, ever, but she could not bring herself to tell him that, not if the thought of marrying her was the only thing keeping him alive. Her mind went numb and she began to cry, not for herself but for the desperateness she had already brought him and would continue to bring him.

He squeezed her hand gently, and his soft voice reassured her. 'There, there, Evelyn, don't cry, love. It'll be all right, you'll see. It'll be all right once I'm out of here and we can settle down.'

When Eve left him she was not sure what else they had said or what promises she might have made other than to visit again tomorrow. She was simply aware of the shock which still numbed her mind and the enormous relief she felt that she *had* left him.

She had a brief conversation with Robert but she was too distracted to make much of that either, except agree that they should keep their plans secret for the moment and meet again in a few days if he could arrange some leave or find an excuse to go absent for a while. Then she went home.

'How's Tom?' her mother asked.

'In terrible pain and dying, Mama, but he reckons that where there's life there's hope.'

'And what's he hoping for, exactly?' her mother asked shrewdly.

'That I'll marry him.'

'And will you?'

'No, but I'm beginning to think I should.' The words came with tears. 'I don't want to marry him, Mama. I never have, apart perhaps from one fleeting moment just after the war started.'

She wanted to tell her mother that she had met Robert again and that she had agreed to marry him but she sensed that was best kept secret for the time being. She also wanted to say that Aunt Lizzie thought she *should* marry Tom, but she did not because she thought it would provoke another family row and she could not face being the source of any more trouble.

Rose studied Eve's face and knew this was the moment to tell the truth if ever she was going to tell it. Now was the time to tell Eve that she had married for the wrong reasons and left her husband for the man she really loved, and explain the repercussions it had caused. Now was the time to explain why Lottie had left home and what had happened to make her leave the country. Now was the time to explain that she was not married to Edward even though she had four children by him, and that Eve and the others were bastards. Now was the time to admit everything, all the hypocrisies.

But she did not, because she could not, especially when her divorce from Hubert was so close that she and Edward could finally think of getting married and making everything all right.

All right? Well, as all right as she could. She could not do anything for Lottie, or for Jamie or for Helen who was worried sick about Joe. Eve was the only one she *could* help, but she sensed she would not help her by making her doubt everything she had been brought up to believe. Not right now. Eve had enough to contend with.

Eve went back to see Tom the next day. Her mind was made up. She had never made any commitment to him and he had to understand that. She knew she could make Robert happy, and knew equally well that she *would* make Tom, and herself, unhappy if she married him.

She visited during normal hours and because she was early she sat down and waited on a bench in the corridor outside the ward.

'Are you Miss Forrester?' Another Sister touched her shoulder. 'You've come to see Corporal Dobbs?'

She nodded, heart thumping, wondering if Tom had died, wondering what her feeling would be if he had.

'You've been nursing in France, haven't you?' the Sister asked pedantically.

'Yes. Why?' she snapped her reply, unsure of the question's relevance.

'Corporal Dobbs has developed another infection in his groin. We're just about to dress and repack it. Normally we wouldn't allow visitors in, of course, but you're an exception considering the circumstances and the fact that you've come a long way. Besides it's very painful for him and it might help him to have you there.'

'Of course. Do you have something I can wear?'

'Evelyn?' Tom said through gritted teeth as a nurse took her to his bed. She bent over him and kissed him on his cheek and this time he did not try to hold her. His hands were gripping the bed covers and his knuckles were as white as the sheets.

'We're just going to do your dressing, Tom, and I'm going to help,' she told him.

He scowled. 'I don't know if I like that idea.'

'Come on Corporal,' the nurse said, and added tactlessly, 'Miss Forrester won't see anything now that she won't see once you're married.'

She heard the nurse's words and looked directly at Tom as he looked back at her. The nurse wittered on for several seconds but they ignored her and did not speak to each other. Not voicing the question somehow made it seem even clearer. Are you going to marry me, Evelyn? She could read the words in his mind, and she tried to divert him so she did not have to answer.

'Let go of the blankets, Tom.' She placed both her hands on one of his and prised his fingers open as the nurse did the same with his other hand.

He released the blankets and transferred his grip to the rail which formed the bedhead. She helped the nurse roll the covers down. She had seen some awful wounds but his were some of the worst.

The nurse removed the old dressing. Eve watched Tom gritting his teeth until he could not stand the pain any more. He screamed. The nurse dropped the dressing. Eve reached across the bed. 'I'll clean the wound and finish the dressing nurse.'

She worked carefully, trying hard not to disturb the silver tube which led into his bladder, but noted there was fresh blood seeping along it. She cleaned him and redressed the wound, and then settled him as best she could, just as she had thousands of men before him.

'Thanks, Evelyn.'

'There's no need to thank me, Tom.'

'It's grim, isn't it?'

'Yes, it's grim.'

'D'you think you can take it? Being married to me?'

She looked away and did not answer, grateful that the nurse had returned and could be used as a distraction.

He tugged at her sleeve and spoke quickly, as though he was using words to control the pain he must be feeling. 'I haven't told you about my plans, have I? I've got a bit put by so we'll use some of it to buy a small shop with accommodation behind and above, and I'll set up as a cobbler. It's the obvious job for a man with no legs because I won't have to walk anywhere. People'll bring their shoes to me to repair and collect them when they're ready. I can sit at a shoe last as easily as stand at one and there's no heavy lifting to be done. The tanners and hardware stores'll willingly deliver what materials I need and people'll always keep wearing out their shoes and needing repairs so there should be a steady income.'

'I'm impressed,' she said, and meant it.

'So, Evelyn, you can see you don't have to marry me out of charity or sympathy. I won't have any legs and I won't be able to give you children, but it'll work in every other way, you'll see. We'll have a nice little house and a business, and you can keep on working if you want to or you can stay at home once we can afford it.'

'You've got it all worked out, Tom. I can see that.' She chose her words carefully, preparing to tell him she was not going to join him in his little cobbler's shop.

'I've always been careful, Evelyn, and known how to get what I wanted. I just keep nibbling away at things until they work out.'

'Yes, Tom, I can see that,' she repeated.

'You don't sound very happy, Evelyn?' he said, and a moment later convulsed with pain.

'Nurse!' She called for help and settled Tom down again, but the pain was too much and he quickly lost consciousness.

She sat by him for a long time but when he did recover he was confused by the powerful pain killers he had been given. He would not have understood her even if she had told him she was not going to marry him, but she was aware that the longer she delayed telling him the greater the shock and the worse the repercussions would be.

She walked back to the Ward Sister. 'He's half conscious but not lucid so I'll leave him to rest.'

Sister nodded. 'Thanks for your help. You wouldn't like to join us, I suppose? We're inundated and they're still flooding in, poor devils.'

'I'm on sick leave at the moment,' she explained. 'I'm hoping to go back to France when I'm fit but I don't know if they'll let me. Anyway, Sister, if you think it's bad here you should see it over there, especially in the winter. I just hope we don't have to fight through another one.'

'So do I, but if you feel like keeping your hand in doing some light work I'm sure we can arrange something. We need all the experienced help we can get and, of course, you could see more of your fiancé.'

'He isn't my fiancé. I've never had any intention of marrying him and he knows that,' she insisted, and added, 'I don't suppose Doctor Braithewaite's coming this afternoon?'

'He should have been here but someone else came in his place. It appears that our Doctor may be transferred up north, just outside Coldstream. Some sort of remedial hospital, I think they call it, but I don't know much. Why don't you telephone him? Come with me and I'll arrange it.'

'Thank you,' she said and followed with a heavy heart. Transferred? Up North? She had the feeling that Fate was determined to keep her and Robert apart.

* * *

'Evelyn? Is something wrong?' Robert's voice crackled in the telephone.

'Not particularly. I wanted to talk to you. To get things sorted out and arrange to spend some time with you.'

'Difficult. I'm being sent up north, just outside Coldstream.'

'When?'

'Tomorrow evening. Look, I'll get over to you tomorrow afternoon. I don't know when, but I'll be there. I must go. 'til then.'

'Bye.'

The telephone crackled. He had gone.

Eve was glad there was no one at home when he arrived. It would have been difficult to explain why he had suddenly reappeared after two years, and even more difficult to explain why she kissed him in the way she did.

'That was rather meaningful,' he said as their lips parted.

'It was meant to be. What's all this about going to Coldstream? I hoped we might finally have some time together.' She led him into the front room

'I've been given an opportunity I don't want to miss, Evelyn. The experience I gained with Jacques has helped me to treat a number of men with serious burns, and I've developed a few ideas of my own to improve conditions for amputees. I'm keen to develop these treatments and to pass what I've learned on to other doctors. There's a hospital near Coldstream that's been doing something similar for years and my CO has arranged for me to go up there.'

'I see,' she could not argue, not with him or the army. 'It's ironic, Robert, that if your mother hadn't been burned you probably would never have become so interested in that sort of treatment. I suppose that once again I can blame her for keeping us apart.'

She meant what she said as a joke but he obviously took her seriously.

'She won't keep us apart any more. She hasn't spoken to me since I began the proceedings to divorce Lydia. It's not that she has any particular affection for Lydia, she simply doesn't want the scandal to get out.'

Eve was astonished. 'You've begun proceedings? When?'

'Two years ago. It'll probably take another three to finalise everything without bringing the whole business out into the open. Perhaps the war'll be over by then and we can get on with our lives.'

'God, I hope so.' Another three years seemed a very long time. 'I don't want to be apart from you all that time.'

'That's what I hoped you'd say. You could come north with me!' He held her hands. 'Look, the so-called offensive's turned the Somme into a bloody slaughter-house and everywhere's inundated with wounded and sick men. I'm sure I could arrange for you to come with me, if you want me to. You'd be ideal, Evelyn. You've served abroad, you've been under fire and you've even been wounded. You'd have much more in common with the men than most nurses and that'd help them because they'd feel much more inclined to talk to you about their own experiences, and all that's a part of my treatment.'

'Someone's already suggested I apply for light duties so I could help nurse Tom. I'm not keen on that idea, but I like yours.' His proposal excited her. She could do what she was good at, and be near him. 'I've to report for an MO's examination in four days. Can you arrange things that quickly?'

He nodded, said he had to go, kissed her, grabbed his cap and left. She watched him being driven away in the army car and remembered how she felt the night she had first seen him driven away by Perkins.

It was too late to visit Tom that day but she went the next, determined to make him understand that she would not marry him, but he was delirious with fever brought on by the infection in his wound. She used the local police station's telephone to call the hospital for the next two days and was told the fever had not subsided. The next day she visited him on her way to her own medical. Tom looked awful, very near the end, and she felt terribly sorry for him.

She was relieved and a little apprehensive when the

doctor who examined her told her he had received an application for a special posting.

'I'll be honest with you, Sister. I don't really approve of people asking for special privileges like this. If we consider one application then we should consider them all, but you do appear to have very rare qualifications for this posting and I see you actually came into the service by a back door and on a recommendation. Tell me one thing, though. There isn't a young man waiting for you up there, in Coldstream is there?'

'A young man, sir?' She tried to sound surprised by the question and obviously succeeded in convincing him that her interest was purely professional.

'All right, you're not fully fit but you're fit enough to do light work so I'll endorse the posting. You know what you have to do to get up there.'

'Yes thank you, sir.' She began to feel guilty about leaving her parents again so quickly, but she was glad to be going because her aunt was still trying very hard to bully her into marrying Tom. They had already exchanged sharp words and the next step would be a full blown row, which was exactly what she did not want.

Eve arrived home in time for the evening meal but there was no meal being prepared and the house was empty. She knocked on Maisie's door. Her father answered it. He looked drawn and unsteady.

'What's the matter, Papa?'

'It's Jamie, Eve.'

'What about him?'

'He's been killed. Maisie heard this afternoon.'

'Oh God!' her heart seemed to stop, then an awful fear swamped her.

'How's Mama?'

'Not very good. Come and talk to her, will you? I don't want to lose her again.'

Eve found her mother comforting Maisie and her aunt trying to comfort them both, and Helen, beautiful Helen, staring out of the window, fingers of one hand thrust into

483

her mouth, consumed by her own imagined horrors.

Eve tried to talk to them all, but she could not because whatever she said sounded hollow even though it was sincere. After several minutes of spouting inadequate words which neither comforted them nor satisfied her she stepped down into the scullery and then into the back garden.

A few minutes later she heard the door open and close behind her and hoped it was her father, but it was Katarina.

'It is not your fault, Evelyn, that you have seen things they have not. But it is not their fault either, so do not blame them for not understanding.'

'I don't blame them, Katarina.'

'It seems to them that you do, Evelyn, because you do not talk about what it is like over there.'

'Only because I didn't want to frighten them, Katarina. Anyway, there won't be much time for talk now. I'm going away in two days. I received a new posting.'

'Where?' Katarina sounded alarmed.

'The north of England. Borders country.'

The next morning she wrote a letter to Tom, explaining why she could not marry him and apologising if she had given him the impression that she would. She did not intend to post the letter, but to leave it with him only if he was still incapable of understanding her when she visited him for the last time.

However, the letter did serve an unexpected purpose in that it helped to clear her mind and organise her thoughts, and that was fortunate because when she arrived Tom had recovered from the fever and was able to have a proper conversation.

She deliberately did not smile or kiss him when she greeted him.

'How do you feel, Tom?'

'Better. Thanks for coming each day. I'm sorry I wasn't well enough to talk.'

'Don't worry, I didn't come every day, actually. Some days I just telephoned.'

'Well, you made the effort,' he said forcibly. 'Have they told you? They're going to try me in a wheelchair next week. So I can wheel myself down the aisle for our wedding.'

'Tom, there isn't going to be a wedding. I'm not going to marry you. In fact I'm not coming again. The MO's signed me fit and I'm taking a posting away from here.' She stood up instinctively and went to smell a rose in a nearby vase of flowers.

'I see,' he said moodily, after a few seconds.

She turned to look at him. 'I never said I'd marry you, Tom.'

He did not answer. He simply turned his head away, quite deliberately, and stared along the ward.

'Tom?' She called out to him but did not move towards him.

He still did not answer, but he used his elbows to shift himself into a more comfortable position, and that single movement confirmed that she was right not to marry him. Tom was behaving exactly as his father had when she had asked him to visit Polly. And he was behaving just as Polly and Lou did when they were so sure they were right that they would not listen to anyone else's point of view.

She suddenly had an overwhelming sense of freedom. She had lived for over two years with the belief that she owed the Dobbs family more than she could ever repay them but now she realised that each one of them in turn had manipulated her into believing she owed them some obligation.

They had all made her feel guilty, in their different ways.

'Look at me, Tom.' She spoke firmly but he did not move and she knew this was a critical moment. 'Look at me.'

He did not move so she walked around his bed and confronted him, but he still fixed his eyes and refused to look up at her.

'You might have tricked me into marrying you by making me feel as though I was responsible for what happened to you and because I felt sorry for you, but you said you did not want that. You didn't want sympathy or charity, you made that quite clear, so that only leaves love, Tom. You wanted me to marry you because I loved you, and I'm afraid I don't. If I married you for any other reason I'd end up hating you, so it's best for both of us if I simply leave you to find someone who really will love you. Goodbye Tom, and good luck.'

She walked away trembling, explained to Sister what had happened, and left without looking back.

One ordeal was over but Eve had another one to face. She had to tell her parents she was leaving the following morning. She knew that her personal circumstances would guarantee her compassionate leave if she asked for it, but she did not want to ask for it. She could not help her parents or Maisie feel any better and she would only antagonise her aunt when she announced that she had told Tom she would not marry him. It was better to go.

She told them all during the evening meal.

'Leaving already?' Her mother began to cry. 'I thought you'd be at home for weeks more.'

'It's the Somme, Mama,' she manipulated the truth, 'there're so many casualties the hospitals are overflowing and they need all the help they can get. I've been posted to light duties so I can relieve a fully-fit nurse for other duties. I would have told you last night but what with one thing and another I didn't think it'd help you to know.'

'I suppose so,' her mother sniffed. 'Where're you going? Not back to France?'

'No, I'm not fit enough for that. I'm not even going into a normal hospital. They're sending me to a special hospital where they treat severely burned and crippled men. It's near Coldstream.'

She started as her mother and Aunt Lizzie both dropped their knives and forks at the same time.

'Why?' Aunt Lizzie asked sharply. 'Why there?'

'Why not, Aunt? They need the sort of skills I have.' She looked at her mother and aunt and noticed their frowns, and when she looked at her father for an explanation she saw he had the same expression. 'Have I said something wrong? Something to upset you?'

'No, lass,' her father said quickly, but in a strained voice. 'It's just something else we've got to come to terms with. Everything's changing and we're having difficulty keeping up with it all. It's the war. This bloody awful war!'

She was stunned. She had never before heard him swear.

'Edward?' her mother asked suddenly, 'would you take me out for a walk this evening? It's so sultry in here.'

'I could take you, Mama,' she offered quickly, eager to be of some use.

'No, thank you, dear. I'd like some time alone with your father.'

The refusal hurt.

Aunt Lizzie squared up to her within five minutes of her parents leaving.

'What about Tom Dobbs, Eve?'

'I told him this afternoon.'

'What, that you're abandoning him?'

'No, Aunt! I told him that I wasn't going to marry him.'

'Although you persuaded him to fight by implying you would marry him? And when you know his marrying you might be the only thing keeping him alive?'

'Aunt Lizzie, I didn't promise to marry him if he joined up. That's something he's either made up or assumed. I don't care what anyone thinks of me, Aunt, but I'm not going to marry him. He's a manipulator, like his sisters Polly and Lou.'

'Well, that's a very convenient opinion after all this time. I remember you saying Polly was everything that was wonderful and we were all lacking because we didn't idolise her the way you did.'

'That's not fair!' Eve blazed back.

The row burned on for five minutes, until Katarina came down to intervene because Paul was upset and crying.

'I'm sorry we seem to argue all the time, Aunt,' Eve said, offering what her preacher father would have termed an olive branch, but her aunt glared at her and turned away, provoking another outburst which Eve was barely able to control. Instead of trying to explain her position once again she asked a question she wanted answered. 'Why's everyone so upset about me going to Coldstream?'

'Your father explained. It's all these changes. Especially so soon after losing Jamie.'

She did not believe the answer, but she did not argue. There had been enough arguments.

As Edward pushed her through their local park Rose looked up at the wisps of cloud catching the last colour from the setting sun.

'I thought that once I'd seen Hubert and he'd agreed to divorce me all our problems would be over. It seems they were only just beginning.'

'Come on, sweetheart, things could be worse.'

'Jamie's dead, Lottie's missing in Russia, Helen's worried sick about Joe and Eve's going to Pincote.'

'Not Pincote. She's going to Coldstream which is miles away, and there's no reason why she should ever go to Pincote,' he said quietly. 'Even if she goes to the same hospital that treated John there's no reason for her to find out he was your brother. Besides, what if she does? She'll only learn what Lottie already knows. Why don't we just tell her and Helen, sweetheart? It'd be so much easier than all this secrecy.'

He was right, of course, as he usually was, but it would take time to explain it all properly and there was not enough time if Eve was leaving tomorrow morning. Besides she felt too tired. Jamie had been a shock and she needed all her energy not to slide back into the half world Edward had dragged her out from just before the war started. But there was one other thing she wanted his views on.

'Lizzie seems to pick on Eve all the time. Why do you think that is?'

'Partly because she blames Eve for your condition, but mainly because she sees so much of herself in Eve, faults as well, and it upsets her.'

Yes, she could understand that. In fact, since Eve had come back from France Rose had found it quite unnerving to see how alike Eve and Lizzie were becoming.

Eve woke early. It was another fine day, a good day for a long train journey, she thought, and wondered how she would feel being on a train again. At least this one would not be shelled by artillery.

She was washed, dressed and packed to leave before anyone had stirred, and was in the kitchen preparing breakfast when her aunt came down.

'I'm glad I caught you alone, Eve.'

'Yes, Aunt?' Perhaps the olive branch she had tried to offer was about to be accepted.

'I'm sure that if you explained the circumstances you could be released from your duties, Eve. After all, there's your mother to think about and you could be an enormous help to her if you stayed here, and then there's Tom. I know you've said you didn't promise to marry him and you don't want to, but have you thought what it would mean to him if you did, and how little it'd cost you? After all, he can't impose himself on you and he's not likely to live that long, is he?'

'That's morbid, Aunt, to expect me to marry him in the hope he'd soon be dead.'

'It's practical. It's a way for you to face up to your responsibilities, both to Tom and your mother.'

'To mother?'

'If you hadn't joined the suffragettes, gone to prison and gone on hunger strike, your mother wouldn't have been knocked down going to visit you.'

Eve thought it was best not to answer, for fear of saying something which would force her and her aunt apart for ever, but her aunt clearly misinterpreted her silence.

'Well, you haven't argued with me so I assume you agree with me. I'm warning you, Eve, that if you run away now you'll regret it for the rest of your life. Once Tom's dead it'll be too late to say you're sorry.'

Eve did not know how to respond, so she thought she should tell her aunt exactly that. 'I'm sorry, Aunt Lizzie, I really don't want to fall out with you but I don't know how

489

to talk to you, not any more. You ignore everything I say, so I think it's best if I don't say anything.'

'Except goodbye?' her aunt asked sharply, and all Eve could do was nod.

The goodbyes were painful, not only because the house had begun to feel like home again but because when she faced up to her real feelings she knew that Aunt Lizzie was right, in part. No matter how much she tried to believe she was not responsible for Tom, she still felt that he would not have been so horribly injured if it were not for her. Not only Tom but her mother, too, and Jamie – would he have joined up if she had not allowed Lady Braithewaite and Cedric Rathbone to out-manoeuvre her?

As she left home her sense of guilt and the worry that everyone thought she was walking away from her responsibilities weighed her down more than the bag she carried, but she smiled through the pain so that her Aunt Lizzie did not know how successful she had been in casting doubts.

A taxi came to collect her from the house and she was thankful for the formality it somehow brought to her leaving.

The train journey north suffered all the frustrations and delays of any journey she had made in France. When night came and she tried to sleep sitting upright in a compartment packed with soldiers and their kit she longed for her hospital train bunk, or even better the comfortable beds she had used while on the American trains. She did not arrive at her destination until noon the following day. She telephoned Robert and he appeared with a motor-car forty minutes later.

'It's good to see you, Evelyn,' he led her to a quiet spot at the side of the station before he kissed her. 'We can't have you seen to be fraternising with officers or they'll transfer you away. They're very proper up here so we'll have to be careful. I've even had to make up an excuse to come to town. Collecting you is an ancillary duty. And so is taking you to lunch.'

490

They ate in the dining room of a small and austere hotel, under the constant gaze of a stern proprietress who did not relax until she had heard enough of their conversation to believe their relationship was strictly professional.

'You see, Evelyn, Jacques taught me a new technique which helps burns to heal slowly and cleanly and with less pain to the patient, but it requires intensive nursing. Also, the patients take longer to recover than they might if traditional methods were used. Unfortunately because the treatment takes longer and needs more nurses it's frowned upon. The trouble is that everyone's working flat out to cope with the number of patients we have and there aren't enough beds.'

'I can understand that, Robert. It's all very well giving a few men better treatment but what about the others who're left waiting?'

'Quite, but there are rarely any setbacks with the new treatment which means that very few patients come back for additional treatment. I need to prove that the overall effect isn't only to ease suffering but also to allow more patients to be treated in the long run.'

'And exactly how will you do that?'

'We're to set up a special ward, which you'll run. We'll treat our patients my way while the other doctors continue with the traditional methods, and we'll constantly compare the results from each method. Now, we'll have to train our own people very carefully, not only in the techniques for the physical treatment but also in how to boost the men's morale. I'm convinced that a patient's mental attitude influences the rate and the degree of their recovery.'

'Well, I hope you can train me in all this because I'm going to be as much a beginner as anyone else,' she reminded him.

'You'll learn fast enough, but you'll also have to learn how to handle the politics. The people up here are used to using some unconventional methods but they think they've gone as far as possible. They think any changes are experimenting for experiment's sake. They're very concerned that I might be using the men to further my own reputation and they're looking for any chance to prove they're right. Unfortunately there is still a level of experimentation and somehow we've got to overcome any problems that causes.'

Everything he said encouraged her to look forward to the challenge and although only four nurses applied to transfer to the new ward from their current positions she was still able to accept the first patients only one week after she arrived at the hospital. Within a month staff had volunteered to come from other hospitals and the ward was full of patients.

Although she was supposed to be on light duties she worked twelve-hour shifts doing anything that was required. Instead of deteriorating, her health seemed to benefit from the high morale which was generated among the patients and the staff as well, and she became a firm believer in Robert's theory that mental and physical welfare were connected.

After a few weeks she even managed to escape from the feeling of guilt which had plagued her, it seemed, for the past two or three years, and at last she could see her relationship with her parents and with Tom in a clearer perspective.

A few days before Christmas she received two letters. The first was a short, almost formal, letter from her mother detailing various family matters and unceremoniously stating that Tom Dobbs had died, and the second letter came from the Sister in Tom's hospital saying that it was a blessed relief that Tom had finally given up the agonising struggle to stay alive and had surrendered to the inevitable.

Perhaps he had, but the feelings of guilt which were never far away surged back and overwhelmed her for several minutes. She had been vulnerable when he asked her to marry him, emotional because she had just closed the White House and she did not know what the future held for her. She was scared of being left alone like her Aunt Lizzie, and that was why she had hesitated, had not told him clearly that she would not marry him. That was why she had allowed him to kiss her.

She could not blame him for thinking that she did feel something for him, that if he persisted she might agree to marry him.

No, she could not blame him which meant she had to blame herself for his misery and his death. Tom Dobbs would remain with her for the rest of her life, something that would always be etched into her conscience.

She suddenly found herself crying for him and Jamie, and for everyone else she felt she had let down over the past few years. Then someone knocked on her door and told her that twenty more injured men were due to arrive later and that she would have to make room for seven more in her ward.

She dried her eyes, blew her nose, and said she would see to the ward in a few minutes.

She put the letters back in their envelopes and looked out at the snow which was falling on the surrounding hills and fields. It seemed a long time since that summer's day in France when her mother had written to tell her that Tom had been injured. She had learned a lot in that time and that was due to two men who had featured in her life for the past three years. Robert had exerted a positive influence which she had learned to benefit from and Tom had exerted a negative influence which she had learned to overcome, but both had taught her to use her strength.

Now, with Christmas coming, she had to find a way to use that strength to close the distance which had developed between her and her family, and in particular heal the rift between her and her aunt. Meanwhile she had to go to work so she put the letters in her pocket to show Robert later, when they could find time to be alone.

Eve was not able to show Robert the letters until late in the afternoon. He read them quickly and handed them back to her. 'How d'you feel about it, Evelyn?'

'I can cope, Robert, don't worry.'

'You will feel it, Eve, when you slow down enough for the shock to get hold of you.'

'Slow down?' she grimaced. 'There's another seven men

arriving today. I don't know where we're going to put them, Robert. We don't have enough room!'

'Talking of room, we've been offered an annex. It's an old manor house and it's some distance away but the owner's offered to convert it into a hospital for us!'

'How far away?' she asked, immediately wary of spreading their thin resources even thinner.

'I don't know exactly. It's in a place called Pincote and it's called Laybourne Manor. It belongs to a man called John Laybourne who was a patient at this hospital some thirty years ago. He'd suffered severe burns and an amputation. After the war started and the hospital treated several of his employees he founded a charity to help rehabilitate patients with burns. He's heard what we're doing and he'd like us to look at the house with a view to taking it over. We'd need to spend a weekend there. How d'you fancy it?'

She was keen to spend a weekend away with Robert, but not as some rich man's guests in a manor house. However she could see that Robert wanted to, and anyway she felt it was part of her duty to the patients and to Robert to do all she could to improve facilities. 'Yes, I'll look forward to it.'

CHAPTER 31

January 1917

The weather turned wet and extremely cold the weekend they were due to visit Laybourne Manor and Eve was pleased Robert had managed to borrow a motor-car so they could drive all the way and not have to wait around in draughty railway stations.

They drove to Pincote Market, a grey stone town with a stern-looking bank and ornate municipal buildings set around a large market square, ate a light lunch and asked directions to the manor. They were told to follow a road which swung out of the Pincote Valley, climbed up to a farmed plain and ran eastwards under the shelter of a high, untamed ridge with an outcrop of bare rock stacked up through its centre. They soon found an estate wall, almost overgrown with rhododendron bushes, and drove alongside that until they reached a pair of fancy wrought-iron gates watched over by a derelict lodge.

She asked Robert to stop the car the moment they drove through the gates and saw the house at the end of the long curved drive.

Laybourne Manor sat at the bottom of the ridge among large old trees. It was almost covered by dense ivy and a creeper which still bore some crimson leaves, and she thought it was the most romantic house she had ever seen.

The manor was grand, two storeys high with attic dormers making a third floor. It had a set of white stone steps leading up to a double front door which seemed strangely off-centre and it was not until they drove close enough to see through gaps in the ivy that she realised one end of the house appeared to have been lopped off and repaired with concrete rather than the stone which made up the other walls.

The moment they stopped outside the house a short, round, elderly man who was dressed in durable country clothes opened the front door and ran down the steps. 'Good afternoon to you. I'm Wilkin, Herbert Wilkin. I'm Mr Laybourne's agent.'

Robert introduced himself first, and introduced Eve as he helped her out of the car. Mr Wilkin frowned. 'Forrester? Not from around here, are you, Miss Forrester?'

'No, from London. Why?'

'It's just that Forrester's a famous name around these parts.' He led them up the steps to the front door. 'Come inside. You'll find the place rather damp and run-down, I'm afraid, but it hasn't been lived in for two years or more.'

'Mr Laybourne doesn't live here, then?' she asked.

'No. Mr Laybourne lives in Devon these days, where it's warmer for him, but he wants this house and the grounds used as a hospital.' Mr Wilkin showed them through a large wood-panelled hall and into a musty-smelling room filled with furniture covered with white dust-sheets and Eve remembered how the White House looked the day she left it. Then she listened as Mr Wilkin explained, 'I'm afraid it's rather dilapidated now, but there've been many alterations carried out to make the house more convenient for someone with Mr Laybourne's disabilities, and he convalesced here so we assume it's suitable.'

'What are Mr Laybourne's disabilities?' She asked because Robert had told her very little.

'He had a very serious accident, Miss Forrester. He was badly burned, lost a leg, was virtually blinded and breathed a lot of hot smoke which damaged his lungs. He should have died years ago, but he's outlived everyone in his own and his wife's family. Mrs Laybourne died three years ago after she contracted typhoid out in Italy, and now he's completely alone.'

'How awful!' she said, feeling sympathy for the man. 'Was his accident anything to do with the end of the house being pulled down?'

'No. Well, not really. Mr John was injured in the 1885 mine disaster which killed dozens of local men, and afterwards a group of miners came out here and tried to burn the manor down. They failed, of course, but Mr John's father died in the fire.' He paused as if he was about to say more, then seemed to change his mind. 'Mr John's circumstances certainly are very sad, Sister, but perhaps some good can come of them if we can establish the hospital. He's instructed me to make it clear that he'll meet all costs to convert the manor to either a suitable convalescent home or a full hospital if possible. If you feel, Doctor Braithewaite, that the proposition is practical we simply need a list of all your requirements for me to make the necessary arrangements with architects, builders and decorators and the firms which can supply all the special equipment you'll need. We'll arrange everything under your guidance and simply hand over a fully equipped hospital.'

She heard a slight concern in Robert's voice as he said, 'That could cost an absolute fortune, Mr Wilkin. Does Mr Laybourne realise—'

'Please don't worry about money, Doctor,' Mr Wilkin interrupted. 'Mr Laybourne owns everything around here. There's a story that an emissary from the King took one of his ancestors up onto the crag on South Ridge, King's Crag, and offered the family everything they could see from horizon to horizon if they could control the bandits that lived up here. By the time Mr John was born the family not only owned the land but they'd sunk coal mines, built railways, founded the bank and dozens of other businesses. Later, Mr John married a very wealthy lady and when she died all her money passed to him so he's a very rich man.'

'I see,' Robert said.

'It's an ill wind, Doctor,' Mr Wilkin said briskly, 'and Mr Laybourne wants the town to benefit from his wealth. There will be some conditions imposed but they're not onerous. Mr Laybourne simply wishes to choose the hospital's name and to give names to several wards. That's all. Now, I'll show you around and then leave you with a spare set of keys so you can come and go at your leisure. We've reserved rooms for you both to stay in the railway hotel tonight, at Mr Laybourne's expense, and I'll meet you back here tomorrow afternoon to discuss matters.'

It took Mr Wilkin nearly two hours to show them through the house and the out-buildings, and after he provided them with oil lamps and left them alone they spent a further three hours looking around the cold and gloomy old house. By the time they had finished it was dark and the wind was hurling sleet against the windows.

'Well, what do you think?' Robert asked when they finished their second tour and she closed the notebook she had used to jot down all her impressions and thoughts.

She shrugged. 'It'd need thorough cleaning, redecorating, a large number of alterations, better plumbing and electricity. We'd certainly have to install a decent heating system to keep all these rooms and corridors warm and we'd also need telephones. I think it'd probably be cheaper to build a new hospital.'

'But it'd be quicker to convert this house. And think about the grounds, Evelyn. They must be wonderful in the summer, level and open with hundreds of shrubs to provide scents for the men who can't see any more. Then, right behind, there's that ridge to offer a challenge to men who'll want to climb it just to see the view from the top.'

She could see he wanted to press ahead and she could understand why, but all she wanted at that moment was to sit down somewhere warm. 'All right, Robert, let's come back tomorrow and make a proper list of everything which needs to be done. Meanwhile can we please leave because I'm slowly freezing to death?'

Outside, she turned her collar up as the wind blew sleet against her with stinging force. They ran hand in hand to the car and within minutes they had driven out of the gates and onto the road back to Pincote Market.

They drove into a moving curtain of sleet which hid the road ahead and forced them to drive slower and slower until eventually Robert stopped, the windscreen completely covered with slush. 'I'll have to turn around and go back, Evelyn. It's too dangerous to drive through this.'

She agreed. They could not see where they were going and it would be foolish to risk an accident on a night like this when they would be unlikely to find help. 'Can you turn around? The road's very narrow?'

'Yes, I can drive onto some level ground on my side,' Robert said and immediately began to turn the car around.

Eve hung on as the car bumped over what had looked like level ground, and was relieved when she felt the front wheels ride up onto the road. Then the car stopped.

Robert cursed, allowed the car to roll back, then tried to reach the road again, but the car would not move forwards at all. 'It's stuck in something, Evelyn. I'll get out and have a look.'

He jumped out and reappeared within seconds, his head and shoulders covered with sleet.

'I'm sorry Evelyn, but it's stuck fast and we'll need something to pull it back onto the road. We can stay here, or walk back to the manor.'

She grimaced. They would freeze if they stayed in the car. 'Back to the house. The estate wall's only just over there. We can climb over it and save ourselves having to walk all the way back to the main gates.'

Robert took their bags from the car and scrambled to the top of the high wall, helped her over, and within minutes they were inside the estate grounds.

It was so completely dark she could not see anything as they stumbled forwards. The wind hurled sleet at them and the long grass and tangled undergrowth caught their feet and ankles. Eve constantly tugged herself off bushes which snagged her cloak as she followed Robert through the shrubbery. It seemed ages before they were able to walk on clear, albeit soggy ground, and they moved forwards hand in hand, the wind against their backs.

There was no moon and the darkness was complete so they blundered forwards in the direction they instinctively thought was right.

The wind kept lifting Eve's cloak, blowing sleet underneath and she was busily trying to keep it down when she took a step and felt nothing underneath her foot. 'Robert!' She clung onto him and they both fell together. Cold water flooded over her, but she scrambled onto her feet with her head and shoulders above the surface.

'Robert!'

'It's all right. We've fallen into a lake.'

They turned and climbed up the bank. She shivered as the wind cut through her soaked clothes. 'Have you still got the bags?'

'Yes,' Robert grunted, 'I picked them up again but they went under when I did.'

They found the house ten minutes later. She felt warmer as soon as she was inside, but she and Robert were both shivering violently and she knew they had to dry themselves and change out of their wet clothes before they became dangerously chilled. Robert found and lit the oil lamps they had used earlier and she opened their bags.

'All our spare clothes are soaked, Robert, but there are towels and clothes upstairs. They'll be damp and musty but they'll be a lot better than the things we're wearing.'

They ran to the adjoining rooms where she had seen the clothes. She found several towels, peeled off her wet, clinging clothes and dried herself vigorously, rubbing hard until her skin glowed. Then she wrapped herself in the quilt from the bed and tried to find clothes which would fit her but she could not find any. 'Mrs Laybourne must have been incredibly thin, Robert. Nothing of hers goes even halfway around me.'

'There're plenty of shirts and things in here. I've finished, so come and look. I'll go downstairs and try to light a fire.'

She did as he suggested, dressed herself from neck to toes in a pair of John Laybourne's woollen combinations which fitted her quite well, borrowed one of his shirts and a waistcoat, pinned one heavy woollen shawl from Mrs Laybourne's room around her as a skirt and wore another around her shoulders.

She found Robert trying to light the fire in the music room and he spoke without looking up at her. 'I thought we'd stay in here because it's smaller to heat and there's the chaise-longue and a settee for us to sleep on. There's also plenty of brandy in a cupboard over there. I've just used some of it to help light the fire. Terrible waste but we need warmth from without as well as within.' The fire caught as he spoke and he watched it for a few moments before he turned to look at her. 'Good God, you look like a gypsy.'

He laughed and passed her a glass half filled with brandy. She sipped it and enjoyed the warmth which spread through her. 'You're not trying to get a poor servant girl drunk, are you, sir?' she joked lightly.

'That wasn't my intention, but here's to our first night alone together, Evelyn,' he smiled, and chinked his glass against hers.

They settled onto the settee in front of the fire and drank brandy, gradually slipping together as the warmth of the spirit and the fire combined.

'It's strange, Robert, but I feel quite at home here. Almost as if I belong,' she murmured as the flames entwined around each other and licked at the darkness in the chimney.

'And you just a poor servant girl?' he turned her joke back on her, and squeezed her against him.

'Yes,' she said and snuggled closer against him, 'and very eager to please, sir.'

'Don't forget I'm still married, Evelyn.'

'I know, but I don't care,' she said and kissed him hard.

He responded and pulled her down so she lay across his lap, and seconds later she felt his hands working their way inside the layers of clothing she had painstakingly put on.

They both giggled a lot as they tried to clamber out of the combination of undergarments they had both chosen for warmth, and their laughter overcame the embarrassment and reserve they felt as they lay down together on the floor in front of the fire.

'I love you, Evelyn. More than I can ever tell you or show you.'

She smiled and stroked his face. 'That's how I feel about you. You can't realise how happy I am that we found each other, after all. I know it sounds ridiculous but it seems that I've spent half my life watching you leave me, one way or another.'

'No,' he said quietly, kissing her fingers as they brushed his lips, 'I know what you mean. I seem to have spent too much of my life leaving you. It always made me feel so sad, turning my back on you.'

'We did say, before the war started, that one day we'd have to discuss our sadnesses,' she remembered.

'But not now,' he said and his lips pressed against hers. Then he kissed her throat and neck and his hands caressed her body lightly so that her skin tingled with pleasure.

She remembered the feeling of intimacy which had started when he dabbed rain off her face the first time they met, the feeling which had been reinforced on Hampstead Heath when they had stood alone under the stars, the feelings she had for him a few months earlier when he finally asked her to marry him. In her mind they were married, in spirit if not in law, and she did not resist the new feelings of longing which flowed through her.

'Please,' she reassured him when he hesitated, and her pleasure became more and more intense as her passion unleashed itself. Suddenly she sensed their marriage was complete. She felt wanted and she felt safe and she was overwhelmed by a happiness which seemed to cocoon her.

The act marked the end of the few lingering doubts she had about Robert's commitment to her. It also made her realise how much the war, and danger, had changed her. She was less inclined to be patient and wait for things she wanted. Life could end too quickly. Afterwards they each dressed once more in all the layers of clothes and cuddled for a while before going to sleep.

Eve slept well and did not wake even when thin sunlight sifted through cracks in the window shutters and dimly lit the room. She woke only when the door opened behind her and she heard voices.

'Strange,' a man's voice said, 'fire's been lit. Someone must've been here.'

She shook herself, stood up and turned to look over the settee towards the door.

'Jesus save us!' a woman said sharply.

'Christ!' the man with her said, grabbed at the woman and turned to leave.

'Please don't go! I'm sorry I frightened you. Our car became stuck and we stopped the night,' she explained as she moved towards the couple who cowered away from her. 'I know we shouldn't be here but Mr Wilkin gave us the keys and we couldn't go anywhere else.'

'Who are you?' The man peered at her.

'Evelyn Forrester. I'm a nurse.'

'*Forrester?*'

'Yes. Why?'

'What're you doing here?' the man asked.

Robert had woken up and she introduced him and explained why they were there, then asked the couple why they had reacted in the way they had.

'Well, miss you see—' the man began but the woman cut him short.

'Now then, Henry, you let me explain,' she scowled at him, intimidating him into silence. 'We both used to work here in the old days when Mr Sebastian Laybourne, Mr John's father, was still alive, and it was said then that there was a gypsy curse put on this place. We work the farm across the way now and we came over when we saw smoke coming out the chimney, miss. Even brought some food over in case someone needed it, but we thought the room was empty until you stood up. And looking like you did, like a gypsy's ghost if you don't mind me saying, miss, well it gave us both a turn, like.'

The excuse sounded plausible but she did not believe it. She sensed the couple were not telling her everything but they were obviously eager to leave so she accepted their food, thanked them and watched them go.

'Curious.' Robert said when they were alone.

'You thought so, too?'

'Yes. It was your name which caused a reaction. Mr Wilkin mentioned it yesterday so when we see him we'll have to ask him why.'

Mr Wilkin did not hesitate to explain when they asked.

'Forrester's a well-known local name, although there's none of them left around here now. It's a well honoured name too, and there's a small monument dedicated to Edward Forrester in the market place. He was a miner and he saved dozens of men's lives in the disaster I told you about yesterday. In fact he risked his own life to save Mr John Laybourne's.'

'Edward Forrester?' she asked. 'That's my father's name.'

'Well, isn't that another coincidence, miss, but there's a dark side to this story, too. This Edward Forrester was sent to prison for murdering Mr John's father, Sebastian. He was pardoned a few years later when his sister, Lizzie, found new evidence, but he never came back here. No one knows what happened to him after he was released from prison.'

Her mind wrenched from one thought to another. Edward Forrester? His sister Lizzie? Not Elizabeth, or Beth or Bet or Betty, but Lizzie? And the strange looks her parents and Aunt Lizzie had given her when she said she was coming to the hospital near Coldstream, the hospital John Laybourne went to after Edward Forrester saved him? And the story Helen and Jamie had once told her about not meeting their father until they were three or four years old, a story their mother laughed away as imagination or childish confusion?

It all made a sort of sense, and yet it made none. Perhaps

it was all coincidence? Other than asking her parents which might only make a poor relationship worse, the only way to learn the truth would be to speak with John Laybourne.

'Will Mr Laybourne come to open the hospital, Mr Wilkin?' she asked as innocently as she could manage.

He nodded, and said he was sure Mr Laybourne would travel up for that.

Mr Wilkin had arranged for the motor-car to be recovered and brought to the manor, but before she and Robert left Eve insisted on walking to the top of South Ridge. She was stunned to see the large entrance to a drift mine on the other side of the ridge, and on the slope which rose steeply on the far side of the valley a mass of busy railway sidings below terrace upon terrace of small houses. The ridge marked the difference between an agricultural and an industrial world.

She gazed down on the activity in the valley then turned to look over the peaceful plain. She would have liked to climb up onto King's Crag and stand where the King's emissary once stood, but Robert said there was not enough time so they walked back down the slippery paths and began the drive back to the hospital.

'We'll have to find some very good people to run that place, Evelyn,' Robert said as they turned out of the gates.

'I know,' she said, staring back at the house, and sensing even more that that was where she belonged.

Lottie was sitting at the piano, a blanket wrapped around her shoulders, trying to play the piano in the large drawing room, but she was so cold her fingers stumbled over the keys. Although February was nearly over, they still had several months of winter to endure in the house which was meant only for summer living. The logs they were now burning had not been properly dried and they smoked but did not give out much heat, so there was a thick layer of ice inside every window in the house.

Lottie looked up when Tatiana came in and stood looking at a window she could not see through. 'Is something wrong, Tatiana?'

'Look. From Valerie Vassilievitch,' Tatiana handed her a telegram.

Its message was simple. *'Come home. Now.'*

'Perhaps he wants to see you, Tatiana. You've been apart for two and a half years now.'

'We've been apart for twenty-seven years, Charlotte. Even when we were together we were apart. But I don't understand this message. It's as if he's scared to say anything more. And if that's the case we may be safer here.'

They stared at each other, each wanting the other to answer a question they could not answer, and moments later a maid crept into the room. 'Excuse me, madam, but there's a gentleman called to speak to you. He wouldn't tell me his name but he said it was important.'

Tatiana frowned. 'Charlotte, would you mind dealing with that? I need to think.'

'Certainly.' Lottie followed the maid out into the corridor which led to the large reception hall and saw a huge man wearing a heavy fur hat, tulup and boots. He stood facing away from her and stamping his feet to revive them. 'Can I help you. I'm afraid Mrs Zubova can't see you at the—'

'Krasnaya, you speak Russian like a peasant.' He pulled his hat of.

'Komovsky! Peter!' She flew at him and kissed him hard on his numbed lips. 'How are you? It's been years.'

'I think of you every night, Krasnaya, in the most innocent way.'

'And I think of you. Constantly. Come into the drawing room.'

He hesitated. 'I'm not sure I'm welcome, Lottie.'

At that moment Natasha spoke from the top of the stairs. 'My God! It's the great Russian bear come to life again.'

'And my sweetest compliments to you, too, Natasha,' Peter grinned, and then opened his arms as Natasha rushed down the stairs and threw herself at him. 'Am I forgiven?'

'Of course. I think of Charlotte as my sister so you are my brother-in-law. Well, in a manner of speaking.'

'And how is my brother?' Peter asked Lottie, and when she looked away and could not answer he wrapped her in his arms and they cried together for several minutes.

Natasha had gone to fetch her mother who also welcomed Peter and they all went back to the drawing room together.

Peter read the telegram and looked at Tatiana. 'I hate to admit I would ever agree with your husband, but I think you should go. You may not be safe here for much longer. Parts of the army are in mutiny. The cavalry's supporting the peasants it was sent to put down, and only the Cossacks and the Guards remain truly loyal to the Tsar. Quite frankly I think they may turn, too.' He folded the telegram and handed it back to Tatiana. 'There's nobody here to defend you, so close up, pay the servants, go back to Petrograd and don't expect to come here again. The revolution has started, ladies, and no one'll stop it now. Not until it's run its course.'

Lottie was shocked, and she said so.

'Krasnaya, you go to the British Embassy and explain your situation and they'll find some way to get you home, either on a British ship or through Finland and Sweden. And when you go, wear these and present them to my mother who probably thinks by now that she has two very poor sons.'

She took the small bag he dug out from inside his shirt, and when she opened it she saw his mother's rings, the rings he had recovered in Paris. It suddenly occurred to her that three years had passed since then. 'I will,' she said quietly.

'You promise?' he asked, staring into her eyes, and she nodded. Then he stood up and pulled his coat back on. 'I cannot stop but there'll be a train tomorrow. Be on it. Please.'

Before he left she took him to the nursery. When she opened the door Irina was sitting on the floor on the far side of the room.

'Here's your Uncle Komovsky,' she said.

Irina looked up, grinned, stood up with her arms open

507

wide and took six steps before she fell. Peter picked her up and kissed her. She giggled at him as he held her and murmured when he kissed her.

'How long since she started trying to walk?' he asked.

'That was the first time, Komovsky. There must be something about you that all women like,' she said.

He grinned and said he had to leave. She saw him to the front door, and once again he told her to go to Petrograd in the morning. And once again she promised she would.

Lottie was stunned when she arrived back in the capital. The carriage driver Tatiana engaged was uneasy about accepting her fare when he heard her address, charged three times more than normal and even then was grudging about taking them home. As they drove through the snow-covered streets she could understand why. Siberian Cossacks on their shaggy ponies patrolled the streets around the Tauride Palace and the roofs of most public buildings sprouted machine-gun posts from where heavily-dressed soldiers studied the streets below. She also realised, from seeing well-armed guards standing by entrances, that many of the large buildings around the Zubov's house were barracks occupied by Petrograd's and the Tsar's more fashionable regiments.

A Cossack patrol stopped the carriage and an officer peered inside. Lottie held Irina tightly and placed her free arm around the boys as they moved to her, but the fur-hatted officer smiled and waved the carriage on.

Like Tatiana and Natasha, Lottie stood up as Valerie Vassilievitch entered the room, and she thought he was everything Sasha described. He was handsome and he had an aura of kindness and authority. In some ways he reminded her of Joseph.

He looked surprised to see them.

'You didn't expect us so soon?' Tatiana said.

'So soon?' he frowned.

'Your telegram,' Tatiana explained.

'What telegram? I haven't sent a telegram.' He turned

508

back through the door. 'Olga! Come in here, please.'

Olga appeared and was as surprised as Mr Zubov.

Tatiana smiled. 'Well Charlotte, it appears someone has played a trick on us. Maybe we should return to the country.'

Her husband frowned. 'No. Perhaps it is better you stay here, Miss Forrester also. Sadly things are changing and very quickly, but at least we have regiments of Guards in the capital. They'll protect us if the worst happens.' Then he shook his head. 'But who could have played such a trick on you? And why?'

She watched the expressions on both Tatiana's and Natasha's faces as they assured him they had no idea, and she unconsciously felt the rings she was wearing as she remembered Peter's expedient visit.

That night she heard shots fired in the city, and several days later she was shopping with Natasha when they heard tramping feet and voices singing 'La Marseillaise'. They stood still as a wide procession rounded the corner ahead of them and marched towards them. The procession took ten minutes to pass. Between each chorus of their song the marchers shouted a single slogan: '*Bread and Peace.*'

She learned from a woman standing close by that people in the capital were dying for the want of bread, and she thought about the Estate Irina where the workers who knew how to grow the crops to make flour had been sent away and made to fight battles they could not win. It was madness, even she could see that.

'It's frightening,' Natasha said quietly, 'but at least we have the Guards here. As Papa says, they'll protect us, Charlotte.'

A few days later she heard lorry after lorry roar past the house, and above the noise they made she heard the sound of men singing 'La Marseillaise'. She ran to the window, shaded her eyes against the glare of the bright morning sun, and saw lorries loaded with soldiers pass around the corner. Shots were fired. She could not see what was happening but suddenly the street filled with grey-clad soldiers rushing from the surrounding barracks, and a moment later, without any more shots being fired, the street turned red – not with blood but with flags which the soldiers were waving.

Whole regiments of the Guards who were supposed to be their saviours were not only deserting, they were going over to the people. She watched as an officer jumped out onto a ledge outside a high window and fired a single shot into the air to attract his men's attention. He succeeded. His men turned and silently listened to what he said, then they raised their rifles and their bullets pitched him back through the open window.

She was horrified – and scared. More scared than she had ever been before.

That evening they heard that the Cossacks had sheathed their sabres instead of stopping a starving mob from the people's Petrograd scrambling across the frozen River Neva shouting for bread.

A telephone message told the household that the army was openly fraternising with the revolutionaries and the Courthouse was being burned. A later call told them that the people had smashed their way into the seat of government. Minutes later Lottie and Tatiana rushed to the window and looked down on another mass of marchers. Thousands of men and women were tramping through the snow shouting a new slogan: *'Where is the new Government?'*

The Revolution had begun and thanks to Peter she was in the midst of it, but what did it mean to her?

She asked Olga's advice.

'Very little, I think, Charlotte. The people are very excited tonight but they have had enough fighting and they will not want to fight among themselves as Aunt Tass and Mr Zubov believe. Anyway, tomorrow we'll have a new Government which will listen to the wants of the people.'

Olga was correct. Russia did have a new Government, the violence quickly died down, and she was no longer worried. The blood bath Mr Zubov predicted did not occur and she suddenly had a sense that her Russification was

510

complete. She had seen some of the suffering and a little of the excesses of Russian life.

Now it was safe she took any opportunity which arose to walk around the great city. Although she could appreciate some of the city's beauty she knew enough about its slums for it not to entrance her as it had Sasha. If anything it made her sad, both for itself and for him, and as she stood on a bridge and stared down at the frozen river she remembered how he had told her about coloured lanterns and skaters dancing to bands. His music welled up in her mind and a huge ache began to grow in her.

She wanted to leave the city, and never return.

When she arrived back at the house Tatiana told her that the new Government had forced the Tsar to abdicate.

Valerie Vassilievitch took down his sporting guns, cleaned and oiled them, and prophesied there would be lynch mobs on the streets by morning. Olga was moved from her apartment into the Zubov house. Petrograd held its breath and the two telephones in the Zubov house hardly stopped ringing throughout the night.

The following morning life went on as usual, and Lottie asked Tatiana to help introduce her to someone who could advise her of how she might return to England.

'You wish to leave, Charlotte?'

'Yes, Tatiana. I ache for Sasha. It started yesterday and I can feel it consuming me. I have to get away, from Petrograd, Russia and everything that reminds me of him.'

'And Estate Irina?' Tatiana asked quietly. 'And your memories?'

'No, but—'

Tatiana held up her hand. 'It's grief, Charlotte. I'm afraid you can't hide from it or ignore it, only live through it and grow stronger because of it. Coping with death is a part of life, it prepares you to cope with the inevitability of your own death.'

She smiled. 'That's a very Russian thought, Tatiana.'

'That's because I *am* very Russian, Charlotte.' The comment was heavy with meaning and suggested Tatiana had something more on her mind. A moment later Tatiana coughed, which she sometimes did when she was about to break bad news. 'As is little Irina.'

'What do you mean?'

'Immediately after the Revolution started I spoke with certain friends to ask if I could obtain papers for you to leave Russia with Irina, Leo, Sergei, and perhaps Natasha. No Russians are being allowed to leave, and you would only be allowed to leave if you surrendered all rights to your daughter.'

'I'd never do that!' Even the thought was abhorrent.

'Then, Charlotte, I'm afraid you have no choice but to stay.'

The next day Lottie suggested that as spring was approaching and the country was short of bread she should return to the estate. Tatiana demurred but Natasha agreed that she would like to return. Natasha said she could see the sense in it, and once it was agreed that they would both go Leo and Sergei said it was unfair if little Irina went to the estate and they had to stay in the city. At that point Tatiana also conceded, and Valerie Vassilievitch agreed it was for the best and showed their commitment to their duties as good Russians.

PART 4

CHAPTER 32

Spring–Summer, 1917

Eve was frustrated by the resistance Robert's new ideas encountered, but her attitude mellowed when it was agreed that his team should move into the new Pincote Hospital Annex when it was completed.

Because they were so busy neither she nor Robert found time to make more than one visit to Pincote to see how the hospital was progressing. That visit was so hurried that Eve did not expect to have time to ask anyone about the Forresters, and she was surprised when the hotel manager's wife invited herself into her room and asked if they could talk.

'Well now, Miss Forrester, you can tell me to mind me own business and I'll not take offence, like, but *are* you related to Lizzie Forrester like everyone says you are?'

'Is everyone saying that?' she asked, amazed that anyone should be saying anything at all about her.

'Aye, they are that. Ever since your last visit, 'specially as you went up to the manor, mind.'

'I'm sorry but I'm very confused,' Eve admitted.

'Well, lass, so are we, which is why I've come to talk to you because if you are Lizzie and Edward's daughter we

515

wouldn't want you to think you're not welcome here. Or them for that matter. We'd love to see 'em any time, even if it has been years since they left, like.'

'My father is called Edward, and I do have an Aunt Lizzie, but why do you think I'm Lizzie's daughter?'

'Because you're the image of her, lass. Your ma and da might have grown up as brother and sister but they weren't of course. Lizzie was taken in by Josh and Minty when she was a baby and the folks around here always reckoned Lizzie and your da might get together in the end.'

'You knew them well, in those days?'

'Very well. Lizzie Forrester taught me at the school for years, and me brother and sisters. Me old ma even made some clothes for her. Her and Rose Laybourne, for Rose's eighteenth-birthday ball. You know, when Rose's brother, John Laybourne came back from America? Just before the '85 disaster? They must've told you about it?'

'Bits and pieces,' she lied, keen not to discourage the woman from telling her more, 'but you know what it's like when you're little, you don't really listen. I wish I had now I've come here.'

'Well, I can tell you most things, like. I was only little then, and your parents'd remember me as Alice Darling. Me da was crippled by the mine and we lived just down the road from your folks. Your da taught me brother Billy all about mining.'

Alice Darling, now Alice Bewley, talked for an hour and told stories which convinced Eve that her parents and aunt did come from Pincote, and helped her to understand why they had kept their past lives secret.

'So no one believed my father intended to kill Sebastian Laybourne?'

'No. It was my brother Billy who told him there was a mob going up to the manor to burn it down. Edward didn't even know Mr Laybourne was there. No one did. He only went to calm things down and save your mother. She'd been Miss Rose's Governess until Rose left to get married to Mr Belchester, and then she'd stayed on to look after the house and to be Mrs Laybourne's companion. Well, that was the story, like, but we all knew she and Mr John were very keen on each other even though he was engaged to the McDougall girl.'

'They were keen on each other? What happened?' Eve sensed she might be about to unearth another element of the story.

'The Disaster happened. The big collapse. Your father saved Mr John's life but he could not stop him losing a leg and being burned terrible. And half blinded. Well, your mother pulled him back from the grave, like, and stood by him all the time he was at the hospital you're working in now, and even when he came home. Then, during the Midsummer Fair, must have been in '86, she just left. I suppose she just couldn't face living with Mr John, him being crippled, like. I can't say I blame her. Not seeing what me ma went through with me da, but it shook everyone, including Mr John. He married Miss McDougall but I don't think they were ever that happy, and then he took to drinking and shut himself away, like. We didn't see him for years, and there were some who blamed your ma, but as I said they don't know what it takes to live with someone who's badly crippled like that.'

'Is Mr Laybourne that badly crippled?' she asked.

Alice Bewley thought for a moment, then said in a surprised voice, 'No, I don't suppose he is. Not really.' Then she seemed to realise how long she had been talking for, excused herself and left.

Eve was furious, and confused. She was furious with her aunt for insisting that she should have stood by Tom Dobbs when her aunt had abandoned John Laybourne, who did not seem to be as badly injured as Tom. And she was confused as to how there could be any family resemblance between her and her aunt if Aunt Lizzie was not her father's blood sister.

Robert listened to her story and gave her two pieces of advice. 'We'll meet John Laybourne when he comes to open the hospital and I'm sure he'll notice the resemblance so I wouldn't say anything to your parents or aunt until you've heard what he might have to say. And when you do broach the subject, do it gently. There's been enough trouble between you all as it is. They must have their reasons for keeping all this secret, and you should respect that.'

'That's all very well for you to say but—' she began, but he held his hand up to stop her.

'Haven't you ever kept something secret to save someone's feelings?' he asked, and immediately gave her examples to prove his point. 'You went to prison rather than let the newspaper publish a story which would have hurt your parents and aunt. You tried to protect Lottie by not telling her what your parents were saying about her. You didn't admit that Rathbone had misquoted your views on joining up. You—'

'All right!' She held her own hand up to stop him. 'I accept your point, but something else has just occurred to me.'

'Yes?'

'If my mother married this Mr Belchester in '85 and my father went to prison for several years, how could she have given birth to Helen and Jamie in '87? And what happened to Mr Belchester?'

'I don't know, Evelyn,' Robert said patiently, 'but does it really matter?'

'Yes. It does to me. I want to know what happened.'

A month later Eve spent a few days with her parents but the atmosphere was very strained because she had to be careful not to say anything out of place, particularly when her aunt deliberately antagonised her by voicing an opinion that she would have been better employed looking after Tom Dobbs than nursing strangers. Maisie made matters even worse by avoiding her completely, and after three days Eve decided she could not stay any longer and reported back for duty.

She had wanted to ignore Robert's advice and tell her mother and father what she knew but she sensed that would simply make a bad situation even worse so she decided to wait until she had an opportunity to talk with John Laybourne.

Lottie was glad to leave Petrograd and happy to be back at Estate Irina. They arrived on the day Nikolas began digging over one of the garden plots and he cried when he saw them come along the drive.

Some of the house servants had moved or found other work but there were enough available to staff the house. The women who could help with the crop were delighted to see the family had returned and they set to work immediately.

The spring came early and it was wet and wonderfully warm. Then the summer came early and was hot, guaranteeing a good harvest.

Lottie measured the wheat's growth by standing her daughter at the side of a field. 'Look, Irina, last week it was only this high and now it's taller than you.'

Irina looked at the wheat, pulled down a tip, tickled herself under her chin and laughed.

Olga came for a week in August, and found the family outside the house watching the peasant women as they went into the fields to cut the first of the wheat. 'Good morning, Aunt Tass. That looks like a good crop.'

'Olga!' Tatiana kissed her warmly. 'Yes, and we should thank Charlotte. We mightn't have come back if it hadn't been for her.'

'Well, you should thank her for getting you out of the city. Food's scarce, even for us, and there are demonstrations almost every day. More than ever the people are demanding food and peace.'

'And how's Valerie Vassilievitch?' Tatiana asked and Olga's mood changed. 'I don't know. I'd like you to see him.'

Lottie saw the look Tatiana and Olga exchanged and knew Tatiana would go back with Olga when she returned. Despite the difference in their ages these two women were incredibly close, one a wife and the other a mistress of sorts.

Later that evening, after a long day, when Lottie was dozing in a chair in the drawing room, Tatiana woke her.

'I'd like to talk to you while we're alone, Charlotte.' Tatiana waited until she ha her full attention before she

519

continued. 'I don't like my husband very much but I do love him, unlike Olga who neither loves nor likes him but respects him. I suspected Valerie was ill when he almost totally ignored you earlier this year because that is not in his character. Olga has told me that he is suffering immense strain because of the current political situation and since it is my duty to be with him I intend to return to the capital with her.'

'But Tatiana, I thought everything was under control?'

'It was, but Lenin's exciting the Bolshevik Party to demand greater power and there was an uprising last month. My husband's department failed to infiltrate the revolt and it had to be stopped by the army. Lenin escaped but Valerie Vassilievitch is sure he'll be back. The German army is about to attack the city of Riga. If we cannot defend Riga we might lose Petrograd and Valerie believes Lenin will try to use the threat of the Germans attacking the capital to cause trouble and mount another revolt. I owe it to Russia to be with him at this tine.'

'I understand, Tatiana.'

'No, I don't think you do,' Tatiana said quietly. 'The Russians and *nemets* hate each other. We have been told that as the *nemets* advance they are raping Russian women before murdering them and their men, and they are butchering the children to end the Russian race. This could be a story put about to make our soldiers fight, or it could be true, Charlotte. I have no way of knowing, but you've seen the soldiers run riot in Petrograd. Can you believe they will defend the capital with good hearts?'

'No.' She was glad she was not in Petrograd. God knows what the Germans would do to her as a British Citizen, or what would happen to little Irina.

'I'd like you and Natasha to stay here with the children. I will arrange to send you newspapers to be left at the station with Igor, but you must make other arrangements also. Tomorrow you must go into town, not just the village but right into town, and arrange for a daily delivery of all available newspapers to this house, whatever it costs. You must do everything you can to keep yourself aware of events. Obviously we will try to keep you informed but as things change we might not be able to send telegrams or newspapers to Igor.' Tatiana sighed and bit her lip. 'Before I go I'll show you a safe which contains gold coins. Don't hesitate to abandon the estate if you think it necessary but if you have to leave, take those coins.'

It seemed to Lottie that as soon as the other gold was harvested from the fields it appeared in the skies. The sunsets stretched across the western horizon and back above the estate. The sky was gold and the air was filled with dust, and a strange aura of impending danger settled all over the countryside.

It took six months to convert Laybourne Manor into a full working hospital. It was made to look symmetrical again when a stone-clad extension containing operating theatres was built to replace the end which had been burned, and internally a number of walls were removed to join rooms together to make more efficient ward space. Staff were to be accommodated temporarily in large wooden huts until better accommodation could be built for them.

The opening ceremony was supposed to be simple and attended only by John Laybourne, the staff who were to work in the hospital and a few dignitaries, but in the event most of the townspeople from Pincote Colliery were excused work for the morning and swarmed over South Ridge and down into the estate grounds to see the plaque unveiled.

Eve watched carefully as John Laybourne, thin, grey, elderly, hanging on crutches and with his eyes hidden behind thick-lensed spectacles turned and welcomed the crowd he could hear but could not possibly see.

'The war cannot last much longer,' he gasped, 'especially now the Americans have joined us. When it's over this hospital will serve you all, as its namesake did.'

He pulled a string and a curtain fell off a plaque which read,

The Edward Forrester Memorial Hospital was opened on the

fourteenth of June 1917, to honour Edward Forrester who in 1885 endangered his own life in order to save so many others.

Everyone clapped and Robert, and then Eve were called forwards to meet John Laybourne.

'Miss Forrester I've been looking forward to meeting you. I know you don't come from around here but you must realise that your name is revered in this town?' he said, clasping her hand in both of his and standing rock-steady on his crutches and good leg. He peered closely at her. 'Forgive me, but my eyes aren't good, especially when I'm tired and in this bright sunlight, but you sound very young. However, I can't believe you've been made Matron here simply because your name's Forrester.'

'I hope not, sir,' she said and gave him a brief resumé of her nursing career.

'Very impressive. Very impressive.' He smiled and she noticed the way his face remained stiff where his skin had been burned. 'I know Doctor Braithewaite's Lady Braithewaite's son, but you're no relation to the suffragette woman who ousted her from the Women's League, are you?'

'I am that suffragette woman, Mr Laybourne. That's how I first met Doctor Braithewaite. Do you think that affects my ability to run this hospital?' she did not bother to hide her irritation.

'Goodness gracious, no, dear lady, but however did you manage to conceal your partnership with Braithewaite from the newspapers?'

'I think there were other things happening which diverted them, sir. The war, for example.'

He laughed and they both looked up as three aeroplanes droned high above their heads. She could see them but she knew he could not.

Elizabeth had called to see Bill's wife Gladys, their daughter and grandchildren who were all in their beds with influenza, and as she left the house and closed the door behind her she saw Bill turn the corner and walk towards her. He smiled and she smiled back, glad their friendship had not been harmed by the very temporary silliness they had both indulged in a few years ago. Bill was important to her, he had a very special place in her heart, and their friendship was something she treasured and would never wish to lose.

'I've just been in to see your family, Bill. They all seem a bit better.'

'Thanks, Lizzie. And how are you?'

She did not answer, and his smile disappeared as the air suddenly vibrated with the roar of noisy, throbbing engines.

'Zeppelin?' His lips formed the word but she could not hear what he said because of the noise the engines made.

They walked to the middle of the road and looked up, their hands shading their eyes from the sun, but they could not see anything above the roof-tops.

Front doors banged open as people ran into the street and formed a crowd, staring up into the bright June sky.

'What's happening?' someone shouted from an upstairs window.

'Zeps, I reckon,' Stan Butcher shouted back but she contradicted him.

'No, that's not the noise a Zep makes,' Elizabeth said, sure of herself, and watched Bill walk further down the street to look through a gap between the mission building and a row a houses.

Somewhere in the near distance a heavy gun started to pump shells and moments later she jumped as pieces of shell casings pinged down into the street.

'Christ!' Bill shouted and pointed behind her. 'Get out of the street! Get under cover.'

She turned and saw five aeroplanes coming towards her, low and flying very slowly. The large German crosses painted on their wings and fuselages made her freeze with terror. She could see the Germans in their leather helmets. The enemy was only yards away!

'Lizzie!' she heard Bill call but she still could not move.

Suddenly he grabbed her and dragged her away. She

heard an engine whine and saw an aeroplane falling towards her. Two black things fell from it as it flattened out and climbed away, its engine popping and spluttering. She heard a short high-pitched scream.

Bill dragged her into the mission yard, threw her between two piles of coal and dropped on top of her.

The world turned somersaults, coal, bricks, glass and slates rained down and she heard a roar like a gas jet, but much louder. She looked up and saw daylight through the gable-end and the roof of the mission building, and seconds later coarse red flames with black edges licked out. She felt the heat even though the flames were thirty feet above her.

Bill was still lying on top of her and she looked beyond him and saw his house and the ones either side. Or what was left of them. The top floor of his house was not there and the houses either side had lost their roofs and several courses of brickwork.

The windows suddenly blew out of his home and moments later flames engulfed the whole house.

'Bill!' Gladys and his daughter and grandchildren were in there. 'Bill!'

He stirred, lifted his head slowly and shook it. Blood flicked across her face. He slumped onto her again and she saw the back of his head was badly cut. 'Bill! Pull yourself together.'

She lifted his head. His eyes were rolling and he looked concussed but she turned him over and made him sit up.

'Oh Christ! No!' He clambered up and tried to run towards his home but his legs kept buckling under him. He stopped trying to run and crawled, dragging himself out of the yard and halfway across the street, raking back debris as he moved through it. 'Gladys! Gladys!'

'Come back, Bill,' Elizabeth yelled and ran after him. 'It's no use, Bill, you can't do anything. You can't go in there. Come away, there's nothing you can do.'

He screamed, 'Gladys!' and as the heat from the flames crinkled her hair she had to sit on him to stop him crawling any closer.

She could see through the second-storey windows and saw burning floorboards and joists fold in the middle and collapse. She thought she saw Gladys's iron bed plunge down with the timber and other pieces of furniture. Red sparks rocketed up into the air in a column of black smoke and seconds later the floor below collapsed with an awful splintering noise. Even more sparks rushed skywards. The sparks and pieces of wood floated back down, blazing or smoking or just glowing, but she knew they could still cause bad burns so she tried to get Bill under cover. He did not want to go but she shouted and pulled at him and finally he relented. She led him, half dragging him away from the disaster, and he came, doubled-up and broken, still staring at what had been his home.

Katarina appeared, white and shaking.

'Hold on to him. Don't let him move from here. I'm going to see what I can do.'

The street was littered with people, most of them stunned or not badly hurt, but Stan Butcher was dead, bleeding from his ears and nose, and an elderly woman who had just moved into the street tried to stand up, gave an enormous twitch, and collapsed, dead.

Fire bells rang urgently and a few minutes later the fire-engine turned into the bottom of the street and stopped. She told the firemen that Bill's family had been in the house which was totally destroyed and the men shook their heads and did what they could to stop the flames spreading to the other houses.

'Anyone in the mission?' The senior fireman asked.

'No, they're all out working. In the munitions factory in Silvertown,' she said, not immediately aware of the irony.

Another fire-engine arrived ten minutes later but it was too late to save the mission. The building she had worked in for thirty-one years was a huge bonfire, but that did not matter, not when Bill's Gladys and his family were dead.

The Midsummer Fair was an annual Pincote Market event. It was usually held on the Friday, Saturday and Sunday nearest Midsummer's Day, but this year it had been brought forward by a week to follow on from the opening of the new hospital.

Eve and Robert were too busy at the hospital to attend the fair itself but John Laybourne had invited them to join him at an open-air concert in the town's Victoria Gardens on Sunday evening.

Eve had taken special care to look as attractive as she could for Robert's sake, and had been pleased with his compliments, but she was taken aback by John Laybourne's reaction when he saw her.

She was standing in clear sunlight, while he was sitting with his back to the evening sun, a wide-brimmed hat shading his eyes from whatever glare was left.

'Good God!' He looked shaken, and reminded her how the man who had come into the music room had looked when he first saw her. 'Good God.'

'I'm sorry,' she apologised quickly, 'have I done something to upset you?'

'No, my dear, not at all.'

'Are you sure?'

'Yes, Miss Forrester. Just come and sit down beside me. The music'll start quite soon,' he said quietly and in a distracted voice.

His reaction suggested he might be willing to answer some of the questions she wanted to ask, and she found it difficult to sit through the concert. The way John Laybourne fidgeted suggested he was also finding it difficult to sit there. His hands never stopped moving, and every so often she saw him glance towards her, frown, and quickly look away.

The orchestra played the National Anthem at the end of the concert and as soon as it was over she felt him grip her arm. 'I've arranged dinner for us at the hotel, but would you mind if first my driver and I gave you a short conducted tour of the Pincote towns? Starting at the 1885 Monument?'

'Not at all,' she said before Robert could speak. 'We'd both enjoy it, wouldn't we, Robert?'

'Forgive me, Miss Forrester,' John Laybourne smiled at

her, 'but am I correct in detecting a certain familiarity between you and Doctor Braithewaite?'

She was not sure how to answer but she did not need to speak because Robert answered for her. 'Miss Forrester and I plan to get married but we haven't made any definite arrangements yet and we don't wish to make the news public for personal reasons.'

'I quite understand, and I admire you both for your discretion. I was once in a very similar situation.'

They stopped in the market-place and he showed them the 1885 Monument, the memorial raised to commemorate what Edward Forrester had done to save so many men from dying in a pit disaster.

He explained his own part in that and how Edward Forrester saved his life and Edward's sister, Elizabeth, helped him to come back from the dead by reading to him and talking to him every day for months even though he did not react.

'My own mother had a similar experience, sir.' She explained what had happened and how her father had helped her to recover even though everyone else thought he was hoping for the impossible.

'You said he recited Shakespeare to her?'

'Yes. From *Henry V*,' she confirmed, and watched him mull over what she had said.

'It wasn't King Henry's speech to his troops before the battle of Harfleur?' he asked, and when she nodded he added, 'Once more unto the breach? Yes it would be. It would be.'

He knew? She was puzzled, but put that aside while she asked him about the names he had given to the various rooms, the small wards, in the hospital. 'What made you choose those particular names, sir? John, Edward, Rose, Catherine, Elizabeth and Charlotte?'

'Well, John and Edward are obvious. Rose was my sister, Catherine my half sister, Elizabeth was Edward's sister and my saviour and Charlotte was my mother's name.'

'Most of the names are just as relevant to me, Mr

Laybourne,' she said and trembled as she told him what the names meant to her.

He looked puzzled. 'Your mother's name is Rose, not Elizabeth?'

'Yes, sir? Why?' She was surprised that he, like everyone else, had assumed she was Aunt Lizzie's daughter.

'I think we should be open with each other, Miss Forrester. The last time I saw my sister Rose, she was living with Elizabeth Forrester in a small house in north London.'

'Angel Street? In Islington?' she asked.

'Yes. You know it?'

'I grew up there.'

'I see,' he said, and paused and seemed to think for a long time before he spoke again. 'Miss Forrester, I'm a little confused. I know this must appear to be a very odd question, but are you sure Rose is your mother, not Elizabeth?'

'Yes, sir, I'm absolutely sure. My brother and older sister remember Lottie and me being born, and Aunt Lizzie had lost her baby only a few months earlier when her husband was killed. I know I look like her and I'd always assumed I'd inherited that side of the family's appearance through my father, until a few weeks ago when someone told me my aunt had been taken in by my father's family. Now, like you, I'm confused. I don't understand how I can possibly look like my Aunt Lizzie.'

He stared at her and did not speak, then he smiled as if a long-time mystery had been solved satisfactorily, and said kindly, 'No, Miss Forrester, I don't suppose you do, but when you next see your aunt will you please wait until you're alone with her and tell her you've met me, that I'm quite well, and that now I've met you I understand.'

'Of course, Mr Laybourne, but can you explain it all to me?'

'Miss Forrester, do you think we might dispense with the formalities as it appears I'm your long-lost Uncle John. Can we all simply use each other's Christian names?'

'Of course, but until now I didn't know I even *had* an Uncle John.'

'No I don't suppose you did, and until now I didn't know

Elizabeth was my half sister,' John smiled a little sadly. 'I heard rumours, after my father's death, that he cast his seed far and wide, shall we say, but it never occurred to me that he fathered Elizabeth. I assume she found out and that was why she ran off instead of staying here to marry me. It actually makes sense of something our old coachman told me just before he died. He said I wasn't to go on blaming Elizabeth, that she had no choice.'

'Oh God!' Eve gasped. 'I've been blaming her for everything. For abandoning you and for expecting me to look after Tom Dobbs, and for trying to stop me coming north to work, but now I can guess why she wanted me to stay away. She was trying to keep her secret.'

'Yes, Evelyn,' John said, 'and I'm not sure that I should have told you as much as I have but as Fate has brought you to Pincote I think you should know what really happened. There are many stories told about your parents and I wouldn't want you to hear and believe one which isn't true, Evelyn.'

'Come on. I'll show you the house where Edward and Elizabeth grew up and the school where Elizabeth taught, and then we'll go to the hotel and I'll finish the story over dinner.'

Eve was astounded by John's story.

'It all goes back to 1885, Evelyn. Rose and Edward had fallen in love even then, but it was an apparently hopeless situation because he was a miner and she was the owner's daughter. Our father, Sebastian, forced her to become engaged to Hubert Belchester because it suited his business. When the mine collapsed shortly afterwards Edward lost his temper and threatened to kill my father, so when the police discovered my father's body and saw Edward running away they assumed he was the murderer.'

'Did he kill him?' she asked quickly, keen to know the truth.

'Yes, but in self-defence, although that was not proved until years after your father had been tried and sent to prison for murder.'

She told him she did not understand how her mother could have carried Helen and Jamie if her father was in prison and she was married to Mr Belchester.

'Your father escaped from the police and they might never have found him if he hadn't surrendered himself a year or so later. Meanwhile your mother had run away from Belchester because he treated her badly. They obviously found each other, but I don't know exactly what happened, although I imagine Elizabeth does.'

Another realisation struck her. 'Of course, Aunt Lizzie'd be Mama's half sister, wouldn't she?'

'I suppose she is, Evelyn, but she might not know. Your father mightn't know the truth either, so you'll have to be careful what you say when you see them and talk about all this.'

'I'm not sure I ever will tell them that I know what happened. I'll tell Aunt Lizzie, as you said, because I think it's important that we sort out our differences, but I don't see any reason to tell Mama and Papa. It's their life, isn't it? And it all happened a long time before I was born?' She looked at Robert and saw him nod.

John also nodded. 'Yes, it was all a long time ago, but you should hear the rest of the story. Rose went back to Belchester and he very nearly drove her mad before he tried to kill her. She ran away again, with your brother and sister, and Elizabeth hid her. Even though it took them several years they managed to find proof that Edward had killed my father in self-defence and he joined them in Angel Street. They've been hiding from Hubert Belchester ever since. That's probably why they've tried to keep everything secret. You see, your mother's still married to him.'

'I wondered if she was,' she admitted, and shrugged. 'Not that it matters as far as I'm concerned. They're still my mama and papa whether they're married or not.'

'Yes,' John said in a matter-of-fact way, 'of course they are. What's ironic is that you should have come here to live on the estate where your mother grew up – even if you are living in a hut in the grounds rather than in the house itself. Still, it must give you an added interest, knowing that in effect you're working in your ancestral home.'

'Yes. I hadn't thought of it like that,' she said.

Later that night, when she was lying awake in her bed, she could not stop thinking. Now she knew why her parents and Aunt Lizzie were trying to lead quiet and private lives she could understand why they did not want her to become a suffragette and risk exposing them. Now she could understand all they must have been going through as she attracted more and more attention. Then she wondered if she was the reason Lottie was followed? Perhaps that was something to do with her mother's legal husband.

Although she knew she was not being rational she blamed herself for everything, and decided then that she had to go home and make some sort of peace with her aunt, but she felt she needed a reasonable excuse if she was to invite herself to their home.

The following day she read a three-day-old newspaper and found the excuse she needed. The mission had been bombed by German aeroplanes, the first attack of its kind that London had sustained. More important than the mission, Gladys Crabb and her family had all been killed.

Robert helped her arrange compassionate leave and she sent her parents a telegram to say she had read the news and was coming home for a few days.

It was not until she was actually at the railway station the following morning that she realised she had used the words *coming home* in her telegram. She wondered what her parents might make of that.

Once again the journey was slow because the train was hauled into sidings while troop trains rattled past on the way to the docks, and she did not reach London until Wednesday evening, thirty-six hours after she left Pincote.

Her father opened the front door and immediately wrapped his arms around her. 'Welcome home, Eve. It's been months since we saw you.'

'How are you, Papa? And Mama and Aunt Lizzie? How're Helen and Maisie and have you heard from Joe or

Lottie?' The questions raced out and he answered them patiently as he took her bag and told her to go into the kitchen, but she held back and quietly asked the most awful question. 'And Mr Crabb? How's he?'

'He's in there with the others. It's the funerals tomorrow. You will come?'

'Of course. Did they find enough to bury?'

'Bits, but there's a coffin for each person.'

'It's better than the Front, Papa. They don't often get coffins there.'

'Now they've started dropping their bombs on women and children, Eve, this is the Front. One of them, anyway,' he said quietly and gripped her arm. 'I'll tell you what it has done for us, though. It's made a lot more sense of Jamie's death. We can see now that he was fighting for us, too, and not just for a lot of foreigners.'

Everyone welcomed Eve warmly and she sensed that Mr Crabb's loss, unwanted and unequal though it was, had somehow been her gain, but she decided not to tell her aunt about John Laybourne until the next day, or even the day after.

The funeral was stark, simple and awful. Four coffins buried together in ground that crumbled in the summer heat.

There were dozens of mourners, all still chilled by the shock of Germans killing neighbours *in their own street* but sweating under a June sun that did not know or care what had happened.

Bill was the last one left of his small family; his son-in-law had been one of the Somme's first victims.

There was no customary wake. The family gathered at home and tried to comfort Bill as best they could but it was not possible to ease the grief which had already settled on him.

'Thanks for coming all the way down here, Evelyn,' he said, and she felt guilty about using his misery as an excuse to come.

'It's a terrible thing, Mr Crabb.'

'Yes,' he said blankly and she thought he looked smaller than she remembered him.

She wandered out into the back garden and stood in the centre of the small lawn with her back to the house and the sun on her face. Helen followed her and asked how things were in the hospital, and they talked for a while. Helen looked worn out and admitted that she was hardly able to sleep for worrying about Joe, and then Aunt Lizzie came out and Helen went back indoors.

'Have you heard the news, Eve? Yesterday the Government gave the vote to married women over thirty.'

'No, I hadn't heard,' she said absently, her mind on matters which, for the moment, seemed more important. 'What'll Mr Crabb do now, Aunt Lizzie? I can't imagine him wanting to go back to his house even if it was rebuilt.'

'Bill? He'll stay on here for a while, and then we'll have to see.'

'That's a good idea. At least it'll be more like a home for him,' she said, closed her eyes and enjoyed the warmth that had built up in the sheltered little garden. Everything was quiet and she suddenly realised that now was the right time to tell her aunt about Pincote. 'Can we talk, Aunt? Without having a row?'

'I imagine so. What about?'

'John Laybourne?'

'Oh.'

'He asked me to give you his best wishes and to tell you he's well, and that now he's seen me he understands why you left.'

'Oh, Eve!' her aunt cried out. 'I loved him so much! I'd have done anything for him – I did! And then I found out I was his sister. Half sister! God! I've bottled it up all these years.'

Eve suddenly realised that she was holding her aunt, they were holding each other, and they were both sobbing for things that could not be changed.

'I'm sorry Aunt, if only I'd known I wouldn't have done or said half the things I have.'

'I know, and I don't blame you, Eve, not really. If anything I'm jealous of you for being so much like me and doing so much that I'd like to have done.' Her aunt stepped back and wiped her eyes. 'How much did John tell you?'

'Most of it, I think. All about Hubert Belchester, the way he treated Mama, Papa being in prison, you proving his innocence. I don't suppose I know everything but I don't have to. It's Mama and Papa's secret, and they don't have to know that I know. I'm not going to tell them. I'm not even going to tell them I'm working in Pincote. That's my secret.'

'You're working in Pincote?'

'At the Edward Forrester Memorial Hospital. John's converted the manor. We've knocked it about quite a lot so we can treat a hundred and forty men at a time, and we're expecting to extend it to take two hundred. Robert's the Senior Consultant and I'm Matron. Our own little hospital, and there's a ward named after each of you.'

'Good God! And the lodge? Is that still there?' her aunt asked.

'It's there, but it's derelict. I asked John why he'd never improved it and he said it was his folly. Another memorial to the past,' she said, and hesitated while she wondered if she should say more. 'John's offered to renovate it and give it to Robert and me as a wedding present.'

'You're getting married?'

'Not yet. We're waiting for his divorce.' She explained all about Robert and his situation.

'Oh, Eve, you do lead such a complicated life. John and I talked about living in the lodge. Will you take it on?'

'No. We'd quite like to live in there but it wouldn't be fair on Mama and Papa. Once the war's over and we can apply for our discharge we'll either move back to London or possibly even try to buy the White House and set up a specialist clinic there. But that's all secret for the moment. I don't want Mama and Papa to know I'm even thinking about marrying Robert. Not for a while.'

'Secrets, Eve? There've been too many in this family for too long.'

'Perhaps, but they haven't done any real harm, have they?'

'Yes, Eve. I think they have.' Eve listened as her aunt told her what Hubert Belchester had done to Lottie to drive her away, and they were both so engrossed in the story that neither of them noticed Bill as he walked up to them.

'Thought I'd come out and see if you two were all right. You've been out here an hour, now. You both friends again?'

She noticed the way her aunt took Bill's arm in hers. 'I think so, Bill. Aren't we, Eve?'

'I hope so, Aunt Lizzie, I really do.'

Her aunt smiled at her, and then at Bill. 'We've been telling each other our secrets, Bill.'

'Oh yes?' he said in a concerned voice.

'Not all of them, Bill. Not yet, anyway,' her aunt said quickly.

Eve enjoyed her visit and would have been sorry to leave if she had not been missing Robert so much. She travelled back to the north on a train which was loaded with soldiers home on short leave. When she told them she had also served in France and knew what conditions were really like they dropped their reserve and told her things no one in the services would admit to any civilian. They also told her how much they dreaded having to fight through another winter.

She tried to cheer up the men by reminding them that the Americans had come into the fight and that might mean it would be over before the winter set in, but the men told her there were no Americans in France and the official view seemed to be that they would not be ready to go into action until after the winter.

She arrived back at the hospital in a depressed mood and even seeing Robert did not make her feel much happier.

'It's the war, Robert. From what I've heard it could go on for another year. We've already been fighting for nearly three years and the battle fronts haven't changed much from when I first went out to France. The only thing that's really changed is that we've killed and maimed a few million men and wiped villages and whole towns off the map.'

'How are things at home?' he asked, ignoring her mood.

'Much better, thank you. I told Aunt Lizzie everything and we're friends again. I even told her about our plans, and I suspect she's some of her own. I think she'll marry Bill.'

'So there're no distractions there?' he confirmed.

'No. Why?'

'Because, dear Evelyn, for the first time since we've known each other you don't have a great cause to fight. The suffrage issue is being resolved, you don't have to prove yourself to your family any more and this hospital's been established so we don't have to fight for that or our right to heal in our own way. I think you're depressed because you have nothing to distract you, Evelyn. You might have to start enjoying your life!'

She told him he was talking rubbish, but she wondered if there was an element of truth in what he said.

July passed into August and Eve could not settle, then in September she received a letter inviting her and Robert to her aunt's wedding in September.

Robert could not leave the hospital but she went to London for a week.

She was delighted to find Joe was home on leave and they talked easily about the conditions in France, but like all those who had experienced active service they did not allow anyone else to know how bad things were for fear of frightening them too much. Joe told her that he had given Helen a straight talking to and she found that Helen was far more friendly and their relationship was almost back to normal. Maisie rather sheepishly introduced Eve to a young man whose hand had been blown off. He had been evacuated in a hospital train and was full of praise for all the medical and nursing staff he had met, and that also helped Eve feel less out of place.

Aunt Lizzie and Bill asked if she thought they were marrying too soon after Gladys's death and she did not hesitate to tell them that she had not even thought about that.

'Life's for the living, Aunt, and I'm sure Gladys would give you her blessing if she could.'

'Thanks, Eve.' Bill kissed her. 'And what about you? Any thoughts of getting married?'

'No, not yet,' she said, and wished she had not been quite so crisp, but marriage was a difficult subject to face. Especially now, but she did not want to discuss that with anyone but Robert. Not until she was sure.

Katarina looked gaunt, and with the growing troubles in Russia it was easy to see why. Sasha, Peter and Lottie had disappeared completely and it was impossible to guess how they were or what dangers they were facing. Paul was very tall now, a young man and the image of Sasha.

The wedding was held in the church at the end of the road and Eve was pleased that her father was allowed to play a part in the service. Her aunt looked very pretty dressed in a simple pale-green dress which hung like a loose, long-sleeved blouse until it reached her waist where it was tailored to hang straight down to a hem three inches below her knees. The shortage of material had dictated a change in fashions and Eve wondered if the ankle-length skirts she had grown up with would ever return.

However, although her aunt was the main attraction of the wedding day, her mother caused the greatest stir the following day by temporarily abandoning her wheelchair for a pair of crutches.

After an enjoyable week Eve knew she should have returned to Pincote in a buoyant mood, but she could not relax and another train journey spent talking to disillusioned soldiers made her even more depressed than the last time she had returned.

Then, when she arrived back at the hospital she found it was overrun by German soldiers.

She went straight to Robert's office. 'Robert! What's going on? What're all these Germans doing here?'

'Good afternoon, Evelyn,' he said brightly. 'I'm very well, thank you for asking. No we didn't have any problems we couldn't handle while you were away, and yes, on a personal level I did miss you.'

537

'I'm sorry. It's just that I've spent the last day and a half with men who're just home from killing Germans and I arrive here and find the place running with them.'

'They're prisoners of war, Evelyn, sent here to work. They're tidying up the gardens and laying concrete paths so the men stuck in wheelchairs can get out even when the ground's wet. We don't want them getting bogged down in the mud, do we?'

'I'm sorry, I didn't think, but how do the men feel about it? Rubbing shoulders with the enemy? The men who might have put them in here in the first case?'

'They're not as upset as you seem to be. In fact most of them like to get out and talk to the Germans, as best they can, and they certainly keep the enemy generously supplied with cigarettes. They feel sorry for them, miles from home, not knowing when, or even if, they'll see their families again.'

His words struck a chord with her. She remembered how she felt when she went to prison for the first time. 'Yes, I'll make sure I talk to them, too. How long are they here for?'

'Until they've finished the work or the war ends. Whichever happens first.' Robert grinned and came around his desk to hold her and kiss her. 'I'm glad you're back. I have missed you.'

They walked on the Ridge that evening, and climbed up to King's Crag, using the steel steps which had been fastened to the rocks. When they reached the top they stood and looked over the farming plain to the south and west. Eve stood in front of Robert and when he put his arms around her she leaned her head back against his shoulder and gave a deep sigh.

'What's wrong?' Robert asked. 'Wish you could lay claim to this as your ancestors did?'

'No, not particularly. If my mother, John and their parents are anything to go by this did not give them any great happiness, did it? I don't even feel I'm associated with it, apart from working here.'

'Then what is wrong? You've been edgy since you came back today?'

'It's because I want the war to be over, Robert. And because I love you.'

'Is there a particular connection between those two statements?'

'Yes, there is. I'm expecting your baby.' She had suspected it for a few weeks, but the last week had made her sure.

He did not answer and his silence made her tense because she knew a baby would not only complicate their lives but might cause difficulties with his divorce. She turned around and looked at him.

He had not spoken because he was smiling too much.

They stood on the crag and watched the sun set, and then, sure they would not be disturbed, they made love again under a sky which was full of pink and golden light.

The following morning Eve had an unexpected opportunity to talk to the enemy soldiers when one of them was brought to her because he had cut his hand badly. She could not speak German and he could not speak English, but they were both surprised to find the other spoke fluent French.

'The part of Germany I come from used to be in France. No doubt, if we lose the war, it will go back to being in France and I suppose I will then become a Frenchman,' he said philosophically, but he made her realise how utterly stupid the situation was.

'What did you do before the war started?' she asked him.

'I was a painter. Not an artist, you understand? I painted houses and hung wallpaper.'

'My father's a painter and decorator,' she said excitedly, 'and so was my brother. Before he was killed.'

'In France?' the enemy soldier asked.

'Yes.'

'My three brothers were also killed there, by a mine exploded in tunnels dug under their trenches. I wonder, sometimes, if it was dug by men from this town.'

'Perhaps it was,' she said, and apologised for hurting him as she stitched his cut.

'If you saw what it's like over there you'd realise how

'pointless the war is,' the man said and did not flinch as she pushed the needle through his skin.

'I've been over there. I worked on a hospital train for nearly two years.'

'So you know?' he said, thanked her for her help and kindness, turned to leave but hesitated. 'You know, then, that it's the people who choose the uniforms who make the war. If we all wore the same uniforms, or no uniforms at all, no one would know who the enemy was.'

Although she knew he had oversimplified his argument she still believed he was not too wrong, and she wondered if being pregnant was anything to do with her growing need to stand up and campaign for an early end to the slaughter.

Eve did not know whether it was a biological coincidence or an unconscious desire to get away from the hospital but the next day she suffered her first morning sickness, and each subsequent morning she felt worse and worse until it was clear that she would not be able to continue working.

The realisation made her feel even more depressed, and she blamed herself for letting Robert and the team down. In his usual practical manner Robert said it might be better for the team if she left because everybody had guessed they were seeing each other secretly and her leaving would remove that distraction.

It was surprisingly easy to obtain her discharge and on the bright October morning she was due to leave Pincote she and Robert climbed up to King's Crag to look at the autumn view.

'It's beautiful, Robert, but I'm not sorry to leave.'

'I thought you liked it here.'

'Only because you're here. Otherwise it just reminds me of so much misery and misunderstanding. And it reminds me, every day, that I'm deceiving my parents by not telling them I'm here and I know all about their secrets. Secrets! I hate them.'

'So you'll tell your parents the truth about me?' he asked openly.

She patted her stomach. 'I don't have much choice, do I? Besides, I want to get everything out into the open. I told you, I don't want to live with secrets. Not any more.'

'Or dishonesty?' he asked astutely.

'What do you mean?' She always felt uncomfortable when she sensed he could read her mind.

'Eve, you're going to live with Maisie, who's always been against the war, and you've suddenly developed pacifist tendencies . . .'

'That's not fair, Robert!' she said sharply, deliberately interrupting him. 'I was never a great supporter of this war, and you know that. I did think there was some need for it when we heard the stories about all the atrocities which were supposed to have happened, but I don't believe we'll solve any problems by killing and maiming even more men or destroying even more towns and villages. It's time it was stopped, and that's up to the politicians. They were the ones who started it.'

'And you're going to try to make them stop it?' he asked calmly.

'I'll do what I can, Robert. I have to.'

He shook his head and smiled at her. 'So you have another grand campaign to occupy yourself with?'

'I suppose I have.' She smiled back at him.

'Well, I wouldn't want to be in the Government's shoes when you're let loose on them, but just remember you're pregnant and our baby comes before everything except you. That means no more demonstrations, no more going to prison and no more hunger strikes.'

'No, Robert,' she grinned, 'but lots of speeches and letters to the newspapers.'

He kissed her, and looked across the plain which spread out below them. 'Your ancestors were content just to bring law and order to the land we can see, Evelyn, but you want to bring it to the whole world. Just leave a little time for living, as well.'

She had not seen the sadness in his face for a year, but now she heard it in his voice. She hugged him. 'Don't worry, Robert. I'm not being totally unselfish. The sooner

541

this war's over the sooner we can be together and begin to live a normal life.'

He nodded and said quietly, 'I'll look forward to that. Meanwhile I'd better take you to that station or you'll miss your train.'

'My final train home, Robert. Trains have played a big part in my life over the past few years.'

She kissed him goodbye on the station platform, a long and passionate kiss. Now she was a civilian it did not matter if anyone saw them.

CHAPTER 33

Newspapers were delivered to Estate Irina whenever they became available. They came irregularly, they were often a week or more out of date and they tended to be scant because of a paper shortage, but they were informative enough. Lottie always saw them coming because they were brought by an old man in a small cart and he trailed dust for two hundred yards or more, a huge grey feather hanging from the back of his cart.

He came via the station and when he arrived at Irina he always stopped for tea and a talk with Nikolas who was a skilled gossip and soon learned the intimate details of people he had never met. 'That devil Testov's put up the price of meat again!' he would say, or 'Sychkin, the grain merchant's supporting his new mistress by charging more for a sack of flour.'

Nikolas always knew precisely the prices being charged, but the details did not matter to her. The important thing was that the prices were going up and people with little money were having to pay more if they did not want to starve.

The estate had barns full of wheat and grain, the mill was

working to its maximum ability to grind it, there were cattle with full bellies and good skins in the fields and paddocks. How long would it be before the members of the new revolutionary society thought it had a right to take what it wanted? And who was going to stop them?

Nikolas drove her to the station the following day and she sent a telegram pleading with the grain merchant who bought all the Zubov product to come and agree a price and arrange collection. She did not care about bartering for the best price, she simply wanted the crop moved.

In the third week of September the news-sheet reported that Riga had fallen. The German Army was within three hundred and fifty miles of the capital, Petrograd and the seat of government. She started to read the lurid details of the obscenities the *nemets* were supposed to have committed but she threw all the newspapers into the fireplace and burned them before Natasha could read the stories. Natasha was already frightened enough for both of them.

Lottie asked Nikolas to find some clay she could model into a chess set. 'I can carve you a chess set, Miss Charlotte. I would be very happy to do so as I have nothing else to do.'

'Thank you, Nikolas, but I have little to do and I would like to model one from clay.' She saw him shrug and wander off and she hoped he would find enough somewhere on Irina's fertile land.

He came back hours later with a bucket-load of sticky, grey clay and put it in the scullery. 'Wood looks nicer, and it's less heavy,' he said grumpily as he clomped out of the room.

She smiled and guessed he was thinking that she was also a *nemets*, and the English always did have peculiar habits.

She modelled her chess pieces and thrust a gold coin into the base of each one before she placed them in the oven to harden, at cook's expressed disgust.

The following day Nikolas drove her to the station again to send a second telegram to the Zubov's grain merchant and also one to Mr Zubov asking him to help sell the grain.

Some days later she received a telegram from Tatiana

telling her to sell the grain to Sychkin in the town, and told her the lowest price she should accept, but when she went to see him he offered her less than half the lowest price. A further exchange of telegrams with Tatiana instructed her not to sell to Sychkin but to give all the peasants as much grain and flour as they wanted and to keep the rest for cattle feed or for anyone else who wanted to buy it. Tatiana indicated there were still shortages in the capital and she would try to find a Petrograd merchant who would collect the crop.

She was relieved that the barns would soon be emptied, not only because she was worried about attracting thieves but because she was conscious that Irina's barns held enough flour to make tens of thousands of loaves which would alleviate the misery of so many people who were starving.

Lottie was also relieved when she read that the Russian soldiers did not abandon Petrograd. Maybe it was because the potential invaders were the hated *nemets* or perhaps there was still some feeling of national pride, or perhaps because they did not want their wives, daughters and mothers submitted to the treatment the *nemets* were famed for? She did not know, but the soldiers fought hard and only conceded ground after heavy losses. But, as she read day after day, they were conceding and the Germans were fighting their way closer and closer to the capital.

Then Olga came for several days and told her the Tsar and his family had been moved to Siberia to protect them from the Bolsheviks and the political situation was becoming desperate. No one would buy the crop or even pay to have it taken to Petrograd so Mr Zubov would have it collected when he had time to make arrangements.

On a cold November day when there was ice in the wind, the newspapers stopped coming and the telegraph system stopped working, and the old man who came to say there were no newspapers told them some of the rumours which had started to circulate.

The Germans had taken Petrograd. The Kaiser had made Lenin the new Tsar. The Bolsheviks had taken over the

Government. The Kaiser had brought his cousin back as a puppet ruler.

She did not think any of the stories seemed very probable, but Natasha, clearly worried about her mother and father, and Olga, asked 'Do you think the Germans have captured the capital?'

'I don't know.'

'What are we going to do, Charlotte?'

'I don't know, but for God's sake don't let the children or Nikolas know we're frightened.'

'Do you think the Germans will come here?'

'I expect we'll be among the first to know if they do,' she said shortly and walked out of the room.

She had to think. Were the Germans really likely to invade deep into Russia with all its vastness when they were still fighting in France and Belgium? What would encourage them? What would stop them?

She sat down and made lists, determined to think of every possibility, because if she led the children and Natasha away from Irina they would have to go somewhere suitable for small children to live and that had to be planned. They could not simply run and hope to live where ever they could find accommodation, or off the land, because winter was coming.

Yes, winter was coming!

She called for Natasha. 'What's the weather like in the capital at this time of year?'

'Awful. It's cold and foggy and rains heavily and non-stop for two or three months. The days are very short. Dawn comes about ten o'clock and it's dark again by three.'

'And later in the year it freezes and snows and the cold fog comes down from Finland?' she said triumphantly.

'Yes!' Natasha obviously understood what she was thinking. 'Not good weather to fight, especially to conquer a big city like Petrograd!'

'In which case, Natasha, I think we're safe to spend the winter here and we'll worry about next year when it comes,' she said calmly, amazed how happy she felt about not having to move.

A few days later she was sitting in the drawing room when she heard the maid answer the front door. Minutes afterwards something resembling a wild animal strolled into the room.

'Krasnaya, I thought I told you to leave?'

'Peter!' she called and rushed to him. 'How are you? Where have you been?'

'I'm well and I've been in Petrograd. Did you know there's been a Revolution?' he spoke calmly, almost sarcastically, and she felt irritated.

'Yes, thanks to you I was there when it happened. I think Irina and I were in more danger there than we were here.'

'No, my lovely but stupid beauty, you weren't. You saw the opening rounds, but the *real* revolution took place a week ago. Lenin returned and the Bolsheviks have stormed the Winter Palace and taken power by force. Kerensky and his provisional government are out of power.' Peter sighed, then turned on her and added angrily, 'If you'd still been in Petrograd I could have got you and little Irina out and to safety but I can't do anything now. The country's about to fall into chaos! Why didn't you listen, Krasnaya?'

'Because I listened to other people who seemed to make more sense. Why should I have believed you knew more than them?'

'Because I'm Colonel Grinevetsky of Lenin's new Bolshevik Red Army and I've been helping to plan all this for years. I even had a fake telegram delivered. Didn't you wonder why?'

'Oh God!' Everything suddenly seemed so obvious. 'Grinevetsky? Isn't that the man you said was employing you to kill yourself?'

'Yes, and as far as everyone else is concerned Peter Komovsky is dead.'

'Both you and Sasha?' she said sadly.

'Sasha's alive.'

'What?'

'My last information is that he's alive. That's two weeks old but there's no reason to think that's changed. He's a prisoner of war and he's playing a damned piano in a prison camp. Both for Germans and Russians. At last he's learning to survive and, like me, he'll do business with anyone who can help him.'

She began to laugh. She had spent three years either worrying about him or assuming he was dead and there he was playing piano in complete safety! She had probably been exposed to more danger than he had.

'Why didn't he write?'

'The Germans aren't obliged to allow prisoners to write letters and in this particular camp the commander doesn't believe in such privileges.'

'How do you know all this?'

'I've been to Germany to negotiate the handover of surplus arms once an armistice is signed. I asked a lot of people a lot of questions, and I must say I actually found the Germans very helpful and quite charming. And, of course, once the armistice is signed in a few weeks' time Sasha can go home, where ever that is.'

'A few weeks? Really?'

'If everything goes as we hope, but don't tell anyone I told you.' He made a sign as if he was cutting his throat. 'But you can reckon on seeing Sasha before the new year starts.'

She looked past Peter and saw Natasha had come into the room and was staring at him. 'It is you, you bear!' She kissed him. 'Sasha? I heard you mention Sasha.'

She explained what Peter had told her and Natasha was in tears within seconds. 'That's wonderful. But what about Petrograd?'

Peter heaved his coat off and told her what had happened to the Government, and then turned to more personal matters. 'I also have bad news, Natasha. Your father's very ill. Dying.'

'I must go!' she said quickly but Peter grabbed her by both arms and looked at her very steadily.

'No! He's too far gone to know if you were there, anyway your mother told me she doesn't want you to see him.'

'Why not?'

'Because he looks a mess. He thinks he's failed in his work and he tried to kill himself but his gun misfired, or something. He shot his jaw off instead of blowing his brains out.'

'Peter!' Lottie said to warn him not to continue so brutally, but Natasha shrugged.

'Don't blame him, Charlotte. It was my father who sent Peter's father to prison. I think Papa may have hoped the grieving widow would go to his bed for comfort, or for help, but Olga told Peter what he had done, and warned him that their apartment was to be raided.'

'But Olga still sleeps with him?' She remembered Tatiana saying Olga did not love him but it still seemed a very cold thing to do.

Peter grunted. 'How do you think I got so much of my information, Charlotte? Olga was very useful.'

'And you knew about this, Natasha?' she asked, stunned by the thought that Olga was a Bolshevik spy and unhappy about the divided loyalties.

'Only since you arrived three years ago. You must understand, Charlotte, that my father and I have different political views. Very similar to the stories you have told me about your father and your sister.'

It may have been similar but the degree of deception was different, and she could not approve, whatever the needs or demands were. The rest of it all made sense, of a sort, but Lottie found it difficult to think of Peter as a Colonel until he explained that it was a political rank given to him as authority to do business on behalf of the Bolshevik Party. Whenever he wanted to impress people he now called himself Colonel Grinevetsky of Lenin's Order of Ordnance.

Lottie laughed and said it sounded like a suitable title for a man who bluffed his way through life but what it really meant was that he was a bandit with an official title, which made him laugh.

He stayed for three days, gave them several revolvers and boxes of ammunition, told them to get rid of their crop before it attracted the wrong sort of visitors, and said goodbye after giving her an official letter signed by him and two better known Bolsheviks, instructing all Comrades to give them every possible assistance.

'You take care, Krasnaya. The law is collapsing fast, but one rule must collapse before a better one can take its place. In the meantime, I suppose there will be some looting and murders and rapes. Stay here if you can but don't die defending the place. Leave if it becomes too dangerous. Sasha'll find you where ever you go, but go home to your parents if you can. I'm sure the other thing can be sorted out, if anyone in England even remembers after all this time.'

'And you take care, Komovsky. I hope I'll see you again.'

'You will, Krasnaya. I promise you. In better times. I love you.' He swung up onto his horse, blew her a kiss in true bandit-style, and left.

'And I love you, Komovsky, Grinevetsky. Whoever you are,' she said softly, too softly for him to hear. Then she watched him for as long as she could still see him, and cried. For him, for her, and because if he had not told her Sasha was alive she would have made love to him, and that would have been wrong.

Then she turned away and cursed the fact that the harvest they had all worked so hard to produce was still sitting in the barns, and from what Peter had told her it was an even more dangerous liability than she thought.

They came in the evening gloom a week later, as the frost was falling, and hammered on the front door with rifle-butts. The maid ran to answer but Lottie grabbed her and told her to go back to the warm scullery and stay there. Then she told Natasha to go upstairs and sit with the children who had been moved so they all slept in one room.

'Try to keep them quiet, don't let any of them come down here, and don't leave them under any circumstances. No matter what you think you hear.' She pushed the trembling Natasha towards the stairs and when the door was hammered again she called out in coarse Russian and told the callers not to be so noisy and she was on her way.

She opened the door to Sychkin and a deputation, and

saw they had brought eight wagons with them.

'Good evening, Comrade. We are Representatives of the People's Soviet for this area and we have come on behalf of the New Republic to re-allocate some of the reserve cereal you are storing.'

She answered spontaneously, 'Very well Comrade Sychkin. However, I will require your written authority to re-allocate this product as it has already been claimed by the Republic as a war reserve for the official Red Army. Colonel Grinevetsky of Lenin's Order of Ordnance has already comissioned the entire stock. You must have known he was here for three days to audit the stock and write up accounts? Here, read this.'

She showed Sychkin Peter's letter and enjoyed the look of shock and then horror that crossed his face as he signalled his thieves to leave.

When they had gone she closed the door and leaned against it, trembling. She was sure they would be back, or someone would, but next time they would not knock, they would simply steal the sacks. Tomorrow she would distribute more grain and flour to all the people who helped grow and harvest the crop. That would be her policy, and for every one distributed they could put one in the cellars.

It rained hard for two days and made it impossible to distribute the crop and when she went to the barns the following day she found them empty. She walked to the flour store behind the mill and found the doors ripped open. The flour had also been taken.

Sychkin had sent his thieves in the night, and there was nothing she could do about it, but she consoled herself by believing that the danger had gone with the crops.

Although the newspapers were only delivered sporadically over the next few weeks she read that the Bolsheviks had signed a truce with Germany in preparation for a full armistice and an end to a war that had dragged on for more than three years. But she also read that another war had started.

The Bolsheviks, who called themselves the Reds and

claimed they were in power, were now being challenged by the anti-Bolsheviks, the Whites, and both had formed armies. The civil war Peter and Tatiana had predicted had come.

She was too weary to bother with it all. She simply wanted an armistice signed with Germany so Sasha could come home.

In February the old man who brought the newspapers all the way from town or sometimes telegrams from the station said he would not come any more. 'Igor stopped me as I passed the railway station and asked me to give you this telegram but I have no newspapers, and if you need them in future you must come to collect them.'

'Why?' she asked. 'Don't we pay you enough to come out here every day and drink our tea and vodka and eat our food?'

'You pay handsomely, madam, but not enough to risk my life for.'

'What do you mean?' she asked sharply, her tense nerves tightening even more.

'You haven't heard of the Cossacks who are coming, looting and killing everyone they can find?'

'Don't be ridiculous!' she said sharply, aware that Natasha and Nikolas were listening and they were already scared enough. 'You shouldn't spread such rumours, you old gossip.'

'They're not rumours, madam. I do not come all this way only to deliver newspapers to you. I deliver all sorts of things, to a number of houses and stores. This morning I found the Pavenkov family hanging from the trees outside their house. I rode past quietly as the wind blew the snow about, and I was careful not to disturb the Cossacks who were loading the family's furniture and pictures onto wagons.'

'How do you know they're Cossacks?'

'By their ponies, and what they did to the bodies. They had hung and butchered them just as they did Sychkin and his mistress three nights ago. I have heard of this before, but

552

I did not believe it myself, not at first.'

'Sychkin? The grain merchant?'

'Yes.' She felt ill as he told her how the couple had been caught in the remote house Sychkin's mistress owned. 'Sychkin always was a greedy and stupid man. The barns at his mistress's place were bulging with grain and flour which is very very valuable on the black market in the cities. That's what the Cossacks wanted so you were very clever to empty your stores so quickly. Also, there was fine furniture for the taking, quality paintings and silver pieces. They say there is a market for these things now our money is worthless and the rich people no longer trust the banks to look after their interests.'

She listened to the old man and thought that now the brigands were fighting the brigands Sychkin may have saved her and the children by stealing their crop. However, she was still worried by what the old man said about the attraction of fine art and furniture now that money was virtually worthless. Everyone for miles around knew the house was filled with valuable objects, and anyone who did not know what the house contained would rightly assume it offered rich pickings. The house would attract trouble sooner or later. It was inevitable.

The old man obviously guessed what was on her mind.

'I'd leave this grand house, madam, before they come also for you.'

'Thank you for your advice.' She could see Natasha and Nikolas were both trembling, and she tried hard not to show her own fear. Perhaps their one chance was if the Cossacks were with the Red Army, the Bolsheviks. She could show them the official letter Peter gave her. 'Do you know if these men were Reds or Whites.'

'I don't know,' the old man shrugged. 'They could even be Greens. They're the new scourge. They issue proclamations and say they are for the people, but the only people they are for is themselves.'

Yes, she thought, like Sychkin. Until now she had understood why Peter hated the Secret Police so much, but now she had seen how quickly the country had become lawless and disrupted by fighting she could understand why Mr Zubov felt his work was so important.

There were so many conflicts, so much confusion that she did not know what to do. The official advice was that it was more dangerous to travel than to stay in one place, especially in the depths of winter, but she was sure the old man was telling the truth about the marauding Cossacks in which case it would be safer to leave.

Distractedly, she glanced at the telegram the old man had brought. It was from Olga and she could see it had been sent from Mr Zubov's office.

She frowned as she read it. Tatiana was on her way to Irina with three more children. Why?

'Do you think Igor's safe out at the station?' she asked the old man, concerned about the one member of the Zubov staff who lived alone at the railway station which was used only a few times each year.

'He is a poor man who has nothing, so he is safe. It is all of you, madam, and the children who live in this grand house that I fear for.'

She stared at the frost on the window and thought about the snow outside. She felt imprisoned, and that made her think of Sasha. How would he find her if she left?

After the old man had gone she remembered how Peter had once hidden away in a loft in his house and she asked Nikolas to make up beds in the attic so they might all hide up there at night. He seemed to work at it all day, and when she went up to ask if he had nearly finished she could not find him.

'Nikolas? Are you here?'

'Yes, Miss Charlotte,' his voice answered.

'Where? I can't see you.'

'Behind you,' he said, and when she turned she saw him standing in a doorway which had been hidden behind an old wardrobe. 'I remembered there was a store room up here so I've cleared everything out and used the junk to hide the wall. There are beds for all of you, and Mrs Zubov and the new children. I will hide you each night by pushing the wardrobe across the door.'

'Thank you, Nikolas, but I think we'll only do that if needed, and I'll sleep in my room as usual and call you if there's trouble. And I think you should have one of these, too.' She handed him one of the belted holsters and revolvers which Peter had left. 'It's heavy, but wear it at all times, as I will do from now, but keep it under you jacket. I don't want to frighten the children.'

He disappeared later that evening and when she went to look for him she found him in one of the large out-buildings, setting the traces on the Zubov's large troika. 'Forgive me, Miss Charlotte, but I think perhaps I should teach you how to drive the small sleigh tomorrow, and then we should try the troika, with everyone loaded onto it.'

She nodded. 'Yes, Nikolas, I think we should.'

After an anxious and thankfully uneventful night Nikolas showed her how to harness up two horses to the small sleigh, and then gave her an hour's tuition on the flat snow which covered the fields.

'You have a natural grace, Miss Charlotte,' he grinned as she raced the horses and brought them back towards the house in a sweeping curve. 'I think that this afternoon we should try the large one with two horses, and perhaps tomorrow with three.'

'I agree!' she shouted with the joy of smooth motion and steered the horses around the house in time to see another sleigh coming along the drive.

It had to be Igor, he was the only one who insisted on following the drive even when the world seemed to be covered in snow.

'Charlotte!' Tatiana shouted as Igor pulled his sleigh alongside hers. 'Learning how to drive?'

'Yes, I'll explain later, but first introduce me to our new guests,' she said calmly, not wanting to alarm the three children who sat silent in the back of the sleigh.

'My nieces, Helena and Alexandra, and their brother Lev.'

All three, huddled in their furs, smiled a little warily, but stood as they were introduced. She guessed the girls were about five and six years old and Lev was probably eight, a little younger than Leo. So now, in addition to Irina, she had responsibility for five children ranging from five years old to nine. And four adults, also, considering how tired Tatiana looked and sounded.

Later, when she was alone with Tatiana, she explained about the Cossack Greens who were looting the surrounding estates and murdering the occupants.

Tatiana shrugged. 'I know. There is lawlessness all over and the estates are the most vulnerable. Our people, the Whites, are mostly in control down here but the Reds are in control in the north and they are making inroads. I think we may soon see full-scale battles taking place, especially because the railway is near and that is the fastest way to move armies.'

'Then why have you brought more children here?'

'Because my sister and her husband have disappeared and their house has been taken over by Bolsheviks. Our house has also been occupied and I would have been murdered if Olga hadn't hidden me in her apartment. I have brought them here because the capital is no place for children, especially highborn children. Also the Germans are advancing very quickly.'

'But the truce? I thought the war was over?'

'The Germans have grown tired waiting for the Bolsheviks to agree the terms of an armistice and have started fighting again.'

'So the prisoners of war won't be released?'

'I'm afraid not, Charlotte.'

Her heart fell, and she could not think what to do.

That afternoon she drove the troika with gusto. Tatiana said the Reds, the Bolsheviks, were in control in the north and she had a letter almost guaranteeing her safety when she was under their rule. She had to go north as soon as possible, certainly before the Cossacks returned to plunder Estate Irina, and the only ways were by railway or by sleigh. The railway went to Petrograd and the advancing Germans so her only choice was to go by sleigh.

As she brought the troika back to its shelter Nikolas smiled. 'It's fortunate you worked in the fields and grew muscles as well as wheat, Miss Charlotte. I think that tomorrow we should try with three horses, which is very different.'

'I think we'll try with three this afternoon, Nikolas. And tomorrow we'll try with three and with the sleigh fully loaded with everything we might need for a long journey.'

'In this weather? It's winter, and the children—'

'I know,' she said sharply. 'Please set the traces for three horses.'

The wind carried flecks of snow which made her walk with her head down as she jumped off the sleigh and trudged back towards the house. She did not see the six men ride out from behind the folly until it was too late to warn Nikolas. She was wearing a white fur coat and hood and they obviously had not seen her but they rode up behind Nikolas and one of them booted him in the back.

'Hey, old man working in the snow. What are you doing?'

She inched out of sight and listened to Nikolas's nervous reply.

'I'm resetting the traces on this troika,' he answered truthfully.

'I can see that, fool. Why? This isn't weather to go out driving?'

'Don't tell me!' Nikolas retorted in a complaining voice. 'Look at me. My beard is already frozen to my chin from going backwards and forwards since dawn, but no one cares about poor old Nikolas. Not when there's wine and food to be saved from these damned Cossacks who are terrifying all the estates around her. I have a cellar-full to be hidden and I'll freeze solid before I've finished.'

'Let us help you, old man. Draw up the sled and we'll help you. Where's this cellar?'

'It's hidden. I tell them that it's safer where it is but they think someone who maybe has a grudge is going to tell all Russia about their secret.' She watched Nikolas walk to the folly and quickly push the seat back so the men would not realise that was the first time it had been moved that day. 'Look, all of you, come up here and tell me if you'd have known there was a cellar here. And then come and see how warm it is below.'

She watched him go down first leading the others, and then come back and almost drag down the last man who obviously thought he should mount guard. Then she heard whoops of joy as the men saw the wine. Several minutes later Nikolas reappeared with the pole which could be used to open and close the cellar from inside. He quietly pushed the seat back in place, closing the trap-door, and she watched him wedge the pole against the seat in a way which would stop it being moved, trapping the men in the cellar.

Then he calmly walked to the horses and hitched each rein to the troika. She waited until he had finished before she walked back to him.

'That was very brave, Nikolas, and very clever.'

'No, it was simply necessary, but that's only six men. They said there's another dozen coming.'

Her mouth dried up. 'When? Did they say?'

'Tonight, tomorrow?' He shrugged and turned to look into the snow which was coming down heavier. 'We cannot leave today. This will become a blizzard by tonight. The children would freeze to death.'

Lottie gave Tatiana the third revolver Peter had left because she thought Tatiana would use it if needed, which Natasha would not. What courage Natasha had was used up and she was no more use than any of the children. Lottie insisted everyone sleep in the attic, and she and Nikolas took turns to sleep or sit up listening. She wondered how quickly the men entombed in the cellar would die, but she had no impulse to let them out. At least, with all that wine, they could die oblivious.

The blizzard Nikolas predicted came at four o'clock the following morning and she felt that it probably offered them some protection. The other Cossacks had surely found somewhere to spend the night, and she could not think they would be in any hurry to leave when they saw what the weather was like.

The wind dropped at about eight o'clock and at nine Nikolas pulled the troika up in the shelter of the house and they loaded it with the supplies Lottie had prepared during the night.

'Your chess set?' Nikolas complained. 'We'll have enough to take without—'

She interrupted him and explained why she had to take it, and he suggested if that was the case she should take a chess board as well so it looked more normal. He had dispersed the Cossacks' ponies after removing their gear, and he carefully stacked the Cossacks' rifles under the troika's driving seat, arguing that even if they did not use the rifles they could sell them.

The troika held her, Nikolas, the six children and half the necessary luggage. Tatiana and Natasha were to follow on the smaller sleigh with the rest of the luggage, but that was not yet loaded.

She walked back into the house to check all the children were dressed in as many layers as possible and that they had all eaten a full and warming breakfast.

'Where are we going, Mama?' Irina asked, and the other children turned interested faces towards her.

'We're going on a sleigh ride through the snow. A long one,' she said and was relieved to hear the general enthusiasm, even though she knew it would not last once the children had become bored with it. Also, she knew this was going to be a long and wearing journey, both physically and mentally, and it was important to make sure everyone was comfortable before they set off. 'Tatiana, before we leave Nikolas and I would like to test the troika with all this weight. We may need to put more on your sleigh.'

Tatiana nodded. 'Please go. I'm not quite ready anyway.'

Lottie helped all the children onto the large troika and seated them so they all faced backwards and were kept out of the wind. Then she sat up beside Nikolas who was driving, and adjusted her coat and hood so very little of her face was left exposed.

'Go!' she shouted, pretending a gaiety she did not feel, and whooped with pretend joy as the sleigh jerked into motion.

They ran for twenty minutes, over the brow of a low hill and until they reached the edge of the forest which bordered the cultivated part of the estate. This was the pretty forest, Tatiana said, which changed its colours with the seasons. At the moment the trees were bare, without even buds. North of this were the pine forests, and that was where they were going.

'Whoa!' Nikolas reined in his central horse and the other two obeyed moments later.

And as the troika stopped creaking they heard shots.

'Should we turn back?' Nikolas asked.

'No. Go on. There's nothing we can do and we need to move fast. Don't forget they can follow our tracks.' She clenched her fists and tried hard not to cry. Why did life have to be like this? She instinctively moved to feel the pendant which always comforted her and realised she had left it in the house along with Sasha's music. 'Go on, Nikolas. Quickly!'

She concentrated on holding on as Nikolas urged the horses across the frozen surface. He turned through a gap in the trees, reassured her he knew exactly where he was and eventually came out on an iced up road that led to a village where they stopped to eat, and drink hot tea.

'When are we going home?' Sergei asked as they settled back in the sleigh.

'We're going home now, but to our new home and it'll take a long time so you'll all have to be patient,' she said, unwilling to tell them outright that they were not going back to Estate Irina.

They spent each night under cover in hostels or sharing cottages, cabins or farm buildings with the owners. She was careful not to attract too much attention and always haggled over the cost of accommodation when charges were discussed.

During the days they navigated by advice, instinct and luck, and they were stopped by every patrol that saw them.

She always spoke on their behalf, usually acting as though she was both a hag and a nag, and Nikolas simply sat still and nodded in agreement with whatever she said. She was travelling with her uncle and six children because her husband had gone missing in the war and their home had been burned in a Red raid, or a White raid, depending on which side she was talking to. Both sides searched the sleigh and looked at everything they carried. The first patrol they encountered very nearly stole the chess set and might have done if they had not been distracted by Nikolas's collection of rifles, which they preferred.

After that scare she told the children she wanted them each to play with a few chess pieces every time they were stopped. She believed that if she told the men the chess pieces were all the children had as toys they would be unlikely to steal them.

Her story was well-practised by the time they reached a new lumber camp safely inside the area controlled by the Bolshevik Red Army. They had been travelling for two months and although they had changed horses more times than she could recall, they could not change the troika and it was worn out. Pieces had been breaking or falling off for the past two weeks and it was clearly beyond repair. All they could do now was work to live. That, and staying alive, was all that mattered in this mad and chaotic country.

'Name?' The woman who registered new arrivals asked, without looking up from her book.

'Family Komovsky and Nikolas Grinevetsky,' she lied, proudly.

'Relationship?'

'My uncle and my six children.'

'Home town?'

'London, England.'

The woman's head snapped up. 'Answer truthfully, please.'

'I have. My husband's Russian and my six children are

Russian, but my home town is London. But then we lived in Petrograd.'

'Petrograd District,' the woman said blandly, and continued with the other questions on the form. The last question was, 'Identification?'

'I only have a letter from Colonel Grinevetsky of the Red Army.'

'Let me see it.'

Lottie held out the precious letter and the woman took it, grimaced to show she was impressed and said she would have to keep it for processing.

'No,' Lottie argued. 'I might need it.'

'You do need it. You need it to get a cabin and work. To get those you have to give me the letter for processing. It's the same everywhere. It's your choice.'

Lottie surrendered the letter.

They were allocated a log cabin and she and Nikolas were given jobs.

The cabin had two rooms and was kept warm by a large wood-burning stove. The rooms were large enough to house her family in reasonable comfort and the children all slept on sawdust-filled sacks in one room while she and Nikolas slept in the other, with a curtain hung between them. They shared clean communal toilets and wash rooms in nearby blocks and ate communal meals in a large canteen.

She and Nikolas did whatever duties they were allocated, from cutting down or trimming trees, to sawing them or helping in the canteen and sometimes, in her case, helping to teach in the school.

The work was hard and although the living conditions did not compare with Estate Irina they were far better than Maxim Suvarin's house in the capital. Lottie realised as soon as they arrived that many people who worked in the camp had only known houses such as Suvarin's.

She knew that the children would talk to neighbours' children and there was no possibility of keeping her secrets, but since they had been allocated a cabin she was not too worried. She and Nikolas found, in fact, that they and the children were welcomed by everyone and Nikolas was treated as a hero when people heard how he had trapped the six marauding Cossacks.

She noticed that Irina, especially, became very clinging and always wanted special treatment from Mama, and she found it painful to keep refusing her own daughter extra cuddles or time, but she had five other children to think of and she knew she had to be fair to them. After all, they had lost more than her daughter. They were all orphans, and they were old enough to remember their parents and miss them terribly.

Nikolas settled down happily to the family life he had never known, and lavished an uncle's care and love on each child quite indiscriminately. She thought there were worse ways to spend a year or two, and wondered what Sasha and Peter, and her family were doing, and whether they had given up all hope of ever seeing her again.

They worked throughout the summer when the sun beat down into the clearings, and throughout the winter even though the air was thick with cold and there was almost no daylight. The demand for timber was high so they continued cutting. During the winter they sometimes had to heat the saw blades to stop them cracking, but somehow they managed.

At the end of a long day in the sawmill, she celebrated the start of 1919 in the canteen with a heaped plate of cabbage and the secret thought that it was her twenty-sixth birthday. Then she pulled her coat on, donned fur hat and gloves and stepped out into the utter darkness.

The camp had grown since she had arrived and there were probably five hundred cabins or more, all neatly arranged in rows to make streets. As she reached the end of her street she sensed someone was following her.

An old, forgotten fear rose, and died in a moment. She was strong now, as strong as many men, and she had seen and done so much that she was rarely scared for herself, only what might happen to the children if she was hurt or killed. She did not stop at her cabin but she realised that whoever was following her had halted, so she turned back and walked towards the huge shadow which loomed darker than the dark grey snow.

'Are you looking for someone?' she asked bluntly.

'Yes.'

'Who?'

'I know what she looks like but I don't know what she calls herself. I believe she had an old man and six children with her? She could call herself Grinevetsky, or Komovsky, or something English. I think she was here but she might have moved on by now.'

'Who are you?'

'My name's Suvarin. Maxim Suvarin.'

She gulped, and stammered, and that gave her away.

An enormous hand clamped around her neck and paralysed her while his other hand yanked off her hat and then flicked a cigarette lighter close to her face. His finger and thumb were holding her so tight she could not move as he ran the light over her, inspecting all the details of her face. She could feel the heat and smell the petrol as it burned.

'So it is you,' he said gruffly. 'The Colonel sent me to get you.'

'What Colonel?' she asked uneasily.

'He calls himself Grinevetsky. The English are in the north. He told me to find you and take you to them.'

'The English?'

'And the Americans. We are chasing them away so you must come quickly.'

'I have six children.'

'Bring them, too.'

'To the north? How far north?'

'To Archangel.'

'No. It's too dangerous for the children.'

'They're Russian children. They'll live. Be ready in two weeks, or you'll die in this God-forsaken country, and from what I remember you have the will to live.'

'What about Nikolas?'

'Leave him.'

'I'll think about it.'

'You will be ready, or the Colonel will cut off my nose. He has not forgiven me for not taking better care of you last time we met.'

'How would we travel?'

'Truck and train. It's comfortable.'

'Did he say anything about Sasha? His brother? The Germans were holding him?'

Suvarin shook his large head. 'No, though if he was a soldier there's a good chance he still is. In either the Red or White armies.'

This time she shook her head. 'No, he wouldn't have volunteered for another fight. He didn't much want to go to the first one.'

'It's not a matter of volunteering. You don't think these armies are made up of volunteers, do you? Half the so-called soldiers are kids and most of the rest are only there because they got forced into it and can't get out. If deserters get caught they get shot, and if they don't they usually freeze to death or starve. They don't let anyone except officers know they're within a hundred miles of a town.'

'Of course you must go,' Nikolas said firmly, and made her cry. 'You must look after the little ones. They, and you, are all that matter.'

'I could try to take you with us,' she offered, but he shook his head and said he was too ancient and did not have many winters left in him.

He was not there when she woke up on the morning Suvarin was coming for them. She dressed and washed the children and took them to the canteen for their *kasha*, their breakfast gruel, and waited back at the cabin, but Nikolas did not come home.

She left him a present, two pieces of the chess set. She left the white King and Queen because she thought he would appreciate that and it would remind him of them. She thought he might one day find the gold useful if he could ever bring himself to smash the pieces to get at it.

And then, as her eyes iced up with tears which froze in the cold, she collected the children and marched them to Suvarin's lorry which was waiting.

She did not look back when they drove away because if Nikolas was there to watch them leave she did not want to see him crying too.

Lottie sat in the seat next to Suvarin and the children had to sit as best they could in the cramped driver's cab. They took turns to sit on her lap or squeezed on the seat between her and the locked door. Otherwise they had to lie on a small ledge behind the two seats or on the floor beside the sheet of metal which covered the engine.

The lorry was part of a convoy of twenty, and it ground slowly and noisily up hills and around the twisting snow-bound forest roads. It was almost impossible to talk above the noise the engine made and she did not have the opportunity to ask Suvarin about the plan to evacuate them until the convoy stopped at the top of a hill to allow the lorries to cool down and the drivers to drink tea.

The children all sprang away, glad of the chance to stretch cramped muscles, and she asked Suvarin what the plan was.

'It's very simple. We travel like this for two days until we reach the Moscow to Archangel railway north of Vologda. Then we take a train as far north as possible. Then I'll have to find some way to deliver you to the British.'

'Do you mean that's not been planned?' she asked incredulously.

'It's impossible to plan that far in advance,' he said, 'because, of course, things change.'

She wondered what she had done, how much danger she had placed the children and herself in, but it was too late now. They were miles from the camp and she had no means of getting back.

They drove throughout the short day and well into the night, stopping frequently to allow the lorries to cool down and to rest the drivers who found it hard to keep staring into the blackness ahead, aware of very little other then the tail-light of the lorry in front. The children soon became bored and after a while she could not think of anything to suggest they do, so she asked them all to sing. She was grateful when they all fell asleep because she was beginning to feel unusually irritable with them, but she assumed that was a mixture of fear and her own boredom, and the thought of leaving Nikolas after all he had done to help them.

They stopped overnight at a camp meant to accommodate men. When she walked through a vast canteen she realised she was the only woman among several thousand men and she unconsciously slipped her hand beneath her coat and touched the revolver which was still strapped around her waist.

A few men stared at her in a way she found both unsettling and offensive, but most either ignored her or smiled and talked to the children. She tried to eat the food Suvarin bought for her, but she did not feel hungry and pushed it away. The children had no problems in dividing it up and finishing it all, happy that it tasted better than anything they had eaten in the camp.

She did not sleep well, even with her gun tucked under her mattress, and she was glad when morning came and they could continue with the journey. Things were coming to a head. Now she simply wanted to get it all over with, and combine her new life with her past, if the English police allowed her to.

The following night, after all the children had fallen asleep in the cramped lorry cab, Suvarin stopped the lorry under fierce arc lights in something that resembled a railway goods yard, and a few minutes later what appeared to be a battleship on rails steamed up to a wooden platform.

'Our train,' Suvarin said and pointed to the grey painted iron clad monster. It bristled with machine-guns that poked through loop holes, and small cannon mounted in turrets which could turn to fire in several directions.

They woke the children and climbed onto a wooden platform. Suvarin helped them to step up into a carriage which had rows of seats running across it and a central aisle which served the whole length. The carriage had been completely encased by steel and the windows were covered with a strong grill which looked dense enough to stop most bullets, but also had a solid cover which could be pulled down.

Minutes later the carriage filled with soldiers and the train steamed out of the station. First Sergei, and then Irina, and moments later Helena and Alexandra began to cry.

'Whatever's the matter?'

Helena explained, 'Sergei asked Leo when he'd see Uncle Nikolas and Leo told him we won't see him again because we're going away and we won't see anyone again. Ever.'

She comforted Helena as she broke down into fresh sobs, and then she felt Irina tug at her skirt. 'It's not true, is it, Mama? I love Uncle Nikolas and he tells me stories and it'll break my little heart if I never see him again.'

'Oh, Irina.' She clutched her tightly and could not bear the thought of her 'little heart' being broken, and seconds later she was crying with them. 'I have to take you away to keep you safe. We'll go to another country where there's no fighting and no soldiers.'

'Can I come too?' one of the soldiers asked and several others murmured in agreement. 'I was dragged in to fight the Germans in '14, taken prisoner in '17, released in '18 and didn't even get home before me and me pals were rounded up and told that now we weren't fighting the Germans we had to fight other Russians. Now, in '19 we're told we've got to fight the British and Americans who were our allies until a few months ago. I don't understand how this Bolshevism works if all we're going to do is keep fighting people. All I want is to go home to my wife and kids, if I can find 'em, if they're still alive.'

She nodded and agreed that she still didn't fully understand it either. When he turned away she looked closely at him and realised that although he looked old he was probably no older than her, and she wondered what Sasha looked like now, and where he was, and whether or not he was thinking of her.

568

The children were huddled together on one seat and the train's motion and monotonous sound lulled them to sleep. She and Suvarin sat opposite them and she heard him snoring shortly afterwards, and then she dozed, half aware of what was happening around her and half dreaming.

Suddenly she woke up fully, realised it was almost daylight, and saw the soldier she had talked to last night was sitting among the children with Irina on his lap. He was telling them stories. The last story he told them was that he was another Uncle Nikolas, and as they grew older they would meet lots of uncles who would tell them stories for a while and then disappear, because that was what uncles were famous for. That was their magic trick.

This kind stranger, a lost soldier, had solved one of her problems.

'Thank you, Nikolas,' she murmured and smiled, and he winked at her.

An hour later she heard him answer to the name Anton, but the children did not notice, or did not hear. He was Uncle Nikolas to them and he answered to that every time they called him.

The train stopped at midday.

Suvarin nodded to her as the soldiers opened the carriage door and jumped down beside the rails. 'It could get a little sticky from here. We're getting close to the areas held by the British so the carriage'll be closed down, and a hundred men who haven't washed for weeks can smell a bit so I suggest we get some air while we can. And stretch our legs.'

'No, it'll be too cold for the little ones and they can run about in here now the soldiers have—' she said firmly, and then saw the look on Suvarin's face.

'We will get out and stretch our legs,' he said and fastened the coats Helena and Alexandra were wearing. 'You take care of Irina and the boys.'

He picked up the girls and carried them to the door, jumped out and lifted them down to the track. She followed, Irina and the bag containing the chess set in her arms, Leo and Lev following.

Suvarin lifted them all down and told the five older children that if they could climb up the embankment and stay hidden at the top he had a prize for them, but only if they did it without making any noise.

'There'll be two sleds at the top,' he said with certainty. 'Come on.'

'How did you know the train would stop here?' She handed him Irina so she could climb more easily.

'It always does. It's the last safe place before it's likely to run into the British or Americans. I didn't tell you before because I didn't want the soldiers to know or guess we might try to leave. In case they tried to stop us.'

'Why are the British here, Maxim?'

'That's what Lenin keeps asking. The British and Americans are frightened of Bolshevism and they're trying to kill it before it gets a hold. They're trying to join up with the Whites, the old Tsarists, the anti Bolsheviks.'

'Is the White Army around here?' She asked as they reached the top of the embankment.

'Difficult to know. Bands of them turn up everywhere. There are also whole divisions of renegade Red soldiers who do not necessarily follow the true Bolshevik cause. How do you tell one Russian from another? Especially in this cold.'

She saw his breath had frozen to ice on his moustache and beard, and she took Irina back from him as he led them away from the embankment edge.

'Eat these now children. They'll help keep you warm.' He handed them all a bar of chocolate, then pointed to a gap in the trees and told them to follow him.

They found the sleds and drivers about a hundred yards into the forest, and within minutes they were loaded aboard and the ponies were pulling them at a slow trot.

'The drivers'll leave us at a cabin where we'll find some useful papers and stay overnight, and tomorrow we'll make our way down to Shenkursk which is occupied by the British. And they'll take you home. It's easy.'

It was dusk when they reached the cabin. The sled drivers

showed them a primitive stable which sheltered a strong pony and a shed which housed a strong sled, and then they left.

As she entered the cabin the first thing she noticed was a framed photograph of Sasha, in a suit, playing the piano. She picked it up and found a letter from Peter was stuck to the back of the frame, but she did not read it until after she had settled the children and helped Suvarin to prepare food.

When she did read it she found Peter had written in English, and she assumed he thought that might prevent the sled drivers possibly reading and understanding it. After the usual comments and courtesies he apologised for having kept the plans secret from her, and told her to introduce herself as Komovsky to the British Headquarters when she reached Shenkursk and to inform them that she had an official appointment with a Mr Andrews in Archangel. By the time she reached Shenkursk he would have informed the Headquarters there that she was expected and had important tactical information to pass on.

Once she arrived in Archangel she was to speak to Mr Andrews and he would arrange for her and the children to be sent by ship back to England.

He also said he was trying to find Sasha, and he looked forward to them all drinking vodka together until they fell over. His final words were to give his love to his mother, and he signed the letter, with a flourish – Komovsky.

CHAPTER 34

The children were ready to sleep as soon as they had eaten so she laid them across two palliasses she placed near the wood burner, and she and Suvarin sat and talked.

The smell of the burner and the pine-log cabin reminded her of the camp she had left and she wondered how Nikolas was. She had decided that if ever she gave birth to a boy she would call him after the old man who meant so much to her and had done so much for her.

Suvarin drank vodka from a bottle which he kept offering to her, and she kept refusing. She remembered Peter's warning about Maxim Suvarin and she thought she should keep her wits about her, but the more he drank the more mellow he became and she assumed he had either changed his ways, or possibly now that she had rough hands and a brown face and muscles he thought she was more suited to cooking for him than entertaining him in bed.

They talked long into the night, the children murmuring in their sleep, wood in the burner cracking and shifting and the cabin groaning like a ship at sea. The lamp burned so low the wick smoked and she smelled the fish the lamp oil was pressed from. Suvarin lit a candle just before the lamp died and he disposed of the match very carefully.

'We would not want to set fire to our little house, would we?'

She could see his face in the candle light. He was smiling.

'If you hadn't been so drunk that you allowed those men to attack me you might still have your house.'

'Tch!' he muttered, and shrugged. 'Lose a house and you can rebuild it or get another, but lose a friend and it is forever. I thought you had died and gone to the river. The friends I gave shelter to in that house never came back. Except Komovsky, or that damned silly name he uses now. He came back. He knocked out five more of my teeth, but he came back, and that is why I owe him a big debt. I owe you a debt too, one that is impossible to repay, except perhaps with my life. I learned much from that house, but you suffered most from it, I think.'

'I also learned a lot from that house. I faced up to misery and disgust and fear and learned how strong I can be. Up until that night when I was nearly raped I had always had someone who insisted on protecting me. First it was my family, and then a lovely man called Joseph, and then Peter, whom I love next to Sasha. But that night I called on everyone, including you, but no one came and so I learned that *I* was responsible for *myself*. And then I realised I could be responsible for others too, and that meant I had finally grown up.'

'Being grown up is not always a pleasure,' he grumbled. 'I would like to go back to dreaming a child's dreams, to think that there is really magic and anything is possible. That is instead of seeing men and the world crumbling and knowing nothing can be done. Instead of feeling hungry and cold and stiff in my joints, and knowing it won't get better.'

She watched him swig the last of his vodka and look sorrowfully at the empty bottle. In the silence a wolf howled and another, farther away, answered, and prompted her to say, 'At least we have full stomachs and a warm house for tonight.'

'Yes,' he said and his head dropped stupidly, so she

573

helped him to his palliasse and laid him down, then settled herself a few feet away.

Several minutes passed and she thought he was asleep when he suddenly said, 'Yes, and it's warmer than my new house.'

'Where's your new house?'

'In the city. Not the best part, but very respectable. I bought it from a German merchant who wanted to sell it quickly when the war started. It's just what I always wanted, a big house in a square, my own little bit of paradise, but it's always cold. I can't get it warm, not even in summer. It's always winter in my new house. In my little paradise.'

'Who lives there with you?'

'No one. I live all alone.' He turned over and grumbled, drunk and morose. 'All alone. I've got my big house and some new friends, but not real friends. No one loves me and that's why it's always winter in paradise square.'

She lay still and listened to him snore and the children, *her children*, snuffle. It was strange to think that a man like him should have the same dream as her. But he had his cold house, his wintry house in paradise square, and she had her warm children. And she thought herself lucky.

The following morning Maxim set the pony to the sled, loaded on the children and her bag with the chess set, and they set off for Shenkursk.

Maxim used the single track timber trails but they were not meant for visitors and the map he had was barely adequate so they constantly found themselves in dead ends and had to turn around and retrace their steps. Eventually they thought they had found the right trail and Maxim put the pony into a fast trot, while the children settled down under several rugs and furs and Lottie made sure no one fell off.

They soon found a road surfaced in the middle with iced snow, which suggested it had been well used quite recently but which was deserted all the while they trotted along in the soft snow which formed its verge.

They stopped each hour to stretch their muscles and make tea to keep them warm. The light faded about four o'clock and the temperatures dropped even lower. They still had not seen any sign of Shenkursk and Lottie began to worry that if anything happened to the pony or sled, or if they became lost again, they would have to spend the night in the open. Without shelter the children might become dangerously chilled or even die.

She knew Maxim also realised the dangers because he was driving the pony fast in spite of the poor light.

The cold and the constant wind made her eyes water and freeze so she could not open them and she could not see why Maxim slowed the sled to walking pace. She took a glove off and furiously rubbed her eyes with her fingers, trying to melt the ice which stuck her lashes together.

Then her stomach churned as she heard the snap of a rifle bolt.

'Halt! Who goes there?' said an English voice in the time-honoured way.

Shenkursk stood on the sandy bank of a frozen river. It was a city built of sand-coloured bricks, and in the summer it was a popular resort for the wealthy who demanded good hotels.

Maxim took her to one of the best and helped her to book a suite for herself and the children. She asked him if he would stay as her guest for the night or for a few days but he said he had a train to catch in two days and he would change the pony, go back along the road and spend the night in a shelter he had seen.

She gave him the revolver Peter had given her, thanked him for all his help, told him she had forgiven him for not helping her when she was attacked in his old house and said she hoped he would soon find some warmth in his new home.

They said goodbye in the hotel's reception. He kissed each of the children before he left, hugged and kissed her, and turned away, a huge fur bear going out into the night. He waved as he drove the sled away, but he did not look back.

* * *

It was too late to report to the British headquarters and she
desperately wanted to buy the children some of the clothes
the hotel displayed in glass cases. She also wanted each
child to bathe, dress properly, and sit down to eat a civilised
meal before they went to their warm and comfortable beds.

The hotel manager had already been charmed by the
sight of several gold coins taken from the chess set, and
nothing was too much trouble.

The children were bathed, dressed in their new clothes, and
resting before being taken to the hotel restaurant, and Lottie
was enjoying her first proper bath for nearly two years. The
piping-hot water was relaxing, the scent of lavender soap
was soothing, and the luxury of not being cold and
frightened was intoxicating.

Something told her Peter would find Sasha, just as he had
found her, and Sasha would escape just as she would. It
seemed to be ordained that she would go back to England
as Mrs Sasha Komovsky and with a ready-made family,
and if she was only half as careful as she had learned to be
no one would even associate her with Charlotte Forrester
who had once killed a man in self-defence.

She wondered, now, why she had not simply gone directly
to the police and explained what had happened? The
answer, of course, was that she was a different person then,
and because her parents thought she might be a little mad,
and because Joseph had been there to help and advise her.

She lay back, closed her eyes and ran water over her
head, washing her hair, and she did not hear or notice
Alexandra until she felt the girl's hand touch her shoulder.

'What's the matter, little one?'

'Irina's scared and she's crying.'

'Why?' she stood up and reached for a towel.

'It's the bangs. The big bangs.'

'The what? The big bangs?' She frowned and began to
towel herself dry. 'What big bangs?'

There was a sudden explosion, the window smashed and
the hotel shifted sideways.

576

'Oh God!' She saw her blood in and on the mirror, the way her shoulder had been opened up, and saw herself duck as another shell screamed over the hotel.

She twisted a small towel around her shoulder and grabbed Alexandra. 'Are you hurt?'

'No,' she trembled.

'Let me see,' she said sharply, turned her about and saw she was not harmed. 'Go and stand in the corridor, but don't go any further. Go on!'

She wrapped herself in a large towel and pushed Alexandra into the corridor where there were no windows, then rushed into the sitting room. 'Come on, out here. Away from the glass.'

A deafening screech and heavy thud. A roar and instant flame. The big window hung several inches inside the room and fell to the floor, propping itself against the wall. Air, colder than ice, cut through her.

'Come on!' Helena grabbed Sergei and Lev grabbed them both and pushed them across the room, as Leo picked up Irina. She found herself behind them all, herding them towards the corridor.

A number of guests rushed from their rooms but no one knew what was happening or seemed to care that she was wearing only bloodstained towels.

'Can someone get me a doctor, please? I've been cut, badly. And can someone find out what's happening?'

'We're being shelled, young woman,' an elderly, military-looking man said calmly. 'And I'd say it was from all around.'

Leo stepped forwards. 'Shall I go up to the roof? I may see something?'

'No, Leo, you stay with the others. You're the oldest and you must keep them together and safe. I must dress, and see to my shoulder.'

'I'm a doctor,' another man said. 'Let me look.'

He reached for her but she pushed his hands away. 'In your room or mine Doctor, but not in the corridor.'

'In mine. My bag's there.'

Everyone ducked as two more shells screamed over.

Their blast cracked the ceiling and dust settled on everyone's head and shoulders.

It occurred to her they would all be safer in the basement, if there was one, but she did not want to send the children on their own.

'How quickly can you sort this out, Doctor?'

'Let me see it first!' He grabbed her wrist and pulled her into a room, then slammed the door behind him.

Another shell screamed in but he ignored it and picked up his bag.

'Bathroom. Through there,' he ordered and she obeyed.

She sat on the side of the bath and she heard him grunt as he pulled the towel off her shoulder. 'Is it bad, Doctor?'

'I've seen worse, but yes, it's bad. You've sliced the muscle. You haven't cut any arteries.'

'Good. Can you stitch it?'

'Yes, but it'll hurt and you mustn't move it for a week.'

She looked up as another shell screeched over. 'Just stitch it. Please.'

It did hurt, as if the needle and thread were red hot and had barbs which tore her flesh every time he pricked her skin and dragged the twine through it, but she clamped her jaw shut, closed her eyes and thought the pain could not go on for ever.

A bed sheet ripped into bandages and a sling completed the repair. Lottie thanked him, offered him payment which he refused, and walked back to the corridor. She told the children she would be with them in a few minutes, and asked Alexandra to help her dress.

The hotel did have a basement and the manager packed all the guests in and gave them tea and vodka if they wanted it. She had two glasses to help numb the pain which was throbbing from her elbow to her breast, but she refused any more because she knew she might need a clear head.

The lights flickered, blacked out, and then came on dimly, and she remembered the bag with the gold coins was lying in her bedroom. 'Leo, Lev! I'm going back to our room but I want you both to stay here and look after the others. I won't be long.'

'Mama!' Irina cried out. 'Don't go!'

'I won't be long.' She avoided Irina's outstretched hands.

'Mama!'

Then Sergei started to sob, and Helena.

'Just stay there. I won't be long.'

She pushed her way through the crowd, found the door and ran to the stairs. Then one word seemed to silence all the chaos going on around her.

'Evacuation!'

She ran back down the stairs and grabbed at a man who seemed to know what was happening. 'Did you say evacuation?'

'Yes. The Bolshevik Army's coming and I've heard the British are leaving.'

'They can't be!'

'They are,' her doctor friend appeared. 'I think they're hoping the Reds'll stop shelling if they leave. I think they're going about midnight.'

'What about civilians?'

'They can go too, if they've got transport or can walk.'

'But I've got little children! Irina's barely four and a half. She can't walk, and I can't carry her. I've got a five-, and a six-, and a seven-year-old. My oldest are only eight and nine.'

'Then, unless you can find transport you'll have to wait and see what the Reds do, but with all due respect you'd better try to make yourself look a lot less attractive than you are. The Reds up here are largely made up of two renegade divisions and haven't seen any women for months. I can guess what your fate would be but God knows what'll happen to your children if you're taken away.'

'Thank you for your help.'

Lottie found the chess set, smashed it, and collected the remaining gold coins in a small bag which had a long loop so she could hang it around her neck. She shoved the little Derringer into her pocket and wished she had kept the revolver she had given to Maxim, then collected the children's coats and hats and rushed back down to the basement.

'Children, whatever happens you must all hang on to each other and stay together. Do you understand?'

The nods and murmurs suggested they did, but she knew that children were likely to forget if they were distracted or frightened so she hurried them through the chaotic streets towards the British Army's headquarters. She was thankful that the shelling had stopped, but terrified that it could begin at any moment and she and the children might still be out on the streets.

'You can't go down there,' an English voice warned her.

'Look, I'm English, I've got six children and I need to join the evacuation.'

'We're not taking civilians, Mrs. We ain't even taking the wounded, God 'elp 'em.'

'I've got six children!'

'We don't care if you've got sixty. We're not taking civilians.'

'That's right,' another English voice said, a cultured ladylike voice. 'I've just spent an hour waiting to see the CO, or somebody pretty high up, and he told me the same. We can follow the army if we want to, or we can stay here. The convoy's going to assemble in the street over there so I suggest you try to get yourselves and the children onto a sled, if you can find someone to take you.'

'What'll you do?' Lottie asked.

'Stay here. I've no means of getting away and the children I look after are far too small to take out at night. But good luck to you,' the woman said in a matter-of-fact voice, and walked away.

'Good luck to you, too,' Lottie called after her, and wished she still had the letter of safe passage that Peter had given her. Then she realised that without that letter and the relentless 'processing' that took place, Peter would never have found them and they would still be in the camp.

She gathered up the children and led them to where the civilian convoy was beginning to assemble.

She approached a man with a large sleigh. 'I've six children. Can you help me get away?'

He looked at her, then at the children, and shook his head. 'I'll be fully loaded with my own family.'

She ran to another man and repeated the question. He simply waved her away and loaded his own children on board.

The next four sleds were already overloaded.

The army began to move along the street and she tried to stop them but soldiers pushed her back and several lowered their rifles and frightened her enough to stop her doing anything more.

'Will someone help me? Please?' she yelled as sleds and sleighs moved into the street.

'Try down by the bridge,' a woman shouted. 'They're grouping up there as well.'

'How do I get there?'

'Follow that road,' the woman said and pointed.

'Come on, children.' Lottie called to them and looked over her brood. Her heart stopped. Irina was missing! 'Irina! Irina! Where's Irina?'

She told the other five to stay exactly where they were and ploughed through the growing crowd looking for her little daughter. 'Irina? Irina? Has anyone seen a little girl on her own?'

No one had, or no one cared. They were all too busy saving themselves and their own families to worry about someone else's lost child.

'Oh, Irina!'

Suddenly Lev was pulling at her coat. 'Matushka! Matushka! We've found her. Her legs hurt from walking so she sat down on a wall and we did not see her. We're sorry, Matushka.'

'Oh Lev!' She hugged him tight to her. 'Why are you sorry?'

'Because we know it would be easier for you if it wasn't for us. If it was only you and Irina, Matushka.'

She hugged him tighter and cried as she spoke. 'I hadn't thought about that, Lev because you are all my children, not only Irina. I love you all the same and I'll never leave you.'

'And we all love you, Matushka.' Lev smiled at her and squeezed her gloved hand as they walked back to the others.

'Lev, what's this word, Matushka?'

He looked embarrassed, and after being pressed admitted it was what all the children secretly called her.

'But what does it mean, Lev?'

'It means little mother, and we call you Matushka because you are our mother, and you're very little, like us.'

She hugged him again and hugged Irina when she saw her. Then she found herself hugging them all. 'Come on, we'll go to the bridge. Someone'll help us.'

They had almost reached the bridge when the shelling started again, but the shells were exploding on the far side of the town so she did not make the children take cover.

'I've six children. Can anyone help me?' she asked everyone who looked as though they might be able to help but everyone had excuses not to help, or they simply ignored her.

The army had gone and the first length of the civilian convoy was also moving past. The remaining civilians were setting themselves up, ready to leave.

'Please! Can't anyone help me?'

She heard a single shell explode and saw a huge fountain of sparks, and then the lights went out all over town. The pale moon made the snow glow with a cold grey light.

Somewhere behind her she heard small-arms fire. The Red Army was already on the town's outskirts. That was probably why the shelling had stopped, to give the soldiers time to infiltrate the streets.

'Can anyone take any of my children?' she screamed desperately.

'I can take one,' a man offered.

'So can I,' someone else said.

'And me,' a woman said. 'I've always wanted a daughter. I'll take her.'

Lottie saw the woman grab at Alexandra. 'No! I'm not giving them away to strangers. I just want them taken to the British in Archangel.'

'Of course. That's what I meant,' the woman said and tried to pull Alexandra onto her sled.

'No!' Lottie yanked Alexandra back, and felt the stitches in her shoulder tear open.

'Matushka?' Alexandra wailed.

Lottie looked at her, and realised she would be better off with strangers than left alone in Shenkursk once the Bolsheviks arrived, especially if they were one of the renegade division. Alexandra was a beautiful child. She kissed the girl briefly and told her, 'Go with the lady, Alexandra. It'll be safer for you.'

'And I'll take the other pretty one,' a man grabbed Helena.

'I'll take the little girl and the youngest boy,' someone else offered.

Everything began to spin and Lottie suddenly felt helpless and defeated. Her shoulder was agony and she could feel her blood oozing down her arm and her side. She was not in any condition to make the journey to Archangel even if she could find someone to take her so it was best if she let all the children go.

All the children were crying but Helena's sharp scream pulled her around. The man who wanted Helena had picked her up and slapped her face because she was crying.

'Don't do that! Bring her back here. Now!'

'You can have her,' the man said and dropped Helena immediately.

Lottie looked around her and saw all the children but Alexandra. She turned and saw her a few yards away, looking back from the sled she was seated on. She looked shocked and frightened. 'Alexandra!'

The girl waved, the woman who wanted her pushed her arm down and the man driving the sled cracked the reins so the sled moved away.

'Alexandra!' Lottie screamed. 'Jump! I want you here with me!' Alexandra pushed the woman away and jumped before the sled gathered any real speed.

Lottie ignored the pain in her shoulder, hugged Alexandra tightly and pleaded to be forgiven for what she had nearly done.

Alexandra hugged her back and sobbed, saying just one word over and over. 'Matushka, Matushka.'

Lottie gathered all the children around her and watched the convoy move away. Hundreds of people had gathered, mainly old people who could not manage the journey through the arctic night and the days ahead, and a few desperate people like herself who could not find transport to leave on.

The shells continued to scream down on the far side of the city and at times she could see the flashes from the artillery pieces as the gunners fired into the civilian town.

After the sleds had gone a long column of people who hoped to walk to freedom filed past and she was tempted to join them in the hope that someone might offer to carry the children when they grew too tired to walk, but she was disillusioned. Half the people who said they could not spare space for the children already had their sleds stacked with personal items which they obviously thought were more precious.

'Let's go back to the hotel, children,' she said, and tried to hide her fear.

She shepherded the children away from the crowd which lingered by the bridge and along an empty street which led directly to the hotel. She was half-way along it when she saw her last chance to escape. A man was driving an empty sled towards her.

'Wait here children, and don't say anything or move unless I call you. Understand?' she asked and pushed them into the shadow of a wall.

The sled was travelling quite slowly down the long street and she had enough time to remove the bag from her neck, take out two gold coins, return the bag to safety and then take out her little pistol. She cocked the hammer on the Derringer's first barrel as Olga had shown her to do nearly five years before and stepped into the road in front of the sled.

'Hey! Stop!' she shouted loudly in case the driver had not seen her. 'I'd like to hire your sled. I'll pay you well.'

'Keep your money,' a gruff voice answered from inside a heavy fur skin.

'In gold?' she persisted.

'How much gold?' the driver asked.

'Look,' she jangled the coins and held her hand out. 'But don't try to steal them because I've a gun pointing at your head, and if you try to steal them I'll shoot you and take your sled anyway.'

She cocked the hammer on the second barrel, just to let him know she did have a gun pointing at him.

'You've learned well, Krasnaya,' Peter said, 'but are you going to stop the entire Red Army with your little pistol?'

'Komovsky? Where did you spring from?'

'Where the hell have you been, Lottie? I've been looking all over town for you. I'd planned for Sasha and me to be at the hotel when you arrived. I thought we could all drink vodka until we fell down, but I hadn't reckoned on the glorious Bolshevik Revolutionary Army attacking the place. I wouldn't have sent you here if I'd known.'

She jumped onto the sled and hugged Peter, winced and stepped back.

'What's happened to you, Krasnaya?'

'I've cut my shoulder, badly. It was stitched earlier this evening but I think I tore the stitches a little while ago and now it's bleeding again. I'll live, but where's Sasha?'

'I don't know. He should have met me three days ago but he didn't. Then I heard about the plans to attack the city so I came here to help you rather than wait for him.'

'Will he come here?'

'Not if he's got any sense. Anyway, where are the children? We need to get going ourselves.'

'Get going? Can't we stay now you're here? Surely we'll be safe with you?'

'No. Being caught with me could be your death warrant.'

'What?' She trembled. She had always assumed he could offer safety in this dangerous country.

'Red Terror, Lottie. Late last year the Bolsheviks decided to start executing anyone who didn't agree with them. Hundreds, thousands, who knows? I unwisely suggested that all the Revolution had achieved was to exchange the Tsar for a Dictator. I made enemies. Anyway, we must get going. We need to catch the convoy and get the British medical team to look at your shoulder before you lose too much blood. You can die fast in this temperature.'

Peter loaded the children onto the sled, and Lottie covered them with furs and told Peter he could move off. Alexandra smiled at her as they crossed the bridge where she had almost been given away and mouthed one word – Matushka. Lottie smiled back at her, relieved that she had been forgiven so easily.

Guns boomed all around and shells screamed down into the city which was half hidden by thick smoke. They soon caught up with and passed the stragglers who were trying to walk to safety and Lottie hoped that the British Army had made sure the route they were taking was safe from ambush.

She noticed how white the children's faces were and wondered whether that was the effect of shock or simply the reflection of the snow. Then she noticed how every sound echoed, and how each of the children suddenly had two white faces. Then she realised Alexandra had come to sit beside her and was feeling inside her coat, heard the girl say something to Peter and sensed that the sled was going faster.

Then all she could feel was cold, and then nothing.

When Lottie woke up she saw Peter looking down at her, noticed a dim room, smelled fish and thought they were back in the fish seller's room in St Petersburg. For a moment she had the deflating feeling that everything had been a dream, and then she saw a weather-beaten old woman with a wrinkled face and remembered the panic in Shenkursk.

'Are we safe, Peter?'

He nodded.

'And the children?'

'They're in the next room,' he said quietly. 'There's nothing for you to worry about. Just lie still and get better.'

'Where are we?'

'We're in a cabin in a safe area. You've lost an awful lot of blood and all we can do is stay here until you've made it

586

up again. Once you're fit I can take you across to the railway and you can take a train into Archangel and go home.'

'Just like that?'

'Not quite,' he said, and smiled. 'It's not a regular service but the Americans and British use the railway to carry troops and supplies. I'll take you to one of their outposts and they'll send a train to collect you.'

'I am really that important?'

He laughed. 'You are to me, Krasnaya. You are to me.'

'Thank you,' she said and saw him fade away.

The next time Lottie recovered consciousness she was told Peter had left and would be away for at least two weeks, but that she was not to worry because he had made arrangements for someone else to take her and the children to Archangel if he did not come in time.

She found that although she was still too weak to stand up or do anything she was able to stay awake throughout the day and take an interest in the games the children played. The cabin was quite large, with four rooms. It was owned by an elderly couple who enjoyed having the children around and did not mind looking after her.

She was too weak to become bored and the fortnight spent waiting for Peter passed quite serenely. It was only at the end of the third week that she started to fret. By the time four weeks had passed she was feeling fit and strong and eager to move, and the frustration of being cooped up in the cabin and not knowing when she could leave was becoming intolerable.

Then, during a ferocious blizzard the outer door banged open and a snow-clad figure stamped into the cabin.

'I'm sorry I was so long,' Peter said, as if he had come back from a simple errand a few minutes late. 'You can leave tomorrow. You'll be in Archangel in a day or so and then wait there until the ice breaks and a ship can take you home. How are you feeling?'

'What's wrong, Peter?' she asked, well aware that he was behaving like a parody of himself.

He sighed as he pulled his furs off and dropped them on

the floor, but he did not answer her.

'Tell me, Peter. What's wrong?' She was alarmed.

'Sasha's not coming, Lottie.'

'Why not?'

'Because he's dead.' Peter dug into a pocket and handed her the piano and violin pendant she had left at Irina.

'What happened?' Her throat was dry. She was too shocked to cry.

'Sasha went to the estate when the Germans released him. The house had been looted but he found your pendant had fallen under a table. He went to the station and Igor told him all the workers had run away after the Cossacks had come, killed Tatiana and taken you, Natasha and the children with them.'

'Go on, Peter. I'm all right,' she said, even though she was reeling at what Sasha must have been thinking at that time, and horrified by the way the Cossacks had probably treated Natasha.

'Sasha went to Petrograd. He intended crossing into Finland and making his way back to England but he met Olga who persuaded him it was too dangerous and not to do anything until she'd spoken to me. I knew I was being watched so I dared not go near him or you, but Olga told him I had found you and where he should meet me. A week after he should have met me Olga received a package containing your pendant and Sasha's papers.'

'Are you sure he's dead?'

'He might have lost his papers, but he wouldn't have lost your pendant, Lottie. I think, maybe they thought they were killing me, but don't worry, I will take my revenge,' Peter growled.

'No, Peter. Please don't. Just come home with the children and me.'

'Oh, Krasnaya, how I dream of that, but I can't. Your Government wouldn't allow me to, for one thing. I have to help them in exchange for them helping me.'

'I don't understand?' she said.

'I think you do. I promised certain services if they agreed to take you and the children home without any questions. I still have to deliver those services, Krasnaya, and then I will come.'

'If someone doesn't murder you first.'

His smile frightened her and she clung to him and pleaded with him not to stay behind when she left, and even threatened to stay if he did not go with her.

'Matushka,' he said softly, 'you have to think about the children.'

'Yes, I know.'

'Then you understand that I must stay and do my duty?'

'Yes, but will you sleep with me tonight? Sleep the way we slept in Suvarin's house. Hold me all night?'

'Yes, Krasnaya Matushka, beautiful little mother.'

Peter wrapped Lottie up in his arms and held her firmly, and she thought how cruel it was that after accepting Sasha was dead she should learn he was alive only to be told he had been murdered. It was all so pointless and cruel that she despaired and wished she could cry because she thought that might make her feel better, but she could not cry. She was too miserable to cry.

Then she heard Helena call out and begin to whimper as she often did, and she went to comfort her.

However much grief she might feel, her children had the right to feel much more. They had all suffered far worse than her and she knew she owed a lifetime's care to each one. Somehow she had to find a way of protecting them without making the mistakes her parents had made when they protected her.

She crept back into her bed, snuggled up to Peter and kissed him.

'I love you, Komovsky.'

'And I love you, Krasnaya,' he returned her kiss.

He held her until her shoulder started to hurt, and then they turned their backs on each other and went to sleep.

When she woke up he had gone.

Chapter 35

Spring 1919

Even when she was on board the Royal Navy ship which took her from Archangel Lottie still followed Mr Andrews' instructions to avoid awkward questions about her real identity by pretending she was an influential Russian of high birth who spoke flawless English and French.

She received constant attention from all the ship's officers and when she shaded her eyes to look at the sandy coastline and asked what part of the coast she could see, she received three immediate answers.

'Norfolk, Mrs Komovskaya.'

'North Norfolk, to be precise, Madame.'

'To be really precise we're just off Yarmouth.'

She smiled. 'I once lived just north of Yarmouth. There's a pier there, I believe.'

'There certainly was, Madame, but the suffragettes blew it up just before the war started.'

She smiled. At the time she had been shocked by what Eve and the other suffragettes were doing, and by how much they suffered, but it was nothing compared to the Revolution going on in Russia. She had been terrified by the man who followed her, but now she had escaped from bandit Cossacks and Lenin's Red Army it did not seem quite so terrible. She had been repulsed by the thought of a man touching her or by having to touch anyone else, but now she enjoyed contact. She had been desperate at the thought of insecurity and of possibly losing Albert, but now she valued her freedom and was coming to terms with having lost Sasha.

She had changed a lot in a little more than six years, but so had the world. She watched the coast for a few more minutes, and then made up her mind.

'Would it be possible to put the children and me ashore?'

The question caused confusion and consternation.

'I'll ask the Captain,' one of the officers suggested, and raced off for advice.

The ship changed course within minutes.

The Captain came off the bridge to ask if she simply wanted to go ashore for a short while or whether she intended to leave the ship for good, and when she told him she did not intend to come back he looked downcast.

'We've enjoyed having you and the children on board, Mrs Komovskaya. I've been instructed to afford you all possible assistance but it's rather an irregular procedure to allow passengers to disembark anywhere other than a formal . . .'

'I've led a rather irregular life, Captain,' she said, smiling and touching his arm as she interrupted him.

'So I understand, Madam. So I understand.'

The ship stopped a little way off Yarmouth and lowered a boat to take the passengers ashore. The landing party was very formal and Lottie was embarrassed as a small crowd gathered to watch her and the children being carried the last few yards to the beach.

She thanked the sailors, and watched the boat return to the ship. After it had been hoisted back into its davits she was astonished to see sailors pour out onto the ship's deck and line the ship's railings. Moments later flags were run out and the ship blasted its siren three times. As that sound echoed into silence she saw the sailors raise their caps, and

591

the sound of three cheers floated across the water.

'All for little Lottie Forrester of Angel Street,' she said to herself and encouraged the children to wave back as the ship turned and steamed away.

Suddenly she felt lost.

She was back in England, and it felt as though she was in a foreign country.

Mr Andrews had given her a quantity of English money so she hired a taxi and asked the driver to take her to Joseph's house which was along the coast.

The house had not changed in the six years since she had first seen it. She reminded herself that she had been running away then, but now she was going home, wherever that might prove to be.

She climbed out of the car and wondered if this could be home for her and the children. She had been happy here and there was no reason why they should not be.

An elderly woman came around the corner of the house and called across the front garden. 'Can I help you, madam?'

'Mrs Miller?'

'Not for a long time,' the woman said mildly, screwed up her eyes and peered forwards. 'Who're you?'

'Charlotte. Charlotte Forrester. Or Forest.'

'Well, I don't believe it,' Mrs Miller said and turned as the children, bored with sitting in the motor-car, all began to pile out. 'Are they yours?'

'Yes.'

'How many of them?'

'Six.'

'Good 'eavens. You didn't waste much time, Miss Charlotte. Wait until Joseph hears about this.'

'He's here? How is he?'

'He's getting old, my dear. Getting old.' Mrs Miller paused, then said, 'We've a lot to talk about, all of us. Can you stay for a while or are you in a hurry?'

'We've nothing to hurry for, and nowhere to go, Mrs Miller,' Lottie admitted.

'Then bring all them kiddies indoors. And it's Mrs Belchester now, not Mrs Miller.'

That was a name Lottie had not heard often but she had not forgotten its significance and she was startled to find Mrs Miller using it. 'Mrs Belchester?'

'Yes, Miss Charlotte. That's Joseph's real name. As I said, my dear, we've a lot to talk about, and to admit to.'

Lottie had thought Joseph was dying when she left him and she was amazed to see how well he was now. He looked older, much older, and he was partly paralysed and needed a wheelchair, but the slowness which had plagued him had gone and he seemed to twinkle with energy and good humour.

He and his Bessie, as he called her, had been married four months.

Lottie paid the taxi driver and helped Bessie settle the children with food and drink, and accepted Joseph's invitation to join him in his study.

'I've an awful confession to make, Charlotte. In fact I've several, and I hope you'll listen long enough to hear them, my apologies, and my explanations, although I wouldn't blame you if . . .' He stopped and she saw he had tears in his eyes.

'Whatever's wrong, Joseph?'

'I tricked you into coming with me, Charlotte. I made you believe you killed a man when you hadn't.'

'Mr Grundley?'

'Yes. It wasn't even him who grabbed you. That was one of the men I'd been paying to follow you, to terrorise you into accepting my protection. He pretended he was dead.'

'Joseph?' she asked, not sure she had heard him correctly.

'It's true, Charlotte. Every word. You didn't kill anyone.'

The flood of relief dazed her for several seconds, then she asked, 'Why, Joseph? Why?'

She listened carefully and did not interrupt him once while he explained.

'I'm terribly sorry, Charlotte. I did some awful things to you, my dear.'

'I understand, Joseph, and I've had far worse things happen to me since I left you. My son, John, was born dead. I left two very close friends to be butchered by renegade Cossacks. I was separated from Sasha, my daughter's father, for four years, and then he was murdered before he could find me. And his brother, Peter, whom I love very much, has disappeared and I don't know if I'll ever see him again.'

'You've had a lot to cry over, Charlotte.'

'I don't cry. Not very often. I haven't cried over any of the things I told you about,' she said, and saw him frown. 'So much has happened, Joseph, that I'm scared to start crying in case I can't stop. It's easier just to accept what's happened and shut it out. It's the only way I can cope.'

He sighed and reached out to hold her hand. 'You should cry, Charlotte, otherwise you'll become as hard and bitter as I used to be. Crying doesn't mean you're weak, my dear, it means you're human.'

She looked into his eyes and wanted to cry, but she could not; perhaps because she did think of it as a sign of weakness and she was determined that no one should ever again think she was weak.

She had wanted to cry when the men attacked her in Maxim Suvarin's house, but she sensed that would not stop them doing whatever they wanted to do to her and she was not prepared to humiliate herself in front of them. She did not cry for long when baby John was born dead because she was determined to show everyone that she was strong enough to withstand the worst of shocks. She did not cry when she told Nikolas not to go back to Estate Irina because she did not want to upset the children, and she did not cry when Peter told her Sasha was dead because suddenly she could no longer feel anything deeply enough to make her cry.

Abandoning Nikolas made her cry because she felt exactly as she had when she left Joseph.

'This brother, Peter? Will you marry him if he comes to find you?'

'Oh, yes! Of course I . . .' She did not finish what she was going to say.

Peter clearly loved her as she loved him. He had risked his life for her, protected her, *looked after her*, just as Joseph had, her father had and Albert would have. But that was not what she wanted.

She remembered the first time Joseph had her followed and how she felt. She did want to be protected and looked after, *she had wanted to look after herself and others*.

'Matushka! Matushka.' Sergei appeared at the door, tears streaming down his face.

'Come here,' she said in Russian and held out her arms, and as he ran to her she asked softly, 'Whatever's the matter, little man?'

'I was scared you'd gone, like everyone else.'

'No, I'll never leave you. I was simply talking to my old friend.'

'Is he another Uncle Nikolas?' Sergei asked, tears already drying on his face.

'Yes,' she said uncertainly. 'But you'll have to talk to him in English or French because he can't speak Russian.'

Sergei giggled. 'Don't be silly, Matushka, everybody can speak Russian. Even little children.'

In order to prove he was right Sergei spoke to Joseph in Russian and when Lottie translated and Joseph responded only in English and French the boy thought it was great fun and left to tell the others that their new Uncle Nikolas was pretending he could not speak Russian and they all had to try to catch him out.

Lottie told Joseph what Sergei was saying and the old man laughed loudly, then asked, 'Can you stay here for a while, Charlotte?'

'Do you really want us to? The children can be exhausting.'

'I'd like you to stay. We have so much to talk about, and to tell you about. While I wouldn't say I'm a friend of your parents, I would say we're reasonably friendly and there are things you should know before you go to see them. I assume you do plan to see them?'

'Of course. Them and Katarina. I'd like Irina to know her grandfather and grandmothers.'

* * *

Any uncertainties Lottie had about Joseph being another Uncle Nikolas were dispelled the following morning. The children constantly tried to trick him into speaking Russian and fell about laughing when he gave them nonsensical answers in English or French. The smaller ones begged to sit on his lap and be taken for rides in his wheelchair and they enjoyed pushing him down to the beach and hauling the chair through the soft sand so he could organise them into playing games.

Afterwards they sat quietly and listened to him tell stories about his magic castles in Spain.

Every night, after the children had gone to bed, Lottie sat with Joseph and Bessie and talked about what had happened to her, or listened to them tell her about her own family.

She was shaken when they told her how ill her mother had been, and how she could now leave her wheelchair and walk a little way on sticks. She was even more shaken when they told her Jamie had been killed, but she was pleased when they said Maisie had remarried. Maisie and her husband, who only had one hand, lived above a grocer's shop they had bought.

They said Helen was having great difficulty with Joe who had been sent home in one piece, physically, but was severely shell-shocked and trembled constantly, so much that he could not work.

'Your aunt's also remarried, Charlotte,' Joseph said. 'Big chap. Was a policeman. Bill Crabb.'

'Did his wife die, then?' she asked. She remembered Gladys had been ill for years, but she was stunned when they told her how Gladys had died and how close Bill had been when the house was bombed.

'And, Eve?' she asked.

Bessie answered before Joseph could say anything. 'Got herself into a bit of trouble campaigning for the war to end and probably ruined any hope she ever had of going into politics, but she married too. A doctor. Robert Braithewaite. They took over Maisie's house when she left. Bought it from

596

the landlord and set up a surgery there although he still works down by the docks, too. They've a son and daughter. The girl's called Charlotte.'

Lottie smiled, and asked, 'And their son?'

'John.'

'Oh,' she said, her heart falling, 'that's what Sasha and I called our son.'

Bessie reached out and touched her hand. 'Cry for him, Charlotte. He deserves that, at least.'

Lottie sighed. 'I can't. It's all too long ago and I can't even cry for his father, but at least I know they're together.'

After a week Lottie reminded Joseph and Bessie that she had to think about leaving before the children became too settled there. She had realised that her immediate thoughts of living in the house were totally impractical because she had to find a way to support herself and six growing children, and she could not do that if she lived in such a remote house.

'What will you do, Charlotte?' Joseph asked. 'It won't be easy for you.'

'I'll manage, Joseph. Over the past five years I've done all sorts of things I'd never dreamed I could do, and I do have a little capital behind me.'

'May I ask how much?' Joseph asked.

'You may, but I couldn't tell you the precise amount because it's in gold. Twenty-eight gold coins.'

Joseph nodded, then said, 'You'll need a big house for all the children, Charlotte, and I'd like you to have the house in Leinster Place. You always said it was your idea of paradise.'

'I couldn't!'

Bessie snorted at her. 'Of course you could. If you'd have married him instead you'd have had it, and we don't want it, do we Joseph? It's empty and going to waste, which is a crime.'

'I insist you take it off my hands, Charlotte,' Joseph said firmly. 'It was always a cold house. It needs lots of children to warm it up.'

'That's settled, then,' Bessie said briskly, 'but how will you earn your keep?'

'Well, I speak several languages now and I thought that perhaps I could work as a translator or even teach.' She hesitated, unsure if she should tell them about her other idea. 'I've always had a strong imagination, and I've seen and done a lot over the past few years, and I thought I might try to write.'

'Your father did,' Joseph said immediately. 'Fairy stories. I always rather envied him that.'

Lottie stayed one more week, then a car took her and the children to Norwich station and she began the last leg of her long journey back from Estate Irina to Angel Street.

She walked up Mile Hill, past the costers' barrows, and was surprised that she did not see any of the young men she had known since she was a girl. The barrows were all run by their fathers or mothers, or in some cases their wives, and it was not until she stopped and looked back down the hill that she realised why.

The young men were all dead, or so badly injured they could not work their barrows any more.

The shock of what the war had done to Britain spread through her, and made her want to hurry home and throw herself into her father's arms, something she had not done since she was tiny.

Irina was pointing up at the angel, calling it a pretty icon, and Lottie suddenly realised that her daughter would soon be five years old, and was living in a foreign country. Irina, like the others, was Russian.

'Come on children, follow me.'

'Where are we going?' the chorus was general.

'To meet some people.'

'Are they nice people?'

'They're very nice people. Very nice people indeed,' she said and looked back to make sure there were no stragglers. She smiled when she saw they had paired themselves up as they always did. Sergei and Irina held hands and walked in front of the others, Alexandra followed with

Helena, and Lev and Leo walked at the rear.

Lottie heard a door bang and saw a tall woman carry a baby to a perambulator. Eve!

'Eve! Eve!' she began to run and heard the clatter of small feet following her.

Eve looked up, left her baby in the pram and started to run towards her. 'Lottie!' she squealed excitedly. 'Oh, Lottie!'

They collided rather than met and squeezed each other tightly for several minutes before a small hand diverted Lottie's attention.

'Matushka! Matushka!' Sergei cried urgently.

'Yes, Sergei, what is it?'

'Matushka. You're crying.'

'I know, it's because I'm happy.'

'You cry because you're happy?' Sergei shrugged and walked back to hold Irina's hand. 'Matushka cries because she's happy, Irina?'

Irina shrugged, too, obviously thinking that adults had a lot to learn.

'Eve, I'd like to introduce you—'

'Let's go indoors first, Lottie. Mama and Papa would want to—' Eve broke down into tears and virtually carried Lottie to the house.

The children followed them and crowded together on the path as Eve rapped the door-knocker, then stepped back.

The door opened and Lottie saw her father for the first time since she had run away from him six years earlier.

'Oh my God,' he said. 'Lottie!'

'Papa! I love you and I'm so sorry for what I did.' She threw herself at him and he caught her and swung her off her feet as he hugged and kissed her.

'No, girl, I'm sorry. We all are. Come in. Come home.'

Then she heard the piano.

'He's been here three days, Lottie,' her father said.

'Sasha?'

'Yes. He got out through Finland and Sweden.'

'SASHA!' She rushed to the front room and touched the door as he opened it.

They stood, staring at each other. His head had been shaved and he was thin and gaunt and his eyes were well back in their sockets, but he was the most beautiful thing she had ever seen.

'Lottie! You look wonderful.'

He hugged her and kissed her and told her how much he loved her. Her tears flooded out of her, and when she felt her mother's arms come around her she sobbed so hard she could not talk properly, only gasp out single words.

'How? Sasha? How?' She pulled the pendant out of her blouse for him to see.

'Olga betrayed me, but the man they sent to kill me was an old friend who also plays piano. He took the pendant and my papers to prove he had killed me but then I had to hide for his sake.'

'Peter?'

'Olga betrayed him too, and Maxim Suvarin. Maxim was killed but Peter escaped. I found him. We bought guns and tried to escape across the frozen gulf to Finland. The ice was breaking and dangerous so we were slow. Very easy targets for the guards along the coast. They were catching us and Peter said one of us should take both guns and try to stop the guards while the other escaped. He said I should go because I write pretty tunes for the piano, and because you love me more than you love him.'

'He's dead?'

'Yes. He dropped flat and they pushed him into the water just before the fog rolled in.'

She burst into fresh floods of tears, and murmured, 'Komovsky, Komovsky.'

'Mama?' A hand tugged at her coat.

'Oh, God! Irina! I'd forgotten all about you.' Lottie picked her up and passed her to Sasha who sat down on the piano stool, Irina on his lap.

'You've grown since I last saw you, little princess,' he said in Russian.

Irina tinkled with the piano keys for a moment, then turned and stared at him.

'Are you another Uncle Nikolas?'

'No precious, I'm your Papa.'

'Matushka?' Leo called out from the front door. 'May we all come in, also?'

'Of course, all of you. Come in.'

She saw her parents eyes grow wider and wider as each child made polite introductions in Russian. Then she saw panic on her mother's face.

'Lottie! Where are we going to put them all? There's no room here, not now we're sharing with Lizzie and Bill and Katarina and Paul.'

Lottie turned to Sasha. 'Do you still want to see big skies?'

'America?' he asked, and shrugged. 'Maybe, one day, but not yet. I think our children have been moved enough. We don't want them thinking they're Russian gypsies. Anyway, I'd like to see the big skies you told me about in England.'

'So we'll stay?'

He nodded. Lottie turned to her mother.

'I've been given a house, Mama, if you don't mind me living there,' she said cautiously. She wanted to accept Joseph's offer, but not if it meant causing more trouble between her and her parents.

'Leinster Place?' her mother asked, and Lottie nodded. Her mother smiled. 'No Lottie. I've exorcised all the ghosts I knew in that house, but would you want to live there? Hubert said you always complained that it never seemed like home, that it had a cold atmosphere.'

'Yes, I did, Mama.' She remembered how she used to feel, and she remembered what Maxim Suvarin said to her in the cabin the night before they reached Shenkursk. He said it always felt like winter in his house because there was no love in it. 'But when the house is a home for Sasha and me, and Katarina and Paul if they want to come, and Sergei, Leo, Alexandra, Helena, Lev and Irina, there simply won't be any room for the cold to get in. One day I'll write it all down and explain what I mean, Mama, but I know it'll never be winter in my Paradise Square.'